Guilty of Dancing the Chachachá

· G. CABRERA INFANTE ·

Guilty of Dancing the Chachachá

TRANSLATED FROM SPANISH

BY THE AUTHOR

Welcome Rain Publishers

New York

Guilty of Dancing the Chachachá by Guillermo Cabrera Infante

Delito por bailar el chachachá

First Spanish publication

by Santillana, Madrid, 1995

© Santillana, 1995

Translation © 2001 by Guillermo Cabrera Infante

Library of Congress Cataloging-in-Publication Data

Cabrera Infante, G. (Guillermo), 1929–

   [Delito por bailar el chachachá. English]

   Guilty of dancing the chachacha / G. Cabrera Infante ; translated from Spanish
by the author.— 1st ed.

     p. cm.

   ISBN 1-56649-187-8

   I. Title.

PQ7389.C233 D4513 2001

863'.64—dc21   2001026248

Text design by Fritz Metsch

Printed in the United States of America by HAMILTON PRINTING CO.

First Edition: October 2001

1 3 5 7 9 10 8 6 4 2

To Miriam too

· CONTENTS ·

"But—Your Honor,

my only crime was

dancing the chachachá."

—CUBAN SONG POPULAR AROUND 1956

"*Chachachá* Dance that swept Cuba '53, became a fad in USA later."

—*Penguin Encyclopedia of Popular Music*

THE SHORT STORIES YOU ARE ABOUT TO READ SHOULD COM-prise a reader. The three are trying to become, like the Trinity, one. This is not a demented holy writ, but the stories do form an anthology of sorts. They seem to converge because they actually share the same space at the same time: an impossibility in physics but not in fiction. Two are set in a Cuban restaurant at the end of the fifties. The third restaurant, more prestigious and more expensive, could cater to a coy and cozy clientele—richer yet poorer. The anecdotes I dote on tend to move from dining room to table to terrace in some sort of triple play: from thinker to ever to chance.

Suddenly the narration changes from the third person singular to a singular first person. It is the narrator who has the last laugh now: funny fights phoney. As with Paris (but not in France) the woman in question is a Helen too frequent, but the latter-day narrator is more of a Faust than a Paris. And not only because he thinks that this Helen, who was the spleen of Paris, would make him immoral with a kiss.

His thirst for knowledge will be quenched by the little book he carries with him everywhere. It is the book of his life which, according to Mallarmé, Hamlet reads aloud. Like all books, this one is not made with ideas but with words—a printed *fons et origo*. He won't burn it but it will be burnt eventually by a local Mephistopheles.

It would have been easy, believe me, to change the grammatical persona, and this book would be then more coherent. But I wanted to see it as a modulation. That is to say, a digression of the main mode in music: all arts aspire to the condition of popular music. Though it so happens that Cuban music is full of modulations that are contrasts of the musician's inner ear, an invisible but sonorous metronome called the *clave*—not to be confused with the *claves*, plural not singular, a leading instrument in Cuban orchestras in the past.

The magic weight that carries the *santería* ritual (all dancing, all singing, but never secular) in the first short story is not a ballet but a ballast for the female character. The background music in the second story should sound like a true bolero—a song with a faint rumor of drums because it is the lyric that matters. In the third and last story, the dance—a chachachá—carries the tune.

The women seem to come out of Greek mythology and Roman religion, but I knew and loved them. Though I never understood them: they were as complicated for me as they were for Freud. So I needed Ovid to be my Virgil, though this was life, not hell. Perhaps the two ill met by moonlight when Dante called the girl next to me by another name and said somewhat in jest: "Trivia laughs among the nymphs eternal." It gave some meaning to *The Art of Love*, addressed by Ovid to an alter ego: "Our theaters have always held dangers for pretty girls." Though he added, perhaps meaning me, "An overwritten style/Repels girls as often as not."

This trio of short stories is made out of things past. Two of them happen when the bolero was king, though it has been defined as a ballad with a dish of black bean on the side. In the third story, the protagonist jumps in character from his field of vision—to fall into history's deep abyss. The narrative is informed by that old witchcraft called memory. After all, nostalgia is a sometime thing, and in spite of his musing the narrator is always looking into a rearview mirror. All his literary reflections come from the same book found in the Lost and Found Department. And the city is always the City.

Do I have to tell you that it is called Havana?

*The Great Ekbó**

*Ekbó, a gathering of gods in *santería*.

IT WAS RAINING. THE RAIN HIT HARD THE OLD AND SICKLY columns. A man and a woman were out of reach of the rain because they were sitting in a restaurant. The man was staring at the white tablecloth as if it had patterns. The woman was wearing white, even the waiter wore white. He came to take the order in a florid flurry of pen and pad. The man thought: "I bet he's new in the job." He, who was not wearing white, asked her:

"What are you going to have?"

She looked up from the menu. The dark brown cover bore an inscription that was either a promise or a tautology: *La Maravilla—Menu.* Her eyes seemed lighter now with the limelike light that came from the squalid square in the rain. "The light that comes from nowhere, according to Da Vinci," he thought. He heard her talking to the waiter in a stage whisper blurred by the sound of the rain.

"And you, sir?"

The waiter was waiting on him now. "Ah, the waiter that came from abroad. Or is he really good-mannered?"

"Any meat?"

"No sir. Today it's Friday, sir."

"Catholics! Obsessed with rules and regulations." He thought it over for a second or two.

"No dispensation?"

"Beg your pardon?" asked the waiter.

"Bring me red snapper then, grilled. And mashed potatoes. Oh yes, and a *malta*." As he was not Irish he didn't mean whiskey but a light beverage made in Havana of burnt brown sugar and malt.

"Would you like something to drink?" he asked her.

"You bet," he thought and she said she would have a beer. "She ain't like a little girl."

While lunch was coming, he looked at her. "But she ain't just like a woman." She looked up from the plain tablecloth at him. "The defiant dame," he thought. "Why don't you look beat today? You ought to, you know."

"What are you thinking about?" she asked and her voice sounded strangely softly calmly.

"If only you knew, little girl." But he said: "Nothing. Nothing in particular."

"Were you examining me?" she asked.

"I was looking at your eyes."

"Eyes of a Christian in a Jewish face," she quoted him.

He smiled. In fact he was slightly bored.

"When do you think it'll stop?" she asked. "I mean the rain."

"I know but I don't know," he said. "In a coon's year maybe. Perhaps in a minute or two. You never know in Cuba."

He always spoke as if he had just come back from a long voyage abroad. Trip or trek. Or as if he had been brought up somewhere else. Or even as if he were a tourist passing through. As a matter of fact, he had never been out of Cuba. He was a tourist in his own country, an alien.

"Do you think we will be able to go to Anabacoa?"

"Guan-abacoa," he corrected her.

"Yes, that. Do you think we'll go there?"

"I do." Was he marrying her? "Though I don't know if there'll be anything going on just yet. It's not raining violets, you know."

"I know." She smiled.

They stopped talking by mute mutual agreement. He looked at the square beyond the wounded pillars, along the colonial street still cobbled in bluish stones made abroad, at the old green-hued moldy church beside the square with its scarce thin trees. It was a livid landscape in the rain.

Now he realized she was staring at him.

"What are you thinking about?" he said. "Remember we swore we would always tell each other the truth?"

"I would have told it to you anyway. I—"

She stopped. She bit her lips and then opened her mouth wide. She did this often. He had advised her not to: it didn't suit her.

"I was thinking." He wondered if she was thinking what she was thinking about now or earlier. "I don't know why I love you. You are exactly the opposite of the man of my dreams. But all the same I can look at you and feel I love you. Moreover, I like you."

"Thank you," he said petulantly.

"Don't!" she said, upset. It was her turn to stare at the tablecloth. Then she looked at her hands, at her fingers rather, with unpainted nails. She was tall and slim and she looked elegant in the white dress she had on, with its wide, square décolletage. Her breasts were in fact small but the curve of her chest made her appear to have a larger bust. She wore a long strass necklace and had her hair coiffed in a chignon. Her lips were full and even and pink. She had no makeup, except perhaps for some mascara that made her eyes bigger, her pupils lighter. She was really put off now and they didn't speak again before the meal was over.

"It's not stopping," she said, meaning the rain.

"Indeed it isn't," he said.

"Anything else?" said the waiter, coming back.

He looked at her, deferentially.

"No thank you," she said to the waiter.

"I just want a cup of coffee and a cigar," he said.

"Certainly, sir," said the waiter.

"And the bill."

"Yes sir!"

"Are you going to smoke?"

"Yes," he said. She loathed cigars.

"You do it on purpose."

"You know I don't. I do it because I like it."

"It's not good to do everything one likes."

"Sometimes it is."

"And sometimes it isn't."

He looked at her and smiled. She didn't smile back.

"Now I wish it hadn't happened."

He knew what she meant.

"Why?"

"What do you mean, why? Because I do. Do you think everything is so easy?"

"No," he said. "On the contrary. Life is complicated and hard. Everything is hard. Even the good life is hard."

"It's especially hard to go on living," she said. He could follow her train of thought. She was back on the old dark subject. At the beginning she had spoken of death all day, all night. All the time in fact. Then he made her forget the idea of death, but right now he thought that to die was almost an anagram of idea. Yesterday, yesterday evening to be exact, she began to talk of death again. Not that he found the topic unpleasant, but as you can see he was more interested in the literary aspects of it, and although he thought a lot about it, he didn't like to talk about it—especially with her.

"Dying is no problem," she said finally. "The cat is out of the bag," he thought. Then he looked at the street. It was raining very hard indeed now. "Just like the beginning of *Rashomon*," he was still thinking. "All we need is an old Zen sage to come out of the pillars to say: 'I don't understand, I don't understand . . .'"

"I don't understand," he said aloud.

"You don't understand that I'm not afraid to die? I'm not."

He smiled at his own slip and at her confusion afterwards.

"You look like the Mona Lisa," she said. "All smiles and no mystery."

He didn't say anything. He looked at her eyes, her mouth, her cleavage—then remembered. He liked remembering. Nothing was better than remembering. Sometimes he believed that he found things interesting only if he could remember them again. Like all this now. This moment exactly. And her. Her of course. Her eyes, her long lashes, the yellow-olive color of her eyes, the light reflected from the tablecloth on her face, her eyes, her lips, the words they revealed or hid, the quiet, caressing sound of her voice, her teeth as white as the light, her tongue, redder than her livid lips now, that at times reached the edge of her mouth and was quickly withdrawn, the running rain, the tinkling glass and the rattling cutlery drumming metallic on the crockery, a remote and barely heard incidental music coming from nowhere, Muzak making a musing, the steel blue of the cigar smoke as if coming from a fired gun, the fruity, fresh air from the terminally ill square. He was deeply moved by wondering what the exact recollection of this moment would be like tomorrow. Or even better, the day after tomorrow.

"Let's go," he said, suddenly standing up.

"But it's still raining," she protested.

"And it's going to go on raining all afternoon, evening, and night. It's three o'clock already."

She hesitated.

"Come on, the car is just outside."

They ran to the car and they got in. For a moment he felt that the rarified air pocket inside the car was going to smother him. But he settled himself in the small driver's seat and started the engine. He pulled out.

The car left behind the narrow, meandering streets of downtown Havana, the old handsome houses, some of them mercilessly, crassly demolished and turned into car parks, even the Plaza Vieja destroyed to dig under it just one more car park, the intricate ironwork of the balconies ("This is a city of baroque balconies and flat rooftops," he thought), the huge solid and stately Customs House, the *muelle de* Luz and La Machina, giant wharfs both, and La Lonja the stock exchange, then the Paula Promenade, prominent in the eighteenth century and now a faultless pastiche of itself, and the old church of Paula, its south end looking like a half-built Roman temple (or a preserved ruin) and the crumbling segments of the city wall with a tree growing on top, nature conquering the remnants of a fortress, the Tallapiedra powerhouse with its corrupt stench redolent of sulphur mines to give light to night life, and the Elevado, the elevated structure for toy trains, and Atares Castle looming in the rain, and the flyover, dull and dour, let him see the amazing crisscross of railway lines down below and the electric cables and the telephone wires up above running like a horizontal rain, a maze without a Daedalus—and at last he came onto the open road, so propitious to flight for an Icarus without wings.

"I would like to see the photos again," she said suddenly. "Now?"

"Yes."

He fished out his wallet and gave it to her. She looked at the photographs silently in the dim light of the car. She didn't say anything when she returned the wallet to him. Then, when the car left the main road to turn into a side road, she said:

"Why did you show them to me?"

"Because you asked to see them, darling," he said. "What else?"

"I don't mean now."

"I don't know." He smiled. "I suppose it was the marquis de Sade in me."

"No, it wasn't that," she said. "It was vanity. Vanity and something extra. You did it to get hold of me completely, to reassure yourself that I was yours above everything. Above desire and remorse. Remorse above all."

"And now?"

"Now we're living in sin."

"Is that all?"

"Don't you think it's enough?"

"And remorse?"

"Where you'll always find it."

"And pain?"

"Where you'll always find it."

"And pleasure?"

It was an old charade they had played many times. Now she was supposed to say where exactly pleasure was to be found—but she didn't say anything.

He insisted.

"And pleasure?"

"There's none to be had," she said with finality. "We're living in sin."

He pushed the waterproof transparent wing back a little and threw what was left of his cigar away. Then he said to her:

"Open the glove compartment, please."

She did so.

"There's a book in it. Take it out."

She did so.

"Open it at the bookmark."

She did so.

"Read what it says."

She saw it said in capital letters: "NEUROSIS AND GUILT FEELINGS." And she closed the book and put it back in the compartment and closed it. For good.

"I've no need to read anything to know how I feel."

"But," he said, "it's not supposed to tell you how you feel but why you feel how you feel."

"I know quite well why I feel the way I feel and so do you."

He laughed.

"Of course I do."

The small car bounced and then turned off to the right.

"Look," he said.

Ahead of them, to the left, a small graveyard shone all white and wild through the rain. Its sterilized symmetry belied any thoughts of maggots and foul corruption.

"Isn't it beautiful!" she said.

He slowed down.

"Why don't we get out and walk around it for a few minutes?"

He gave her a brief, half-taunting look.

"Do you know what time it is? It's four already. We're going to get there when the party's over."

"You're a bore," she grumbled.

That was the other half of her personality: the little girl. She was a monster, half woman, half child. "Borges should include her in his fantastic fauna," he thought. The infant female. Along with the catoblepas and the amphisbaena. The female child.

He saw the village and stopped the car at a fork in the road.

"Could you tell me where the baseball ground is, please?" he asked a group of people and two or three of them described the way in a way that he knew he would get lost. At the next crossing he asked a policeman, who showed him the road.

"Aren't people obliging here?" she said.

"Serf-service. Man on foot and man on a horse. Nowadays the car is the horse."

"Why are you so arrogant?"

"Me?"

"Yes, you!"

"I don't think I am really. It's just what people think but I have the courage to say it."

"It's the only kind of courage you have . . ."

"Perhaps."

"Never perhaps. You know yourself . . ."

"All right, I do! I warned you from the beginning, though."

She turned around and looked at him closely.

"I don't know how I can love such a coward!" she said.

They had arrived.

They ran through the rain to the building. At first he thought there wasn't going to be anything on because he couldn't hear anything but the rain and—among some buses and a few old cars—saw nothing but a bunch of boys dressed as baseball players. But when he went in he felt as if he had penetrated all of a sudden a magic domain: there were a hundred or two hundred blacks dressed in white from head to toe: white shirts and white trousers and white socks and white shoes and their heads covered with white caps which made them look *"Just like a convention of colored cooks,"* he thought, and the women were also dressed in white and there were a few white-skinned women among them and they were all dancing in a ring to the rhythm of the drums and in the middle a huge black man who was already old but still powerful and wore dark glasses so that only his white teeth could be seen perhaps as another part of the ritual dress and who thumped on the floor with a long wooden staff that had a carved black's head made of wood with human hairs for a handle and this old black man with the dark glasses sang and the others answered as he shouted *olofi* and paused while the holy word resounded against the walls and the rain and he shouted *olofi* again and then sang *tendundu kipungule* and waited as the chorus repeated *olofi olofi olofi* and in that atmosphere so strange and turbulent yet cool and damply lit the black master of ceremonies sang again *nani masongo silanbasa* and the chorus repeated *nani masongo silanbasa* and again his slightly guttural and hoarse voice sang out *sese maddie silanbaka* and the chorus repeated *sese maddie silanbaka* and again

She came up close to him and whispered in his ear:

"Divine!"

"Damned theater slang!" he thought. But he smiled because he felt her breath on the back of his neck and her chin resting on his shoulder.

the black man sang *olofi* and the chorus answered *olofi* and he said *tendundu kipungule* and the chorus repeated *tendundu kipungule* all the time keeping the rhythm with their feet and going endlessly round in a circle in a close group knowing they were singing to the dead and praying that the dead might rest in eternal peace and that those still alive might be comforted and waiting for their leader to say *olofi* again so that they could say *olofi* and begin again with the invocation *sese maddie* and then *olofi*.

"*Olofi* is God in their language," he explained to her.

"What does the rest of it mean?"

"For me to explain what *Olofi* means is bad enough," he thought. Then:

"They're hymns to the dead," he said. "They sing to the dead so that they may rest in peace forever."

Her eyes shone with curiosity and excitement. She clutched his arm. The dance went on round and round, tirelessly. Young and old alike were frantically dancing. One small black man wore a white shirt completely covered with white buttons in front.

"Look!" she said into his ear. "He's got *hundreds* of buttons on his shirt!"

"Hush!" he said, because the man had looked up.

silanbaka bica dioko bica ndiambe and the old black man humped his staff rhythmically against the floor and great drops of sweat ran down his arms and face and made faintly dark patches on the immaculate whiteness of his shirt and the chorus said after him again *bica dioko bica*

ndiambe and close to the man in the middle other ring-
leaders were dancing and repeating the chorus's response
and when the black man in the dark glasses murmured take
it! one of them chanted *olofi sese maddie sese maddie* and
the chorus repeated *sese maddie sese maddie* while the
black man in the dark glasses thumped his staff against the
floor vigorously as he wiped away the sweat with a hand-
kerchief that was of the purest white linen—

"Why do they dress in white?" she asked.

"They are worshipping Obbatala, the goddess of the
pure and unblemished."

"Then I can't worship Obbatala," she said perhaps as a
joke.

But he looked at her reproachfully and said:

"Don't talk nonsense."

"It's true."

She looked at him and then turned her attention to the
old black man and said, ridding what she had said before of
all insinuation:

"Besides, it wouldn't suit me. I'm much too pale for
white."

"But you are wearing white!"

"It's not pure white."

and at his side another black swayed in time to the music and something indeterminate which went against the rhythm and interrupted it with his fingers on his eyes and he opened his eyes extremely wide and pointed to them again and emphasized the sensual and somewhat disjointed and mechanical movements of his body which nevertheless seemed possessed by an unseen power and now the chanting reverberated against the wall *olofi olofi sese maddie sese maddie* and invaded the whole building and reached two black boys in baseball caps who listened and looked on as if unwilling to embrace something that was theirs and reached the other spectators and drowned the noise of the beer bottles and the glasses in the bar at the back and flowed down the steps of the stands and danced among the puddles in the baseball field and went on over the sodden outer fields and through the rain reached the aloof and distant palm trees and went on further into the wild country and seemed to want to surmount the far-off hills and climb them and crown their summits and go on higher still *olofi olofi bica dioko bica dioko ndiambe bica ndiambe ndiambe y olofi y olofi y olofi* but again *sese maddie* but again *sese maddie* but again *sese* but again *sese*

"That man's being sent," he said, pointing to the mulatto who had his fingers in his huge popping black eyes.

"Is he really?" she asked.

"Of course he is. It's only the hypnotic effect of the drums, but they don't seem to realize it."

"Would I be affected by it, do you think?"

But before telling her that she would, that she could be intoxicated by that rhythm, he became afraid that she would rush off and dance with them so he said:

"I don't think so. It's only for the benighted. Not for people like you who have read Ibsen and Chekhov and know Tennessee Williams off by heart. We're the heathen in this temple."

She felt slightly flattered but also flustered. Now she said:

"They don't seem benighted to me. Primitive, I agree, but not benighted. They believe. They believe in something neither you nor I can believe in and they are guided by their belief and live and die according to its rules and afterwards they sing songs to their dead. I think it's wonderful!"

"Superstition, girl, superstition," he said pedantically.

"It's something barbaric and remote and alien, as faraway as Africa, where it comes from. I prefer Roman Catholicism with all its sham."

"That's remote and alien too," she said.

"Yes, but there's the Bible and Saint Augustine and Saint Thomas and Saint Teresa and Saint John of the Cross and Bach's music . . ."

"Bach was a Protestant, wasn't he?"

"A Protestant is only a Catholic who can't sleep at night."

He felt good now because he felt he was witty and capable of talking above the drums and the chanting and the dancing, and because he has overcome the fear he had felt when he came in.

and *sese* but again *sese* and *olofi* and *olofi sese olofi maddie olofi maddie maddie olofi bica dioko bica ndiambe olofi olofi silanbaka bica dioko olofi olofi sese maddie maddie olofi sese sese* and *olofi* and *olofi* and *olofi*

The music and the singing and the dancing suddenly stopped as they witnessed how two or three blacks grabbed the mulatto with the frenzied eyes by the arms and prevented him from knocking his head against one of the pillars.

"He's gone," he said.

"You mean he's been sent?"

"Yes."

They all gathered round the man in a trance and carried him to the end of the hall. He lit two cigarettes and offered one to her. When he had finished his cigarette he went over to the wall and threw the stub out on the damp field. It was then that he saw the black woman coming up to them.

"If you'll allow me, sir," she said.

"Of course," the man said, without knowing what it was he had to allow.

The old black woman said nothing. She could have been sixty or seventy. "But you never know with black people," he thought. Her face was small and fine-boned, her skin was intricately wrinkled and glistened about the eyes and mouth, but was taut over the prominent cheekbones and pointed chin. Her eyes were keen and merry and wise.

"If you'll excuse me, sir," she said again.

"What is it?" he said but thought: "I'm sure she wants some money off me."

"I should like to speak to the young lady," she said. He thought: "So she thinks she can touch her more easily. She's right, you know."

"But of course!" he said, standing back a little and wondering uneasily what the old black woman really wanted.

He saw the girl listening carefully at first and then lowering her earnest gaze from the old black woman's face to the ground. When they had finished talking, he came up again.

"Thank you very much, sir," the old woman said.

He didn't know whether to offer her his hand or bow slightly or smile. He chose to say:

"Not at all. I must thank *you*. By all means."

He looked at the girl and noticed that something had changed.

"Let's go," she said.

"Why? It's not over yet. It goes on till six. They must go on singing till sunset."

"Let's go," she said again.

"What's going on?"

"*Please*, let's go."

"All right, all right! Let's go by all means. But first tell me what's going on here. What's happened? What was that old nigger on to you about?"

She looked at him dourly.

"That old nigger, as you put it, is a great woman. She has

lived a lot and knows a lot and if you really want to know she has just taught me something."

"Really?"

"Really."

"And may I know what the pedagogue had to say?"

"Nothing!"

She moved away toward the door, finding her way with her graceful courtesy through the groups of faithful. He caught her up at the door.

"Wait a minute!" he said. "I did bring you here."

She said nothing and let him take her arm as far as the car. As he was unlocking it, a boy came up to him and said:

"Hey, mister, can you settle an argument? What sort of car's that? German?"

"No, it's English."

"It's not a Renault, is it?"

"No, it's an MG."

"Just like I said," the boy said with a satisfied smile and rejoined his friends.

"Always the same thing," he thought. "Never say thank you. And they're the ones who breed most!"

He saw it had stopped raining and the air was fresh and

he drove carefully until he found the road back to the highway. She hadn't broken her silence and when he looked into the driving mirror he saw that she was crying.

"I'm going to stop and put the roof down," he said.

He pulled over to the side of the road and saw that he had stopped close to the little graveyard. As he lowered the roof and fastened it down behind her he wanted to kiss the nape of her neck—but he felt as if he was being repulsed now as strongly as he had been welcomed on other occasions.

"Were you crying?" he asked her.

She lifted up her face and showed him her eyes without looking at him. They were dry, but very bright and slightly red at the rim.

"I never cry, darling. Except on stage."

He was hurt but said nothing.

"Where are we going?" he said.

"Home," she said. "*My* home."

"You're quite sure?"

"Surer than you might think," she said. Then she opened the glove compartment, took the book out, and turned toward him.

"Here you are," she said shortly.

When he looked he saw she was handing him the two photos—the one of the smiling, solemn-eyed woman and the one of the little boy, taken in a studio, with huge, solemn eyes and no smile on his lips—and realized that he was taking them automatically.

"I'd rather you kept them."

A Woman Saved from Drowning

IT WAS RAINING AGAIN. THE RAIN HIT HARD AT THE OLD sickly columns across the street. A man and a woman were out of reach of the rain because they were sitting in a restaurant, but the windowpanes were made opaque by rain and steam. The dining room was done all in white: white walls, white tables, white waiters. Except for them the restaurant was empty, but music was being played at full tilt, in invisible waves, a surf of sound. Now they were broadcasting "Pecado," a bolero taken perhaps too fast. The woman was looking at the plain white tablecloth as if it had a pattern. Suddenly the man said:

"Don't look now but they're playing our song."

"What did you say?"

He pointed at the ceiling.

"*Pecado*, the song of sin."

"You and your silly play on words."

Before he could say anything a waiter came to them. He was ready to take the order with a florid flurry of pen and pad. He looked unctuous but slightly sinister too—perhaps because he needed a shave.

"What are you going to have?"

"You must be new in the job."

"I beg your pardon?"

"You heard me."

"As a matter of fact I'm not."

"Then you must know that the menu comes first, then the order."

"Ah yes. Just a minute."

The waiter went to a nearby stand to take out two menus and came back to the couple. He handed one menu to the man.

"Sir?"

"In my country women come first."

The waiter gave the woman her menu. She took it, but looked at the man, then she buried her head in the menu. On the cover it said *La Maravilla*—the name of the restaurant. She looked up from the menu. Her eyes seemed lighter, more opal than olive-yellow in the limelike light that came from the windows. He looked at her and said to himself: "The light that comes from nowhere, according to Leonardo."

"What are you going to have?" he said aloud.

She didn't answer but talked to the waiter instead—in a stage whisper he was not able to decipher.

"And you, sir?"

"Any meat?"

"Today is Friday, sir."

"Shit! Catholics! Always obsessed with rules and regulations."

"No dispensation then?"

"I beg your pardon?"

"Number two."

"Never mind. Bring me some lamb chops."

"Lamb is off."

"What did you say?"

"Lamb is off season."

"Do they hunt electric sheep in here?"

"What I meant to say is that we don't have any lamb today."

"You meant it but you didn't say it."

"I beg your pardon, sir."

"Number three."

"What do you have?"

"Only fish. It's *Friday*, sir."

"You already said that," he said and took a look at the menu.

"I'll have red snapper—"

"I'm sorry, sir, but we don't do the snapper."

"It's off season," he said sarcastically.

"No, it isn't, but they didn't have any left at the fish market today."

"What *do* you have, then?"

"Like fish? We don't have red snapper but we have gray mullet, grouper—"

"That's a nice grouping."

"—tuna or tunny, bonito, marlin or swordfish—"

"Bravo!" he said, clapping once. "That's white of you."

But the waiter was not disturbed by the man's remark.

"What are you having, sir?"

"Swordfish. Grilled."

"Are you sure you don't want it fried? Fried it's very tasty, sir."

"I want my swordfish grilled, if you don't mind. I'm sure you won't mind."

"No, sir. I don't mind. What do you want with it?"

"What do you mean?"

"Any tubercle?"

"You mean *tuber*, the potato is a tuber."

"How do you want your potato?"

"Mash, mash. Can't you see I'm a masher? Ask the lady if you don't believe me."

"Is that all, sir?"

"Yes, that is all."

When the waiter went away, she said:

"Carry on like that and he'll spit in your soup."

"But I didn't order any soup."

The woman turned to the tablecloth for comfort. After a while she looked up at him.

"The defiant dame. Why don't you look beat today? You should, you know."

Now she speaks strangely softly calmly:

"What are you thinking about?"

"If only you knew, little girl," he thinks. "Nothing. Nothing in particular."

"Were you examining me?"

"I was looking at your eyes."

She quoted: "Eyes of a Christian in a Jewish face. Is that it?"

He smiled but he was in fact slightly bored. He exclaimed wanly, "That's my girl."

She looked at the window, then at the man.

"When do you think it will stop? I mean the rain."

"I know but I don't know."

"Is that one of your riddles?"

"In a coon's year maybe. Perhaps in a minute or two. You never know in Cuba. Bear in mind she is the pearl of the Antilles."

"Do you think we will be able to go today after all?"

"It's not raining violets, you know."

She smiled.

"It's raining cats and dogs."

"That's a stupid saying, unworthy of you."

Both stopped talking by mutual consent. But you could see he was vexed.

"When is that luncheon coming? It's impossible to have a decent meal in this country."

"You speak like a tourist."

"But I'm not a tourist. I am an alien. I'm the man who fell from the sky and into a hole."

Meanwhile, subdued but ever present, the Muzak was

playing now "Perfidia," a sentimental bolero sung in Spanish by Nat King Cole. The song was becoming pertinent to the scene as it pleaded to a woman to talk to God himself about a man's predicament of unrequited love.

"I'll vouch for that," said the woman and fell silent. Then the two of them were not talking to each other anymore. The song vanished but the sentiment lingered on as a sound track for the livid landscape in the rain. He came back from the sight to the sound to think: "It's a fucking Utrillo." Then he noticed the woman staring at him.

"What are you thinking about now?"

"Actually—" she started evasively.

"We swore we would always tell the truth to each other, remember?"

"You don't have to tell me. I would have told you anyway. I—" She stopped to bite her lips.

"I was thinking—" She stopped again but didn't bite her lips anymore. "I don't know why I love you."

"Here she goes again."

"You are exactly the opposite of the man of my dreams. But all the same I like you." Finally she said, "There."

But the man answered petulantly:

"Thank you." Then: "I like you too."

"Please don't!"

She turned her attention to the tablecloth, then she looked at her hands—at her lovely fingers, rather. "Dainty, almost perfect hands," he thought, and then took a good look at her. She was tall and slim and she looked elegant in her white dress with the square décolletage. Her breasts were small and placed high on her chest and her lips were full and even and pink. She was not wearing any makeup except for some mascara.

The meal arrived to rescue her from his greedy gaze. She was having a Cuban meal: black beans, white rice, fried green plantains, and an avocado salad. The color of it all— black, green and yellow—contrasted with the whiteness of the restaurant and the table and the gray slab of a fish the man was eating. All the while they did not speak to each other.

The woman diverted her gaze from the remnants of the lunch to look at the windows all steamed up with the vapor condensed on the panes. Behind them the rain didn't let up.

"It's not really stopping, you know."

"Indeed it isn't."

Now the waiter came back again.

"Anything else?"

"No, thank you kindly."

"I want a cup of coffee and, yes, an *Ecce homo*."

The waiter was dumb.

"What?"

"An H. Upmann, a cigar."

"Very good, sir."

"And the check."

"Yes sir!"

After the waiter went back inside, she said to him, looking uncomfortably:

"Are you going to smoke?"

"You bet."

"You do it on purpose. You know I loathe cigars."

"I like them a lot."

"It's not good to do everything one likes."

"Sometimes it is."

"And sometimes it isn't. You should know."

He smiled but it was not a winsome smile. She did not smile back. She looked deadly serious.

"I wish it hadn't happened."

"I know what you mean, but why do you mean it?"

"What do you mean, why?"

GUILLERMO CABRERA INFANTE

"Dear, it takes two to tango or to do the mambo. Or whatever couples do."

"You're being flippant."

"Of course I am."

"Do you think that everything is so easy?"

"On the contrary. Life's not easy. Life is complicated and hard. Even the good life is hard."

"Dying is not hard."

"You are right. Dying is not hard, what is hard is comedy."

"Why do you have to say that?"

"I didn't say it first. Who said it first was one of your ancestors, Kean the tragedian."

As a full stop he smiled wanly like an updated Cheshire cat.

"You look like the Mona Lisa, all smiles and no mystery."

The man stopped smiling to look out the window. "Not Utrillo but Pizarro. Bizarre!" Now he looked at the reflection of his face and drew an invisible mustache with his finger.

The couple were sitting at an empty table. It had been recently emptied except for the salt and pepper shakers and an ashtray. The man smoked a big black cigar. From somewhere the Muzak was piping "Frenesí," a frenzied bolero. The man tried to recover his lost ground.

"I wish I were twins."

"You a twin? Don't make me laugh."

"Not me. I'm nonpareil. I mean the music. It's a jazz bolero, whose title is 'I Wish I Were Twins.'"

"Again?"

"I wish I were twins again," he said mockingly. He smoked his cigar contentedly; the woman was still staring at him.

"You know what?"

"What?"

"You're beginning to sound like a DJ."

"Touché rather than touched."

"To think that my mother predicted I would marry a small dark man who smoked cigars!"

"Your mother's a *soot*sayer. All she got right was the cigar bit. For I'm not small but short and definitely not the marrying kind."

She was really put off and she didn't speak. Only the sound of cutlery on china mixing with other voices in the room and above and underneath, as a matter of fact the whole dining room, flooded by the melody from the Muzak. Later, when lunch was finished and the waiter had removed the utensils and come back again to sweep the table with a small broom and a tiny silver spade and after he rolled up the cloth to replace it with a fresh tablecloth rolled out very daintily, the man took out a pen and started drawing on the spotless surface what looked like a modern house designed by a mediocre follower of Le Corbusier in the tropics.

"Don't get too complicated, will you?" he said without looking at her. "When a woman gets complicated, she's unhappy, and when a woman is unhappy, she cries and spoils her makeup."

"I'm not wearing any makeup."

"I know."

He kept on drawing, unconcerned. Now the drawing looked like some sort of blueprint.

"Anything else?" said the waiter, coming back once more. He frowned at the man who was still drawing on the otherwise spotless tablecloth.

"No thank you," she said to the waiter.

"And the bill."

"Yes sir!"

"What's that?" she asked, paying closer attention to the man's laborious drawing. After a second he looked up at her. Muzak was now an incidental music coming from nowhere—just like the movies. The smoke of the cigar, or half of it, steel blue as if coming from a smoking gun in the hand of the murderer, his victim not yet on the floor but falling—falling down as all dead bodies fall. The fruity fresh air from the terminally ill square reached him through the shroud of rain, Havana in the rain, the world in the rain. Boring rain, boring place, boring world.

"What is that?"

"What is what?"

"What you've designed."

"*Drawn,*" he corrected her. "What I've drawn. Drawn but not drowned."

"It looks like a house." Obviously she was trying to mend fences.

"It is a house, dear. It's a dull house or a house for a doll."

"I don't see the doll."

"That's because there is no doll."

He ceased talking, but the rain and the Muzak went all around. She was visibly bored, even stopped a yawn with her hand.

"Shall we go?"

He would not stop his drawing. "Can't you see it's still raining?"

"And it will go on raining all afternoon, evening, and night."

She stood up. He shouted at her from his drawing:

"Sit *down! Please.*"

He stopped drawing to look at her.

"Please sit down and listen. Listen carefully, little girl."

She sat again. The man stopped drawing for good and put his pen into his jacket inside pocket. He smiled as she stifled another yawn. "The second," the man thought.

"Shall we go?"

"Can't you see? It's still raining. There's only cant and rain."

She stood up.

"Sit down!" he shouted again and then hissed: "*Please. Pretty please.*"

She sat down.

"And listen. Listen carefully."

She didn't yawn again.

"As you must know, El Presidente, the hotel, has always been favored by tourists. Perhaps because it's an Edwardian building, red bricks, brown stone, and all. Anyway, not many years ago an American couple stayed at the hotel."

He placed the salt and the pepper closer to each other and then he put down his cigar butt in the ashtray.

"Now they were leaving the hotel to catch the plane back to New York, the big apple of her eyes. But they were late. Or rather, she was. She was very impatient to go out the front door, but the doorman advised her very firmly not to leave the hotel. Not just yet. Though the rain had stopped, the street was flooded. 'But I have to leave!' said the woman. 'We must!' Those were her famous last words."

He stopped for an effect.

"Both husband and wife started to wade the flooded street. The woman discovered that the floodwater was only knee-deep. They waded on, the woman bringing up the rear. Suddenly—she disappeared."

The woman, our woman, sat on the edge of her chair.

"What do you mean, disappeared?"

"She disappeared. For good." The man, her man, snapped his fingers. "Just like that."

"I can't believe it!"

"Believe it. The eager woman stepped into a lidless manhole underwater and disappeared through. The body was never found. She simply went down the manhole. A tidal wave had blown its cover—and down she went. Not to hell but to sea and surf. Remember the shore is only two blocks away from El Presidente—and three blocks from this cozy corner." As an end to his story he pushed the white salt shaker flat on the table and down to the floor. She stared at the fallen salt shaker disappearing.

"Did she truly disappear?"

"Vanished. Forever. Like Lot's wife. Not petrified in salt but into salt water anyway."

"What was it? A dream? It is a dream."

"No, it's not a dream."

"W-what was it, then? One of your sick drawings?"

"It is not an invention of mine, believe me."

"An allegory, then."

"It was in all the papers at the time. It even made the front page of *The New York Times*. It is of course *hubris*."

"What?"

"*Hubris*. It's Greek for arrogance, pride become fate."

"It suits you to a T."

He smiled. "But it's the woman who disappeared, not the man."

"We're not man and wife."

"Not yet. But we will be. Eventually."

He smiled again.

"Smiling. That's your Hebrew."

"Hubris."

"Hebrew, *hubris*—who cares?"

She threw her napkin on the table like a fighter a towel on the canvas, in the ring. End of fight. The napkin almost covered the drawing.

"I'm leaving."

"Are you? All by yourself?"

"All by myself and all alone."

"The street is still flooded."

"I don't care. I'm doing my disappearing act right now, right here."

She stood up finally. She grabbed her handbag. It was white. She was leaving now, pushing forward one of the glass doors and going into the terrace and out of the restaurant—to step into a mirror. For a moment her image was reflected on the pane as if she was trespassing into a looking glass. Still smiling, the man looked at her double and thought: "Parallax." On the pane, in the pain. From his seat and at the floating body in the glass surface, he shouted in a whisper:

"Don't step into a manhole."

She didn't hear or pretended that she didn't. She crossed the wet terrace and went down the three steps onto the sidewalk—but she stopped before stepping down. The water was still flooding the street and overflowing the sidewalk. She was about to turn back, to look back at least—as if asking for help with her eyes. But she didn't. She stood motionless for a second, like a momentary statue of salt. But then she steeped one foot gingerly in the water, murky and grim, and she saw it reached her instep. Then she tried again with her right foot. The water didn't reach the whole of her shoe. It was dark but shallow. Finally she stepped decidedly onto the sidewalk—to walk down the street.

The nearby avenue, called Calle Linea, the street straight like a line, looked even more flooded. She didn't wear a raincoat or have an umbrella because they were useless: when it rains in Havana, it rains. On the tarmac, in the dark, in the night, darker than the asphalt, she saw a manhole. But it had kept its cover by making a pothole around it, ordinary and yet not looming. Then, chance playing a winning hand with fate, she saw a car coming: an obvious taxi even in a city where taxis are not obvious. She hailed the providential taxi, and when it stopped by the curb, she opened a drenched door: opaque but the sheet of water reflecting the streetlights above—which shone like chaste stars. She got in, slammed the door to talk softly to the driver, and the taxi sped ahead in the relentless rain, two tires bumping in and out of the manhole.

Guilty of Dancing the Chachachá

SHE LOOKED AT ME WITH OPAL EYES—OPAL WHEN THE STONE
is the color of oil or urine. She looked at me while she was
eating. She was smiling now. Her table manners were
almost perfect. (Or perfect for the American custom of
switching the fork from one hand to the other.) To anyone
like myself who cares for the small perfections in everyday
life (the well-trimmed lawn, socks without clocks, an
unjeweled hand), it was a pleasure to watch her eating, wit-
nessing her table manners—with her bed manners in
mind.

We had ordered the same meal. A soup of black beans, a
creole *picadillo* (*picadillo* not peccadillo: minced meat not a
minor sin), and white rice, plus fried green plantains. On
this occasion we were both drinking beer: very cold, the tall
glasses sweating. The food was on the table, near the nap-
kins. There was also on the table an avocado pineapple

salad, two glasses of icewater, and a bread basket. But that was not all. Between us there was on one side a stainless steel cruet and an épergne with salt and pepper, and on the other side a heavy cut-glass ashtray and a sugar bowl and a pottery vase containing two large decaying *girasoles*, the sunflower living like us by night. The tablecloth was spotlessly white. She was looking at me, still smiling, and I returned her gaze across the bric-à-brac but not the smile. Secretly I tried to play a guessing game, trying to guess her thoughts in silence, furtively, futilely ignoring what was going on at the next table, engrossed as I was in my mute or moot point.

what are you thinking about
about you
about me and what about me
about both of us together
where in a lifeboat or in a spaceship or in bed
no please dont joke about it please about us and about
you and about being together always and truly
truly
yes truly yes together

why dont we get married

till the bed us do part

no never ever

speak now or forever hold your peace

I gave up playing. But I was not talking. How could anyone expect me to talk through that junkyard of a table? It's a grim gewgaw, that's what it is. Better to take a look around the room. What about the next table? Forget the next table. But the big boys at the next table had finally tired of watching (particularly the one who was trying to look like a vicarious Valentino) and were tapping on the table (a bongo player's apprentice, blond, with acne) and spitting on the floor (the leading man of the trio) and all of them swigging beer. Then they were footing the bill and they were leaving. Good riddance. But as they left, the one who used the floor as a spittoon scratched himself between the legs, loose pants over the scrotum, scratching as he went out. One by one all of them scratched themselves, monkeys at my back: all scratching, all swaggering. The cream of Cuban youth, spitting, beating imaginary drums, scratching their crotch, their *güebos*. Each one having a ball. They were wearing *verde-olivo* fatigues and I can hardly imagine why they have been served beer. It is prohibited to drink in uniform—or is it? Anyway, prohibition is in the hand of the beer holder. So out they went. Not without looking once more at our table with the eyes of silent actors: Valentino and Novarro and Gilbert all in the same movie—*The Three Horsemen of the Anaphrodisiac.*

I looked at her and asked her (daring that I am) what was she thinking while I was sinking.

"How late it is."

A sigh of relief: mine.

"There's plenty of time."

"What time is it, please?"

"Early."

"Please tell me what the time is or I'll be late."

"Nine. I just heard the cannon blast."

"It's more than nine, isn't it?"

I looked at my watch but I read the date not the time.

"Finish your meal. You have plenty of time."

"I've finished already."

She stood up with her bag in her hand. I looked at her as though I had just seen her for the first time. I always saw her as though for the first time. The first time I saw her naked, the first time I slept with her. I was pleased with the simple way she dressed and with her elegant slim figure.

I should marry her.

"Are you going just like that?"

"Yes."

She stooped to kiss me.

"Is this your dessert?"

She laughed. Her laugh was sweet and soft.

"Will you wait for me here?"

"Yes of course. Now I'll have my dessert and a cup of coffee. Why don't you have some coffee now?"

"When I get back."

"Good. In the meantime I'll have a cigar and read a bit and hope that the time won't be really mean."

"See you later, darling."

She looked like Kay Kendall, my favorite actress: she is always the reluctant bride.

"Come back when you're through."

My last sentence was tantamount to her Will you wait for me here? With such tautologies one conducts conversation—and life as well. I saw her going out into the dark night: tall and thin and dressed in white, with her swift walk, gracefully briskly directly going to the theater with a sense of duty that always moved me. At the time, she was appearing in two different small parts (the ingenious device of an imported Argentine stage director straight out of the Berliner Ensemble: actually a copycat of Helene Weigel, the Widow in Red) in a mediocre opus by Bertolt Brecht after Maximus Gorky, that was apparently not meant to be merely seen or admired but rather venerated as though it was a mystery play—and who is going to tell me it is not religious drama? Certainly not Brecht. He's dead.

But it was not Brecht I wanted to talk about. For I indeed wax openly about Bertolt, that odious Brechtian who said that to be impartial in art is to side with the faction in power—he of all people. It is hardly of this Shakespeare of the trade unions that I want to speak, but of *her*. She who had to make those feeble exercises in propaganda as if she were Cordelia and Miss Julie in one single role, wan waxworks. She rebelled only over a minor point of personal ethics. After the curtain fell, she did not join in the *Internationale* with the rest of the cast as a choir. That old anthem preserved in mothballs like the clapping actors aping or echoing the applause of their audience, like the *pioneritos*, the little pioneers, presenting bouquets of roses both to actresses and actors (and in Cuba, my God!, where to give flowers to a man has always been to imply that he is a queen without a throne but with a scepter, oh so sodomite), like the whole atmosphere of the theater, with the captive audience singing revolutionary songs and rocking and rolling in a Slavonic tidal wave, everybody joining hands and swaying left, center, and left, like Mao-thinking reeds. All of it, the whole surf scene imported from the Soviet Union, from China, maybe even from Albania, for the play is a carbon copy of Brecht's *Modellbuch*, which means precisely an annotated libretto plus a film of the original performance in East Berlin sent out to Havana to program our mise-en-scène of *Die Madre*, sometimes also titled *La Mütter*. She declined, atta girl!, to sing the line, *"ni César ni burgués ni Dios habrá."* And when the assistant director asked her why, she replied simply, with a smile, *"Porque creo en Dios."* Because she believed in God, she said. Which was after all not an excuse but the truth. That's why she was spared the purge. Or was it the purgative? The political castor oil originated in the tropics or atropine from the deadly nightshade to anesthetize the body politics.

I was left alone in the restaurant, waiting. Smoking, taking sips of coffee, first warm as the evening but then tepid: cool, finally cold, until, without noticing, I used the

GUILLERMO CABRERA INFANTE

cup as an ashtray and when I came to drink again I found the dead taste in my brew, the anti-taste of destruction. I remembered I had sipped ashes before but *impavidum ferient ruinae.*

I opened my book. I always carry a book with me: armpit knowledge. But it is actually like a priest with his breviary. Only any book is my breviary: my missal for the masses. I had often thought that had I not been born in Cuba, had I been educated in the humanities, had *el maestro* Varona died before changing the *humanidades* into a common *bachillerato,* the tepid baccalaureate, thirty years earlier, I should have been able to inscribe the moment, any moment, this very moment with some *jeux de mots* in Greek, though I'm a Latin from Havana and I call my pains *Dolores.* Greeks don't bring me any gifts of tongues. In any case, a master typographer told me that in Cuba there was never a single set of matrices in Greek. Not a single fount, not a single fons, not a single *foné*—soon not a single voice either. And I left resting in peace the memory of *el buen* Varona, philosopher of the Caribbees, the insulated educator, *magister,* to try to read. And could not.

Don't be alarmed. This often happens to me: reading a

line twenty, thirty times and even reading it over once again aloud—understanding nothing. Because the meaning is lost beyond cloudy, or rather foggy distractions, reading only words, designs full of sound and sans serif signifying nothing. It was *The Unquiet Grave* now. A book which quietly ungraved itself, popping out of treatises of Roman law and novels by forgotten French authors of the last century and manuals of canon law bound in black. It happened in an old antique shop that now sold largely secondhand books bought wholesale from those who are fleeing the country. It surprised me to find such a modern binding with its pretentious paperback look and the bold blurb by Hemingway ("It's a book, which, no matter how many readers it will ever have, will never have enough") that I decided to buy it (a fatal folly) for ten Cuban centavos! Thus I became another of the many useless readers who go down unquietly to an early grave trying to attain the limits of the impossible (all in all we will never make enough), while falling prey to the timeless spell of the book.

The mistake which is commonly made about neurotics is to suppose that they are interesting.

I was sitting outside on the terrace to get away from the

air conditioning, once the cold of the rich after Sartre, now nationalized. I sensed the approach of the invading forces of a summer cold through each antrum. It would at once occupy all my sinuses and then they will attack both pharynx and rhyming larynx, taking bronchial tubes and pneumatic lungs in a blitzkrieg of infection, smothering me in their blitzfieber. *Achtung! Gesundheit!*

I glanced over the empty tables (almost empty, more than empty: there was a solitary couple at the back) and along the surrounding garden hedge that adorns the terrace while discreetly preventing the customers from being seen by pedestrians crossing. I looked across the shrubs of privet and over the parapet, and then I could see into the street beyond, letting my myopic glance pass further, into the square, the plaza filled with ficus. Does that singular tree have a plural? Romantic Cubans called them *jagüeyes*, Cuban classicists *laureles*. The plaza, called *parque* with a hyperbole, with its fountain forever empty watched over by a dethroned Neptune, Poseidon exiled from the waters, who was nevertheless prominent on another site in Old Havana, at another time and in a forgotten Cuban novel. At the place there was an evening colonnade on either side of the gardens vaguely reminiscent of the grove of Academe. But instead of Plato and his rent boys, there are now Alexander nighttime bands and Epicurean partisans (also called *sans parti*), *milicianos*, militias in wonderland, more adepts of Democritus than of democracy. Before, there had been turbulent terrorists and still earlier in the suave or ardent island by night, in these "invisible gardens" infested with the barbaric soldiers of Batista, and before that there were pre-Socratic constitutionalists listing as they passed by: *"Nacer aquí es una fiesta innombrable."* To be born here is an unnamable feast, and by here they meant the park, Havana, the island. There were now Sophist parking attendants always on the lookout for a place, Pythagorean *billeteros* selling lottery tickets to Lot without his wife and with a pi in the sky, sleepy Cynics walking dogs that leave behind turds as if cast on the stone edge. And that character who most resembles Aristotle among us: the Peripatetic taxi driver from the stand nearby chatting with a philosopher friend (Plotinus at the steering wheel) on all possible subjects between fares. *It is not interesting to be always unhappy.*

I remembered how once I had written a short story of

longing and belonging set in this restaurant-café, bodega bar for the *nueva clase* or maybe one or two rich left behind and for a few *café-concert* conspirators. And I thought about the gulf, not about the stream but about the abyss that opens up between life and literature, which is a void between too distinct realities. *A mistake/ It is not happy, engrossed with oneself. Malignant.* It was then not now that my friend Benigno Nieto said to me in his drawling voice over drinks: "Chico, the terrible thing is that no sooner do we adjust ourselves to the bourgeoisie, to having a place in the sun, as they say, than the bourgeoisie suddenly disappears and we have to start all over again." *Maligno Nieto,* did I ever tell you?, that's what Mao calls the Great Leap Forward. *Ungrateful, and never quite in touch with reality.* Poor Benigno! Where have you gone with your seven velars that were actually a case of lambdacism and your hilarious story about a mounted mare that I published, which was instantly labeled pornographic by the scandalized *Kulturalny Apparat* headed by two ladies from the *bobería* wearing glasses: "I am sick and tired of the police of sex pushing me around and culture managers and Marxist dames in eyeglasses." What about your theory that in order to be a writer one must forever abandon (insular) life? Joyce, Aímé Cesáire—even Carpentier, born in Switzerland. Have you forgotten Sappho?, I asked—or did I think I asked? We'll never know. By then a blonde interrupted my Sapphic variations and I forgot Benigno's literary isles to concentrate on coasting around this floating island of flesh.

No man is an island—maybe. But women are an archipelago. Of medium height, broad in the hips, wearing the Cuban version of the chemise: tight at the waist and tailored like a glove over bust and buttocks. I describe her so because she exhibited such anatomical candor in walking (in sandals) with a sensuality that nobody found surprising. She was pushing the glass doors by first putting one hip forward between the transparent swinging sheets as though the ministry of sex were waiting inside and not the familiar dining room where the all too evident common people turned around to look at her, all at once, in the very moment that she went up the three little steps—tip, tap, toe—onto the terrace, with some coyness and with more customary but affected difficulty, little of which came now naturally to her through the tightness of the silk. Shanghai (pronounced "Changai") was not only porno pictures and not from Peking opera buffa in the Chinese *barrio*, but perhaps the producers of this Cuban *cheong-sam* sheltered in there.

Then I remembered an item that I had read in the *Grave*, but hardly an epitaph. It was at the beginning of the book and I began to look for it. *How many books did Renoir/* the painter or his son the filmmaker?/ *What are masterpieces?* (interesting)/ *Let us name a few. The "Odes" and the "Epistles" of Horace.* Hey, Palinurus, I've read them and I can even quote *el viejo Horacio* in Spanish. In Russian I can stage a Horace show. *Las ruinas me encontrarán impávido. "Ruins will find me unmoved."* How about that for a double play? *The "Eclogues" and "Georgics"* (I read some and soon forgot) *of Virgil/* (the *Aeneid* is boredom bound), *the "Testament" of Villon.* I cited but not recited "La Ballade du Concours de Blois"—"I only trust in things uncertain." Too many books I have not read are the coming attractions. Forget it! Or rather, forget 'em./ *There is no pain in life equal to that which two lovers can inflict on one another/* True too true./ *Communism is the new religion which denies original sin, yet we seldom meet a Communist who as a man seems either complete or happy.*

(How can you possibly read or transcribe *this, now?* Palinurus, you're risking my life, man. Cuban overboard!) Happy or hapless? The Chinese are always pictured with a smile on their face. Laughing gas, for sure. Someone, the Cuban ambassador to Peking, told me that Mao ordered every Chinese who has his photo taken to be the picture of happiness by a grin on his face. That's more than a billion smiles a year! Mona Lisa versus Malthus. *My friends in the first period: Horace, Petronius, and Virgil.* (My first friend, my first accomplice, my first procurer was Petronius: I masturbated at twelve with the *Satyricon* in one hand. That's what classics are for: such decadence, such cadences.) *In the second: Rochester/ Jesus was a petulant man/ "Repose, tranquility, stillness, inaction—these were the levels of the universe, the ultimate perfection of Tao," Chuang Tzu* (a quotation of a quotation of a quotation). *The secret of happiness (and therefore of success) is to be happy with existence, to be always calm. But is it the secret of art?/ The moment a writer puts pen* (what about the typewriter?) *to paper he is of his time./ A man who has nothing to do with women is always incomplete/ London pigeon can fly/ Pascal (or Hemingway, Sartre, or Malraux)/* (why not Raymond Chandler, Nathanael West, or William Burroughs?), *ora te pro nobis.* (There follows a list of four suicides and as I was not going to hang myself tonight I carried on looking— back to the beginning.) *The more books we read, the sooner we perceive that the true function of a writer is to produce a masterpiece and that no other task is of any consequence.* FULL STOP

(What's the point of going on searching? Depression is often called recognition. Master Bates was the first translator of the *Satyricon* into Papiamento.) Well, after all, gents, the quotation is the one that alludes to a girl who walks in sandals, with charmingly flat feet, her legs displaying their timeless beauty. But I hardly think this quotation will suit me, since I am not following this woman, it is not daytime and the sun can give no life to the scene. In fact, I am rather condemned to this artificial, electric life, surrounded by these flashes futilely pitched against the dark.

I thought, when I saw the girl sit down, at the back, face turned toward me, that I should marry her! Even if she does not walk in beauty, night.

But I didn't have to marry her to discover she was not a natural blonde. Nor strip her. Nor meet her. Not even go near her for God's sake! She had a broad face with high cheekbones and a square chin. In the strong Latin face, a large protruding mouth and a short nose with a high bridge in profile might seem Greek (Greek and Latin, Latin and Greek, Greek to me, glib to you), with big, almost colloidal eyes. Now, ordering, she smiles at the waiter and shakes her head, her hair, to mean no, while she shows a neck with which old Count Biela would have performed ancestral transfusions back in Transylvania. I should marry her. Even if she had square knees. *Stekel: "All neurotics are at heart religious. Their ideal is pleasure without the guilt. The neurotic is a criminal without the courage to commit a crime."* (I was thinking of Pavese, who said just before killing himself: "Suicides are shy homicides.") *Every neurotic is playing a particular scene.* (Further down!) *It is the disease* (down!) *of a bad conscience.* (Down! Shit!)

A mistake which is commonly made about neurotics is to suppose

I see the foyer of the Auditorium (now called Amadeo Roldán Theater) is all lit up. What's on today? A concert, surely. In a moment this place will fill up with people in a strong interlude. A long time ago, somebody said the *bon bourgeois* came to the concerts at the Auditorium to see and be seen during the *entr'actes* at El Carmelo. Will this wag say the same of the socialist in the Amadeo Roldán? *Pour épater les socialistes.* Is opium the religion of the Chinese? Poppycock.

She came walking between tables, through a roomful of men, past the glances of both sexes, among the books. Before, there was a newsstand here selling *Time* and *Life* and *Look, Collier's,* the *Saturday Evening Post, Newsweek, See, Coronet, Pageant, Fortune, U.S. News & World Report, True Detective, Ellery Queen's Magazine, Mad, Tru Confessions, Confidential, Photoplay, Screen Stories, Police Gazette, Saturday Revue, Atlantic Monthly, Life en Español,* and *Selecciones del Reader's Digest;* and now it is a bookstall selling *The Tale of the Shark and the Sardines, The Communist Manifesto, Panfilov's Men, The Road to Volokoplanks, Night and Day* (by Simonov not Cole Porter), *A Real Man, The Steel Was Forged,* and what next? *The Complete Works (abridged) of V. I. Lenin,* that's what. And Mao's *Little Red Reading Book.*

Another *exempli gratiae?* In 1929, tens of thousands of Cubans decorated Havana and filled with paper roses the

streets of the city through which a pilot was to ride in triumph—an airman who had achieved only a human exploit
but who presented himself like a Greek hero. Hundreds of
placards, posters, and handbills read:

WELCOME LINDBERGH

And for four days the city had a fiesta staged for the procession and ceremony of the tall, reserved, disdainful (they
claimed he was shy) American aviator. In 1961, hundreds of
thousands of Cubans decorated Havana, filling with ban-
ners and buntings every avenue of the city through which
another pilot was about to ride in triumph—a flying man
who had piloted some sort of craft but who presented himself as a Greek god:

DOBRO POSHALOBAT GAGARINU

That was not Greek but Russian, on thousands of placards,
posters, handbills, streamers, and for four days the city had
a fiesta, indulging in the ceremony & procession of the
small, extrovert, disdainful (and he was short but not shy)
Soviet cosmonaut.

I almost felt her stilettos piercing through the door and

up the stairway to paradise: to the ladies I could only guess, alas! She was tall, with high round breasts, springy thighs, and large buttocks that almost burst her dress, which was more like a cast of the shape of sex than a vestment. She was seen through the glass panels, echoing on the granite floor, her image to be gloated over down to the crudest detail, so Cuban, of a midriff bulge like one of Cranach's potbellies, displayed as much by her as the long Latin legs and as her heavily made-up protruding mouth and as the black eyes and dark hair perhaps dyed black and as the nostrils that flared rhythmically as she moved. I could marry her right now!/ *Engrossed with oneself, ungrateful and malignant*, that's Benigno, *and never quite in touch with reality*, that's me! *Neurotics are heartless.* Newrotten.

Then all of a sudden people were beginning to leave the concert hall. An ordinary interlude. The rather provincial calm of the night imploded into the noise of the public and more than imploding the night had its natural peace devoured by the paulo-post future of the human Leviathan. It should come from Shakespeare and I was at once so embarrassed that my train of thought must have been so loud that I was sure it showed on my face. Correction: aping Shakespeare like a monkey on his back. But it's too late, the die is cast, *hubris* has been committed. Now the punishment of a thundering voice and a thunderbolt of slap on my back almost floored me. It was not the Bard but the People.

"Shakespeare!"

This mouthpiece of the proletariat just said quite clearly, "Chah-keh-spe-a-reh." He mispronounces all the words which do not belong to the workers' vernacular now in use. It's all a party fad. But I didn't really have to turn around. In fact I didn't.

"Quiay," meaning more or less or less than more a hello.

"What's that supposed to mean? Don't you remember me anymore?"

"How could I ever forget."

"Now let's see. Who d'you think I am, then?"

"Ludwig Feuerbach."

"Not so high, brother."

"Offenbach."

He was laughing.

"Bach?"

"You're goofing!" He was still laughing. "You've not

changed any, have you? Always the same tricks, the same old treats, the same word cracks. When are you gonna get some changes made, man? I would of thought socialism would slow you down."

He almost said "socialismus."

"Ah, you are a socialist?"

"Trying to be funny?" He was not a wag. "Marxist-Leninist." He was a party hack. *"Patria o muelte!* and *Venceremo!"*

"I'm happy for you."

"Not for socialism," I thought.

"And you?"

"How do you mean?"

"Happy-Happy de Ulacia"; he meant a popular *orquesta de sones.*

I thought of replying that for a long time Groucho, Harpo, and Chico were the only Marxes possible. I meant that I had no idea then that Zeppo and Gummo even existed. I thought of telling him what a sign of the time it was that one of the most loved men of the century had the same last name as the most hated one. Indeed, I meant this most beloved clown whose name meant a double curse. He was christened—did he really?, well, his name was Adolph

Marx. But I didn't mention Harpo, my prompter whispered in my good ear, called Vincent.

"Didn't you give me your diagnosis already? You're the medico." I should have said the quack. "Not I."

He laughed again. Villains laugh first and last. He tried to laugh me away. But it was true. I met him first in high school. From there he went to the university, to medical school. He left a postmortem examiner with a forensic degree, to establish himself as (and this was the name he called himself as a specialist) an abortionist. To him it made no difference whether death was at the beginning or the end of a life. He is still laughing. I almost did the decoy: quack, quack.

"Nobody's gonna hold nothin' against you, Shakeprick. Not for the time bein', anyway. We still need a few old bourjoy inteleckchuals. But wait till we form our own caterers." He probably meant "cadres"—and perhaps not. "Most of those B.C. writers will have to learn—yes—to swim the strait."

B.C. meant "Before Castro," and by the strait, he didn't mean straight but the Gulf Stream. I suppose I was one of the bourgeois intellectuals. I shouldn't have to outline the story of my life. That kind of biostrip makes me puke. Particularly in front of this notable socialist savant, whose mere presence is obscene. Were I talking to anyone else, I shouldn't account for my life. Not in the class-conscious terms now in fashion. But I could have told him that I was a bourgeois who lived in a small town until I was twelve. Who moved with his Communist parents to Havana, physically, spiritually, and socially underdeveloped. Undafrivolous, as somebody said. With bad teeth in a poor mouth and with only the clothes I stood up in. Who lived the ten most important years of a man's life—his adolescence or the beginning of my puberty that was an extension of my poverty—in a miserable tenement sharing with father, mother, brother, two uncles, a cousin, and a grandmother, plus the occasional visits from relatives from home town, a single room (rather like Groucho's cabin) our only home. Where all the available comforts of civilization could be obtained within a hand's reach: built-in kitchen, built-in bathroom, an open-plan b.r. & svrl. oth. unimg. mod. con. A young man who had his first suit (secondhand) given him by a kind-hearted alien. Who could not even dream, at twenty, of having a girl because he was too poor to afford that luxury of the sexes—just a palindrome. Whose first reading was from books begged, borrowed, or stolen. Who first went to theaters, concerts, and the ballet by sneaking in. Who lived for seven years with a consumptive brother whose illness destroyed his talent as a painter. Who married and had to share a two-room apartment with all his old family—and his new one too.

That is almost all the life story on this bourgeois intellectual, decadent and cosmopolitan, of course, who had to give up hope of a university career because the only salvation possible for his family depended on his taking a poorly paid, oppressive job: proofreading for a right-wing newspaper. Corrupt and reactionary, of course. I should finish by saying that I got a divorce eventually.

Were this Cuban wise guy a different person, I should have told him all this—or perhaps I would shut myself up as always. Proofreading is an excellent training for reading without moving your lips. Were he of another kind, I should have invited him to sit down and have a smoke or a cup of kindness yet. But my uninvited guest had at least one flash of prescience. He was ready to leave.

"Where them don't wan' me—"

"Goodbye."

"See you soon, *compañerito*."

He meant "little comrade," literally. Diminutives are dangerous as they can also mean something mean. Could that be a threat? Or something wicked my way come. I didn't really have time to think so—party paranoia being eclipsed now by erotic schizophrenia, ideology displaced by erotomania. Or as the Japanese say, I will win the erections. Some beautiful girls had come all in a row and happiness intruded once more. Beauties are raining in!

At the other side of the glass was this fabulous little blonde, her long hair done in a thick plait, with the neck, arms, and pose of a ballerina. She and not the book made the evening really Connollyan. At my left was a stunning *mulata*, her hair severely cut, but her stern looks and my swift regard were betrayed by that wild, wide mouth, which lent her face an aspect of some forbidden fruit. I look into the tree—actually a dwarf palm in a pot—of lewd knowledge for some serpent to introduce me. I would have married even Eva.

Then there was another beauty that I could have married if only there had not appeared the one person whom I least wanted to see. Even the last visitor would have been welcome by comparison. He kept walking toward me. Here comes a commissar of art and letters. The comic czar of culture. He was dressed, as usual, in Italian-made loafers (to describe him one had to begin with his feet: he was mad about shoes) in dark blue suede. He had on a charcoal gray silk suit, a celeste shirt and a cobalt blue tie (perhaps by Jacques Fath, apparently bought on one of his trips to Paris) with three thin black horizontal stripes. His jacket was thrown around his shoulders Italian-style—and I should have said he came Bette Davising toward me. Finally he got to my table, smiling: recently barbered, shaved, and doused. He smelt nice. Guerlain, Diorissimo, or even better, L'Air du Temps.

"Hello."

"*Quiay.*"

This was my most civilized greeting of the evening. But he sat down anyway, earnestly smiling. Had he not been so fat because of his gourmandise, he would have been quite good-looking. At times he was almost *bonitillo*—not to be confused with *boniatillo,* a dessert made with sweet potatoes. He spoke with winsome unctuousness—to alien ears, that is. There was nothing obsequious about him. Once a bad Spanish playwright wrote a line about his heroine that she was silk outside, iron inside. Valle Inclán, a rival writer from the first-night audience, cried out: "That's no woman, that's an umbrella." End of play flooded by laughter.

This man was no woman. He was an umbrella, since he knew how to shut up and be stiff in dire circumstances and how to shelter himself in raw silk. He was his own umbrella. I remembered Mark Twain's remark that a banker is somebody who lends out his brolly when the sun shines and reclaims it when the weather gets rough. I can think of nobody more like a banker than a commissar. Now he was an umbrella on a fine day. Or night.

Before he began his little speech (he loved to spawn speeches), I had the waiter bring more coffee and a clean ashtray, please. He would not drink anything. Yes—one moment: mineral water. In public he was so virtuous that he became a virtuoso. It was common knowledge that in private his behavior was something else. But I do insinuate in excess. My guest drank neither too little nor too much and only dared visit clean, well-lighted places. His great vice was like Gide's love of Arab boys, a Proustian *carnet de bal*, the ways of a superior spirit in the Wildean sense. My guest had (and still must have) a fancy (or craving) for beautiful young men. This was a secret so well known in Havana that his private vice became almost a public virtue—for a time. He spoke with the memory of a lisp.

"And there was I, searching in the most unusual places for just you." In fact of fiction he was no Wilde, only Wilder.

"For me?" I could play it coy and cozy if I wanted to.

"Yes, you—oh the nerve! For days I've been leaving messages for you with everybody but just everybody."

"I got none." I stonewalled myself behind a stone face.

"Yes, you did, and well I know it. But as always you prefer to avoid me, evasive as you can be because—" and he broke off, leaving the word hanging in midair. Was I grateful. Because I took advantage of the word because to look at a well-ripened woman (almost an adolescent by Balzac standards: she was not yet thirty) who was an habituée. She came every evening to El Carmelo with her husband, a doctor or a hairdresser of consequence, even perhaps a dentist dressed accordingly in a white jacket. They sat together alone. But soon there was a group surrounding her. She was laughing (she laughed a lot), and from time to time turning to her escort. I was taken with her laugh, with her pleasant face, with her well-shaped legs (a trifle plump, if you see what I saw), but more than anything her main attraction was that she was so generous with herself. She was generous with her smile, her charm, her body—which she showed off to absolutely everyone. Once in a while I felt a little pity for White Jacket. But only a little. For I began to think how that couple should have pleased Maupassant e*n mot passant.* Even though his pleasure would not have been as evenly distributed as her figure. Chekhov would have liked neither of them, while Hemingway, as a young writer, would have been pleased with her husband as a hero.

"Why?"

"Because," and he paused again—like a musician, he was very sparing with his silence chords—"you are frightened of me."

"Of you?"

I almost burst out laughing. But my face was kept straight by the appearance of twin girls, the Verano sisters, May and June. I did not laugh because I was figuring out how to get married with both of the twins. I was sorry they weren't Siamese, Enga and Chana, welded together by a promising promiscuous cartilage and joined to me by the liturgical cord of the blessed sacrament. Can the church marry one to Siamese sisters? One would do.

"Not of me. Of what I represent."

"What do you represent?"

"My immodesty prevents my saying it."

"That line is mine."

"Well, it shouldn't be I who has to say it."

"And I'm not going to, either."

"Come on! With all that I strive for."

"What's that?"

"To win men like you over to my side." The lisp became a lilt. Perhaps some of my friends were right after all. (With emollients, Serge Lifar would say, rounding off his opinion in accented French: *"À quoi bon la force, si la vaseline suffit?"*) It would have insured me against all the unpleasantness to come. But my antagonist corrected himself, quickly, self-criticism gaining the upper hand to style.

"I mean, over to *our* cause. We need your kind of intellect."

"But you don't need me, only my intelligence. Herr Doktor Viktor Frankenstein was indeed a materialist—he wanted no more than the brain."

He smiled wanly. He was a man who knew how to smile, even if coldly. Could this man be one of the cold spirits that Mac Yavelly spoke of as if spirits could be bottled? Those who then liberated like the djinny would dominate the world? Stalin should have been a cold spirit before becoming a frozen mummy.

"You realize we are not in agreement on many subjects. But we could be in accord over other issues."

En garde.

"Like what?"

"You can't"—can't or cant or Kant—"represent the only cultural policy in the Revolution." Policy or the police? I looked to see if any other delectable dishes had come into the restaurant. May I see the menu, please?

"I represent no policy, let alone that creature of the red pond."

"If not you, your magazine. It seems to appropriate revolutionary culture all to itself."

He was referring, Your Honor, to the literary supplement that I and a number of friends put about. It was then nothing more than an unremarkable weekly, idly done in the small hours of each Friday, making Crusoes of us all. It was made quickly, shoddily, edited in an amateurish fashion and put to bed half asleep—but which time would change into a historical tissue-*issue.*

"The magazine wants *all* culture to itself."

No use arguing. I would have been better off finishing my Upmann by myself: singing, dubbed by Fred Astaire, "I want to be by myself," and looking at the little girls, at the young girls, at the old girls, and continuing to gloss over my glass darkly those six Palinurian sentences. To top it all off, my cigar went out when it was only half finished to become a stub. I lit it again and burned my little finger a little, while watching the woman who had just arrived. I should have married this one. I decline to describe her. I could never be *le roi Candaule* for State Security. I shall only say as a concupiscent pointer that if a Cyd cherished body were grafted to the fonder face of Jane, Comrade Lysenko would be unable to produce such a delectable graft hybrid. I watched her whole figure in every one of her movements and mourned not having Marey's gun to shoot to record and store her image like a latter-day Coppelius. But she vanished into the maddening crowd.

"Did you know that once *compañera* X criticized me for writing that *mulatas* were more to my taste than eyes scream. I mean than ice cream?"

I was referring to a female ideologue of the party that was already transforming itself, silently, deviously, into the Party. He seemed uncomfortable and changed position in his seat, and I was able to see his socks hideously azure with black clocks.

"Why? What did she say?"

He was eager to know the opinion of this woman who spoke equally badly of him as of me—though for quite opposite reasons. Curiously, she too had particular tastes as well known in the Party as abroad. One of the Party anecdotes told of her triangular relationship with a piano, a dark dikish beauty—and the music of Ravel. I won't tell the whole story, but for the solace and amusement of connoisseurs suffice it to say that before the end of a party some comrade or other found both in a secluded music room. It happened in Old Mexico, and the Indian girl, seated naked on top of the Steinway, was holding the score between her dusky legs! It was the solo part for the Concerto for the Left Hand.

"She said that I was putting women on equal footing with perishable products."

"And what did you say?"

"That it was better to place a woman as a sometime thing—than as a music stand."

He laughed spontaneously, heartily for the first and only time that night. His laugh was loud, rather rusty, and it had a falsetto ring—more like a rat's squealing than a mousy squeak.

"Returning to our topic—"

"Tropics."

"—for whom are you making this magazine?"

"For oneself."

"Seriously. No *boutades*, please."

"For myself by myself."

"There! You see? That is exactly where I cannot *possibly* be in accord with your group."

I thought: "Be in discord, then." But I said:

"Don't say my 'group,' please. It hurts."

"You're all a clique!"

"And a *claque*."

"You and your puns!"

Were puns more dangerous than guns? Have pun, will travel. But he was the second to make such implications that evening. *Les visiteurs du soir.* Since everything happens in threes, I was then ready for the true third. Don't worry. It will come.

"I warn you! I'm speaking of something very serious."

"I know. You have the gravity of mousyleum in Pink Square."

He became very pale. I realized that he was controlling himself badly. He kept fingering his tie. He ordered another mineral water. Is he trying to drown himself? I doubt it. Commissars are seldom suicidal. I asked for another coffee, another Upmann, and another ashtray. I always fret about ashtrays. Smoke and ashtrays. That's what smoking is all about. While the waiter was coming and going, while I sipped my fresh coffee and while I lit my fresh cigar, he did not say another word—dark as the grave. And was I thankful. Six or seven women came in, some together, others alone. I decided to arrange one of those collective *mariages à la mode,* suddenly in fashion. The only problem would be to convince the people's magistrate of my platonic substance, like in the *Parmenides:* one, many, etc. A great religion, Islam, and quite a jump. I should have been born in Arabia Felix or in Arabia Petrae—even in Arabia Deserta. But would not this rabid

Lawrence of Bessarabia also be there? Apart from the one thousand and one tales of his sexuality, my visitor of the evening had other patterns of history branded on his soft skin. A brave university leader, a demagogue, a forceful Communist, a consumptive through striving for a proletarian cause, a perpetual prisoner under the past tyranny, a coward beyond redemption, a saint of the Revolution minus a miracle or two, an erratic *maquisard* who used revolutionary parties as communicating blood vessels, laborious and tenacious outlaw working single-minded for the triumph of the rebels, a fugitive expelled from old Party, a full member of the revolutionary gov ment-in-exile, an architect of the agrarian reform informer for *Seguridad*, the Cuban Stasi, an adv politicians and leaders, a confidant of the women Revolution, possibly a legislator of the new Cons and rumored to be the first minister of culture So much history, perhaps all of it true. He made of Caligula. Wasn't he the one who said he wa heads of Rome to be only one? More practi modest, this commissar wanted all the brai to be only one. I thought how it would plea

t
k
w

El Carmelo (which was then, like Roma, the whole world) had a single warm inviting umbrella that I could go under myself to pass a better night. Ah vast vagina! Totalitarian reality jerked me out of total dreams.

"Your group is promoting abstract art."

He pronounced it ax-tract, rather menacingly.

"Myself, *personally*, I am not against abstract art, mind you. It doesn't disturb me at all. But you and your group must realize that abstract painting flourished here at the time of maximum penetration," a bugger word, "of imperialist influence. It didn't coincide gratuitously with the worst years of the Batista regime. Abstract painting, this literature you push, and public, beatnik," which he pronounced biknik, "hermetic poetry, formalism, jazz. All of it together with the prostitution of popular music and folklore," which sounded like fucklore, "and language, mind you, has to be attributed to the nefarious domination of imperialism."

"As well as Malthusian practices. Or Balthus too."

"*What?*"

"At the time of the toughest imperialist penetration, con-traceptives were introduced, from the humble condom to all kinds of dildos. All evil come to us from the vile North where we are despised."

Even cold weather and little girls. He couldn't have read *Lolita*, could he?

"Make fun of it and see what happens to you."

My God, what a woman had just appeared! I came out in a cold sweat and vertigo. Once, as a boy, I had the same sensation in a toyshop. Toys, tits—who cares? I do.

"I mean it. I'll tell you something else, too. Do you remember the heyday of the *danzón*?"

"Yes, everybody knows that. From the turn of the century almost up to the twenties." Dance on to the music of time.

"That is to say that the *danzón* came to the fore with the throes of colonialism. To put it in medical terms, as my doctor friend would say, with the gestation of the Republic and the uterine cyst of the American intervention—"

"North American intervention. Twice."

"And the *son*?"

That's another Cuban dance, not the son of *danzón*.

"It coincides with the republican struggle and its apogee was reached at the time Machado was overthrown."

"Right. Now they play mambo."

This was more like a dance contest, really.

"Music impregnated by Yankee influence, by the way."

"By jazz."

"You put it one way, I another. The mambo belongs to that period of graft and corruption under Presidents Grau and Prío."

Everything was going swimmingly. He didn't really know he was treading in deep water.

"Now we come to the chachachá."

Just as we came to the chachachá I saw a big girl who had caught my eye a moment before and was now getting up to go. She hesitated for an instant (that's how long happiness lasts, pal) between sitting and standing, almost with her back to me. I was not thinking of Ingres, for this tropical odalisque was alive and there was nothing marble about her flesh. It occurred to me that there was no greater pleasure than being aware of the existence of women, that to die without it would deprive me of peace in the grave. Only here, in the forms of a paragon, beauty, aesthetic pleasure, and nature's masterpiece became something real that could be appreciated with all the senses, not only with the mind, in a synthesis of body and soul that is the beginning and end of all desire. I asked myself if anybody would have thought of that lately. Maybe chaste Chaucer back in the fourteenth century did. My *contrebasse d'Ingres* was already gone by then.

"What about the chachachá?"

He was tense when he asked me—or was it the bubbles in the mineral water?

"Que es un baile sinigual!"

I answered him by singing him the famous chachachá of the same title, but I'm not much of a singer.

"Seriously."

"Seriously then. It was tremendously popular everywhere."

"Agreed."

"This dance made by the people, for the people, and of the people. This Lincoln-like dance that makes Negroes rock while it moves whites to try it, came into being about 1952, about the year Batista gave one of his *trois coups*. The last to be exact," which I pronounced ex-act. But he didn't see my point.

"This national dance, negro, popular, not only suffered the disgrace of being born at the same time as Batista's dictatorship, as you know, time of the greatest penetration, etc. But it had its brilliant heyday when Batista also had neither his apogee nor his decline, but was still shining on with the brightness of a five-star general."

Now he saw it and fell silent.

"You ought to ask me what I mean, so that I can answer that the chachachá, like abstract art, like beatnik literature, like hermetic poetry, like jazz, of course—all are guilty art forms. Why? Because in a Communist state, everything and everybody is guilty. Nobody, nothing is free of guilt. Not even art, especially not art."

He seemed about to break down but did not do so. I did not guess it that night, but six months later, when his political machinations and his skill in lobbying and his Florentine ability for intrigue in high places finished off the magazine and many other things besides. Among them all hope, hope above all. In a leap from the concrete to the abstract that might not please old Hegel but would have made Marx rush in where Engels fears to tread.

As for that night, I seemed about to collapse and I acted as if I were demolished—not by him but by Her. Soon there appeared the tallest most beautiful most desirable woman in the whole Western World, and she sees me and almost bows her perfect head, charming me with the hint of a smile. She came back to me as on page one.

I should have proposed to her there and then. But I remained seated, wanting all not to be real, believing her an illusion, a mirage in the desert of a harem, wishing she had not happened at all—for I fell in love. Should I marry *Her?*

GUILLERMO CABRERA INFANTE was an editor and film reviewer in pre-Castro Cuba. Although he was a supporter of the revolution and a cultural ambassador under Fidel's regime, his journal was censored, then shut down by the government. Cabrera Infante went into exile in 1965 and became one of the earliest and most outspoken of Castro's Cuban critics. He is the author of such highly acclaimed works as *View of Dawn in the Tropics, Holy Smoke, Mea Cuba, Three Trapped Tigers,* and *Infante's Inferno.* He lives in London, where he claims to be "the only English writer who writes in Cuban." In 1997 he was awarded the Cervantes Prize, the Nobel of the Spanish language.

Bridges over Water

Understanding Transboundary Water Conflict,
Negotiation and Cooperation

World Scientific Series on Energy and Resource Economics

(ISSN: 1793-4184)

World Scientific Series on Energy and Resource Economics — Vol. 3

Bridges over Water

Understanding Transboundary Water Conflict, Negotiation and Cooperation

ARIEL DINAR
The World Bank and Johns Hopkins University, USA

SHLOMI DINAR
Florida International University, USA

STEPHEN MCCAFFREY
University of the Pacific, USA

DAENE MCKINNEY
University of Texas-Austin, USA

 **World Scientific**

NEW JERSEY · LONDON · SINGAPORE · BEIJING · SHANGHAI · HONG KONG · TAIPEI · CHENNAI

Published by

World Scientific Publishing Co. Pte. Ltd.

5 Toh Tuck Link, Singapore 596224

USA office: 27 Warren Street, Suite 401-402, Hackensack, NJ 07601

UK office: 57 Shelton Street, Covent Garden, London WC2H 9HE

British Library Cataloguing-in-Publication Data
A catalogue record for this book is available from the British Library.

World Scientific Series on Energy and Resource Economics — Vol. 3
BRIDGES OVER WATER
Understanding Transboundary Water Conflict, Negotiation and Cooperation

ISBN-13   978-981-256-893-9
ISBN-10   981-256-893-X

Typeset by Stallion Press
Email: enquiries@stallionpress.com

Printed in Singapore by Mainland Press Pte Ltd

FOREWORD TO THE FIRST EDITION

Our interest in authoring this textbook is anchored in our active engagement in the subject of transboundary (international) water and negotiation. Each of us has been involved, in one way or another, with teaching this subject in the classroom, conducting research, and participating in international forums. Some of us have even acted as consultants to governments involved in transboundary water decisions. In our work on the subject, we have come to realize that despite conflicting interests among riparians over a shared water body, the interactions among neighboring states have largely lead to cooperative outcomes.

Since the study of conflict and cooperation over freshwater has proliferated in academic and professional settings, a guiding textbook on the subject is imperative. To our knowledge, there is no such textbook and this volume is an attempt to fill that void. In addition, the study of conflict and cooperation over freshwater often requires an interdisciplinary approach, considering the topic's political, economic, legal, environmental, and hydrological nuances. To that extent, we feel this textbook speaks of the multidisciplinary facets of freshwater, by bringing together a group of scholars from the aforementioned fields to analyze these important points. The lessons learned and issues raised in this volume are applicable to the student or the practitioner, regardless of the disciplinary background they prescribe to.

This volume also hopes to provide the reader with a somewhat positive assessment regarding the future of the world's water. Often heard are gloomy scenarios citing "water-wars" as making up future conflicts. Media reports, as recent as 2006, have predicted that armies are on stand-by to tackle wars over water.[1] Even respected international leaders have predicted that water scarcity will lead to interstate violence. Most notable have been expressions made by United Nations Secretary General Kofi Annan citing that "Fierce competition for fresh water may well become a source of conflict and wars in the future."[2] Similarly, Ismail Serageldin, at the time Vice-President of the World Bank, was cited that "If the wars of the twentieth century were fought over oil, the wars of this century will be fought over water."[3]

---

[1] Russel, B. and Morris, N. "Armed Forces are Put on Standby to Tackle Wars over Water," *The Independent*, February 28, 2006, p. 2.

[2] Association of American Geographers (AAG), (March 1, 2001). "United Nations Secretary General Kofi Annan addresses the 97th Annual Meeting of the Association of American Geographers" [Transcript of speech]. Association of American Geographers. Retrieved November 2, 2004, from http://www.aag.org/News/kofi.html (Last visited on September 5, 2005).

[3] Serageldin was quoted in Crosette, B. "Severe Water Crisis Ahead for Poorest Nations in the Next Two Decades," *The New York Times*, August 10, 1995, Section 1, p. 13.

While such predictions are well suited to capture headlines and turn heads, they are marred with sensationalist and populist appeal. Conflicts indeed proliferate over transboundary water, yet cooperation among states usually ensues. Examples of cooperation far outnumber armed incidents. This volume is dedicated to assessing these phenomena.

The book's main readership are graduates in economics engineering, water law, international relations, and practitioners in water resource management, international water and water policy.

The book comprises 11 chapters, allowing adjusting the sequence of issues into a 13-week semester course. The book also includes a series of annexes with supporting material, and software that allows the reader to have hands-on experience with the various concepts that have been discussed and demonstrated in the book. It is planned that the set of case studies and the scope of the hands-on analysis will be expanded in future editions.

Ariel Dinar, Washington DC
Shlomi Dinar, Miami FL
Stephen McCraffey, Sacramento CA
Daene McKinney, Austin TX

July 2007

ACKNOWLEDGMENTS

We would like to acknowledge the research support and encouragement we received from our students who participated in our various international water classes at Johns Hopkins University in Washington, DC, Florida International University, University of the Pacific in California, University of Texas at Austin, and the students of the University of Economics in Prague, the Czech Republic.

We received useful comments on an earlier version of the manuscript from Elcin Caner, Pothik Chatterjee, Max Du Jardin, Abigail Goss, Haik Gugarats, Andrea Semaan, and Nicholas Smith.

We are very thankful for the permission to use artwork that we received from the following organizations: Transboundary Freshwater Dispute Database at the University of Oregon, United Nations Environmental Programme (UNEP), United States Climate Change Science Program, and the World Bank.

The following individuals were instrumental in obtaining for us high quality maps and diagrams: Becci Anderson, Caryn Davis, Jeff Lecksell, and Nick Sundt.

We would also like to pay special tribute to the editorial team of World Scientific Publishers who worked with us for their risk-taking ability, flexibility, patience, professional support and good sense of humor. This beautiful book could not have been produced without the dedication and undivided attention of Juliet Lee Ley Chin, Sandhya Venkatesh, Sharon Ho, Yolande Koh, and Hooi Yean Lee.

Stephen McCaffrey would like to thank the governments and international organizations with which he has worked for all that he has learned from them about international watercourses.

Ariel Dinar would like to place the regular disclaimer that the views expressed in this book should not be attributed to the World Bank.

CONTENTS

1. INTRODUCTION: STATE OF WATER AND INTERSTATE WATER RELATIONS

Objectives

This chapter sets the stage for most of the concepts and jargon a "water person" uses. It considers global water issues, sectoral use patterns, and other water-related concepts such as water scarcity. The chapter will likewise demonstrate the link between a basin's water situation and the potential **conflict** that can arise between the riparians. You will also be introduced to concepts relevant to international water agreements. Finally, you will note the distribution of international river basins and the nature of various **conflicts** over water.

Main Terminology

Access to water; Acre-foot (af) ($1\,\text{af} = 1235\,\text{m}^3$); Brackish water; Conflict; Consumptive use; Cooperation; CuSec (cubic meters per second); Desalinization; Downstream riparian; Electrical conductivity (EC); Evaporation; Externality; Fresh water; Ground water; International water; Irrigation; m^3 (cubic meter); Nonconsumptive use; Parts per million (PPM); Peace; Recycling (Water reuse); Salt water; Treaties; Upstream riparian; War; Water cycle; Water in circulation.

This chapter will set the basis for understanding the problem of water availability in the world, its regional distribution, and how humankind may affect it with human interventions. We will link in this chapter the notion of water scarcity to the evidence on water **conflicts** among nations and try to set the stage for the remaining chapters of the book. The chapter helps in establishing some of the language and concepts to communicate without getting too wet. The reader will not only be able to get a "free access" to the rest of the book's chapters but also to other literature on water.

THE STATE OF WATER IN THE WORLD

Our world witnesses several phenomena that individually and jointly have led to an increase in water dependency among sectors and segments of society, as well as among nations. Population growth, increase in urbanization and industrialization, and technological progress, just to name a few, have led to deforestation, water quality deterioration, and this affects the availability of water for human uses and ecological needs. As the, more or less, fixed amounts of the world's natural resources, such as land, water, forests, and other environmental amenities, have to be shared by a larger number of humans over time, increased competition and strategic decisions become more apparent at all levels of decision-making, starting with the household and ending with state level water managers.

How Much Water Is There and How Is It Used?

There is plenty of water in our globe. The problem is that it is either hard/expensive to extract or is available at the "wrong time" and/or at the "wrong places." Countries that share the same water source may have different levels of access and this, alone, could be a source of **conflict**.

Box 1.1: **Access to water.**

What does "access" mean? For example, a river that is shared by two countries may constitute an upstream country with a steep terrain. Consequently, reasonable use of the water for production of any benefit is made difficult. Nevertheless, the water flows across the border and reaches the flat terrain of the **downstream riparian**, where it can be fully utilized. A good example is the case of the Blue Nile and two of its major riparians, Ethiopia and Egypt. While 85% of the water originates upstream, Ethiopia's terrain makes utilization of the resource difficult. For several decades, the two riparians have been conflicting over the amount of water allocated to Egypt in a water treaty. Alternative, approaches other than the allocation of the water among the riparian states have to be considered.

Most of the available water is generated in a continuous process called "the **water cycle**." Figure 1.1 notes the many water-consuming sectors, interactions among them, and physical relationships that affect the **water cycle** — the way that water is generated, moves, and stored. In addition, Fig. 1.1 points to many interdependencies, or what economists term externalities, among sources, users, and locations. In other words, what one user does affects the availability of water to others. This makes water unique relative to other natural resources.

Since water can be transported, ownership becomes an issue and may affect relationships between riparians. Figure 1.2 demonstrates the contribution of oceans, rivers, and vegetation, and lakes to the global **water cycle**. In addition, it explains the transport of water from one place to another, not via the traditional conduits (of pipes and rivers) but rather through space.

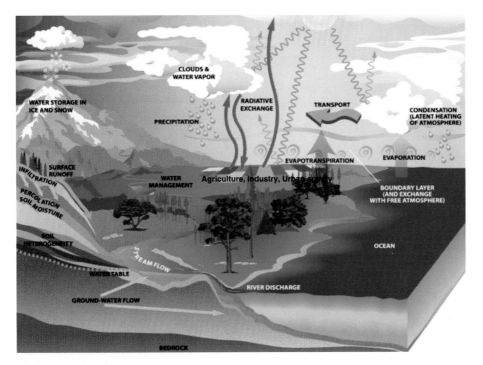

Fig. 1.1: The **water cycle**.

Source: Modified from US Climate Change Science Program (with permission to use), http://www.usgcrp.gov/usgcrp/images/ocp2003/ocpfy2003-fig5-1.htm (visited on July 7, 2006).

What are the main sources of water available for extraction, and how is water stored? There are four major water sources for human use: surface (rivers, lakes); **ground water** (renewable, nonrenewable, fossil, **brackish**); reused treated wastewater; desalinized water (sea and **brackish ground water**).

What are the water-using sectors and how do they utilize water? We will see that the distribution of water use by sectors across continents and countries varies a great deal. The composition of sectoral use of water may affect the relationship (**conflict/cooperation**) among riparian states. This happens for various reasons. First, time of use varies across sectors. While agriculture requires water for **irrigation** mainly during the summer season, hydropower utilizes the available water during the winter. Second, quality of water needs varies across sectors. While agriculture can use water of relatively low quality, residential uses are quite sensitive to water quality standards. In addition, water "quality" is actually a vector of various components, and may differ in nature among sectors. For example, level of minerals in the water affects the "salinity" of the water and its suitability for **irrigation** of salt-sensitive crops. For residential uses, quality takes into consideration stricter standards such as level of nutrients, and other chemical elements that make water harmful for residential use.

In the following paragraphs, we provide a very general description of water use by sectors. But first, take a look at the information in Table 1.1.

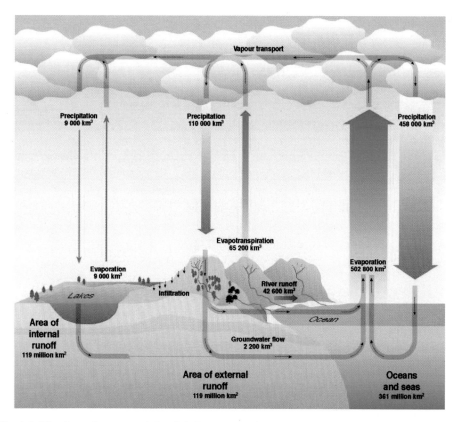

Fig. 1.2: The dynamic nature of the global **water cycle**.

Source: United Nations Environmental Programme (with permission to use), UNEP (2002) http://www.unep.org/vitalwater/03-water-cycle.htm (visited on August 20, 2006).

Table 1.1: Sectoral water withdrawals by region, rounded numbers (%).

Region	Residential	Industry	Agriculture
Africa	7	5	88
Europe	14	55	31
North America	13	47	49
Central America	6	8	86
South America	18	23	59
Asia	6	9	85
Oceania	64	2	34

Source: World Resources Institute (1998).

One immediate observation from Table 1.1 is the unequal distribution of water withdrawals among the continents, especially the share of agriculture. One rule of thumb is that the higher the share of agricultural use in the economy, the less developed the country. In addition, to the implications based on the share of water used by agriculture, as is explained below, the shares of water withdrawals also imply the sectoral power relations and the status quo solutions, which may not necessarily be the most efficient ones.

Irrigation consumes the lion share of the available water, depending on the country. Therefore, **irrigation** dictates many of the characteristics of the water situation in the world. Soil is watered using various application methods such as flood, furrow, sprinkler, and drip, just to name a few. Some of the **irrigation** water is consumed by the plants, the reminder percolates, and evaporates. In most locations, 50% of the water that is being "sent" to the fields is lost to percolation and **evaporation** even before reaching its destination. **Irrigation** may cause many negative consequences, e.g., soil and **ground water** pollution by pesticides and fertilizers. Although the **irrigation** season could be long, most of the **irrigation** demand for water occurs during the summer months. **Irrigation** water use is consumptive in nature because the entire applied amount is used and may be removed from the water system. Consequently, some part of the **irrigation** water is returned to the water system at a different location or modified in quality. Therefore, it is important to correctly account for the water actually used by the plants when one calculates comparative water use efficiencies.

Residential customers use about 5–10% of the available amount, depending on the country. Water is used for drinking, bathing, gardening, swimming pools, and other related functions. In many countries, up to 60% of the water pumped into the residential system is unaccounted for, either due to leaking or illegal connections. Sewage is a result of urban water use, and requires disposal. If disposal is not undertaken appropriately, negative externalities affect other users and sources (e.g., **ground water**). Demand for residential uses is distributed over the year with some peaks during the summer months. The main uses are (Clarke and King, 2004) flushing and toilet (30%), cleaning (5%), cooking and drinking (10%), laundry (20%), and bathing and showering (35%). Urban water use is **consumptive**.

Industry uses about 5–10% of the available amount, depending on the country. Water is used in manufacturing processes, and especially for cooling or cleaning. Similar annual distribution features of demand are observed for industrial water use as for residental water use. Industrial water use is **consumptive**.

Hydropower uses stored water behind dams. Water runs through turbines to create electricity in a **nonconsumptive** manner. Then it returns to the river for other **consumptive uses**. Most of the demand for electricity is high during the winter months. Hydropower use may create changes in the composition of the water when it returns to the river, due to erosion and sediment removal, and thus affects the environment downstream.

Ecological (environmental) uses, also called environmental flows, utilize about 0–10% of the amount of the water system, depending on the country. Water is intentionally left in waterways, such as rivers and lakes, to support ecological functions in a **nonconsumptive** manner.

In the context of international water it is important to recognize the manner in which water is used by different sectors in each country. This may help in explaining the sources for possible or existing **conflicts** over water and, more importantly, the possible ways of solving such **conflicts**.

How do we measure water availability? Water flows, stored, and changes quality. Therefore, we use both velocity and quantity units, and several measures of quality:

- In units of stock (**cubic meter**; cubic kilometer, **acre-foot**).
- In units of flow (**cubic meter per second, cubic meter** per hour, **cubic meter** per annum).
- Water quality affects availability. Water that is too polluted is unsuitable for consumption by people, plants, and machines. Level of pollutants in the water is measured in units of concentration (**parts per million** — ppm, or billion — ppb; salinity is also measured by **electrical conductivity** — EC).

The total amount of water on earth is very large. However, as was mentioned earlier, most of it is not available. Therefore, we need to introduce some vocabulary, and familiarize ourselves with several notations:

- Total water is the amount of all forms of water, some of which is not accessible at all.
- Renewable water is the amount that is being renewed either annually or along longer durations.
- Available water is the amount that humans can access and use for their consumption.

In addition to the natural differences in water availability, there are differences in availability that result from various aspects other than natural causes, such as man-made, population growth effects, technologies, and impact of quality deterioration.

Clarke and King (2004) estimate that water consumption per person per year was $350\,\text{m}^3$ in 1900 and $642\,\text{m}^3$ in 2000. These figures reflect only improved living standards (e.g., family swimming pools), advanced home technology (e.g., washing machines), and increased **access to water** (e.g., home connection to city water) in many countries. These increases coupled with population growth rates are one of the major sources for increased consumption of **fresh water** resources in the world.

Let us now view some of the information on the availability of global water resources. The amount of available water to the world today is relatively the same as it was when the Mesopotamian civilization prospered, even as global demand has steadily increased. Estimated values vary according to the source, but differences are not significant. Total water on earth is estimated to be $1,386$ million km^3 (Clarke and King, 2004). Of this amount, 97.5% is **saltwater** (e.g., oceans and seas). The remaining 2.5% is **fresh water** [34.65 million km^3 according to Clarke and King

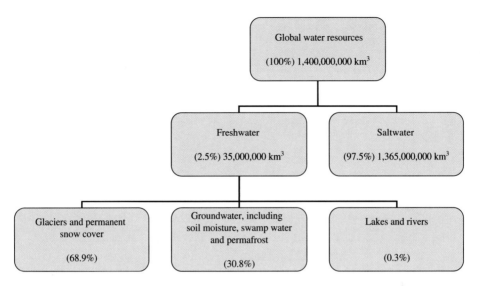

Fig. 1.3: Distribution of global water resources.

Source: Based on estimates in Shiklomanov (1996, 1999).

Note: As indicated in the text, a somehow similar estimate is provided by Black (1991) and Clarke and King (2004).

(2004) and 35.03 million km^3 according to Shiklomanov (1993), or 27 million km^3 according to Black (1991)].

As Fig. 1.3 demonstrates, of the 35 million km^3 of water on earth (Black cites 27 million), only 0.3% is considered easily accessible for human use. (Black cites 0.6% and Clarke and King cite 0.4% as available, but since they refer to a larger base amount — 34.65 million km^3 — the total available amount is very similar.) The remaining water is either technically or economically unreachable. Water is also stored in the soil and **ground water** aquifers, which could be extracted, depending on temporal economic considerations.

As was mentioned earlier, the increased water use per person per year has led to increased total annual water withdrawals [579, 1,382, 3,973 km^3, in 1900, 1950, and 2000 respectively, according to Clarke and King (2004)]. The sector using the lion' share of **fresh water** resources — **irrigation** — has expanded during this period by more than fivefolds — to nearly 250 million hectare (ha) (1 ha = 2.5 acre), as can be seen in Fig. 1.4.

However, it is clear from Fig. 1.4 that starting in the mid-1990s the irrigated area per capita in the world began to slightly decrease (from 47 ha per 1000 people in 1980 to 43 ha in 2000). This does not mean that food per capita is decreasing. On the contrary, FAO (2005) suggests that food per capita (measured in calories per capita) is increasing. With technological and management improvements, the water required to produce food may therefore decrease over time.

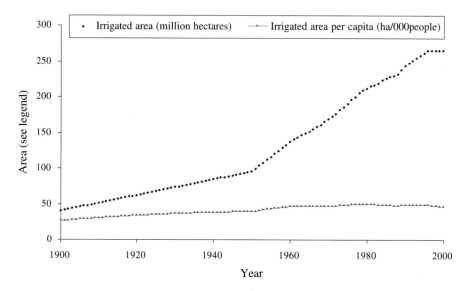

Fig. 1.4: Irrigated area of the world and irrigated area per capita 1900–2000.

Source: Modified (with corrections) based on data compiled by Worldwatch Institute from Postel (1998).

Box 1.2: How much water is needed to produce our food, cloth and computers?

Water (m^3) needed to produce 1 kg of various foods: Potatoes 0.5; wheat 0.9, rice 1.9, poultry 3.5, and beef 15 (Clarke and King, 2004).

Water (m^3) needed to produce 1 cup of various beverages: milk 0.25, coffee 0.14 (Waterfootprints, 2006), tea 0.034 (Chapagain and Hoekstra, 2003).

Water (m^3) needed to produce 1 medium size cotton T-shirt 4.1, one computer microchip 0.032 (WWF, 2006).

HOW DO WE MEASURE WATER SCARCITY?

Having said all the above, and considering just one parameter, the rate of population growth, water availability per capita[1] has been reduced by 60–80% over the last 50 years, as can be seen in a sample of countries. The declining trend of per capita water availability will continue so long as population is forecasted to grow (United

---

[1] There are also other indexes that represent water availability (or scarcity) in a given country. For example, the ratios between rainfall (mm/year) or runoff (m^3/s) to **evaporation** (mm/year) are used as well. However, such indexes are stochastic in nature and are affected by annual climatic conditions in the country or the river basin. One index that has been used in the project on freshwater assessment of the WMO (1997) is the ratio between water withdrawal and availability in a country; see also Bjorklund and Kuylenstierna (1998).

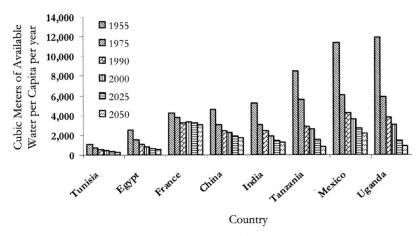

Fig. 1.5: Decrease in water availability per capita (m^3/year) between 1955 and 2050, using UN medium population prediction rates for 2000–2050.

Source: Authors' calculation based on data from Population Action International, 1993, 1995, 2004; United Nations Population Division, 2000.

Nations Population Division, 2000; Population Action International, 1993, 1995, 2004) at alarming rates in countries that face severe water scarcity (Fig. 1.5).

What is the common trend in almost all countries in the world (Fig. 1.5 includes only eight representative countries) and what does it mean in terms of future water scarcity and possible **conflict**? Well, it is clear that the water availability per capita decreases in a hyperbolic fashion decreasing from left to right. This is driven by the increase in population and the, more or less, stable water resource availability in the country. There are only a few countries in the world (e.g., Italy) where the water availability per capita is actually increasing because of decline in population growth over time.

The water availability per capita index, although very rough and controversial, provides a good upper limit to the state of water scarcity in a country. Are all countries, that face severe water scarcity, affected in the same way? What are the other factors that could be considered to either alleviate or reduce water scarcity in a country? There are three factors that affect the ability of a country to cope with water scarcity.[2] First, water quality is an important dimension of water scarcity. The available water in a country that is polluted is consequently no longer part of the usable quantity. Second, the standard of living in a country is a major factor affecting the way humans will consider water scarcity. Higher living standards are usually associated with elevated levels of water consumption (e.g., washing machines, swimming pools). Finally, the technological level of a country may allow its citizens

---

[2]Falkenmark and Widstrand (1992) suggested ranking of water shortage measure in m^3 per capita per year: (a) < 1000 is a water-scarce country; (b) 1000–1700 is a water-stressed country; (c) 1701–3000 is a water-insufficient country; 3001–10000 is a water-sufficient country; and > 10000 is a water-abundant country.

to live quite well on relatively small amounts of water (e.g., **recycling**, seawater **desalinization**[3]). At the country level, we witness several cases of inter-basin water transfers (e.g., China, California, Israel) to ease local water scarcity situations.

Now that we have gained additional knowledge about the state of water, its regional and sectoral distribution and use patterns, and availability in various countries, we can introduce the concept of international river basin and discuss the **conflicts** that may take place over scarce water.

For Further Discussion. Consider the likely impact of future global warming on water supply across several riparians in a given basin. What could be the physical as well as the political–economical consequences? Consider further the sectoral water use (such as in Table 1.1). Would extreme use patterns exacerbated by global warming impacts be manageable? Are there mechanisms that the basin riparians may be able to consider in order to find a stable regional solution to the water scarcity in the basin?

THE STOCK OF INTERNATIONAL RIVER BASINS

What is an international water body — basin, lake, or an aquifer? A detailed answer can be found in Chapter 3. However, for the time being we will consider the straightforward definition to mean that it spans over the territories shared by two or more independent states.

Why has the number of international river basins grown over time?

Wolf *et al.* (1999) suggest three reasons for that:

1. national basins became international given the political changes;
2. appropriate tools were not available to delineate all existing basins and
3. previous counts (e.g., the 1978 FAO register) ignored many island nations.

The creation of new states, a result of **wars** or political changes, means that a basin is no longer categorized as domestic but rather considered international. But this is not the only change. Another change ensues the new riparian states may be *a priori* hostile to each other based on their pre-independence relations so that the level of **conflict** in the basin is quite likely to be elevated (e.g., nonwater, historical **conflicts** can likewise drive the **conflict** over water). Therefore, in addition to an increase in the number of the international basins, there is also an increase in the

---

[3]Israel is one of the most water scarce countries. However, with technological advances, it has been able to recycle about 250 million m[3] per year and replace **fresh water** by treated waste waters for **irrigation**. Recently, the biggest water **desalinization** plant has been in operation, injecting 120 million m[3] to the drinking water system. Saudi Arabia also extended its water supply ability by investing in many **desalinization** plants.

number of **conflicts**, both water-related and nonwater-related (that can indirectly be associated with water issues).

Examples of Newly Created International River Basins and Ensuing Conflict

The Aral Sea Basin, which is home to the Syr Darya (River) and Amu Darya, was part of the Soviet Union until 1992. With the collapse of the Soviet Union and the creation of the independent states of Kazakhatan, Kyrgyzstan, Tajikistan, Turkmenistan, Uzbekistan, the Aral Sea Basin became international, consequently instigating dispute among the riparians. While related basin problems were internalized during the Soviet era and hence managed by a higher authority — Moscow — issues such as water allocation, pollution and **externality** impacts became international in nature after the collapse of Soviet Union.

Another illustrative example the 1999 **war** in the former Yugoslavia is created several new states and several new international river basins. Among these basins the Neretva and Trebisjnica River Basins shared by Bosnia and Herzegovina and Croatia. Although not yet declared a **conflict**, there are signs of looming problems in the management of the shared resource. The main problem is the pollution of the downstream tourist areas of the Adriatic Sea region of Bosnia and Herzegovina by industrial and urban wastes in Croatia.

While there has been an increase in the number of river basins due to geographical changes, international basins have actually "disappeared" due to the unification of a nation. Examples include Yemen (Northern and Southern Yemen) and Germany (East and West Germany). In general the net increase in the number of international basins between 1978 and 1999 amounts to 47 "new" international basins (Table 1.2).

While the number of international river basins in the various continents varies little, Africa is by far the continent with the highest share of land constituting international river basins (Table 1.3). Despite this finding, Africa is by far the continent with the least number of international **treaties** signed among international basin riparian states (see also Chapters 3, 7, 8, and 9).

Table 1.2: Number of international river basins by continents and sources of documentation.

Region	Barrett (1994)	1978 Register	Wolf *et al.* (1999)
Africa	55	57	60
Americas	60	69	77
Asia	40	40	53
Europe	45	48	71
Total	200	214	261

Source: Wolf *et al.* (1999).

Bridges Over Water

Table 1.3: Percentage of land area within international basins.

Continent	1999 Update (%)
Africa	62
Asia	39
Europe	54
North America	35
South America	60
Total	45

Source: Wolf *et al.* (1999, Table 2).

For Further Discussion. Based on Table 1.2, the number of transboundary watercourses increased from 214 to 261 between 1978 (or before) and 1999. Globally, this is about a 20% increase, which indicates either better delineation of basin boundaries or results of political struggle, leading to independent states, or both improved cartograpical tools and political unrest. If we look at regional distributions of such changes, we may come up with additional hypotheses. For our present discussion, let us focus on newly established states that must suddenly share a river basin. Would this be a factor in instigating more, or less, **conflicts**? Using the Aral Sea assess the problems, the five republics have had to contend with since independence and comment on their ability to contend with such issues. What type of differences in conflict or cooperation would you expect when comparing the Aral Sea Basin with the Tigris-Euphrates Basin, which is shared by only three states? While we have not studied yet any of these basins, still let us use our *a priori* knowledge.

A list of international basins and the number of countries that share them (except basins that are shared by 2, 3, and 4 countries) is presented in Table 1.4.

A visual documentation of the location, size, and distribution of the various transboundary river basins and lakes in the form of maps delineates the recent boundaries of all known basins (Maps 1.1–1.6).

WATER AND CONFLICT — GROUND FOR DESPAIR OR REASON FOR HOPE?

Whatever the situation regarding water scarcity may be, the overarching message, in many of the existing analyses and statements made by leading world experts is that our world is on the verge of a water quantity and quality crisis. Some are also sending alarming messages. For example, places on the front cover of his edited book Ohlsson (1995) quotes a statement by Ismail Serageldin (at the time Vice President of Environmentally and Socially Sustainable Development Vice Presidency at the

Table 1.4: Number of riparian states and the basins they share.

Number of countries	The shared basins
17	Danube
11	Congo, Niger
10	Nile
9	Rhine, Zambezi
8	Amazon, Lake Chad
6	Aral Sea, Ganges–Brahmaputra–Meghna, Jordan, Kura–Araks, Mekong, Tarim, Tigris and Euphrates, Volta
5	La Plata, Neman, Vistula
4	17 basins
3	49 basins
2	176 basins

Source: Wolf *et al.* (1999, Table 6).

World Bank) predicting that "The **wars** of the next century will be over water." The United Nations Secretary General, Kofi Annan, has declared that "Fierce competition for **fresh water** may well become a source of **conflict** and **wars** in the future" (AAG, 2001). A featured article on preventing **conflict** in the next century (The Economist, 2000:52) includes a blurb on water violence. It argued that "Water shortages will grow even more serious; the stuff of future **wars**. ... With 3.5 billion people affected by water shortages by 2050, conditions are ripe for a century of water **conflicts**." The 2004 Nobel **Peace** Prize winner, Wangari Maathai (Int'l Herald Tribune, 2004:6) suggests that "...we face [the] ecological crises of deforestation, desertification, water scarcity and a lack of biological diversification. Unless we properly manage resources like forests, water, land, minerals, and oil, we will not win the fight against poverty. And there will not be **peace**. Old **conflicts** will rage on and new resource **wars** will erupt unless we change the path we are on." Finally, on the cover of their book Clarke and King (2004) placed a slightly modified version of the excerpt used by Ohlsson (1995). Clarke and King use the statement, "If the **wars** of the twentieth century were fought over oil, the **wars** of this century will be fought over water." The quote is attributed World Bank. Whether or not the world will experience water **wars** is to be seen, but the fact is that scarcity and water **conflicts** have been there for centuries and will be with us for years to come.

Is the future that gloomy? Have there been only **conflicts** over water? Or are there also "reasons for hope" (Elhance, 2000)? To be able to make educated arguments about the state of "future **wars**" over water, we invite the reader to consider the following chapters, gaining both information and analytical tools to consider the realm of transboundary freshwater. We believe that after reading the book the reader will be better equipped, and to assess the likelihood of future **cooperation**, **conflicts** or **wars** over water. Before we provide a synopsis of the

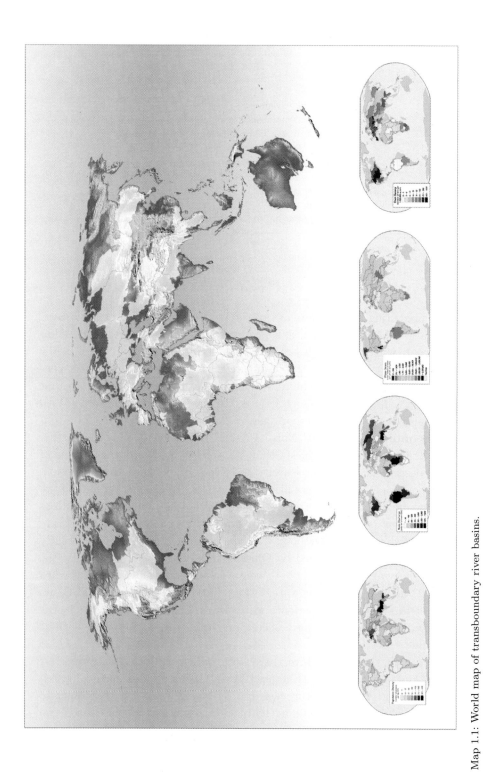

Map 1.1: World map of transboundary river basins.

Source: Transboundary Freshwater Dispute Database, http://www.transboundarywaters.orst.edu (Permission granted to reproduce maps from the Transboundary Freshwater Dispute Database).

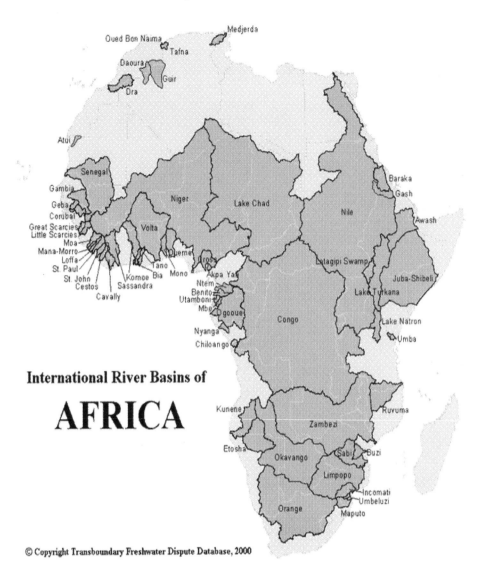

© Copyright Transboundary Freshwater Dispute Database, 2000

Map 1.2: Africa map of transboundary river basins.

Source: Transboundary Freshwater Dispute Database, http://www.transboundarywaters.orst.edu
(Permission granted to reproduce maps from the Transboundary Freshwater Dispute Database).

book's chapters, a glance into several important works which will set the tone for
this volume, is essential.

Background Information on Water Conflict and Cooperation

Wolf and Yoffe (2001) record a total of 1831 conflictive and cooperative events
between 1949 and 2000 in 263 international river basins. As can be seen in Fig. 1.6,
the number of cooperative events surpass the number of conflictive events.

Map 1.3: Asia map of transboundary river basins.

Source: Transboundary Freshwater Dispute Database, http://www.transboundarywaters.orst.edu (Permission granted to reproduce maps from the Transboundary Freshwater Dispute Database).

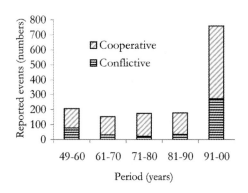

Fig. 1.6: Conflictive and cooperative water events over the last 50 years.

Source: Authors, based on Wolf and Yoffe (2001).

Map 1.4: Europe map of transboundary river basins.

Source: Transboundary Freshwater Dispute Database, http://www.transboundarywaters.orst.edu (Permission granted to reproduce maps from the Transboundary Freshwater Dispute Database).

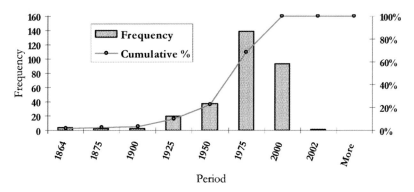

Fig. 1.7: Distribution of bilateral **treaties** during 1864–2002.

Source: Based on data in Dinar (2007).

In a recent work, Dinar and Dinar (2005) show that it is scarcity that drives the process of **cooperation** among riparians to rivers that are shared between two riparian states. A descriptive statistics (Fig. 1.7) of the 300 **treaties** (between 1896 and 2002) that were analyzed in their work suggest a similar pattern that

Map 1.5: North America map of transboundary river basins.

Source: Transboundary Freshwater Dispute Database, http://www.transboundarywaters.orst.edu (Permission granted to reproduce maps from the Transboundary Freshwater Dispute Database).

was depicted in Fig. 1.7, namely, **cooperation** (measured by treaty formation) has increased significantly in the last two decades. Thus, the claim that the next century will be characterized by **wars** over water is simply erroneous.

Conflict and **cooperation** over scarce water resources has taken a variety of forms. From the extremes of full **cooperation** to full-scale **conflict**, one always wonders 'why a **conflict** ensues', and 'how **cooperation** may be enhanced.' Sharing of water resources is a global problem, as international river and lake basins comprise nearly 50% of the world's continental land area (United Nations, 1978). The economic and political costs of lingering international water **conflicts** are significant. Specifically, the economic development of river basins is likely delayed or halted. Short- and long-term damages to parties occur as a result of a unilateral action taken by another party. Finally, additional indirect social costs may also be the result of such **conflicts**.

For example, there are several ways in which cooperative international river development offers possibilities for mutual gain (Krutilla, 1969). An **upstream riparian** may wish to undertake measures on the domestic reaches of the stream to provide some protection from flood hazards and some improvement of flows during low-flow seasons. According to Krutilla (1969), documenting the Columbia River

International River Basins of

SOUTH AMERICA

Map 1.6: South America map of transboundary river basins.

Source: Transboundary Freshwater Dispute Database, http://www.transboundarywaters.orst.edu
(Permission granted to reproduce maps from the Transboundary Freshwater Dispute Database).

case, cooperative participation in design and scale, and mutually planned sharing
of costs and attendant benefits, are likely to lead to more effective exploitation
of the river's potential than if each party were to take an independent course of
action, ignoring off-site effects. In general, where inter-dependencies exist, pooling
the resource potential of an entire river system offers a wider range of technically
feasible alternatives, and by avoiding duplication, pooling resources provides an

opportunity for selecting the most economical combination of sites and measures for attaining mutually desired objectives.

> **For Further Discussion.** Can technology and trade ease water scarcity? At this entry point in this course, address the following scenarios: (1) Can a water-scarce, technologically-advanced country trade water saving technology for water and ease water scarcity and likely **conflict** among the two basin riparians? and (2) Can trade in commodities replace the need to manufacture or grow water-intensive commodities in countries or regions where water is a scarce resource? These two questions will open for us the way to the rest of the discussions in the book.

SUMMARY AND THE STRUCTURE OF THIS BOOK

This chapter is intended to set the tone for this book. Two initial observations have been made: (1) We noted that both the amount of water available, globally, per person and its quality are declining over time albeit not at the same rate in all locations; and (2) We argue that riparian states may adapt to water scarcity situations also by signing **treaties** that address their scarcity problems. Whether or not these two processes complement each other and provide solutions to water scarcity **conflicts** remains to be seen. The book will consider various approaches that will assist in addressing this quandary.

Chapter 2 provides a comprehensive literature review that is organized, more or less, by the main disciplines that are relevant for describing and analyzing water **conflict** and **cooperation**. The reader is exposed to the fields of economics, an hydrology and engineering, and international relations and other disciplines and is introduced to the methods used by each to address the issues of transboundary water. Chapter 3 provides the basis for understanding the development and application of international water law, providing several examples from various transboundary rivers around the world. Chapter 4 introduces principles of **cooperation** and demonstrates how they are implementing in international water management. Chapter 5 introduces various principles and solution concepts from the field of cooperative game theory. In Chapter 6, the reader is guided through a series of applications of these concepts to practical issues of water resource investment and management. Chapter 7 builds on the previous chapters and discusses **conflict** and **cooperation** over international water from an international relations and negotiations point of view. Chapter 8 serves as a primer for the legal aspects of international water **treaties** by providing an overview of selected international cases in their geographic and political contexts. Chapter 9 focuses on a framework that addresses the generic characteristics of treaty analysis. The first part of the chapter provides a descriptive exploration of the substance of **treaties** while the second part suggests a theory for considering how water agreements can sustain participation by the relevant parties and promote **cooperation**. Chapter 10 demonstrates how river basin models can be used to assess and quantify **conflict** and potential **cooperation**. Furthermore, the chapter affirms that river basin models are crucial for providing data for the calculating certain solution concepts introduced in Chapters 5 and 6. Chapter 11 concludes the book, drawing lessons from the various chapters, and suggesting directions for future research work and teaching.

Practice Questions

1. When describing the global water situation, we have used several indexes. Some indexes are human neutral and some take into account human decisions. Which are the indexes used and which of them are human neutral?

2. How is it possible for people to live on $< 100 \, \mathrm{m}^3$ of available water per year, in some countries, while minimum standards for water consumption are 100 liters per day per person?

3. It is estimated that both water per capita and irrigated area per capita are declining over time. Do you really think that we are facing a food crisis?

4. How do you explain the relatively low number of **treaties** signed among basin riparians in the late 1800s and early 1990s, compared with the relatively high number of **treaties** signed in the mid to late 1990s?

REFERENCES

(AAG) Association of American Geographers (2001). "United Nations Secretary General Kofi Annan addresses the 97th Annual Meeting of the Association of American Geographers" [Transcript of speech]. Association of American Geographers. Retrieved November 2, 2004, from http://www.aag.org/News/kofi.html (Visited September 5, 2005).

Barrett, S. (1994). "Conflict and Cooperation in Managing Internal Water Resources", World Bank Policy Research Working Paper 0-860.

Bjorklund, G. and J. Kuylenstierna (1998). The comprehensive freshwater assessment and how it relates to water policy world wide, *Water Policy*, 1, 267–282.

Black, P. (1991). *Watershed Hydrology*. Engelwood Cliffs, NJ: Prentice-Hall.

Chapagain, A.K. and A.Y. Hoekstra (2003). "The water needed to have the Dutch drink tea", Value of Water Research Report Series No. 15, UNESCO-IHE, P.O. Box 3015, 2601 DA Delft, The Netherlands.

Clarke, R. and J. King (2004). *The Atlas of Water*. London: Earthscan.

Dinar, S. and A. Dinar (2005). "SCARPERATION: The Role of Scarcity in Cooperation among Basin Riparians", Paper presented at the 2005 International Study Association Convention, Honolulu, Hawaii March 1–5, 2005. http://convention2.allacademic.com/one/isa/isa05/index.php?cmd=isa05 (Visited on July 28, 2006).

Dinar, S. (2007). *International Water Treaties: Negotiation and Cooperation along Trans-boundary Rivers*. London: Routledge.

Elhance, A.P. (2000). Hydropolitics: Grounds for despair, reasons for hope, *International Negotiation*, 5(2), 201–222.

Falkenmark, M. and C. Widstrand (1992). Population and water resources: A delicate balance, *Population Bulletin*, Population Reference Bureau.

Food and Agriculture Organization of the UN (FAO) (2005). *The State of Food Insecurity in the World*. Rome: FAO.

Int'l Herald Tribune (2004). Page 6, December 11–22.

Krutilla, J. (1969). The Columbia River Treaty — The Economics of an International River Basin Development. Published for the Resources For the Future by the John Hopkins University Press, Baltimore, MD, 1969.

Ohlsson, L. (ed.) (1995). *Hydropolitics: Conflicts over Water as a Development Constraint*. UK: ZedBooks.

Population Action International (1995). *Sustaining Water: An Update*. Washington, DC: Population and Environment Program.

Population Action International (1993). *Sustaining Water: Population and the Future of Renewable Water Supplies*. Washington, DC: Population and Environment Program.

Population Action International (2004). *Sustaining Water: Population and the Future of Renewable Water Supplies*. Washington, DC: Population and Environment Program.

Postel, S.L. (1998). Water for food production: Will there be enough in 2025? *BioScience*, 48(8), 629.

Shiklomanov, I.A. (1993). World fresh water resources. In: Gleick, P.H. (ed.), *Water in Crisis*, Chapter 2. New York: Oxford University Press.

Shiklomanov, I.A. (1996). *Assessment of Water Resources and Water Availability in the World*. St. Petersburg (Russia): State Hydrological Institute.

Shiklomanov, I.A. (1999). *World Water Resources: An Appraisal for the 21st Century*. IHP Report. Paris: UNESCO.

The Economist (2000). Preventing Conflicts in the Next Century. In: A Special Publication The World in 2000: 51–52.

United Nations Population Division (2000). *World Population Prospects*. New York: The United Nations.

United Nations (1978). *Register of International Rivers*. Oxford, UK: Pergamon Press.

(UNEP) United Nations Environmental Programme (2002). *Vital Water Graphics An Overview of the State of the World's Fresh and Marine Waters*. Nairobi, Kenya: UNEP (ISBN: 92-807-2236-0).

Waterfootprints website, http://www.waterfootprint.org/Index.htm (Visited on July 28, 2006).

Wolf, A. and S. Yoffe (2001). Basins at Risk. A DESC Study on International Waters. Final Draft, March. TFDD: Basins at Risk, Department of Geosciences, Oregon State University, Corvallis, OR.

Wolf, A., J. Natharius, J. Danielson, B. Ward and J. Pender (1999). International river basins of the world, *International Journal of Water Resources Development*, 15(4), 387–427.

World Meteorological Organization (WMO) (on behalf of other participating agencies) (1997). *Comprehensive Assessment of the Freshwater Resources of the World*. Geneva: WMO.

World Resources Institute (1998). *World Resources 1998–99, A Guide to the Global Environment.* New York: Oxford University Press.

WWF (World Wildlife Fund) (2006). Rich Countries Poor Water, http://assets.panda. org/downloads/rich_countries_poor_water_final_170706.pdf (Visited on august 17, 2006).

ADDITIONAL READING

(FAO) Food and Agriculture Organization of the United Nations (2003). *Review of World Water Resources by Country.* Rome: FAO.

Gleick, P.H. *et al.* (2004). *The World's Water 2004–2005.* Washington, DC: Island Press.

Postel, S.L., G.C. Daily and P.R. Ehrlich (1996). Human appropriation of renewable fresh water, Science, 271 (February 9), 785–788.

(UNDP) United Nations Development Program (2006). Human Development Report 2006, Beyond Scarcity: Power, Poverty and the Global Water Crisis. New York: UNDP.

(UNEP) United Nations Environmental Programme (2002). *Atlas of International Freshwater Agreements.* Nairobi, Kenya: UNEP.

World Bank (2005). *World Development Indicators.* Washington, DC: World Bank.

(WWC) World Water Council (1998). *Water in the 21st Century.* Paris: WWC.

2. OVERVIEW OF LITERATURE ON CONFLICT NEGOTIATION AND COOPERATION OVER SHARED WATERS*

Objectives

While the literature on transboundary water is relatively young, the depth and scope of issues it has been covering has grown over the years. The chapter covers the main disciplines involved in analyses of transboundary water, namely law, geography, economics, negotiation. After reading this chapter you will have (1) a good understanding of the approaches used by each discipline, (2) a recognition of the issues that are central to transboundary water, and also some good grasp of the various hot spot basins around the world.

Various works on conflict, negotiation, and cooperation over shared international fresh waters (shared waters) have been published over the years. However, the end of the Cold War and renewed interest in water and environment, around the Dublin and Rio conferences,[1] in 1992, also had much influence in fostering interest in shared water issues, specifically as it pertained to the spheres of politics, security, and international relations. The past 15 years have seen much more work on international water and this will be reflected in this chapter as well.

While studies regarding conflict and cooperation over water have varied in scope, work on shared waters can nonetheless be distinguished by three unique categories — theoretical, empirical, and case studies.[2] The literature has also both embodied and benefited from the tools, lessons and underpinnings provided by different academic disciplines. Four such fields have been most instrumental: economics, international law, international relations, and negotiation theory. Other disciplinary approaches, such as geography and hydrology, have made significant contributions and will be incorporated as well.

---

*A revised and updated version of Dinar and Dinar (2003).
[1] The conferences highlighted the importance of water as an "economic good" with "basic human need" in national and international arenas.
[2] We intentionally do not report on the rich literature that focuses on individual basin case studies. These can be found in Dinar and Dinar (2003). An additional source of updated work can be found in the Water and Conflict Bibliography website (http://biblio.pacinst.org/conflict/) by the Pacific Institute.

DISCIPLINARY APPROACHES

The different fields introduced above have all been invaluable in contributing to the work done on shared waters. Economics has brought to bear such concepts as regional cooperation, game theory, and institutional economics. International Water Law, rich in its history but relatively juvenile in its codification status as of 1997, has introduced particular important legal principles such as *equitable utilization* and the *obligation not to cause significant harm*, paramount in contributing to future resolution of conflicts over shared waters. The field of international relations has likewise sharpened ideas on conflict and cooperation over water, employing variables and concepts such as state power, interdependence, and domestic politics. This discipline has also been instrumental in guiding discussion on water and international security issues and institutional and organizational approaches. Negotiation studies have introduced concepts such as party motivation, third party mediation, linkage, culture, and other important tools to understand different bargaining outcomes.

Economic Aspects of International Water Conflict Negotiation and Cooperation

Although economics is one of the building blocks of cooperation over shared waters, it is surprising that the economic literature is not sufficiently endowed with works related to international water. Since the seminal work by Krutilla (1967) on the economics of the agreement between the USA and Canada over the Columbia River, there have not been many works of this magnitude.

Economic studies of cooperation over shared water usually take either the central planning approach or the market approach. The first approach assumes the existence of a central planner that makes decisions regarding the allocation of water and other factors of production, and resulting benefits among the riparian states (e.g., Giannias and Lekakis, 1996; Kally and Fishelson, 1993). The second approach, driven by market considerations, assumes that riparian states behave as agents in the market, responding to price and value signals and driven by profit maximization (e.g., Dinar and Wolf, 1994; Zeitouni *et al.*, 1994; Becker *et al.*, 1996). Such approaches assume politically neutral considerations. However, as is well acknowledged (see the section on international relations), this assumption is not well suited with reality of international water. As with many other scarce common pool resources (Ostrom *et al.*, 1994), strategic behavior is more common among parties sharing common water resources. Incorporation of strategic behavior into water-sharing approaches brings us to game theory.

Game theory has been applied to international water conflicts only sporadically. Rogers (1969) applied a game theoretic approach to the disputed Ganges–Brahmaputra Basin that involved different uses of the water by India and Pakistan. The results suggest a range of strategies for cooperation between the two riparian nations, which will result in significant benefits to each. In a more recent paper, Rogers (1991) further discussed cooperative game theory approaches applied to water sharing between the USA and Canada in the Columbia Basin, among Nepal, India, and Bangladesh in the Ganges–Brahmaputra Basin, and among Ethiopia, Sudan, and Egypt in the Nile Basin. An in-depth analysis is conducted for the Ganges–Brahmaputra case, where a joint solution improves each nation's welfare more than any noncooperative solution (Rogers, 1993). Dufournaud (1982) applied game theory to both the Columbia and the Lower Mekong to show that "mutual benefit" is not always the most efficient criterion to measure cooperation in river basins.

While game theory has been very useful in explaining water allocation among international basin riparian states, lately, pollution and water quality aspects of transboundary water sharing have become increasingly important. Here too, game theory may help in understanding potential for cooperation among basin riparians. Fernandez (2002) developed and applied a differential game using data of abatement costs, environmental damages, trade flows, and pollution dynamics to transboundary water pollution problems along the border between the USA and Mexico. The framework offers a way to compare pollution control when the USA and Mexico coordinate efforts and when they act independently. In another recent work, Umanskaya *et al.* (2006) develop a differential game to examine the effects of international lobbying on the solutions for transboundary pollution stock control involving two trading countries. The model explores (at the theoretical level) optimal pollution regulation strategies and the evolution and equilibrium levels of pollution stock in both countries under two different scenarios: in the presence and in the absence of international lobbying. Comparison of the outcomes of these scenarios shows that international lobbying may lead to a laxer regulation of the transboundary pollution externality and degradation of environmental quality.

Application of metagame theory, which is a nonnumeric method to analyze political conflicts, has been applied to water resources problems by Hipel *et al.* (1976) and Hipel and Fraser (1980). The resulting outcome of a conflict is a set of strategies most likely to occur and their payoffs to each participant. Becker and Easter (1995) analyze water management problems in the Great Lakes region among different US states and between the United States and Canada. A central planning solution is compared to a game theory solution with the results favoring the solution found through game theory.

Using a game theory approach, Dinar and Wolf (1994) evaluate the idea of trading hydrotechnology for interbasin water transfers among neighboring nations. They attempt to develop a broader, more realistic conceptual framework that addresses both the economic and political problems of the process. A game theoretic model is then applied to trade in the Middle East involving Egypt, Israel, the West Bank, and the Gaza Strip. The model allocates potential benefits from trade among the cooperators. The main findings are that economic merit exists for water transfer in the region, but political considerations may harm the process, if not block it entirely. Part of the objection to regional water transfer might be due to unbalanced allocations of the regional gains and, in part, to regional considerations not directly related to water transfer.

Incorporation of economics of conflict and cooperation into international shared-water problems has become more used in recent years (Dinar and Wolf, 1997; Just and Netanyahu, 1998a). Just and Netanyahu (1998a) for example, include various works that apply game theory and other economic concepts (e.g., regime theory, contract theory, water markets, bargaining theory). Other examples include Netanyahu *et al.* (1998) that apply game theoretical approaches to the dispute over the Mountain Aquifer between the Israelis and the Palestinians.

Additionally, Bennett *et al.* (1998) demonstrate the application of interconnected games (addressing issue linkage) to the Aral Sea Basin and to the Euphrates River Basin. They conclude that issue linkages — such as trade and air pollution (for the Aral Sea Basin) and the Kurdish ethnic dispute and the Orontes River conflict (for the conflict over the Euphrates) — may be a more efficient approach than using side-payments — which are subject to instability due to the Victim Pays principle[3] — in the formation of cooperative agreements. But Just and Netanyahu (2004) suggest that the linkage between negotiated issues other than water will actually eliminate a solution in the case of the Mountain Aquifer between the Israelis and Palestinians. Still with the Israeli–Palestinian conflict, Yaron (2002) applies game theory models to assess the economic value of cooperation and non-cooperation between Israelis and Palestinians over their shared-water resources. He concludes that whether or not a solution to the regional water problem will be of a cooperative or noncooperative nature will depend on several political, institutional, and economic considerations that may or may not be in place.

Finally, Just and Netanyahu (1998b) discuss cooperation in the context of a multiriparian river basin. According to the authors, coalitions are more sustainable when they incorporate a smaller number of players rather than a larger number. This may be relevant in cases where cooperation is lacking in a river basin, yet a large number of riparians may make treaty formation difficult. The authors argue that multilateral coordination in river basins with a large number of riparians may have to be preceded by bilateral agreements first — since they are easier to sustain.

This approach is also advocated by Swain (2003), who argues for a sub-basin approach to cooperation in the context of the Nile Basin. Swain contends that while the basin is composed of 10 states, Egypt, Sudan, and Ethiopia hold within their territory the largest portion of the river flow and have the largest stakes in the conflict. Since a multilateral initiative addressing the concerns of all 10 riparians will most likely not transpire, solid cooperation at the sub-basin level should take priority. The arguments of Swain and Just and Netanyahu are still to be tested in light of the on-going regional Nile initiative, led by the World Bank.

Taking a basin-wide approach, Rogers (1997) argued that externalities can either create conflicts or hamper cooperation. According to Rogers, however, if there is a way to internalize such externalities, a basis for cooperation may exist. Several

---

[3]The Victim Pays principle suggests that the party that suffers from externalities created by the other party pays to mitigate or to adapt for its suffer or damage. The Victim Pays principle can be compared with the Polluter Pays principle, which argues that the creator of the externality pays for the cost imposed by it.

principles are of specific interest such as pareto-admissibility (compensation possible) and superfairness (for all parties), both of which are a basis for cooperation. Using three cases, the Columbia, the Ganges–Brahmaputra, and the Nile Rivers, Rogers applies a game theoretic approach to demonstrate the use of such concepts. Another game theoretic approach is applied to the Great Lakes Basin by Becker and Easter (1999). Alternative diversion restrictions and coalition structures are applied to evaluate potential for basin-wide cooperation and noncooperation among the federal governments of Canada and the United States and the relevant provinces.

An interesting linkage between domestic water pricing policies and basin economy is addressed by Roe and Diao (1997). They argue that depending on the relative size of the water sector, different water pricing policies of the river riparians may either have negative or positive effects on the domestic economy as well as the international economy of the basin. The authors show that the economies of the two riparians are interlinked and affected by the price policies of the other.

Another angle through which one can learn about efforts to assess economic benefits and costs that are associated with a basin wide utilization of water is via the optimization models and cooperative game theory models. Our book addresses to some extent the optimization and modeling approaches in Chapter 10 and the principles of cooperation in Chapters 4–6.

For Further Discussion. Surprisingly, both the number and the scope of economic studies (including game theory) of transboundary water are quite small. One can attribute it to various factors, such as complication of the problems that provided disincentives to economists, or the case-study nature of such problems that might be of less interest to economists. What would you suggest as new paradigm for economic work on transboundary water that could be of interest to economists in this field?

Regional Optimization Models

Optimization models provide solutions that, economically, are preferable to the entire basin. They are usually seen as if a social planner took responsibility for the preferences of the parties in the basin and suggested solutions that they "could not resist." A class of optimization models applied to resource allocation problems can be found in the literature.

Chaube (1992) applies a multilevel, hierarchical modeling approach to international river basins in order to evaluate possible resolution arrangements of the India–Bangladesh–Nepal–Bhutan conflict over the Ganges–Brahmaputra river basin water. That modeling approach allows the utilization of existing models and institutional frameworks for the analysis of large-scale, real-life problems. By breaking the overall problem into hierarchical stages, it can carry a robust analysis of physical, political, economic, and institutional systems. As opposed to Chaube (1992), who used a static framework, Deshan (1995) presents a large-system, hierarchical dynamic programming model, which is applied to the Yellow River in China.

By incorporating intertemporal effects, this approach allows for the testing of likely future impacts of water availability scenarios on the urban, storage, and hydropower sectors that compete over the scarce water of the river. Having the intertemporal effects built into the regional framework allows a careful evaluation of potential cooperation arrangements as well.

Another tool is the multiple objective planning approach. North (1993) applies a multiple objective model (MOM) to water resource planning and management. MOMs are particularly important in water-related conflicts, since water conflicts may arise because each party has a different set of objectives (that may conflict with other parties' objectives) in using the scarce resource. MOMs can compare the results of various optimization problems in terms of incommensurate values for economic, environmental, and social indicators.

Kassem (1992) develops a river basin model driven by water demand at each of the nodes (stakeholders, users, countries, etc.) in the river basin. This comprehensive approach takes into account both the available water resources and the characteristics of water use by each of the use sectors. In addition, the model allows for policy interventions directed at each of the river basin parties, in order to affect water use efficiency. Pricing, storage, and administrative quota restrictions are among such interventions.

The similarity among these planning models is that they provide a wide set of alternatives for consideration by the parties, but they do not create a mechanism flexible enough to respond to changing local and global situations (e.g., relative power, economic conditions) affecting the parties involved.

LeMarquand (1989) suggested a framework for developing river basins that are economically and socially sustainable. At the core of the approach is a river basin authority to coordinate basin-wide planning and execution of multipurpose projects, including water and other regional development. In the case of developing countries, the approach also includes a component to coordinate donor activities. Especially in international rivers. LeMarquand suggests the following conditions for successful water sharing agreements: (1) similar perceptions of the problem, (2) similar characteristics of the welfare functions of the parties, (3) similar water production functions, (4) existence of some level of dialogue, (5) a small number of parties involved, and (6) at least one party having the desire to resolve the conflict.

Sprinz (1995) investigated the relationships between local (state) production and pollution and international pollution-related conflicts. Although very specific to international environmental pollution conflicts, there are some features in this work that can be adapted to international water conflicts. The move from closed economies to a situation that allows international trade, international pollution regulation, and global environmental problems produces a more stable and acceptable solution.

While the economics, game theory, and planning approaches provide an overall framework for basin-wide arrangements for regulating flows, pollution, and benefit allocations, it is quite obvious that without amending such allocation solutions with a sound legal and institutional framework, they will not be practical under many real-world situations. Therefore, one should immediately address the vast literature on international water laws and its applications.

International Water Law[4]

The evolution of International Water Law provides a useful insight into the context of the legal aspects of water conflicts and their resolution. The literature includes not only a general assessment of international legal clauses but also application to particular river basins' conflicts and their resolution. In the context of both these approaches, it is especially interesting to note the controversy between upstream and downstream countries. In addition to reviewing key works on surface water, we will also address issues related to groundwater.

International Law for Surface Water

In 1997, the *UN Convention on the Non-Navigational Uses of International Water Courses* was adopted by the United Nations — considered to be an international framework agreement for use by states in negotiating water disputes (for more in-depth discussion, see Chapter 3). Perhaps most notably the Convention has officially put to rest the historic conflict between the two extreme principles of *absolute territorial sovereignty* (the right of an upstream state to do as it wishes with the waters in its territory regardless of the adverse affect on downstream states) and *absolute territorial integrity* (the right of a downstream state to an uninterrupted flow of a fixed quantity of usable water from upstream states). Instead, it adopted the *limited territorial sovereignty* principle, which introduces *equitable utilization* and *the obligation not to cause significant harm*. The Convention was adopted by a vote of 103 for and 3 against, with 27 abstentions and 33 members absent. However, the Convention has yet to be ratified by a sufficient number of countries to enter into force — the ratification deadline (May 20, 2000) has passed. The 1997 Convention is seen as the modern international law, replacing several attempts to arrive at rules and laws in the past 200 years (Salman and Uprety, 2002; McCaffrey, 2001).

Much work on International Water Law has, of course, preceded the 1997 Convention, comparing it with previous frameworks. Three comprehensive studies (Salman *et al.*, 2002; McCaffrey, 2001, 2007) provide a comprehensive review of the process leading to an analysis of the content of the 1997 Convention. A more in-depth analysis of the Convention and its various clauses can be found in Chapter 3. In this context, let us only mention two other recent works. One recent publication (Subedi, 2005) provides a comprehensive view of the existing challenges facing the International Water Law, with a special focus on the Ganges Basin in comparison with the Rhine and Mekong Basins. The works in Subedi (2005) challenge international law applications in basins with high

---

[4]A more detailed and focused review of international law literature is provided in Chapters 3 and 9.

scarcity, high risk of environmental pollution, and sustainable development. In addition, the interaction between national laws and international law is used to demonstrate potential difficulties. The work by Nolkaemper (2005) is very representative of challenges brought about in the 21st century that have to be addressed by the international law. Issues such as industrial chemical pollution, salinization, and rehabilitation of ecosystems in the Rhine, and the regional EU Water Framework Directive that was imposed on European countries after the International Water Course Law was adopted, may affect its implementation, indicating that states may not be ready yet for its full implementation.

A major work reviewing the 1997 UN Convention by Tanzi and Arcari (2001) not only takes the reader through a historical context of how International Water Law has developed and evolved but also reviews the entire Convention, its principles and articles. Their survey reveals and emphasizes several important points: (1) The *equitable utilization* principle and the *no harm* rule, rather than competing with each other, are part of the same normative setting. This applies to both water allocation and pollution. One does not prevail over the other. (2) While the Convention is primarily interested in the economic exploitation of water, its reference to general rules and standards of environmental law constrains the freedom of co-riparinas. While the no harm principle does not necessarily refer to pollution issues, pollution is one of the mainstays of the principle. Thus the "subjectivism inherent in the unilateral or agreed assessment of the equitable character of a use finds a limit in the objective requirements of protection and preservation of the watercourse" (Tanzi and Arcari, 2001). (3) The authors also argue that it is this balance inherent in the Convention that makes it a suitable reference in actual or potential negotiations. And while the Convention has not entered into force, its authority is not subject to codification. Rather the authors argue that its relevance is demonstrated in the way it is used in other international agreements as a catalyst and impetus for ending disputes.

We turn now to a quick mention of works that were published prior to the adoption of the 1997 Watercourses Law. McCaffrey (1993) reviews an array of rules of international law that concern shared water resources. Focusing on the two main principles — *equitable utilization* and the *obligation not to cause significant harm* — he compares draft resolutions of three highly authoritative international legal organizations, which reflect evidence for state practice and customary law. McCaffrey clearly shows that interpretation of the concepts of *equitable utilization* and *prevention of harm* put different degrees of weight on both principles. Despite the differences, McCaffrey argues that the work of such organizations is most welcome and will, without question, contribute to the resolution of international water controversies (McCaffrey, 1993:99).

Kliot (1994) attempts to apply the 1991 Draft Rules of the International Law Commission (ILC)[5] and the 1966 Helsinki Rules to three Middle Eastern river

---

[5]The ILC is the body associated with the United Nations, which was responsible for drafting the Articles that culminated in the 1997 Convention.

basins. Kliot chose perhaps some of the most politically-charged river basins in the
world for applying a still growing and evolving International Water Law. Her analysis not only demonstrates how particular rules apply to particular positions and
realities in each river basin, but also speaks about some of the deficiencies in the
Draft Articles and the Helsinki Rules, making recommendations of how they can
be improved upon when applied to actual river basins. Another account of international law in the context of the Middle East is provided by Ahmed (1994). Perhaps
most interesting about Ahmed's analysis is his stipulation that the 1929 and 1959
Agreements signed between Egypt and Sudan, and ignoring the other Nile River
riparians, continue to be valid despite the changing geopolitics in the region. These
two agreements have been quite controversial among the other Nile river riparians
but Ahmed bases his contention on international law, in general, and Articles 11
and 12 of the 1978 Vienna Conventionon Succession of States in respect of Treaties
and the 1969 Vienna Convention on the Law of Treaties, in particular, which recognize the legality of such treaties. Ahmed also applies the 1966 Heslinki Rules to the
Nile Basin. Waterbury (1994) reviews the Nile River, Tigris–Euphrates, and Jordan
River Basins. Like Kliot, Waterbury analyzes the hydropolitics of each basin and
the positions of each state in the context of International Water Law. Waterbury
provides a descriptive and brief overview from various reports and newspaper articles of the interests and principles advanced by Middle Eastern riparians to defend
their claims of transboundary waters. These are based on principles such as equity,
reason, and appreciable harm.

Dellapenna (1996) also reviews the hydropolitics of the Jordan and Nile River
Basins in the context of International Water Law. He demonstrates how the positions and subsequent favored legal principles of the riparians have evolved over the
years. Despite their evolution, Dellapenna describes how the principles have been
opposed at their core, depending on the geographical location of the states, and
argues that the tension between opposing principles can only be managed if the
water is cooperatively managed by the respective states in such a way as to assure
equitable participation in the benefits derived from the water from all communities
sharing the basin. Like Kliot and Waterbury, Hillel (1994) considers the Nile, the
Jordan, and the Euphrates–Tigris. Hillel's work includes a deep historical and religious analysis transcending the link between the basins' ancient civilizations and
subsequent modern state system with water. Most interesting is the analysis on
legal criteria (Hillel, 1994:269) for sharing international waters and a small section
describing how antecedents to rules regulating water allocation can be found in the
Middle East itself. Islamic law and edicts issued by medieval Jewish sages, Hillel
argues, had also evolved a sophisticated set of principles to regulate water management in order to minimize conflict. These traditions, however, have not been
extended to international rivalries over water rights.

In another work touching upon the connection between individual treaties and
the 1997 Convention, Ramoeli (2002) reviewed the South African Development
Community (SADC) Protocol on Shared Water Courses. While the SADC Protocol was originally signed in 1995, it was recently (in 2000) modified and expanded
to align itself with the UN Convention on the Law of Non-Navigational Uses of

Shared Watercourses. Ramoeli explains how the harmonization process between a general international convention and a regional protocol took place. Interestingly, harmonization is discussed and encouraged in Article 3 of the UN Convention. The modified SADC Protocol can provide an appropriate lesson for other river basins considering the same procedure.

Perhaps the most comprehensive, not to mention a convenient compilation, of pre-Convention writings can be found in two, Spring and Summer, 1996 special issues of *Natural Resources Journal.*[6] The two volumes include some of the key thinkers on International Water Law. The writings reveal some of the developments and evolution of International Water Law in the 1990s — specifically the clash between Articles 5 and 7 in the context of the ILC alluded to above by McCaffrey. Again, we offer much more details on international law in Chapter 3.

International Law for Groundwater

Groundwater, the "unexplored resource," has received cursory attention and has often been considered the "poor cousin" to surface water. The issue of groundwater and international law is reviewed by Biswas (1999). An out-of-sight, out-of-mind mentality has resulted in its contamination and overuse, both in domestic and international aquifers. Increasingly, however, it is realized that the issue is of high priority. Both McCaffrey (1999) and Freestone (1999) discuss the issue of groundwater in the context of International Water Law and International Environmental Law. McCaffrey reviews the relevance of the 1997 Convention to groundwater issues and international agreements and finally looks at the work of international legal non-governmental organizations and expert groups in the field of groundwater. Both McCaffrey and Freestone indicate that surface water and groundwater are not alike, and thus international groundwater law has to be developed. The law of international groundwater is still in its embryonic stages.

In an effort to apply International Water Law to a specific groundwater aquifer, Eckstein and Eckstein (2003) discuss the Mountain Aquifer shared between the Israelis and Palestinians. After reviewing some of the entailed hydrogeological and hydropolitical issues, the authors consider the 1966 Helsinki Rules and 1986 Seoul Rules as they apply to groundwater. Most interesting about the authors' analysis, however, is their discussion of the 1997 UN Convention. The authors argue that under the definition of a "watercourse" and "groundwater" set forth by the Convention, the Mountain Aquifer cannot be accounted for and the authors provide specific examples. Given that the Convention does not account for the Mountain Aquifer, Eckstein and Eckstein discuss other legal principles that may be relevant for the management of the Mountain Aquifer.

Kemper *et al.* (2003) also discuss the applicability of International Water Law to groundwater and review the case of the Guarani Aquifer system, shared by

---

[6] *Natural Resources Journal*, 36(2), Spring 1996, Part 1; *Natural Resources Journal*, 36(3), Summer 1996, Part 2.

Argentina, Brazil, Paraguay, and Uruguay. The authors review the legal principles required for appropriate use of the aquifer, considering different legal clauses and texts assessed by international organizations and legal societies, culminating their discussion of International Water Law with the 1997 UN Convention. Like Eckstein and Eckstein, Kemper *et al.* consider the definition of "watercourse" and "groundwater" and argue that applying the 1997 UN Convention to the Guarani Aquifer may be problematic. The authors also point to the Bellagio Draft Treaty as a possible outline for aquifer management in the Guarani case but realize that, given groundwater law's embryonic development, the riparian states will have a challenging task ahead.

We will conclude with a recent work by Daibes-Murad (2005), which offers a new legal framework for managing international groundwater, with an application to the Mountain Aquifer conflict. Using a wealth of existing treaties, including the Ballagio Draft Treaty Framework (all are provided in Appendix 1 to that work), and extrapolating from existing international treaties, Daibes-Murad suggests a "Progressive Framework" to take into account (1) the asymmetry among the parties, (2) the opposed riparian priorities over rights vs. needs, and (3) the lack of cooperation and coordination, and existing water institutions and practices. We should indicate here that many of the components proposed in the "Progressive Approach" are very similar to the principles of the Joint Management institution proposed by Feitelson and Haddad (2001), and the suggested framework to address the "Victim Pays" principle by Just and Netanyahu (2004), using a game theory model to assess various solutions to that conflict.

International Relations

Although an array of disciplines have influenced the study of conflict and cooperation over water, the international relations discipline has had much bearing. Topics such as scarcity, interdependence, domestic politics, geography, and state power have set the context for analyzing river basin hydropolitics. Other important issues and approaches, under the guises of the international relations discipline, have also shaped the hydropolitics field. These include: the security-water nexus and the water-war debate, institutional and organizational approaches for analyzing conflict, and cooperation over shared international waters. While a detailed and focused analysis of hydropolitics and international relations can be found in Chapter 6, the following section summarizes and categorizes some of the important literature as it is related to the above topical issues.

Topical Issues

There is no better place to start this literature review, pertaining to the international components of hydropolitics, than with Elhance (1999), who provides one of the most recent and comprehensive analyses of conflict and cooperation over water in the context of six river basins. He considers elements such as geography, hydrology, and politics, and argues that the geographic and hydrological nature of an international river basin creates a complex network of environmental, economic, political, and security interdependencies between its riparian states. These interdependencies, however, may lead to either conflict or cooperation over shared waters. Understanding how conflict ensues and abates and how cooperation comes about has been the main focus of the nexus between hydropolitics and international relations.

What are some of the factors and variables that either facilitate cooperation or prolong conflict? Gleick (1998) argued that the intensity of the conflict and the need for cooperation over freshwater is determined by several factors: (1) the degree of scarcity, mismanagement, or misallocation of water in various regions; (2) the interdependence of states regarding common water resources, which respect no political boundaries; (3) the geographic and historic criteria of water ownership vis-à-vis states; (4) whether a protracted conflict underlies the water dispute; (5) the existence of alternative sources of water or options for a negotiated agreement and the desperation of the parties to an agreement; and (6) the relative power of the parties. Some of these factors are considered below.

On the one hand, scarcity, and the interdependent character of environmental issues such as water, has been argued by some scholars to contribute to conflict, and possible violent conflict, between states (Mathew, 1999; Falkenmark, 1992; Gleick, 1993; Homer-Dixon, 1999). On the other hand, other scholars have argued that those same variables are just as likely to contribute to cooperation (Deudney, 1991; Brock, 1992; Wolf and Hamner, 2000a). Thus while the variables under consideration have been uniform, the assumptions about their propensity for conflict or cooperation have been opposing.

Domestic politics and the overall relationship between the respective countries have also been argued to contribute to either conflict or cooperation. If domestic political sentiments reject cooperation and the overall relationship between the riparians is poor, conflict is likely to arise. However, if domestic political sentiments favor cooperation and the overall relationship between the riparians is warm, cooperation is likely to ensue. Lowi (1993), Elhance (1999), and Giordano *et al.* (2002), to name a few, have provided examples of domestic sentiments that have explained the conflictive scenario while LeMarquand (1977) has provided examples of domestic political workings that have facilitated the cooperative scenario.

Power and geographic location have also been touted as important variables in understanding conflict and cooperation over international rivers. Depending on whether the river basin's hegemon is upstream, and thus occupying the geographically superior position, or downstream, and thus occupying the geographically inferior position, scholars have come to different conclusions on whether conflict or cooperation shall ensue (Frey, 1984, 1993; Lowi, 1993; Naff, 1994; Homer-Dixon, 1999; Amery and Wolf, 2000). Others have considered only the relative power capabilities, as the key variable, among the river basin's riparians to analyze the propensity for conflict and cooperation (Hillel, 1994; Allan, 2000).

Issues and Approaches

The above topics and debates have also helped shape the environmental security field as it pertains to freshwater issues. The water-war debate has taken center stage in this water-security nexus. The core argument of the water-war school has been that wars have been fought over water in the past and will be fought even more intensely in the future (Cooley, 1984; Starr 1991; Bulloch and Darwish, 1993; Soffer 1999; Myers, 1993). Critics argue that while water installations have been a target of military attack, the water-war prediction has been alarmist at best. The reasons include lack of evidence of past wars over water, the ability of states to contend with scarcity through trade and technology, armed interstate conflicts being caused by a multitude of political and economic factors, and water being an element of cooperation and not armed conflict (Allan 1996; Ohlsson 1999; Wolf 1999; Dolatyar and Gray 2000; Wolf and Hamner 2000a, 2000b; Wolf, 2000; Turton, 2000; Lowi, 2000; Allan, 2001; Lonergan, 2001; Uitto and Wolf, 2002).

There are some conclusions that can be made regarding this fascinating debate. Conflict over water — in some cases political and in some cases prone to armed exchanges — may indeed take place. In many cases, water is used as a military tool or target in a war over unrelated issues. Most of the time, however, either the status quo of stalemate and conflict ensues or the parties realize that cooperation is more rational and cost-effective and engage in negotiations over the resource. Similarly, the rich history of cooperation over water, demonstrated in thousands of documented treaties, not only outweighs the few examples of water-wars and military skirmishes over water, but also demonstrates that shared-water resources may ultimately induce cooperation rather than conflict. Finally, the security and scarcity dimension of water, as a whole, may require some scrutiny. Countries may employ different strategies to cope with water scarcity or may over time develop room in their national discourse for economic and environmentally conscious solutions to their domestic and regional water problems. Until then, they will choose to make it a security matter.

> **For Further Discussion.** The literature on international relations applications in transboundary water seems to miss a significant volume of work that is not related to water, but is very relevant at the basin level. What can we presumably add from other known conflicts, and how can that be used in the case of water conflict and cooperation?

Institutional and Organizational Aspects

The aforementioned remarks about cooperation provide a good transition for discussing institutional and organizational approaches to hydropolitics. Indeed, disputes over water may require a basin-wide solution whereby institutional and other organizational mechanisms are employed to foster collaboration among the respective riparians.

Two works, Nishat and Faisal (2000) and Kibaroglu and Unver (2000), emphasize the importance of institutional mechanisms for cooperation over shared waters in the context of the Ganges–Brahmaputra–Meghna and Euphrates–Tigris River Basins, respectivey. Nishat and Faisal (2000) discuss the role of the Joint Rivers Commission (JRC) in the context of the agreements and memorandums of understanding signed between India and Bangladesh, primarily for sharing the Ganges. According to the statutes of the JRC, the parties are to discuss mutual water issues within the auspices of the Commission and find effective solutions to these problems in its institutional capacity. But the authors argue that while the JRC has been instrumental in the cooperative framework between the two countries, it requires more authority in identifying and implementing effective solutions. It should therefore engage in regular collection and sharing of data and should be extended in scope to include other water issues that have emerged over time. Kibaroglu and Unver (2000) analyze the history and implications for future negotiations and cooperation over the Euphrates–Tigris within the boundaries of the Joint Technical Committee (JTC). The authors suggest particular principles, rules, norms, and decision-making procedures for a more effective JTC. The two works admit or imply, however, that despite the utility of the institutions created, political constraints such as lack of political will on the part of one of the parties and the relative power discrepancies among the countries combined with their distinct underlying interests may scuttle the effectiveness of the institution.

Duda and La Roche (1997) discuss the importance of basin-wide institutions and international organizations in the management of transboundary water conflicts and the facilitation of cooperation. Using the case of the Danube River Basin, the authors argue that states that experience bigger political conflicts should cooperate over issues such as water and environment. Such cooperation may help ameliorate the political conflict. Another important point is that nations should try to develop and test out joint management mechanisms of shared freshwater resources rather than employ compensation or allocation mechanisms. International institutions such as the Global Environmental Facility (GEF) have the capacity to facilitate both of these recommendations. Similarly, Uitto and Duda (2002) consider the role of the GEF in promoting cooperation in the Aral Sea Basin, Bermejo River, and Lake Tanganyika.

Jagerskog (2002) also discusses the role of regimes and institutions, such as the 1955 Johnston negotiations, which culminated in a water-sharing scheme that was never recognized by the states. He argues, however, that this unrecognized agreement actually helped regulate the relations between Israel and Jordan and has facilitated more friendly relations. The author recognizes the limitation of regime theory, arguing that water is sometimes subordinate to other more contentious areas of dispute. The author also discusses the 1994 Agreement between Jordan and Israel, which included an agreement on the disputed water. He then assesses the quality of the regime by looking at its effectiveness, robustness, and resilience in relation to actual events. He applies similar tools to the Joint Water Committee established between Israel and the Palestinian Authority.

Also praising the role of institutions and rules, Henwood and Funke (2002) address the importance of institutions in managing Southern Africa's transboundary water. According to the authors, if water-related problems are perceived to develop into a threat, the water issue will become "securitized." The chances of this taking place increase if a water dispute or regional water issue is part of the foreign policy paradigm of the countries rather than the international relations paradigm. Foreign policy is much more limited. It is more about the national interest of the state. International relations, on the other hand, are more inclusive and broader in scope referring to all forms of interactions, including interactions between governments and nongovernmental organizations over trade, values, ethics and communication — issues that will not create undue tensions. The situation unique to Southern Africa vis-à-vis water places the issue in the foreign policy sphere, which is not good for regional development and stability in Southern Africa. Cooperation rather than conflict must be the basis for the states' interaction and the "desecuritization" of water can only be achieved through provisions that create and institutionalize the capacity to manage shared watercourse systems effectively.

Turton and Henwood (2002) extend the notion of hydropolitics, arguing that Arun Elhance's definition of hydropolitics as "the systematic analysis of interstate conflict and cooperation regarding international water resources" does not take into account the rich literature on water, the environment, society, and culture. Instead, Turton and Henwood (2002) argued that hydropolitics should cover all political interactions over water and thus it should be defined as: "the authoritative allocation of values in society with respect to water." This is similar to the proposals made above by Dolatyar and Gray (2000). Turton and Henwood (2002) also include works that suggest moving away from the river basin as a unit of reference and instead allow for interbasin analysis. To a certain extent, the notion of interbasin could be considered as a unit of analysis assuming that cooperation is possible and that externalities from such expansion are internalized. A compelling example of interbasin transfers of water between SADC countries is provided by Heyns (2002). The work outlines, in our view, all the necessary items for consideration for policy-makers in evaluating the feasibility of interbasin transfers. Since interbasin transfers within the jurisdiction of one country have recently become rather "popular," the suggested framework could be applied to assist in the analysis of transboundary interbasin transfers. Still, international transfers are more complicated and more is needed in the suggested framework to address it.

Giordano and Wolf (2003) provide another assessment of the importance of institutions. The authors argue that the difference between conflict over water and cooperation over water is attributed to the degree of institutions embodied in a river basin. Specifically, evidence of how institutions can serve to defuse tensions is seen in basins with large numbers of water infrastructure projects. In fact, co-riparian relations are more cooperative in basins with established water treaties — by extension higher levels of institutional development. In addition to reviewing international legal principles and conventions that have refined principles of shared water management, the authors cite the actual treaties states have negotiated over shared waters. The authors' broad approach to treaty analysis allows them to make specific recommendations for fostering higher levels of institutionalism in different river basins via several key factors such as equitable distribution of benefits, flexible criteria for water allocation, and water quality and conflict resolution mechanisms.

A new framework based on network analysis is of interest in shared water as it allows comparison of various management systems across states and cultures. Blatter and Ingram (2001) employ new approaches for the study of water such as network analysis, discourse analysis, historical and ethnographic analysis, and social ecology analysis. According to the authors, the meaning of water and other water policy issues are not fully captured in the context of the nation state or other modern approaches, which is "beyond human control and rational calculation" (p. 4). Blatter (2001) explores the notions of network analysis and discourse analysis — phenomena also associated with the notion of epistemic communities in the international relations lingo of the constructivist persuasion — in the context of Lake Constance. Blatter considers the influence of ideas, institutions, and cross-border networks in transboundary water policies. Accordingly, this is a new political landscape where political actors, communities, and organizations are embroiled in the process of change and reconstruction — symbolic meaning and shared issue framing become extremely important. These nontraditional influences led to the development and success of cross-border cooperation in regulating boating and pollution on Lake Constance (p. 94).

In the context of the Black Sea, DiMento (2001) argues that even in a watercourse where riparians are divided by nationalist fervor, ethnic conflict, exclusionary ideologies — elements that divide actors — cross-boundary networks, discourses on cooperation, institutions, and legal regimes can emerge. This example provides additional tools for the analysis and management of water bodies. In fact, DiMento concludes that despite the claims of many of the Black Sea riprains that they cannot be environmentally sensitive given their difficult economic state and needs, efforts have emerged pointing to a new understanding of transboundary interaction and institutionalizing procedures essential for international cooperation to combat the Sea's degradation. DiMento specifically points to the role of the Black Sea Environmental Program (BSEP), developed under the auspices of the United Nations Environment Program and the Global Environmental Facility, in bringing together international legal principles and technical and financial instruments to support efforts by the riparian countries in their ongoing efforts at rehabilitation and protection of the Black Sea. The challenges are plenty, DiMento admits, but the institutionalization of particular principles and values makes the process more amenable to success.

Meijerink (1999) also developed a unique approach — a framework for decision-making on international river issues. The basin for which this framework is applied is the Scheldt Basin that lies within France, Belgium, and The Netherlands. Meijerink focuses on the process of the negotiations among the riparians and attempts at predicting the direction at which the negotiation process will develop. The analysis covers the period 1967–1993 that includes 14 rounds of negotiations and the final agreement that has been reached.

Another new approach to cooperation over water is offered by Kuffner (1998) who advocates a concept of sharing international rivers by jointly managing them to the maximum mutual benefit through an international agency, instead of dividing the waters and managing them separately. Kuffner criticizes the traditional solutions to water division among parties that are often stipulated in agreements on the account that they are based on a rather rigid allocation formula and do not provide for adjustments to changing conditions. Kuffner suggests the interconnection of water systems between states, with the aim of buying and selling water when the need arises, or allowing the transfer of water surplus in one system to an adjacent system. The solution would require a physical conveyance system and agreements regarding water trade, specifying the price and quality of water. He cites the example of the Lesotho Highlands Project as a possible case to emulate in the Jordan River Basin. Implied in Kuffner's analysis is a challenge to the notion of state sovereignty, and a neglect of the fact that rights to the water will still have to be assigned to companies by, most likely, governments, which means that water quantities will still have to be divided among countries. A similar approach — joint management of the resource — is suggested by Fitelson and Haddad (2001) who developed a joint management scheme for the Mountain Aquifer shared by the Israelis and the Palestinians. However, while Kuffner suggested an international agency to manage the shared resource, Feitelson and Haddad's (2001) management scheme consists of a committee that is based on experts from the two riparians.

Negotiation

In this section, we discuss the relationship between hydropolitics and negotiation theory. In addition to Chapter 7, Chapter 9 will also consider these elements in a more detailed fashion. Nonetheless, in this section we review and categorize some of the main literature pertaining to such concepts as prenegotiation, third-party intervention, culture and negotiation, the position of states along a river as a form of power in a negotiation process, asymmetrical negotiations, and economic discrepancies among the parties.

Faure and Rubin (1993) introduce perhaps one of the less analyzed concepts in the process of negotiations over water — culture. The work includes river basins from across the globe. Specifically, Deng (1993) analyzes the conflict over the construction of the Jonglei Canal between North and South Sudan; Slim (1993) considers how the clash of political cultures between Turkey, Syria, and Iraq and between Iraq and Syria has contributed to the conflict over the Euphrates; Lowi and Rothman (1993) argue that given the intractable conflict between the Arabs and Israelis, it is only when the larger political issues (e.g., identity, recognition, and security) are discussed seriously that cooperation on water can advance in a more meaningful manner and at the same time help the negotiation on the larger issues gain more momentum.

Another element of the negotiations process is power, which was discussed in the context of conflict and cooperation in the previous international relations section.

According to Zartman and Rubin (2000), however, the conventional definition of power, where the state with the mightiest military and the strongest economy will have its way in negotiations, or will have overwhelming influence, should be scrutinized. In the negotiation process, power is better understood as being issue-specific rather than static and aggregate. The example of the Indo-Nepali water relations is analyzed by Gyawali (2000) who considers the overwhelming aggregate power of India (military and economic might) versus the issue-specific power of Nepal (owning the sites where hydroelectric plants can be built). Relying on negotiation concepts and tactics developed by Habeeb (1988), Gyawali argues that while India and Nepal have negotiated agreements that have been perceived by Nepal to have overwhelmingly benefited India, the issue of hydroelectric generation has not been permanently settled. Only a fraction of the benefits that can accrue, if large storage dams are built deeper in Nepal, have so far been attained. Gyawali reviews some of the inner political workings of the India–Nepal water relationship, arguing that Nepal has been able to increase its bargaining power.

Kremenyuk and Winfried (1995:8–9) also discuss location and geography as an element of power in environmental negotiations. The authors argue that a downstream nation is more likely to ask for strict controls of water pollution than an upstream nation. In that context, Faure and Rubin (1995:22–23) argue that when it comes to pollution issues, for example, the upstream interest may be far less inclined to take the problem seriously, let alone to bear responsibility for devising an appropriate solution, than the downstream interest. To support it, Matthew (1999:171) contends that downstream states are more likely to be concerned about the future and more willing to participate in a collective management scheme than upstream states. In such a scenario, parties differ in their dependence on an agreement as well as their motivation to negotiate one.

Economic discrepancies among states are also a factor in negotiations over water. The literature deals with the limited resources and assets that a poor nation can bring to bear relative to a richer nation. As a negotiating tactic, a bargaining strategy held by the weaker party is to deprive the stronger actor of what it desires. According to Sjostedt and Spector (1993:311–312), cooperation from the poorer country will ensue if the richer country provides economic and financial incentives. Weak states may use their incapacity, relative to stronger states, to comply with certain provisions desired in a cooperative management, as a leverage to receive benefits.

Barrett (2002) developed a theory for interstate cooperation over shared resources and considered the notion of asymmetries as an element of international environmental agreements. The theory is applied to global shared resources such as the ozone layer and to regional water resources such as the Aral Sea and the Rhine in Europe. In the context of asymmetrical negotiations, Barrett argues that to encourage participation in and enforcement of a treaty, concessions can be extracted and financial and technological aid can be guaranteed in return for compliance. Similarly, according to Young (1994:134–135) and Underdal (2002), those states which believe that they have been treated fairly and that their core demands have been addressed will be more inclined to make agreements work and will stand by their commitments.

Economic differences among the parties reflect their attitudes toward the environment. Richer nations and poorer nations may value the same resource in completely different ways. Poor countries may have more of a propensity to pollute to the detriment of wealthier countries with higher pollution standards. According to Compte and Jehiel (1997:64), mutually beneficial agreements between states with heterogeneous preferences may require side payments. Similarly, Martin (1995:73) argues that heterogeneities in capabilities and preferences create possibilities for tradeoffs among international actors. For example, states that have intense interests in environmental protection are willing to make economic sacrifices. In essence, this is a kind of *exchange* whereby a state may agree to forgo benefits on some issues in return for concessions on others (pp. 81–82).

The literature, therefore, provides us interesting insight into water and negotiations. To induce cooperation, in general, or pollution abatement, in particular, in asymmetric situations — whether it is positional or economic asymmetry — side-payments may have to be employed or issue linkage will have to be the strategy. The geographical upper hand of upstream states may thus give it an advantage in negotiations with downstream states. At the same time, the relative economic disparity of one country and its propensity to pollute, relative to another country, may win it some concessions in negotiations over pollution abatement. This is investigated in Dinar (2007) and to some degree in Lemarquand (1977).

GLOBAL STUDIES

A recent trend in transboundary water research includes efforts by geographers, economists, and international relations scholars to focus on global analysis of water treaties, and other aspects of cooperation among basin riparians. This trend follows a similar branch in international economics that addresses peace–war relationships among states and determinants of cooperation (e.g., Polachek, 1980, 1997; Reuveny and Kang, 1996).

Giordano *et al.* (2002) suggest that the international level of water conflict among riparian states and domestic water and nonwater events in each of these states are linked. Using three case studies in the Middle East, South Asia, and Southern Africa, the authors apply both cooperation/conflict indexes and contextual analysis to make their point. A similar proposition except for using a wider set of observations and a more comprehensive set of variables can be seen by Hensel *et al.* (2006). They add an interesting angle to the cooperation theory, arguing that cooperation is more likely where basin level institutions exist, and also, where riparian-level institutions are supporting cooperation. A similar argumentation has been made by Giordano and Wolf (2003), but the work by Hensel *et al.* (2006) is also supported by empirical analysis of treaty data.

Both Giordano *et al.* (2002) and Hensel *et al.* (2006) do not use the global river basin data set. Several studies utilize the treaty data set of Oregon State University (OSU). Song and Whittington (2004) and Espey and Towfique (2004) explain differences in treaty making among riparians of transboundary river basins, using geographical, economic, political, cultural, and trade variables. It is also interesting to point to the work by Sigman (2004), who assessed econometrically the role of trade among riparian states in achieving better pollution control arrangements. We also note an article by Toset *et al.* (2000), which attempts to explain conflict over water among basin riparians and across a large number of river basins based on similar variables.

The literature also provides some antagonistic theories as to the linkage between scarcity (of resources) and conflict/cooperation. Giordano *et al.* (2005) suggest that at highly scarce and highly abundant situations, the likelihood of conflict is relatively low, but at medium level of abundant/scarcity levels, the likelihood of conflict is higher. The authors amend their argument of resource scarcity with the role of scarcity, of proper institutions, and the role of trade. No empirical support to their propositions is provided. A somewhat different theory is suggested by Hensel *et al.* (2006). They claim that resource-poor basins form environments that are highly competitive, leading to inability to create institutions or ineffective institutions to handle conflict over these scarce resources. In resource abundant basins, the opposite is the case. Therefore, their theory suggests that more cooperation will be more evident in resource-abundant locations. Using a subset of 57 transboundary basins, the authors attempt to demonstrate that as the level of scarcity increases, conflicts are more likely. In a third theoretical development, Dinar (2006a) suggests the term "Scarperation" to argue that at low levels of scarcity (abundance) and at high levels of scarcity, riparians are less likely to cooperate, for different reasons. In the case of the low scarcity, they have no reason to cooperate as each has sufficient amount of the resource. At high scarcity levels, there is so little or nothing to share that their cooperation may not be effective. Cooperation will be most effective and thus most likely in the moderate scarcity zone. Thus the cooperation curve displays a hill-shaped behavior with regard to scarcity level. Dinar *et al.* (2007) apply this theory to a dataset of 226 bilateral basins, as is reported below.

Dinar *et al.* (2007) investigate the determinants of cooperation between riparians of bilateral rivers. They prove the hill-shaped behavior of scarcity-cooperation interaction. In addition, international trade and governance in the basin affect the likelihood of cooperation. Geography was found less important in explaining levels of cooperation, but the authors suggest that geography explains treaty arrangements rather than likelihood of treaty formation or level of cooperation. Addressing the structure of bilateral rivers' treaties, Dinar (2005; 2006b; 2007) shows the interaction between the geography of the transboundary river and the nature of agreement over scarce resources. In particular, the author assesses the impact of geography and economic variables on side-payment and cost-sharing patterns in 271 recorded bilateral treaties.

A very useful study has been conducted by Wolf *et al.* (2003) who assemble a Geographical Information System database in order to identify basins at risk of eruptible conflicts. Using GIS technology, a data set that includes historic events of biophysical, socio-economic, and geopolitical events are compiled and used to identify basins at risk for the future.

> **For Further Discussion.** So far, this chapter has reviewed works from quite a number of disciplines. If you are a manager of a consulting firm that was awarded a contract to study a water conflict in a river basin and to suggest solutions, how would you recruit your consultants and how would you prioritize the sequence of the work?

CONCLUSION

Shared water resources are subject to conflict and, at the same time, are also a source for cooperation. Our much-focused review in this chapter does not cover the entire list of works in the field, but it provides the necessary mix of the disciplines we include in the book: law, international relations, economics, and planning.

While we focus in our review on a subset of disciplines, we are aware that the field of conflict and cooperation over shared waters has come a long way in the last decade. In addition to the sources referred to in footnotes 1 and 3, various publications that represent these different disciplines can be found in Beach *et al.* (2000), which includes both earlier publications and an extended list of journal publications in an annotated format.

We also note an extensive compilation of international water treaties found in the Atlas of International Freshwater Agreements (UNEP and OSU, 2002) and the Transboundary Freshwater Dispute Database of Oregon State University (OSU).[7] One can also refer to the Food and Agriculture Organization for earlier treaties and other depositories, such as the United Nations Treaty Collection and the International Water Law Institute of the University of Dundee, to locate treaty texts.[8]

The literature on international law is very rich, but also focused. Only recently, with the adoption of the 1997 UN Convention on the Non-Navigational Uses of International Water Courses did work in international law take a step toward a

---

[7]http://www.transboundarywaters.orsu.edu

[8]Systematic index of international water resources treaties, declarations, acts and cases by basin, *Food and Agriculture Organization*, Legislative Studies, V I N 15, 1978, Systematic index of international water resources treaties, declarations, acts and cases by basin, *Food and Agriculture Organization*, Legislative Studies, V II, N 34, 1984; Food and Agriculture Organization, WATER-LEX, http://faolex.fao.org/waterlex/; United Nations Treaty Collection, http://untreaty.un.org (subscription required); International Materials, International Water Law Research Institute, University of Dundee, http://www.dundee.ac.uk/law/iwlri/Research_Documents_International.php

more comparative analysis of international disputes and agreements. This is a trend that we tried to capture in the review and will further address in Chapter 3.

International relations literature is not rich in work that is comprehensive, but focused more on cases rather than on explaining sources of differences among cases. A synthesis work is needed to facilitate better understanding of processes and trends. The emerging globalization is surely a field that should be more investigated by international relation experts to explain opportunities for better cooperation over shared water.

The field of economics is underrepresented in the literature reviewed in this book. This is not to say that economics is not important or that economists are not interested in international water issues. It is probably a combination of several factors, including difficulty in obtaining accurate data and information, and the ability to communicate the results to the decision-makers in the respective river basins. Therefore, economists should develop models that do not rely on sophisticated approaches, which necessitate accurate data that is probably as scarce as the water in the basin they are investigating. Regardless, economic analysis for identifying conditions for cooperation in various basins is greatly needed. Economic justification of cooperative arrangements and development options is the first step toward the initiation of a negotiation process that hopefully will lead to an agreement.

And finally, while each of the disciplines we reviewed has a legacy and potential, it is clear from the review that each discipline by itself cannot provide sufficient explanation to the spectrum of issues and cases in the field of shared water. What we hope we were able to show is that the various approaches are actually complementary and jointly provide better explanations and more useful solutions to shared water problems. This observation or belief is reflected in the rest of the book.

Practice Questions

1. Provide a critical evaluation of the strong and weak aspects of International Water Law, addressing fairness, efficiency, and sustainability of the resource allocation principles.

2. Review and discuss at least two approaches that have been suggested in the literature for managing transboundary water.

3. In their papers, Giordano *et al.* (2005), Hensel *et al.* (2006), and Dinar *et al.* (2007) suggest a certain relationship between level of resource abundance/scarcity and conflict/cooperation. (a) Draw the suggested relationships and discuss the theory used in each paper to explain the proposed relationship. (b) What in your opinion are the strong and weak parts in each theory?

REFERENCES

Ahmed, S. (1994). Principles and precedents in international law governing the sharing of Nile Waters. In: Howell, P. and J.A. Allan (eds.), *The Nile: Sharing A Scarce Resource*. Cambridge and New York: Cambridge University Press.

Allan, A.J. (2000). *The Middle East Water Question*. London and New York: I.B. Tauris Publishers.

Allan, A.J. (2001). *The Middle East Water Question: Hydropolitics and the Global Economy*. London and New York: I.B. Tauris Publishers.

Allan, A.J. (1996). The political economy of water: Reasons for optimism but long term caution. In: Allan, J.A. and Court, J.H. (eds.), *Water, Peace and the Middle East: Negotiating Resources in the Jordan Basin*. London and New York: I.B. Tauris Publishers.

Amery, H. and A.T. Wolf (2000). Water, geography and peace in the Middle East: An introduction. In: Amery, A. and A.T. Wolf (eds.), *Water in the Middle East: A Geography of Peace*. Austin: University of Texas Press.

Barrett, S. (2002). *Environment and Statecraft: The Strategy of Environmental Treaty-Making*. Oxford: Oxford University Press.

Beach, H., J. Hamner, J. Hewitt, E. Kaufman, A. Kurki, J. Oppenheimer and A. Wolf (2000). *Transboundary Freshwater Dispute Resolution: Theory, Practice and Annotated References*. Tokyo: United Nations University Press.

Becker, N. and K.W. Easter (1995). Cooperative and noncooperative water diversion in the Great Lakes Basin. In: Dinar, A. and E. Loehman (eds.), *Water Quantity/Quality Management and Conflict Resolution*. Westport, CT: Praeger.

Becker, N. and K.W. Easter (1999). Conflict vs. cooperation in managing international water resources such as the great lakes, *Land Economics*, 75(2), 233–245.

Becker, N., Z. Naomi and S. Mordechai (1996). Reallocating water resources in the Middle East through market mechanisms, *Water Recourses Development*, 12(1), 17–31.

Bennett, L., S. Regland and P. Yolles (1998). Facilitating international agreements through an interconnected game approach: The case of river basins. In: Richard, J.E. and S. Neyanyahu (eds.), *Conflict and Cooperation on Trans-Boundary Water Resources*. Boston: Kluwer Academic Publishers.

Biswas, A.K. (1999). Water crisis: Current perceptions and future realities. In: Salman, S. (ed.), *Groundwater: Legal and Policy Perspectives*, Proceedings of a World Bank Seminar, World Bank Technical Paper, No. 456, November 1999.

Blatter, J. and H. Ingram (ed.) (2001). *Reflections on Water: New Approaches to Transboundary Conflicts and Cooperation*. Cambridge and London: The MIT Press.

Blatter, J. (2001). Lesson from Lake Constance: Ideas. Institutions and advocacy coalitions. In: Blatter, J. and H. Ingram (eds.), *Reflections on Water: New Approaches to Transboundary Conflicts and Cooperation*. Cambridge and London: The MIT Press.

Brock, L. (1992). Security through defending the environment: An illusion? In: Boulding, E. (ed.), *New Agendas for Peace Research: Conflict and Security Reexamined*. Boulder: Lynne Rienner.

Bulloch, J. and A. Darwish (1993). *Water Wars, Coming Conflicts in the Middle East*. London: Victor Gollancz.

Chaube, U.C. (1992). Multilevel hierarchical modeling of an international basin. In: *Proceedings of the International Conference on Protection and Development of the Nile and Other Major Rivers*, Volume 2/2, Cairo, Egypt. 3–5 February.

Compte, O. and P. Jehiel (1997). International negotiations and dispute resolution mechanisms: The case of environmental negotiations. In: Carraro, C. (ed.), *International Environmental Negotiations: Strategic Policy Issues*. Glos, United Kingdom and Vermont, United States: Edward Elgar Publishing.

Cooley, J. (1984). The war over water, *Foreign Policy*, 54 (Spring).

Daibes-Murad, F. (2005). *A New Legal Framework for Managing the World's Shared Groundwaters, A Case Study from the Middle East*. London Seattle: IWA Publishing.

Dellapenna, J. (1996). Rivers as legal structures: The examples of the Jordan and the Nile, *Natural Resources Journal*, 36(2), Spring, Part 1.

Deng, F. (1993). Northern and Southern Sudan: The Nile. In: Faure, G.O. and J. Rubin (eds.), *Culture and Negotiation: The Resolution of Water Disputes*. Newbury Park, London, New Delhi: Sage Publications.

Deshan, T. (1995). Optimal allocation of water resources in large river basins: I theory, *Water Resources Management*, 9, 39–51.

Deudney, D. (1991). Environment and security, *Bulletin of Atomic Scientists*, 47(3).

DiMento, J. (2001). Black Sea environmental management: Prospects for new paradigms in transitional contexts. In: Blatter, J. and H. Ingram (eds.), *Reflections on Water: New Approaches to Transboundary Conflicts and Cooperation*. Cambridge: The MIT Press.

Dinar, A. and A.T. Wolf (1997). Economic and political considerations in regional cooperation models, *Agricultural and Resource Economics Review*, 26(1), 7–22.

Dinar, A. and A.T. Wolf (1994). International markets for water and the potential for regional cooperation: Economic and political perspectives in the Western Middle East, *Economic Development and Cultural Change*, 43(1), 43–66.

Dinar, S. and A. Dinar (2003). Recent developments in the literature on conflict and cooperation in international shared water, *Natural Resources Journal*, 43(4), 1217–1287.

Dinar, S. (2006a). *Scarperation*: A theory of scarcity and cooperation over transboundary rivers, Working paper, Department of International Relations and Geography, Florida International University, Miami, Florida.

Dinar, S. (2006b). Assessing side-payment and cost-sharing patterns in international water agreements: The geographic and economic connection, *Political Geography*, 25(5).

Dinar, S., A. Dinar and P. Kurukulasuriya (2007). SCARPERATION: An empirical inquiry into the role of scarcity in fostering cooperation between international river riparians. Paper presented at the AERE Session (*Environmental Conflict and Cooperation*) of the 2007 ASSA Winter Meetings, Chicago, IL January 5–7, 2007.

Dinar, S. (2005). Patterns of engagement: How states negotiate international water agreements, Processes of International Negotiation, International Institute for Applied Systems Analysis (IIASA), Laxenburg, Austria, 2005, http://www.iiasa.ac.at/Publications/Documents/IR-05-007.pdf

Dinar, S. (2007). *International Water Treaties: Transboundary River Negotiation and Cooperation*. London: Routledge.

Dolatyar, M. and G. Timothy (2000). *Water Politics in the Middle East: A Context for Conflict or Co-operation?* New York: St. Martin's Press.

Duda, A. and D. La Roche (1997). Sustainable development of international waters and their basins: Implementing the GEF operational strategy, *International Journal of Water Resources Development*, 13(3).

Dufournaud, C. (1982). On the mutually beneficial cooperative scheme: Dynamic change in the payoff matrix of international river basin schemes, *Water Resources Research*, 18(4), 764–772.

Eckstein, Y. and E. Gabriel (2003). Groundwater resources and international law in the Middle East peace process, *Water International*, 28(2).

Elhance, A.P. (1999). *Hydropolitics in the 3rd World: Conflict and Cooperation in International River Basins*, Washington, DC: United States Institute of Peace Press.

Espey, M. and B. Towfique (2004). International bilateral water treaty formation, *Water Resources Research*, 40.

Falkenmark, M. (1992). Water scarcity generates environmental stress and potential conflicts. In: James, W. and J. Niemczynowicz (eds.), *Water, Development, and the Environment*. Boca Raton, Ann Arbor, London, and Tokyo: Lewis Publishers.

Faure, G.O. and J. Rubin (1995). Organizing concepts and questions. In: Sjostedt, G. (ed.), *International Environmental Negotiation*. Newbury Park, London, New Delhi: Sage Publications.

Faure, G.O. and J. Rubin (eds.) (1993). *Culture and Negotiation: The Resolution of Water Disputes*. Newbury Park, London, New Delhi: Sage Publications.

Feitelson, E. and M. Haddad (eds.) (2001). *Management of Shared Groundwater Resources: The Israeli Palestinian Case with an International Perspective*. Kluwer Academic Publishers.

Fernandez, L. (2002). Solving water pollution problems along the U.S.-Mexico border, *Environment and Development Economics*, 7(4), 715–732.

Freestone, D. (1999). International environmental law: Principles relevant to transboundary groundwater. In: Salman, M.A.S. (ed.), *Groundwater: Legal and Policy Perspectives*, Proceedings of a World Bank Seminar, World Bank Technical Paper N456.

Frey, F. (1984). Middle East water: The potential for conflict or cooperation. In: Naff, T. and R. Matson (eds.), *Water in the Middle East: Conflict or Cooperation*. Boulder and London: Westview Press.

Frey, F. (1993). The political context of conflict and cooperation over international river basins, *Water International*, 18(1).

Giannias, D. and J.N. Lekakis (1996). Fresh water resource allocation between Bulgaria and Greece, *Environmental & Resource Economics*, 8, 473–483.

Giordano, M.F., M.A. Giordano and A.T. Wolf (2005). International resource conflict and cooperation, *Journal of Peace Research*, 42(1), 47–65.

Giordano, M.A., M.F. Giordano and A.T. Wolf (2002). The geography of water conflict and cooperation: Internal pressure and international manifestation, *The Geographical Journal*, 168(4), 293–312.

Giordano, M. and A. Wolf (2003). Sharing waters: Post-Rio International Water Management, *Natural Resources Forum*, 27.

Gleick, P.H. (ed.) (1993). *Water in Crisis*. Oxford University Press.

Gleick, P.H. (1998). *The World's Water: The Biennial Report on Freshwater Resources 1998-1999*. Washington, Covelo and London: Island Press.

Gyawali, D. (2000). Nepal-India water resource relations. In: Zartman, I. and J. Rubin (eds.), *Power and Negotiation*. Ann Arbor, Michigan: The University of Michigan Press.

Habeeb, W. (1988). *Power and Tactics in International Negotiation: How Weak Nations Bargain with Strong Nations*. Baltimore: The Johns Hopkins University Press.

Hensel, P.R., S.M. Mitchell and T.E. Sowers II (2006). Conflict management of riparian disputes, *Political Geography*. 25, 383–411.

Henwood, R. and N.N. Funke (2002). Managing water in international river basins in Southern Africa: International relations or foreign policy. In: Turton, A. and R. Henwood (eds.), *Hydropolitics in the Developing World: A Southern African Perspective*. Pretoria: Centre for Political International Studies, University of Pretoria.

Heyns, P. (2002). Interbasin transfer of water between SADC countries: A development challenge for the future. In: Turton, A. and R. Henwood (eds.), *Hydropolitics in the Developing World: A Southern African Perspective*. Pretoria: Centre for Political International Studies, University of Pretoria.

Hillel, D. (1994). *Rivers of Eden: The Struggle for Water and the Quest for Peace in the Middle East*. New York and Oxford: Oxford University Press.

Hipel, K.W. and N.M. Fraser (1980). Metagame analysis of the Garrison conflict, *Water Resources Research*, 16(4), 627–637.

Hipel, K.W., R.K. Regade and T.E. Unny (1976). Political resolution of environmental conflicts, *Water Resources Bulletin*, 12(4), 813–827.

Homer-Dixon, T. (1999). *Environment, Scarcity and Violence*. Princeton, NJ: Princeton University Press.

Jagerskog, A. (2002). Contributions of regime theory in understanding interstate water cooperation: Lessons learned in the Jordan River basin. In: Turton, A. and R. Henwood (eds.), *Hydropolitics in the Developing World: A Southern African Perspective*. Pretoria: African Water Issues Research Unit.

Just, R.E. and S. Netanyahu (eds.) (1998a). *Conflict and Cooperation on Trans-Boundary Water Resources*. Kluwer Academic Publishers.

Just, R.E. and S. Netanyahu (1998b). International water resource conflicts: Experience and potential. In: Richard, J.E. and S. Netanyahu (eds.), *Conflict and Cooperation on Trans-Boundary Water Resources*. Boston: Kluwer Academic Publishers.

Just, R.E. and S. Netanyahu (2004). Implications of 'Victim Pays' infeasibilities for interconnected games with an illustration for aquifer sharing under unequal access costs, *Water Resources Research*, 40(5), W05S01.

Kally, E. and G. Fishelson (1993). *Water and Peace: Water Resources and the Arab-Israeli Peace Process*. Westport, CT: Praeger.

Kassem, A.M. (1992). The water use analysis model (WUAM) a river basin planning model. In: *Proceedings of the International Conference on Protection and Development of the Nile and Other Major Rivers*, Vol. 2/2, Cairo, Egypt, 3–5 February.

Kemper, K., E. Mestre and L. Amore (2003). Management of the Guarani aquifer system: Moving towards the future, *Water International*, 28(2).

Kibaroglu, A. and O. Unver (2000). An institutional framework for facilitating cooperation in the Euphrates-Tigris river basin, *International Negotiation: A Journal of Theory and Practice*, 5(2).

Kliot, N. (1994). *Water Resources and Conflict in the Middle East*. London and New York: Routledge.

Kremenyuk, V. and L.W. Winfried (1995). The political, diplomatic and legal background. In: Sjostedt, G. (ed.), *International Environmental Negotiation*. Newbury Park, London, New Delhi: Sage Publications.

Krutilla, J. (1967). *The Columbia River Treaty: The Economics of an International River Basin Development*. Baltimore: The Johns Hopkins University Press.

Kuffner, U. (1998). Contested waters: Dividing or sharing? In: Scheumann, W. and
   M. Schiffler (eds.), *Water in the Middle East: Potential for Conflicts and Prospects
   for Cooperation*. Berlin, Heidelberg and New York: Springer-Verlag.

LeMarquand, D. (1989). Developing river and lake basins for sustained economic growth
   and social progress, *Natural Resources Forum*, (May), 127–138.

LeMarquand, D.G. (1977). *International Rivers: The Politics of Cooperation*. Vancouver:
   University of British Columbia, Westwater Research Centre.

Lonergan, S.C. (2001). Water and conflict: Rhetoric and reality. In: Diehl, P. and
   N.P. Gleditsch (eds.), *Environmental Conflict*. Boulder and Oxford: Westview
   Press.

Lowi, M. (2000). Water and conflict in the Middle East and South Asia. In: Lowi, M.
   and B. Shaw (eds.), *Environment and Security: Discourses and Practices*. New York:
   St. Martin's Press.

Lowi, M. and J. Rothman (1993). Arabs and Israelis: The Jordan River. In: Faure, G.O.
   and J. Rubin (eds.), *Culture and Negotiation: The Resolution of Water Disputes*.
   Newbury Park, London, New Delhi: Sage Publications.

Lowi, M.R. (1993). *Water and Power: The Politics of a Scarce Resource in the Jordan
   River Basin*. New York: Cambridge University Press.

Martin, L. (1995). Heterogeneity, linkage and common problems. In: Keohane, R. and
   E. Ostrom (eds.), *Local Commons and Global Interdependence: Heterogeneity
   and Cooperation in Two Domains*. London, Thousand Oaks, New Delhi: Sage
   Publications.

Matthew, R. (1999). Scarcity and security: A common-pool resource perspective. In:
   Barkin, J.S. and G.E. Shambaugh (eds.), *Anarchy and the Environment: The Inter-
   national Relations of Common Pool Resources*. Albany: State University of New York
   Press.

McCaffrey, S. (1993). Water, politics and international law. In: Gleick, P. (ed.), *Water in
   Crisis*. Oxford: Oxford University Press.

McCaffrey, S. (1999). International groundwater law: Evolution and context. In: Salman,
   S. (ed.), *Groundwater: Legal and Policy Perspectives*, Proceedings of a World Bank
   Seminar, World Bank Technical Paper N456.

McCaffrey, S. (2001). *The Law of International Watercourses: Non-Navigational Uses*.
   Oxford University Press.

McCaffrey, S.C. (2007). *The Law of International Watercourses*, 2nd edn. Oxford,
   New York: Oxford University Press.

Meijerink, S.V. (1999). *Conflict and Cooperation on the Scheldt River Basin*. Kluwer
   Academic Publishers.

Myers, N. (1993). *Ultimate Security: The Environmental Basis of Political Stability*. New
   York and London: W.W. Norton & Company.

Naff, T. (1994). Conflict and water use in the Middle East. In: Rogers, P. and P. Lydon
   (eds.), *Water in the Arab World: Perspectives and Prognoses*. Cambridge: Harvard
   University Press.

Netanyahu, S., J.E. Richard and H.K. John (1998). Bargaining over shared aquifers: The
   case of Israel and the Palestinians. In: Richard, J.E. and S. Neyanyahu (eds.), *Conflict
   and Cooperation on Trans-Boundary Water Resources*, Boston: Kluwer Academic
   Publishers, pp. 41–60.

Nishat, A. and I. Faisal (2000). An assessment of the institutional mechanisms for water
   negotiations in the Ganges-Brahmaputra-Meghna System, *International Negotiation*,
   5(2).

Nolkaemper, A. (2005). The evolution of the regime for the River Rhine. In: Subedi, S.P. (ed.), *International Watercourses Law for the 21st Century, The Case of the River Ganges Basin*. Hapshire: Ashgate.

North, R.M. (1993). Application of multiple objective models to water resources planning and management, *Natural Resources Forum*, (August), 216–227.

Ohlsson, L. (1999). *Environment, Scarcity and Conflict: A Study of Malthusian Concerns*, PhD Dissertation, Department of Peace and Development Research, University of Goteborg.

Elinor, O., J. Walker and R. Gardner (1994). *Rules, Games, and Common-Pool Resources*. Ann Arbor: Michigan University Press.

Polachek, S.W. (1980). Conflict and trade, *Journal of Conflict Resolution*, 24(1).

Polachek, S.W. (1997). Why democracies cooperate more and fight less: The relationship between international trade and cooperation, *Review of International Economics*, 5(3), 295–309.

Ramoeli, P. (2002). The SADC protocol on shared watercourses: Its origins and current status. In: Turton, A. and R. Henwood (eds.), *Hydropolitics in the Developing World: A Southern African Perspective*. Pretoria: Centre for Political International Studies, University of Pretoria.

Reuveny, R. and H. Kang (1996). International trade, political conflict/cooperation, and granger causality, *American Journal of Political Science*, 40(3), 943–970.

Roe, T. and X. Diao (1997). The strategic interdependence of a shared water aquifer: A general equilibrium analysis. In: Parker, D. and Y. Tsur (eds.), *Decentralization and Coordination of Water Resource Management*. Dordecht: Kluwer Academic Publishers.

Rogers, P. (1969). A game theory approach to the problem of international river basins, *Water Resources Research*, 5(4), 749–760.

Rogers, P. (1991). *International River Basins: Pervasive Unidirectional Externalities*. Italy: Universita di Siena.

Rogers, P. (1993). The value of cooperation in resolving international river basin disputes, *Natural Resources Forum*, 15, 117–131.

Rogers, P. (1997). International river basins: Pervasive unidirectional externalities. In: Dasgupta, P., K.G. Maler and A. Vercelli (eds.), *The Economics of Transnational Commons*. Oxford: Oxford University Press.

Salman, M., A. Salman and K. Upretti (2002). *Conflict and Cooperation on South Asia's International Rivers: A Legal Perspective*. Washington, DC: The World Bank.

Sigman, H. (2004). Does trade promote environmental coordination? Pollution in international rivers, *Contribution to Economic Analysis and Policy*, 3(2).

Sjostedt, G. and B. Spector (1993). Conclusion. In: Sjostedt, G. (ed.), *International Environmental Negotiation*. Newbury Park, London, New Delhi: Sage Publications.

Slim, R. (1993). Turkey, Syria, Iraq: The euphrates. In: Faure, G.O. and Rubin, J. (eds.), *Culture and Negotiation: The Resolution of Water Disputes*. Newbury Park, London, New Delhi: Sage Publications.

Soffer, A. (1999). *Rivers of Fire: The Conflict over Water in the Middle East*. Rowman & Littlefield Publishers.

Song, J. and D. Whittington (2004). Why have some countries on international rivers been successful negotiating treaties? A global perspective, *Water Resources Research*, 40.

Sprinz, D. (1995). Regulating the international environment: A conceptual model and policy implications. Prepared for the 1995 Annual Meeting of the American Political Science Association. Chicago, IL, 31 August–3 September.

Starr, J. (1991). Water Wars, *Foreign Policy*, 82.

Bridges Over Water

Subedi, S.P. (2005). *International Watercourses Law for the 21ˢᵗ Century. The Case of the River Ganges Basin.* Hapshire: Ashgate.

Swain, A. (2003). Managing the Nile River: The role of sub-basin cooperation. In: Chatterji, M., S. Arlosoroff and G. Gauri (eds.), *Conflict Management of Water Resources.* Hampshire and Burlington: Ashgate.

Tanzi, A. and M. Arcari (2001). *The United Nations Convention on the Law of International Watercourses: A Framework for Sharing.* London, the Hague and Boston: Kluwer Law International.

Toset, H.P.W., N.P. Gleditsch and H. Hegre (2000). Shared rivers and interstate conflict, *Political Geography,* 19.

Turton, A. (2000). Water wars in Southern Africa: Challenging conventional wisdom. In: Solomon, H. and A. Turton (eds.), *Water Wars: Enduring Myth or Impending Reality,* Africa Dialogue: Monograph Series, N 2, African Center for the Constructive Resolution of Disputes, South Africa.

Turton, A. and R. Henwood (eds.) (2002). *Hydropolitics in the Developing World: A Southern African Perspective.* University of Pretoria.

Uitto, J. and A. Duda (2002). Management of transboundary water resources: Lessons from international cooperation for conflict prevention, *The Geographical Journal,* 168(4).

Uitto, J. and A.T. Wolf (2002). Water wars? Geographical perspectives: Introduction, *The Geographical Journal,* 168(4), 289.

Umanskaya, V.I., E.B. Barbier and C.F. Mason (2006). Trade, transboundary pollution, and international lobbying. Department of Economics and Finance University of Wyoming Department 3985, 162 Ross Hall 1000 E. University Ave., Laramie, WY 82071. Downloaded from http://www.economics.ucr.edu/jobs/VictoriaUmanskaya.pdf. Visited on March 15, 2006.

UN Environment Programme and Oregon State University (UNEP and OSU) (2000). *Atlas of International Freshwater Agreements.* UNEP Press.

Underdal, A. (2002). The outcomes of negotiation. In: Kremenyuk, V. (ed.), *International Negotiation: Analysis, Approaches, Issues,* 2nd edn. San Francisco: Jossey-Bass.

Waterbury, J. (1994). Transboundary water and the challenge of international cooperation in the Middle East. In: Rogers, P. and P. Lydn (eds.), *Water in the Arab World: Perspectives and Prognoses.* Cambridge: Harvard University Press.

Waterbury, J. (2002). *The Nile Basin, National Determinants of Collective Action.* Yale University Press.

Wolf, A.T. (1999). Water Wars' and water reality: Conflict and cooperation along international waterways. In: Lonergan, S. (ed.), *Environmental Change, Adaptation, and Security.* Dordtecht, Boston and London: Kluwer Academic Publishers.

Wolf, A.T. (2000). Hydrostrategic territory in the Jordan Basin: Water, war, and Arab-Israeli peace negotiations. In: Amery, H. and A. Wolf (eds.), *Water in the Middle East: A Geography of Peace.* Austin: The University of Texas Press.

Wolf, A.T. and H. Jessy (2000b). Trends in transboundary water disputes and dispute resolution. In: Lowi, M. and B. Shaw (eds.), *Environment and Security: Discourses and Practices.* New York: St. Martin's Press.

Wolf, A.T. and J. Hamner (2000a). Trends in transboundary water disputes and dispute resolution. In: *Water for Peace in the Middle East and Southern Africa.* Green Cross International.

Wolf, A.T., Y. Shira and G. Meredith (2003). International waters: Identifying basins at risk, *Water Policy,* 5.

Yaron, D. (2002). An approach to the problem of water allocation to Israel and the Palestinian entity. In: Dinar, A. and D. Zilberman (eds.), *The Economics of Water Resources: The Contributions of Dan Yaron.* Boston: Kluwer Academic Publishers.

Young, O. (1994). *International Governance: Protecting the Environment in a Stateless Society.* Ithaca and London: Cornell University Press.

Zartman, W.I. and J. Rubin (2000b). Symmetry and asymmetry in negotiation. In: Zartman, W.I. and J. Rubin (eds.), *Power and Negotiation.* Ann Arbor, MI: The University of Michigan Press.

Zeitouni, N., B. Nir and S. Mordechai (1994). Two models of water market mechanisms with an illustrative application to the Middle East, *Resources & Energy Economics Journal*, 16(4), 303–330.

3. THE DEVELOPMENT AND APPLICATION OF INTERNATIONAL WATER LAW

Objectives

After reading this chapter you should have a general understanding of how International Water Law has developed and how it fits within the field of international law. You should also have gained a basic understanding of some of the ways in which countries have attempted to use International Water Law to serve their interests.

Main Terminology

Customary international law; International watercourse; Riparian state or simply riparian; Shared freshwater resources; State; The law of international watercourses.

International Water Law has developed at an accelerating pace over the last century, in parallel with growing competition between countries for this precious and increasingly scarce resource. For the sake of terminological consistency and precision, this body of norms will generally be referred to as **the law of international watercourses**, to distinguish it from the other branch of international dealing with water, the law of the sea.[1] It should also be noted at the outset that we deal here chiefly with the use, protection, and management of **shared freshwater resources**[2] for purposes other than navigation; the latter activity, while it may of course interact with nonnavigational uses, is governed by a separate body of rules.

One of the overriding realities of the early 21st century is the growing competition between countries for increasingly scarce water resources. At the turn of

---

[1] International Watercourse: A system of surface waters and groundwaters, parts of which are situated in different states, constituting by virtue of their physical relationship a unitary whole. This expression is sometimes also applied to a border-straddling aquifer that has no hydrologic connection to surface water.

[2] Freshwater, whether surface water or groundwater or a combination of the two, that is shared by more than one state. This expression is potentially broader than "**international watercourse**", but in most cases bears an equivalent meaning.

this century, over one billion people lacked access to safe water and some 2.4 billion were without adequate sanitation facilities, according to the World Health Organization (WHO, 2000). Moreover, while the amount of freshwater on Earth remains constant, the global population continues to increase. The world currently has over 6.5 billion inhabitants, a figure which is projected to climb to over 9 billion by 2050 (UN Population Division, 2005). The result is less water on a per capita basis and growing competition for increasingly scarce water supplies.

An aspect of this problem that is not always appreciated is that much of Earth's freshwater is shared by two or more **riparian states**.[3] According to a United Nations study, the world's 263 international drainage basins account for some 60% of global river flows (UNEP Atlas, 2002). The study indicates that around 40% of the world's population lives in these river basins, which form at least a part of the territory of 145 countries. When the decreasing availability of freshwater is combined with the extent to which it is shared internationally, the potential for disputes between countries over this precious resource becomes obvious.

How will states deal with these disputes? Are there relevant principles of international law that can be of assistance in resolving them? What guidance can be derived from past and ongoing disputes? This chapter will offer an introductory treatment of these questions. But our understanding of the development and role of International Water Law will be enhanced if we have at least a basic understanding of the international legal system within which it operates and of which it forms a part. The following paragraphs therefore offer a very brief overview of the international legal system.

At its most basic level, international law is the law governing the relations between sovereign "states," as countries are referred to in international law parlance. It governs their rights and duties vis-à-vis each other in a host of areas. International law consists, for the most part, of treaties and **customary international law**, which comprises the unwritten rules of international law formed through the practice of states that is engaged in out of a sense of legal obligation.

While international law is similar in many respects to domestic law in that it has counterparts to many domestic law subjects, there are important differences. Perhaps the most fundamental of these is that international law is a *decentralized* system. This feature has pervasive consequences, affecting everything from how international law is made to how it is enforced. For some, it even raises questions about whether international law can properly be characterized as "law." Let us look briefly at these overarching questions after first considering what it means for international law to be a decentralized normative order.

We are used to a legal system in which there are executive, legislative, and judicial branches. These have only rough counterparts in the international legal system. There is no international president or prime minister. While the U.N. Secretary General may appear at first blush to fill this role, in fact the U.N. Charter does

---

[3] A **riparian state** is a state in whose territory part of an **international watercourse** is situated.

not give him or her executive powers. Obviously, the Secretary General may have much greater influence than that, but this depends upon the incumbent's personal qualities more than his or her legal authority. The United Nations Security Council does have limited — though very important — executive powers in the field of international peace and security.

Similarly, there is no international legislature, *per se*. The U.N. General Assembly may appear to have some of the features of a legislative body but in fact the Charter gives the Assembly only powers of study and recommendation. (The sole exception is that the Assembly has the power to set the U.N.'s budget and apportion expenses as between member states.) It is only the Security Council, again, that may be said to have legislative powers on the universal level, but once more those relate to the narrow albeit crucial area of international peace and security.

A search for international counterparts to domestic courts will yield comparable results. There is no court with compulsory jurisdiction, or authority, over states. Jurisdiction is consensual in international tribunals, which means that states may generally decide for themselves whether they wish to submit a dispute to a neutral third party. The U.N.'s main judicial body, the International Court of Justice (ICJ) or World Court, adjudicates cases that states bring to it by mutual consent. A state may express its consent specifically, in a treaty provision, or generally, by means of a declaration to that effect filed with the court (some 65 states have filed such declarations). There are, of course, specialized international tribunals, as well. The International Criminal Court (ICC), which tries individuals for crimes under international law, has received much attention of late, as have the *ad hoc* international criminal tribunals set up to deal with the situations such as those in the former Yugoslavia, Rwanda, and Cambodia. In addition, states have established tribunals or dispute resolution processes to adjudicate disputes in such sectors as the Law of the Sea and international trade.

If there is no international legislature, how is international law made? It is made directly by its subjects, which are chiefly states. The two main sources of international law are treaties and **customary international law**. States participate voluntarily in the process of making law in each of these ways and accept the results as binding. The processes themselves are, of course, quite different: treaties are negotiated, signed, and ratified, while customary rules develop much less formally over time on the basis of state conduct. But states accept the processes as legitimate ways of making law. Refusal to do so, or to accept treaties or customary norms as binding, would make it very difficult for a state to function in the international community. A few words about each of these sources of law may be of assistance in understanding them.

A treaty may be called many things: treaty, convention, agreement, protocol, accord, covenant, charter, exchange of notes, even memorandum of understanding (MOU). Whether the instrument is actually a "treaty," in the international law sense of the term, depends chiefly on whether the parties intended to create legal obligations by entering into it. Treaties may serve a variety of purposes, from the sale of land (Russia's sale of Alaska to the United States), to the establishment of rules governing a particular field (such as diplomatic relations or **international**

watercourses) to the establishment of an international organization (the UN Charter). The importance of the treaty as a source of law — or obligation — continues to increase as states rely on treaties to an ever-greater extent to give their international relations in a wide variety of fields greater stability.

Customary international law, or simply custom, is composed of norms accepted by states through their conduct. The fact that customary rules are unwritten does not affect the influence they have on state behavior. One need only think of the power of unwritten social norms developed and accepted by individuals for evidence of how such norms can affect conduct. While a social norm will usually be unwritten, it will nevertheless generally exert a strong pull to compliance, often much stronger than a statute or other form of law such as a speed limit or stop sign. This is the case with customary norms as well. States accept **customary international law** as a legitimate law-creating process. They may derogate from most customary norms through treaties, but to the extent they have not done so customary law will continue to apply and will even fill gaps in treaties and provide rules for their interpretation.

As with its creation, the enforcement, or implementation, of international law is unlike that of law on the national level (see also Chapter 8). This is due largely to the fact that, as we have seen, international law is a decentralized system. There are exceptions, of course, but in general the international legal system relies to a much greater extent than national ones on unilateral recourse to self-help for enforcement. The exceptions have to do largely with self-contained regimes, such as that of the U.N. Charter concerning the use of force and the World Trade Organization (WTO).

Enforcement of international law may thus be viewed as being either centralized, in the sense that the enforcement measures are taken or authorized by an international body, or decentralized, in the sense that such measures are taken unilaterally. Centralized enforcement is typically limited to issues of great importance to the international community, such as the use of force or the commission of crimes under international law. Decentralized or unilateral enforcement may take such forms as economic sanctions, diplomatic measures or even, in extreme cases, the use of force (although this is unlawful under the U.N. Charter except in self-defense or as authorized by the Security Council).

For Further Discussion. Some nonlegal experts criticize International Water Law as ambiguous and not effective. However, given the track record of the treaties and the fact that International Water Law is in the basis of all negotiations among basin **riparians**, one has to conclude that there is not yet a better alternative. Still, room for improvement exists. With what we know so far, what are the stronger and weaker aspects of existing International Water Law in terms of equity and enforcement of transboundary water use arrangements?

It is perhaps more helpful to think in terms of compliance with international law rather than its enforcement. To paraphrase one noted authority, most countries observe most of their international obligations most of the time (Henkin, 1979).

Why is this, given the lack of an international police force or courts with compulsory jurisdiction? The answer is that it is generally in their interest to do so. States participate directly in lawmaking and thus ordinarily accept the rule of law in question. They observe the rules in part out of considerations of reciprocity: I will treat your citizens in my territory fairly because I expect that you will do the same for my citizens in your territory. But efforts to bring a state back into compliance with its obligations often do not involve the taking of reciprocal measures — e.g., raising a tariff on the violator's exports in response to its having exceeded an agreed tariff level. Instead, states often take advantage of particular areas of strength they enjoy vis-à-vis the other state — for example, agreeing to open a market for a particular product in exchange for returning to compliance with a water treaty. Countries generally do not want to be viewed as law-breakers for fear that other states would not deal with them. States accused of breaching an international obligation do not respond that they are not bound by international law. Instead, they assert some form of defense or challenge the factual basis of the accusation. In other words, they make arguments based on international law.

It should be obvious from the foregoing that the international legal system is rather rudimentary in comparison with those on the domestic level. When there is a lack of symmetry in the power of the states involved in a particular dispute, it can be difficult to achieve resolution. But it is important not to lose sight of the fact that violations are the exception, and when they occur they are most often resolved peacefully and satisfactorily.

Against this background, we may examine the development and application of International Water Law. The chapter will begin by tracing the historical development of International Water Law. It will then offer an overview of the most basic principles of **the law of international watercourses**. Finally, the chapter will illustrate how these principles have been interpreted and applied in selected disputes between nations. Treaties relating to **shared freshwater resources** will be dealt with in Chapter 8.

HISTORICAL DEVELOPMENT OF THE LAW OF INTERNATIONAL WATERCOURSES

This section is introduced by two historical case studies intended to illustrate how political units related to each other regarding **shared freshwater resources** in ancient times and in the "modern" era, in this case the 19th century. It then looks at the evolution of International Water Law, from three perspectives: subject matter; approaches; and legal principles.

Two Historical Case Studies

Ancient Times

It is perhaps not surprising that since the dawn of history, social or political units of humans have been cooperating or competing with each other over **shared**

freshwater resources. In fact, the vital role of water in human life has led people to congregate near sources of fresh water since time immemorial. Rivers nourished the great ancient societies, which have come to be known as the fluvial, or hydraulic civilizations, and drove their economies. A well-known work argues that the bureaucratic structures needed for extensive irrigation works in Asia led to the formation of certain forms of government (Wittfogel, 1957). These ancient societies flourished not only in the Old World river basins of the Nile, Tigris–Euphrates, Indus, Yellow, and Yangtze, but also in the New World regions of Mexico and coastal Peru (Teclaff, 1967). But even before the rise of these civilizations, evidence of early canals and dikes suggests that small communities in places such as predynastic Egypt and Mesopotamia had found it necessary to cooperate in order to control and utilize effectively the waters of major rivers (Teclaff, 1985). Breakdowns in these cooperative relationships resulted in conflicts, with the victor sometimes absorbing the vanquished, leading eventually to the formation of empires.

But historical evidence also suggests that conflicts over water between ancient city "states" or principalities at least sometimes resulted in the conclusion of formal agreements concerning water boundaries, allocation, or similar matters in dispute. The best known of these is the earliest recorded treaty of any kind (Nussbaum, 1954). It was concluded in approximately 3100 B.C. following hostilities between the Mesopotamian city states of Umma, the upper **riparian**, and Lagash (known today as Telloh), the lower **riparian** (Nussbaum, 1954; Teclaff, 1967). These cities appear to have been in almost constant conflict over water supplies. The dispute in question erupted when Umma violated a previous allocation of waters and ended with a victory by Lagash, the laying of a boundary stone and the digging of a boundary canal into which Euphrates waters were diverted (Nussbaum, 1954; Teclaff, 1967). The treaty memorializing these terms is recorded on the well-known "Stela of the Vultures," which is housed in the Louvre (Teclaff, 1967). Unfortunately, however, the agreement did not end the dispute over irrigation water between the two city-states. With a view to finally settling it, a later ruler ordered that a new canal be dug to bring water to Lagash from the Tigris. This canal, known today as Shatt-al-Hai, is still in use (Lloyd, 1961).

Both the fact that the observance of the agreement was provided for and the manner in which this was done are of present interest. The boundary stone was laid not by the ruler of the victorious party, Lagash, but by the king of an upper **riparian** city state that exercised hegemony over both Umma and Lagash. In addition, the citizens of Umma — the city that had precipitated the conflict — swore to uphold the treaty in the name of the most powerful Sumerian gods, which both parties worshipped. The deities would in effect be guarantors of the agreement and would punish any violation (Nussbaum, 1954).

This case study demonstrates that literally for thousands of years, political units have been involved in conflicts over **shared freshwater resources**. It further shows that the contesting parties have attempted to resolve those disputes through recorded agreements couched in specific terms that were guaranteed by reference to some normative order, even if that was represented by a higher temporal or spiritual power. In tracing the development of **the law of international watercourses**, it is impossible to ignore these early arrangements, even though they precede by hundreds and sometimes thousands of years the rise of the modern nation state and international law as we know it today.

The very fact that co-**riparian** social and political units have found it expedient and even necessary to enter into cooperative relationships with regard to their shared water resources since ancient times provides valuable insight into the way in which groups of humans have been brought together by and have interacted with regard to rivers throughout history. The simple fact is that the importance of water to humans, individually and in organized groups, has led them to seek stability in their relations concerning shared watercourses through the development and acceptance of customs, as well as through more formal acts such as agreements. These customs and agreements form what we know today as international law.

The Modern Era

While navigation had been the subject of international agreements and claims for some time, what has been characterized as "the first diplomatic assertion of any rule of international law" concerning the non-navigational uses of **international watercourses** was made by Holland in 1856 (Smith, 1931). The claim concerned the River Meuse, which rises in France, flows through Belgium and into the Netherlands where it forms a common delta with the Rhine. The Dutch government in 1856 protested against Belgian diversion of water from the Meuse into the Campine Canal. Holland contended that the diversion caused it harm in three ways: diminished navigability of the Meuse; increased velocity of a related watercourse; and flooded land (Smith, 1931). The position of the Dutch government was stated as follows:

"The Meuse being a river common both to Holland and to Belgium, it goes without saying that both parties are entitled to make the natural use of the stream, but at the same time, following general principles of law, each is bound to abstain from any action which might cause damage to the other. In other words, they cannot be allowed to make themselves masters of the water by diverting it to serve their own needs, whether for purposes of navigation or of irrigation." (Translation of the letter in the original Dutch in Smith (1931), where the original may also be found.)

This statement is interesting in several respects, including the references to "natural" use and "damage" to another state. What would qualify as a "natural" use? A dam? Or only use for domestic, agricultural, and municipal purposes? As to "damage," is Holland using this term in its absolute sense, so that no damage whatsoever would be permitted in its view? Or did it have in mind a meaning more in line with today's concept of prohibited harm, which would include only "significant" harm or the like? We do not know the answers to these questions, but the questions do arise when one looks at the text of this claim through today's lenses. The two governments ultimately settled the dispute in treaties of 1863 and 1873 (UN Treaty Collection, Nos. 157 and 158).

The Evolution of the Law of International Watercourses

The way in which **the law of international watercourses** has evolved may be viewed from several perspectives (McCaffrey, 1993). In this subsection, we will look at evolution of the subject matter covered, approaches to regulating the subject matter, and the legal principles themselves.

Subject Matter

When political units have decided that they need to regulate their uses of **shared freshwater resources**, what kinds of uses have they been concerned about? Have these, or at least the emphasis given to them, changed over time?

As we have already seen, the earliest recorded agreement regarding shared freshwater concerned its allocation for irrigated agriculture. Along with use for domestic purposes, irrigation and navigation were most likely the principal uses of freshwater in ancient times, and even well into modern times. There is evidence that people traveled in boats on the Tigris and Euphrates Rivers of Mesopotamia in the fifth millennium B.C. and on the Nile in the fourth millennium (Teclaff, 1991). There were evidently no general rules applicable to navigation on these rivers in ancient times, the freedom to navigate on a river depending on obtaining the permission of the ruler who controlled it. Navigation developed later in Western Europe but during the Roman Empire was open to the public, except for commercial activity, on rivers within the Empire's borders. After the fall of Rome, cities gradually asserted dominion over stretches of rivers in their territories and even entered into agreements allocating exclusive control among themselves.

The Peace of Westphalia in 1648, consisting of the Treaties of Munster and Westphalia, is generally regarded as marking the emergence of the modern nation-state and thus the beginnings of the international legal system we know today. The Treaty of Munster granted the Dutch Republic independence from Spain and opened the lower Rhine to free navigation. However, it also declared the Scheldt River in the Spanish Netherlands closed to navigation as a concession to Amsterdam in its commercial rivalry with Antwerp (Wescoat, 1996). Given the steady growth in the economic importance of navigation in Western Europe, it is not surprising that the major peace treaties of the 19th and early 20th centuries addressed the subject.

The chief purpose of the Congress of Vienna of 1815 was to establish a balance of power in Europe to maintain the peace following the Napoleonic Wars, though Napoleon's final defeat, at Waterloo, did not come until 9 days after the signing of the Congress's Final Act. The latter instrument established freedom of navigation for commercial purposes on the Rhine and other rivers of Western Europe (Congress of Vienna, 1815). This was followed by the General Treaty of Peace of 1856 ending the Crimean War, which established freedom of navigation on the Danube for all countries, following the model of the Congress of Vienna. An innovative feature of both the Congress of Vienna and the 1856 treaty was the establishment of river commissions charged with administering the rivers concerned (Wescoat, 1996). Such commissions are increasingly a feature of treaties relating to **international**

watercourses and play an important role in international river basin management. Finally, the 1919 Treaty of Versailles, ending the First World War, declared certain important rivers of Western and Eastern Europe, including the Rhine, Meuse, Elbe, Oder, and Danube, to be international, opening them to commerce and trade (Treaty of Versailles, Articles 331–362 and 378; Wescoat, 1996).

The Treaty of Versailles is perhaps even more noteworthy for its provisions, few though they are, on non-navigational uses — hydropower, irrigation, fishing, and water supply (Treaty of Versailles, Articles 358, 359; Wescoat, 1996). This was the first time a major peace treaty — and peace treaties were the principal multilateral treaties of the time — dealt with such uses and reflects their growing significance in Europe. The importance of non-navigational uses is underscored by the Versailles Treaty's recognition that they may, under certain circumstances, take precedence over navigational uses — something that was virtually unheard-of up to that time. It soon became evident that accordingly, an absolute priority for navigation over other uses was inconsistent with the optimal use and management of a watercourse. Non-navigational uses had become too important, economically and socially, to be trumped automatically by navigation. Accordingly, it is generally recognized today that navigation should be treated like any other use in resolving a conflict between uses of an **international watercourse**.

Since at least the early 20th century, an increasing number of treaties have addressed quantitative allocations of water rather than, or in addition to, navigation rights. The treaties establishing these allocations usually seek to adjust competing demands by **riparian** states for irrigation water. Since irrigated agriculture accounts for 70–80% of a state's total water use in most cases, where more than one state on a given river uses water for this purpose, it is important that they establish the quantities they are entitled to use.

A final step in the evolution of subject matter areas covered by international water law concerns protection of the ecosystems and environment of **international watercourses**. While the capacity of humans to pollute watercourses increased immensely in the West with the industrial revolution, even in the Middle Ages freshwater was polluted to the extent that it may have been responsible for such epidemics as the Black Plague of the 14th century. Treaty approaches to the prevention of water pollution evolved from those aimed at the protection of fisheries (for human consumption) to those setting water quality standards or objectives, or regulating the discharge of specified pollutants. Treaties embodying the latter approach are often aimed not only at protecting the resource for human use, but also at protection of the aquatic ecosystem *per se*. Indeed, the general treaty on the use of **international watercourses** adopted by the United Nations in 1997 goes so far as to require that the parties "protect and preserve the ecosystems of **international watercourses**" (UN Convention, 1997, Article 20).

Regulatory Approaches

As with the kinds of uses regulated, the very approach to regulating the uses of **international watercourses** has itself evolved. We look briefly here at two of the principal aspects of this development: the definition of the freshwater that is being regulated; and the manner in which it is regulated.

As to the definition, or even conception, of the freshwater being regulated, this has changed significantly over time as understanding of hydrology has improved. In addition, of course, older agreements that were concerned with navigation seldom found it necessary to define what was meant by "river" or "watercourse" at all. It was enough to refer to navigable rivers that "separated or crossed" the states concerned, or words to this effect (Congress of Vienna, 1815, Article 108). Agreements typically applied to a "river" or "lake" but seldom mentioned tributaries or, even less, groundwater or entire drainage basins.

However, as uses of shared freshwater intensified, knowledge of freshwater systems grew and the subject matter covered expanded, watercourse agreements increasingly moved away from a narrow conception of their scope of coverage (McCaffrey, 1993). This trend has been matched by the work of expert groups and learned societies, discussed in the following subsection (ILC Draft Articles, 1994; Helsinki Rules, 1966). Today, it can be said that watercourse treaties generally tend to take a holistic approach, regulating the use and management by the parties of entire drainage basins or watercourse systems.

The second aspect of this trend concerns the manner in which shared freshwater is regulated. While earlier treaties generally focused on the resolution of a particular dispute or problem between the states concerned — often involving navigation or fishing — modern agreements exhibit more of a tendency to lay down systems for the integrated management and development of the **international watercourse** in question (McCaffrey, 1993). These systems typically envisage multiple kinds of uses and are often administered by institutional management mechanisms established by the **riparian states** to assist them in implementing their commitments to cooperate in the use of common water resources. The emphasis is thus on planning, management, and integrated development — a proactive approach rather than the more reactive one followed in the past.

Legal Principles

This subsection considers the evolution of the legal principles governing the use of **international watercourses**. The idea that there are legal restrictions on a state's use of **international watercourses**, apart from those contained in treaties, has been traced to the practice of the constituent entities of the Holy Roman Empire (Berber, 1959) and is supported by the writings of commentators dating at least from the 19th century (e.g., Caratheodory, 1861; de Martens, 1883–1887; Farnham, 1904). This concept has been endorsed by learned societies since as early as 1911. In that year, the Institute of International Law (IIL), a highly respected group of experts in the field of international law, adopted the Madrid Resolution on International Regulations regarding the Use of **International Watercourses**. The Madrid Resolution's "Statement of reasons" contains the following passage: "**Riparian States** with a common stream are in a position of permanent physical dependence on each other which *precludes the idea of the complete autonomy* of each State in the section of the natural watercourse under its sovereignty" (IIL Madrid Resolution, 1911, emphasis added). The IIL and other organizations of high repute have continued to produce drafts reflecting rules of international law in the field as those rules have developed through state practice during the 20th century. These efforts include the IIL's 1961 Salzburg and 1979 Athens Resolutions, the International Law Association's 1966 Helsinki Rules on the Uses of the Waters of International Rivers (Helsinki Rules, 1966), and the Draft Articles on the Law of the Non-navigational Uses of **International Watercourses** adopted in 1994 by the U.N. International Law Commission (ILC Draft Articles, 1994). A mere review of the dates of these instruments shows the increasing frequency with which the subject has been treated by expert groups and, in the case of the UN Convention, the international community. This growing attention in turn reflects the expanding importance of the law governing **shared freshwater resources** and the need to develop and clarify it to prevent disputes and promote cooperation.

The two latter drafts deserve particular emphasis. The Helsinki Rules constituted the first effort at a comprehensive codification of the law in the field and are still referred to for guidance by governments, organizations, and scholars. The ILC Draft Articles were prepared by the United Nations' foremost body of experts in the field of international law. The U.N. General Assembly established the ILC in 1947 and has since called upon it to prepare drafts that codify and progressively develop rules of international law on various topics. Its drafts often form the basis for the negotiation of multilateral treaties on the subjects they address. The ILC's draft articles on **international watercourses** formed the basis of a general, multilateral treaty on the subject, the 1997 U.N. Convention on the Law of the Non-navigational Uses of **International Watercourses** (UN Convention, 1997), which we will consider in the following section. Both these drafts take an expansive approach to the scope of the subject-matter, defining the physical scope of coverage broadly (international drainage basin in the case of the Helsinki Rules and **international watercourse** system in the case of the ILC Draft Articles). They cover all the principal uses of **international watercourses** and contain procedures for the avoidance and settlement of disputes. While the main rules reflected in these instruments will be discussed in the following section, it can be stated here that those rules represent a distillation of state practice over the years in relation to **shared freshwater resources**. Since the instruments are designed to cover any **international watercourse** in the world, the rules they contain are quite general. But the fact that the international community now accepts that there are such general rules in itself constitutes considerable progress over the situation prevailing a century, or even a half-century, ago.

A BRIEF OVERVIEW OF PRINCIPLES OF INTERNATIONAL WATER LAW

As we have seen, states sharing freshwater resources have developed basic rules governing the use of those resources in their practice over many years. These rules form part of **customary international law**, which as noted earlier is a body of unwritten law that is binding on all states. Countries sharing freshwater may also wish to enter into treaties applying and adjusting rules of customary law to suit their specific situations and the watercourses they share. Many states have done this; over 400 such international agreements have been concluded since the early 19th century (UNEP Atlas, 2002) and the pace seems to be quickening.

In 1997, the United Nations General Assembly adopted the Convention on the Law of the Nonnavigational Uses of **International Watercourses** (UN Convention, 1997). The U.N. Convention was negotiated by a special working group of the General Assembly open to all U.N. member states. The negotiations were based on a draft prepared by the U.N. International Law Commission, an expert body charged with the codification and progressive development of international law. Because of the process by which it was produced as well as its content, the U.N. Convention is widely regarded as reflecting in a number of respects rules of **customary international law** relating to the use by states of **international watercourses** for purposes other than navigation. The most basic of these rules are those relating to equitable and reasonable utilization; prevention of significant harm; and notification and consultation regarding planned measures. These rules apply to all forms of shared freshwater, including both surface water and groundwater. Each will be discussed briefly in the following paragraphs.

Perhaps the most fundamental rule of **the law of international watercourses** is that of equitable and reasonable utilization of **shared freshwater resources** (UN Convention, 1997, Articles 5 and 6). This rule requires that states use and protect international freshwater in a manner that is equitable and reasonable vis-à-vis other states. Equitable and reasonable utilization requires that each **riparian state** take into account all relevant factors, ranging from physical ones to those relating to the use by itself and other states of the watercourse and their dependence upon it. The object of this rule is to achieve a fair balance among the uses of an **international watercourse** by the states sharing it. In the *Gabčíkovo-Nagymaros Case*, discussed below, the International Court of Justice referred to what it described as the "basic right" of a state to "an equitable and reasonable sharing of the resources of an **international watercourse**" (*Gabčíkovo-Nagymaros Case*, 1997, p. 54).

The second obligation of states sharing freshwater resources is to prevent the causing of significant harm to other states through activities related to an **international watercourse** (UN Convention, 1997, Article 7). This obligation means that states must take all appropriate measures to avoid such harm and, if it is nevertheless caused, to do their best, consistent with their rights and obligations of equitable utilization, to eliminate or mitigate it.

The third basic obligation under **customary international law** relating to **international watercourses** is that a state planning a new project that may adversely affect other states sharing an **international watercourse** must provide timely advance notice of those plans to the other states (UN Convention, 1997, Articles 11–19). The state in which the new measures are planned must then, if requested by the notified state, enter into consultations and, if necessary, negotiations concerning the planned measures and any necessary modification of them to avoid violation of the rights of the latter state. This rule applies to all projects that have the potential to change the regime of the watercourse in a way that would be prejudicial to other **riparian states**.

These are the three most fundamental rules of **customary international law** regarding the use of **international watercourses** and other conduct that affects them. Other obligations may be derived from these rules, notably obligations to prevent and control pollution and to protect and preserve the ecosystems of **international watercourses**. The latter may be regarded as an emerging obligation under **customary international law** but it is in fact implicit in the obligations of equitable utilization and prevention of significant harm.

> **For Further Discussion.** Let us discuss the three rules of **customary international law** regarding the use of international law. Do you see any way they can contradict each other? Can they be enforced in a reasonable way? Can they be interpreted differently by different **riparians**? Could you suggest additional means to make them more complementary to each other?

A SURVEY OF SELECTED INTERNATIONAL WATER DISPUTES

Having reviewed briefly the most fundamental obligations of **customary international waters law** relating to **shared freshwater resources** as they have developed over the years, we will now look at a selection of disputes over **international watercourses** to see whether and how these rules have evolved and how they have been applied. This section will focus on illustrative disputes from four regions: North America, Asia, Europe, and Africa.

North America

The Rio Grande

The Rio Grande rises in Colorado, flows through that state and New Mexico, then forms the border between the United States and Mexico from the vicinity of the sister cities El Paso, Texas and Ciudad Juárez, Chihuahua, Mexico, to its mouth at the Gulf of Mexico. The river has been the subject of disputes between the United States and Mexico since at least the late 19th century. At that time, Mexico complained that diversions in Colorado and New Mexico were reducing the Rio Grande to a dry bed at Ciudad Juárez, where the river begins to form the border between the two countries. Mexico contended it had a right to the water, its use of it being prior to that of the United States by hundreds of years (McCaffrey, 2001, Chapter 4). The United States attributed the low flows to drought but the State Department asked the Attorney General for a legal opinion on the respective rights of the two countries to Rio Grande water. The Attorney General, Judson Harmon, responded in 1895 with an opinion that has since become known as reflecting the "Harmon Doctrine" (Harmon Opinion, 1895). In that opinion, Harmon stated that on the basis of his examination of all available evidence of international law, because the United States enjoyed "absolute sovereignty" within its territory, it was free to use the waters of the Rio Grande regardless of the consequences for Mexico.

Interestingly, as we will see in Chapter 8, the United States ultimately entered into a treaty with Mexico in 1906 whose purpose was to allocate Rio Grande water "equitably" between the two countries (Rio Grande, 1906). In the treaty, the United States agrees to construct a large storage reservoir in New Mexico and to deliver specified quantities of water to Mexico. This case thus illustrates a situation in which the parties began by taking extreme positions but ultimately concluded an agreement that both viewed as achieving an equitable apportionment.

The situation was reversed a century later, with the United States complaining that Mexico was failing to deliver certain quantities of water into the lower Rio Grande as required by a later treaty. A prolonged drought in a region that is already semi-arid, coupled with population growth as well as expanded industry and agriculture, has resulted in critical water shortages on both sides of the border. The Rio Grande is in fact so over-utilized that it has often not reached the Gulf of Mexico in recent years. A 1944 treaty between the United States and Mexico (Rio Grande, 1944) specifies the quantities of water each country is allocated from the lower Rio Grande. From 1992 to 2002, Mexico accumulated a debt to the United States under the treaty of over 1.5 million acre feet of water (1.8 billion cubic meters, or 1.85 cubic kilometers).

In the same 1944 treaty, the two countries entrusted the International Boundary and Water Commission, or IBWC, with the settlement of all disputes arising between them under the agreement. Decisions of the IBWC are recorded in the form of "Minutes," which become binding upon the parties if not disapproved within 30 days. This novel procedure, which is particularly valuable in treaties dealing with shared freshwater, effectively permits the basic agreement to be amended so that it is kept up to date and the parties are able to respond to current problems.

After months of difficult negotiations over Mexico's water debt, the commissioners of the IBWC signed Minute 308 in June 2002, providing that Mexico is to provide 90,000 acre-feet (111 million cubic meters) of water to the United States by October 2002, the last year of the current five-year payment cycle under the treaty (Minute 308, 2002). In March 2005, Mexico and the United States announced that Mexico's water debt would be eliminated by the end of September 2005 through a combination of water transfers and additional deliveries (IBWC, 2005).

While Minute 308 does not purport to guarantee a long-term solution to the problem of water shortages in the lower Rio Grande, it at least illustrates the advantages of institutionalized cooperation, of having a forum in place that can assist the states concerned with the solution of their water problems when they arise. The case also shows what is possible when the countries sharing an **international water-course** enjoy good, even if not perfect, relations.

Asia

The Euphrates

While as we have seen, the waters of the Euphrates have been the subject of disputes for thousands of years, a current controversy was sparked by Turkey's massive GAP (Guneydogu Anadolu Projesi — Southeast Anatolia Development Project) project in southeastern Anatolia, which affects both lower **riparian states**, Syria and Iraq. It has been predicted that this project, which involves over 20 dams and massive irrigation schemes, will drastically reduce flows to the two downstream states at a time when their water needs are increasing. For example, Lowi estimates that the share of Euphrates water available to Iraq after 2000 will be 4,473 million cubic meters per year, down from 29,351 from 1986 to 1990 (Lowi, 1995). For international relations aspects of this conflict, see Chapter 7.

There are bilateral treaties and joint mechanisms between the parties, but no basin-wide agreement or joint mechanism. At one point, Turkey threatened to cut off the flow of Euphrates water unless Syria ceased to provide sanctuary to the Kurdish Workers' Party (PKK), which has waged a violent independence campaign against the Turkish government. The legal positions advanced by Turkey and Iraq, the uppermost and lowermost **riparians**, are similar to those espoused by the United States and Mexico in the late-19th century dispute over the Rio Grande. Iraq has based a claim to 700 cubic meters of water per second on what it termed its "acquired rights" to the use of Euphrates water for irrigation, based on thousands of years of use for that purpose. Turkey, on the other hand, has stated that it has no legal obligations vis-à-vis the lower **riparian states** concerning the Tigris and Euphrates. Yet at the same time, Turkey has said it has taken all measures necessary to avoid causing significant harm to the downstream states and that it will guarantee a flow of 500 cubic meters per second below the GAP project (McCaffrey, 2001). The latter statements may indicate a recognition by Turkey that it does in fact have legal obligations, even if for political reasons it does not want to admit this.

The situation is thus potentially volatile. Given the present situation in Iraq, it does not seem likely that the Iraqi government will be in a position to focus on negotiations with its upstream neighbors in the near future. It seems inevitable that Turkey's continued development of the Euphrates will constrict water supplies available to Syria and Iraq. It is, however, possible that the European Union, which Turkey aspires to join, may use its influence to try to convince Turkey to come to a water sharing agreement with Syria and Iraq or perhaps to submit the question of equitable allocation among the basin states to a third party for resolution. Win–win solutions are doubtless possible, but without regular communication and institutionalized cooperation they will be difficult for the countries to find.

Europe

The Danube

The case concerning the *Gabčíkovo-Nagymaros Project* between Hungary and Slovakia involved a treaty concluded in 1977 by Hungary and Czechoslovakia providing for the construction of a major project consisting of a series of dams and other works on a 200-kilometer stretch of the Danube River, most of which forms the border between the two countries (*Gabčíkovo-Nagymaros Case*, 1997). Concerns relating to the project, including its possible environmental consequences, began to surface in Hungary in the 1980s, resulting eventually in Hungary's decisions to suspend, then abandon work on the project, and to announce in May 1992 that it was terminating the 1977 treaty.

Czechoslovakia rejected Hungary's purported termination of the agreement as ineffective because it did not comply with the law of treaties. Czechoslovakia had already completed construction of most of the works for which it was responsible under the treaty when Hungary abandoned the project and was confronted with a difficult decision regarding how to proceed. It ultimately decided to put the project into operation to the extent that it could by acting alone, without Hungary's participation. Czechoslovakia therefore dammed the Danube in October 1992 at a point on the river upstream of where it begins to form the border, and where it lies entirely within what was then Czechoslovak territory. This dam and related works, known as Variant C (because it was one of the possible variants of the original project considered by Czechoslovakia in response to Hungary's withdrawal), enabled Czechoslovakia to channel much of the flow of the Danube — between 80% and 90% — through the project's bypass canal, on Czechoslovak territory, and thus to put the upstream portion of the project into partial operation. But this also meant that the stretch of the Danube between the dam and the point at which the bypass canal rejoins the Danube — much of which forms the border between the two countries — contained only 10–20% of the water it had formerly.

Slovakia became an independent state on 1 January 1993 and succeeded to Czechoslovakia's interest in the project by agreement with the Czech Republic. (The court later held that Slovakia succeeded to the 1977 treaty vis-à-vis Hungary, as well.) By Special Agreement of 7 April 1993, Hungary and Slovakia submitted the dispute to the International Court of Justice (ICJ) in The Hague.

Among Hungary's contentions in the suit was that Czechoslovakia, which was in the position of an upstream state, had no right to divert through the bypass canal on its territory the quantity of Danube water it was unilaterally diverting by means of the Variant C dam. According to Hungary, this was in part because the diversion by Czechoslovakia violated the principle of equitable utilization of shared water resources and the prohibition of causing a co-**riparian** significant harm. For its part, Slovakia argued that it was implementing the treaty to the extent it could without Hungary's participation, and that the reduction in the flow of the Danube in the stretch in question was merely what was envisaged by the treaty. The ICJ held that Hungary had not lawfully terminated the treaty and in fact had breached it, but that this could not mean that Hungary had "forfeited its basic right to an equitable and reasonable sharing of the resources of an **international watercourse**," which was the effect of Slovakia's Variant C (*Gabčíkovo-Nagymaros Case*, 1997, para. 78).

This case is a recent one, involving two European states, and their arguments were made in the context of a proceeding before the International Court of Justice, the principal judicial organ of the United Nations, rather than in a political context involving diplomatic exchanges. This might account for the fact that neither party took an extreme position. Instead, the arguments of both parties relating to International Water Law were well grounded in generally recognized principles. And the ICJ itself, in deciding the case, also relied in part on well-recognized principles of **the law of international watercourses**, in particular that of equitable and reasonable utilization.

The Rhine

The Rhine is Western Europe's longest river. It passes through or forms the borders of Switzerland, Liechtenstein, Austria, Germany, France, and the Netherlands. The basin is home to some 60 million people and the river provides drinking water to approximately 20 million. The Rhine serves one of the most highly developed regions on Earth.

Pollution of a watercourse that is so heavily relied upon is therefore a source of concern. While it was once called Europe's biggest sewer, from which the famed Rhine salmon had disappeared by the late 1950s, much progress has been made — even if it has been slow — since the International Commission for the Protection of the Rhine against Pollution (ICPR) was established in 1950 (ICPR, 1950). The first salmon had returned by 1993 but whether they are fit for human consumption is an issue due to heavy metal concentrations. In its latest incarnation, the ICPR serves as the principal forum for cooperation between Rhine **riparians** in their efforts to protect and sustainably develop the Rhine ecosystem.

The case we will focus upon here, however, involves pollution of the Rhine by chlorides, largely from Mines de Potasse d'Alsace (MDPA), a French state-owned potassium mining concern. While Rhine chloride levels are now declining, and potash mining in Alsace ended in 2002 due to exhaustion of the deposits, for many years discharges of waste salts into the Rhine by MDPA was a serious irritant in relations between France and the Netherlands, the country most harmed by the chloride pollution.

Chloride pollution of the Rhine had been a major problem since levels began to rise rapidly in the middle of the 20th century. In 1986, the Rhine **riparians** attempted to address the issue by concluding the Convention for the Protection of the Rhine from Pollution by Chlorides (Rhine, 1986). This agreement called for a progressive reduction of Rhine chloride levels, beginning with the injection, at a depth of 1500–2000 m below Alsatian ground level, of 20 kg/s of salts in the form of brine. In an effective reversal of at least one interpretation of the "polluter-pays principle," costs of this means of disposal were to be borne as follows: France and

Germany, 30% each; the Netherlands, 34%; and Switzerland, 6%. The cost-sharing formula reflects economic reality more than principle or law, namely, that it is cheaper for a victim of pollution to pay for prevention than for clean-up. In the case of the Netherlands, clean-up means treating the water to make it suitable for, *inter alia*, horticultural and domestic uses.

Implementation of the Convention has been problematic, however. First, concern on the part of Alsatian residents that the injections would pollute groundwater delayed French ratification. Then in 1991 the parties agreed in an additional protocol to the Chlorides Convention that injection would not be used as a disposal method. Instead, France was allowed to discharge waste salts into the Rhine, up to a level of 200 mg/l. Amounts above that level could be stored temporarily on land, but France was permitted to increase discharges during high river flows. The costs of temporary storage were to be shared according to the above-mentioned formula.

This case demonstrates that even in Western Europe, a region that prides itself on protecting the environment and following international law, prevention of transboundary pollution can be difficult. This may be especially true in democracies, in cases in which pollution abatement could threaten the jobs of significant numbers of people. The case also shows that while none of the countries involved would be likely to dispute the principle that a country should not cause transboundary pollution harm, economic and political concerns may lead them to agree on a different regime in the interest of putting an end to the problem. A solution to this problem proved elusive despite the fact that the dispute involved a politically, socially, and economically homogeneous group of co-**riparian states**. Other factors would also have indicated the likelihood of a positive outcome: good political relations, and economic integration, as between the **riparians**; an applicable agreement; and a joint institution within which the problem could be discussed. But the source state evidently concluded that the domestic, political, and economic cost of instituting alternate disposal methods would be greater than the cost — both economic and diplomatic — of failing to cease causing harm to the Netherlands. The result might have been different if the pollution had been of a toxic character, posing serious health risks to downstream residents.

Africa

The Nile

The Nile River consists of two branches, the White and Blue Niles. The White Nile originates in the region of Lake Victoria and flows north to Khartoum, Sudan, where it is joined by the Blue Nile. The Blue Nile flows from Lake Tana, in the Ethiopian highlands, to its confluence with the White Nile. The Nile then flows north through Egypt and empties through its vast delta into the Mediterranean Sea. The Blue Nile supplies over 80% of the water reaching Egypt but its flow is torrential, in contrast to the slow and steady flow of the White Nile, making storage crucial. For discussion on international relations aspects, see Chapter 7.

While Egypt and the grandeur of its history are synonymous with the Nile in the minds of many, it is but one of the 10 states in the Nile River Basin (the others are Burundi, D.R. Congo, Eritrea, Ethiopia, Kenya, Rwanda, Sudan, Tanzania, and Uganda). Moreover, it is entirely dependent for its water supply upon other Nile **riparians**. For centuries, even millennia, this gave rise to no difficulties since Egypt was the only territory in the basin using significant amounts of water. But as Egypt's population and level of development, and thus its water needs, increased, and as other states in both the Blue Nile and White Nile basins became independent and began using more water, tensions over the Nile began to rise.

The first potential conflict arose beginning in 1920 between Egypt and Sudan, over the Gezira cotton scheme south of Khartoum and the associated Sennar Dam on the Blue Nile in Sudan. This was a classic problem involving a downstream state that had long-established uses and an upstream state that planned new ones. The pattern is repeated around the world because downstream states tend to have a flatter terrain that lends itself to agricultural development, while upstream states — especially those at a river's headwaters — tend to be more mountainous. The latter have more limited possibilities for water resources development, especially until the technology was developed to construct large dams for water storage and hydroelectric power production. A downstream state's long usage of a river's water often prompts it to argue that it has acquired the right to use the quantity of water that it has been using. According to this theory, such historic uses would trump any new uses by upstream states that conflicted with them. This could put the upstream state in a difficult position if its proposed new use would adversely affect the downstream state. An absolute reading of the obligation to prevent harm (the "no-harm" rule) would protect the downstream state against its upstream neighbor. However, a more flexible interpretation of that rule, or even more so the doctrine of equitable utilization, would allow a reasonable balance to be struck between the existing uses downstream and the new uses upstream.

British influence in the basin at the time allowed the issue to be resolved in the 1929 Nile Waters Treaty (Nile, 1929). The agreement was concluded between Egypt and Britain because the latter administered Sudan. It allocated specific quantities to each country, in a 12:1 ratio in favor of Egypt. The treaty further protected Egypt by requiring its previous agreement before any works were implemented on waters in the Nile system, "so far as all these [waters] are in the Sudan or in countries under British administration," if those works would affect Nile waters to the prejudice of the interests of Egypt (Nile, 1929, para. 4(b)). To this day, Egypt maintains that this clause binds the Nile equatorial lakes states, including Kenya, Tanzania, and Uganda, as successors to Britain; those states vehemently reject this contention.

After its independence in 1956, Sudan stated that it did not consider itself bound by the 1929 Agreement. For its part, Egypt in 1952 adopted plans for what became the Aswan High Dam, which would create a reservoir extending some 250 km into Sudan. Sudan protested, complicating Egypt's efforts to obtain financing for the High Dam, but eventually the two countries concluded the 1959 Nile Waters Agreement (Nile, 1959). This treaty revised the allocations under the 1929 treaty to produce a 3:1 ratio, again in favor of Egypt, and protected Egypt's "established rights," and those of Sudan, in the amount of water each was using as of the date of the agreement (48 billion cubic meters for Egypt and 4 billion for Sudan, the 12:1 ratio under the 1929 Agreement) (Nile 1959, Article I(1)). Entitled "Agreement for the Full Utilization of the Nile Waters," the 1959 treaty indeed allocated the lion's share of the total flow of the Nile as between the two countries (74 billion cubic meters out of an estimated total natural flow of 84 billion). It also authorized the reservoir created by the High Aswan Dam (the Sudd el Aali Reservoir, known today as Lake Nasser). Through this agreement, then, Egypt did consent to a substantial re-allocation of Nile water as between itself and Sudan, at least in terms of the proportion each country would receive. But in return it received water security in the form of recognition of its "established rights," the immense storage of Lake Nasser and agreement, with Sudan at least, on the quantity of water to which it was entitled.

This is all well and good, but the picture becomes more cloudy when it is enlarged to include the upper **riparian states**. Neither Ethiopia, which contributes some 85% of the water reaching Egypt, largely via the Blue Nile, nor the equatorial lakes states of the upper White Nile, were parties to either of these agreements and none recognizes either treaty as binding upon them. There is as yet neither a basin-wide agreement accepted by all **riparian states**, nor a permanent joint mechanism for the management of the Nile Basin. As discussed below, however, the Nile Basin states have recently established a transitional institution, the Nile Basin Initiative (NBI), which will continue to operate until it is replaced by a permanent mechanism, and are close to finalizing a Nile River Basin Cooperative Framework Agreement.

The most heated recent disputes over Nile waters have been between Egypt and Ethiopia, with Egypt being wary of Ethiopia's plans to develop the river. The reverse is also true, however: Ethiopia fears that Egypt will attempt to use the massive irrigation projects currently being developed there, such as the Toshka, or New Valley project, to restrict the development that Ethiopia may rightfully undertake of its water resources. According to Waterbury, the Toshka project involves bringing some 200,000 ha under irrigation by diverting Nile water via a canal beginning on the west bank of Lake Nasser and running some 70 km to oases west of the Nile. Another project of major proportions is the so-called "Peace Canal," which would pass under the Suez Canal and deliver Nile water to the Sinai Peninsula (Waterbury, 2002). Again, these existing and planned projects illustrate the tension between the "no-harm" and equitable utilization principles and demonstrate why downstream states will usually rely on the former while upstream states typically assert the latter.

Until recently there has been no mechanism within which Egypt and Ethiopia could communicate on a regular basis and attempt to identify win–win solutions to their Nile water problems. But beginning in the late 1990s, Nile Basin states have established a process, and now a transitional international organization head-quartered in Uganda (Nile Headquarters Agreement, 2002), known as the Nile Basin Initiative (NBI). Through this process, Egypt and Ethiopia, as well as the other Nile Basin states, are identifying projects of mutual benefit. Subsidiary Action Plans for the Blue and White Niles have been established, and the states involved in each meet together regularly (NBI website). These efforts hold promise and offer hope that the countries of the Nile River Basin will soon formalize their cooperation in a basin-wide agreement containing principles and obligations, and establishing a permanent joint institution.

While in their draft agreement, the Nile Basin countries have accepted in principle the obligations of equitable utilization and prevention of significant harm, until the agreement is finalized and enters into force they are likely to rely on their historic positions: acquired or historic rights and the "no-harm" rule in the case of Egypt; and equitable utilization, interpreted to allow the use of significant quantities of water, in the case of Ethiopia and other upstream states. But progress on the projects being planned jointly by these countries should go a long way to reconciling their respective positions.

CONCLUSION

In this chapter, we have looked at the way in which International Water Law has evolved and illustrations of how it has been applied in selected disputes. We have seen that the law in this field has developed largely in the 20th century, at least with regard to nonnavigational uses. We have also seen that states sometimes take extreme legal positions, perhaps as negotiating tactics, and that these positions have in certain cases given way to more balanced approaches agreed to in treaty form by the states concerned.

Whether or not the countries involved in a dispute over shared water resources are able to reach agreement on a treaty, principles of international law will always be in the background of their relations, influencing their arguments as well as the shape of any ultimate agreement. For this reason, the progressive achievement of clarity regarding the rules of international law applicable to shared freshwater should help to prevent disputes and, when they arise, to facilitate their resolution.

Practice Questions

1. Does a state have absolute sovereignty over its portion of an **international watercourse**?
2. Is a state required to notify other **riparian states** of a planned project that may have adverse effects on those other states?
3. Can a project such as a large irrigation scheme in a downstream state cause harm to an upstream state?
4. Does the legal concept of an "**international watercourse**" include groundwater that is related to surface water?
5. State the three most important rules of law governing **international watercourses**.

REFERENCES

Agreement between the United Arab Republic and the Republic of Sudan for the Full Utilization of the Nile Waters, Cairo, 8 Nov. 1959, 453 UNTS p. 51.

Berber, F.J. (1959). *Rivers in International Law*. London: Stevens & Sons.

Caratheodory, E. (1861). *Du droit international concernant les grands cours d'eau*. Leipzig: Brockhaus.

Case Concerning the Gabčíkovo-Nagymaros Project (1997) I.C.J. 7.

Congress of Vienna, 9 June 1815, Consolidated Treaty Series, Vol. 64, p. 453.

Convention on the International Commission for the Protection of the Rhine against Pollution, Bern, 29 April 1963, 994 UNTS 3, formalizing the body that had initially been established in Basel on 11 July 1950 by an exchange of notes between France, Germany, Luxembourg, the Netherlands, and Switzerland. The Bern Convention of 29 April 1963 will be superseded upon the entry into force of the new Bern Convention of 12 April 1999. See the website of the ICPR, www.iksr.org/icpr.

Convention on the Protection of the Rhine Against Pollution by Chlorides, Bonn, 3 December 1976, 16 ILM 265 (1977), commonly known as the Rhine Chlorides Convention.

Convention concerning the Equitable Distribution of the Waters of the Rio Grande for Irrigation Purposes, 21 May 1906, UNTS No. 455.

de Martens, F.F. (1883–1887). Traite de droit international, 3 vols., transl. from the Russian by Alfred Léo. Paris: Chevalier-Marescq et cie.

Exchange of Notes between the UK and Egypt in regard to the Use of the Waters of the River Nile for Irrigation Purposes, Cairo, 7 May 1929, 93 LNTS p. 44.

Farnham, H.P. (1904). *Law of Waters and Water Rights*. Rochester: Lawyers Co-operative Publishing Co.

Headquarters Agreement between the Government of the Republic of Uganda and the Nile Basin Initiative, Kampala, 4 Nov. 2002 (copy on file with author).

Helsinki Rules on the Uses of the Waters of International Rivers (1966). *International Law Association*, Report of the 52nd Conference, Helsinki. London: International Law Association, p. 484.

Henkin, L. (1979). *How Nations Behave*. New York: Columbia University Press.

http://www.ibwc.state.gov/PAO/CURPRESS/2005/WaterDelFinalWeb.pdf

Institute of International Law (IIL) (1911). Resolution on International Regulations regarding the Use of International Watercourses, Annuaire de l'Institute de droit international, Madrid Session, April 1911, vol. 24, pp. 365–367, Paris.

International Boundary and Water Commission, United States and Mexico, Minute 308, 28 June 2002, available at http://www.ibwc.state.gov/NEW/what_s_new.htm

International Law Commission of the United Nations (1994). Draft articles on the law of the non-navigational uses of international watercourses, *Y.B. Int'l L. Comm'n*, Vol. 2, pt. 2, p. 89.

Legislative Texts and Treaty Provisions concerning the Utilization of International Rivers for Other Purposes than Navigation, U.N. Doc. ST/LEG/SER.B/12 (1964).

Lloyd, S. (1961). *Twin Rivers*, 3rd edn. London: Oxford University Press.

Lowi, M.R. (1995). *Water and Power: The Politics of a Scarce Resource in the Jordan River Basin*. Cambridge: Cambridge University Press.

McCaffrey, S.C. (1993). *The evolution of the law of international watercourses*, Austrian Journal of Public International Law, 45, 87–111.

McCaffrey, S.C. (2001). *The Law of International Watercourses: Non-Navigational Uses.* Oxford: Oxford University Press.

Nussbaum, A. (1954). *A Concise History of the Law of Nations,* revised edition. New York: Macmillan.

Opinion of U.S. Attorney General Judson Harmon, 21 Op. Att'y Gen. 274 (1985).

Smith, H.A. (1931). *The Economic Uses of International Rivers.* London: P.S. King & Son.

Teclaff, L. (1967). *The River Basin in History and Law.* The Hague: Martinus Nijhoff.

Teclaff, L. (1985). *Water Law in Historical Perspective.* Buffalo, New York: William S. Hein.

Teclaff, L. (1991). Fiat or Custom: The Checkered Development of International Water Law, *Nature Resources Journal,* 31(1), 45, 72–73.

Treaty Relating to the Utilization of the Waters of the Colorado and Tijuana Rivers, and of the Rio Grande (Rio Bravo) from Fort Quitman, Texas, to the Gulf of Mexico, 3 Feb. 1944, 3 UNTS 314.

Treaty of Peace between the Allied and Associated Powers and Germany, Versailles, June 28, 1919, G. Martens, Recueil de traitẽs 11, 3rd ser.

United Nations Convention on the Law of the Non-Navigational Uses of International Watercourses, 21 May 1997, U.N. Doc. A/RES/51/229, 21 May 1997, 8 July 1997, 36 ILM 700 (1997).

United Nations Environment Programme, Food and Agriculture Organization & Oregon State University, Atlas of International Freshwater Agreements, UNEP (2002).

United Nations Department of Economic and Social Affairs, Population Division (2005). *World Population Prospects, The 2004 Revision,* U.N. Doc. ESA/P/WP.193, 24 Feb. 2005 at p. 1. The report is available on the Population Divison's website, http://www.un.org/esa/population/publications/WPP2004/WPP2004Highlights_final.pdf

Waterbury, J. (2002). *The Nile Basin: National Determinants of Collective Action,* New Haven and London: Yale University Press.

Wescoat Jr., J.L. (1996). *Main currents in early multilateral water treaties: A historical-geographic perspective, 1648–1948, Colorado Journal of International Environmental Law and Policy,* 7(1), 39–74.

Website of the Nile Basin Initiative, http://www.nilebasin.org

World Health Organization (WHO) (2000). *The Global Water Supply and Sanitation Assessment 2000.*

Wittfogel, K.A. (1957). *Oriental Despotism: A Comparative Study of Total Power.* New Haven: Yale University Press.

ADDITIONAL READING

Caponera, D.A. (1996). Conflicts over International River Basins in Africa, the Middle East and Asia, Review of European Community & International Law, 5(2), 97–106.

McCaffrey, S.C. (2006). *Understanding International Law.* Atlanta: LexisNexis Publishers.

McCaffrey, S.C. (2007). *The Law of International Watercourses,* 2nd edn. Oxford, New York: Oxford University Press.

4. PRINCIPLES AND PRACTICES OF COOPERATION IN MANAGING INTERNATIONAL WATER

Objectives

This chapter is a nontechnical introduction to understanding and analyzing cooperation with a focus on international river basins. Starting with several definitions of cooperation, this chapter considers how cooperation succeeds and fails. After reading this chapter you will be familiar with various principles of cooperation, with their strengths and weaknesses, and preview to several examples of river basins where cooperation unfolded or failed.

Main Terminology

Autonomy principle; Cooperation; Democracy principle; (Dis)economies of scale; Economically optimal arrangements; Efficiency requirement; Equity principle; Grand coalition; Group rationality; Individual rationality; Joint cost; Market failure; Strategic choice; Step-wise agreement; Universality principle; Value of cooperation; Voluntary principle.

The availability of natural resources such as water, forests, and land throughout the world has decreased over time (both in terms of quantity and quality) as a result of development, urbanization and expansion of agriculture. Forests have been converted to agricultural lands, land erosion has increased, surface water bodies have been polluted by industrial and urban wastes, and aquifers have been contaminated by agricultural wastes (such as pesticides) and salt water intrusion (resulting from over pumping groundwater).

The inevitable consequences of increased demand for, and decreased supply (including deteriorating quality) of various natural resources, especially water, is an increase in the value of these scarce resources and their services, leading to increased competition over their allocation. Consequently, there is a greater need for comprehensive and stable arrangements of a sustainable nature, that will satisfy all parties involved, directly and indirectly.

Regional conflict, negotiation, and **cooperation** are three possible steps in a process that results in an economic and institutional system that may, under certain conditions, lead to regional arrangements dealing with resource allocation and management. In this chapter, we discuss the conditions under which a regional cooperative arrangement is possible, and to what degree economic considerations alone provide the basis for **cooperation**.

Economic concepts are extremely applicable in the case of resource conflicts arising from **market failure**. Such concepts can be used to design institutions and organizational solutions in terms of rules and structures that are socially desirable. Likewise they identify solutions associated with gains to all parties involved in the conflict (Loehman and Dinar, 1995). The literature provides several methods that may be adapted to identifying cooperative solutions. After familiarizing ourselves with cooperative principles in the next section, we will briefly review several approaches and demonstrate how they have been applied to water resource-related cooperative analyses. This section will be followed by several examples of actual cases of **cooperation** over water from various parts of the world. The lessons learned are summarized in the concluding section.

(ECONOMIC) PRINCIPLES OF COOPERATION

Cooperation, in a general sense, is defined as a process through which individuals and groups may move up from one level of social development to the next more prosperous one (Bogardus, 1964). Several principles of **cooperation** are described in the literature. The most important include: (1) the **democracy principle** of managing the cooperative arrangement, (2) the **voluntary principle** of joining and leaving the cooperative arrangements, (3) the **autonomy principle** of self-sustainability, (4) the **equity principle** of participating and sharing benefits, and (5) the **universality principle** of having a set of goals that attract all participants (e.g., Bogardus, 1964). In addition, **economically optimal arrangements** of a cooperative nature have to fulfill an economic **efficiency requirement**. Such arrangements should be associated with additional gains to the participants. They also have to address issues of justice and fairness associated with the allocation of the resulting benefits or the **joint cost**. These points will be demonstrated and elaborated later.

Cooperative participation in design and scale, and mutually planned sharing of costs and benefits, are likely to lead to more effective exploitation of a resource. This is in contradistinction to unilateral undertakings by the parties, exhibiting no coordination. In general, where inter-dependencies exist, pooling the resource potential of an entire river system, for example, offers a wider range of technically feasible alternatives. In addition, by avoiding duplication of investment, the cooperative strategy provides the parties with an opportunity to select the most economical combination of physical sites along the basin for joint utilization of the river.

Cooperation Difficulties

Given the apparent advantages inherent in the cooperative development of an international river, why have such undertakings proceeded slowly? There are several reasons: (1) technical complexity of the cooperative project (e.g., Waterbury, 2002; Just and Netanyahu, 1998), (2) ill-defined rights and responsibilities of each riparian (e.g., Dinar, 2004), (3) the existence of differing goals that cannot be represented by a simple balance of costs and gains to the riparians concerned, and (4) the existence of additional considerations (nonwater related issues, such as economic and political) among the riparians and other stakeholders (Kibaroglu, 2002).

For example, in the Nile Basin, there are a number of factors making **cooperation** more difficult (Waterbury, 1996, 2002). They include: (1) high rainfall variability over time and across the basin states, (2) divergent economic growth rates, (3) high population growth rates, and (4) growing water-related needs necessitating immediate action rather than a long-term vision. Also, potential nonsignificant contributions of various basin states may diminish their role in a cooperative arrangement, because they will have very little to offer.

Contrary to the perception that a "**grand coalition**" (the group of all parties that can cooperate — all riparian states that share the river basin) is associated with the highest total benefit from **cooperation**, Just and Netanyahu (1998) observe that basin-wide multilateral agreements are less common than agreements among only a subset of the riparians (see also Chapter 2). Their observations that (1) the performance of multilateral organization is negatively correlated with the number of signatories and (2) that negotiations over international water resources tend to yield bilateral arrangements in higher frequency than multilateral arrangements, lead them to challenge the **grand coalition** perception. According to the authors, a grand coalition imposes transaction costs on each coalition member, due to inner coalition monitoring problems, and the free rider problem. Hence the authors support a "partial coalition" since it may offer greater net economic benefits to be shared between the parties and a higher level of sustainability in **cooperation** over time (Just and Netanyahu, 1998). Consequently, one may expect some dis-economies of scale in enforcement costs of larger group arrangements and economies of scale in benefits accrued from bigger water investments stemming from larger coalitions (see Chapter 5).

According to the above indicators, the likelihood of a cooperative arrangement is affected by the behavior of the net benefit obtained from adding additional riparians. One scenario could be that the likelihood may increase with the number of participating parties up to a point where the difference between benefits and costs is in its maximum level and thereafter the likelihood decreases. Another possibility is that enforcement costs exceed benefits up to a point where, as with additional participants, the benefits become so significant that they surpass enforcement costs and **cooperation** is justified.

These points are important and should be considered carefully. The only question that arises is whether or not many partial agreements provide a more stable environment for regional **cooperation** than one grand multilateral agreement. In terms of time gained during negotiations, and better resource management in the short run, several partial agreements may be better. However, a long-term analysis is needed as well. A possible compromise includes a sequential pattern in which initially partial cooperative arrangements are attained followed by a higher-level coalition arrangement. For example, if at first, only bi-lateral **cooperation** arrangements were established in a basin with three riparians, a second phase could include a **grand coalition** of all three riparians.

An attractive and economically sustainable regional cooperative arrangement must fulfill, what are known in economics as, individual and **group rationality**. That is, the regional cooperative outcome is preferable to the noncooperative outcome for each participant (individual rationality). In addition, the regional cooperative outcome for each participant is preferable to outcomes from any partial cooperative arrangement that includes a subset of the regional participants (group rationality). The regional cooperative arrangement also requires that all costs or gains are allocated or accounted for. This means, at least in theory, that all costs — direct and indirect, internal and external — that are associated with **cooperation** can be identified and included in the cooperative agreement. We will address these points in more detail in Chapters 5 and 6.

To further demonstrate the potential role of economic principles in regional **cooperation**, we can borrow from the field of international trade and investment (Moran, 1996), although water and water-related activities are not as easy to trade or handle as other commodities. Since globalization of economic activity can be a source of benefit and harmony among trading nations on the one hand, this can also create conflicts because of unfair trading practices. As domestic trade and production policies can affect international trade, other domestic policies can impact the stability of water-sharing arrangements as well.

Economics and politics play interactive roles in the evaluation of regional **cooperation**. Just as political considerations can effectively veto a joint project with an otherwise favorable economic outcome, a project with potential regional-welfare improvements might influence the political decision-making process to allow the necessary **cooperation**. Therefore, economic and political considerations should be incorporated into regional **cooperation** evaluations. Several works demonstrate these issues.

Dinar and Wolf (1994a, 1994b, 1997) argue that economic efficiency alone is not sufficient for **cooperation**, especially when it is related to the allocation of a scarce resource, such as water, among hostile potential cooperators. Furthermore, the authors develop a framework for analyzing economic and political aspects of **cooperation** and demonstrate, using the case of trading Nile water, how regional cooperative arrangements based only on economic considerations are inferior to arrangements that likewise take into account political considerations.

LeMarquand (1977) provides a general conceptual framework for considering international river **cooperation**, taking into account hydrologic, economic, and political aspects. The conceptual framework identifies three sets of factors, each containing several variables that establish general patterns of incentives and disincentives for **cooperation**. The three sets are the Hydrologic–Economic relations among the potential cooperators, the Foreign Policy of each potential cooperator (regarding relevant issues), and each potential cooperator's Domestic Policy and Consensus. The Hydrologic–Economic set can be viewed as a necessary condition for **cooperation**. Consequently, Foreign Policy, which is affected by Domestic Policy and Consensus, may decay or enhance **cooperation**. However, this framework does not include an important set of factors: the power of a potential cooperating party to prevent the establishment of other coalitions. Another potential drawback to this approach is its lack of quantitative measurements for the various factor sets and variables used.

Few studies address the sustainability of a cooperative arrangement once an agreement has been reached. Morrow (1994) identifies four problems associated with sustainability of cooperative solutions: sanctioning, monitoring, distribution, and information. All four activities are varied as to their impacts on the stability of the cooperative arrangement. A distributional problem arises when the actors have different preferences regarding the cooperative arrangement. An information problem likewise occurs when the actors are uncertain of the value of the different cooperative arrangements, and may benefit by sharing knowledge if they are not in or status quo. Assuming that the parties reveal their true interests by signing a cooperative agreement, there is no need, in theory, to enforce and sanction. However, problems with monitoring, enforcing, and sanctioning (in cases of defection) in a cooperative environment, which are subject to the *ex post* noncooperative behavior of some parties, are very relevant yet difficult to resolve as well. For example, monitoring and enforcing a cooperative agreement may be expensive and difficult because it requires acquiring complicated information. The distribution of relevant information among the signatories is one of the key factors in the effective implementation of a cooperative agreement.

STRATEGIC BEHAVIOR AND COOPERATION

Cooperation may also be associated also with strategic behavior. Clearly, international water issues depend on interactions among states where one player's decision depends, to some extent, on the choice of another player (or other players). This is often called a "**strategic choice**." By working out the logic behind purposeful behavior of actors involved in some strategic interaction, it is possible to determine how individuals ought to make choices in a particular interaction if they adhere to principles of rationality. The principles of rational choice require that the players' behaviors are motivated by their own personal or group goals and values. These, in turn, may be modified by the parties' updated expectations (as situation changes) and constrained by the available resources and the rules of the institutional context in which they operate. In the jargon of game theory, a game's outcome depends upon the set of feasible outcomes, participants' choices, and the rules of the game (see also Chapters 5 and 6).

When the demand of a population for water in a river basin begins to approach its supply, the inhabitants have three choices. These options are equally applicable to the problems facing inhabitants of a single basin that includes two or more political entities. Each of these options can also be modeled (Falkenmark, 1989;

LeMarquand, 1977):

1. The inhabitants may work unilaterally within the basin (or state) to increase supply — through wastewater reclamation, desalination, or increasing catchment or storage — or decrease demand, through conservation or greater efficiency in agricultural practices.
2. The inhabitants of a basin may cooperate with the inhabitants of other basins for a more efficient interbasin distribution of water resources. This usually involves a transfer of water from the basin with greater water resources.
3. The inhabitants may essentially do nothing and face each cycle of drought with increasing hardship. This is the option most often chosen by countries that are less developed or are wracked by military strife.

Although the last alternative may seem unreasonable, game theoretic models can help explaining how nations may make choices, which lead to such choice due to the nature of their underlying interests and the strategic structure of the game itself. The modeler can then try to make prescriptions in such cases to change the contexts, leading to more efficient and welfare-enhancing outcomes.

The principles described above address **cooperation** and focus in particular on issues such as time consideration, **grand coalition**/partial **cooperation**, and expansion of the scope of cooperative activities. The following sections show that cooperative strategies almost always address such issues. Questions such as when to activate a certain feature in the **cooperation** arrangement, whether or not to wait for the entire set of parties to agree on **cooperation** (as was discussed earlier in this chapter), and whether or not to address the issue under dispute or to involve more issues that may enhance **cooperation** are taken into consideration by basin states in an attempt to deal with a water dispute.

COOPERATION IN MANAGING WATER AND NATURAL RESOURCES

Both conflict and **cooperation** combine a mix of economic and political variables. Some scholars see conflict as the norm and consider **cooperation** to be rare. Others believe that relations between various interest groups resemble a variety of rules, norms, and a wide spectrum of political interests, all of which facilitate a cooperative environment (Stein, 1990). Analyses of conflict situations and cooperative solutions suggest that the general observations made by Stein (1990) hold for the case of water as well, which is a source for conflict, but likewise be a basis for **cooperation**. For a detailed analysis, see Chapter 9.

Sharing water resources is a global problem, since international river and lake basins comprise nearly 50% of the world's continental land area (United Nations, 1978). In Africa, Asia, and South America, this proportion rises to at least 60% (Barrett, 1994). The economic and political cost of unresolved international water conflicts are very significant. Economic development of river basins may often be delayed or halted. In addition, short-term and long-term damages (such as pollution) to the parties may occur as a result of a unilateral action taken by another party. Finally, indirect social costs may also be the result of such conflicts.

There are several ways in which cooperative international river development offers possibilities for mutual gain (Krutilla, 1969). For example, an upstream riparian may wish to undertake flood-control measures on its reaches of the river so as to provide protection from floods and likewise improve the river's flow. In documenting the Columbia River case, Krutilla (1969) argues that, cooperative participation in design and scale, and mutually planned sharing of costs and attendant benefits, are likely to lead to more effective exploitation of the river's potential than if each party were to take an independent course of action, ignoring off-site effects. In general, where interdependencies exist, pooling the resource potential of an entire river system offers a wider range of technically feasible alternatives, and by avoiding investment duplication, an opportunity arises to select the most economical combination of sites and measures for attaining mutually desired objectives.

Although, conflicts over water resources are very common, there are a large number of cases where solutions were found, either among all the basin riparians or only some of them. They include one case involving 12 of the 15 riparian countries (Danube), three cases involving nine (out of ten) (Nile), and eleven riparians (Niger, Congo), three cases involving four of six riparians (Chad, Volta, Ganges, Brahmaputra, Mekong) two cases involving two of five riparians (La Plata, Elbe), nine of four riparians, 30 of three and at least 148 of two (Source: Panel of Experts on the Legal and Institutional Aspects of International Water Resources Development (1975), quoted by Barrett on page 2, Annex VII).

An important empirical example of the value of basin-wide **cooperation** in the Ganges is provided in Rogers (1969, 1993) in relation, to the Ganges–Brahmaputra. Using a game theoretical model, the study shows Nepal, India, and Bangladesh should be better off cooperating over a set of possible regional water-related projects. In reality, **cooperation**, as attractive as it seems in models, has not been practiced in that region for reasons related to trust and regional politics. Only recently, in December 1996, was a water treaty signed between India and Bangladesh, which addresses water-sharing issues at the Farakka Dam.

Even when **cooperation** does transpire, it does not always proceed smoothly and in some cases fails altogether. Failure to cooperate is usually explained by (a) technical complexity of the cooperative project, such as the data collection and sharing project by the ten Nile Basin riparian countries; (b) ill-defined rights and responsibilities of each riparian, such as the United States and Mexico dispute over the Colorado water where the quantity aspects were well defined but the water quality issues were left undefined; (c) existence of differing goals that cannot be represented by a simple balance of costs and gains to the riparians concerned, such as the ground water issues — that actually transcend ground water extraction rules — between the Israelis and the Palestinians; and (d) existence of wider considerations among the riparians and other stakeholders, such as the case of Chad and Nigeria over the Lake Chad water islands.

The above examples demonstrate that the effective joint management of international waters often depends on the opportunities embodied in **cooperation** and collaboration vis-à-vis water development and management, and other related regional issues of interest to the countries. In addition, it is becoming increasingly clear that a variety of factors tend to preclude cooperative management within basins. (Here we use the term cooperative management also to address the resolution of conflicts, which need some degree of **cooperation**.) These factors may include unequal power and hostile political relations between riparians, or an especially large number of riparian states. For sure, any successful basin-wide arrangement evolving in the face of these factors has been a result of strong NGO or other third-party involvement, roles that have been taken up with increasing reluctance (Bingham *et al.*, 1994).

Even though it is suggested that the likelihood of a basin-wide arrangement is less attainable because of existing externalities affecting the riparians' levels of utility (Just and Netanyahu, 1998), there are two issues that need further attention. First, mechanisms can be put in place that will reduce and even eliminate the externality impacts, hence promote basin-wide cooperative water arrangements. Such mechanisms may include river basin authorities, or **step-wise agreements** — such as was the case in the Danube River Basin (Linnerooth, 1990), or in the cases of the Mekong and the Aral Sea Basins (Kirmani and Le Moigne, 1997), and information collection and dissemination systems that are becoming more and more affordable and acceptable in various parts of the world (Kilgour and Dinar, 1995). Second, even if a partial **cooperation** arrangement is more likely to develop in the basin in the short- and medium-run, the longer-term prospect for such arrangements are gloomy in light of previous empirical evidence (Kaufman *et al.*, 1997). For that reason, it is important, in case of less-than-basin-wide arrangements to identify preconflict symptoms that may or may not develop, and that their dynamics is not expected.

Kally (1989), while evaluating the potential for **cooperation** in water resources development between Middle East countries, examines a particular approach that is based on individual water-related projects among two or more parties in the region. It should be noted that in Kally's approach, the water-related projects cut across basins and do not focus on a particular basin. The author suggests that it is possible to envisage different combinations of various projects of potential interest to the particular parties as well as to all parties in the region. However, political considerations other than those related directly to water are likely to determine the level of **cooperation** in the region and the particular subset of projects to be selected.

For Further Discussion. The sets of principles for **cooperation** suggested by Bogardus, Krutilla, and LeMarquand include items that are unique to each set, items that are similar across these three sets, and items that are complementary to each other. Compare the sets along the lines of that typology.

CASES OF COOPERATION

There are a variety of successful and less successful experiences of **cooperation** between riparian countries over the development and management of a river basin. Several examples detailing the experience of various river basin organizations from Africa are found in Rangeley *et al.* (1994). One successful and long standing example of international river basin **cooperation** in Africa is that of the Senegal River (LeMarquand, 1990). The dispute began during the French colonial era yet and continued after the independence of three of the Basin states: Mali, Mauritania, and Senegal.

Despite the Senegal River's importance for understanding cooperation over water, we shall briefly discuss the following cases: the Mekong River Basin, the Danube River Basin, the Aral Sea Basin and the Jordan Basin. The Mekong example demonstrates the value of **cooperation** even during times of war. The Danube Strategic Action Plan is an example of how the riparian states of the Danube River Basin established an integrated program for the basin-wide control of water quality. This was the first large scale initiative known for its activity and success. The Aral Sea Water and Environment Program is the least mature of the four examples, but is in itself a major achievement. The Jordan Basin is an example of riparian states' ability to sign a cooperative agreement over water allocation in a region with highly variable water supplies and a long history of political hostility.

The Ganges–Brahmaputra–Meghna Basin

The Ganges–Brahmaputra–Meghna Basin (see also Case Study 2) spans about 1.2 million square kilometers and is inhabited by 500 million people. It includes Bangladesh, Bhutan, Nepal, and India. This region appears to have exceptional opportunities for development. It is richly endowed with natural resources. It boasts of one of the world's largest sources of rich water resources, hydropower, coal, gas, and land, and a network of water ways for international transportation.

Following some empirical work on the **value of cooperation** in water resources management (Rogers, 1993), the World Bank, in 1996, initiated a study to assess the transboundary opportunities for regional development (ASTEN, 1997). Table 4.1 presents an outline of the issues and cooperative options facing the region. Following recent developments in transboundary water and energy arrangements (Salman, 1997; Rogers and Harshadeep, 1997), a window of opportunity has been created for promoting cooperative approaches and planning a shared vision for sustainable regional development including poverty alleviation.

Although water is the principle disputed resource among three of the region's countries (Bangladesh, India, Nepal), the World Bank study adopted the "expanding the cake" approach, which takes into consideration other resources than water to facilitate **cooperation**. Table 4.1 provides the set of issues that were included in the negotiations, such as energy, logistics, and the environment.

Table 4.1: Outline of the issues and options for regional **cooperation** in the Ganges Basin.

Focus area	Primary transboundary Problems	Primary options (examples) Hardware	Primary options (examples) Software	Recent events
Water	Low-flow augmentation needs to meet increasing domestic, industrial, and agricultural demands, Flood control, Hydropower, Cost recovery, Navigation, Fisheries, Siltation, Pollution, Cost of subsidies	Dams in Nepal and India Groundwater pumping (conjunctive use), Interbasin transfers/distribution systems/Embankments, Demand-side management & pollution control mechanisms, Dredging, Watershed conservation measures, Increasing conveyance, distribution, and use efficiency	River basin approaches, Negotiations/Agreements, Regulations, Pricing and other economic instruments, Stakeholder participation, Cropping patterns/sectoral, spatial and temporal water allocation, Institutional setup/ reorganization/strengthening	Ganges Water Sharing Agreement — India & Bangladesh, Nepal–India joint studies and energy agreements, Mahakali River Agreement (India and Nepal), Bhutan–India joint studies and agreements hydropower and low-flow augmentation
Energy	High demand (current and future) and deficits, esp. in India; Energy constraints on development; Financing; Cost of subsidies	Tapping hydropower potential in Nepal, Bhutan, & NE India (dams and run-of-the-river); Additional power generation (coal, gas, oil); Regional energy grid (incl. electricity links, gas pipelines between Bangladesh and India); Increasing generation, transmission, and use efficiency	Integrated approach to sustainable regional energy resources management Encouragement of power/energy trade, Pricing Private sector investment, Coordinated international lending/Joint implementation, Institutional setup/reorganization/ strengthening	Nepal–India joint studies and energy agreements, Encouragement of private investment

(*Continued*)

Table 4.1: (*Continued*)

Focus area	Primary transboundary Problems	Primary options (examples) Hardware	Software	Recent events
Logistics	Major infrastructural constraints to regional trade — roads, railways, inland waterways, pipelines, electricity grids, air and sea ports and links, Highly bureaucratic systems for regional and multi-modal transport, Low level of intra-regional and global trade	Targeted construction and rehabilitation of roads, railways, bridges, and inland waterways and other links (pipelines, grids), Trans-Asian Highways and Railways	Integrated transport planning and management, Policy reform (streamlining customs, transit, standards), Institutional setup/reorganization/ strengthening, Free-trade zones, Automated systems, Transit routes through Bangladesh for NE India and Nepal access to sea	SAARC and ESCAP studies and recommendations, Preferential trade agreements (SAPTA), SAARC free trade area (SAFTA), Discussions on trade facilitation between Bangladesh and India, Jamuna Bridge in Bangladesh
Environment	Relative global, regional, and local environmental impacts of various energy and water resource management options, Transboundary pollution — air, water, trade in 2-stroke engines, etc., Saline intrusion, Arsenic in groundwater, Biodiversity protection	Input/product substitution, Cleaner processes, Waste reduction, treatment and reuse, Other low-environmental impact, "Hardware" options for water, energy and transport	Integration of environmental concerns into development planning process, Institutional setup/reorganization/ strengthening, Regional coordination in environmental protection	Ganga/National River Action Plan in India, "Judicial Activism", Concern for the Sunderbans, fragile mountain ecosystems, "cradle of rivers"

Source: Adapted from ASTEN, (1997).

The Mekong Basin

The Mekong River (see also Case Study 1) rises in China and flows through Myanmar, Laos, Thailand, Cambodia, and Vietnam. The Mekong case reveals the successful application of a comprehensive development approach in an international river basin. That being said, it is one of the least developed major rivers in the world, in part because of difficulties inherent in implementing joint management among its diverse riparian states.

Specifically, China and Myanmar located upstream have had little interest in regional **cooperation**. At the same time, their individual development plans did not overly trouble the downstream riparian states (although today China's prospective projects on the Mekong are raising concerns). The downstream countries, though acknowledging the potential benefits to be drawn from the river, could not find the financial resources for joint development or a mechanism to overcome their divergent interests. Nonetheless a formal international basis for **cooperation** was established in 1957 when the Mekong Committee was created, comprised of representatives from the four downstream riparian states. Programs for developing the resources of the Mekong for irrigation, navigation, power, and flood control were advanced with support from the United Nations, Asian Development Bank, the World Bank, and other donor countries.

The Committee's mandate is to prepare and submit to participating governments plans for coordinated research, study, and investigation. In addition, the committee is charged with making requests on behalf of the governments for special financial assistance and for receiving and administering these funds. Finally, the Committee is responsible for drawing up and recommending governments criteria for use of the water for development purposes. All four representatives must attend all Committee meetings, and any decision must be unanimous. Meetings are held three to four times a year, and leadership is rotated annually in alphabetical order by name of country.

With agreement among the riparians on priority issues, extensive international support was forthcoming. Along with the collection of physical data and the establishment of hydrographic networks, the Committee encouraged undertaking of economic and social studies and a regional training activity, including, programs for aerial mapping, surveying, and leveling. Navigation has also been improved along the river due to the Committee's work. The Committee also helped overcome mistrust among the riparians through increased integration. Consequently, Laos and Thailand signed an agreement on developing the power potential on one of the Mekong tributaries inside Laos (Nam Ngun). This project provides electricity to Thailand and was financed by international funds. As a sign of the Committee's viability, the supply of electricity from Laos to Thailand and the payment in hard currency by Thailand to Laos was never interrupted, despite hostilities between the two countries.

During the 1970s, the Committee's momentum started to fade, and international support decreased. There were several reasons for this change, including: (1) political and financial obstacles that impeded the shift from data collection and studies to actual development projects; (2) the departure of Cambodia from the

Committee in 1978, paralyzing its activity — it rejoined in 1991; (3) the divergent development objectives of the members, and (4) over-ambitious projects that were at times inconsistent with long-term needs (Bingham *et al.*, 1994; Kirmani, 1990).

The Strategic Action Plan for the Danube (DSAP) River Basin, 1995–2005

The Danube River is shared by a number of riparians that for decades were allied with hostile political blocks, and consequently locked in tense ideological disputes. During the period of centralized planning, the central and eastern European countries did not develop full environmental protection policies to respond to the degradation of the river. Legal standards for environmental quality were often unenforced or unenforceable. Apart from Germany and Austria, all other Danube countries are currently undergoing fundamental transformation of their political, legal, administrative, economic, and social systems. For additional information on legal aspects relating to water management, see Chapter 3.

Recognizing the increasing degradation of water quality, in 1985 the (at that time) eight riparians of the Danube signed the "Declaration of the Danube Countries to Cooperate on Questions Concerning the Water Management of the Danube," also known as the Bucharest Declaration. It committed the riparian states to a regional, integrated approach to river basin management. Basin-wide coordination was strengthened at a meeting in Sofia in September 1991, in which the riparians elaborated on a plan for protecting the water quality of the Danube. At that meeting, the countries and interested international institutions, including the World Bank and UNDP, met to draw up an initiative to support and reinforce national actions for the restoration and protection of the Danube River. The countries and donors established a Task Force to oversee the program, which covers monitoring, data collection and assessment, emergency response systems, and preinvestment activities. A Program Coordination Unit was likewise established to monitor the day-to-day activities of the Environmental Program.

In 1991, as part of the overall Danube Environmental Program, each riparian country identified a country coordinator and a person to serve as a country "focal point". These individuals would be the liaisons to the Program Coordination Unit in Brussels (now in Vienna). Both the coordinator and focal point were also members of the Task Force. The country coordinator was usually from a ministerial or other political position. The focal point was a technical person who handled the day to day issues of the country team that included representatives of various sectors and government agencies.

The public consultation process that was designed to guide and support the development of the DSAP in 1994 required a facilitator from each country who had some technical background either in water or environment. The local facilitator organized and ran the local public consultation meetings in each of the nine countries, based on an agreed design. The World Bank designed and initiated the format of the consultation process, including training sessions.

A major accomplishment of the Danube public consultation was the development of a Strategic Action Plan for the Danube River Basin, which was adopted
by the Task Force in October 1994, and ratified by the countries' respective water
or environment ministers in December 1994, in Bucharest. In late 1993 and early
1994, another major Danube River activity was being carried out in the basin —
the Convention on **Cooperation** for the Protection and Sustainable Use of the
Danube (the Danube River Protection Convention). The Danube River Protection
Convention aims to achieve sustainable and equitable water management in the
basin and was ratified in June 1994, in Sofia (Task Force for the Programme, 1995).

Water and Environmental Management in the Aral Sea Basin

The Syr Darya and Amu Darya Rivers constitute The Aral Sea Basin (see also
Case Study 4). The Basin covers parts of Kazakhstan, the Kyrgyz Republic, Turkmenistan, Tajikistan, Uzbekistan, and a small area of Afghanistan. River water has
played a vital role in the economic and social life of these arid Central Asian countries. In the 1960s, resulting from Soviet irrigation projects, water was withdrawn
from the Amu Darya and Syr Darya before being discharged into the Aral Sea and
was conveyed to remote desert areas in Kazakhstan, Turkmenistan, and Uzbekistan.
The water has been used mainly for irrigation of cotton and rice, using very inefficient irrigation technologies. This has resulted in decreasing water level, a reduction
in the lake's area, and increased salinity levels in the water (Ayres *et al.*, 1996).

The marked reduction in the lake's size has resulted in significant climatic
changes in the region, including lower temperatures, reduced snowfall (thus reduced
snowmelt), and further diminished river flow. Additional effects include wind erosion
and salt deposits, which cause damage to crops, power lines, concrete structures,
and land fertility, as well as severe health problems among the region's population.
Specifically, the water level of the Aral Sea has dropped from 53.3 to 39 m above
sea level, and salinity content tripled from 10 to 28 g/l between 1960 and 1989.
If no action is taken, the water level is expected to fall to 32 m, and the salinity
content will increase to 65 g/l in the mid 1990s (Ayers *et al.*, 1996) (No updated
observations beyond the year 2000 are available. See also Case Study 4 (Aral Sea)
for water quantity and quality information.) In addition aquifer levels have dropped,
and aquifer water quality has deteriorated significantly. Forest areas have declined,
and in many places disappeared. Navigation of the lake is impossible now, and fish
stocks have practically disappeared. All the fish for the region's canning industry,
once brought from the Aral Sea, is now imported from other regions.

The basin countries recognize the gains to be realized from a basin-wide effort to
address the causes of the crisis. The five states — Afghanistan does not participate
in this effort — are exploring means for deepening interstate **cooperation**. Some
of the cooperative endeavors considered include rehabilitating and stabilizing the
environment of the Aral Sea, improving the management of the international waters

of the basin, and building up the capacity of regional institutions to deal with water management in the region (World Bank, 1997).

A detailed regional water resource management strategy was agreed upon by the basin states. The strategy includes interstate water-sharing agreements, sharing of information, and monitoring of the international water ways in the Basin. The expected benefits from regional **cooperation** are substantial and drive the actions of individual states.

The Jordan River Basin

Water is one of the major issues addressed in the 1994 peace treaty between Jordan and Israel. In fact, the treaty could likely be used as a possible model for other river basins.

Cooperation between the two states is based on mutual recognition of their reliance on different joint sources (Jordan and Yarmouk Rivers' and the Arava ground waters) and that "... water can form the basis for the advancement of **cooperation** between them ..." (Jordan Times, 1994:6). Water-related **cooperation** between Jordan and Israel is also based on the understanding that any joint undertaking of management and development of these water resources will not harm the water resources of the other party. The agreement also stipulates the need to explore water augmenting options due to the inadequate availability of existing water resources.

The alternative options that the two riparians considered for advancing cooperation and alleviating water shortage include: (1) development of existing and new water resources; (2) prevention of contamination of water resources; (3) mutual assistance in the alleviation of water shortages; and (4) transfer of water-related information and knowledge.

The 1994 treaty ensures proper implementation of the various items by including a description of various steps and actions that acknowledge both historical usage, present needs, and water origin. Examples include: (1) allocation rules for water from the Yarmouk and Jordan Rivers during various seasons; (2) operation and maintenance schemes of sources in one state's jurisdiction supplied to the other state; (3) development and operation of joint storage systems; (4) joint monitoring of water quality, and (5) joint management of ground water wells in the Arava Valley, recognizing existing pumping schemes.

In his book *Diplomacy on the Jordan*, Haddadin (2002:442) provides telling evidence for the state of water **cooperation** between Israel and Jordan: "...the **cooperation** between Israel and Jordan, in general, was going downhill because of the Likud policy toward peace and the Palestinians. Water, on the other hand, continued to flow and proved to be an element of **cooperation** for the benefit of both sides. The water that the treaty brought saved Jordan from devastating effects of drought that lasted from March 1998 to January 2000. Israel honored most of her commitments to Jordan, at a time when she badly needed the water herself (The Israeli Water Commissioner announced, in April 1999, that he was cutting irrigation water to 40% of the usual quantities. He went to say that he did not have water to give Jordan either. But the flow to Jordan continued until the level in Lake Tiberias got to the Red Line.)"

For Further Discussion. Referring to the Rio Grande and Euphrates Basins that were presented in Chapter 3, using the set of principles suggested by Bogardus, Krutilla, and LeMargquand, explain which of the principles function and which does not function in each of the two basins.

SUMMARY AND SUGGESTED STRATEGIES FOR COOPERATION

Several variables form the basis for international **cooperation** over natural resources. They include: (1) developing incentives for voluntary **cooperation**, (2) developing monitoring and enforcement mechanisms to ensure compliance with **cooperation** arrangements, (3) creating institutional structures for managing potential conflicts, and (4) addressing third-party effects.

The lessons learned from past experience suggest that integrated international resource management will be best implemented before conflict develops. Cooperative development plans will also be more stable if they link as many components as possible (e.g., linking water quality with quantity and surface with groundwater sources. Annex A4 to this chapter proposes generic strategy for regional **cooperation** on transboundary water.)

Creating incentives for voluntary **cooperation** among riparians in an international river basin may be accomplished either by targeting a broad set of issues of interest to all riparians, or by ensuring an attractive outcome, or by providing linkages to out-of-basin activities. The role of a third party in the process of resolving existing conflicts, or preventing potential future conflicts, is crucial.

A list of rules of thumb (Bingham *et al.*, 1994) for reducing the likelihood of conflicts and laying the foundation for international river basin cooperative management may include:

1. focusing on interests underlying each riparian's position;
2. sharing information;
3. developing strategies for joint fact finding;
4. expanding the set of alternative development options;
5. preventing asymmetrical outcomes;
6. developing mechanisms for transparent and fair allocation of joint gains from **cooperation**.

When the negotiation of a grand coalition is not viable, an alternative approach to achieving regional **cooperation** is the creation of partial-coalition agreements.

This may either be an interim or ultimate option. The partial coalition arrangement is challenged, however, by more likely negative third-party effects relative to the **grand coalition** arrangement.

Practice Questions

1. Contrary to "common sense," there is evidence that **cooperation** among a subset of basin riparians is more common than a **grand coalition** agreement. Support and use examples of various river basins around the world.

2. What are the principles of **cooperation** suggested by Bogardus (1964)? Discuss each principle with regard to its relevance to the political, institutional, and economic realities in a given river basin selected from the set in this chapter.

3. In his conceptual framework of international rivers **cooperation** over international rivers, LeMarquand (1977) suggests several sets of conditions that may inhibit or facilitate **cooperation**. (a) Enumerate all of these conditions and articulate their effect on river basin cooperation. (b) Apply LeMarquand's framework to one of the basins discussed in this chapter and assess how well the framework pertains to that basin. (c) Specify the variables included in each set and discuss how they affect **cooperation** in a river basin. (d) Apply the framework to one of the basins in this chapter and discuss how well does the framework apply in the case of that basin.

ANNEX A4: A POSSIBLE STRATEGY FOR REGIONAL COOPERATION IN INTERNATIONAL RIVER BASINS

Based on practical experience (World Bank, 1996), a general strategy framework to deal with regional **cooperation**, including and focusing on international rivers can be proposed. The main strategic imperatives are:

1. Long-term vision and planning;
2. Utilization of instruments underpinning the problems;
3. Comprehensive approach and cross-sectoral and international coordination.

Key strategic interventions for achieving goals of sustainable and equitable water resources are included in Table A4.1.

Table A4.1: Strategies for river basin **cooperation**.

Strategic goal	Specific items
Strengthening policy and regulation, both domestic and international	(1) Building and strengthening local capacity
	(2) Strengthening and improving data and information collection and analysis systems, and sharing of data and information
	(3) Increasing awareness and involving stakeholders in decision-making processes, both domestic and international
Support long-term national and regional programs	(1) Adoption of a basin wide approach
	(2) Promote consensus on importance and urgency of international water problems
	(3) Promote harmonization of water regulation among the basin countries
	(4) Encourage participation of all subsectors
Evaluate basin-wide development alternatives	(1) Identify, modify and promote successful regional shared water agreements
	(2) Facilitating exchange between riparians
	(3) Hydrological data services — data and information sharing
Expanding areas of interaction and joint interest	(1) Promote joint water-related and nonwater related projects benefiting all countries in the basin
	(2) Establishing dispute-resolution mechanisms
	(3) Include out-of-basin expertise

REFERENCES

ASTEN (Asia Technical Department) (1993). Environment and natural resources division, South Asia Development Triangle Newsletter, The World Bank, March.

Ayers, W.S., A. Busia, A. Dinar, R. Hirji, S.E. Lintner, A. F. McCalla and R. Robelus (1996). Integrated lake and reservoir management. World Bank Technical Paper No. 358, Washington, DC.

Barrett, S. (1994). Conflict and cooperation in managing international water resources. Policy Research Working Paper 1303, The World Bank, Washington, DC.

Bingham, G., W. Aaron and Wohlgenant (1994). *Resolving Water Disputes: Conflict and Cooperation in the United States, the Near East and Asia.* Arlington: (ISPAN).

Bogardus, E.S. (1964). *Principles of Cooperation.* Chicago, IL: The Cooperative League of the USA.

Dinar, S. (2004). Patterns of engagement-how states negotiate water. Paper Presented at the 2004 ISA Annual Convention, Montreal, Canada, 17–20 March.

Dinar S. and A. Dinar (2003). Recent developments in the literature on conflict and cooperation in international shared water, *Natural Resources Journal,* 43(4), 1217–1287.

Dinar, A. and A. Wolf (1994a). International markets for water and the potential for regional cooperation: Economic and political perspectives in the western middle east, *Economic Development and Cultural Change,* 43(1), 43–66.

Dinar, A. and A. Wolf (1994b). Economic potential and political considerations of regional water trade: the western middle east example, *Resources and Energy Economics,* 16, 335–356.

Dinar, A. and A. Wolf (1997). Economic and political considerations in regional cooperation models, *Agricultural and Resource Economics Review,* 26(1), 7–22.

Falkenmark, M. (1989). Fresh waters as a factor in strategic policy and action. In: *Population and Resources in a Changing World.* Stanford University: Morrison Institute.

Haddadin, M. (2002). *Diplomacy on the Nile.* Boston: Kluwer Academic Publishers.

Just, R.E. and S. Netanyahu (1998). International water resource conflict: Experience and potential. In: Richard, E.J. and S. Netanyahu (eds.), *Conflict and Cooperation on Trans-Boundary Water Resources.* Boston: Kluwer Academic Publishers, pp. 1–26.

Kally, E. (1989). The potential for cooperation in water projects in the Middle East at peace. In: Fishelson, G. (ed.), *Economic Cooperation in the Middle East.* Boulder, CO: Westview Press, pp. 303–325.

Kaufman, E., J. Oppenheimer, A. Wolf and A. Dinar (1997). Transboundary fresh water disputes and conflict resolution: Planning an integrated approach, *Water International,* 22(1), 37–48.

Kibaroglu, A. (2002). *Building a Regime for the Waters of the Euphrates-Tigris River Basin.* Kluwer Academic Publishers.

Kilgour, M.D. and A. Dinar (1995). Are stable agreements for sharing international river waters now possible? Policy Research Working Paper No. 1474, The World Bank, Washington, DC.

Kirmani, S. (1990). Water, peace, and conflict management: The experience of the Indus and Mekong River Basins, Water International, 15(4), 200–205.

Kirmani, S. and G. Le Moigne (1997). Fostering riparian cooperation in international river basins. World Bank Technical Paper No. 335, World Bank, Washington, DC.

Krutilla, J. (1969). *The Columbia River Treaty — The Economics of an International River Basin Development.* Published for the Resources For the Future by the John Hopkins University Press, Baltimore, MD.

LeMarquand, D. (1976). Politics of international river basin cooperation and management, Natural Resources Journal, 16, 883–901.

LeMarquand, D. (1977). *International Rivers: The Politics of Cooperation.* Vancouver, BC: Westwater Research Center, University of British Columbia.

LeMarquand, D.G. (1990). International development of the Senegal River, *Water International,* 15(4), 223–230.

Linnerooth, J. (1990). The Danube River Basin: Negotiating settlements to transboundary environmental issues, *Natural Resources Journal,* 30, 629–660.

Loehman, E.T. and A. Dinar (1995). Introduction. In: Dinar, A. and E.T. Loehman
   (eds.), *Water Quantity/Quality Management and Conflict Resolution: Institutions,
   Processes, and Economic Analyses.* Westport, CT: Praeger, pp. xxi–xxx.
Moran, T.H. (1996). Trade and investment dimensions of international conflict. In: Crocker,
   C.A., F.O. Hampson and P. Aall (eds.), *Managing Global Chaos, Sources of and
   Responses to International Conflict.* Washington, DC: United States Institute of Peace
   Press, pp. 155–170.
Morrow, J.D. (1994). Modeling the forms of international cooperation: Distribution versus
   information, *International Organization*, 48(3), 387–423.
Rangeley, R., B.M. Thiam, R.A. Andersen and C.A. Lyle (1994). International river
   basin organizations in Sub-Saharan Africa. World Bank Technical Paper Number
   250, Washington, DC, September.
Rogers, P. (1969). A game theory approach to the problem of international river basins,
   Water Resources Research, 5(4), 749–760.
Rogers, P. (1993). The value of cooperation in resolving international river basin disputes,
   Natural Resources Forum, May, 117–131.
Rogers, P. and N. Harshadeep (1997). The Farakka Ganges Water Sharing Treaty, Some
   Implications for India and Bangladesh, Mimeo, World Bank, ASTEN, 22 January.
Salman, S. (1997). The Ganges River Treaty of 1996: A comparative analysis. World Bank,
   Legal Department, Washington, DC, 25 March, Preliminary Draft (Permission to
   quote was awarded).
Sprinz, D. (1995). Regulating the international environment: A conceptual model and
   policy implications. Prepared for the 1995 Annual Meeting of the American Political
   Science Association. Chicago, IL, 31 August–3 September.
Stein, A.A. (1990). *Why Nations Cooperate.* Ithaca: Cornell University Press.
Task Force for the Programme (1995). Strategic Action Plan for the Danube River
   Basin (1995–2005), Environmental Programme for the Danube River Basin, Vienna,
   Austria.
United Nations (1978). *Register of International Rivers.* Oxford, UK: Pergamon Press.
Waterbury, J. (1979). *Hydropolitics of the Nile Valley.* New York: Syracuse University
   Press.
Waterbury, J. (1996) Socio-economic development models for the Nile Basin. Keynote
   Paper Presented at the 4th Nile 2002 Conference, Kampala, Uganda, 26–29 February.
Waterbury, J. (2002). *The Nile Basin, National Determinants of Collective Action.* New
   Haven and London: Yale University Press.
World Bank (1996). African water resources: Challenges and opportunities for sustainable
   development, World Bank, Washington, DC, Draft, January.
World Bank (1997). Water and environmental management in the Aral Sea Basin. Draft
   Project Document, Rural Development/Environment Sector Unit, Europe and Cen-
   tral Asia Region, World Bank, Washington, DC, 30 September.
Yoffe, S. (2002). Basins at risk: Conflict and cooperation over international freshwater
   resources. PhD Dissertation, Department of Geosciences, Oregon State University,
   Corvallis.
Yoffe, S., G. Fiske, M. Giordano, K. Larson, K. Stahl and A.T. Wolf (2004). Geography
   of international water conflict and cooperation: Data sets and applications, Water
   Resources Research, 40, W05S04, doi:10.1029/2003WR002530.
Zeitouni, N., N. Becker, M. Shechter and E. Luk-Zilberman (1994). Two models of water
   market mechanisms with an illustrative application to the Middle East. Nota Di
   Lavoro, 12.94, Fondazione Enrico Mattei, Milano, Italy.

5. COOPERATIVE GAME THEORY AND WATER RESOURCES — PRINCIPLES

Objectives

Our main focus in this and the next chapter is the application of Cooperative Game Theory (CGT) models to international water resource issues. In this chapter we will justify the use of CGT in water resource problems, and in particular, in international conflict-cooperation cases. The chapter reviews several important CGT concepts and demonstrates their use and calculation. After reading this chapter you will have a good grasp of basic CGT concepts and be able to apply them at both conceptual and empirical levels to simple cases.

Main Terminology

Alternate cost avoided (ACA); Arbitration; Asking price; Bargaining/negotiation set; Characteristic function; Constant-sum game; Core; Defecting; Dominant; Economic goods; Efficiency; Egalitarian non-separable cost (ENSC); Extreme points of the core; Feasibility; Game in a matrix form; Generalized Shapley; Grand coalition; Group rationality; Imputation; Individual rationality; Inessential coalition; Marginal cost; Mixed strategies; Nash/Nash-Harsany; Nash equilibrium; Negotiation; Non-cooperative coalition; Non-zero sum game; Nucleolus; Partial coalition; Payoff; Players; Possibility frontier; Prisoner's dilemma (PD); Proportional use; Pure strategies; Riparian; Stability; Status quo; Shapley value; Separable costs remaining benefits (SCRB); Strategy; Superadditivity (subadditivity); 2-person cooperative matrix form game; Willingness to pay; Zero-sum game.

We shall first discuss the concept of game theory (GT), so that we feel comfortable with it as we progress in its application to water resources. As it may sound strange, Game Theory has many definitions used in the literature, but all of them aim at the same main concepts. Von Neumann and Morgenstern ([1944] 2004:48–49), in their seminal work "Theory of Games and Economic Behavior" define game theory as a method of describing interactions between agents that is subject to rules which dictate the possible moves for each agent and a set of outcomes for each combination of moves. Myerson (1997:1) defines GT as the study "of mathematical models of conflict and cooperation between intelligent rational decision makers... that will influence one another's welfare." And Osborn (2004:1) asserts that Game Theory aims to help us understand situations in which decision-makers interact. We actually combine the various definitions to come up with one that will be very relevant to our international water context: Game Theory is the study of mathematical modeling of strategic behavior of decision makers (**players**), in situations where one player's decisions may affect the other **players**. The basic assumption of GT is that decision makers are rational **players**, that they are intelligent, so, while pursuing well-defined objectives, they take into account other decision-makers' rationality and, accordingly, build expectations on their behavior.

According to Parrachino *et al.* (2006:2):

> "GT consists of a modeling part and a solution part. Mathematical models of conflicts and of cooperation provide strategic behavioral patterns, and the resulting **payoffs** to the **players** are determined according to certain solution concepts. There are two branches of GT. The first is the non-cooperative Game Theory (NCGT) and the second is the cooperative Game Theory (CGT). The main distinction between the two is that NCGT models situations where **players** see only their own strategic objectives and thus binding agreements among the **players** are not possible, while CGT actually is based mainly on agreements to allocate cooperative gains (solution concepts)."

We will focus mainly on CGT approaches and solution concepts in this book.

STRATEGIC CONSIDERATIONS IN AQUIFER WATER SHARING

To start, we will refer to a problem of non-cooperation, known as the **Prisoner's Dilemma (PD)** problem, which is typical to situations in the water sector. We will show how this PD problem can be converted into a cooperation problem. Then we will introduce several basic cooperative game theory concepts and their application to water resources.

The Groundwater Game

Consider a case where there are two **riparian** states, A and B, sharing one transboundary (international) aquifer (Fig. 5.1).

Assume for simplicity that the economy of each country is based only on the aquifer water. Water is pumped and then sold in the international market (say, bottled water). The international market does not distinguish between the water that is sold by A or B (same product). The international demand function recognizes just the total amount of water (from A and B) in the market. To be more realistic we could instead describe water as an input to a production process of a given good that is then sold in the international market. But this is not necessary for demonstrating our point. The international market is limited in its capacity to consume water.

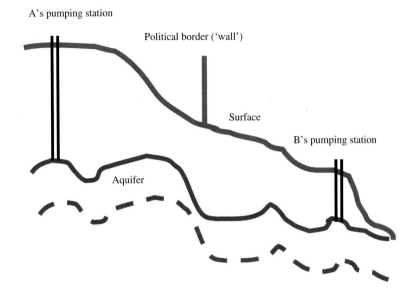

Fig. 5.1: Illustration of the regional joint aquifer between countries A and B.
Source: Authors.

Table 5.1: The demand schedule for
water in the international market.

P (US\$/m^3)	W (billion m^3)
32	2
16	4
9	6
4	8

Quantities of water in that market range between 2 billion and 8 billion m^3 per year. The demand schedule for water in the market is given in Table 5.1.

As is the case with other **economic goods**, the market responds to the quantities supplied (W) such that the price (P) per unit of water is a decreasing function of W. The demand function (5.1) shows the relationship between P and W (based on the data in Table 5.1).

$$P = 51.75 - 11.425W + 0.6875W^2 \tag{5.1}$$

The demand function in the market for water is shown in Fig. 5.2 (based on Eq. (5.1)).

While there is a border between A and B, the aquifer does not recognize that border, as is the case in almost all international water bodies. The geography of the regional terrain is such that country A has to pump the aquifer water from depth that is much deeper than that of country B. For simplicity assume that the cost of pumping water for country A is $C_a = \$0.6/\text{m}^3$ and that for country B is $C_b = \$0.2/\text{m}^3$. (This cost ignores, for simplicity, the fact that the water table in the aquifer will fall as more water is pumped and, therefore, the pumping cost will

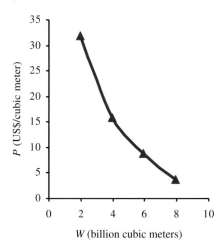

Fig. 5.2: The demand function for water sold in the international market.

Source: Authors.

increase.) Assume further for simplicity that each country has only two strategies regarding the annual pumping volume from the aquifer. That is either to pump 2 or 4 billion m^3 per year. Pumping 0 is not considered by any riparian, therefore, the amount of water sold in the international market could be 4 (2 + 2), 6 (2 + 4 or 4 + 2) or 8 (4 + 4) billion m^3, depending on the combination of strategies each country will choose.

From here on, the rest of the analysis is quite technical and simple, but the interpretation is quite interesting and important. We calculate revenue and cost and thus **payoff** to each country for each combination of pumping strategies. We present these **payoffs** as a **game in a matrix form** in Fig. 5.3 below.

The game that was described and summarized in Fig. 5.3 is called a **Prisoner's Dilemma** game. Why is that? A **prisoner's dilemma** game, originally designed by Albert Tucker in 1950 (Poundstone, 1992:117), is a conflict situation where **players**

			Country B	
			Water pumping **strategy** (billions of m³/year)	
			2	4
Country A	Water pumping **strategy** (billions of m³/year)	2	30.8 31.6	16.8 35.2
		4	33.6 17.6	13.6 15.2

Fig. 5.3: The **strategy/payoff** matrix of the water pumping **prisoner's dilemma** game.

Note: The values to the upper left of each cell are of country A and those to the lower right of each cell are of country B.

(usually two), consider cooperating or not cooperating (**defecting**). (We use the notion "player" to represent the entity — individual, corporation, state — involved in the strategic interaction we capture in a game.) Because of the structure of the **payoffs** associated with each of these strategies, and also because of lack of communication among themselves, the **players** end up facing the worst joint and individual **payoffs**.

Notice that in our water pumping game, there is a "wall" between the two countries and each makes a decision independently of the other country. Returning to Fig. 5.3, country A's preferred **strategy** is to pump 4 billion m^3 per year because the **payoff** associated with this **strategy** is the highest it can get — 33.6 billon dollars. Using the same rational, country B's preferred **strategy** is also to pump 4 billion m^3 because the **payoff** associated with this **strategy** is 35.2 billion dollars. However, when both countries select to pump 4 billion m^3/year $(4 + 4 = 8)$, they "dump" the international market and the price per unit of water is the lowest, resulting in the lowest individual and joint **payoff** for the countries. The non-cooperative strategies **payoff** can be called the **status quo** of the **prisoner's dilemma** game.[1]

What is going on here and how can that situation be improved? There are several proposed improvements of the **prisoner's dilemma** situation described earlier (Poundstone, 1992; Dixit and Nalebuff, 1993; Axelrod, 1985, 1997). We will refer here only to one, namely, improving the communication between the two countries — in our case, removing the "wall" between them. If the two countries could be convinced to select the cooperative **strategy**, and to pump 2 billion m^3 each, then the joint **payoff** would be 62.4 billion dollars and it would be preferred over any combination of strategies in the game, especially over the **status quo** joint payment of 28.8 billion dollars. Once the countries are convinced to select the cooperative **strategy**, the remaining problem is how to allocate the joint **payoff** in the amount of 62.4 billion dollars among themselves. The remainder of this chapter and Chapter 6 will focus on the answer to this question.

For Further Discussion. Let us be realistic. Can we find examples from the cases reviewed in Chapters 3 and 4, where a situation such as in the groundwater game (not necessarily related to groundwater) can be described? What are the additional assumptions one has to consider in order to apply game theory to solve such conflicts?

2-Person Cooperative Matrix Form Games: Bargaining Solutions

So far we assumed that the **players** do not communicate with each other, and thus do not cooperate. As we already noticed, the **players** of a **prisoner's dilemma**

---

[1]We should add that similar games can be designed where the payoff to one player is exactly the loss of the other (**zero-sum game**); or when the two **players** share a given amount (pie) of the resource (**constant-sum game**). The groundwater game we discuss here is **non-zero sum game**, where the **payoffs** can change, depending on the two strategies selected by the **players**.

game can improve their individual **payoff** levels if they can find agreeable allocation of the joint **payoff**. One way they may reach a fair, acceptable and equitable
agreement is by **negotiation**, where they offer each other help on how to allocate
the highest **payoff** cell. If the communication process is made via a third, neutral
party, it is called **arbitration**.

A simple example of such a game is the seller-buyer game. The seller and the
buyer have a common interest — to exchange the good one has and the other desires.
Each has a departure point — **asking price** and **willingness to pay** price. The
seller **asking price** is the upper limit and the buyer **willingness to pay** price is
the lower limit for a negotiated agreement. If the sale takes place, the price will be
in the feasible region that is between these two price values. The no-sale outcome
is called the **status quo**.

A bargaining game can be represented by the following matrix (Fig. 5.4):
Player I has two strategies, A and B. Player II has also two strategies, a and b.
The sum of their joint **payoffs** in cell aB is the highest — (8 + 3 = 11).

As we can see, this game has two pure **Nash equilibrium** solutions at (aB)
and (Ba), where player II prefers (aB) and player I prefers (bA).

Definition: Two strategies are in **Nash equilibrium** if neither player gains by
changing their **strategy** unilaterally.

The two **Nash equilibrium** strategies suggest also that if player I sticks to
strategy A and player II to **strategy** a then Aa will be selected, which allocates 1
to player II and 2 to player I. This is quite significantly less than 8,3 or 4,4 that the
players could get. Figure 5.6 depicts the area ((8,3); (2,1); (4,4); (1,2)) which is the
feasible region for the game **payoff**. But assuming that the **players** are rational,
they will have to find ways to increase their joint **payoff** and then to negotiate
how to allocate it such that they will be better of compared to the lowest **payoffs**
(1,2 and 2,1) they face. One way they can do it is by deciding to move away from
the **pure strategies** (selecting only one **strategy** all the time).

Mixed Strategies

The vertical and horizontal dotted lines in Fig. 5.6 are the maximum that
the **players** can secure for themselves if the play **mixed strategies**. The
region that is confined between the dotted lines can be obtained only if the
players will cooperate, through bargaining and **negotiation**. It is called
the **bargaining/negotiation set**. **Players** are also allowed **mixed strategies**.

		Player I	
		A	B
Player II	a	1,2	8,3
	b	4,4	2,1

Fig. 5.4: A bargaining 2-player game.

<u>Definition:</u> A **mixed strategy** is a combination of strategies that can be used if the game is played a number of times. A player facing K strategies decides to play **strategy** i α_i of the time, $i = 1, \ldots, K$, and $\sum_{i \in K} \alpha_i = 1$.

Let p and $(1-p)$ be the probabilities that player II assigns to the a and b strategies, respectively, and that q and $(1-q)$ are the probabilities that player I assigns to the A and B strategies.

To find the values of p and q, and to find the **Nash equilibrium** solution associated with the **mixed strategies**, we solve the equations (Fig. 5.5) for player II and player I, respectively:

Player I	Player II
$2q + 4(1-q) = 3q + 1(1-q)$	$1p + 4(1-p) = 8p + 2(1-p)$
$2q + 4 - 4q = 3q + (1-q)$	$p + 4 - 4p = 8 + 2 - 2p$
$3 = 4q$	$2 = 9p$
$q = 3/4$	$p = 2/9$
$(1-q) = 1/4$	$(1-p) = 7/9$

Fig. 5.5: The procedure to calculate the probabilities of the **mixed strategies** in the cooperative game.

With that in mind, we can now calculate the new **Nash equilibrium** in the following way:

For Player I: $2q + 4(1-q) = 2(3/4) + 4(1/4) = 6/4 + 4/4 = 10/4 = 5/2$
For Player II: $p + 4(1-p) = 2/9 + 4(7/9) = 2/9 + 28/9 = 30/9 = 10/3$.

This is a unique, stable solution. In the case of a **2-person game**, where the **negotiation** set equation is $y = f(x)$ and the **status quo** point (has to be known) is (xo, yo), then the solution (x, y) is found by maximizing the product $(x - xo)$ $(y - yo)$, which creates a rectangle over the two **players' possibility frontier**. The solution to the **negotiation** game is presented in Fig. 5.6. The red-edges hexagon is the **negotiation** possibilities locus. The **players** would be better off if they select any equilibrium **strategy** that brings them to end up on the line $[(8,3; 4,4)]$ and a **Nash equilibrium** solution will be in point D. Point D is where the utility substitution curve between the two **players** tangents to the **negotiation possibility frontier**. It is also the intersection between the 45° line and the **negotiation possibility frontier**.

While we started this chapter with an example that is based on a "water economy," we moved to a game that is not related to water. While the **mixed strategy** game has no connotation to water, one aspect, which is the fact that the game is repeated, is mainly a characteristic of water related games. But since we want to stick to water, and in particular transboundary/international water, we will focus in the next section on the question of use of Game Theory in water resources, starting with the general question: "What makes water resources issues fit the game theory context?"

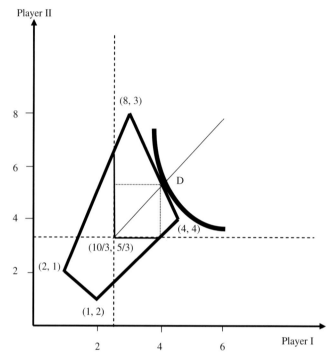

Fig. 5.6: Determining the **negotiation** space of a 2-player **negotiation** game and the **Nash equilibrium**.

Source: Authors.

For Further Discussion. The concept of **mixed strategies** is very attractive. It allows **players** to adjust their strategies to a rigid structure of the game and to obtain **payoffs** that otherwise would not be possible. Let us further discuss the **mixed strategy** game concept and its suitability to water resources. What are the pre requisites, the setups, the behavioral patterns, and the physical water patterns that need to be in place? Can we still recommend **mixed strategies** for addressing transboundary water problems?

WHAT MAKES WATER RESOURCES A CANDIDATE FOR COOPERATIVE GAME THEORY?

Indeed this is a question that intrigues many scholars in the field. First, water-related conflicts involve usually a small number of stakeholders (**players**) that are interrelated to each other (see also Chapters 3, 4 and 7). Therefore, there is a greater scope for strategic behavior among **players** in water-related conflicts. Second, the level of externalities associated with water utilization is a big incentive for cooperation. Externalities include: (a) the **zero-sum** (or **constant-sum**) outcomes of unilateral use of the resource (e.g., if party B uses more of the resource in the aquifer, less is left to party A, and also the cost of pumping party A faces is much more substantial due to the depth to the water table); and (b) the negative impact of water quality degradation that party A — the upstream — imposes on party B — the downstream (in the case of a river). Third, the great economies of scale associated with water infrastructure make it more attractive to build bigger rather than smaller water projects, hence, providing incentives to joint considerations. Fourth, water projects are in many cases multi-objective ones, leading to inclusion interests. Therefore, a major issue of water projects investment and management is the allocation of the cost and benefits among the various stated project objectives (e.g., sub-sectors and groups of beneficiaries). And fifth, many water problems are transboundary in nature, leading to inter-jurisdictional, interregional, or international conflicts. Since the **players** and the problems will last, it is likely that cooperation may be attractive for part of or all the **players** (see additional discussion in Chapters 4, 7 and 10).

Most of the CGT applications are about sharing benefits. Benefits can be created both from saving on investment and operational cost and from increasing welfare that is associated with the utilization of the resource — e.g., new opportunities that are not available when no cooperation is in place.

Several extensions to the allocation solutions will also be addressed. Specifically, we will touch upon the concepts of **stability** and upon the impact of uncertainty of the preferred solution. What CGT offers in most cases, is an allocation of the benefits from cooperation that, depending on the solution concept, fulfills certain requirements. However, in many cases, the issue of **stability** of the solution is not addressed. We will discuss several **stability** concepts and demonstrate their use.

> **For Further Discussion.** So far the analysis relies on cooperative approaches and demonstrates the usefulness of CGT. However, we know very well that in many water-related problems, the parties adopt non-cooperative strategies. Using examples from Chapters 3 and 4, can we conclude that non-cooperative approaches may better describe transboundary water problems?

THE COOPERATIVE GAME THEORY FRAMEWORK

The theory of games is composed of two main branches, a descriptive theory and a solution theory. We will focus in this book on various solutions concepts. In this chapter we will introduce concepts such as **Imputation**, the **Core** and the **Characteristic Function**, and will demonstrate their calculation and use. Solution concepts list will be extended in Chapter 6 to include: the **Core**; the **Shapley Value**; the **Nucleolus**; the **Generalized Shapley**; **Nash/Nash-Harsanyi**; and others. We will also include some Non CGT allocations, such as **Egalitarian Non-Separable Cost (ENSC)**; **Alternate Cost Avoided (ACA)**; **Separable Costs Remaining Benefits (SCRB)**; **Marginal Cost**; and **Proportional Use**.

We will focus on one basic solution concept — the **Core**. But we will first introduce basic concepts needed for CGT analysis — the **Characteristic Function**, the Pareto Set and the Space of **Imputations**. These will be called pre-solutions.

The Characteristic Function of a Cooperative *N*-person Game

When cooperation is possible among **players**, there is then a possibility for creating coalitions among various subsets of the group of **players**. That is, if the group of **players** agrees to form a coalition, they must reach some sort of equilibrium or **stability**. When group members cooperate, it is implicitly assumed that there is a utility transfer between them. In the case of the game presented in Fig. 5.4, for example, an agreement could be that the sum of 11 $(8+3)$ is divided such that player II gets 7 and player I gets 4.

This being said, we have to make several assumptions regarding the perception of the level of utility embedded in the joint benefits. We assume that the utility functions of the various coalition members are such that the rate of transfer of utility among any two of the members is 1:1. What does this mean from a practical point of view? It means that we must assume that all members of a coalition value the marginal utility of one additional unit of **payoff** (say \$1) at the same rate, which implies that we do not allow in a coalition for the "too rich" to live side by side with the "too poor."

Definition: The **characteristic function** of an *n*-person game is a real-value function v defined on the subsets of N **players**, which assigns to each coalition $s \subset N$ the maximum value to s, of the game between s and $N - s$, assuming that these two coalitions form.

Here N is the set of all **players** in the **negotiation** game; S $(S \subseteq N)$ is the set of all feasible coalitions in the game; s $(s \in S)$ is a feasible coalition in the game; the **non-cooperative coalitions** are $\{j\}$, $j = 1, 2, \ldots, n$; the **grand coalition** is $\{N\}$; the number of possible coalitions between a group of n **players** is $2^n - 1$; $v(j)$ is the value of **non cooperative coalitions** — what each player may obtain if he or she continues to act on his or her own (**status quo**); $v(s)$ is the value of **partial coalitions** — what subgroups of **players** may obtain if they form these subgroups; and $v(N)$ is the value of the **grand coalition** of all **players** in the **negotiation**.

Therefore, a **characteristic function** (v) of a group (coalition) captures in a single numerical index the potential worth (value) of that group of **players**. This means that $v(s)$ is the amount of utility that the members of s can obtain from the game, whatever the remaining **players** may do.

Several qualities of v are as follows:

For the empty set $\emptyset$ (meaning no players exist),
[1] $v\{\emptyset\} = 0$,
and for any coalitions Q and T, we get
[2] $v(Q \cup T) \geq v(Q) + v(T)$, if $Q \cap T = \emptyset$.

The latter relationship implies that v is superadditive. It means that any set of **players** can do at least as well in coalition than in a subcoalition.

<u>Definition</u>: By an n-person game in **characteristic function** form it is meant a real-value function v, defined on the subsets of N, satisfying conditions [1] and [2].

Suppose that the normal form of the game is **constant-sum**. The game between s and $N - s$ is then strictly competitive, and it follows, if it is finite, that the minimax theorem holds. Thus we have

[3] $v(s) + v(N - s) = v(N)$. This leads to the following definition.

<u>Definition</u>: A game in the **characteristic function** form is said to be **constant-sum** if for all $s \subset N$, $v(s) + v(N - s) = v(N)$.

We are now interested in the particular **payoff** vectors that the **players** in a **constant-sum game** with $v(N)$ can divide among themselves. There are many ways to divide $v(N)$ among the n **players**. However, it is clear that no player will accept payment that is less than the minimum that this player can attain by himself or herself. In addition, there are other conditions, but they will be discussed at a later stage.

Imputations

There are many (allocation) solutions to the same game. Uniqueness of the solution is always a desirable property, but it is one of many desired properties. Other properties that one would request from a solution include enforceability, **stability**, derivability (from a social process), and compatibility with experimental evidence. Unfortunately, these and other properties of desired solution may be in conflict with one another, so compromise is desirable in selecting among allocation solutions.

Three conditions, namely **efficiency**, Pareto optimality, and **individual rationality**, are always necessary to obtain. Solutions that obtain these three properties are called **imputations**.

<u>Definition</u>: An **imputation** for the n-person game v is a vector $x = (x_1, \ldots, x_n)$, satisfying:

(i) **Efficiency**: $\sum_{j \in N} x_j = v(N)$ (it allocates all benefits or cost without leaving any slack);

(ii) **Individual rationality**: $x_j \geq v(\{j\})$ for all $j \in N$ (it makes every one better off compared with their non-cooperative (**status quo**) situation); and

(iii) Pareto optimality: $\sum_{j \in N} x_j \leq v(N)$ (this condition means **feasibility** — that all allocations are contained within what the **grand coalition** may obtain), and $\sum_{j \in N} x_j \geq v(N)$ (it is such that no player can be better off without affecting the other **players**' welfare).

The Core

The **Core** is a very important concept in CGT. We will define it, demonstrate its use, and calculate several of its relationships to other solution concepts.

<u>Definition:</u> The **Core** of an n-cooperative game in the **characteristic function** form is a set of game allocation gains (**imputations**) that is not dominated by any other allocation set. The **Core** provides a bound for the maximum (or minimum in terms of cost) allocation each player may request.

In this respect, the **Core** is an overall solution for many allocation schemes that are contained within the **Core**. The **Core** fulfills requirements for **individual** and **group rationality**, and for joint **efficiency** (Shubik, 1982). While the first and the last conditions have been explained earlier, **group rationality** will be explained hereafter. We also have to make several additional clarifications to bring the CGT concepts to be in line with the practical issues we are familiar with.

CGT assumes that **players** are economically rational; that the decision of each player to join a given coalition is voluntary; and a coalition speaks in one voice. Ω_j is player j's **Core** allocation of the coalition gains/savings. The **Core** equations are (this specification is for a game where the **players** have to share a common cost. The equations for sharing common benefits will be similar, but only the inequality signs will be reversed):

$\Omega_j \leq v\{j\}$ $\forall j \in N$. This equation fulfills **individual rationality** condition — that is the cooperative allocation for each player is preferred (cheaper) to the non-cooperation case.

$\sum_{j \in s} \Omega_j \leq v(s)$ $\forall s \subseteq S$. This equation fulfills the **group rationality** condition — that the cooperative allocation to any combination of **players** is preferred (cheaper) to any allocation in any sub-coalition they can establish.

$\sum_{j \in N} \Omega_j = v(N)$. This equation fulfills the **efficiency** condition — that the value of the entire set of **players** will be fully allocated/paid for by the **grand coalition** participants. As was indicated before, the system of the 3 sets of equations is called the **Core**. It provides a range for possible allocation solutions, some of which will be described later. As a matter of fact the **Core** can also be empty, meaning that there is no allocation solution that fulfills the set of conditions that defines the **Core**.

Examples of Use of Core Allocations

The simple river game. A river's water is worth 100 (units of money) if used by country A (upstream) for irrigation, 200 if used by country B for hydropower, and 300 if used by country C for navigation. What should be the best negotiated solution to this water allocation problem?

The possible *a priori* coalitions among the three countries are:

Individual coalitions: A, B, C

Sub coalitions: AB, BC, AC

Grand coalition: ABC

In the case of no cooperation, the value of the **characteristic function** for each individual coalition is $v(A) = 100$, $v(B) = 0$, $v(C) = 0$ because A is the upstream country and it will use all the water in the case of non-cooperation.

In the case of **partial coalitions**, the value of the **characteristic function** is (assuming that **players** obey the rule of property rights): $v(AB) = 200$, because B will use the water to generate $200 > 100$, then A will get P_B from B. If this coalition works, A gets P_B and B gets $200 - P_B$; $v(AC) = 300$, because C will use the water to generate $300 > 100$, then A will get P_C from C. If this coalition works, A gets P_C and C gets $300 - P_C$. Here we assume for simplicity that A will not allow any water used by a coalition that does not include itself, and that B has no means of preventing the water flow to C.[2]; $v(BC) = 0$, because A will not let B and C use the water without sharing with A their benefits. In the case of the **grand coalition**, the value of the **characteristic function** is $v(ABC) = 300$.

The **Core** equations are:

$v(A) = 100$
$v(B) = 0$
$v(C) = 0$
$v(AB) = 200$
$v(AC) = 300$
$v(BC) = 0$
$v(ABC) = 300$.

An illustration of the **Core** of this game is presented in Figs. 5.7a and 5.7b.

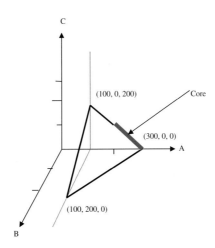

Fig. 5.7a: The **Core** of the river game.

Source: Authors.

---

[2]Clearly, such assumptions lead to a specific **Core**. By changing the assumptions regarding the possible interactions among the **players** will lead to different **Core** solutions.

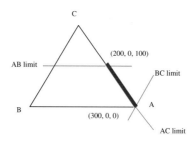

Fig. 5.7b: The **Core** (focusing on the triangle) of the river game (b).
Source: Authors.

Here the coalition {AB} can improve on any allocation above the dashed line (AB limit), which is the line on which they receive exactly 200. But between that line and the bottom edge (on which they would share 300) AB is ineffective.

In contrast, coalition {AC} is a stronger coalition that is satisfied (unable to improve its worth) only along the right edge of the triangle.

{BC} is an **inessential coalition** that can do nothing that B and C could not do individually.

By inspection of Fig. 5.7b we see that the **Core** is the thick line segment on the lower right, having end points of (200, 0, 100); (300, 0, 0).

Extreme Points of the Core

Because the **Core** is a locus of **imputations** of the game gains, it is very useful to be able to assess whether or not the **Core** is small or big, or even if it is empty. A method to calculate the **extreme points of the Core** of a convex game can help in identifying possible allocations and their relationship to the **Core**. The essence of the method, suggested by Shapley (1971), is to refer to a sequence of establishment of any feasible coalition and to allocate the incremental gain generated by each player's entry into an existing coalition. The method of calculating the **extreme points of the Core** is also useful in future calculations of the **Shapley value** (which will be introduced and demonstrated in Chapter 6).

We will start now with an empirical example that will demonstrate the calculation of the various solution concepts we introduced so far. This example is based on Dinar and Howitt (1997). They applied CGT to a region facing water quality problems. In particular, they evaluated a regional cooperative solution in the form of a water treatment facility. Assuming that the location of the facility is pre-determined, the focus of their approach was on the comparison between various solution concepts, and between states of nature. They estimated a cost function of the joint facility. The cost function has strong economies of scale in the capacity of the treatment facility, thus regional cooperation in the form of joint treatment is economically preferable to individual actions (given that all collective costs are accounted for in the cost function they used).

For purposes of this chapter we modify the data and the context of the example used by Dinar and Howitt (1997) by applying it to a river basin that includes 4 **riparian** states. Assume that the river flows through 4 states. Assume that there is in place a treaty that allocates the water among the **riparian** states but the only way to realize the benefits of the water is by building dams, either by each country, or by subsets or the full set of states in the basin. It is assumed that the incremental coordination cost of the regional cooperative solution is negligible. Notice that the basin geography is not factored here (as it was in the simple river game above).

Assume that all participating states will use the same dam technology, so that the only important parameter is the size of the dam. Because the water in the river is allocated according to the share of flow, consideration must be given to high and low flows in building the dam. Of course, the objective of the player states is to reduce their cost (no other political considerations are included).

The Allocation of the Dam Cost among the 4 Riparian States

The dam cost function is: $C = e^{0.377}Q^{0.789}$ where the first component on the right hand side is the fixed cost and the second is the annual capacity of the dam. Assume two water flow scenarios — Low and High. The use of water by each state is presented in Table 5.1.

Using the dam cost function and the possible coalition formation between the **riparian** states, a cost can be assigned to each coalition of states as demonstrated in Table 5.2.

The **Core** equation (inequality) system for the two states of nature scenarios is:

	High flow	Low flow
$\Omega_A \leq$	1,112	699
$\Omega_B \leq$	1,208	807
$\Omega_C \leq$	1,013	586
$\Omega_D \leq$	5,610	2,722
$\Omega_A + \Omega_B \leq$	2,005	1,303
$\Omega_A + \Omega_C \leq$	1,836	1,112
$\Omega_A + \Omega_D \leq$	6,172	3,099
$\Omega_B + \Omega_C \leq$	1,921	1,208
$\Omega_B + \Omega_D \leq$	6,233	3,173
$\Omega_C + \Omega_D \leq$	6,110	3,025
$\Omega_A + \Omega_B + \Omega_C \leq$	2,645	1,664
$\Omega_A + \Omega_B + \Omega_D \leq$	6,780	3,536
$\Omega_B + \Omega_C + \Omega_D \leq$	6,720	3,392
$\Omega_A + \Omega_C + \Omega_D \leq$	6,660	3,464
$\Omega_A + \Omega_B + \Omega_C + \Omega_D =$	7,257	3,820

The systems of the above inequalities may have more than one solution. Solving this system is done via a mathematical programming procedure. We will not solve this system here. One possible solution that is obtained by solving the above system

Table 5.1: Annual water utilization for
high and low water flow scenarios.

State	Low flow	High flow
A	2,500	4,000
B	3,000	5,000
C	2,000	4,000
D	14,000	35,000
Total	21,500	48,500

Source: Dinar and Howitt (1997).

Table 5.2: Dam cost for the high and low flow scenarios (billions of US$).

Coalition of riparian countries	High flow		Low flow	
	Water dammed	Dam cost	Water dammed	Dam cost
{A}	4,500	1,112	2,500	699
{B}	5,000	1,208	3,000	807
{C}	4,000	1,013	2,000	586
{D}	35,500	5,610	14,000	2,722
{AB}	9,500	2,005	5,500	1,303
{AC}	8,500	1,836	4,500	1,112
{AD}	39,500	6,172	16,500	3,099
{BC}	9,000	1,921	5,000	1,208
{BD}	40,000	6,233	17,000	3,173
{CD}	39,000	6,110	16,000	3,025
{ABC}	13,500	2,645	7,500	1,664
{ABD}	44,500	6,780	19,500	3,536
{ACD}	43,500	6,660	18,500	3,392
{BCD}	44,000	6,720	19,000	3,464
{ABCD}	48,500	7,257	21,500	3,820

Source: Dinar and Howitt (1997).

(for the high flow case) is $\Omega = (797, 1208, 477, 4775)$. This solution fulfills the **Core** conditions of **individual rationality**, **group rationality**, and **efficiency**.

The **characteristic function** values for all possible coalitions are presented in Table 5.3.

Table 5.3 is the procedure to calculate the **characteristic function** for coalitions in the dam cost game. Columns (1)–(4) are simply the dam cost for each individual state when acting alone (**non-cooperative coalition**) {A}, {B}, {C}, and {D}. Column (5) is the cost of the dam for the coalition of states that is indicated on the left hand side of the table (values are taken from Table 5.2). For example, in the case of high flow, coalition {A} has an incremental cost of 1112 and this is also the value of the **non-cooperative coalition** {A}. Coalition {AB} can put the dam for a cost of 2008, while each player can do it for 1112 and 1208 respectively for {A}

Table 5.3: **Characteristic function** values for different coalitions.

Coalition	Incremental cost for state				Value of coalition s	$\sum_{j \in s} v\{j\}$	Incremental gains for coalition s
	A	B	C	D			
	(1)	(2)	(3)	(4)	(5)	(6)	(7) = (6) − (5)
High Flow							
{A}	1112				1112	1112	0
{B}		1208			1208	1208	0
{C}			1013		1013	1013	0
{D}				5610	5610	5610	0
{AB}	1112	1208			2005	2320	315
{AC}	1112		1013		1836	2125	289
{AD}	1112			5610	6172	6722	550
{BC}		1208	1013		1921	2221	300
{BD}		1208		5610	6233	6818	585
{CD}			1013	5610	6110	6623	513
{ABC}	1112	1208	1013		2645	3333	688
{ABD}	1112	1208		5610	6780	7930	1150
{ACD}	1112		1013	5610	6660	7735	1075
{BCD}		1208	1013	5610	6720	7831	1111
{ABCD}	1112	1208	1013	5610	7257	8943	1686
Low Flow							
{A}	699				699	699	0
{B}		807			807	807	0
{C}			586		586	586	0
{D}				2722	2722	2722	0
{AB}	699	807			1303	1506	203
{AC}	699		586		1112	1285	173
{AD}	699			2722	3099	3421	322
{BC}		807	586		1208	1393	185
{BD}		807		2722	3173	3529	356
{CD}			586	2722	3025	3308	283
{ABC}	699	807	586		1664	2092	428
{ABD}	699	807		2722	3536	4228	692
{ACD}	699		586	2722	3464	4007	543
{BCD}		807	586	2722	3392	4115	723
{ABCD}	699	807	586	2722	3820	4814	994

Source: Dinar and Howitt (1997).

and {B}. Column (6) is the sum of the individual costs of the members of the coalition. For example in the case of {AB} it is the cost for {A} (in column 1) plus the cost for {B} in column 2. Column 7 is the gains from cooperation, which is calculated as the difference between the value in column (6) and that in column (5). The values in column 7 are what drives the cooperation between the **riparian** states. The higher these values the more incentives the states will have to join a cooperative arrangement.

How do we compare between the various possible **Core** allocations? A method (Shapley, 1971) that calculates the possible extreme **Core** allocations is based on

Table 5.4: **Extreme points of the core** for the case of high flows.

Maximum incremental allocation								Coalition formation sequence
High flows				Low flows				
A	B	C	D	A	B	C	D	
1112	893	640	4612	699	604	303	2156	ABCD
1112	893	477	4775	699	604	284	2233	ABDC
1112	809	724	4612	699	552	413	2156	ACBD
1112	597	724	4824	699	428	413	2280	ACDB
1112	608	477	5060	699	437	284	2400	ADBC
1112	597	548	5060	699	428	293	2400	ADCB
797	1208	640	4612	496	807	361	2156	BACD
797	1208	477	4775	496	807	284	2233	BADC
721	1208	713	4612	456	807	401	2156	BCAD
537	1208	713	4799	356	807	401	2256	BCDA
547	1208	477	5025	363	807	284	2366	BDAC
537	1208	487	5025	356	807	291	2366	BDCA
823	809	1013	4612	526	552	586	2156	CABD
823	597	1013	4824	526	428	586	2280	CADB
724	908	1013	4612	456	622	586	2156	CBAD
537	908	1013	4799	356	622	586	2256	CBDA
550	597	1013	5097	367	428	586	2439	CDAB
537	610	1013	5097	356	439	586	2439	CDBA
562	608	477	5610	377	437	284	2722	DABC
562	482	603	5610	377	428	293	2722	DACB
547	623	477	5610	363	451	284	2722	DBAC
672	623	487	5610	356	451	291	2722	DBCA
550	597	500	5610	367	428	303	2722	DCAB
537	610	500	5610	356	439	303	2722	DCBA

Source: Dinar and Howitt (1997).

incremental contributions of states joining existing coalitions. The results for the case of high flows are presented in Table 5.4.

Let us provide an explanation to how the **extreme points of the Core** are calculated. We refer to the sequence of ABCD (the first line in Table 5.4). State A is the first one to form a "coalition." State A joins coalition $\{\emptyset\}$ (the empty set) to create coalition $\{A\}$ that is associated with a value of 1112. Therefore, $\Omega_A = v(A) - v(\emptyset) = 1112 - 0 = 1112$. Then, state B joins $\{A\}$ to create coalition $\{A, B\}$, whose associated cost is $v(A, B) = 2005$. Therefore, $\Omega_B = v(A, B) - v(A) = 2005 - 1112 = 893$. Next, state C joins coalition $\{A, B\}$ to form coalition $\{A, B, C\}$, whose cost it $v(A, B, C) = 2645$. Therefore, state C's share in the joint cost will be $\Omega_C = v(A, B, C) - v(A, B) = 2645 - 2005 = 640$. Finally, state D joins coalition $\{A, B, C\}$ to form the **grand coalition** $\{A, B, C, D\}$. The cost of the **grand coalition** is $v(A, B, C, D) = 7257$. Therefore, D's share in the joint cost is $\Omega_D = v(A, B, C, D) - v(A, B, C) = 7257 - 2645 = 4612$. Notice that the allocation suggested by the solution of the equation system above matches the extreme point resulting from the sequence BACD. Notice that the highest and lowest values of

Table 5.5: Distance of the states from the desired allocation, in the Ω_{BACD} allocation.

State	Desired allocation	Allocation in Ω_{BACD}	Absolute difference	Relative difference (%)	Likely satisfaction
A	537	797	260	48	Not satisfied
B	482	1208	726	150	Furious
C	477	477	0	0	Very satisfied
D	4610	4775	165	3.5	Satisfied/Very satisfied

Source: Based on Dinar and Howitt (1997).

calculated extreme points for each player are shaded in Table 5.4. For example, State A's range should be between 537 (desired) and 1112 (least desired, but acceptable).

The **extreme points of the Core** provide an ordering of the states' preferences. State A is likely to prefer allocations closer to 537 than to 1112. State B will prefer allocations closer to 482 than to 1208. State C will prefer allocations closer to 477 than to 1013, and state D will prefer allocations closer to 4612 then to 5610.

What do the **extreme points of the Core** tell us about a given **core** allocation, say $\Omega_{BACD} = (797, 1208, 477, 4775)$? We can immediately assess the level of satisfaction of each state from any allocation. Although we will get to the related issue of **stability** of the allocation solution at a later stage, let us just calculate the "distance" of each state from the desired allocation (in this case it is Ω_{BACD}). The calculated values are presented in Table 5.5.

We can also assess the **stability** of the coalitions, based on the results in Table 5.5. However, we will leave this part for the next chapter. In the next chapter we highlight several principles that help us understand **stability** in the context of cooperative game theory.

For Further Discussion. The **Core** seems complicated to calculate. However, it is easier applied as a concept. To justify the importance of making efforts to estimate **cores** and the **extreme points of the Core**, let us look at the **Core** from another angle. What is the analogous of the **Core** in **negotiations**? What are the signals the **extreme points of the Core** send? Who should be the prime user of this information? With answers to these questions we may have better incentives to invest in calculation of **Cores** and **extreme points of the Core**.

SUMMARY

In this chapter we demonstrated how a transboundary water situation is expressed using game theory concepts. Moreover, we presented a groundwater extraction as a **prisoner's dilemma** game and demonstrated how it can also be transformed from that to a cooperative game that will lead to preferred **payoffs** to the parties involved. Making the analogies between the groundwater game to other transboundary water conflicts, we introduced the necessary conditions for cooperation and demonstrated how certain cooperative allocation concepts such as **imputations** and the **Core** can be described and calculated, using a real life transboundary water allocation problem.

Practice Questions

1. The game in Fig. 5.3 is a **prisoner's dilemma** game if the **players** stick to the game outcomes/**payoffs** that are indicated in the cells. However, if the **players** agree to share the **payoffs** in a way different from the prescribed ones in the cell, they may end up in a "cooperative" solution, where they will share in one way or another the total **payoff** in the cell that represents strategies 2,2. Propose an allocation that in your opinion will be preferred on the two **players** and explain your selection of such values.
2. Analyze a possible regional arrangement in the GW game where one of the riparians (A or B) suggests not to pump any amount and offers the other riparian to pump alone (2,4,8) and to share the payoff among the two.

   a. Which will be the riparian that will likely pump? Why?
   b. Would it be a good joint strategy to have only one riparian pumping and share the payoff?
3. What are the differences between an **imputation** and the **Core**? What are the relationship between the **Core** and **imputations**?
4. Prove that the allocation $= (797, 1208, 477, 4775)$ in the dam cost game is in the **Core**.
5. Refer to the dam cost game. It includes two states of nature — low flows and high flows. By extrapolation try to make an educated guess (and explain it) about the relative **stability** of allocation solutions under low flows and high flows.

REFERENCES

Axelrod, R. (1985). *The Evolution of Cooperation*. Cambridge, MA: Basic Books.

Axelrod, R. (1997). *The Complexity of Cooperation*. Princeton, NJ: Princeton University Press.

Dinar, A. and R. Howitt (1997). Mechanism for allocation of environmental control cost: Empirical tests of acceptability and stability, *Journal of Environmental Management*, 49, 183–203.

Dixit, A.K. and B.J. Nalebuff (1993). *Thinking Strategically*. New York: W. W. Norton & Company.

Myerson, R.B. (1997). *Game Theory Analysis of Conflict*. Cambridge, MA: Harvard University Press.

Osborn, M.J. (2004). *An Introduction to Game Theory*. New York: Oxford University Press.

Parrachino, I., S. Zara and F. Patrone (2006). Environmental and Water Resource Issues: Basic Theory. World Bank Policy Research Working Paper 4072.

Poundstone, W. (1992). *Prisoner's Dilemma*. New York: Anchor Books.

Shapley, L. (1971). Cores of convex games, *International Journal of Game Theory*, 1, 11–26.

Shubik, M. (1982). *Game Theory in the Social Sciences Concepts and Solutions*. Cambridge, MA: The MIT Press.

Von Neumann, J. and O. Morgenstern (1944; 2004). *Theory of Games and Economic Behavior, Sixtieth-Anniversary Edition*. Princeton: Princeton University Press.

ADDITIONAL READING

Davis, M.D. (1983). *Game Theory: A Nontechnical Introduction*. Mineola (NY): Dover Publications.

Kreps, D.M. (1990). *Game Theory and Economic Modelling*. New York: Oxford University Press.

Poundstone, W. (1992). *Prisoner's Dilemma*. New York: Anchor Books.

6. COOPERATIVE GAME THEORY AND WATER RESOURCES — APPLICATION OF SOLUTION CONCEPTS

Objectives

In this chapter, we focus on basic Cooperative Game Theory solution concepts, explain their foundations (including assumptions), and demonstrate their empirical application (calculation and interpretation). You will understand the principles used to construct several commonly used CGT solution concepts, such as the Shapley Value and the Nash Equilibrium, and get some acquaintance with additional CGT and other solution concepts, although to a lesser extent. You will also be introduced to an important aspect of CGT, namely the power of the players in the game and the stability of the solution. These are very important concepts that have not been always an integral part of cooperative solutions applications. The chapter explains several of the power and stability concepts and applies them to the game that is being carried over from Chapter 5.

Main Terminology

Alternative cost avoided; Banzhaf power index; Characteristic function; Dummy player; Efficiency; Egalitarian allocation; Egalitarian nonseparable cost; Equitability; Income transfer; Least core; Nash solution/equilibrium; Nash–Harsanyi solution; Nonnormalized Banzhaf index; Normalized Banzhaf index; Nucleolus; Ω-core; Pareto optimal; Propensity to disrupt; Proportional allocation; Relative welfare; Separable costs remaining benefits; Shapley-Shubik power index; The Shapley value; The generalized Shapley value; Total welfare; Utility.

While the Core and its derivatives that were introduced in the previous chapter provide a "range" for possible game outcomes, it is necessary in many instances to have a single payoff vector that expresses the value of the game for each of the players. This is desirable not only for academic purposes, but also and mainly for practical purposes of writing contracts among parties on allocation of costs

---

Notations in this chapter correspond to those used and explained in Chapter 5, unless otherwise indicated.

and benefits. More important, decision-makers have to minimize uncertainty with regard to quantities and qualities that are available for the simple reason that they need to make quite substantive investments that necessitate full information. One of the main problems in interpersonal compensation or monetary transfers is the issue of our ability to evaluate the value of sums of money that exchange hands from one person or group to another. Addressing such difficulty will be discussed in the first section, although we do not expect to solve it. Then we introduce and interpret several CGT solution concepts that have been used in water (including transboundary water) conflicts.

INTERPERSONAL UTILITY COMPARISONS

Bargaining and agreements are one form of solutions to n-person cooperative games. An important issue in cooperative solutions is the interpersonal comparisons of preferences — **utility** comparisons and transfers. It refers to the marginal value of additional unit of **utility** transferred from one player to another and it addresses the question of whether or not players i and j assign the same value to a unit of **utility** (or money) that they exchange among themselves. This issue is critical in the case of CGT solutions because one of the principles of an allocation solution is the ability to share gains among the players — **income transfer**. We are concerned first with **relative welfare**, which is the incremental welfare a unit of **utility** (or income) will be worth for two different players. Second, we are concerned with **total welfare**, which is the additional value to each player from the proposed allocation. We can term these concerns **equitability** and **efficiency**, respectively.

We use an example (Fig. 6.1) to describe the **utility** comparison in the case of two players (after Shubik, 1982). Two players can have any payoff vector on the curve AA′ if they agree, but must take the point O if they disagree. Utilities are assumed to be cardinal but nontransferable and not extrinsically comparable. Assume that point C on AA′ was proposed as a solution. The respective utilities of C are (≈ 0.3; 0.6). The utilities of O are (0; 0). Therefore, C implies **equitability** comparison weights in the ratio of 2:1, and before comparing the solution C, we must change the ratio between their **utility** units by defining $U_1' = 2U_1$ and $U_2' = U_2$. This rescaling gives C new coordinates (≈ 0.6; 0.6) and leaves O at (0; 0). The new slope of the line OC is +1 (similar argument can be made for the **efficiency** argument at O — see analysis at B). The outcome B, in contrast, implies **efficiency** comparison weights in the ratio of 1:3. Therefore, before claiming that the players maximize the value at B, we must rescale by $U_1'' = U_1$ and $U_2'' = 3U_2$. In the new coordinates, the slope of the tangent at B is –1, and B indeed maximizes $U_1'' + U_2''$.

For Further Discussion. Let us spend some time discussing the relevance of interpersonal **utility** comparison to transboundary water resource cooperation.

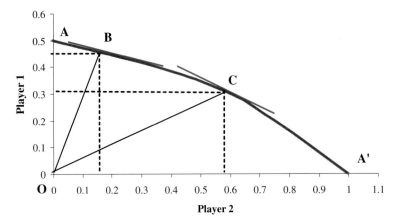

Fig. 6.1: Interpersonal **utility** comparison.
Source: Adapted from Shubik (1982, p. 190).

What does it mean in a practical world when we say that the parties that share the basin differ in valuing benefits from an additional unit of the resource, or an additional unit of payoff? Does that mean that rich countries should be compensated in larger share than poor countries in the basin? Or may be that the opposite prevails? How practically can one incorporate such considerations into a negotiated solution?

Value Solutions

The Value theory was developed from two different directions. One direction is based on the objective to maximize the product of the players' gains in a two-player game (e.g., Zeuten, 1930; Nash 1950, 1953; Harsanyi, 1956, 1959); the other direction is based on the **Shapley Value** formula for n-person game (Shapley, 1951, 1953).

c-Games with Transferable Utility

When an n-person game is represented by a **characteristic function** (Chapter 5), then the value payoffs to the players can depend only on the $2^n - 1$ coalitional permutations leading to the various $v(s)$'s.

The value formula should be invariant with respect to the choice of zero points on the individual **utility** scales and the **utility** scales of the players (meaning that the **utility** of the players can be compared). The value formula is also linear, feasible, and **Pareto optimal** (Chapter 5). The value function is set such that a **dummy player** — defined as player d such that $v(s) = v(s - \{d\})$ for all $s \cap d$ — gets nothing. A **dummy player** is an inessential player that does not add to the value of a coalition when joining it.

The value is determined, based on the above conditions, as

$$\phi_j = \frac{1}{n} \sum_{S=1}^{n} \frac{1}{c(s)} \sum_{\substack{j \in S \\ |S|=s}} [v(s) - v(s - \{j\})], \tag{6.1}$$

where $c(S)$ is the number of coalitions of size s containing player j:

$$c(s) = \binom{n-1}{s-1} \equiv \frac{(n-1)!}{(n-s)!(s-1)!}. \tag{6.2}$$

A proposed procedure (Shapley, 1971) to realize the value of the vector ϕ is: (1) arrange the players in a random order; (2) pay player j its marginal worth to the coalition (the additional gain to the coalition realized when j joins it), consisting of those who came before j. (See Table 6.1 for illustration of a simple example, and Table 6.2 for a more complex example.)

The Least Core and the Nucleolus

The core of a cooperative game in the **characteristic function** form may be empty because certain coalitions provide greater incentive than the grand coalition, and thus the grand coalition will not be formed (empty core). Conversely, conditions may arise where the core does exist but it is too large and leaves the cost/benefit allocation problem open for further bargaining. These two situations are very common in real life and imply no cooperation, or long negotiations to secure cooperation. What the analyst (or the mediator) wants is a unique solution, or, at least, a very narrow set of possible solutions.

A possible approach, in both cases, for obtaining a unique solution, is by reducing the core (if too loose) or expanding the core (if empty). The core that is obtained by adding or reducing the borders of the empty or too-big core is called the Ω-**core** (Ω is the value by which the core was reduced or expanded). Then, obtaining the "**least core**," which is the intersection between all nonempty Ω-**cores**, and if the core is nonempty, it still satisfies the conditions of individual and group rationality (Chapter 5).

The **least core** can be generated by solutions to (6.3)–(6.5), which can be interpreted as a tax or a subsidy to change the size of the core. If the core is empty then Ω ($\Omega < 0$) is an organizational fee for the players in the subcoalitions, so they prefer the grand coalition. If the core is too big, Ω might reduce it ($\Omega > 0$) by subsidizing subcoalitions.

The **Nucleolus** (Schmeidler, 1969) is a single point solution that always exists (if the core is not empty), and minimizes the dissatisfaction of the most dissatisfied coalition. To obtain the **Nucleolus**, we define the Ω-**core** of the game v to be the set of allocations that would be in the core if each coalition were given a subsidy at the level of Ω. By varying Ω, one can find the smallest nonempty Ω-**core** (called the **least core**). The **least core** is the intersection of all Ω-**cores**. A solution to (6.3)–(6.5) can be obtained by applying a linear programming method, which is difficult to demonstrate here.

$$\sum_{j \in S} \omega_j \leq v(s) + \Omega \quad \forall s \in S, \tag{6.3}$$

$$\sum_{j \in N} \omega_j = v(N), \tag{6.4}$$

$$\Omega >=< 0. \tag{6.5}$$

The solution to (6.3)–(6.5) may provide the **Nucleolus**, as a single solution, but it may also provide several individual cost allocations $\underline{\omega}_j$ for the same value of Ω for each coalition s. In this case, we define the excess function $e(\omega, s)$ for each s (that measures how much less it costs a coalition to act alone), and in a lexicographical process obtain the **Nucleolus**, for which the value of the smallest excess $e(\omega, s)$ is as large as possible.

The Shapley Value

The **Shapley Value** is a uniquely defined solution value to an n-person cooperative game in the **characteristic function** form (Shapley, 1953). The **Shapley Value** scheme allocates Φ_j to each player based on the weighted average of their contributions to *all* possible coalitions and sequences. In the calculation, an equal probability is assigned for the formation of any coalition of the same size, assuming all possible sequences of formation.

Definition: A carrier for a game v is a coalition T such that, for any s, $v(s) = v(s \cap T)$.

The definition suggests that any player who does not belong to a carrier is a dummy — i.e., contributes nothing to any coalition when joining it.

Definition: Let v be an n-person game, and let π be any permutation of the set N. Then by πv we mean the game u such that for any $s = \{j_1, j_2, \ldots, j_s\}$,

$$u(\{\pi(j_1), \pi(j_2), \ldots, \pi(j_s)\}) = v(s).$$

The definition says that the game πv is exactly the game v with the role of the players interchanged by the permutation π. Three axioms need to be satisfied:

$$\sum_s \Phi_j[v] = v(s).$$

For any permutation π and $j \in N$ $\quad \Phi_{\pi(j)}[\pi v] = \pi_j(v).$
If u and v are any games $\Phi_j[u + v] = \Phi_j[u] + \Phi_j[v].$

The **Shapley value** is calculated as:

$$\Phi_j = \sum_{\substack{s \subseteq S \\ j \in s}} \frac{(n - |s|)!(|s| - 1)!}{n!} [v(s) - v(s - \{j\})] \qquad \forall j \in N, \qquad (6.6)$$

where Φ_j is the allocation to player j, n is the number of players in the game, and $|s|$ is the number of members in coalition s. The **Shapley Value** is a unique allocation, and is in the core.

The **Shapley Value** is very popular in empirical applications of CGT. Following Zara *et al.* (2006), consider a 3-person game with the following values for each coalition

$$V\{1\} = V\{2\} = V\{3\} = 0,$$
$$V\{1,\ 2\} = 4;\ V\{1,\ 3\} = 7;\ V\{2,\ 3\} = 15,$$
$$V\{1,\ 2,\ 3\} = 20.$$

The calculation of the **Shapley Value** is demonstrated in Table 6.1.

The average contribution of each player over the six possible coalitional permutations is actually the **Shapley Value** (Eq. (6.6)).

The Generalized Shapley Value

The **Shapley Value** assumes equal probability for the formation of any coalition of the same size, which is theoretically possible, and also considers all the possible sequences of formation. Loehman and Whinston (1976) criticized this assumption on the basis of the **Shapley Value** and they proposed **the Generalized Shapley Value**.

Table 6.1: A procedure for calculation of the **Shapley Value**.

Permutation/coalition	Marginal contribution of player j to the coalition			Total for coalition
	Player 1	Player 2	Player 3	
{1, 2, 3}	0	4	16	20
{1, 3, 2}	0	13	7	20
{2, 1, 3}	4	0	16	20
{2, 3, 1}	5	0	15	20
{3, 1, 2}	7	13	0	20
{3, 2, 1}	5	15	0	20
Total contributions	21	45	54	120
Average contribution	21/6	45/6	54/6	20

Source: Adapted from Parrachino *et al.* (2006).

The Generalized Shapley Value differs from the **Shapley Value** in two aspects:

1. It refers only to coalitions that are practically possible, rather than possible from a theoretical combinatorial point of view, and
2. The probability of a coalition occurrence depends on the logical sequence of its formation.

The Generalized Shapley Value assigns, in a similar manner, to each player the weighted average of his contributions to all realistically formed coalitions:

$$\Theta_j = \sum_{\substack{s \in S \\ j \in s}} P(s,\ s - \{j\})[v(s) - v(s - \{j\})] \quad j \in N, \tag{6.7}$$

where

$$P(s,\ s - \{j\}) = P(s|s - \{j\})P(s - \{j\}), \quad \text{and} \quad p(s) = \sum_{j \in s} p(s,\ s - \{j\}).$$

$P(\cdot)$ is a conditional probability, which is interpreted as the probability of a certain player, j, joining a certain coalition, $s - \{j\}$, given the structure of the coalition that existed without that player. Conditional probabilities are determined from "decision trees," which result from the coalition formation process. An example, based on a case analyzed by Loehman *et al.* (1979), is presented in Fig. 6.2. The example is about four municipalities that consider a wastewater treatment plant. Owing to physical (landscape) constraints, some of the coalitions among the four

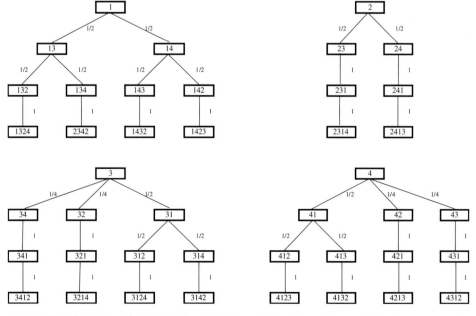

Fig. 6.2: The derivation of conditional probabilities assigned to various coalitional arrangements. *Source*: Adapted from Loehman *et al.* (1979).

municipalities are impossible. The numbers in the boxes are the players (1, 2, 3, 4) and the values along the lines between the boxes are the conditional probabilities that a given coalition (box) will be created, where another coalition (box) exists.

Calculating **the Generalized Shapley Value** is straightforward, and follows a similar procedure as the **Shapley Value**. We will not provide an example in this chapter.

> **For Further Discussion.** The **Shapley Value** is a very popular solution concept. We will use it also in the computer software that is available on the CD. Because the **Shapley Value** is used so often, we should discuss further its limitations. The **Shapley Value** assumes equal probabilities for formation of each possible coalition. Let us take a case from Chapter 3 or 4, where more than two riparians share one basin. The extreme case with the Nile is a good starting point. Let us compare the theoretical coalitional combinations and the actual coalitional possibilities. Then, let us answer the question: Under what strict assumption one can assume that all the coalitional combinations are possible?

The Nash and Nash–Harsanyi Solutions

Following the discussion on **utility** comparison we started earlier, let us turn first to the more theoretical aspects of the **Nash Solution**, which are based on a set of axioms. Some criticize the **Nash solution** as being not realistic; however, it is widely used.

Nash Solution to a 2-Person Bargaining Problem

Nash axioms for a unique solution of a bargaining game:

1. Individual rationality — Each player should receive additional payoffs compared with the status quo.
2. Feasibility — The payoffs should be within the feasible region of possible payoffs.
3. Pareto optimality — There is no other solution that both players consider to be as least as good as the optimal solution.
4. Independence of irrelevant alternatives — If irrelevant pairs of payoffs are deleted, this should not affect the optimal solution.
5. Invariance under positive linear transformations — The solution is stable with regard to different currencies (scales).
6. Symmetry — The solution should not be affected if the players change roles. This means that if player 1 gets y and player 2 gets x, then there must be a **Nash solution** that has an outcome x for player 1 and an outcome y for player 2. Thus, the **Nash solution** should have the same **utility** for both players.

A solution that satisfies these six axioms is the Nash Bargaining Solution (**Nash Equilibrium**). This is a unique, stable solution. In the case of our notation, a cost allocation e_j that satisfies the following maximization problem is a **Nash equilib-rium** solution.

$$\max_{e_j} [C(\{1\}) - e_1] \cdot [C(\{2\}) - e_2], \tag{6.8}$$

subject to the core conditions.

The graphic exposition of achieving a **Nash Solution** is presented in Fig. 6.3.

To demonstrate the calculation of the **Nash Solution**, let us use the following example. Assume two states, 1 and 2, sharing the same water source of 100 m^3. In the status quo, state 1 and state 2 were not able to utilize the water, so that they could not benefit from the water [$U_1^0 = 0$, $U_2^0 = 0$; here the index zero represents the status quo]. To be able to utilize the water, the two states have to cooperate and then allocate the benefits among themselves. Assume that W is the amount of water (m^3) allocated to state 1, and thus $100 - W$ is the amount allocated to state 2. Assume further that state 1 is more efficient in utilizing the water so that each unit of water used by state 1 produces 3 units of **utility** (or payoff). State 2 is less efficient and each unit of water produces only 2 units of **utility**. Note that we assume here a linear relationship between water and payoff.

An allocation corresponding to a **Nash Equilibrium** will be obtained by solving the following problem:

$$\max_{W} \left(U_1^1 - U_1^0\right) \cdot \left(U_2^1 - U_2^0\right) = [3 \cdot W - 0] \cdot [2 \cdot (100 - W) - 0].$$

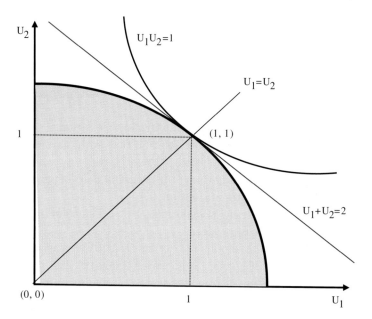

Fig. 6.3: The **Nash Equilibrium**.

Source: Authors.

Subject to $0 \leq W \leq 100$ and to Core conditions.

The solution (can be found using a simple spreadsheet) that maximizes the above problem, subject to the constraints is an equal allocation of the water among the states, which yields $W = 50$; $U_1^1 = 150$; $U_2^1 = 100$; and $(U_1^1 - U_1^0) \cdot (U_2^1 - U_2^0) = 15,000$ (remember that in our example $U_1^0 = U_2^0 = 0$). Notice that in this example we allowed only allocation of the water but not **utility** (income) transfer. Allowing that may change the **Nash solution** values.

The Nash–Harsanyi Solution to an n-Person Bargaining Problem

The **Nash–Harsanyi** (NH) **solution** (Harsanyi, 1959) to an n-person bargaining game is a modification to the 2-player **Nash solution** (Nash, 1953). This solution concept maximizes the product of the grand coalition members' additional utilities (income, or savings) from cooperation compared with the noncooperation case, subject to core conditions, by equating the additional **utility** gains of all players. The NH solution satisfies the Nash axioms (Nash, 1953), it is unique, and it is contained in the core (if it exists). The solution to the Nash and the NH allocation might provide unfair allocations if there are big **utility** differences between the players (e.g., very rich player and very poor player).

$$\text{Max} \prod_{j \in N} \left(C(\{j\}) - h_j \right) \tag{6.9}$$

subject to core conditions.

Where h_j is the NH allocation that satisfies **efficiency** and individual rationality conditions.

Non-CGT Allocation Solutions

There are a wide variety of cost allocation schemes for collectively operated facilities proposed in the accounting and engineering literature. Biddle and Steinberg (1985) provide a comprehensive review, but for this chapter, we include only three main types of allocation solutions. While these allocation solutions refer mainly to cost associated with joint facilities, it is as well relevant to any arrangement of allocation of joint resources and investment in their utilization. In the following section, the terms player and user are used interchangeably.

Egalitarian Allocation

The egalitarian allocation method suggests equal shares of cost or benefits among the users $[\beta_j = \frac{1}{N}]$. The method can be applied also to portion of costs, such as separable or non-separable costs, as one can see later.

Allocation Based on Proportional Use

This allocation scheme simply suggests that each user of the joint facility will be charged in proportion to the volume of the services it uses (i.e., the volume of water it receives from the dam, or the amount of wastewater it sends to the facility for treatment). Thus, the cost to user j is

$$P_j = C(N)\frac{q_j}{\sum_{j \in N} q_j}, \tag{6.10}$$

where P_j is the cost allocated to user j; $C(N)$ is cost of the joint facility; and q_j is the volume of services consumed by user j. This scheme allocates all the joint cost among all N users. Application of this formula is straightforward and will not be demonstrated here.

Allocation Based on Marginal Cost

Allocation on the basis of the marginal cost of the joint facility cost takes into account the marginal quantities consumed by each potential user. Since economies of scale in the joint cost function exist (concave cost function with regard to capacity of the joint facility), the revenues generated by this allocation scheme will not cover the total cost. Therefore, an additional procedure is necessary to account for the remaining uncovered costs. Usually, this can be done using any proportional rule (such as use volume, as we apply here). The formula for this scheme is:

$$B_j = \frac{\partial C(N)}{\partial q_j} \sum_{j \in N} q_j + \left\{ C(N) - \left[\sum_{j \in N} \frac{\partial C(N)}{\partial q_j} C(N) \right] \right\} \frac{q_j}{\sum_{j \in j} q_j}, \tag{6.11}$$

where B_j is the allocation of the joint cost to user j; $\partial C(N)/\partial q_j$ is the marginal cost associated with user j; and $\left\{ C(N) - \left[\sum_{j \in N} \frac{\partial C(N)}{\partial q_j} C(N) \right] \right\}$ is the remaining uncovered cost, which is allocated based on proportional use. The calculation of this allocation scheme is straightforward and will not be demonstrated here.

Separable Cost Allocation Methods

The next set of cost allocation formulas distinguishes between separable and non-separable costs (NSC). Separable costs (SC) equal to the total change in the cost of a joint project from adding user j to the project already designed for $N - j$ users. Such costs include mainly direct costs, and the additional costs associated with changing the size of the project. A general formula is:

$$\Gamma_j = SC_j(C) + \alpha_j NSC(C), \tag{6.12}$$

where

$$SC_j(C) = C(N) - C(N - \{j\}) \quad \forall j \in N,$$
$$NSC(C) = C(N) - \sum_{j \in N} SC_j(C),$$

and

$$\sum_{j \in N} \alpha_j = 1.$$

The values for α_j may be determined in various ways, as will be demonstrated below.

Egalitarian Nonseparable Cost (ENSC)

This allocation method suggests simply that $\alpha_j = 1/N$.

Alternate Cost Avoided (ACA)

Here, the share of user j is determined in the following way:

$$\alpha_j = \frac{C(\{j\}) - SC_j(C)}{\sum_{j \in N} C(\{j\}) - SC_j(C)}. \tag{6.13}$$

Separable Costs Remaining Benefits (SCRB)

This method provides a full allocation and not only a formula for the calculation of α_j. The separable cost of user $j \in N$ is the incremental cost $m_j = C(N) - (C(N - \{j\})$. The alternate cost for user j is the cost $C(\{j\})$ it bears while acting alone, and the remaining benefit to user j (after deducting the separable cost) is $r_j = C(\{j\}) - m_j$. The SCRB assigns the joint cost according to the following formula (Young, 1985)

$$\kappa_j = m_j + \frac{r_j}{\sum_{j \in N} r_j} \left[C(N) - \sum_{j \in N} m_j \right]. \tag{6.14}$$

In other words, each user pays its separable cost, and the "nonseparable costs" $C(N) - \sum_{j \in N} m_j$ are then allocated in proportion to the remaining benefits, assuming that all remaining benefits r_j are nonnegative for each player.

POWER, ACCEPTABILITY, AND STABILITY

The fulfillment of the core conditions for an allocation scheme is a necessary condition for its acceptability by the players. Thus, solutions not included in the core are also not stable. Although an allocation scheme may fulfill the core requirements, some players that might view it as relatively unfair compared with another allocation still may not accept it. Allocations, which are viewed as unfair by some players are less stable. Some players might threaten to leave the grand coalition and form subcoalition because of their critical position in the grand coalition. The stability of any solution is important given the existence of fixed investments that have to be repaid over time, and thus a more stable solution might be preferred even if it is harder to implement. A useful comparison among various allocation schemes is the measure of the stability of the solution. We will review here several power indexes and use them in calculating the stability of a game.

The **Banzhaf power index** was developed (Banzhaf, 1965) to deal with coalitional battles. Here we shall discuss the version that is developed for games in the **characteristic function**. The main element of the Banzhaf index is the swing. A swing is a pair of sets $\{S, S - \{j\}\}$, such that S is a winning set and $S - \{j\}$ is not. For each player j in the set of all players N, we can calculate a number $\eta_j(v)$ that represents the number of swings for j in the simple game with the **characteristic function** v. Let $\overline{\eta}(v) = \sum_{j \in N} \eta_j(v)$ be the number of swings in the game. A player with $\eta_j(v) = 0$ is a *dummy* in the game, since his help is not needed to make a coalition win. A player with $\eta_j(v) = \overline{\eta}(v)$ is called a *dictator*.

The swing numbers form the **nonnormalized Banzhaf index**. We are interested in the relative power, so we define the **normalized Banzhaf index**:

$$\beta_j(v) = \frac{\eta_j(v)}{\overline{\eta}(v)}. \tag{6.15}$$

Shapley and Shubik (1954) suggest a method for measuring power in voting games. "... the power of an individual member depends on the chance that member has of being critical to the success of a winning coalition." Loehman *et al.* (1979) used an *ex post* approach to measure power in a cooperative game. Their index can be interpreted in a similar way as the **Shapley–Shubik Power Index**. The Loehman *et al.* power index $(\mathcal{L}_i)$ compares the gains to a player with the gains to the coalition. The power index $(\mathcal{L}_i)$ is:

$$\mathcal{L}_j = \frac{\Theta_j - v(\{j\})}{\sum_{j \in N} (\Theta_j - v(\{j\}))} \quad j \in N, \quad \sum_{j \in N} \mathcal{L}_j = 1, \tag{6.16}$$

where Θ_j is the allocation solution for player j. This index is also used in Williams (1988) in the equation that calculates the allocation using the **Alternative Cost Avoided** method (Ransmeier, 1942).

The power index can also be used to calculate a measure of stability for the various solutions under various states of nature. The power index is calculated separately for each state of the nature. If the power is distributed more or less equally among the players, then the coalition is more likely to be stable under various states of nature. The stability measure $(\nabla_\Theta \equiv \sigma_\Theta / \overline{\Theta})$ is simply the coefficient of variation calculated over all players in a given allocation solution $(0 \leq \nabla_\Theta \leq 1)$ and state of the nature. The greater the value of ∇_Θ the larger the instability of the allocation solution.

A simple measure for stability of an allocation scheme is *the number of players that prefer it over other schemes.* In the cost allocation game, a player will prefer a scheme that assigns them the least cost. Therefore, the percentage of the satisfied players in the game reflects the level of stability.

Gately (1974) introduced the concept of "**propensity to disrupt**" the grand coalition as the ratio of how much the other players would lose if player j refuses to cooperate to how much player j would lose. Gately (1974) also applied the concept to a problem of investment in electric power in India. The concept was modified and applied (for $n > 3$) by Straffin and Heaney (1981) to the case of the Tennessee Valley.

The Gately **propensity to disrupt** of player j is calculated as the ratio between its gains and the coalition gains from a given allocation $(x_1, \ldots, x_n)$:

$$G_j = \frac{v(\{j\}) - x_j}{\sum_{i \in N} v(\{j\}) - v(N)} \quad j \in N. \tag{6.17}$$

According to Straffin and Heaney, the propensity of j to disrupt an allocation $(x_1, \ldots, x_n)$ is:

$$SH_j = \frac{\sum_{i \neq j} x_i - v(N - j)}{x_j - v(\{j\})} = \frac{v(N) - v(N - j)}{x_j} - 1, \quad j \in N. \tag{6.18}$$

SH_j measures the loss to members in coalition $N - j$ compared to player j's loss, if player j disrupts the grand coalition. Negative values reflect enthusiasm for the allocation. When this ratio is positive and large, player j has a powerful threat to disrupt the grand coalition unless his allocation is improved. Using this concept, one can reduce the set of mutually acceptable distributions by eliminating any core imputations for which player's **propensity to disrupt** are higher than a certain value.

APPLICATION (WITH COMPARISON AMONG SOLUTION CONCEPTS)

We turn now again to the modified example from Dinar and Howitt (1997) — that we named the dam cost game. We apply now various allocation schemes and present and compare their results, using various criteria. We selected several cooperative game theory allocation solutions as well as several engineering and accounting methods. We do not present the detailed calculations here.

Comparison of the Allocation Schemes

Three conventional allocation methods and four game theory solutions were applied to the problem of allocating the joint cost of a joint dam. The objective is to allocate the joint cost such that the solution will be acceptable to all players (users) and that the **efficiency** condition will hold, resulting in a stable collective agreement. Table 6.2 summarizes the allocation schemes.

The **Shapley Value**, and the SCRB suggest allocations that are very much similar to the case of the high water flows scenario and the Shapley and the **proportional allocation** suggest similar values in the case of low water flow scenarios. Using these allocations, players A, B, and C pay very similar shares of the joint cost and their relative reduction in cost compared with the noncooperation situation is also similar. Player D is probably less satisfied with the Shapley and Proportional use allocations. This player "gains" only 7% in lower fees from cooperation compared with 40% for each of the other player in the game. Player D would prefer the marginal cost allocation where that player's contribution to the game is less substantial compared with the other allocation solutions.

Table 6.2 presents the ratios of the cost allocation in the grand coalition compared with the noncooperation. It is clear from the results in the table that players A, B, and C gain more from cooperation, in terms of percentage cost reduction, than player D in all allocation schemes, except the Marginal cost. So, player D, who contributes the most to the cooperation gains may consider defection. Comparison of the high and low water flows scenarios suggest that player D's share in the joint cost always increases when capacity increases. For players B and C it happened in three out of five allocations, and player A's share decreases as capacity increases. Similar results can be obtained from an analysis of the extreme points of the core that were calculated and discussed earlier in the course (Chapter 5). Testing for core conditions (Table 6.2) reveals that the marginal cost allocation is not included in the core in the case of high water flows (one of the conditions does not hold). All allocation solutions fulfill core requirements in the case of low water flow. Using the core argument, the marginal cost allocation will not be accepted by the players.

Acceptability and Stability

Table 6.3 presents the power indexes for the players, and the stability index for the different allocation schemes. In both the high and low water flow scenarios, the least stable scheme is the marginal cost and the most stable scheme is the **proportional allocation**. The other schemes consistently keep the same order of stability over both water flow scenarios, with Shapley, SCRB, and the **nucleolus** being in the middle between the **proportional allocation** and the marginal cost allocation.

Comparing the different schemes for the reduction in the cost share of each player suggests that in the case of high water flow, players A, B, and C prefer the **proportional allocation** scheme for its least cost share (60, 62, and 59%, respectively, of the cost compared with noncooperation), and player D prefers the marginal cost allocation (81% compared with noncooperation). In the case of low water flows, players A and C prefer the **proportional allocation** (63 and 60%, respectively, compared with noncooperation), player B is indifferent between the Shapley and the proportional (66% compared with noncooperation), and player D prefers the marginal cost (79% compared with noncooperation).

Table 6.2: Comparison of allocation schemes used in the dam game (in parentheses are cost shares relative to noncooperation).

Allocation scheme	Player				In core
	A	B	C	D	
High Water Flows					
Shapley	745.7 (66)	822.1 (68)	627.7 (62)	5061.5 (90)	Yes
Nucleolus	797.0 (71)	855.0 (71)	735.0 (72)	4870.0 (87)	Yes
Nash–Harsanyi	690.5 (62)	786.5 (65)	591.5 (58)	5188.5 (92)	Yes
Proportional use	673.3 (60)	748.2 (62)	598.5 (59)	5237.0 (93)	Yes
Marginal cost[a]	904.9 (81)	980.3 (81)	821.3 (81)	4550.5 (81)	No
SCRB	755.6 (68)	829.3 (69)	680.7 (67)	4991.4 (89)	Yes
Low Water Flow					
Shapley	502.9 (72)	543.6 (66)	389.3 (66)	2384.2 (87)	Yes
Nucleolus	562.0 (80)	552.0 (68)	417.0 (71)	2289.0 (84)	Yes
Nash–Harsanyi	450.5 (64)	558.5 (69)	337.5 (57)	2473.5 (91)	Yes
Proportional use	444.2 (63)	533.0 (66)	355.3 (60)	2487.5 (91)	Yes
Marginal cost[a]	554.1 (79)	639.6 (79)	465.4 (79)	2161.0 (79)	Yes
SCRB	484.6 (69)	570.1 (70)	397.2 (68)	2368.1 (86)	Yes

[a]With adjustments.
Source: Dinar and Howitt (1997).

Table 6.4 presents the **propensity to disrupt** calculations for each player using the six allocation schemes. In general, all players have an interest in keeping the grand coalition. Among all four players, D is the one with the highest propensity to keep the coalition under all allocation schemes and water flow scenarios. Other players vary in their stability of **propensity to disrupt** index. Player C has the lowest values of **propensity to disrupt**, so this player is more likely to consider defection under certain conditions.

Figure 6.4 compares the changes in stability for the two water flow scenarios. Any point below the 45° line indicates a decreased stability as capacity increases, and points above it indicate decreased stability as capacity decreases. It is interesting that the **proportional allocation**'s stability is quite insensitive to the capacity of the joint facility. The two game theory allocations (Shapley and **Nucleolus**) increase in their stability as capacity increases, and the other engineering schemes' (marginal cost and SCRB) stability decreases as capacity increases.

The analysis provides clear empirical evidence that the different allocation schemes have different outcomes in terms of their acceptability to the players, and the derived stability. The allocation schemes can be ranked by the players for their fairness in different ways. However, the Nash–Harsanyi, and **proportional allocation** are always ranked first and the marginal cost is always ranked last. The regional problem has also been analyzed for two representative state of nature water flow scenarios. Among the allocation schemes, Nash–Harsanyi, proportional, Shapley, and SCRB were found to be more stable in both water scenarios

Table 6.3: Power and stability indexes.

Allocation scheme	Player				Stability index
	A	B	C	D	
High Water Flows					
Shapley	0.217	0.229	0.228	0.325	0.175
Nucleolus	0.188	0.209	0.165	0.439	0.427
Nash–Harsanyi	0.250	0.250	0.250	0.250	0.000
Proportional use	0.260	0.273	0.246	0.221	0.077
Marginal cost	0.122	0.135	0.113	0.628	0.876
SCRB	0.211	0.224	0.197	0.366	0.268
Low Water Flows					
Shapley	0.197	0.265	0.198	0.339	0.234
Nucleolus	0.138	0.256	0.170	0.435	0.461
Nash–Harsanyi	0.250	0.250	0.250	0.250	0.000
Proportional use	0.256	0.276	0.232	0.236	0.070
Marginal cost	0.145	0.168	0.122	0.565	0.730
SCRB	0.216	0.238	0.190	0.356	0.254

Source: Dinar and Howitt (1997).

Table 6.4: Propensity to disrupt values as calculated for the various allocation schemes.

Player	Allocation scheme					
	Shapley	Nucleolus	Nash–Harsanyi	Proportional use	Marginal cost	SCRB
High Water Flows						
A	−0.30	−0.28	−0.17	−0.15	−0.36	−0.24
B	−0.25	−0.28	−0.22	−0.10	−0.37	−0.26
C	−0.15	−0.27	−0.09	−0.10	−0.35	−0.21
D	−0.80	−0.79	−0.81	−0.81	−0.78	−0.80
Low Water Flows						
A	−0.46	−0.52	−0.40	−0.39	−0.51	−0.44
B	−0.18	−0.19	−0.28	−0.16	−0.30	−0.21
C	−0.22	−0.27	−0.10	−0.15	−0.35	−0.24
D	−0.76	−0.75	−0.77	−0.77	−0.73	−0.76

($\nabla < 0.25$) while the **nucleolus** and the marginal cost allocations were less stable ($0.40 < \nabla < 0.90$).

The stability of game theory allocations (Shapley, **Nucleolus**) increases as water flows increase; however, the stability of the traditional cost allocation methods (SCRB, marginal cost) decreases as water flows increase. The **proportional allocation** method and the **Nash–Harsanyi solution** have the same degree of stability in both water flows scenarios analyzed.

The **propensity to disrupt** index suggests that the players in the game do not consider defection from the grand coalition. Several players have higher levels

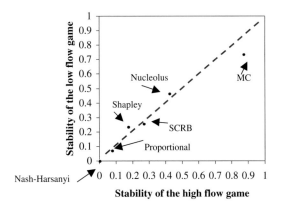

Fig. 6.4: Stability index of various game solutions in the high and low flow games. *Source*: Dinar and Howitt (1997).

of (negative) **propensity to disrupt** values than others, but in general it can be said that all six allocation schemes are pretty stable.

> **For Further Discussion.** What is analogous to acceptability and stability in the context of transboundary treaties? Using the examples from Chapters 3 and 4, identify the various problems related to acceptability and stability in existing treaties as well as in treaties that never materialized. How can we quantify some of the existing problems in certain treaties and express them in terms of game theory?

CONCLUSION

This chapter, a very condensed one, has the aim of introducing CGT and other solution concepts for games where a grand coalition may have advantage over individual actions and subcoalitional arrangements. The chapter attempted at providing a balanced view of the usefulness and relevance of CGT for transboundary water issues. The immediate set of conclusions that one can derive from this chapter is that CGT is a proper framework to analyze cooperation options in transboundary water problems. However, it is very clearly noticed that there is quite a wide range of results that one has to consider, using various criteria. While some of these criteria are met, others are not, and this adds an important dimension to the evaluation and prioritization of solution concepts that are presented in the chapter. We believe that the approach used in this chapter, where a set of solution concepts have been calculated and compared, is a plausible answer to such concerns. Analysts working on complicated transboundary water issues, have to take into account not only the political-economic aspects of the problems, but also the objective physical aspects, by itself complicated and hard to model or assess. Therefore, we do think that the best way to provide decision-makers and analysts useful tools is to apply several of them and to critically compare the results. Clearly some tools are more relevant under some situation and others, under other situations.

Practice Questions

1. (After Dinar *et al.* (2008)): For the following (Kat watershed) game, determine if the Core is empty or not, and calculate the **Shapley Value**:

$v\{A\} = 336{,}060; v\{B\} = 1{,}758{,}946; v\{C\} = 1{,}185{,}693$
$v\{A, B\} = 2{,}341{,}140; v\{A, C\} = 1{,}521{,}753; v\{B, C\} = 2{,}944{,}639$
$v\{A, B, C\} = 3{,}552{,}913$

2. Demonstrate why the allocation by the marginal cost rule in Table 6.2 does not lie in the core.

REFERENCES

Banzhaf, J.F. (1965). Weighted voting doesn't work: A mathematical analysis, *Rutgers Law Review*, 19.

Biddle, G.C. and R. Steinberg (1985). Common cost allocation in the firm. In: Peyton Young, H. (ed.), *Cost Allocation: Methods, Principles and Applications*. New York: North-Holland, pp. 31–54.

Dinar, A. and R. Howitt (1997). Mechanism for allocation on environmental control cost: Empirical tests of acceptability and stability, *Journal of Environmental Management*, 49, 183–203.

Dinar, A., S. Farolfi, F. Patrone and K. Rowntree (2008). To negotiate or to game theorize: Evaluating water allocation mechanisms in the Kat Basin, South Africa. In: Dinar, A., J. Albiac and J. Samchez-Soriano (Eds.), *Game Theory for Policy Making in Natural Resources and the Environment*. London: Routledge Publishers.

Gately, D. (1974). Sharing the gains from regional cooperation: A game theoretic application to planning investment in electric power, *International Economic Review*, 15(1), 195–208.

Harsanyi, J.C. (1959). A bargaining model for the cooperative n-person game. In: Tucker, A.W. and R.D. Luce (eds.), *Contributions to the Theory of Games*, Vols. 1–4. Princeton University Press, pp. 325–355.

Harsanyi, J.C. (1956). Approaches to the bargaining problem before and after the theory of games: A critical discussion of Zeuten's, Hick's and Nash's theories, *Econometrica*, 24, 144–157.

Loehman, E., J. Orlando, J. Tschirhart and A. Whinston (1979). Cost allocation for a regional wastewater treatment system, *Water Resources Research*, 15(2), 193–202.

Loehman, E. and A. Whinston (1976). A generalized cost allocation scheme, In: Lin, S. (ed.), *Theory and Measurement of Economic Externalities*. New York: Academic Press.

Nash Jr, J.F. (1950). The bargaining problem, *Econometrica*, 18, 155–162.

Nash Jr, J.F. (1953). Two-person cooperative games, *Econometrica*, 21, 128–140.

Parrachino, I., S. Zara and F. Patrone (2006). Cooperative game theory and its application to natural environmental and water resource issues: 1. Basic theory. World Bank Policy Research Working Paper 4072.

Ransmeier, J.S. (1942). *The Tennessee Valley Authority: A Case Study in the Economics of Multiple Purpose Stream Planning.* Nashville (Tennessee): Vanderbilt University Press.

Schmeidler, D. (1969). The nucleolus of a characteristic function game, *SIAM Journal on Applied Mathematics*, 17, 1163–1170.

Shapley, L.S. and M. Shubik (1954). A method for evaluating the distribution of power in a committee system, *American Political Science Review*, 48, 787–792.

Shapley, L.S. (1951). *Notes on the N-person Game: II. The Value of an N-person Game.* RAND Publication RM-641.

Shapley, L.S. (1953). A value for *n*-person games. In: Kuhn, H.W. and A.W. Tucker (eds.), *Contributions to the Theory of Games, n. II, Annals of Math. Studies, 28.* Princeton University Press, pp. 307–317.

Shapley, L.S. (1971). Cores of concave games, *International Journal of Game Theory*, 1, 11–26.

Shubik, M. (1982). *Game Theory in the Social Sciences Concepts and Solutions.* Cambridge, MA: The MIT Press.

Straffin, P. and J. Heaney (1981). Game theory and the tennessee valley authority, *International Journal of Game Theory*, 10, 35–43.

Williams, M.A. (1988). An empirical test of cooperative game solution concepts, *Behavioral Science*, 33, 224–230.

Young, H.P. (ed.) (1985). *Cost Allocation: Methods, Principles and Applications.* New York: North-Holland, pp. 31–54.

Zeuthen, F. (1930). *Problem of Monopoly and Economic Welfare.* London: Routledge & Kegan Paul.

ADDITIONAL READING

Dinar, A., A. Ratner and D. Yaron (1992). Evaluating cooperative game theory in water resources, *Theory and Decision*, 32, 1–20.

Parrachino, I., A. Dinar and F. Patrone (2006). Cooperative game theory and its application to natural, environmental and water resource issues: 3. Application to water resources. World Bank Policy Research Working Paper 4074.

7. HYDROPOLITICS AND INTERNATIONAL RELATIONS

Objectives

The history of hydropolitics does not support the claim that the next war shall be about water. The chapter considers a set of variables, including scarcity, geography, relative power, domestic politics, and international water law, to explain the onset of conflict and initiation of cooperation over transboundary waters. Strategies and tactics for promoting cooperation, and eventually an agreement, between riparians are also discussed. After reading this chapter, you will understand that while political disputes over water do take place (and may become most volatile in otherwise unstable regions) they rarely become violent. You will be equipped with evidence showing that for the same reasons that conflict may arise over a shared-water body, cooperation may also come about. You will gain knowledge of several elements that facilitate both conflict and cooperation over transboundary waters. Finally, you will learn about different tactics used to facilitate cooperation and negotiation over transboundary waters, and understand that the intricacies of conflict and cooperation are of highest importance in otherwise precarious regions where a water dispute may aggravate the already tense political environment.

Main Terminology

Constructivism; Domestic politics; Epistemic communities; Functionalism; Geographical configurations; Hydropolitics; Interdependence; International water law; Liberalism; Linkage; Neoliberal institutionalism; Neorealism; Protracted conflict; Realism; Reciprocity; Scarcity; Third-parties.

Chapter 2 provided a compelling history of conflict and cooperation over transboundary water bodies. Chapter 3 examined the development of **international water law** and the manner by which disputes over water may be analyzed in the context of international legal principles. Chapters 4–6 considered several economic approaches, including game theory, in demonstrating how cooperation and conflict over water come about. This chapter will build on the previous chapters and will discuss conflict and cooperation over water from an international relations and negotiations perspective.

Hydropolitics, or the politics of water, is often associated with violent disputes between states, at least in the popular press and policy-related publications. The claim that violent conflict over international shared rivers is a *fait accompli* resonates due to its sensationalist appeal. In its most acute form, the assertion reasons that "the wars of the next century will be about water."[1] Given that water is crucial for basic survival, irreplaceable, transcends international borders, and scarce, it follows that states will take up arms to defend access to a shared river. As water becomes increasingly scarce, such as in the Middle East, North Africa, and Central Asia, a water war is more likely (Cooley, 1984; Starr, 1991; Bulloch and Darwish, 1993). In general, when national capabilities (including resources) cannot be attained at a reasonable cost within national boundaries, they may be sought beyond (Choucri and North, 1975, p. 16).

As mentioned in earlier chapters, the last time water has played the main role in instigating a war was 4,500 years ago. This was the case of two city states, Lagash and Umma, battling over rights to exploit boundary channels along the Tigris River in modern day Iraq. Since the beginning of the 1900s, water has played a role only in initiating armed — or near armed — skirmishes between states. There have been only seven such recorded incidents between 1918 and 1994 (Wolf and Hamner, 2000, p. 57). Not surprisingly, the majority of these episodes have taken place in the Middle East where water is scarce and the political atmosphere tense.

To argue that conflict is an anomaly in the realm of **hydropolitics** would be a distortion of reality. Political disputes regularly arise over shared rivers. In fact, this is the case in regions known for having limited water availability and historically tense relations between the riparians but also in regions with relatively more ample water and cordial relations between the riparians. Surely, water disputes in regions with historically tense relations between the states and scarce water resources have tended to be more volatile. In such regions, like the Middle East, water is evolving into an issue of high politics and the probability of water-related violence is increasing (Gleick, 1993, p. 80).

Despite the sensationalist appeal of the "water wars" thesis, researchers have argued that major violent incidences over scarce water resource have not only been absent in the past but are unlikely in the future. Several explanations have been offered. Allan has claimed that states experiencing water **scarcity** import food commodities from abroad. Through trade in "virtual water," states are able to aug-ment their inadequate water resources (water resources they would have otherwise needed for their own irrigation) rather than wrangle with fellow riparians over a shared-water body. By extension, the incidence of violent conflict with fellow ripar-ians is reduced (Allan, 1998). Another explanation has claimed that a state's insti-tutional capacity (or second-order resources) is able to assuage the ramifications

---

[1]The prediction, made by Ismail Serageldin, Vice President of the World Bank at the time, was quoted in Crosette (1995).

of physical water **scarcity** (first-order resource). Second-order resources account for a state's economic well-being, stable political institutions, and technological know-how and innovation. Second-order resources can often make up for deficiencies in the first-order resource, allowing a state to adapt to the economic and political implications of water **scarcity** (Ohlsson and Turton, 2006).

For Further Discussion. Given the above dichotomy, of first-order resources and second-order resources, how many scenario combinations result and what are they? What countries would you place under each combination?

Another explanation holds that states themselves have tended more toward cooperation over water than violent conflict. That is, the history of **hydropolitics** has been rather one of cooperation and negotiation than conflict (Wolf and Hamner, 2000, p. 66; Chapters 3 and 8). Compared to the small number of militarized episodes involving freshwater, history has recorded over 3,600 water agreements and declarations with one of the earliest dating back to 805 AD (UN Food and Agricultural Organization, 1978 and 1984).[2] Interestingly, for the same exact reasons that water has been a source of dispute between states, it has also become a foundation for collaboration among them. So while conflict over water seems most bothersome in arid and otherwise politically precarious regions, disputes have rarely turned violent. Nonetheless, understanding the means by which conflict ensues and cooperation evolves is most instrumental in such unstable regions.

UNDERSTANDING CONFLICT AND COOPERATION OVER WATER

Several theoretical schools within the international relations discipline provide an appropriate basis for considering how conflict and cooperation come about. While these writings have rarely been directly applied to transboundary rivers, several deductions can be made. **Realism** and **neorealism**, for example, have argued that international politics always takes place in the shadow of war. A constant state of fear from destruction fosters not only distrust among states but also inhibits cooperation. Similarly, since no world government exists, states essentially co-exist in an anarchic environment of self-help (Waltz, 1979; Morgenthau, 1948; Gilpin, 1975; Greico, 1990, p. 38). According to neorealists, states are also preoccupied with the gains of other states, relative to their own gains, in addition to their concerns about survival (Greico, 1990, p. 28; Snidal, 1991; Powell, 1991, p. 315;

---

[2]In 805 AD Emperor Charlemagne granted a charter to a monastery, guaranteeing freedom of navigation on the Rhine River. Chapter 3 cites an even earlier agreement concluded in approximately 3100 BC. Other databases or works that have compiled freshwater treaties and acts include: Dinar (2007); United Nations, Food and Agriculture Organization, WATERLEX; Oregon State University, International Freshwater Treaties Database; and United Nations, United Nations Treaty Collection.

Waltz, 1979, p. 105). Cooperation among states may produce a situation where one country attains more than another, allowing it to use these gains to inflict harm on the other state. A state may, therefore, decline to join a cooperative arrangement if it believes that the discrepancies in otherwise mutually desirable gains favor its treaty partners (Greico, 1990, p. 10). This may be especially true in regions where access to freshwater is considered a national security issue and the relations between the states are already tense.

The hydrology of an international river basin links all the riparian states, requiring them to share a complex network of environmental, economic, political, and security interdependencies (Elhance, 1999, p. 13). Therefore, in addition to the general state of nature which promotes conflict among states, **realism** and **neorealism** would contend that the interdependencies that bind fellow river riparians, highlight not only the sensitivities between them but more importantly their reciprocal, mutual vulnerabilities. This tends to make cooperation difficult and tension more likely (Waltz, 1979).

While disputes indeed occur among river riparians, conflict ultimately opens the way to cooperation, and cooperation is almost always codified in international treaties. It is perhaps of little surprise that, to date, thousands of international agreements have been recorded. Therefore, the security, political, economic, and environmental interdependencies in which an international river binds its riparians, is also a cause for cooperation and coordination.

Contrary to **realism** and **neorealism**, **liberalism** and **neoliberal institutionalism**, do not consider cooperation an anomaly. Conflict is not a constant global phenomenon nor does anarchy automatically presuppose conflict (Keohane, 1989, p. 10). Conflict may take place but it is usually a function of misunderstandings between the parties (Ferguson and Mansbach, 1988, pp. 91–97). Similarly, conflict and cooperation are usually a function of the prevailing expectations between the states. Cooperation emerges as self-interested actors, co-existing in an anarchic environment, reach autonomous and independent decisions that lead to mutually desirable cooperative outcomes. States are "rational egoists" and will therefore cooperate if they have mutual interests and stand to gain from cooperation (Hollis and Smith, 1991, p. 19; Keohane, 1989, p. 18). While an interdependent relationship between actors may indeed exacerbate the vulnerabilities between them, as **neorealism** would contend, it also means that the actors may have more reason to cooperate on the particular issue they are mutually dependent on. In other words, countries are able to realize joint gains and pursue cooperative arrangements when it is in their interest to do so. In the context of international rivers, where interdependency among the riparians is intrinsic to the physical river, cooperation may be more efficient than unilateral action and conflict.

As the discussion above reveals, the nature of international **hydropolitics** is that of conflict and cooperation between states. Below, a set of variables that consider conflict and cooperation over transboundary rivers is enumerated. **Scarcity** is considered first.

Scarcity

Aggravating the **interdependence** of river riparians, **scarcity** may bring parties to the brink of conflict as states often compete with one another for the limited resource. As argued, environmental decline occasionally leads to conflict, especially when scarce water resources must be shared (Mathews, 1989, p. 166; Homer-Dixon, 1999, p. 139).

Countries may suffer from **scarcity** in water supply, energy, flood prevention facilities, or pollution control and may be, therefore, inclined to exploit an international river. As far as water quantity is concerned, Falkenmark has argued that environmental stress results when the population grows large in relation to the water supply derived from the global water cycle. In consequence, conflicts may easily arise when users are competing for a limited resource to supply the domestic, industrial, and agricultural sectors (Falkenmark, 1992, pp. 279–280). The same author has also argued that 1,000 cubic meters of water per capita per year constitutes the minimum amount necessary for an adequate quality of life in a moderately developed country (1986, pp. 192–200). When water availability drops below this figure, **scarcity** problems grow intense. As water **scarcity** becomes more acute, violent conflict becomes increasingly probable. This link embraces such issues as constrained agricultural and economic activity, migration, greater segmentation of society, and disruption of institutions (Homer-Dixon, 1999, p. 80). Various conflicts can develop, whether at the individual, or the national level (Falkenmark, 1992, p. 292; Gleick, 1993, pp. 79–105, 105–110; Gleick, 1998, p. 4; Homer-Dixon, 1999, pp. 67–69; Myers, 1993; Samson and Charrier, 1997, p. 6). In the case of pollution, for example, the cost of water contamination is often borne by the downstream riparians, abetting a further lack of bilateral cooperation (Kratz, 1996, p. 26).

Scarcity can just as well lead to cooperation. The need to tackle **scarcity** brings the riparians together to realize integrated and coordinated projects. As Dokken argues, in some cases environmental scarcities and environmental problems may be considered the starting points for cooperation (Dokken, 1997). In short, attempting to ameliorate **scarcity** or to exploit a river so as to satisfy a particular need, whether water quantity or hydroelectricity, can encourage states to cooperate for their mutual benefit. In other words, resource **scarcity** based on environmental degradation tends to encourage joint efforts to halt such degradation (Deudney, 1991, p. 10). Environmental disparities modify the meaning of ecological **interdependence** whereby "states and groups of states will try to seek alliances as they seek to exploit, or to escape, these disparities" (Brock, 1992, p. 99).

While **scarcity** is an important element for explaining conflict and cooperation, it is not sufficient. With respect to conflict, Elhance has cautioned that by itself **scarcity** of natural resources does not necessarily lead to interstate disputes. Rather, it is when such a resource is rightly or wrongly perceived as being overexploited or degraded by others at a cost to oneself, that states may become prone to conflict (1994, p. 4). Geography may be partly to blame.

Geography

With regard to the **interdependence** of the parties vis-à-vis the common resource and the geographical criteria of water ownership, some scholars have argued that certain **geographical configurations** of rivers may be more prone to disputes. This is the case especially in upstream-downstream situations in comparison to cases where, for example, the river straddles the border (Gottmann, 1951, p. 159; Falkenmark, 1990, p. 184; Just and Netanyahu, 1998, p. 11; Toset *et al.*, 2000, pp. 980–981; Amery and Wolf, 2000). Dinar (2006, 2007) has labeled these configurations as *through-border* and *border-creator*, respectively. The *through-border* configuration constitutes a river that flows from one country into another, crossing the border only once. The *border-creator* river constitutes a river that flows in its entirety along the border, separating the countries. Figure 7.1 diagrams these configurations.

A geographically asymmetric relationship exists in the *through-border* configuration. The upstream state can pollute producing a unidirectional externality in the downstream direction. Similarly, the upstream state may impound water in its territory to the detriment of the downstream state. In short, the assumption is that upstream country A can harm downstream country B's part of the river but not vice versa.[3] A geographically symmetric relationship exists in the *border-creator* configuration. In this instance, any state that engages in a harmful activity may harm itself as well as its neighbor. Also, harm can be reciprocated (Dinar, 2006, p. 416). It is by no means certain that conflict in the exploitation of *border-creator* rivers can be avoided (Falkenmark, 1986a, b, p. 96), but the geography of *border-creator* rivers helps by simplifying both retaliation and **reciprocity** (Dinar, 2006, p. 429).

LeMarquand has utilized slightly different labels to describe similar river configurations. According to LeMarquand (1977, p. 8), "successive" rivers (i.e., the upstream-downstream configuration) and "contiguous" (i.e., rivers where the river forms some part of the border between the two states) produce different incentives

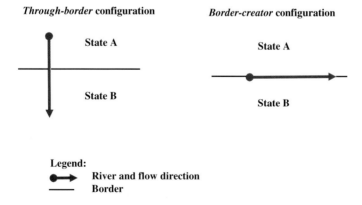

Fig. 7.1: *Through-border* and *Border-creator* configurations.

---

[3]This is a prototypical case. Yet there are instances where dams built downstream cause inundation or environmental damage upstream.

for cooperation (1977, p. 8). According to LeMarquand, when the river is contiguous, there is significant incentive for cooperation. The incentive to attain such cooperation is to avoid the "tragedy of the commons" (LeMarquand, 1977, p. 9). Alternatively, cooperation finds no incentive when the upstream country uses the river's water to the detriment of the downstream country and that country has no reciprocal power over the upstream country (LeMarquand, 1977, p. 10). Relative power may, therefore, act as another element explaining conflict and cooperation.

Relative Power

In considering the relative power of the parties, conflict may be most likely when the most powerful country in the river basin is located in the upstream position. According to Lowi, the interest of the hegemonic state along a river is often a prerequisite to cooperation. Based on the realist and neorealist contention that cooperation can only be sustained if a powerful country desires it and imposes it on another state (otherwise known as *hegemonic stability theory*), Lowi has argued that cooperation is more likely to ensue if the hegemon is located in a strategically inferior position — downstream — and if the hegemon's relationship to the water resource is that of critical need. Lowi considers the 1959 Nile River Agreement between Egypt and Sudan as a prime example for her hegemonic stability contention. In contrast, argues Lowi, river basins with upstream hegemons, evincing an ongoing water dispute between the riparians, are the least likely to witness an end to that conflict (Box 7.1).

Box 7.1: Hegemonic stability theory and the case of the Euphrates–Tigris River Basin

According to Lowi, the case of the Euphrates–Tigris River fits the aforementioned criteria. Upstream Turkey is also the hegemon in comparison with midstream Syria and downstream Iraq. A comprehensive water agreement has not been forthcoming in the Basin largely due to Turkey's intransigence. In short, Turkey's upstream and hegemonic position will continue to dissuade her from giving up the status quo she benefits from (Lowi, 1993, p. 199).

Other scholars have disagreed with the above claim and explain the occurrence of conflict in a different manner. Homer-Dixon has argued that violent conflict between upstream and downstream riparians is likely only when the downstream state fears that the upstream state will use water as a form of leverage and believes it has the military power to rectify the situation (Homer-Dixon, 1999, p. 139).[4] Therefore, the situation is most dangerous when (a) the downstream country is

---

[4]Homer-Dixon considers the outbreak of war.

highly dependent on the water for its national well-being, (b) the upstream country is threatening to restrict substantially the river's flow downstream, and (c) the downstream country believes it is militarily stronger than the upstream country (Homer-Dixon, 1999, p. 193). Homer-Dixon cites the Nile River as a ripe arena for conflict between downstream Egypt and upstream Ethiopia.

Fredrick Frey and Thomas Naff also estimate how states size up to one another through an assessment of the riparian's geographical position along the river, projectable power or brute ability to impose its will on its rivals, and need for water (Frey and Naff, 1985; Frey, 1993; Naff, 1994). Although not developed beyond its illustrative purposes, the authors' *power matrix model* attempts to measure the intensity of a water conflict in a given river basin based on assigning a weighted value for each of the above three factors. With this model, a given power calculation for each riparian, and the potential for conflict intensity in the region, is subsequently surmised. In applying their model to the Jordan, Euphrates, and Nile Rivers, the authors conclude that the greatest potential for conflict exists when a lower riparian is more powerful than the upstream riparian and perceives its need to be deliberately frustrated. In fact, conflict is least likely when the upstream riparian is most powerful since the asymmetry in power inhibits conflict potential. Finally, in a river basin with relative power symmetry among the riparians but with asymmetry in geographic position and need for water, the potential for conflict is moderate. Note that the first and second assessments are directly in opposition to Lowi's conjectures yet in agreement with Homer-Dixon's conclusions.[5]

Protracted Conflict and Domestic Politics

An existing **protracted conflict** between river riparians could also intensify the particular water conflict and impede cooperation. That is, when a water dispute unfolds within the context of a more comprehensive political conflict between the parties (such as over identity, territory, or religion) the former cannot be effectively isolated from the latter. Such a **protracted conflict** often produces enemy images that are adopted by the parties and become deeply rooted, resistant to change, and an obstacle to conflict resolution (Stein, 1996, p. 96).

Lowi has utilized the example of the Israeli–Palestinian, and the larger Arab–Israeli, conflict to argue that without the resolution of the broader political dispute (status of Jerusalem, Israeli settlements, Palestinian refugees, territory, and borders) between the parties, an agreement on water issues will be difficult to achieve. In this particular view, water is relegated to the status of low-politics while the aforementioned issues are considered in the realm of high-politics (Lowi, 1993, p. 196).

A **protracted conflict** of this type, together with the resulting enemy images, often promotes, among the parties, a distributive outlook vis-à-vis the issue at hand.

---

[5]Homer-Dixon discusses the case of the Euphrates River to demonstrate the small chance for violent conflict when the upstream state is stronger (1999, p. 140).

Negotiation scholars argue that with regard to a distributive orientation held by the parties, the goals of one party, and the attainment of those goals, are in fundamental and direct conflict with the goals of the other party (Underdal, 1991, pp. 107–108; Lewicki and Litterer, 1985, p. 76). The parties see the matter under contention in zero-sum terms. The amount of resource available is limited and one party's gain is the other party's loss.

Functionalism, represents another stream of thinkers within the international relations discipline. Functionalists object to the above contention regarding the effects of a protracted conflict on the negotiation process and argue that parties to a given conflict can, and should, utilize a specific issue that binds them together so as to build trust on other more complex issues. The argument is that cooperation on transnational issues, such as trade and environment, will spill-over to other more difficult issues (Mitrany, 1975, pp. x, xviii, 255–256, 261). In applying this same thinking to water issues, given that all parties are dependent on the same water source and must share it in a mutually beneficial and fair manner, cooperation on the water issue could not only be easier to achieve, than other more political and protracted issues, but also may form the basis for trust and cooperation on more difficult issues (Carius *et al.*, 2004, p. 1). Since the resolution of transnational issues and problems often requires cooperation and coordination among the parties, an integrative outlook vis-à-vis the issue is advanced. With an integrative orientation at hand, both parties have an interest in employing negotiation tactics that will provide them with positive results. This attitude stems from an attempt to emphasize the commonalities between the parties and interdependencies of the parties in terms of one another (Lewicki and Litterer, 1985, p. 108; Hopmann, 1996, p. 60).

Domestic politics may also explain the inclination for conflict or cooperation. Stemming from the liberal school of the international relations discipline, the argument is that states represent some subset of domestic society, on the basis of whose interests state officials define state preferences and act purposively in world politics (Moravcsik, 1997, p. 518). In short, shifting and differing interests of domestic elements reflect how states formulate their initial position regarding a given issue (Iklé, 1964, p. 122; Hopmann, 1996, p. 155; Putnam, 1998, p. 434; Gourevitch, 1978, p. 911). Therefore, if a set number of interest groups are able to influence and manipulate government policy, their interest will be the one articulated by the government, at least initially.

Applying this line of thinking to water issues, Frey has argued that: "a nation's goals in transnational water relations are usually the result of internal power processes, which may produce a set of goals that does not display the coherence, transitivity or "rationality" assumed in many analyses of transparent national interest" (1993, p. 63). Elhance has also argued that **domestic politics** has a robust effect on water issues between river riparians. Because water is considered a national security concern in some reaches of the world, it is understandable how a natural resource may be embroiled in nationalistic and identity issues, such as in the case of the Ganges–Brahmaputra–Meghna River Basin (Box 7.2).

Box 7.2: Water, domestic politics and national security in the
Ganges–Brahmaputra–Meghna River Basin

The nexus among water, domestic politics and national security is especially
salient between Hindu India and Islamic Bangladesh along the Ganges. Despite
recent democratization, Bangladesh remains vulnerable to Islamic fundamental-
ism and other domestic political factions that accuse their government of compromising the nation's sovereignty and national interest if they pursue negotiations
with India. Such posturing often curtails cooperation and undercuts the would-
be benefits (Elhance, 1999, pp. 169–171). Another example from Southern Asia is
that of Nepal–India **hydropolitics**. In the future, the parties may seek to transcend their limited agreements for exploiting their shared waters. Nonetheless, a
sector of Nepalese society regards some of the water agreements, already negotiated with India, as providing that country with great benefits at the expense
of Nepal. As such, desires for pursuing additional cooperation with India have
been tainted with domestic skepticism that has culminated in the incorporation
of a clause in the country's constitution which requires any treaty pertaining
to the exploitation of Nepal's natural resources to be ratified by the National
Assembly with a two-thirds majority (Verghese, 1996, pp. 39–40; Shrestha and
Singh, 1996, p. 87; Gyawali, 2000, p. 140). Future cooperation among the parties
will, therefore, be subject to strong domestic scrutiny and final approval.

The above discussion seems to support a general claim that domestic political support for hydropolitical cooperation is often hard to generate and sustain
(Elhance, 1999, p. 237). However, the large number of cooperative instances over
transboundary rivers, combined with the importance of domestic factors in explaining conflict and cooperation, suggest that domestic support also plays a positive
role in facilitating cooperation.

One such example is the dispute between the United States and Mexico over the
Colorado River salinity problem. In the early 1960s, Mexico protested to the United
States that water it was entitled to under a previous agreement was highly saline.
Despite the negotiation of interim solutions, the United States and Mexico agreed
to a definitive solution in 1973. Essentially, the United States would construct a
desalting plant that would deliver less saline water to Mexico. Interestingly, the
solution was shaped to a large part by **domestic politics** and influences. The
desalting plant built in the United States was not one of the cheaper alternatives
that could have been used to improve the water quality going into Mexico. However,
the desalting plant, funded by the federal government, not only satisfied the desires
of all the Colorado River riparians within the US, but also the concerned government
offices and departments. As LeMarquand has argued:

> ... *the basin-wide salinity control program satisfied the Environment Protec-
> tion Agency (EPA) by making its standards more politically acceptable; the
> Bureau of Reclamation. . . has found new opportunities to employ its talents*

*in salinity control; the Department of the Interior now has the opportunity
for the first time to implement the expertise and technological advances
developed by its office of Saline Waters in a grand showpiece desalting plant;
the lower basin states gain some assurances of a slower rate of increase in
salinity concentration; the upper basin states will not have future water
resource development curtailed.* (1977, p. 44).

International Water Law

Conflict over water also takes place because property rights are not clearly defined
and this is largely due to vague legal principles. While the history of **international
water law** has already been considered in Chapter 3, the following discussion shall
only briefly discuss some of the major merits and faults of the most recent legal
document, the 1997 Convention on the Law of the Nonnavigational Uses of International Watercourses. Such attributes may either instigate conflict or facilitate
cooperation.

The Convention, which was adopted by the UN General Assembly, provides
a general framework agreement containing numerous articles developed for use by
states in resolving their common water disputes. However, as of October 2006,
only 14 out of the 35 countries needed for the Convention to enter into force have
ratified, accepted, approved or acceded to it. The deadline for signatures has long
since passed.

Despite the Convention's uncertain status, three of its Articles in particular
should be noted. The principle of *equitable and reasonable utilization*, Article 5, was
an attempt to foster a compromise between two notable and opposed principles:
absolute territorial sovereignty and *absolute territorial integrity*. The former extreme
principle states that an upstream state can essentially do what it wants regardless
of harm to the downstream state. Conversely, the latter principle states that the
downstream state has a right not to be harmed by the upstream riparian. The
principle of *equitable and reasonable utilization* establishes that a state both has a
right to utilize its waters in an equitable and reasonable manner and, at the same
time, the duty to cooperate in the river's protection and development. In other
words, a state has a right to an equitable and reasonable share in the beneficial uses
of the waters of the basin, yet that state should not use these waters in such a way
as to unreasonably interfere with the legitimate interests of other states (Bilder,
1976, p. 18).

Article 6 provides a nonexhaustive list of how equitable utilization may be
determined. The list includes factors such as "effects of the use or uses of the
watercourses in one state on other watercourse states," as well as such factors as
"existing and potential uses of the watercourse." These factors are also equal to one
another in significance. That is, no factor has priority over another.

Article 5 is balanced by Article 7, which imposes an *obligation not to cause
significant harm*. According to Article 7, states are obliged to undertake all necessary measures to ensure that their utilization of a shared watercourse does not
significantly harm another riparian state. Despite the seeming balance between

Articles 5 and 7, international scholars have argued that Article 5 takes precedence over Article 7, even subsumes it in its broad principles of *equitable* and *reasonable* utilization (Dellapenna, 2001, p. 285; McCaffrey, 2001, pp. 308–310 and 370–371).

In short, the Convention has attempted to do a lot for states in helping them resolve their water disputes. It has aspired to strike a compromise between extreme principles. It has made these two compromise principles — which incidentally have characterized contenting claims between upstream and downstream states — the corner stone of its legal agenda. Finally, legal scholars responsible for drafting the Convention have even gone farther and suggested that one article takes precedence over another.

Despite such feats, the Convention has stirred much controversy between states. The precedence Article 5 takes over Article 7, for example, has been of no consequence to states. The emphasis only suggests increased support for reconciling the various interests of river basin states in the development of their shared waters (Wouters, 1997, p. xxiv). It does not say which state has the property right or which use by one state subordinates a different use by another state.

To be fair, **international water law** does not attempt to provide countries with specific guidelines for dispute resolution. Rather it attempts to codify customary law in the most general terms. As an umbrella agreement, it does not pretend to replace individual agreements negotiated between countries over specific disputes. In a way, once countries agree to a specific formula, codified in an international water agreement, they have agreed on the compromise principle of *equitable and reasonable utilization*. As such, it is through existing agreements that we may better detect how states go about reconciling conflicting interests in developing water resources or solving transboundary pollution problems. Property rights are essentially negotiated, and water treaty observations have made clear the ability of states to develop systems of property rights and liability rules in the absence of an overarching international body. The next section will focus on these treaty observations and consider some of the strategies and tactics states may use to turn conflict and deadlock into a negotiated venture.

For Further Discussion. What other variables may help explain conflict and cooperation over transboundary water? How might they interact with other explanatory elements to provide a clear assessment of the hydropolitical dimensions of a given case(s)?

NEGOTIATING AGREEMENTS: TURNING CONFLICT INTO COOPERATION

When considering tactics and strategies used for making cooperation come about, neoliberal institutionalists have much to say. According to neoliberal institutionalists, states are motivated by absolute gains rather than relative gains, as **neorealists** contend. According to this view, states pursue self-interested goals and are not concerned with what the other party is gaining (Axelrod, 1984, p. 14; Lipson, 1984, pp. 2 and 5; Stein, 1990, p. 46). However, while mutual interest to cooperate may exist (such as **scarcity**), cooperation is not certain. Setting aside the other variables for explaining conflict and cooperation discussed in the previous section, neoliberal institutionalists claim that cooperation may be curtailed and mitigated due to a general fear of cheating. In other words, states mistrust one another to honor a cooperative agreement. As their name suggests, neoliberal institutionalists believe that through institutional arrangements, such as agreements or treaties, states can overcome such cheating and mistrust. Institutions provide information, lower transaction costs, increase transparency between the parties, and reduce uncertainty (Keohane, 1982, p. 338; Oye, 1986, pp. 20–22; Keohane, 1989, pp. 2, 4 and 14; Keohane and Martin, 1995, p. 42; Stein, 1983, p. 123).

At the same time, the pay-off structure of the parties interested in cooperation may need to be altered to facilitate cooperation. As Barrett has argued, regimes must be self-enforcing so that no party to the cooperative agreement may gain by withdrawing and so that no party may gain by not complying. Finally, regimes must also be considered fair and legitimate. In short, a successful regime must be self-enforcing and should have the effect of restructuring the incentives of the parties in order to conform their behavior to the tenets of the institutional arrangement (Barrett, 2003, pp. xii–xiv).

Recall the discussion in the previous section on the **geographical configuration** of a river and the relative power an individual state may boast in the context of conflict over transboundary rivers. Though upstream states may obviously be in a position not to cooperate, they do not always exploit their strategic location on a river or their aggregate power to the detriment of the downstream state. Nor are powerful downstream states more inclined to dictate a given water regime with a weaker upstream state according to that state's sole desires. Rather cooperation can come about relatively effectively and efficiently as incentives to cooperate are altered and created.

Foreign Policy Considerations and Linkage

Cooperation is facilitated by foreign policy and **linkage** considerations. The Colorado River salinity issue, mentioned earlier, can best illustrate this point. The United States is at the same time the hegemonic and the upstream state, and should have had no immediate economic incentive to cooperate with Mexico or come to an agreement over the polluted waters entering Mexico. Contrary to the predictions of Lowi's (1993) argument, however, the United States not only entered into an agreement with Mexico but also paid the lofty costs of desalinating the waters of the Colorado that flow into the territory of its southern neighbor. However, not only did the United States not want to be considered a belligerent bully by its southern neighbor, and the rest of Latin America, by rejecting cooperation, but also considered cooperation on the water issue a form of gaining cooperation and support on other fronts (LeMarquand, 1977, p. 46).

For one, the United States did not want to taint its regional and international image — a foreign policy consideration. Second, the United States believed that cooperation on water issues with Mexico would allow it to "cash in" such goodwill on other matters (such as immigration and drug trafficking) at a later point in time — **linkage**.

Reciprocity

Considerations of **reciprocity** may also dampen a country's desire to utilize its geographical position to act strategically. Countries that share more than one river may be upstream on some rivers yet downstream on others. As such, countries may not wish to exploit their strategic location on the first river to the detriment of the other state, setting precedent for the other state to act in the same manner on the second river where it is more strategically located. Utton (1988) has argued that although the Colorado River may flow from the United States into Mexico, several rivers flow from Mexico north to the United States, and the United States requires Mexico's help in maintaining their water quality.

A nation may follow a similar strategy when it shares several rivers, each with a different neighbor. It will not want its strategic behavior on one river, shared with one country, to affect its hydropolitical relations with another country on a different river. This has often been Syria's dilemma relative to the Yarmouk and the Euphrates Rivers. On the Yarmouk/Jordan River Basin, Syria is upstream of Jordan and Israel while on the Euphrates it is downstream of Turkey. Any strategic behavior employed on the Yarmouk could weaken its position with Turkey on the more important Euphrates River (Elhance, 1999, pp. 106 and 145).

Third-Parties

Third-parties such as super-powers or large states (Zartman and Touval, 1996), small states, international organizations, nongovernmental organizations (Wapner, 1995; Weinthal, 2002; Raustiala, 1997; Litfin, 1997), **epistemic communities** (Haas, 1989; Haas, 1990, p. 55; Haas, 1992) and individuals also play an instrumental role in facilitating cooperation and international agreements. Each of the above players can facilitate cooperation in a different manner. Each has their particular strengths and weaknesses. For example, super-powers or large states may be able to engage in arm-twisting, compelling the parties to a cooperative solution. Super-powers and large states may also be able to provide lucrative incentives to parties. Nongovernmental organizations (NGOs) and even small states may not have the resources to do so.

While state actors play an important role as third-party mediators, this section focuses only on nonstate actors, specifically international organizations, NGOs and **epistemic communities**. Such actors are often needed to overcome the many barriers to interstate cooperation in **hydropolitics** and to persuade and enable the respective states to view cooperation as a win–win situation for all concerned (Elhance, 1999, p. 7). These organizations often build consensus, define the negotiating agenda, and create a problem-solving atmosphere (Hopmann, 1996, pp. 234–235; Litfin, 1997, p. 192; Rubin, 1993; Aall, 1996; Young, 1993, pp. 432–433; Victor *et al.* 1993, p. 471). They may also provide financial assistance that might make an agreement more attractive by changing the payoffs for cooperation. The UNDP, in the Mekong River negotiations, and especially the World Bank, in the Indus River negotiations, for example, played instrumental roles in facilitating cooperation between the parties and financially contributing to large projects necessary to make the cooperative agreement work (Radosevich, 1996; Browder, 2000; Pitman, 2000; Alam, 2002).

To understand how transnational organizations, and specifically **epistemic communities**, are able to foster cooperation, it is necessary to look beyond their technical efforts, financial assistance, and even institutional role by considering their *constructivist* functions. According to **constructivist** scholars of international relations, **epistemic communities** are professional and knowledge-based groups that believe in the same cause and effect relationships, test truths to assess them, and share common values and a common interpretive framework (Haas, 1992, p. 3). **Constructivists** argue that world politics is socially constructed. That is, normative and collective understandings have consequences for the physical and social worlds. This involves two basic claims. Namely, that the fundamental structures of international politics are social rather than strictly material, and that these structures shape the actors' identities and interests rather than just their behavior (Wendt, 1995, pp. 71–72). **Constructivists** subscribe to the view that the manner in which the material world shapes and is shaped by human action and interaction depends on dynamic, normative, and epistemic interpretations of the material world.

Since knowledge-based networks, such as **epistemic communities**, are often consulted on technical issues that require expertise that regular politicians and diplomats do not have, they are able to affect policy with their authority. **Epistemic communities**, the theory goes, are able to exert influence on policy innovation, policy diffusion, policy selection, and policy persistence (Adler and Haas, 1992, pp. 375–385). By so doing, they play a role in creating norms, social realities, and perceptions among the policymakers. In turn, nation states will exert power on behalf of the values and practices promoted by **epistemic communities** and will thus help in their international institutionalization (Adler and Haas, 1992, p. 372).

That being said, the influence of **epistemic communities** in fostering cooperation or swaying governments is often subject to the political will and interest of those governments and the domestic support they are able to muster for their ideas. In fact, the political will of governments to cooperate, and the gains they anticipate from cooperation, is an essential component of agreements, often overshadowing the role of expert groups or transnational organizations. However, ideas fostered by **epistemic communities** are often important in shaping agreements and negotiating agendas, especially regarding issues where experts are required to negotiate a particular matter.

While the political tensions on the ground have made negotiating a final peace agreement between Israelis and Palestinians quite difficult, and has consequently also affected a final deal on the water dispute, Israeli and Palestinian water experts and scientists have been heavily involved in shaping a future water agreement between the two sides. While some specifics remain to be concluded, a general agreement exists. Naturally, the larger political atmosphere will have to improve for such an agreement to materialize (Dinar, 2004, pp. 197–198, 224–225).

CONCLUDING REMARKS

According to Elhance (1999, p. 3), **hydropolitics** is the systematic study of conflict and cooperation between states over water resources that transcend international borders. Indeed, the international and transborder characteristics of shared water bodies make them a compelling test case for the analysis of conflict and cooperation. River riparians are physically interdependent because water bodies respect no political borders. Such a relationship promotes not only sensitivities between riparians but also vulnerabilities. But just as shared water resources may be a source of conflict, it is often conflict that provides the impetus for cooperation. Thus, while the sensationalist appeal of the "water wars" thesis still dominates the popular press, the reality of **hydropolitics** is different. While disputes over utilizing the water of a shared river for hydropower, flood control, and water consumption have been common, cooperation has usually followed.

The purpose of this chapter was fourfold: (1) debunk the "water wars" thesis, (2) affirm the history of cooperation that **hydropolitics** exemplifies, (3) investigate some of the main variables that explicate conflict and cooperation, and (4) consider a variety of tactics and strategies that make an international water agreement possible. Considering the main elements that drive conflict, cooperation, and negotiation over transboundary rivers provides the analyst not only with a better understanding of **hydropolitics** but also with some prescription for tackling ongoing conflict in any given river basin. Most importantly, however, understanding the intricacies of conflict and cooperation may be most instrumental in river basins where existing or future water disputes may aggravate the overall political environment.

Practice Questions

1. What is **hydropolitics?**
2. What can the history of **hydropolitics** tell us about the speculation that the next war will be about water?
3. In general, why is shared transboundary water not only a source of conflict but also a source of cooperation?
4. Taking some of the specific variables discussed (**scarcity**, geography, relative power, etc.) explain how each may contribute to both conflict and cooperation.

5. In negotiations of international agreements, what are some of the incentives and tactics that can be used to bring about cooperation?
6. How may third-parties help in fostering negotiation and cooperation?

REFERENCES

Aall, P. (1996). Nongovernmental organizations and peacemaking. In: Crocker, C., F.O. Hampson and P. Aall (eds.), *Managing Global Chaos: Sources of and Responses to International Conflict.* Washington, DC: United States Institute of Peace Press.

Adler, E. and P. Haas (1992). Conclusion: Epistemic communities, world order, and the creation of a reflective research program. In: Haas, P. (Guest Editor) Special Issue: Knowledge, Power, and International Policy Coordination, *International Organization*, 46(1).

Allan, A. (1998). Watersheds and problemsheds: Explaining the absence of armed conflict over water in the Middle East, *Middle East Review of International Affairs*, 2(1).

Alam, U. (2002). Questioning the water wars rationale: A case study of the Indus Waters Treaty. In: Uitto, J. and A. Wolf (Guest Editors), Special Issue: Water Wars? Geographical Perspectives, *The Geographical Journal*, 168(4).

Amery, H. and A. Wolf (2000). Water, geography and peace in the Middle East: An introduction. In: Amery, H. and A. Wolf (eds.), *Water in the Middle East: A Geography of Peace.* Austin: University of Texas Press.

Axelrod, R. (1984). *The Evolution of Cooperation.* New York: Basic Books.

Barrett, S. (2003). *Environment and Statecraft: The Strategy of Environmental Treaty-Making.* Oxford: Oxford University Press.

Bilder, R. (1976). The settlement of international environmental disputes, University of Wisconsin Sea Grant College Program, Technical Report No. 231.

Brock, L. (1992). Security through defending the environment: An illusion? In: Boulding, E. (ed.), *New Agendas for Peace Research: Conflict and Security Reexamined.* Boulder: Lynne Rienner.

Browder, G. (2000). An analysis of the negotiations for the 1995 Mekong Agreement. In: Dinar, S. and A. Dinar (Guest Editors), Special Issue: Negotiating in International Watercourses: Water Diplomacy, Conflict and Cooperation, *International Negotiation*, 5(2).

Bulloch, J. and A. Darwish (1993). *Water Wars: Coming Conflicts in the Middle East.* London: Victor Gollancz.

Carius, A., G. Dabelko and A. Wolf (2004). Water, conflict, and cooperation, *Policy Briefing Paper for United Nations & Global Security Initiative*, United Nations Foundation.

Choucri, N. and R. North (1975). *Nations in Conflict: National Growth and International Violence.* San Francisco: W.H. Freeman and Company.

Cooley, J. (1984). The war over water, *Foreign Policy*, 54.

Crosette, B. (1995). Severe water crisis ahead for poorest nations in the next two decades, *The New York Times*, 10 August, Section 1, p. 13.

Dellapenna, J. (2001). The customary international law of trans-boundary fresh waters, *International Journal of Global Environmental Issues*, 1 (3 and 4).

Deudney, D. (1991). Environment and security: Muddled thinking, *Bulletin of Atomic Scientists*, 47(3).

Dinar, S. (2004). Environmental preventive diplomacy, international relations, conflict resolution, and international water law: Implications for success and failure of the Israeli Palestinian water conflict, *International Journal of Global Environmental Issues*, 3(2).

Dinar, S. (2006). Assessing side-payment and cost-sharing patterns in international water agreements: The geographic and economic connection, *Political Geography*, 25(4).

Dinar, S. (2007). *International Water Treaties: Negotiation and Cooperation Along Transboundary Rivers*. London: Routledge.

Dokken, K. (1997). Environmental conflict and international integration. In: Gleditsch, N.P. (ed.), *Conflict and the Environment*. Dordrecht: Kluwer Academic Publishers.

Elhance, A. (1999). *Hydro-Politics in the 3rd World: Conflict and Cooperation in International River Basins*. Washington, DC: United States Institute of Peace Press.

Falkenmark, M. (1986). Fresh water: Time for a modified approach, *Ambio*, 15(4).

Falkenmark, M. (1986b). Fresh waters as a factor in strategic policy and action. In: Westing, A. (ed.), *Global Resources and International Conflict: Environmental Action in Strategic Policy and Option*. Oxford and New York: Oxford University Press.

Falkenmark, M. (1992). Water scarcity generates environmental stress and potential conflicts. In: James, W. and J. Niemczynowicz (eds.), *Water, Development, and the Environment*. Boca Raton: Lewis Publishers.

Falkenmark, M. (1990). Global water issues confronting humanity, *Journal of Peace Research*, 27(2).

Ferguson, Y. and R. Mansbach (1988). *The Elusive Quest: Theory and International Politics*. Columbia: University of South Carolina Press.

Food and Agriculture Organization (1978 and 1984). *Systematic Index of International Water Resources, Treaties, Declarations, and Cases by Basin*. Rome.

Food and Agriculture Organization. *WATERLEX*; http://faolex.fao.org/waterlex/. Last visited on June 2002.

Frey, F. (1993). The political context of conflict and cooperation over international river basins, *Water International*, 18(1).

Frey, F. and T. Naff (1985). Water: An emerging issue in the Middle East. In: Naff, T. and M. Wolfgang (Guest Editors), Special Issue: Changing Patterns of Power in the Middle East, *The Annals of the American Academy of Political and Social Science*, 482.

Gilpin, R. (1975). *US Power and the Multinational Corporation: The Political Economy of Foreign Direct Investment*. New York: Basic Books.

Gleick, P. (1993). Water and conflict: Fresh water resources and international security, *International Security*, 18(1).

Gleick, P. (1998). *The World's Water: 1998–1999*. Washington, DC: Island Press.

Gottman, J. (1951). Geography and international relations, *World Politics*, 3(2).

Gourevitch, P. (1978). The second image reversed: The international sources of domestic politics, *International Organization*, 32(4).

Grieco, J. (1990). *Cooperation Among Nations: Europe, America, and Non-Tarrif Barriers to Trade*. Ithaca, NY: Cornell University Press.

Gyawali, D. (2000). Nepali-India water resource relations. In: Zartman, W. and J. Rubin (eds.), *Power and Negotiation*. Ann Arbor: The University of Michigan Press.

Haas, P. (1989). Do regimes matter? Epistemic communities and mediterranean pollution control, *International Organization*, 43(3).

Haas, P. (1990). *Saving the Mediterranean: The Politics of International Environmental Cooperation.* New York: Columbia University Press.

Haas, P. (1992). Introduction: Epistemic communities and international policy coordination. In: Haas, P. (Guest Editor), Special Issue: Knowledge, Power, and International Policy Coordination, *International Organization,* 46(1).

Hollis, M. and S. Smith (1991). *Explaining and Understanding International Relations.* Oxford: Clarendon Press.

Homer-Dixon, T. (1991). *Environment, Scarcity, and Violence.* Princeton: Princeton University Press.

Hopmann, T. (1996). *The Negotiation Process and the Resolution of International Conflicts,* South Carolina: University of South Carolina Press.

Iklé, F. (1964). *How Nations Negotiate.* New York: Harper and Row.

Just, R. and S. Netanyahu (1998). International water resource conflicts: Experience and potential. In: Just, R. and S. Netanyahu (eds.), *Conflict and Cooperation on Trans-Boundary Water Resources.* Boston: Kluwer Academic Publishers.

Keohane, R. (1982). The demand for international regimes, *International Organization,* 36(2).

Keohane, R. and L. Martin (1995). The promise of institutionalist theory, *International Security,* 20(1).

Keohane, R. (1989). *International Institutions and State Power: Essays in International Relations Theory.* Boulder: Westview Press.

Kratz, S. (1996). International conflict over water resources: A syndrome approach, *Wissenschaftszentrum Berlin Fur Sozialforschung (WZB),* FS II 96-401.

LeMarquand, D. (1977). *International Rivers: The Politics of Cooperation.* Vancouver: Westwater Research Center.

Lewicki, R. and J. Litterer (1985). *Negotiation.* Homewood: Irwin.

Litfin, K. (1997). Sovereignty in world politics, *Mershon International Studies Review,* 41(2).

Lipson, C. (1984). International cooperation in economic and security affairs, *World Politics,* 37(1).

Lowi, M. (1993). *Water and Power: The Politics of a Scarce Resource in the Jordan River Basin.* Cambridge: Cambridge University Press.

Mathews, J. (1989). Redefining security, *Foreign Affairs,* 68(2).

McCaffrey, S. (2001). *The Law of International Watercourses: Non-Navigational Uses.* Oxford: Oxford University Press.

Mitrany, D. (1975). *The Functional Theory of Politics.* New York: St. Martin's Press.

Morgenthau, H. (1948). *Politics Among Nations: The Struggle for Power and Peace.* New York: Knopf.

Moravcsik, A. (1997). Taking preferences seriously: A liberal theory of international politics, *International Organization,* 51(4).

Myers, N. (1993). *Ultimate Security: The Environmental Basis of Political Stability.* New York: W.W. Norton & Company.

Naff, T. (1994). Conflict and water use in the Middle East. In: Rogers, P. and P. Lydon (eds.), *Water in the Arab World: Perspectives and Prognoses.* Cambridge: Harvard University Press.

Ohlsson, L. and A. Turton (2006). The turning of a screw. Paper Presented in the Plenary Session of the 9th Stockholm Water Symposium *Urban Stability through Integrated Water-Related Management,* hosted on 9–12 August by the Stockholm International Water Institute (SIWI) in Sweden. Also available as MEWREW Occasional Paper

No. 19; http://www.soas.ac.uk/waterissues/occasionalpapers/OCC19.PDF. Last visited on August 2006.

Oregon State University. *International Freshwater Treaties Database*; http://www.transboundarywaters.orst.edu/projects/internationalDB.html. Last visited on May 2004.

Oye, K. (1986). Explaining cooperation under anarchy: Hypotheses and strategies. In: Oye, K. (ed.), *Cooperation Under Anarchy*. Princeton, NJ: Princeton University Press.

Pitman, K. (2000). The role of the World Bank in enhancing cooperation and resolving conflict on international watercourses: The case of the Indus Basin. In: Salman, S. and L. Boisson de Chazournes (eds.), *International Watercourses: Enhancing Cooperation and Managing Conflict*. Proceedings of a World Bank Seminar, World Bank Technical Paper, No. 414.

Powell, R. (1991). Absolute and relative gains in international relations theory, *American Political Science Review*, 84(4).

Putnam, R. (1998). Diplomacy and domestic politics: The logic of two level games, *International Organization*, 42(3).

Radosevich, G. (1996). The Mekong — A new framework for development and management. In: Biswas, A. and T. Hashimoto (eds.), *Asian International Waters: From Ganges-Brahmaputra to Mekong*. Bombay: Oxford University Press.

Raustiala, K. (1997). States, NGOs and international environmental institutions, *International Studies Quarterly*, 41(4).

Rubin, J. (1993). Third party roles: Mediation in international environmental disputes. In: Sjöstedt, G. (ed.), *International Environmental Negotiation*. Newbury Park: Sage Publications.

Samson, P. and B. Charrier (1997). *International Freshwater Conflict: Issues and Prevention Strategies*. Geneva: Green Cross International.

Shrestha, H.M. and L.M. Singh (1996). The Ganges-Brahmaputra system: A nepalese perspective in the context of regional cooperation. In: Biswas, A. and T. Hashimoto (eds.), *Asian International Waters: From Ganges-Brahmaputra to Mekong*. Bombay: Oxford University Press.

Snidal, D. (1991). Relative gains and the pattern of international cooperation, *American Political Science Review*, 85(3).

Starr, J. (1991). Water wars, *Foreign Policy*, 82.

Stein, A. (1983). Coordination and collaboration: Regimes in an anarchic world. In: Krasner, S. (ed.), *International Regimes*. Ithaca: Cornell University Press.

Stein, A. (1990). *Why Nations Cooperate: Circumstances and Choice in International Relations*. Ithaca: Cornell University Press.

Stein, J.G. (1996). Image, identity, and conflict resolution. In: Crocker, C., F.O. Hampson and P. Aall (eds.), *Managing Global Chaos: Sources of and Responses to International Conflict*. Washington, DC: United States Institute of Peace Press.

Toset, H.P.W., N.P. Gleditsch and H. Hegre (2000). Shared rivers and interstate conflict, *Political Geography*, 19(8).

Underdal, A. (1991). The outcomes of negotiation. In: Kremenyuk, V. (ed.), *International Negotiation: Analysis, Approaches, Issues*. San Francisco: Jossey-Bass.

United Nations, United Nations Treaty Collection; http://untreaty.un.org/

Utton, A. (1988). Problems and successes of international water agreements: The example of the United States and Mexico. In: Carroll, J. (ed.), *International Environmental Diplomacy*. Cambridge: Cambridge University Press.

Verghese, B.G. (1996). Towards an eastern Himalayan rivers concord. In: Biswas, A. and T. Hashimoto (eds.), *Asian International Waters: From Ganges-Brahmaputra to Mekong*. Bombay: Oxford University Press.

Victor, D., A. Chayes and E. Skolnikoff (1993). Pragmatic approaches to regime building for complex international problems. In: Choucri, N. (ed.), *Global Accord: Environmental Challenges and International Responses*. Cambridge: The MIT Press.

Waltz, K. (1979). *Theory of International Politics*. Reading, MA: Addision-Wesley.

Wapner, P. (1995). Politics beyond the state: Activism in world civic politics, *World Politics*, 47(3).

Weinthal, E. (2002). *State Making and Environmental Cooperation: Linking Domestic and International Politics in Central Asia*. Cambridge: The MIT Press.

Wendt, A. (1995). Constructing international politics, *International Security*, 20(1).

Wolf, A. and J. Hamner (2000). Trends in trans-boundary water disputes and dispute resolution. In: *Water for Peace in the Middle East and Southern Africa*. Geneva: Green Cross International.

Wouters, P. (ed.) (1997). *International Water Law: Selected Writings of Professor Charles B. Bourne*. London: Kluwer Law International.

Young, O. (1993). Negotiating an international climate regime: The institutional bargaining for environmental governance. In: Choucri, N. (ed.), *Global Accord: Environmental Challenges and International Responses*. Cambridge: The MIT Press.

Zartman, W. and S. Touval (1996). International mediation in the post-cold war era. In: Crocker, C., F.O. Hampson and P. Aall (eds.), *Managing Global Chaos: Sources of and Responses to International Conflict*. Washington, DC: United States Institute of Peace Press.

8. AN OVERVIEW OF SELECTED INTERNATIONAL WATER TREATIES IN THEIR GEOGRAPHIC AND POLITICAL CONTEXTS

Objectives

This chapter focuses on legal traits of treaties and the interaction between political and geographic context of the transboundary basins on the nature of the treaties signed between their riparians. You will have a clear understanding of what treaty is, what the treaty components are, and how states have used treaties to deal with allocation and management issues in a variety of political and geographical settings. You will also be familiarized with the post-treaty arrangements such as the frequently established joint commissions to facilitate states' cooperation with regard to shared freshwater resources, and the mechanisms that can be used to permit a treaty to evolve to suit changed conditions or unforeseen problems.

Main Terminology

Bilateral treaty; Contiguous watercourse; Framework agreement; Limitrophe section of a river; Multilateral treaty; Run-of-the-river hydroelectric power plant; Specific watercourse agreement; Successive watercourse; Treaty.

The **treaty** is a cornerstone of the relations between the countries of the world. It is an agreement between countries creating binding legal obligations. It would not be impossible for them to coexist without treaties but it would be difficult. Chapter 3 contains an overview of the international legal system. As we saw there, the two main sources of international law are treaties and customary international law. The present chapter focuses on treaties. It should be borne in mind, however, that even if a particular question is governed by a **treaty**, customary international law may still come into play in filling gaps in the **treaty** or providing rules for its interpretation. This has been true in virtually every case involving a watercourse agreement that has come before an international tribunal.

Treaties have long played an important role in stabilizing relations between states sharing international watercourses. As we saw in Chapter 3, what appears to be the earliest recorded **treaty** of any kind was an agreement concluded between the Mesopotamian city states of Umma and Lagash (today's Telloh) in 3100 B.C. following hostilities between them over Euphrates waters (McCaffrey, 2001). Today, there are well over 400 agreements concerning shared freshwater resources. These treaties are as varied as the watercourses they deal with and the reasons that motivated the states parties to enter into them. Treaties may be **multilateral** (more than two parties) or **bilateral** (two parties). The majority of freshwater treaties are probably **bilateral** but again, much depends on the factual setting and the subject matter of the agreement in question.

Freshwater treaties may be further classified as being either **framework agreements** or **specific watercourse agreements**. As their name implies, **framework agreements** provide a general structure for states to follow in concluding treaties concerning specific watercourses. They typically include principles and obligations of a general character that may be applied and adjusted by countries formulating specific agreements. Examples of **framework agreements** relating to shared freshwater are the 1997 United Nations Convention on the Law of the Non-navigational Uses of International Watercourses (UN Convention, 1997); the 2000 Revised Protocol on Shared Watercourses in the Southern African Development Community (SADC) (SADC Revised Protocol, 2000); and the 1992 Helsinki Convention on the Protection and Use of Transboundary Watercourses and International Lakes (Helsinki Convention, 1992). **Specific watercourse agreements** are treaties relating to specific international watercourses. See also Chapters 3 and 7, Basin Case Studies 1–4, and Treaties Annex.

In considering freshwater agreements, the following analytical framework, which is really a series of questions, may be helpful:

1. How many parties are there to the **treaty**?
2. Does the **treaty** deal with one watercourse, with all that are shared between the parties, or some combination of these?
3. What is the subject matter of the **treaty** (e.g., allocation of water; prevention of pollution; navigation; establishment of a joint management mechanism; a number of different topics)?
4. What is the **treaty**'s object and purpose (this can sometimes be determined from the **treaty**'s preamble)?
5. How old is the **treaty**?
6. What were the historic and political contexts in which the **treaty** was concluded?
7. Does the **treaty** reflect, expressly or in effect, the principle of equitable and reasonable utilization?
8. Does the **treaty** reflect, expressly or in effect, the principle of the prevention of significant harm to other riparian states?

9. Does the **treaty** establish processes or mechanisms for the regular exchange of data and information relating to the watercourse, or otherwise provide for this?

10. Does the **treaty** require that a state planning new measures relating to an international watercourse provide notification of the plans to other riparian states that may be adversely affected by the planned measures?

11. Does the **treaty** contain provisions relating to the protection of water quality and the ecosystems of the international watercourse in question?

12. Does the **treaty** establish a joint management mechanism, or make use of one already formed by the parties, to assist with its implementation?

13. Does the **treaty** contain mechanisms to allow the parties to keep it up-to-date?

14. Is the **treaty**'s duration limited?

15. Does the **treaty** contain provisions for its termination?

16. Does the **treaty** contain a dispute resolution mechanism or mechanisms? If so, are they compulsory, in the sense that one party may invoke them without the separate consent of the other party? Is the result of the dispute settlement process binding on the parties?

These are general questions of necessity, but may be of use in focusing upon the salient features of a given freshwater **treaty**.

In this chapter, we will consider six examples of **specific watercourse agreements**. Each is very different from the others, which is not surprising since they relate to different watercourses, are designed to deal with different problems, and were concluded in different political contexts. Still, some of the treaties have common features. Try to identify these as you read through the descriptions that follow.

THE 1906 RIO GRANDE TREATY (MEXICO–UNITED STATES)

In Chapter 3, we saw that disputes between the United States and Mexico concerning the Rio Grande continue virtually up to the present day. In this section, we will consider a **treaty** that ended the first major dispute between the two countries involving that river. Some information will be repeated here for ease of reference.

The Rio Grande, called the Rio Bravo in Mexico, rises in the San Juan Mountains of southwestern Colorado, flows for some 645 miles through Colorado and New Mexico then, in the vicinity of El Paso, Texas and Ciudad Juárez, in the State of Chihuahua, Mexico, becomes the boundary between the United States and Mexico. From that point the course of the river stretches for some 1,000 miles to the Gulf of Mexico (official estimates of the length of this portion of the river vary depending on the method of measurement). In fact, the boundary portion of the river dwindles to a trickle until it is joined by its major tributary in the boundary stretch, the Rio Conchos. The latter stream rises in the Sierra Madre Occidental in Mexico and joins the Rio Grande just upstream of the sister cities of Ojinaga, Chihuahua, and

Presidio, Texas. Even with the contribution of the Rio Conchos, in some years Rio Grande waters fail to reach the Gulf of Mexico.

In the late 19th century, Mexico complained to the United States that diversions in Colorado and New Mexico were reducing the river to a dry bed by the time it reached Ciudad Juárez. The United States responded that this was probably due to a drought in the region and that in any event it could not stop private citizens from diverting water. (The diversions were probably a result of recently enacted U.S. legislation encouraging the settlement and development of arid lands in the West.) Moreover, in an opinion of the U.S. Attorney General, Judson Harmon, that has since become infamous as the "Harmon Doctrine," the United States at one point argued that because it was absolutely sovereign over the waters of the Rio Grande within its territory, it was free to use them however it wished regardless of the effects on Mexico (McCaffrey, 2001).

The dispute was resolved some 10 years after it came to a head, in the 1906 Convention concerning the Equitable Distribution of the Waters of the Rio Grande for Irrigation Purposes (Rio Grande, 1906). The **treaty**'s title alone shows how far the United States came from its position of absolute territorial sovereignty. However, in provisions of a kind that are sometimes found in treaties, the parties recite that in consideration of the delivery of water to Mexico described below, Mexico waives any claims to Rio Grande waters and declares fully settled past or existing claims; and that the United States by entering into the **treaty** does not concede any legal basis for Mexican claims or the establishment of any general principle or precedent (Rio Grande, 1906, Articles IV and V). (Does such a provision prevent the **treaty** from being taken into account as evidence of state practice?)

To even out the irregular flow of the Rio Grande, the United States agreed in the **treaty** to construct a storage dam near Engle, New Mexico, and to deliver to Mexico in the bed of the Rio Grande, at a point just above Juárez, 60,000 acre-feet (74 mcm) of water annually according to a monthly schedule (Rio Grande, 1906, Articles I and II). The **treaty** states expressly that it covers only the portion of the Rio Grande from the head works of the Acequia Madre, or the Old Mexican Canal, just above Ciudad Juárez, to Fort Quitman, Texas (Rio Grande, 1906, Article V), some 80 miles downstream of El Paso. The **treaty** discussed in the next section covers the portion from Fort Quitman to the Gulf of Mexico.

It should be underscored that the United States accepted some rather weighty obligations under this **treaty**. These include the construction and maintenance of a dam and reservoir in its territory, the obligation to deliver a certain annual quantity of water to Mexico according to a specific monthly schedule, and the assumption of all costs relating to these obligations (Rio Grande, 1906, Article III). The United States obviously considered it to be in its interest to accept these obligations, even though it had earlier made statements in diplomatic exchanges with Mexico denying any obligation at all to allow water to flow to that country.

For Further Discussion. To what extent was the United States' willingness to enter into this agreement, and to construct the storage dam in New Mexico at its own expense, influenced by a desire to assist its own citizens as well as to address Mexico's complaint? Would the outcome have been different if the Rio Grande had not become a border river but had flowed entirely into Mexico?

THE 1944 TREATY CONCERNING THE RIO GRANDE AND THE COLORADO RIVER (MEXICO–UNITED STATES)

In 1938, negotiations — which had begun in the 1920s but had not borne fruit — resumed between the United States and Mexico concerning both the Lower Rio Grande and the Colorado River (Meyers, 1967). As to the Lower Rio Grande, the fact that the water in that portion of the river is largely provided by Mexican tributaries that enter the river below Fort Quitman necessitated the negotiation of an agreement on its apportionment since the 1906 **Treaty** did not deal with that issue. The United States wished to protect then existing uses while Mexico was more interested in securing the possibility of possible future uses. Mexico was of the view that uses on the U.S. side were "immoderate" and pointed out that it would eventually begin to make use of the water in the Mexican tributaries, which it said contributed three-fourths of the volume of the river (Meyers, 1967). Mexico insisted on including both the Rio Grande and the Colorado in the negotiations, believing that this would give it leverage it would not have — especially with respect to the Colorado River — if they were dealt with separately.

The outcome of the talks was the 1944 **Treaty** Relating to the Utilization of the Waters of the Colorado and Tijuana Rivers, and of the Rio Grande (Rio Bravo) from Fort Quitman, Texas, to the Gulf of Mexico (Rio Grande-Colorado, 1944). The agreement specifies the quantities of water each country is allocated from the relevant portion of the Rio Grande. For example, under the **treaty** the United States is to receive one-third of the flow reaching the Rio Grande from specified Mexican tributaries, provided that this is not to be less than 431,721,000 cubic meters annually "as an average amount in cycles of five consecutive years" (Rio Grande-Colorado, 1944, Article 4(B)(c)). (Mexico's recent failure to meet this average resulted in the "water debt" to the United States discussed in Chapter 3.) Mexico is allocated two-thirds of the flow of those tributaries, subject to the minimum amount just mentioned that must be received by the United States (Rio Grande-Colorado, 1944, Article 4(A)(c)). The **treaty** also assigns to each country the entire flow of certain of its tributaries and makes other provision for allocation of Rio Grande waters.

As to the Colorado River, except for a short stretch of some 20 miles in which it forms the boundary (the **"limitrophe"** section),[1] it is essentially a

---

[1]The section of a river that forms, or is situated on, a boundary between two states.

"**successive**" **international watercourse**, meaning that it flows successively from one country into another.[2] The river rises in Wyoming and Colorado and flows some 1,450 miles through the United States and Mexico before emptying into the Gulf of California (though today, like the Rio Grande, it barely reaches the sea). The great majority of the Colorado's basin is located in the United States; the river flows through Mexico for only around 100 miles. In the United States, the Colorado's basin drains seven western states: Arizona, California, Colorado, Nevada, New Mexico, Utah, and Wyoming. These states entered into a compact in 1922 apportioning the river's water among them. The 1944 Treaty "guaranteed" 1.5 million acre-feet of water per year for Mexico, which amounts to some 10% of the Colorado's average annual flow.

One of the serious difficulties faced by the U.S. states among themselves and as between the United States and Mexico is that because of a series of abnormally wet years preceding the conclusion of the Colorado River Compact in 1922, that agreement was based on an average flow of the river that was significantly overestimated. The interstate allocations under the compact assumed an average flow of 16.4 million acre-feet (maf) per year. It now appears more likely that the average flow is actually between 13 and 15 maf per year, although for the future even this figure is in some doubt due to the possible effects of climate change. Thus it may well be that the river's water has been over-allocated. Only the two immense storage reservoirs in the United States, Lake Mead (formed by the Hoover Dam) and Lake Powell (formed by the Glen Canyon Dam), have prevented serious shortages in lower basin states and in Mexico in times of drought (see generally NRC Study, 2007).

Article 2 of the 1944 **Treaty** renames and expands the functions of the International Boundary Commission that had been established by an 1889 **Treaty** between the two countries. The new body, the International Boundary and Water Commission, United States and Mexico (IBWC), continues to function today, overseeing the implementation of the 1944 **Treaty** as well as other boundary and water treaties between the U.S. and Mexico and settling disputes relating to those agreements. It is composed of a U.S. and a Mexican Section, each headed by an Engineer-Commissioner appointed by the president of the country concerned.

One of the disputes settled by the IBWC had to do with water quality. While the 1944 **Treaty** guarantees an annual quantity of water to Mexico, as indicated above, it says nothing about the quality of that water. When Arizona's Wellton-Mohawk Irrigation District began discharging saline water into the Colorado near the border with Mexico in 1961, Mexico complained that the resulting high salinity of Colorado River water made it unusable for irrigation — the chief use of the water in Mexico. The problem was resolved in 1973 in a "Minute" to the 1944 **Treaty** formulated by the IBWC.

---

[2]The other type, the **contiguous watercourse**, flows on or along a boundary and is thus "**contiguous**" to two states.

For Further Discussion. Why did the two countries not deal with the entire Rio Grande in the 1906 **Treaty**? Would it have been better if they had? Do you think Mexico struck a good bargain in the 1944 **Treaty**? Was it smart of Mexico to insist on including both the Rio Grande and the Colorado River in the negotiations? What lessons does the experience of the parties to the 1944 **Treaty** hold for riparian states in other international drainage basins? As we saw in Chapter 3, the 1944 **Treaty** allows the IBWC to adopt "Minutes," which become binding on the parties if not disapproved within 30 days. They are effectively amendments to the **Treaty**. This device permits the parties to adapt the agreement so that it is kept up-to-date and responds to current problems. This is not a feature of most freshwater treaties. Is the possibility of amending the **Treaty** through the adoption of "Minutes" something that should be considered for other international watercourses?

THE 1959 NILE WATERS AGREEMENT (EGYPT–SUDAN)

This is a **treaty** we have encountered already, in Chapter 3. To recall the Nile's basic characteristics briefly, it is considered the longest river in the world, flowing for over 4,000 miles from its sources around Lake Victoria to the Mediterranean. It drains one-tenth of the continent of Africa, its basin including all or part of 10 countries. Its two branches are the White Nile, flowing north from Lake Victoria, and the Blue Nile, which flows in a more westerly direction from its source in Lake Tana in the Ethiopian highlands to its confluence with the White Nile at Khartoum, Sudan. While the flow of the White Nile is slow and steady, that of the Blue Nile — which is twice as great — comes largely in a torrent in the months of July to September. Thus the famous Nile floods, upon which Egyptians have relied over the millennia for irrigation, originate chiefly in the Ethiopian highlands.

The Nile's irregular flow regime made storage of its waters desirable, leading Egypt to construct the original Aswan Dam in 1902. Designed and built by British contractors, this dam was raised twice but still did not prove equal to the task of containing the Nile's largest floods. Early British studies had concluded that Nile waters should ideally be stored in the upper portions of the basin to prevent enormous losses from evaporation in the lower basin, among other reasons. But given that it is entirely dependent upon the Nile for its water supply, Egypt's policy in the years following World War II, especially after the Nasser revolution in 1952, was that all important Nile works should be situated in Egypt. Accordingly it constructed the Aswan High Dam, some four miles upstream of the original and smaller dam, which was completed in 1970. The dam forms a reservoir with a storage capacity of some 157 km^3 of water which backs up into Sudan. The larger portion of the reservoir in Egypt is called Lake Nasser while Sudan refers to the section in that country as Lake Nubia.

As we saw in Chapter 3, Egypt and Britain, acting for Sudan, entered into a **treaty** in 1929 allocating portions of the Nile waters between them in a 12:1 ratio in favor of Egypt (Nile, 1929). But political changes in Sudan — including its independence in 1956 — and its expanding water needs led to pressure to revise the 1929 agreement. Protracted negotiations between the two countries eventually resulted in the 1959 Nile Waters Agreement (Nile, 1959). The full title of this **treaty** — Agreement for the Full Utilization of the Nile Waters — provides an apt description of its purpose and effect. The **treaty** recites that the parties' "established rights" consist of the quantities they were actually using as of the date of its conclusion: 48,000 mcm for Egypt and 4,000 mcm for Sudan (the 12:1 ratio referred to above). It then apportions the 32,000 mcm the 1929 **Treaty** did not allocate. The result was that from a total natural flow of 84,000 mcm per year, Egypt received 55,500 mcm and Sudan 18,500 mcm, a ratio of 3:1. The **treaty** also authorized construction of the Aswan High Dam (to "stop the flow of any excess [water] to the sea") and a dam on the Blue Nile in Sudan. Finally, the agreement established the Permanent Joint Technical Committee between the two states to coordinate its implementation.

> **For Further Discussion.** Should the eight upstream states have any reason to be concerned about an agreement between the two most downstream riparians allocating the full flow of the river between them? How might such an agreement harm upstream states, if at all? Is there anything they can do about it? The 10 Nile Basin states have been attempting for the better part of a decade to negotiate a new, basin-wide agreement on the use and management of the Nile River Basin. How should such an agreement take into account the 1959 **Treaty** between Egypt and Sudan?

THE 1960 INDUS WATERS TREATY (INDIA–PAKISTAN)

The Indus River rises in Tibet and flows for some 1,800 miles through India and Pakistan to the Arabian Sea. Conflict erupted over its use shortly after the partition of British India into India and Pakistan in 1947, which left a portion of the basin in each of the new dominions. East Punjab, now in India, cut off water flowing through canals to West Punjab in Pakistan, giving rise to a protest from the Prime Minister of Pakistan to his Indian counterpart. This and subsequent disputes led the World Bank to propose a comprehensive plan for the apportionment of Indus waters. After nearly 10 years of negotiations mediated by the Bank, India and Pakistan concluded the Indus Waters **Treaty** in 1960 (Indus, 1960).

The **treaty** is remarkable in that rather than apportioning the water in each of the six rivers in the Indus system as between the parties, it assigns the entire flow of three of the rivers to each of them. Thus, the **treaty** allocates the waters of the "Eastern Rivers" (the Sutlej, the Beas, and the Ravi) to India and those of the "Western Rivers" (the Indus, the Jhelum, and the Chenab) to Pakistan. This solution necessitated the construction of extensive engineering works to ensure that Pakistan, the downstream state, would receive water to replace that which it had formerly received from the Eastern Rivers. The Bank was able to arrange for the participation of other countries in the funding of the needed works. With specified exceptions, the **treaty** prohibits each party from interfering in any way with the rivers allocated to the other. Overall, the **treaty** is quite detailed, leaving very little margin for flexibility or interpretation. This, along with the method of apportioning Indus waters, was thought necessary to make up for the lack of trust between the parties.

The **treaty** establishes the Permanent Indus Commission, which consists of a Commissioner for Indus Waters appointed by each country. The **treaty** provides that the commissioners should ordinarily be high-ranking engineers competent in the field of hydrology. It also provides that "each Commissioner will be the representative of his Government for all matters arising out of this **Treaty**, and will serve as the regular channel of communication on all matters relating to the implementation of the **Treaty**" (Indus, 1960, Article VIII(1)). The two commissioners, who together form the Permanent Indus Commission, are to "meet regularly at least once a year, alternately in India and Pakistan" (Indus, 1960, Article VIII(5)).

For Further Discussion. Is this solution, of allocating entire rivers to one or another country, *sui generis*? Or can the Indus Waters **Treaty** serve as a model for other international watercourses? Does the Permanent Indus Commission correspond with your image of a river commission? Should it have its own premises and staff, as some such commissions do? Should it be required to meet more frequently than once a year?

In 2005, Pakistan invoked the dispute-settlement procedure under the Indus Waters **Treaty** (the first time either party has done so) in respect of a **run of the river hydroelectric dam** being constructed on the Chenab River by India about 100 km upstream from the border with Pakistan. (In essence, a **run of the river plant** operates on the natural flow of a stream without storing water.) The **treaty** permits the construction of this type of dam by India on rivers allocated to Pakistan so long as detailed specifications set forth in the **treaty** are complied with. The dispute involves whether the dam in fact complies with those specifications. Pursuant to the **treaty**, it was submitted to a "Neutral Expert," whom the **treaty** requires to be a "highly qualified engineer." Why do you suppose this method of dispute resolution was chosen? Why not confine dispute settlement procedures to the more conventional means of arbitration or adjudication? (Arbitration is also provided for in the **treaty**).

THE 1995 MEKONG AGREEMENT
(CAMBODIA–LAOS–THAILAND–VIETNAM)

The Mekong River rises in the Himalaya Mountains of Tibet and flows for some 4,500 km through China, Myanmar, Thailand, Cambodia, the Lao People's Democratic Republic (Lao PDR), and into Vietnam, where it empties into the South China Sea through a vast delta. Until recently, the Mekong has been relatively undeveloped, the population of its basin relying principally on fishing and agriculture for their food and livelihoods.

The four states of the Lower Basin, the Lao PDR, Thailand, Cambodia, and Vietnam, have a history of cooperation with regard to the river going back to the 1950s. Their well-known "Mekong Spirit" has prevailed and kept them meeting with each other despite numerous conflicts in the region. Yet they lacked a comprehensive agreement for the use, management, and sustainable development of the river. This came in 1995 with the signing of the Agreement on the Cooperation for the Sustainable Development of the Mekong River Basin (Mekong, 1995).

The agreement sets forth general principles governing the use and development of the river and establishes the Mekong River Commission (MRC) to assist with its implementation and further elaboration. The latter was necessary because of an interesting technique adopted by the four parties: instead of prolonging the negotiations until every last detail was settled, they locked in what they could agree upon in the 1995 **Treaty** then provided that further details regarding certain issues (e.g., procedures for notification, prior consultation, and agreement in respect of proposed uses) would be worked out in the context of the Commission established by the agreement.

The MRC is a robust institution, but relies largely upon external funding from the international donor community (international development banks and bilateral donors) for its support. A national of one of the donor countries, rather than one of the basin states, serves as chief executive officer of the Commission. But these somewhat unusual conditions are clearly accepted by the parties to the 1995 **Treaty**, who doubtless perceive that the benefits of them outweigh any detriments they may entail.

Areas of cooperation identified in the agreement include irrigation, hydroelectric power production, navigation, flood control, fisheries, timber floating, recreation, and tourism. The parties agree to cooperate with regard to these activities "in a manner to optimize the multiple-use and mutual benefits of all riparians and to minimize the harmful effects that might result from natural occurrences and man-made activities" (Mekong, 1995, Article 1). They further agree to protect the environment and ecological balance of the Mekong River Basin, and to "utilize the waters of the Mekong River system in a reasonable and equitable manner" (Mekong, 1995, Articles 3 and 5). Other substantive provisions relate to such issues as maintenance of flows on the mainstream, state responsibility for damage, freedom of navigation, and emergency situations.

While the 1995 Agreement is an advanced one, two issues, both relating to the construction of dams, threaten to undermine its effectiveness, at least to some extent. The first is a result of the **treaty** itself: it requires only notification to other parties, not their approval, prior to the initiation of projects on tributaries of the Mekong. Already three hydroelectric projects are either under construction or on line on Mekong tributaries in the Lao PDR, dams that will affect the flow of the Mekong downstream. The Lao PDR will not use significant amounts of the power generated by these dams itself but will sell it to Thailand.

The second issue arises because China is not a party to the 1995 Agreement (although both China and Myanmar have been invited to participate as observers in the MRC, and in 2002 they became "Dialogue Partners" of the MRC). China's rapidly growing need for electrical power has led it to plan a series of eight hydroelectric dams in the upper reaches of the Mekong, in Yunnan Province. Two of these dams are in operation, three are under construction, and three are in the planning stages. These dams, and China's blasting of rapids to improve navigation for its trading vessels, are already having an effect on the flow regime and ecosystem of the Lower Mekong. They are apparently responsible for a greatly reduced fish catch there, in Thailand and Cambodia, in particular (Perlez, 2005). In the latter country, the operation of the dams in China has altered the river's natural rhythms that have fed the great lake, the Tonle Sap, since time immemorial, cutting deeply into the essential fish catch there. In the Lower Basin as a whole the fish catch dropped by almost half in 2004, according to the MRC. Erosion of river banks, due to more rapid flow as a result of the blasting, has also become a serious problem.

For Further Discussion. Can a freshwater **treaty** be viable if it does not include the country or countries at the headwaters of the river? Are the four Lower Basin countries better off with the agreement or without it? Should China be obligated to compensate the downstream countries for the losses they have sustained as a result of China's dams and its blasting? What are the advantages and disadvantages of a commission that relies principally on external support and is headed by a national of one of the donor countries?

THE 2002 SENEGAL WATER CHARTER (MALI–MAURITANIA–SENEGAL)

The Senegal River rises largely in the Fouta Djallon mountains of Guinea in West Africa and drains territory in four states: Guinea, Mali, Mauritania, and Senegal. Efforts at cooperation began shortly after the four countries achieved independence in 1962. The first agreement between these states, the Convention relating to the Development of the Senegal River, was concluded in 1963. While short-lived, it set patterns that have been followed since: it provided for cooperation in relation to development of the river; established a joint institution (the Inter-State Committee); internationalized the entire Senegal River, including its tributaries and subtributaries, so that no single basin state could utilize its waters unilaterally, exclusively for its own purposes; provided for freedom of navigation for all basin states; and subjected the exploitation of the river to the control of the Inter-State Committee. A series of political crises led to the effective demise of the Inter-State Committee but it was succeeded by the Organization of the Senegal River States (OERS), which was established in 1968 and had an ambitious mandate extending to economic and even military matters. Political difficulties again intervened, however, resulting in the paralysis of the Organization (Godana, 1985).

In 1972, the three lower riparian states denounced (terminated) the earlier agreements relating to the Senegal River and entered into two new treaties: The Convention Relating to the Status of the Senegal River (Status Convention, 1972); and the Convention establishing the Organization for the Development of the Senegal River (OMVS Convention, 1972). A third agreement, the Convention Relating to the Status of Common Works, was concluded in 1978. While Guinea was not a member of the OMVS or the legal regime of the Senegal River until recently, it has now taken steps to join both the organization and the basic treaties.

Like the earlier regime, the Status Convention internationalizes the river and provides for, among other things, freedom of navigation and close cooperation in the use and development of the river. The OMVS Convention establishes that organization and confers upon it responsibility for setting policy regarding the management of the river, and for the establishment of priorities for development projects. Importantly, the agreement further provides that the organization must approve any development program of concern to one or more of the member states prior to its execution. These powers are unusual, and are clear indications of a high degree of integration among the states parties to the convention. Finally, the 1978 **Treaty** offers additional evidence of the integrated approach taken by the three states. It provides in essence for joint ownership of works on the river undertaken pursuant to the Status and OMVS Conventions. These works include the two dams constructed on the river, a hydroelectric dam at Manantali, Mali (completed in 1988), and a dam to prevent salt water intrusion at Diama, near the mouth of the Senegal River where it forms the border between Mauritania and Senegal (completed in 1986).

While the agreements drew praise and the projects implemented pursuant to them held out great hope (Parnall and Utton, 1976), the works unfortunately gave rise to unforeseen and serious problems. These included a large increase in water-borne diseases, especially in the vicinity of the Diama dam, destruction of native fish stocks and the elimination of traditional flood-recession agriculture (Vick, 2006). It was in part to address these problems that the three states concluded the Senegal Water Charter in 2002 (Senegal, 2002). The Water Charter supplements and updates the other treaties that form the Senegal River legal regime. It is a thoroughly modern instrument that adds principles of environmental protection and stakeholder participation to those of integrated water management and development established by the prior agreements (Vick, 2006).

The Water Charter seeks to address the problems identified above while allocating water equitably among the different sectors, principally agriculture, fishing, navigation and power production. It provides that "distribution of water between the uses is based on the following general principles:

- The obligation to guarantee a balanced management of the water resource.
- The equitable and reasonable use of the River's water.
- The obligation to preserve the environment.
- The obligation to negotiate in case of conflict.
- The obligation of each riparian state to inform other riparian states before engaging in any activity or project likely to have an impact on water availability and/or the possibility to implement future projects" (Senegal, 2002, Article 4).

This provision ends with a unique, fundamental safeguard, which appears to be intended to protect the populations relying on and affected by the river, regardless of competing economic demands: "The guiding principles of any distribution of the River's water will guarantee to the populations of the riparian States the full enjoyment of the resource, with respect for the safety of the people and the works, as well as the basic human right to clean water, in the perspective of sustainable development." The reference to the human right to water is particularly significant, as it is the first such reference in a freshwater **treaty**.

Annexes to the Charter contain Operational Manuals for the Manantali and Diama dams. An important and unique innovation of the Charter is its provision that the dams be operated so as to guarantee an annual artificial flood to mimic conditions that existed before the dams were constructed (Senegal, 2002, Article 14). This is designed to restore the conditions necessary to flood-recession agriculture, relied upon by the residents of the Senegal River valley, and to address the circumstances that led to the rise in water-borne diseases.

As noted earlier, Guinea is at this writing in the process of taking the legal steps necessary to join the Senegal River regime. This will mean that all of the states in the basin will be included in the management system that has been developed over more than 30 years. Whether and how the addition of Guinea might affect the progress that has been made, especially in the form of the Water Charter, is unknown. But it is in principle highly desirable for all states in a basin to participate in, and accept, decisions concerning its use, management, protection, and development. We have seen in the context of the Mekong what can happen if river development is not coordinated. From this perspective, the inclusion of Guinea, especially as it is the ultimate source of the Senegal system, would seem to be another positive step in the evolution of the Senegal River management regime.

For Further Discussion. What lessons can be drawn from the Senegal River experience? Will it always be possible for all kinds of uses — hydroelectric, navigational, agricultural, fishing, other traditional uses — to coexist on a river like the Senegal? Is it possible to provide for the unanticipated? How can legal regimes adapt to deal with changing conditions relating to an international watercourse?

CONCLUSION

In this chapter, we have considered treaties relating to international watercourses in three different regions of the world: Africa (the Senegal and Nile Rivers), Asia (the Mekong and Indus Rivers), and North America (the Rio Grande and Colorado Rivers). We have seen that while the six treaties we have looked at all deal with the same vital substance, water, they do so in different ways. Some of the treaties allocate water while others allocate entire rivers and still others attempt to achieve a balance between different kinds of uses of the shared resource. All of the treaties reviewed in the chapter either establish a joint institutional mechanism — usually called a commission — or utilize one already in existence. Yet the purposes, powers, and characteristics of the mechanisms vary considerably. Some of the **treaty** regimes have evolved while others remain as they were on the date the treaties were initially signed.

These **treaty** regimes illustrate that all such arrangements concerning international watercourses are different from one another. Yet by studying these regimes one can gain an appreciation of some of the tools and techniques at the disposal of states wishing to formalize their relations with respect to shared freshwater resources. You should ask yourself, what has succeeded, what has failed, and why? Which of these regimes can serve as models and which are efforts that should not be repeated but from which lessons can be learned? And finally, is the **treaty** the best way to deal with the management of an international watercourse? Can you think of a better alternative or alternatives?

Practice Questions

1. Why do the United States and Mexico have more than one **treaty** relating to the Rio Grande?
2. Do all the treaties considered in this chapter contain provisions on both water quantity and water quality? Should they?
3. What are some of the disadvantages of not including all states in a river basin in a **treaty** concerning that river?
4. Is it possible, or desirable, to have a **treaty** between two or more states that share a watercourse but between whom there are tense relations?
5. Does the state **treaty** practice considered in this chapter indicate that states never modify their treaties concerning shared freshwater resources?

REFERENCES

Agreement on the Cooperation for the Sustainable Development of the Mekong River Basin (1995). 5 April, 34 ILM 864.

Agreement between the United Arab Republic and the Republic of Sudan for the Full Utilization of the Nile Waters, 8 November 1959, 453 UNTS 51.

Charte des Eaux du Fleuve Sénégal [The Water Charter of the Senegal River], 18 May 2002, official French text available at http://lafrique.free.fr/traites/omvs_200205.pdf, unofficial English translation on file with author(s).

Convention Portant Creation de L'Organsation Pour la Mise en Valeur de Fleuve Senegal [Convention establishing the Organization for the Development of the Senegal River — OMVS], 11 March 1972, modified by the Convention portent amendement du 17 novembre 1975, Senegal-Mali-Mauritania, LEX-FAOC016003, available at http://faolex.fao.org/docs/texts/mul16003.doc

Convention Relative au Statut du Fleuve Senegal [Convention on the Status of the Senegal River], 11 March 1972, Senegal-Mali-Mauritania, LEX-FAOC016004, available at http://faolex.fao.org/docs/texts/mul16004.doc

Convention concerning the equitable distribution of the waters of the Rio Grande for irrigation purposes, 21 May 1906, 34 U.S. Statutes at Large 2953, Treaty Series 232.

ECE Helsinki Convention on the Protection and Use of Transboundary Watercourses and International Lakes (1992). Helsinki, 17 March, 31 ILM 1312.

Exchange of Notes between the United Kingdom and Egypt in regard to the Use of the Waters of the River Nile for Irrigation Purposes, 7 May 1929, 93 LNTS p. 44.

Godana, B.A. (1985). *Africa's Shared Water Resources*. London: Frances Pinter.

Indus Waters Treaty (1960). 19 September, 419 UNTS 126.

McCaffrey, S.C. (2001). *The Law of International Watercourses: Non-Navigational Uses*. Oxford: Oxford University Press.

Meyers, C.J. (1967). The Colorado Basin. In: Garretson, A., R. Hayton and C. Olmstead (eds.), *The Law of International Drainage Basins*. Dobbs Ferry, NY: Oceana, p. 486.

National Research Council of the National Academies of Science (2007). *Colorado River Basin Water Management: Evaluating and Adjusting to Hydroclimatic Variability*. Washington, DC: The National Academic Press.

Parnall, T. and A.E. Utton (1976). The Senegal Valley Authority: A unique experiment in international river basin planning, *Indiana Law Journal*, 51, p. 235.

Perlez, J. (2005). In life on the Mekong, China's dams dominate, *New York Times*, 19 March 2005, p. A1.

Revised protocol on shared watercourses in the Southern African Development Community (SADC), Windhoek, 7 August 2000, copy on file with author(s).

Treaty between the United States of America and Mexico relating to the utilization of the waters of the Colorado and Tijuana Rivers, and of the Rio Grande (Rio Bravo) from Fort Quitman, Texas, to the Gulf of Mexico, 3 February 1944, 3 UNTS 314.

1997 United Nations Convention on the Law of the Non-Navigational Uses of International Watercourses, 21 May 1997, UN Doc. A/RES/51/869, 36 ILM 700 (1997).

Vick, M. J. (2006). The Senegal River Basin: A retrospective and prospective look at the legal regime, *Natural Resources Journal*, 46(1), 211–243.

ADDITIONAL READING

Baxter, R.R. (1967). The Indus Basin. In: Garretson, A., R. Hayton and C. Olmstead (eds.), *The Law of International Drainage Basins*. Dobbs Ferry, NY: Oceana, p. 443.

Caponera, D. (1985). Patterns of cooperation in international water law: Principles and institutions, *Natural Resources Journal*, 25, p. 563.

Garretson, A.H. (1967). The Nile Basin. In: Garretson, A., R. Hayton and C. Olmstead (eds.), *The Law of International Drainage Basins*. Dobbs Ferry, NY: Oceana, p. 256.

McCaffrey, S.C. (2007). *The Law of International Watercourses*, 2nd edn. Oxford, New York: Oxford University Press.

Okidi, C.O. (1980). Legal and policy regime of Lake Victoria and Nile Basins, *Indian Journal of International Law*, 20, 395.

Parnall, T. and A.E. Utton (1976). The Senegal Valley Authority: A unique experiment in international river basin planning, *Indiana Law Journal*, 51, 235.

9. GLOBAL ANALYSIS OF INTERNATIONAL WATER AGREEMENTS

Objectives

The availability of hundreds of international water agreements provides a good understanding of how states resolve property rights disputes over a shared river in practice, permitting a systematic investigation of why certain property right solutions arise as opposed to others. This chapter provides a theory and testable hypotheses to test these questions. After studying this chapter you will be able to infer property rights solutions from state practice. Furthermore, you will understand how side-payments and cost-sharing schemes may both be used to promote cooperation between riparians and also indicate how a property rights conflict is solved. Finally, you will ascertain how the geography of a river and the economic asymmetries between the countries explain the variance in monetary regimes.

Main Terminology

Cost-sharing; Economic asymmetries; Existing uses approach; Needs-based approach; Polluter pays principle; Property rights; Reciprocal externalities; Rights-based approach; Side-payments; Unidirectional externalities; Victim pays regime; Willingness to pay.

Chapter 7 explained that when rivers and other bodies of water transverse or divide countries, transboundary externalities often result in interstate conflicts. As suggested, the cause of the conflict may be attributed to several variables but scarcity provides the most basic grounds. That being said, scarcity and the dispute that ensues also provide the impetus for cooperation and coordination among river riparians. Cooperation and coordination are almost always formally codified in international treaties.

Vague international legal principles or weak **property rights** regimes may also facilitate conflict. Despite this drawback, river riparians have been quite successful in negotiating agreements over shared rivers and the thousands of documented agreements over shared rivers are an indication of this (Chapters 3 and 8). This chapter explores the nature of conflicts over a river water, and the treaty remedies open to river riparians. Water agreements that have been documented by several sources, from 1864 to 2002, are under scrutiny. The main aim of this chapter is to demonstrate that only through the analysis of actual water agreements, clear property rights regimes can be detected. Since broad legal principles obtain meaning in actual negotiations, exploring the intricacies of the water treaties states negotiate may reveal how such canons are expressed in practice.

This analysis not only explores the intricacies of the actual water treaties states have negotiated but also considers how stable agreements may come about. The first part of the chapter will be dedicated to a descriptive exploration of the substance of treaties while the second part will suggest a theory for considering how water agreements can sustain participation by the relevant parties and promote cooperation. The latter section is based on Dinar (2006, 2007).

Understanding the intricacies of international water agreements is important for several reasons. First and foremost, institutional capacity, which treaties and agreements embody, help to coordinate the utilization and exploitation of the river desired by the respective parties. Second, agreements help to assuage future disputes and tensions over the river since rules and regulations are already in place. A track-record of cooperation and coordination is also fostered. Finally, treaties may provide some prescriptive value. Successful agreements may be used as models for river riparians currently in dispute or undergoing negotiations.

DESCRIPTIVE CHARACTERISTICS OF INTERNATIONAL WATER AGREEMENTS

Perhaps one of the first studies to consider actual water agreements was conducted by Wolf (1999). He undertook a qualitative analysis of 49 treaties relating solely to water allocation. Naturally, Wolf (1999) was interested in how vague and conflicting international legal principles are reconciled and moderated in actual negotiations among states.

Wolf's (1999) qualitative analysis uncovered several findings. Most importantly, he demonstrated that quantifiable concepts such as the **needs-based approach** for water allocation often emerge in some negotiations rather than the extreme and often intangible **rights-based approach**. In other words, extreme legal principles, such as *absolute territorial sovereignty* and *absolute territorial integrity*, seldom hold and the parties often agree to a compromise based on their actual water requirements rather than "abstract" water rights. As international legal scholars would contend, such water allocation agreements codify the compromise principle of *equitable utilization* through the **needs-based approach**. In fact, this approach is mentioned in the 1997 UN Convention, in Article 6, as one way to determine equitable utilization.

Second, Wolf also found that in disputes between upstream and downstream states over water allocation, historical uses are almost always protected. As Wolf writes:

> *Since there is more, and generally older, irrigated agriculture downstream on an arid or exotic stream, and since agricultural practices predate more recent hydroelectric needs — the sites for which are in the headwater uplands — the downstream riparian would have greater claim whether measured by needs or by prior uses of a stream system.* (Wolf, 1999: 12.)

This is an interesting point since Article 6 of the 1997 UN Convention also recognizes the right of a state to develop and exploit the "potential uses" of a watercourse — acknowledging the needs of upstream states. Wolf's (1999) findings, therefore, demonstrate that while upstream riparians have the right to develop their water resources, past uses of the downstream states are protected. In fact, Article 6 of the UN Convention likewise recognizes the **existing uses approach** in determining equitable utilization.

Another qualitative and descriptive study that considers international water agreements was conducted by Wolf and Hamner (2000). Unlike the above study by Wolf (1999), this particular analysis considers 145 treaties and observes the multitude of issue topics covered by the different treaties, including hydropower, monitoring, water quantity, water quality, and groundwater. Perhaps one of the interesting findings from this study has to do with what Wolf and Hamner call "nonwater linkages." In this context, the authors are effectively describing the concepts of issue-linkage, articulated in Chapter 7, and compensation, which is addressed in detail by the rest of this chapter. The authors explain that by enlarging the scope of water disputes to include nonwater issues, resolution of a **property rights** dispute may be facilitated. Such nonwater related issues include the provision of land, political concessions, and capital from one riparian to another.

MAKING AGREEMENTS STABLE AND SELF-ENFORCING

Wolf (1999) and Wolf and Hamner (2000) provide a very good starting point from which to identify how riparian disputes are resolved, **property rights** conflicts are managed, and legal principles are reconciled in practice. Both studies, however, lack a precise theory and hypotheses that can be utilized to test why particular outcomes arise, as opposed to other outcomes, and in what frequency.

Therefore, **property rights** solutions need to be considered in a more methodical manner. It is for this reason that a theory and testable hypotheses may be developed and tested across the large number of recorded agreements. Below is one such attempt.

As Chapter 7 argued, cooperation may be difficult to sustain. However, it is not an anomaly as neorealists contend. At the same time, the reasons that neorealists do provide for explaining cooperation, are not satisfactory. In the realm of hydropolitics, the instances of (armed) conflict do not outnumber the cases of cooperation nor does cooperation rely on say, the presence of a hegemonic state — that acts malignly. Rather a type of institutional capacity seems to characterize international hydropolitics between riparian states. In addition, both asymmetric and symmetric states in both economic and military terms forge agreements for the utilization of their common rivers. Explaining such a cooperative phenomenon, therefore, becomes the main aim.

Surely, scarcity is the basic motivator for cooperation and agreements. However, one state may derive different benefits from a cooperative project on a river when compared with its fellow riparian or may be less able to pay the costs of a project. Therefore, agreements must also embody a given character in order to restructure the incentives of states so that they are more likely to comply with it. In Barrett's (2003) terms, agreements must be self-enforcing. Chapter 7 already began motivating this discussion by considering such topics as foreign-policy considerations, linkage, and reciprocity. This section will consider other relevant elements including, **side-payments** and **cost-sharing** schemes. What distinguishes such monetary regimes from foreign-policy considerations, linkage, and reciprocity, is that they are often indicated clearly in the actual text of the agreement. The agreement, thus, becomes the main unit of analysis or the dependent variable and it is for this reason that monetary regimes are investigated in detail in this chapter.

Like the notions of linkage and reciprocity, **side-payments** are often used to "ratchet up," or promote, cooperation. Perhaps more importantly, they also point to the **property rights** solution (Barrett, 2003, pp. 357 and 258). Since international water law only provides hints and suggestions as to how **property rights** conflicts are to be resolved, agreements, via the monetary regimes negotiated, may indicate more clearly, which riparian has a right to take what action. For example, if a downstream state pays an upstream state to abate pollution, we can infer from this agreement that the **property rights** do not belong exclusively to the downstream state and it will have to incur some harm as a result of actions upstream.

Interestingly, not all agreements include a monetary regime. Some agreements are very general in their nature, codifying only the spirit of cooperation rather than instituting a specific project or action plan between the riparians. Monetary regimes are, therefore, scrutinized via the investigation of specific agreements.

In an effort to explain **side-payments** and **cost-sharing** outcomes, geography and economics are considered below. For reasons of simplicity, only agreements governing a river shared by two riparians are investigated. At the same time, only agreements for the two geographical configurations introduced in Chapter 7, the *through-border* and *border-creator*, are investigated. The agreements pertain to an array of issue types except for navigation and fishing. While this study is based on Dinar (2006, 2007), and 44 agreements were analyzed for the two configurations, only a sample of the results is presented below. Naturally, while not all rivers solely exemplify these two pure characteristics, all shared rivers have properties of each of these distinct configurations. Therefore, inferences about **property rights** solutions can also be made for these other river types.

GEOGRAPHY AND ECONOMIC RELATIONSHIPS BETWEEN THE RIPARIANS

Geography

As explained in Chapter 7, geography constitutes another basic element for understanding conflict and cooperation over international rivers. It is for this reason that geography makes up the main independent variable in this analysis.

While conflict is not inevitable in the *through-border* river, retaliation and reciprocity are facilitated in the *border-creator* case and conflict may, therefore, be discouraged. In general, upstream riparians are at a geographical advantage. As mentioned in Chapter 7, upstream riparians are able to pollute the river to the detriment of the downstream state and divert its water, thus affecting the flow downstream. Finally, upstream riparians are often located in areas that constitute prime cites where dams may be constructed for hydropower generation and flood-control purposes. Since geography confers particular advantages on an upstream country, strategic maneuvering may be the result. In pollution cases, for example, the costs of the harming activity are incurred downstream — the hallmark of **unidirectional externalities**. This often means that the upstream state may not have the same interest in abating pollution, compared with the downstream state.

On the other hand, **reciprocal externalities** are the hallmark of common property resources such as *border-creator* rivers. Retaliation and reciprocity are embedded in such a geographical configuration. In cases of pollution, for example, while one country may pollute a river, that pollution not only affects the other riparian but also the polluting riparian itself. The incentive to abate pollution or prevent it before it is discharged into the water is thus intrinsic to the geography of the river. Therefore, pollution may be less of a problem for this kind of geography.

What does the above discussion have to do with a negotiated monetary regime? Given the geographical asymmetry embedded in the *through-border* configuration, it is expected that **side-payments**, from the downstream country to the upstream country, would be used to encourage cooperation and solve a **property rights** dispute in agreements that govern this type of a river.

Through-Border Configuration

Interestingly, the majority of agreements that pertain to water quantity issues do not evince **side-payments** from the geographically weaker downstream state to the geographically superior upstream state. One would suspect that the upstream state's ability to impound water to the detriment of the downstream state would empower it to demand compensation for releasing water. But this seldom takes place in practice. Rather agreements tend to divide the water of a shred river equally among the riparians or, as proposed by Wolf (1999), according to a particular formula such as a **needs-based approach**. The main explanation for this phenomenon is that despite the ability of upstream states to utilize the "strategic local" card, the water flowing through the river belongs to both riparians, and the upstream state recognizes this. In essence, there is some evidence, typified in state practice, for the modern legal assertion that:

> *...a state does not own the waters of an international watercourse that are, for the most part, situated in its territory and is free to do with them as it pleases regardless of the consequences for other riparian states. On the contrary, upper riparians are under an obligation not to prevent such waters from flowing to a lower riparian country.* (McCaffrey, 2001:264).

That being said, there exists a small number of agreements that evince strategic maneuvering by upstream states. Thereby, in some instances, payments for actual water are transferred from the downstream state to secure water allocation. A case study depicting such a scenario is presented in Box 9.1.

Box 9.1: 1973 Helmand River Agreement

> While the actual text of the agreement is not available, an account of the agreement is provided by Abidi (1977). Abidi (1977) is unclear as to whether they were directly included in the agreement, but it is obvious that some form of compensation was provided to Afghanistan, the upstream state. Abidi writes that the Agreement called on Afghanistan to release a set amount of water a year for Iran's use from the Helmand River. As Abidi adds, "Iran offered financial payment and concessional transit rights for Afghan exports through Bandar Abbas in return for more water by Afghanistan" (1977:370).

Unlike the issue of water allocation, the situation is quite different in cases where benefits created upstream are shared. In fact, a major motivation for the upstream country to conclude an agreement with the downstream riparian on projects that provide benefits to both riparians, such as hydropower generation and flood-control, is ardently related to **side-payments**. That is, regulation of the river will generally provide external benefits downstream for which the upstream country will not be compensated unless an agreement is negotiated (LeMarquand, 1977, p. 9). Similarly, if the downstream state perceives that the upstream riparian will go forth with a regulation project and is not interested in being compensated for the downstream benefits it thereby creates, the downstream state will not elect to sign an agreement since it will receive benefits at no cost to itself. While **side-payments** are utilized to motivate the cooperation of the upstream country, they likewise embody recognition of the benefits enjoyed downstream and created upstream. A case study depicting this scenario is presented in Box 9.2.

Box 9.2: 1961 Columbia River Agreement

In this case, Canada, the upstream state chose to cooperate not only out of a desire to exploit the river but also to gain compensation from the United States, the downstream state. Indeed, Canada was initially reluctant to go ahead with its projects (construction of dams for flood-control and hydropower generation) unless it was assured of receiving some compensation for the improved stream flow and regulation the United States would likewise enjoy (LeMarquand, 1976, p. 886). Barrett notes that the United States initially believed that Canada would want to develop the Columbia River on its side of the border anyway, and so felt that it did not need to compensate Canada for going forward with the project. When Canada threatened to construct an alternative project on a different river, which would provide the United States with no benefits, the United States heeded the threat as a credible one and Canada was able to secure a more attractive compensation deal (Barrett, 1994, p. 22).

The incentives to cooperate for the sake of pollution abatement may be quite different from the incentives to cooperate on hydropower generation and flood-control. This is because direct benefits from cooperation cannot be derived by the upstream country in the context of a unidirectional externality. Therefore, if a downstream state wishes to encourage abatement by a polluting upstream state, **side-payments** will most likely have to be provided. If the downstream state provides only a portion of the abatement costs, while the upstream state assumes the remaining portion, then it can be said that neither has the property right to solely pollute, in the case of the upstream state, or solely enjoy not being harmed, in the case of the downstream state. Specifically, such an outcome indicates that despite the normatively accepted **polluter pays principle** (where the polluter should pay the costs of pollution), a **victim pays regime** (where the victim country must assume some or all of the costs for the pollution produced upstream) often characterizes what is negotiated in practice. Box 9.3 discusses such a case.

Box 9.3: 1990 Tijuana River Agreement

To truly understand the 1990 Tijuana Agreement, the 1985 Tijuana Agreement must also be acknowledged. In this earlier agreement, it was decided that the pollution was coming from Mexico, and it was further agreed that Mexico should take action to abate the pollution. While the United States offered assistance if Mexico should require it, the agreement concluded that Mexico was to internalize the costs of abatement and take immediate action — in a way a side-payment in favor of the United States. If the 1985 Agreement alone were to be considered, it might be concluded that the geographical hypothesis first proposed above has just been disproved. In essence, the **polluter pays principle**, rather than a **victim pays regime**, would seem to be the dominating tenet. The agreement signed in 1990 addressed the continued sanitation and pollution problems coming from the Mexican side. However, rather than completing the projects Mexico took upon itself following the 1985 Agreement, it was agreed that an international wastewater plant would be built in the United States so as to treat sewage that would otherwise have continued to flow from Mexico downstream. In essence, the United States, recognizing that the sewage coming from Mexico would only be sufficiently treated in this international wastewater plant (at least according to its standards), agreed to finance the greater part of the project. The United States, therefore, assumed some financial responsibility to assure proper pollution abatement.

Border-Creator Configuration

The opposite outcome is expected in agreements that govern *border-creator* rivers. **Side-payments** are not likely to characterize bilateral agreements, neither for encouraging cooperation nor for solving a **property rights** dispute. The geographical symmetrical relationship between the riparians, at least in comparison to the *through-border* configuration, also implies that development of the shared river will more often require a commensurate participation of both countries. Both share the same stretch of the river and the geography of the river acts as a focal point. Box 9.4 presents such a case study on the issue of joint scenic works.

Box 9.4: 1950/1954 Niagara River Agreement

The 1950/1954 Niagara Agreement signed between Canada and the United States, pertains to scenic works for the river whereby the costs of these works are to be divided equally between the United States and Canada. No-**side-payments** are transferred from one side to the other.

Economics

Geography, while an important variable for explaining cooperation and **property rights**, is not sufficient — especially when **side-payments** or the **willingness to pay** of the parties is analyzed and sought. The **economic asymmetries** that characterize the parties should also matter. Richer riparians not only have a greater capacity to assume particular costs for joint projects, such as hydropower generation, but also embody lower propensities to accept pollution when compared with poorer riparians. In general, richer states have a higher **willingness to pay**. The threshold for this asymmetry is set at two times the difference in GDP per capita (Dinar, 2006, 2007).

Hypotheses derived from the economics variable and geography variable merge on several levels. For example, if for a given river the richer state is located downstream and the poorer state is located upstream, then a pollution problem is sure to be of great concern to the downstream state. While the geography of the *through-border* river makes upstream pollution a salient issue for any downstream state, the matter takes on greater magnitude if the polluting state is poorer. Poorer states tend to have lower pollution standards and different preferences for the long-term sustainability of the environment than richer states (Botteon and Carraro, 1997, p. 27). Therefore, the poorer downstream state may also be able to expect more financial compensation for abating pollution. A similar scenario may be proposed for nonpollution issues such as hydroelectric generation and flood-control facilities. Where regulation of the river for flood control and hydropower purposes, for example, is sought and the majority of the facilities need to be located upstream, upstream states may have the negotiating upper hand. An upstream state may agree to cooperate in exchange for some kind of compensation, whether **side-payments** or in-kind through projects that will be largely funded by the richer downstream country.

For Further Discussion. Poor countries, relative to richer countries, may have an upper hand in environmental negotiations given their economic situation. How might this materialize in the negotiation process and how will their negotiating positions be affected?

In short, to assume, as Lowi (1993) does, that a more powerful (and in this case also richer) downstream country acts as a malign and coercive hegemon is problematic. Along these lines, it is also puzzling how a state might use brute force to coerce a weaker state to cooperate when the stronger state depends on the weaker state to honor an agreement. Rather, in river basins where power and **economic asymmetries** characterize the riparians, and exploitation of the weaker party seems likely, the stronger side may realize that it can do better by giving a sense of equality to the weaker side rather than by taking what it wants by force (Zartman and Rubin, 2000, p. 289). In fact, consent by the weaker upstream state is a prerequisite to a cooperative agreement. Benefits in the upstream direction need follow to consummate the deal. An example is presented in Box 9.5.

Box 9.5: 1974 Chukha Hydroelectric Agreement

In this particular case, both Bhutan and India wish to exploit the Chukha River for hydropower purposes (per capita GDP in this time period favored India two-to-one). India, not surprisingly, lead the charge due to its grave need for energy resources in the northern part of the country. Given Bhutan's strategic location, the hydropower installations were built in its territory. Downstream India, nonetheless, financed the project. In addition, all of the surplus energy that Bhutan was not using was sold to India. Bhutan has been able to reap great economic benefits from the compensation it receives from India for the surplus energy.

The hypotheses derived from both variables diverge when the upstream riparian is rich and the downstream riparian poor. In this scenario, the richer state is in the most geographically advantageous position while the poorer state is in the geographically most inferior position. The geographical hypotheses would suggest that the upstream state would not act until it received a side-payment. Its relatively stronger position, in terms of economic prowess, may also discourage it from having to cooperate with a weaker downstream state. However, the theory argues, that the higher **willingness to pay** of the richer upstream country actually assuages its disincentives to cooperate. In this case, the more developed upper riparian may wish to create "good will" with its neighbors by contributing more to pollution control while [themselves] benefiting less (Linnerooth, 1990, p. 643). The side-payment transfer will, therefore, take place from the upstream state to the downstream state. Likewise, richer upstream states tend to take action in favor of poorer downstream states without monetary compensation — in a way a side-payment. An example is presented in Box 9.6.

Box 9.6: 1958 Carol River Agreement

The dispute culminated between upstream France and downstream Spain when France asserted its right to divert water from Lake Lanoux for hydropower purposes. (Per capita GDP in this time period favored France two-to-one.) Lake Lanoux is indigenous to France but sources the Carol River, which crosses into Spain. Initially, France offered compensation to its southern neighbor. Spain's continued intransigence finally led France to adopt a scheme that would return to the Carol all of the water that it diverted for hydropower purposes. Ultimately, the parties referred their dispute to an arbitration panel. The tribune decided in favor of France's position but argued that France must commit to return the same quantity and quality of water to the Carol before it entered Spain. The decision culminated in the 1958 Agreement. This particular case demonstrated that despite France's strategic local and economic disincentives to bend before Spain's protests, France not only offered to return the same amount of water to the Carol River before it entered Spanish territory, but also agreed that the quality of the water would be the same. France was able to internalize the costs of the diversion back into the Carol River, and the immediate economic disincentives to do so were thus moderated.

In the *border-creator* river, similar circumstances apply. That is, if pollution is less of a concern when the parties are economically symmetric due to relatively similar thresholds for accepting and emitting pollution, the situation is just the reverse when the parties are economically asymmetric. In this regard, the richer state may have to help finance pollution abatement by the poorer state or take on a larger portion of the costs for a joint project, such as the construction of a dam for hydropower or flood-control purposes — in a way a side-payment. In instances where the riparians are economically asymmetric, **side-payments** have to be transferred from the richer state to the poorer state to sustain cooperation.

While an agreement that governs a *border-creator* river with economically asymmetric riparians could not be identified by Dinar (2006, 2007), a treaty that governs a river with similar attributes is presented in Box 9.7.

Box 9.7: 1959 Hermance River Agreement

While the Hermance River originates in France, it then straddles the border with Switzerland. (Per capita GDP in this time period favored Switzerland two-to-one.) The agreement relates to flood-control matters and pertains to the stretch of the river in France, whereby France must assume responsibility for the costs of the works. However, the agreement also concerns works on the stretch of the river flowing along the common border (this is the stretch of the river effectively similar to the *border-creator* configuration). Switzerland takes on the responsibility for all the works on that particular stretch. While France is responsible for maintenance of the part of the river that flows solely in its territory and its part of the river which straddles the border, Switzerland assumes not only maintenance responsibilities of its part of the river that straddles the border but also some maintenance responsibilities on the French side. Switzerland, therefore, assumes a greater portion of the **cost-sharing** burden for works and maintenance on the part of the river that straddles the border — in a way a side-payment in favor of France.

CONCLUSION

This chapter has built on the analysis in Chapter 7 by focusing on the manner in which international freshwater agreements, in this particular case treaties that govern rivers shared by only two states, not only form, but also provide, parties with a satisfactory basis for settling their water dispute. While Chapter 7 considered such notions as foreign-policy, issue-linkage, and reciprocity to explain cooperation, this chapter considered another strategic tool often used in negotiations to foster cooperation — **side-payments** and **cost-sharing** schemes. In fact, **side-payments** and **cost-sharing** patterns were chosen as the dependent variables under investigation not only because they are used to "ratchet up" cooperation but because they also say something compelling about **property rights** solutions. For example, if a downstream state pays an upstream state to abate pollution, it can be deduced that the *no harm* principle does not stand. The downstream state must accept some pollution produced upstream.

What facilitates this particular approach is that **side-payments** and **cost-sharing** schemes regularly occur in specific treaties, where a given project or use is negotiated, as opposed to general treaties that simply call on the parties to uphold the spirit of cooperation. As such, an investigation of specific treaties, and the patterns that emerge, can reveal not only how cooperation comes about but also how general legal principles and **property rights** disputes are reconciled in practice.

While other studies have provided some cursory analysis of how legal principles and **property rights** disputes are resolved in practice, they have lacked a theory and testable hypotheses to suggest when particular outcomes are more likely than others. This chapter, based on Dinar (2006, 2007), has considered the role of geography and economics to explain why particular treaty outcomes arise. Specifically, it was hypothesized that agreements which govern the two extreme geographies, the *through-border* and *border-creator* configurations, should elicit different **property rights** regimes. Similarly, agreements that govern rivers shared by two riparians embodying **economic asymmetries** should elicit a different **property rights** regime than an agreement that governs a river shared by two economically symmetric countries.

Here are some of the general lessons that can be learned from the above analysis. Agreements that pertain to water quantity did not evince a laudable pattern of **side-payments** from the downstream state to the upstream state. Therefore, despite some strategic behavior by upstream states, the physical water flowing through a given river is considered a shared resource, not owned by any country, regardless of its superior geographical location.

The same cannot be said for agreements wherein benefits created upstream, or harm incurred upstream, favored downstream states. The bulk of such agreements evinced **side-payments** — indicating not only that **side-payments** may be used to encourage cooperation from the geographically superior upstream state but also that the compromise of coordinating uses on a river are subject to **side-payments** for benefits enjoyed downstream. In this case, the **property rights** of the river's exploitation belong to both parties but the benefits created upstream are recognized in the form of **side-payments**.

Agreements which governed pollution issues were most compelling. Despite the accepted legal norm, the **polluter pays principle**, it was demonstrated that the victim country must incur, at least some of, the abatement costs. A **victim pays regimes** is thereby affected. Such a monetary transfer to the upstream state is a testament not only to the consequences of the downstream state's inferior geographical location but also to its apparent burden to accept some pollution. Surely, when the polluting upstream state is poorer, there is greater urgency in which the richer state must act. As explained, not only do richer states have a higher **willingness to pay** but poorer states also tend to have weaker pollution standards. As such, they can extract more compensation to abate pollution that affects the richer downstream state.

Where the opposite side-payment scenario was evinced, the upstream state was usually the richer party. As hypothesized, richer states have a higher **willingness to pay**. Similarly, rich upstream states may want to create "good will" with their poorer downstream neighbors and undertake actions, regardless of appropriate compensation. In such cases, the economic relationship produces an opposite outcome to that expected by the geographic hypothesis. Therefore, the higher **willingness**

to pay of the upstream state and its desire to create "good will" downstream, assuages the disincentives to cooperate that might be presumed inherent in its superior strategic location.

Agreements corresponding to the *border-creator* configuration did not evince **side-payments**. Naturally, projects were always to be pursued on the parties' common border and, as expected, equal participation was demonstrated in all cases — even when the benefits were not divided equally among the parties. The symmetry embedded in the river geography does not usually compel one state to induce another to cooperate. Furthermore, the river geography facilitates — and necessitates — the participation of both parties in planning and undertaking a joint project. Solutions to **property rights** conflicts in the *border-creator* configuration, then, rarely require **side-payments**, while the coordination of uses along the shared river often demands the parties' equal participation.

Because there were no agreements for the *border-creator* river that embodied states with an asymmetric economic relationship, the economic hypothesis was tested for rivers with a similar geography. The example provided demonstrated that the richer riparian assumed the largest cost burden of the agreed project — in a way a side-payment to the poorer state.

For the most part, projects and tasks to be undertaken on the part of the river that flows along the common border require the equal participation of both parties. **Side-payments** are not required. That being said, asymmetries between the states matter with the richer country taking up the higher **cost-sharing** burden (a side-payment) most of the time.

To conclude, the policy implications of these findings can be very telling since the same results apply across varying regions and continents. The geography of the river matters but so do the economic differences that characterize the riparians. Despite the unique characteristics that embody each river basin, a set of similar **property rights** solutions seem to hold.

For Further Discussion. Articulate the general policy implications suggested above. Can you think of other cases where this model might fit well, suggesting a possible cooperative outcome?

Practice Questions

1. Why is analyzing water agreements an important exercise in understanding conflict and cooperation over transboundary waters?
2. Other than the main study proposed in this chapter, what have other studies concluded about the characteristics of water agreements and **property rights** solutions?
3. Why should geography matter for understanding **property rights** conflicts?
4. Why are the **economic asymmetries** that embody the riparians important?

REFERENCES

Abidi, A.H. (1977). Irano-Afghan dispute over the Helmand waters, *International Studies*, 16(3).

Barrett, S. (1994). Conflict and cooperation in managing international water resources, Policy Research Working Paper, N 1303, The World Bank, Washington, DC.

Barrett, S. (2003). *Environment and Statecraft: The Strategy of Environmental Treaty-Making.* Oxford: Oxford University Press.

Botteon, M. and C. Carraro (1997). Burden sharing and coalition stability in environmental negotiations with asymmetric countries. In: Carraro, C. (ed.), *International Environmental Negotiations: Strategic Policy Issues.* Glos: Edward Elgar Publishing.

Dinar, S. (2006). Assessing side-payment and cost-sharing patterns in international water agreements: The geographic and economic connection, *Political Geography*, 25(4).

Dinar, S. (2007). *International Water Treaties: Negotiation and Cooperation Along Transboundary Rivers.* London: Routledge.

LeMarquand, D. (1976). Politics of international river basin cooperation and management, *Natural Resources Journal*, 16.

LeMarquand, D. (1977). *International Rivers: The Politics of Cooperation.* Vancouver, BC: Westwater Research Center.

Linnerooth, J. (1990). The Danube River Basin: Negotiating settlements to transboundary environmental issues, *Natural Resources Journal*, 30.

Lowi, M. (1993). *Water and Power: The Politics of a Scarce Resource in the Jordan River Basin.* Cambridge: Cambridge University Press.

McCaffrey, S. (2001). *The Law of International Watercourses: Non-Navigational Uses.* Oxford: Oxford University Press.

Wolf, A. (1999). Criteria for equitable allocations: The heart of international water conflict, *Natural Resources Forum*, 23(1).

Wolf, A. and J. Hamner (2000). Trends in transboundary water disputes and dispute resolution. In *Water for Peace in the Middle East and Southern Africa*. Geneva: Green Cross International.

Zartman, W. and J. Rubin (2000). Symmetry and asymmetry in negotiation. In: Zartman, W. and J. Rubin (eds.), *Power and Negotiation*. Ann Arbor, MI: The University of Michigan Press.

10. THE USE OF RIVER BASIN MODELING AS A TOOL TO ASSESS CONFLICT AND POTENTIAL COOPERATION

Objectives

After reading this chapter, you should have a general understanding of how river basin models are developed and how they are used within the field of international water resources. You should also have gained a basic understanding of some of the ways in which countries have attempted to use river basin models.

Main Terminology

Calibration; Constraint; Economic-based allocation; Emergency water management; Geographic information system; Integrated River Basin Management; Model building process; Multiobjective analysis; Node–link network; Optimization modeling; Priority-based allocation; River basin model; Scenario; Sensitivity analysis; Simulation modeling; Systems approach; Trade-off; Verification.

The allocation of water resources in river basins is a critical issue, especially when multiple riparian countries are involved. River basins are inherently complex systems with many interdependent components (streams, aquifers, reservoirs, canals, cities, irrigation districts, farms, etc.). The sustainability of future economic growth and environmental health in a basin depends on the rational allocation of water among the basin riparians (users sharing the basin's water resources) and sectors (municipal, industrial, agricultural, and environmental, among others). Efficient and comprehensive models are available to make water allocation and water quality decisions that can lead to sustainable water use strategies in many river basins.

This chapter presents an overview of river basin modeling and its use in understanding conflicts and cooperation options. Also discussed are data needs and data manipulations, possible **scenarios** to be used in modeling, and how they can affect conflicts and the prospects for cooperation.[1] In a later chapter, a demonstration

---

[1]Scenario is an alternate future development or course of action depending on various system inputs or decisions taken to control the system.

of modeling a generic river basin is presented, including quantitative results on noncooperation-unilateral extraction, climate change impact, population growth pressure, and optimization-cooperation. More detailed information on river basin modeling can be found in the textbooks: Maass *et al.* (1962), Hall and Dracup (1968), Loucks *et al.* (1981), Viessman and Welty (1985), Mays and Tung (1992), Grigg (1996), Lee and Dinar (1996), and Loucks and van Beek (2006).

HOW MODELS HELP US UNDERSTAND CONFLICTS AND COOPERATION OPTIONS

The principal sources of many transboundary rivers lie in mountainous states where water may be regulated by a cascade of reservoirs for various purposes (e.g., energy production) and compete with water use for other uses (e.g., agricultural production) in downstream countries (e.g., the Syr Darya basin in Central Asia). In these cases, the issues of river basin management are international, and policy solutions often entail regional cooperation among the concerned riparian countries.

If a basin is wholly contained within one country, some sort of locally optimal allocation of water to uses that are most economically efficient can be a good solution. However, in transboundary basins, where countries exert their (limited) sovereignty over water resources on their territory, this is often impossible. In this case, the water allocated to a country by agreement between the basin riparians becomes an upper limit on water available for that country. The allocation of that water share within the country is, by and large, a domestic policy issue for that country. However, the allocation of shares between countries is an international issue faced by all the basin riparians.

In many cases, downstream countries do not have local water sources, but they have developed significant irrigated lands and they must rely on upstream countries for water supply (e.g., Nile, Indus, and Aral Sea basins). An upstream country's goal in river basin management may be to maximize hydroelectric power production, and this could be in conflict with the downstream country, whose goal may be to maximize the utilization of water for irrigated agricultural production. Sometimes the temporal characteristics of the goals of upstream and downstream countries in a basin may lead to international water management problems. For instance, upstream peak power demand may occur in the winter, while in downstream countries, peak demand for irrigation water typically occurs in the summer. Without cooperation, these situations can lead to international conflict over the shared waters of a basin.

River basin models have been used to aid in the determination of fair and equitable long-term water sharing agreements or short-term operational plans in transboundary basins. A **river basin model** is a mathematical model that represents the relevant processes in a river basin and can predict the behavior of the basin under different conditions or management **scenarios**.

These models help decision-makers from the basin states understand the ramifications of different water allocation **scenarios** and operational regimes and the corresponding benefits to themselves and their neighbors. They can be used to understand the **trade-offs**[2] between water releases made for one use (say, agricultural production) versus those made for another (say, hydroelectric power generation).

As an example, consider a transboundary basin where an upstream country's water management goal is power generation and a downstream country's goal is irrigation water supply. Making releases for power generation in the winter will not allow saving that water for summer release for irrigation. The following **scenarios** could be considered by the different countries for this situation:

Upstream country:

- Maximize power generation in the upstream country over the planning period; or
- Minimize power deficits in the upstream country in winter months over the planning period.

Downstream country:

- Maximize water supply for irrigation in the downstream country over the planning period.

Clearly, the upstream and downstream **scenarios** could be in direct conflict with one another. An analysis of modeling results of trying to satisfy these different management objectives can be helpful in determining possible cooperative solutions to water management in the basin (objectives are goals intended to be attained by a stakeholder in managing a river basin). Such results would include deficits of water for irrigation as well as deficits of power delivered under the different management **scenarios**. Economic valuation of the water uses (agricultural production, electricity generated, municipal users served, etc.) can also be evaluated by the model. The application of such a model in the Syr Darya basin of Central Asia is discussed later in this chapter. The results of such a model can be used in the creation of a game theory setting for water management in the basin.

As with any model, certain assumptions are made and **constraints** exist. (A **constraint** in a **river basin model** is a limitation on the values which a variable may take on in a **river basin model**.) Models are always constrained by the available data (e.g., streamflow records, reservoir operations, water demands, etc.) and by the **constraints** of the countries in question. Assumptions must be made about various data input to the model and the **scenarios**, such as, the length of the modeling period and the time step, the environmental flows required at various locations in the basin, and initial storage volumes of the basin reservoirs. To model the uncertain nature of regional climate, various flow sequences should be used, such as sequences of normal, dry, and wet years.

---

[2]Trade-off in the context of a basin model is the amount of one objective value that must be given up in order to increase the value of a conflicting objective.

WHY WE MODEL

River basin models are interactive programs that utilize analytical methods, such as simulation and optimization algorithms, to help decision-makers formulate water resources alternatives, analyze their impacts, and interpret and select appropriate options for implementation. Models are used to simulate water resource system behavior based on a set of rules governing water allocations and infrastructure operation. Models are also used to optimize water resource system behavior based on an objective function and accompanying **constraints**. Models tend to reduce the time for decision-making in these uses, and improve the consistency and quality of those decisions.

In the context of transboundary river basins, models are needed by negotiators, planners, and managers of water resource systems, as well as other stakeholders who may be concerned about the economic or environmental uses of shared water resources. The objective of these decision-makers is, among other things, to provide a reliable supply of water with a quality appropriate for its use, production of hydropower, protection from floods, and protection of ecosystems. In transboundary basins, the allocation of water to various users and sectors is carried out in accordance with the prevailing institutional structure of water rights according to national laws, basin-wide negotiated agreements, and international laws.

River basin modeling requires, to varying degrees depending on the problem under consideration, the following activities (see Fig. 10.1):

- *Data Measurement and Collection* — receipt of various data (e.g., water level and temperature, precipitation, air temperature, concentrations, etc.) from

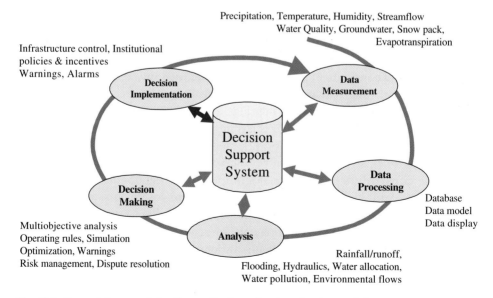

Fig. 10.1: General framework for the application of a **river basin model**.

Source: Authors.

stations throughout a river basin. In addition, various economic and social data are measured and collected.

- *Data Processing* — storage and processing of data related to the processes of interest in the basin, both spatial features as well as time series data. In this context a relational database is used to store the measured data, a data model is used to organize the data in the database according to the "basin" principle, and a **geographic information system**[3] is used to display the data graphically.
- *Analytical Tools* — models designed to predict basin response to various climate and development **scenarios**.
- *Decision Formulation and Selection* — use of results from the models and interaction with users to make decisions on water management in the basin; and
- *Decision Implementation* — dissemination of decisions regarding water use under various conditions.

WHAT WE MODEL

River basin modeling requires the consideration of a wide scope of social, economic, and environmental aspects of resource use and protection. Principal areas of decision-making in water resources management include: **emergency water management**, water regulation, allocation, and quality. Decision-making regimes tend to be different for these areas due to differences in time available for making decisions (hours in the first case, days to months in the second, and years to decades in the third).

Emergency Water Management

We distinguish between river basin management problems dealing with early warning of extreme events, flood management, and accidental chemical spill management.

Early Warning

Early warning systems for floods or accidental chemical spills are information systems designed to send automated hydrologic and water quality data regarding water-related disasters to river basin planners, who combine them with meteorological data and **river basin models** to disseminate hazard forecasts and formulate strategies to mitigate economic damage and loss of human life.

Flood Protection

Protection from flooding events requires higher dimension models and smaller time steps than for many other water resource management models, such as municipal or agricultural water supply, recreation, water quality, etc. Flood flows usually

---

[3]Geographically referenced data in a relational database with a graphical mapping system.

occur over short time intervals (hours to days or weeks) making it impractical to model such events in multipurpose water resource planning models using simple mass balances. Calculating flood inundation as a result of flood wave propagation in a watershed requires two-dimensional modeling, rather than one-dimensional modeling.

Structural measures (e.g., reservoirs, levees, flood proofing) and nonstructural measures (e.g., land use controls and zoning, flood warning, and evacuation plans) are used to protect against floods. Upstream reservoir operators must provide storage capacity for flood protection and emergency warning to populations living in downstream floodplains. These operators need to know how much water to release and when in order to minimize expected flood damage downstream. The flood flow and peak in a basin depend on flood storage capacity and flood flow release policies. These can be determined by simulating flood events entering basin reservoirs. Expected flood damage can be predicted if the distribution of peak flows and the relationships between flood stage and damage, and flood stage and peak flow are known.

Chemical Spills

Accidental chemical spills are a major concern for areas that have vulnerable riverine ecosystems and cities with vulnerable drinking-water supplies and weak spill response capabilities. To protect against accidental spills, studies are performed to determine travel times in river reaches and to plan emergency responses to chemical spills into rivers, including guiding decisions regarding closing and reopening of intakes to drinking-water systems.

Emergency planning for spills in rivers and lakes entails having advective, nonreactive, nonmixing transport models capable of providing quick, worst-case **scenarios** of chemical concentrations at critical points downstream of spill sites. These allow for planning and deciding on alerts to be issued. More detailed, advective-dispersive, reactive modeling of the chemical fate and transport in the river system typically follow after the immediate response actions are taken.

Water Regulation, Allocation, and Quality

River Basin Management

In the area of general river basin management, decision-makers are faced with a myriad of problems, including:

- Operation of reservoirs to supply water for various purposes, including recreation, municipal and industrial water use, environmental flows, irrigation, and hydropower production.
- Examination of the effects of land-use and land-management policies on water quality.
- Assessment of eutrophication in surface water bodies.

- Development of pollution control plans for river basins and estuaries, including hydrodynamic and water quality impacts of alternative control strategies.
- Design and operation of wastewater treatment plants, i.e., what level of treatment is necessary to meet water quality goals under specific flow conditions; and
- Management of river basins, including the evaluation of the interrelationships between economic productivity and environmental degradation in a basin.

Lake and Reservoir Operation

In this area, decisions must be made regarding pollution control, water supply, and hydropower operation, mitigation of climate change effects, reservoir eutrophication, phosphorus control strategies, and operation of multiple reservoir systems. Different types of models are required in this area, such as, water allocation models to determine the distribution of water for economic production and environmental protection in a basin; or two- and three-dimensional models to analyze water quality in lakes.

Nonpoint Source Pollution

Here plans are made for agricultural chemical use or protection of vulnerable water bodies, stream, and aquifers. Modeling and managing agricultural nonpoint source pollution typically requires the use of a distributed parameter watershed model. The data management and visualization capabilities are needed to allow decision-makers identify and analyze problem areas easily.

Conjunctive Use of Surface and Ground Water

Because decision-makers are typically required to consider a multitude of social, legal, economic, and ecological factors, models have great potential for improving the planning and management of conjunctive use (ground and surface water) systems. This can require the integration of a number of simulation and optimization models with graphic user interface capabilities to provide an adequate framework for the discussion of water allocation conflicts in a river basin. Conjunctive use models and multiobjective decision methods can be combined to provide effective interbasin water transfer planning allowing decision-makers to analyze the social, economic, and environmental impacts of water transfers. Models are valuable in facilitating the consideration of a wide range of impacts, allowing decision-makers to incorporate technical information into the decision-making process, and providing output that can be interpreted easily.

For Further Discussion. To what extent do the different areas of water resources decision-making discussed above: **emergency water management**, water regulation, allocation, and quality, have different data requirements? For example, the time periods are different for each area (hours, to days, to months).

Some Issues in River Basin Modeling

There are a number of issues related to water management that must be considered for effective river basin modeling. First, water management takes place in a multidisciplinary and multijurisdictional environment and the problems must be approached from an integrated perspective (McKinney, 2004a). Second, water management must be considered at the scale of the river basin in order to internalize the major, potential externalities between activities of users in different parts of a basin. Finally, the importance of scale effects in trying to model the integrated effects of water uses across an entire basin must be addressed.

Integrated River Basin Management

Integrated River Basin Management are river basin management concepts based on the premise that water is an integral part of the ecosystem, a natural resource and a social and economic good, whose quantity and quality determine the nature of its utilization. River basin management includes both structural interventions and nonstructural rules and policies. *Structural interventions* include the design and construction of physical works under criteria of safety, workability, durability, and economy, including short-term, operation and maintenance activities with existing structures and long-term investments in new structures (McKinney *et al.*, 1999). *Nonstructural interventions* combine optimal operating rules of hydrologic systems, economic optimization of water allocation, and understanding community behavior and institutional processes related to the formation and support of agencies making decisions about water management. These institutional directives, economic/financial incentives, and hydrologic system operating rules have greatly modified the traditional, structural approach to water management. The interdisciplinary nature of water problems requires the integration of technical, economic, environmental, social, and legal aspects into a coherent framework for decision-making purposes. The requirements of users as well as those relating to the prevention and mitigation of water-related hazards should constitute an integral part of the integrated water management process.

Water allocation between competing uses is best addressed at the river basin scale through the use of combined economic and hydrological models. To be effective, **river basin models** must adopt an interdisciplinary approach and a number of barriers must be overcome:

- Hydrological models often use simulation techniques, whereas most economic analyses are performed with optimization procedures.
- Political and administrative boundaries of economic systems are rarely the same as those of hydrological systems; and
- Different spatial development scales, and time horizons are frequently encountered in economic versus hydrologic models.

River basin models are often used to assist planners in answering water policy questions, including socio-economic issues, such as:

- What is the appropriate level of transaction cost for various market-based incentives to improved water use efficiency (e.g., the acceptable level of cost for information, monitoring, contracting, and enforcement of market transactions)?
- How should water be allocated to achieve optimal productivity and net benefits of different water uses (e.g., agricultural, domestic, and industrial use)?
- What will be the demand for and economic value of water (e.g., production costs and willingness to pay) under various management **scenarios**?

River Basin Systems

Figure 10.2 shows the components of a river basin system, including possible sources of water supply (groundwater and surface water), a delivery system (river, canal and piping network), water users (agricultural, municipal, and industrial), and a drainage collection system (surface and subsurface). The atmosphere forms the river basin's upper boundary, and mass and energy exchange through this boundary determines the hydrologic characteristics of the basin. However, the state of the basin (e.g., reservoir and aquifer storage, and water quality) and the physical processes within the basin (e.g., stream flow, evapotranspiration, infiltration and

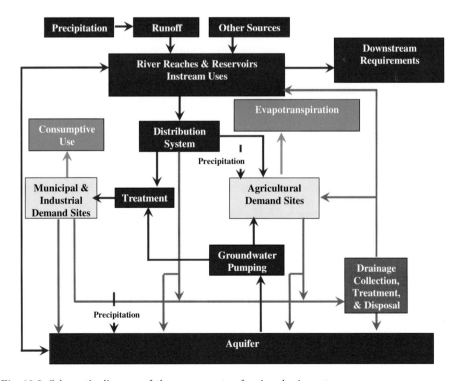

Fig. 10.2: Schematic diagram of the components of a river basin system.

Source: Authors.

percolation) are affected by human actions, including impoundment, diversion, irrigation, drainage, and discharges from urban areas. Therefore, a **river basin model** should include representations of not only the natural and physical processes, but also the artificial "hardware" (physical projects) and "software" (management policies) systems as well. The model should represent human behavior in response to policy initiatives. This may be as simple as a price elasticity of demand coefficient or as complex as a model of farmers' simultaneous choice of optimal water use, crops, and water application technology. The essential relations within each component and the interrelations between these components in the basin must be considered in **river basin models**.

It has been noted by some water resources professionals that there is a tendency for modelers to include too much detail into a model or to neglect important and relevant components of a model. This can lead to inaccurate model results and to inappropriate interpretation of those results. The complexity of a model should be dependent on the problem being analyzed and no more (Ford, 2006).

River basin models need to include interactions between water allocation, agricultural productivity, nonagricultural water demand, and resource degradation to estimate the social and economic net benefits from water allocation and use.

In order for decision-makers to understand critical water management aspects in the basin, the model should represent:

- The underlying physical processes.
- The institutions and rules that govern the flows of water and pollutants in the basin.
- The water diversion, use and return sites in the basin, including consumptive use locations for agricultural, municipal, industrial, and in-stream water uses (incorporating also reservoirs and aquifers); and
- The economic benefits of water use by applying production and benefit functions for water for use in the agricultural, environmental, urban, and industrial sectors.

Scaling of Processes

Figure 10.3 illustrates the scales (basin, district, and user) of relationships and decisions in river basin management. Water is used for instream purposes (hydropower generation, navigation, recreation, environmental flows, etc.) as well as off-stream purposes (agricultural, municipal and industrial (M&I) water uses). Basin planners often attempt to maximize the socio-economic net benefits to the basin stakeholders, such as the economic value of M&I water use, profit from irrigation, and benefits from instream water uses, but also minimize environmental damages due to waste discharges, irrigation drainage, and negative impacts on instream uses.

At one level, institutional policies such as water rights and economic incentives (e.g., water price, crop prices, and penalties on waste discharge and irrigation drainage) constrain or induce system operations and water use decisions. The management of water quantity and quality in a basin is based on the operation of

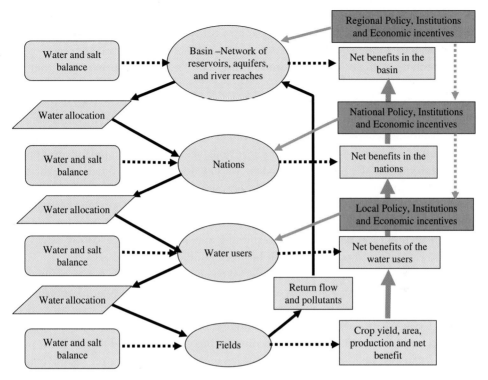

Fig. 10.3: Framework for river basin modeling at various scales.
Source: Authors.

reservoirs, aquifers, and conjunctive surface and ground water systems. The connections between water supply and demand and between upstream and downstream users are important considerations when considering return flows in the basin. The regulation of spatially distributed flows, pollutants, and demands has to be considered in a **river basin model** integrated over the proper scale within the river basin network.

For Further Discussion. Why is scale an important issue in river basin modeling? How does it enter into the formulation of models? What processes are predominant in considering the integrated management of river basins and why are they so important? How has neglecting the integrative nature of river basins resulted in environmental, economic, or social problems in the past?

HOW WE MODEL

Simulation and Optimization Models

Multiobjective, multipurpose, multifacility solutions to problems encountered in river basin management must be not only technically feasible but socially, environmentally, economically, and politically feasible as well. In most river basin management situations, it is hard to see how all the disparate components can be combined into a management plan or design, which meets prescribed and sometimes conflicting objectives and **constraints**. The "**systems approach**," that is, disassembling complex phenomena into smaller, isolated, more readily understood, subsystems, and analyzing the interactions between the subsystems and between the subsystems and the larger environment (Churchman, 1968), can aid in identifying situations where a minimum investment of funds and energies will produce maximum gains in terms of resource allocations, economic development, and environmental welfare. Using this approach, we can focus on the functioning of the components and the relationships and interactions between them under conditions to which the system may be subjected. This provides a means of sorting through the myriad of possible solutions to a problem and narrowing the search to a few potentially optimal ones in addition to determining and illustrating the consequences of these alternatives and the **trade-offs** between conflicting objectives.

Basin-scale analyses are often undertaken using one of two types of models (McKinney *et al.*, 1999): ones that *simulate* water resources behavior in accordance with a predefined set of rules governing water allocations and infrastructure operations, or ones that *optimize* and select allocations, infrastructure, and operations based on an objective function and accompanying **constraints**. Often system performance can best be assessed with simulation models, whereas system improvement can often be achieved through the use of optimization models.

River basin models that simulate the behavior of various hydrologic, water quality, economic, or other variables under fixed water allocation and infrastructure management policies are often used to assess the performance of water resources systems. A distinguishing feature of these simulation models, as opposed to optimization models, is their ability to assess performance over the long term, i.e., decades. Consequently, simulation is the preferred technique to assess water resources system responses to extreme, nonequilibrium conditions, and thereby to identify the system components most prone to failure, or to evaluate system performance relative to a set of sustainability criteria that may span decades. However, sustainability analysis has been accomplished through optimization recently (Cai *et al.*, 2002).

Models that optimize water resources based on an objective function and **constraints** must include a simulation component, however rudimentary, with which to calculate flows and mass balances. A distinct advantage of optimization models over simulation models is their ability to incorporate values (both economic and social) in the allocation of water resources. However, to be adopted by policymakers and system managers, optimal water allocations must agree with an infrastructure operator's perspective. This often requires that models be calibrated not only with respect to physical parameters of the system being modeled, but also with respect to the system management, i.e., the operation and decision-making processes for the system. This latter aspect is often overlooked in model development and application and can lead to poor acceptance of models in practice.

Many **river basin models** tend to have unwieldy input files and cryptic output files, making them useful only to technical specialists. Wide use of these models and the vastly expanded access to data have brought about the need for other technologies (e.g., databases and GUIs) to be integrated with models in order to make data accessible to models and to make inputs and results understandable to analysts and decision-makers. Unfortunately, except in very few cases, most models have yet to utilize the capabilities of modern relational databases.

River basin models have been reviewed by several authors (e.g., Yeh, 1985; Wurbs, 1993; Wurbs, 1994; Wurbs, 1998; Wagner, 1995; Watkins and McKinney, 1995; Labadie, 2004; McKinney, 2004b). Yeh (1985) provided a comprehensive state-of-the-art review of reservoir operation models with a strong emphasis on optimization methods. Wurbs (1993) provided a review of a wide array of reservoir simulation and optimization models and evaluated the usefulness of each approach for different decision-support situations. He hoped that his paper would help practitioners choose the appropriate model from the overwhelming number of models and modeling strategies that currently exist. Labadie (2004) points out the need to improve the operational effectiveness and efficiency of water resource systems through the use of computer modeling tools. He notes that the demand for this is increasing as performance-based accountability in water management agencies increases and as operators and managers come to rely more on modeling tools to respond to new environmental and ecological **constraints** for which they have little experience to draw on.

River basin models range from fully data oriented models to fully process oriented models. Data oriented models are represented by regression models or neural networks (i.e., black box models). Process oriented models are represented by models which have detailed representations of processes, but require few site specific data (i.e., white box models). The choice depends on the quantity and quality of data available and the knowledge of important physical, chemical, biological, and economic processes affecting the system.

For Further Discussion. What are some situations when **simulation modeling** of a basin may be preferred to **optimization modeling** and *vice versa*? How might one go about formulating an appropriate objective for **optimization modeling** of a river basin?

Components of River Basin Models

A typical **river basin model** is developed as a **node–link network**, in which nodes represent physical entities and links represent the connection between these entities (Fig. 10.4). The nodes included in the network are: (1) source nodes, such as rivers, reservoirs, and groundwater aquifers; and (2) demand nodes, such as irrigation fields, industrial plants, and households. Each distribution node is a location where water is diverted to different sites for beneficial use. The inflows to these nodes include water flows from the headwaters of the river basin and rainfall drainage entering the entities. Agricultural water users are assumed to allocate water to a series of

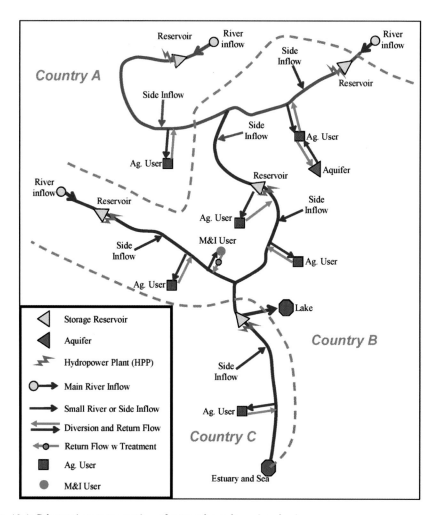

Fig. 10.4: Schematic representation of a transboundary river basin.

Source: Authors.

crops, according to their water requirements and economic profitability. Both crop area and yield may be determined endogenously depending on the model.

To solve the **river basin model** and obtain values for flow and storage in all arc and nodes of the basin network, some solution criterion must be established to provide regulation of the water resources of the basin river under various imposed conditions (**scenarios**). In other words, the model tries to:

- Balance water at the model nodes during each period of a specified planning horizon.
- Satisfy, to the extent possible, the demands of water users in the basin during the planning horizon.
- Follow the operation regimes of the basin reservoirs according to their technical requirements and rules of their operation; and
- Satisfy, to the extent possible, requirements for environmental flows.

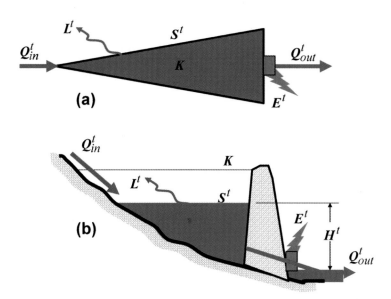

Fig. 10.5: Schematic diagram of a reservoir with power plant: (a) plan view; and (b) side elevation view.

Source: Authors.

The network representation of a river basin in a model is an arrangement of the river reaches, reservoirs and power plants, water users and lateral inflows (see Fig. 10.4). For every reservoir, water balances are calculated as (see Fig. 10.5):

$$S_j^t - S_j^{t-1} = Q_{\text{in},j}^t - Q_{\text{out},j}^t - L_j^t, \tag{10.1}$$

where

S_j^t volume of water in reservoir j at time t (million m^3);

$Q_{\text{out},j}^t$ release from reservoir j in period t (million m^3);

$Q_{\text{in},j}^t$ inflow to reservoir j in period t (million m^3); and

L_j^t loss from reservoir j over time t (million m^3) from seepage or evaporation.

The energy generated at a hydropower plant associated with a dam and reservoir is calculated as (see Fig. 10.5):

$$E_j^t = 2730 * \varepsilon_j * Q_{\text{out},j}^t * H_j^t, \tag{10.2}$$

where

E_j^t energy generated by plant j in time period t (kWh);

H_j^t effective hydraulic head on plant j in time period t (m). For "run-of-the-river" power plants, this value is a fixed constant; and

ε_j efficiency of plant j.

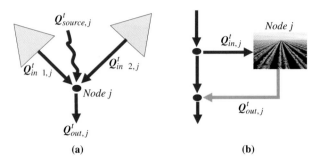

Fig. 10.6: Nodes representing (a) flow at a river confluence with a local source; and (b) return flow from an agricultural water user.

Source: Authors.

For nodes representing confluences of rivers, we have for each node j of this type and for each time period t (see Fig. 10.6)

$$\sum_{\text{out}} Q^t_{\text{out},j} = \sum_{\text{in}} Q^t_{\text{in},j} + Q^t_{\text{source},j}, \tag{10.3}$$

where

$Q^t_{\text{in},j}$ inflow to the node j in period t (million m³);

$Q^t_{\text{out},j}$ outflow from the node j in period t (million m³); and

$Q^t_{\text{source},j}$ source of water for node j in period t (million m³).

For water users, return flow from their diversion can be calculated as

$$Q^t_{\text{out},j} = r_j * \sum_{\text{in}} Q^t_{\text{del},j}, \tag{10.4}$$

where $0 \leq r_j \leq 1$ is the return flow coefficient for node j (dimensionless).

Allocation of Water to Users

Priority-Based Allocation

Such allocation of water to users in a river basin is based on a set of imposed or agree upon priorities assigned to water users. Often, the criterion used to calculate the allocation of water to users in a **river basin model** is to minimize deficits of water delivery to all users in each time period

$$\text{Minimize} \sum_i w_i \frac{Q^t_{\text{dem},i} - Q^t_{\text{del},i}}{Q^t_{\text{dem},i}}, \tag{10.5}$$

where

$Q^t_{\text{dem},i}$ water demanded by user i in period t (million m³);

$Q^t_{\text{del},i}$ water delivered to user i in period t (million m³); and

w_i priority of user i in the allocation process (dimensionless).

This method is used in the Water Evaluation and Analysis Program (WEAP) software discussed in a later chapter. There are different methods that can be used to endogenously or exogenously estimate the demands for water in the basin (primarily agricultural and municipal); however, an exogenous determination is the most common.

In the priority allocation method, for each time step a network flow solver attempts to satisfy the demands of the water users with the highest priority first. Then the lower priority users are satisfied in decreasing order of priority. This is a typical method of solution for several well-known **river basin models**, including WEAP (SEI, 2004), WRAP (Wurbs, 2001), ModSim (Labadie, 2000), and Oasis (Hydrologic, 2004).

River basin simulation models use network flow optimization algorithms to solve large sets of simultaneous equations in order to balance the flows in the network representing the basin. To mimic operating policies, such sets of procedures can be difficult to generate for complex systems, and very different and new rule sets may be needed if structural or significant policy changes are to be investigated. To avoid this, **river basin models** can be formulated as minimum cost capacitated network flow problems solved using network flow solvers, such as the out-of-kilter algorithm (used in HEC-ResSIM) or the more efficient Lagrangian approach (used in ModSim) of Bertsekas (1994). The network flow solver computes the values of the flows in each arc so as to minimize the weighted sum of flows, subject to **constraints** on mass balance at each node and upper and lower flow bounds. The weights are penalties expressing relative priorities in user-defined operating rules (WEAP, 2004). The user must provide lower and upper bounds on diversions, instream flows, and reservoir storage levels and assign relative priorities for meeting each flow requirement and for maintaining target reservoir storage levels. The network solver computes the flows and storage changes in a particular time interval (say, a day or a month), and then uses the solution as the starting point for calculations in the next time interval.

A distinguishing feature of these hybrid simulation/optimization models is the use of optimization on a period by period basis to "simulate" the allocation of water under various prioritization schemes, such as water rights, without perfect foreknowledge of future hydrology and other uncertain information.

Economic-Based Allocation

As an alternative to **priority-based allocation**, economic optimization can be used to allocate water based on economic criteria, such as priority to those uses that return the highest net benefits in the basin. Agricultural water demand can be determined endogenously within such a model using crop production functions (yield vs. water, irrigation technology, salinity, etc.) and an M&I water demand function based on a market inverse demand function. Water supply can be determined through a hydrologic water balance in the river basin with extension to the irrigated areas. Water demand and water supply are integrated into an endogenous system and balanced based on the economic objective of maximizing net benefits from water use, including irrigation, hydropower, and M&I benefits (Rosegrant et al., 2000).

The net benefit (profit) from agricultural water use at a particular site can be expressed as crop revenue minus fixed crop cost, irrigation technology improvement cost, and water supply cost:

$$NB_{Ag} = \sum_{cp} A * Y * p - A * fc - w * p_w, \qquad (10.6)$$

where

NB_{Ag}	net benefit from agricultural water use (US\$);
A	harvested area (ha);
p	crop price (US\$/mt);
f_c	fixed crop cost (US\$/ha);
p_w	water price (US\$/m^3); and
w	water delivered to demand sites (m^3).

A crop yield function, yield as a function of applied water, can be specified as follows:

$$Y = Y_{\max}[a_0 + a_1(w/E_{\max}) + a_2 \ln(w/E_{\max})], \qquad (10.7)$$

where

Y	crop yield (metric tons [mt]/ha);
$Y_{\max}$	maximum attainable yield (mt/ha);
a_0, a_1, a_2	regression coefficients;
w	applied water (mm); and
$E_{\max}$	maximum evapotranspiration (mm).

The net benefit from M&I water use can be derived from an inverse demand function for water (Rosegrant et al., 2000):

$$NB_{M\&I} = w_0 p_0/(1 + \alpha)[(w/w_0)\alpha + 2\alpha + 1] - w \cdot wp, \qquad (10.8)$$

where

$NB_{M\&I}$	net benefit from M&I water use (US\$);
w_0	maximum water withdrawal (m^3);
p_0	willingness to pay for additional water at full use (US\$);
e	price elasticity of demand; and
α	$1/e$.

Net benefits from power generation can be calculated as:

$$NB_{Power} = E * (p_{price} - p_{cost}), \qquad (10.9)$$

where E is the produced hydropower (kWh), p_{price} is the price of power production (US\$/kWh); and p_{cost} is the cost of power production (US\$/kWh).

A **river basin model** based on this development will also include institutional rules, including minimum required water supply for users, minimum and maximum crop production, and environmental flow requirements. In such a case, the objective is to maximize net benefits in the basin from the supply of water to agriculture and M&I water uses, and hydroelectric power generation, subject to institutional, physical, and other **constraints**. The objective is:

$$\text{Maximize } Z = \sum_{j-\text{Ag}} NB_{\text{Ag},j} + \sum_{j-\text{M\&I}} NB_{\text{M\&I},j} + \sum_{j-\text{power}} NB_{\text{power},j}. \qquad (10.10)$$

For Further Discussion. What are the reasons for not using economic allocation of water in a transboundary basin? What are the issues of national sovereignty that must be considered in this case? How can we build these into a **river basin model**?

Multiobjective Analysis Techniques

Water resources problems are inherently multifaceted with conflicting uses of water where **trade-offs** must be made between stakeholders with differing goals. In the previous section, we developed an objective function with three components representing the net benefits from allocating water to agricultural use, municipal and industrial use, and hydropower generation. Using net benefits in common monetary units, these individual objectives are commensurate. When the components are equally weighted, then each component is being given equal priority in the solution process according to its contribution to net benefits. That is, a dollar of agricultural benefit is equivalent to a dollar of hydropower benefit. However, these components or objectives can often be in conflict with one another, such as when agricultural water demand peaks in the summer growing season and hydropower demand peaks in the winter heating season.

Modeling methods that are used to determine the **trade-offs** between various conflicting objectives in water resources problems are used in **multiobjective analyses**. Multiobjective modeling methods have been used for several decades to determine the **trade-offs** between various objectives in water resources problems. Several books devoted to the subject of multiobjective planning, many with applications to water resources problems, have been published over the past three decades, including Haimes *et al.* (1975), Keeney and Raiffa (1976), Cohon (1978), Zeleny (1982), and Steuer (1986).

Examples of multiobjective modeling in water resources planning include Bogardi and Duckstein (1992), who presented an interactive multiobjective analysis method to embed the decision-maker's implicit preference function; Ridgley and Rijsberman (1992), who employed multicriteria decision aid for policy analysis of the Rhine estuary; and Theissen and Loucks (1992), who presented an interactive water resources negotiation support system. In these last two examples, multicriteria evaluation to support group decision-making was emphasized. Other work has focused on integrating technologies to support **multiobjective analysis**. Simonovic *et al.*

(1992) presented a rule-based expert system to facilitate and improve multiobjective programming in reservoir operation modeling.

Model Building Process

The **river basin model building process** consists of several steps (see Fig. 10.7):

- Problem identification — identify the important elements of the basin to be modeled and the relations and interactions between them. That is, a general outline and purpose of the model must be established. The modeler must identify the appropriate type of model for the system and the degree of accuracy needed given the time and resources available for modeling. Generally the simplest model with the least number of parameters which will produce reliable results in the time available is preferred (Ford, 2006).
- Conceptualization and development — establish the mathematical description of the relationships identified previously. In this step, appropriate computational techniques are also determined and implemented for the problem.
- **Calibration** — determine reliable estimates of the model parameters. In this step, model outputs are compared with actual historical or measured outputs of

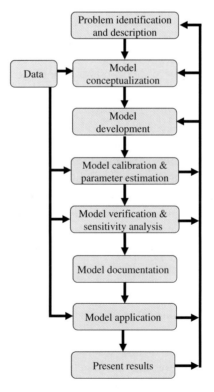

Fig. 10.7: General diagram of the steps in the **model building process**.
Source: Authors.

the system and the model parameters are adjusted until the values predicted by the model agree, to a reasonable degree of accuracy, with the measured values.

- **Verification** — an independent set of input data, i.e., different from that used in the **calibration** step, is used in the model and the model results are compared with measured outputs. If they are found to agree, the model is considered to be verified and ready for use.

- **Sensitivity analysis** — Many of the input data and assumptions that are used to construct a model are inaccurately measured, estimated from sparse data, or poor approximations. Modelers need to know what impact these potential sources of error or uncertainty may have on their model results. **Sensitivity analysis** explores and quantifies the impacts of possible errors in input data on predicted model outputs and system performance indices (Loucks and van Beek, 2005). Sometimes small changes in model parameters can produce large, abrupt changes in model solutions. Often, **sensitivity analysis** is a trial-and-error process of incrementally adjusting model parameters, coefficients, and inputs and subsequently solving the model. In this way, the modeler can see the change in model output values resulting from modest changes in input values and determine the importance of imprecision or uncertainty in model inputs in the modeling process (Loucks and van Beek, 2005).

Geographic Information Systems

Database systems provide comprehensive facilities for storing, retrieving, displaying, and manipulating data essential to the decision-making process. Two common data manipulation and storage tools are the relational database, which relates information in a tabular way so that the rules of relational algebra can be applied, and the geographic database (or **geographic information system**-GIS), which relates information pertaining to fundamental spatial features such as points, lines, and polygons. GIS brings spatial dimensions into the water resources database, and it has the ability to better integrate social, economic, and environmental factors related to water resources planning and management for use in decision-making. GIS offers a spatial representation of water resources systems, but only limited analytical capabilities for solving water resources problems.

There are several strategies for coupling environmental models to GIS (McKinney and Cai, 2002), ranging from loose couplings where data are transferred between models and GIS, and each has separate database management capabilities and systems; to tight couplings where data management in the GIS and model are integrated and they share the same database. Tighter coupling between GIS and **river basin models** has been enhanced by the ArcHydro data model (Maidment, 2002) that can easily represent river basins in GIS.

ArcHydro defines a data structure of classes, such as watersheds, cross-sections, monitoring points, and time series in a manner that reflects the underlying physical watershed. It also defines relationships between the data, so that a river basin (catchment) may know which point represents its outlet, or a monitoring point may be aware of time series records for that location. The ArcHydro data model is being used for water resources planning in the Rio Grande basin shared between the U.S. and Mexico (Patiño-Gomez and McKinney, 2005) and the South Florida Water Management District for the basis of an enterprise GIS database to support flood control, natural system restoration, operations decision support, and regional modeling projects (PBS&J, 2004).

MODELS USED IN TRANSBOUNDARY SETTINGS

Syr Darya Basin

The Syr Darya Basin, with average annual flow of 37.2 billion m^3 and area of about 484,000 km², stretches some 2,337 km from the Naryn River headwaters in Kyrgyzstan through the Fergana Valley shared by Kyrgyzstan, Uzbekistan, and Tajikistan, the Hunger Steppe in Uzbekistan, the Kyzyl Kum desert in Kazakhstan, before finally reaching the Aral Sea. Kyrgyzstan's Toktogul reservoir is the largest in the Syr Darya Basin and the only one with multiyear storage capacity (14 billion m^3 usable storage volume). The reservoir was designed and constructed in the Soviet period to operate in an irrigation mode with minimal winter season releases. Prior to independence in 1991, surplus power generated by summertime, irrigation releases from Toktogul was transmitted to neighboring regions of the Soviet Union. In return for this electricity and irrigation water, those regions sent electric power and fuels (natural gas, coal, and fuel oil) back to Kyrgyzstan for winter heating needs. For a description, the water resources situation in the basin and in Central Asia more generally, see McKinney (2004a).

This situation changed drastically when independent states were established in Central Asia in 1991. Because of complications in intergovernmental relations and account settlements, the introduction of national currencies, and increasing prices of oil, coal, natural gas, the supply of wintertime fuels and electricity sent to Kyrgyzstan from the other Republics was reduced. This created a winter heating crisis to which the Kyrgyz responded by increasing wintertime releases from Toktogul for hydroelectric generation thus depleting reservoir storage during the middle 1990s.

To alleviate these problems, the Syr Darya basin countries authorized the formation of a group to negotiate an interstate agreement on the use of water and energy resources in the Syr Darya Basin. This resulted in an agreement that created a framework addressing **trade-offs** between the competing uses of water for energy and irrigation in the Basin. Under the agreement, compensation is paid for compliance with a Toktogul release schedule that takes into account both upstream (Kyrgyz) winter energy needs and downstream (Uzbek and Kazakh) summer irrigation water demand. To date, the system has remained stable without major conflict and the agreement has entered the second five-year implementation period without major revision.

A critical element in the negotiations of the Syr Darya agreement was helping the parties understand the **trade-offs** between the conflicting objectives of winter electricity releases and summer irrigation releases. A multiobjective optimization model was developed to promote understanding of, and aid in the development of, efficient and sustainable water allocation options for the republics (McKinney and Cai, 1997; Cai *et al.*, 2003). The multiple objectives combined in the model included (1) minimizing upstream winter power deficits and maximizing downstream irrigation water supply. By integrating these objectives with the system's physical, political, and operational **constraints** in an optimization model, the **trade-offs** between the conflicting objectives of satisfying agricultural water demand, and generating hydroelectric power were elaborated and used to develop a number of water allocation **scenarios** to aid decision-making. Further analysis of the economic consequences of the proposed options was prepared using hydroelectric and agricultural input and output costs and prices (Keith and McKinney, 1997).

Rio Grande Basin

The Rio Grande originates in the San Juan Mountains of southern Colorado, flowing 3042 km from its headwaters to the Gulf of Mexico, passing through parts of three U.S. states (Colorado, New Mexico, and Texas) and five Mexican states in (Chihuahua, Durango, Coahuila, Nuevo Leon, and Tamaulipas). The Rio Grande is the international border from the El Paso, Texas area to the Gulf of Mexico. The basin covers an area of about 869,000 sq. km. Of the part of this area that contributes runoff to the river, about half is in Mexico and half is in the U.S. Principal tributaries to the river include the Conchos, San Rodrigo, Alamo, and San Juan Rivers in Mexico, and the Pecos and Devils Rivers in Texas. The Rio Grande water resources are almost entirely allocated and used by the time the river passes El Paso and the river has intermittent flow until it reaches the confluence with the Rio Conchos, flowing out of the Mexican state of Chihuahua.

Mexico and the United States have two treaties and various cooperative regulations that govern allocation of the water resources they share. The two nations signed the "Convention for the Equitable Division of the Waters of the Rio Grande for Irrigations Purposes" in 1906 (IBWC, 1906). This treaty allocated the water in the upper basin above Texas. In 1944, the United States and Mexico signed the Treaty for the "Utilization of Waters of the Colorado and Tijuana Rivers and of the Rio Grande" allocating the water of the lower part of the Rio Grande basin (IBWC, 1944). Under the treaty, each country receives half of the water in the main stem of the river, and full use of the waters in their tributaries (IBWC, 1944). However, the treaty provides that one-third of the flow reaching the river from several named tributaries is allocated to the United States, provided that this is not less than a specified annual amount (averaged over five-year accounting cycles). The vast majority of this water comes from the Rio Conchos basin, as flow in the other tributaries is minimal during much of the year.

Today the Rio Grande supports a thriving agriculture. It also provides water for drinking, hydroelectric power, sewage disposal, industry, and recreation for more than five million people who live in this basin. Current diversions from the river go primarily to agriculture (more than 87%) with Mexico irrigating about 445,154 ha, and the U.S. about 401,852 ha.

Drought has been a persistent problem in the Rio Grande Basin. Indeed, a recent drought event lasted for about 10 years, longer than was ever anticipated in the negotiations of the 1944 treaty, and, as a result, Mexico was unable to deliver the quantities of water required under the 1944 Treaty and accumulated a "water debt" at the end of two consecutive five-year treaty accounting cycles.

The traditional segment-specific approaches to water management planning have been deemed inadequate to meet the challenges of a large transboundary basin such as the Rio Grande. To illuminate strategies to reduce future conflicts over water throughout the entire basin, a comprehensive, model-based planning exercise was undertaken. These strategies include making agriculture more resilient to periodic conditions of drought, improving the reliability of supplies to cities and towns, and restoring lost environmental functions in the river system.

The effort consisted of two parallel, interacting and converging activities, one of which was building a water resources database (Patiño-Gomez and McKinney, 2005) and an associated hydrologic planning model that represents the entire basin (Danner *et al.*, 2006). This model was used to evaluate the hydrologic feasibility of a suite of **scenarios** for improving the management of the limited water available in this system, particularly those opportunities that bridge across management units and jurisdictional boundaries. Hydrologic feasibility includes both physical viability and the ability to provide mutual benefits to stakeholders throughout the system. This enabled the elaboration and understanding of the hydrologic dynamics in the basin such that the **trade-offs** associated with a range of management strategies could be clearly illuminated.

Simultaneously with the development of a basin-wide model, the project generated a set of future water management **scenarios** that respond to the needs and objectives of the basin stakeholders, including water users, planning agencies, environmental organizations, universities and research institutes, and local, state, and national government officials. These **scenarios** were evaluated for hydrologic feasibility by the basin-wide model in a set of gaming exercises. Modeling is necessary to understand how these options will affect the entire system and how they can be crafted to maximize the benefits and avoid unintended or uncompensated effects.

The development of the **scenarios** informed the process of assembling the data to populate the planning model. In constructing the management **scenarios**, a 30–50 year planning horizon was used so that the issue of climate variability and climate change could be considered.

Practice Questions

1. What is "systems analysis" and how can it aid in the planning and design of water resources projects?

2. What is the difference between "simulation" and "optimization modeling"? Give an example when it might be more appropriate to use one rather than the other.

3. In the **model building process**, why is it important to have independent data sets for the **calibration** and **verification** of a model?

4. What is **sensitivity analysis** and how would you use the results of such an analysis to guide data collection efforts?

5. Discuss the circumstances when countries might find themselves with conflicting river basin management objectives.

ANNEX 10A — SOME AVAILABLE RIVER BASIN MODELING SYSTEMS

Some of the more common river basin modeling tools are listed in this Annex, particularly the ones related to water allocation.

Delft-Tools (Delft Hydraulics, 2004) — Delft-Tools is a framework for decision support developed by Delft Hydraulics for the integrating water resources simulation programs. Functions of the system include **scenario** management, data entry, and interactive network design from map data, object-oriented database set-up, presentation, analysis, and animation of results on maps. DELFT-TOOLS integrates the Delft Hydraulics models: SOBEK, RIBASIM, and HYMOS. SOBEK is a one-dimensional river simulation model that can be used for flood forecasting, optimization of drainage systems, control of irrigation systems, sewer overflow design, ground-water level control, river morphology, salt water intrusion, and surface water quality. RIBASIM (River Basin Simulation Model) is a river basin simulation model for linking water inputs to water-uses in a basin. It can be used to model infrastructure design and operation and demand management in terms of water quantity and water quality. HYMOS is a time series information management system linked to the Delft Hydraulics models.

Mike-Basin (DHI, 2004) — MIKE-BASIN couples ArcView GIS with hydrologic modeling to address water availability, water demands, multipurpose reservoir operation, transfer/diversion schemes, and possible environmental **constraints** in a river basin. MIKE-BASIN uses a quasi-steady-state mass balance model with a network representation for hydrologic simulations and routing river flows in which the network arcs represent stream sections and nodes represent confluences, diversions, reservoirs, or water users. ArcView is used to display and edit network elements. Water quality simulation assuming advective transport and decay can be modeled. Groundwater aquifers can be represented as linear reservoirs. Current developments are underway to utilize the functionality of ArcGIS-9 in MIKE-BASIN.

Basic input to MIKE-BASIN consists of time series data of catchment run-off for each tributary, reservoir characteristics and operation rules of each reservoir, meteorological time series, and data pertinent to water demands and rights (for irrigation, municipal and industrial water supply, and hydropower generation), and information describing return flows. The user can define priorities for diversions and extractions from multiple reservoirs as well as priorities for water allocation to multiple users. Reservoir operating policies can be specified by rule curves defining the desired storage volumes, water levels and releases at any time as a function of existing storage volumes, the time of the year, demand for water, and possible expected inflows.

Water quality modeling in MIKE-BASIN is based on steady, uniform flow within each river reach and a mass balance accounting for inputs of constituents, advective transport and reaction within the reach. Complete mixing downstream of each source and at tributary confluences is assumed. Nonpoint pollution sources are handled in the model as well as direct loading from point sources. The model accounts for the following water quality parameters: biochemical oxygen demand, dissolved oxygen, ammonia, nitrate, total nitrogen, and total phosphorus. Nonpoint loads are represented using an area loading method accounting for the nitrogen and phosphorous loads originating from small settlements, livestock, and arable lands assuming certain unit loads from each category.

ModSim (Labadie *et al.*, 2000; Dai and Labadie, 2001) — ModSim is a generalized river basin DSS and network flow model developed at Colorado State University with capability of incorporating physical, hydrological, and institutional/administrative aspects of river basin management, including water rights. ModSim is structured as a DSS, with a graphical user interface (GUI) allowing users to create a river basin modeling network by clicking on icons and placing system objects in a desired configuration on the display. Through the GUI, the user represents components of a water resources system as a capacitated flow network of nodes (diversions points, reservoirs, points of inflow/outflow, demand locations, stream gages, etc.) and arcs (canals, pipelines, and natural river reaches). ModSim can perform daily scheduling, weekly, operational forecasting and monthly, long-range planning. User-defined priorities are assigned for meeting diversion, instream flow, and storage targets. ModSim employs an optimization algorithm at each time step to solve for flow in the entire network to achieve minimum cost while satisfying mass balance at the nodes and maintaining flows through the arcs within required limits. Conjunctive use of surface and ground water can be modeled with a stream-aquifer component linked to response coefficients generated with the MOD-FLOW groundwater simulation model (Fredricks *et al.*, 1998). ModSim can be run for daily, weekly, and monthly time steps. Muskingum–Cunge hydrologic routing is implemented in the model.

ModSim has been extended to treat water quality issues in stream-aquifer systems through an interactive connection to the EPA QUAL2E model for surface water quality routing, along with a groundwater quality model for predicting salinity loading in irrigation return flows (Dai and Labadie, 2001).

ModSim is well documented in both user manuals and source code comments. Model data requirements and input formatting are presented along with sample test applications useful in understanding model set up and operation. Currently, ModSim is being upgraded to use the ".NET Framework" with all interface functions handled in Visual Basic and C#. This will greatly enhance the ability of the model to interact with relational databases and all variables in the model will be available for reading or writing to a database.

ModSim is in the public domain, and executable versions of the model are available free of charge for use by private, governmental, and nongovernmental users. Generally, the source code for the model is not available. However, some government agencies have negotiated agreements with the developer in which the source code is made available to the agency and the agency is allowed to change or modify the source code as necessary for agency-related projects.

OASIS (Hydrologics, 2001; Randall *et al.*, 1997) — Operational Analysis and Simulation of Integrated Systems (OASIS) developed by Hydrologics, Inc. is a general purpose water simulation model. Simulation is accomplished by solving a linear optimization model subject to a set of goals and **constraints** for every time step within a planning period. OASIS uses an object-oriented graphical user interface to set up a model, similar to ModSim. A river basin is defined as a network of nodes and arcs using an object-oriented graphical user interface. Oasis uses Microsoft Access for static data storage, and HEC-DSS for time series data. The Operational Control Language (OCL) within the OASIS model allows the user to create rules that are used in the optimization and allows the exchange of data between OASIS and external modules while OASIS is running. OASIS does not handle groundwater or water quality, but external modules can be integrated into OASIS. Oasis does not have any link to GIS software or databases.

RiverWare (Carron *et al.*, 2000; Zagona *et al.*, 2001; Boroughs and Zagona, 2002; CADWES, 2004) — The Tennessee Valley Authority (TVA), the United States Bureau of Reclamation (USBR), and the University of Colorado's Center for Advanced Decision Support for Water and Environmental Systems (CADWES) collaborated to create a general purpose river basin modeling tool — RiverWare. RiverWare is a reservoir and river system operation and planning model. The software system is composed of an object-oriented set of modeling algorithms, numerical solvers, and language components.

Site specific models can be created in RiverWare using a graphical user interface (GUI) by selecting reservoir, reach confluence, and other objects. Data for each object is either imported from files or input by the user. RiverWare is capable of modeling short-term (hourly to daily) operations and scheduling, mid-term (weekly) operations and planning, and long-term (monthly) policy and planning. Three different solution methods are available in the model: simulation (the model solves a fully specified problem); rule-based simulation (the model is driven by rules entered by the user into a rule processor); and optimization (the model uses Linear Goal-Programming Optimization).

Operating policies are created using a constraint editor or a rule-based editor depending on the solution method used. The user constructs an operating policy for a river network and supplies it to the model as "data" (i.e., the policies are visible, capable of being explained to stakeholders; and able to be modified for policy analysis). Rules are prioritized and provide additional information to the simulator based on the state of the system at any time. RiverWare has the capability of modeling multipurpose reservoir uses consumptive use for water users, and simple groundwater and surface water return flows.

Reservoir routing (level pool and wedge storage methods) and river reach routing (Muskingum–Cunge method) are options in RiverWare. Water quality parameters including temperature, total dissolved solids, and dissolved oxygen can be modeled in reservoirs and reaches. Reservoirs can be modeled as simple, well-mixed, or as a two-layer model. Additionally, water quality routing methods are available with or without dispersion.

RiverWare runs on Sun Solaris (Unix) workstations or Windows based PCs. RiverWare does not have a connection to any GIS software; however, a hydrologic database (HDB) may be available (Frevert *et al.*, 2003; Davidson *et al.*, 2002). HDB is a relational database used by the USBR and developed by CADWES to be used in conjunction with RiverWare. HDB is an Oracle-based SQL database and includes streamflow, reservoir operations, snowpack, and weather data.

Dynamic Simulation Software — Dynamic simulation software has been applied to river basin modeling. This includes the software STELLA (High Performance Systems, 1992), POWERSIM (Powersim, 1966), VENSIM (Ventana, 1995), and GOLDSIM (Goldsim, 2003). These are dynamic simulation packages that stem from the system dynamics modeling method "Dynamo" invented by Forrester at MIT in the 1960s. The latest generation of these packages use an object-oriented programming environment. The models are constructed from stocks, flows, modifiers, and connectors, and the software automatically creates difference equations from these based on user input. These methods all include components for: (1) identification of stocks and flows in a system; (2) graphically representing dynamic systems in "stock-and flow-diagrams"; and (3) a computer language for simulating the constructed dynamic systems. Models can be created by connecting icons together in different ways into a model framework so that the structure of the model is very transparent.

WEAP (Raskin *et al.*, 1992; SEI, 2004) — The Water Evaluation and Planning System (WEAP) developed by the Stockholm Environment Institute's Boston Center (Tellus Institute) is a water balance software program that was designed to assist water management decision makers in evaluating water policies and developing sustainable water resource management plans. WEAP operates on basic principles of water balance accounting and links water supplies from rivers, reservoirs, and aquifers with water demands, in an integrated system. Designed to be menu-driven and user-friendly, WEAP is a policy-oriented software model that uses water balance accounting to simulate user-constructed **scenarios**. The program is designed to assist water management decision-makers through a user-friendly menu-driven graphical user interface. WEAP can simulate issues including sectoral demand analyses, water conservation, water rights, allocation priorities, groundwater withdrawal and recharge, streamflow simulation, reservoir operations, hydropower generation, pollution tracking (fully mixed, limited decay), and project cost/benefit analyses. Groundwater supplies can be included in the WEAP model by specifying a storage capacity, a maximum withdrawal rate, and the rate of recharge. Minimum monthly instream flows can be specified.

WEAP is relatively straightforward and user-friendly for testing the effects of different water management **scenarios**. The results are easy to view for comparisons of different **scenarios**. Changing input data to model newly proposed **scenarios** can be readily accomplished, as long as it is not necessary to make any changes to the ASCII file of historical data.

REFERENCES FOR ANNEX 10A

Boroughs, C. and E. Zagona (2002). Daily flow routing with the Muskingum-Cunge method in the Pecos River RiverWare model. In: Proceedings of the Second Federal Interagency Hydrologic Modeling Conference, Las Vegas, NV.

CADWES (Center for Advanced Decision Support for Water and Environmental Systems), RiverWare Overview, 2004, Accessed 2004: http://cadswes.colorado.edu/riverware/overview.html

Carron, J., E. Zagona and T. Fulp (2000). Uncertainty modeling in RiverWare. In: Proceedings of the ASCE Watershed Management 2000 Conference, Ft. Collins, CO.

Dai, T. and J. Labadie (2001). River basin network model for integrated water quantity/quality management, *Journal of Water Resources Planning and Management*, 127(5), 295–305.

Danish Hydraulics Institute (DHI) (2004a) Mike-Basin Description, Accessed April 2004: http://www.dhisoftware.com/mikebasin/Description/

Danish Hydraulics Institute (DHI) (2004b) TimeSeries Manager Description, Accessed 2004: http://www.dhisoftware.com/mikeobjects/TS_Manager/archydro.htm

Davidson, P., R. Hedrich, T. Leavy, W. Sharp and N. Wilson (2002). Information systems development techniques and their application to the hydrologic database derivation application. In: Proceedings of the Second Federal Interagency Hydrologic Modeling Conference, Las Vegas, NV.

Delft hydraulics (2004) Accessed April 2004: http://www.wldelft.nl/soft/tools/index.html

Fredericks, J., J. Labadie and J. Altenhofen (1998). Decision support system for conjunctive stream – Aquifer management, *Journal of Water Resources Planning and Management*, 124(2), 69–78.

Frevert, D., T. Fulp, G. Leavesley and H. Lins (2003). The watershed and river systems management program — an overview of capabilities, Submitted to the ASCE Journal of Irrigation & Drainage Engineering. Accessed: http://cadswes.colorado.edu/riverware/abstracts/FrevertJIDE2003.html

Goldsim Company (2003). Accessed April 2004: http://www.goldsim.com/

High Performance Systems (1992). Stella II: An introduction to systems thinking, High Performance Systems, Inc., Nahover, New Hampshire, USA, Accessed April 2004: http://www.hps-inc.com

HydroLogics (2004). User Manual for OASIS with OCL, Version 3.4.14, 2001, Accessed April 2004: http://www.hydrologics.net/oasis/index.shtml

Labadie, J. (2004). ModSim: Decision support system for river basin management, Documentation and User Manual-2000, Accessed April 2004: http://modsim.engr.colostate.edu/

Powersim Corporation (1996). Powersim 2.5 Reference Manual, Powersim Corporation Inc., Herndon, Virginia, USA, Accessed April 2004: http://www.powersim.com/

Randall, D. and D. Sheer (1997). A water supply planning simulation model using a mixed integer linear programming engine, *Journal of Water Resources Planning Management*, ASCE, 123(2).

Raskin, P., E. Hansen, Z. Zhu and D. Stavisky (1992). Simulation of water supply and demand in the Aral Sea Basin, *Water International*, 17, 55–67.

Stockholm Environment Institute (SEI) — Boston (2001). Tellus Institute, WEAP Water Evaluation and Planning System, User Guide for WEAP 21, Boston, MA. Accessed April 2004: http://www.weap21.org/downloads/weapuserguide.pdf

Ventana Systems (1995). Vensim User's Guide, Ventana Systems Inc., Belmont, Massachusetts, USA, Accessed April 2004: http://www.vensim.com/

Zagona, E. A., T. J. Fulp, R. Shane, T. Magee and H. M. Goranflo (2001). Riverware: A generalized tool for complex reservoir system modeling, *Journal of the American Water Resources Association*, 37(4), 913–929.

REFERENCES

Bogardi, J. and L. Duckstein (1992). Interactive multiobjective analysis embedding the decision maker's implicit preference function, *Water Resources Bulletin*, 28(1), 75–78.

Cai, X., D.C. McKinney and L.S. Lasdon (2002). A framework for sustainability analysis in water resources management and application to the Syr Darya Basin, *Water Resources Research*, 38(6), 21/1-21/14.

Cai, X., D.C. McKinney and L.S. Lasdon (2003). An integrated hydrologic-agronomic-economic model for river basin management, *Journal of Water Resources Planning and Management*, 129(1), 4–17.

Churchman, C.W. (1968). *The Systems Approach*. New York: Dell Publishing Co.

Cohon, J. (1978). *Multiobjective Programming and Planning*. New York: Academic Press.

Danner, C.L., D.C. McKinney and R.L. Teasley (2006). Documentation and testing of the WEAP model for the Rio Grande/Bravo Basin, CRWR Online Report 06-08, Center for Research in Water Resources, University of Texas at Austin, August 2006.

Ford, D.T. (2006). Tall, Grande or Venti models? *J. Water Resour. Plng. and Mgmt.*, 132(1), 1–3.

Grigg, N.S. (1996). *Water Resources Management*. New York: McGraw Hill.

Haimes, Y., W. Hall and H. Freedman (1975). *Multiobjective Optimization in Water Resources Systems*. Amsterdam: Elsevier Scientific.

Hall, W. and J. Dracup (1970). *Water Resources Systems Engineering*. New York: McGraw-Hill.

HydroLogics, User Manual for OASIS with OCL, Version 3.4.14, 2001, http://www.hydrologics.net/oasis/index.shtml

International Boundary and Water Commission (IBWC) (1944). Treaty between the United States of America and Mexico, http://www.ibwc.state.gov/Files/1944Treaty.pdf

Keeney, R.L. and H. Raiffa (1976). *Decisions with Multiple Objectives: Preferences and Value Tradeoffs*. New York: Wiley.

Keith, J. and D.C. McKinney (1997). Options analysis of the operation of the Toktogul reservoir, Issue Paper No. 7, United States Agency for International Development

(USAID) Environmental Policy and Technology (EPT), Almaty, Kazakhstan, August.

Labadie, J. (2000). ModSim: Decision support system for river basin management, Documentation and User Manual-2000, http://modsim.engr.colostate.edu/

Labadie, J. (2004). Optimal operation of multireservoir systems: State-of-the-art review, *Journal of Water Resources Planning and Management*, 130(2), 93–111.

Lee, D. and A. Dinar (1996). Integrated approaches of river basin planning, development, and management, *Water International*, 21(1), 213–222.

Loucks, D.P., J.R. Stedinger and D.A. Haith (1981). *Water Resource Systems Planning and Analysis*. Englewood Cliffs: Prentice Hall.

Loucks, D.P. and E. van Beek (2005). *Water Resources Systems Planning and Management: An Introduction to Methods, Models and Applications*. Paris: UNESCO.

Maas, A., M.M. Hufschmidt, R. Dorfman, H.A. Thomas, S.A. Marglin and G.M. Fair (1962). *Design of Water Resource Systems*. Cambridge: Harvard.

Maidment, D.R. (2002). *Arc Hydro: GIS for Water Resources*. Redlands: ESRI Press.

Mays, L.W. (ed.) (1996). *Handbook of Water Resources*. New York: McGraw Hill.

Mays, L.W. and Y.-K. Tung (1992). *Hydrosystems Engineering and Management*. New York: McGraw Hill.

McKinney, D.C. (2004a). Cooperative management of transboundary water resources in central asia. In: Burghart, D. and T. Sabonis-Helf (eds.), *In the Tracks of Tamerlane-Central Asia's Path into the 21st Century*, National Defense University Press.

McKinney, D.C. (2004b). International survey of Decision Support Systems for Integrated Water Management, Technical Report, US Agency for International Development, Agricultural Pollution Reduction Activity in Romania, Bucharest, Romania.

McKinney, D.C., X. Cai, M. Rosegrant, C. Ringler and C. Scott (1999). Integrated basin-scale water resources management modeling: Review and future direction, System-Wide Initiative on Water Management (SWIM) Research Paper No. 6, International Water Management Institute, Colombo, Sri Lanka.

McKinney, D.C. and X. Cai (2002). Linking GIS and water resources management models: An object-oriented method, *Environmental Modeling and Software*, 17(5), 413–425.

McKinney, D.C. and X. Cai (1997). Multiobjective water resource allocation model for Toktogul reservoir, Technical Report, US Agency for International Development, Environmental Policy and Technology Project, Central Asia Regional EPT Office, Almaty, Kazakstan, April.

Patiño-Gomez, C. and D.C. McKinney (2005). GIS for large-scale watershed observational data model, CRWR Online Report 05-07, Center for Research in Water Resources, University of Texas at Austin, December.

Ridgeley, M. and F. Rijsberman (1992). Multicriteria evaluation in a policy analysis of a Rhine estuary. *Water Resources Bulletin*, 28(6), 1095–1110.

Rosegrant, M.W., C. Ringler, D.C. McKinney, X. Cai, A. Keller and G. Donoso (2000). Integrated economic-hydrologic water modeling at the basic scale: The Maipo river basin, *Agricultural Economics*, 24(1), 33–46.

Simonovic, S., H. Venema and D. Burn (1992). Risk-based parameter selection for short-term reservoir operation, *Journal of Hydrology*, 131, 269–291.

Steuer, R. (1986). *Multiple Criteria Optimization: Theory, Computation, and Application*. New York: John Wiley & Sons.

Theissen, E.M. and D.P. Loucks (1992). Computer assisted negotiation of multiobjective water resources conflicts, *Water Resources Bulletin*, 28(1), 163–177.

Viessman Jr, W. and C. Welty (1985). *Water Management: Technology and Institutions.* New York: Harper & Row, Publishers.

Wagner, B. (1995). Recent developments in simulation-optimization groundwater management modeling, U.S. National Contributions in Hydrology 1991–1994, *Reviews of Geophysics*, Supplement, 1021–1028, July.

Watkins Jr, D.W. and D.C. McKinney (1995). Recent developments in decision support systems for water resources, U.S. National Contributions in Hydrology 1991–1994, *Reviews of Geophysics*, Supplement, 941–948, July.

Wurbs, R. (1993). Reservoir-system simulation and optimization models, *Journal of Water Resources Planning and Management*, 119(4), 455–472.

Wurbs, R. (1994). Computer models for water resources planning and management, US Army Corps of Engineers, Institute for Water Resources, IWR Report 94-NDS-7, Alexandria, VA.

Wurbs, R. (1998). Dissemination of generalized water resources models in the United States, *Water International*, 23(3), 190–198.

Wurbs, R.A. (2001). Reference and users manual for the water rights analysis package (WRAP). Texas Water Resources Institute, College Station, TX, July.

Yeh, W.-G. (1985). Reservoir management and operations models: A state-of-the-art review, *Water Resources Research*, 21(12), 1797–1818.

Zeleny, M. (1982). *Multiple Criteria Decision Making*, New York: McGraw-Hill.

11. CONCLUSION

Is water becoming scarcer over time? Have the wars of this century been fought over water? Have conflict-solving arrangements been effective? Can various analytical tools developed by various disciplines address water conflict and cooperation? These are some of the questions the book has raised, directly and indirectly, in the various chapters and annexes. In this chapter, we attempt to synthesize some of the conclusions reached with focus on these points.

It is clear that the total amount of freshwater on the planet is relatively constant (so long as desalination of sea water is not considered as an actual source). It is also apparent that population grows over time. However, it is also obvious that what really matters in dealing with water scarcity is not the simple ratio of total available water to total population, but rather the ability of a society to manage available water in such a way that scarcity impacts can be minimized. Therefore, water-related institutions and available technologies matter a great deal and may relieve the impact of scarcity. This is why countries with annual water availability in the range of 250–500 m^3 per capita are being less affected by water scarcity than countries with water availability values of 5,000–10,000 m^3 per capita. The main difference is the existence of proper institutions and advanced technologies to address scarcity. In the context of transboundary water, existence of such differences between riparian states may be either a window for cooperation, or under certain circumstances, a reason for conflict.

We also observe the trend of globalization and international trade, compensating for scarce water. For example, many states have realized that their food security policies have actually led to the excessive use of already scarce water. In essence, under many food security policies, countries would grow their own staple crops, which could otherwise be purchased abroad. With the emergence of international food trade agreements, specialization and relative advantage in food production have reduced water wastage with states importing staples, such as grain, from abroad. Therefore, water availability is much more than just a physical term and can be amended by a plethora of management interventions witnessed in many parts of the world.

Although water is becoming (plainly speaking) scarcer, all the wars that have been fought in this century have never been over water. Is that a good sign? Contrary to the warnings voiced by some world leaders and institutions, we have seen more disputes over water between fellow riparians ending in cooperation. Are the legal conventions and local customary rules playing an important role in such situations?

Are economic incentives associated with benefit sharing, in shared basins, surpassing the likely opportunities attained from unilateral actions? While international law provides the necessary framework for solving transboundary water conflicts, it must be complemented by additional devices, providing a sustainable framework for transboundary water cooperation. In essence, the combination of legal, economic, and institutional components make cooperation most sustainable.

The extensive literature review presented in the book provides the reader not only with background information to the field of conflict and cooperation over international water, but also suggests a different research path. The majority of the analytical works are case-study oriented and variables identified are often appropriate for a single case study. Such an approach narrows the analytical perspective and reduces the possible generalization of the results across a large number of observations. Undoubtedly, empirical works with global relevance and application are lacking. That is, while the theoretical underpinnings of the field have been mainly developed in the context of one, or few, river basins, efforts to test a theory across an extensive set of data are few and far from sufficient in the literature on transboundary water. One would undoubtedly lose important detail by taking this general route. However, one would be able to broaden the basis for conclusions about conflict and cooperation over transboundary water, applying findings to a number of water disputes, and their subsequent resolution.

Another important conclusion gleaned from the book suggests that conflict and cooperation have different time horizons. While conflict may be quick to ensue, the emergence of cooperation is often sluggish. Therefore, the process of negotiation, which leads to cooperation, deserves serious scrutiny. In fact, this topic has not been extensively pursued, thus far, in past literature. That being said, with hundreds of available recorded treaties, there should be sufficient information on the negotiation processes leading to these agreements. Naturally, such investigations will be undertaken as single case studies. In addition, engineers, political scientists, economists, anthropologists, or geographers from the basins in question could work in unison to provide a comprehensive analysis of the agreement's negotiation.

The subject of cooperation is quite complex. However, basin cooperation may be devised around four main factors: providing incentives for cooperation, monitoring and enforcement of the agreement, developing institutional structures for managing potential conflicts, and accounting for (still) likely externality effects resulting from cooperation. Were past experiences successful? In many cases they were. Nonetheless, past experience suggests that integrated international resource management will be efficiently implemented prior to the onset of a conflict. Therefore, a leading consideration in any cooperative arrangement should assume that conflict is likely and needs to be addressed from the outset. Cooperative development plans will also be more stable if they link as many components as possible (the "expanding the cake" principle). Creating incentives for voluntary cooperation among riparians in an international river basin may be accomplished either by targeting a broad set of issues of interest to all riparians or by allowing for side payments (exchanging benefits). The role of trustworthy third party mediators, in the process of resolving existing conflicts or preventing potential future conflicts, is also crucial.

The book afforded considerable import to different quantitative analytical approaches, such as game theory and river basin modeling. Transboundary water is a common property resource and common property resources have long been in the center of public interest regarding efficient and equitable allocation mechanisms used by societies that share them. Cooperative game theory may provide relevant insights and solutions in the case of transboundary water. The perception of fairness plays a crucial role in designing potential allocation rules that are conceived "equitable" and "envy-free" by all parties. The various tools that have been introduced and applied in the various examples (real and stylized) introduced the necessary conditions for cooperation and demonstrated how certain cooperative allocation arrangements can be described and calculated. While cooperative game theory provides a proper framework to analyze cooperation options in transboundary water problems, there is a wide range of results one has to consider, using various criteria. Surely, some of these criteria are met, yet others are not, and this adds an important dimension to the evaluation and prioritization of solution concepts that were presented—it is not only the political-economic aspects of the problems, but also the natural physical aspects that have to be addressed. The importance of accurate river basin modeling as a pre-requisite for any allocation discussion is undoubtedly critical. We will elaborate on it later.

While game theory plays a crucial role in understanding conflict and cooperation over international water, the field of economics (where game theory has been further developed and utilized) is underrepresented in the literature we reviewed in this book. This is not to say that economics is not important or that economists are not interested in international water issues. It is probably a combination of several factors, including the difficulty in obtaining accurate data and information and the ability to communicate the results to the decision makers in the respective river basins. Regardless, economic analysis for identifying conditions for cooperation in various basins is important. Economic justification of cooperative arrangements and development options is the first step toward the initiation of a negotiation process that may lead to an agreement.

The analysis in this book supports the conclusion that just as shared water resources may be a source of conflict, it is often conflict that provides the impetus for cooperation. Past work has focused mainly on water quantity scarcity. However, scarcity related to hydropower, flood control, and pollution works in the same direction as water quantity scarcity. Therefore, all aspects of water scarcity have to be addressed in basin cooperation arrangements and treaties embody these nuances.

A general investigation of treaties will suggest that some agreements allocate water while others allocate entire rivers' resources. Certain agreements even attempt to achieve a balance between different kinds of uses of the shared resource. Some agreements also divide the benefits among the riparians, for a given use of the river. As riparians jointly exploit the river, side-payment and cost-sharing regimes often describe such benefit-sharing arrangements. As suggested in this volume, the geographical configuration of the river and the position of the riparians along that water body matter. Similarly, the economic asymmetries, which characterize certain riparian dynamics are also relevant. In essence, such patterns reveal not only how cooperation comes about but also how general legal principles and property rights disputes are reconciled in practice.

Another important mechanism for the sustainability of the cooperative arrangement, codified in a treaty, is the basin commission. Frequently, the basin commission grounds the cooperative initiative in an institutional setting, which contributes to the durability of the cooperative relationship. A commission may provide the parties with a forum to further discuss the cooperative relationship fostered by the agreement. While a basin commission promotes future cooperation and provides an ideal opportunity for riparians to resolve conflicts of interest, it may not work in different contexts (e.g., geographies, political regimes). One conclusion garnered from the extensive treaty analysis discussed in this volume suggests that there is no one solution that fits all situations. There is also no clear recommendation on how to build a sustainable regime for a given basin.

River basin modeling has shown that there are a wide range of approaches for specifying a model for river basin planning, development, and management. Economic, engineering, biological, political and integrated approaches can all reveal potentially useful information to the river basin planner or the parties to the negotiation. The key to modeling is to discern the most pressing problems, and to decide if the model would be best used to better understand the problem, help identify potential solutions, or be used as an ongoing tool in management and operations. Finally, models can also assess the amount of resources available, and the options to utilize them for producing benefits. One conclusion derived here, and echoes some of our earlier conclusions, is that modeling is a necessary tool for enhancing cooperation. However, to be relevant, a basin model has to be developed by an interdisciplinary team of experts. In addition, the interdisciplinary nature of the issues should be reflected in the model.

The study of conflict and cooperation over transboundary water requires an interdisciplinary approach, considering the economic, political, legal, hydrological, and environmental tones of the topic. The linkage of different disciplinary approaches reflected in this volume is a testament to this reality.

CASE STUDY 1: THE MEKONG RIVER BASIN*

The Mekong River Basin case depicts a number of characteristics important for understanding the field of transboundary water. For example, the basin embodies some of the least developed (tributary) rivers in the world, in part because of difficulties inherent in implementing joint management among a diverse set of riparian states. Related, but not necessarily dependent, the Basin is also an example of uncoordinated international interventions that may or may not be useful in the long run. Most importantly, the Mekong is an example of interstate cooperation in times of war. The 1957 Agreement (Establishment of the Committee for the Coordination of Investigations of the Lower Mekong Basin on 17 September 1957) created the Mekong Committee (the four Lower Mekong riparians of Vietnam, Laos, Cambodia, and Thailand), which existed and acted in various veins despite political, ideological differences, and wars that unfolded in the region. For example, the supply of electricity from Laos to Thailand and in return the payment by Thailand to Laos, was never interrupted, despite hostilities between the two countries.

In 1995, the Mekong River Basin Treaty (1995 Agreement on the Cooperation for the Sustainable Development of the Mekong River Basin) was signed. Nearly 12 years since the treaty was signed it is apparent that the Basin has moved to a new era of cooperation. However, some of the basin riparians are still far from realizing the full potential of cooperation. In this case study, we will analyze the process leading to the 1995 Mekong Treaty and consider the Basin's progress to the present.

FEATURES OF THE BASIN

The Mekong River spans over six countries: China, Myanmar (Burma), Laos, Thailand, Cambodia, and Vietnam, and stretches over 4,800 kilometers (km) with an annual flow of 450–475 billion m^3 (BCM), and with a total drainage area of 795,000 km^2. The Mekong main branch originates in the Tanggula Shan Mountains of the Tibetan Plateau (QinHai Province), traveling for nearly 2000 km through China's Yunnan province, to become the border for 220 km between Laos and Burma's Shan state. The drainage area of this upstream segment of the river basin (Upper Mekong) extends over an area of 174,000 km^2. The total annual runoff from

*This case study benefited from research by Chris Leroy, Steve Rozner, Alexis Gutiérrez, Veronika Stefkova, and Katerina Satavova. It benefited greatly from comments by Greg Browder and George Radosevich. The case study is not aimed at covering all aspects and details.

Map CS1.1: The Mekong Basin.

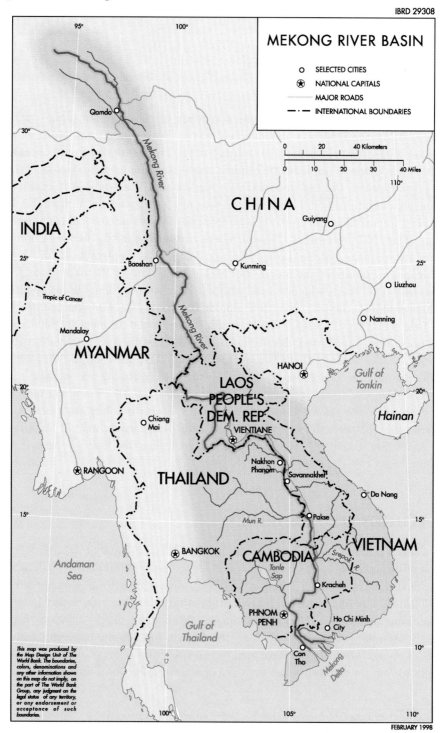

the Upper Mekong is about 80 BCM/year. The Mekong then enters the Lower Basin (Lower Mekong) at the point where Burma, Laos, and Thailand converge (referred to as the "Golden Triangle"). From hereafter, the river flows for another 2,400 km during which it crosses through Laos in an eastward direction, then cuts south to delineate the Thai–Lao border before forming a vast delta area shared by Cambodia and Vietnam — known as the Mekong Delta — where it empties into the South China Sea. The runoff from the Lower Mekong tributaries amounts to 370–400 BCM/year (Hori, 2000; Elhance, 1999; Browder, 2000).

Most of the Mekong's tributaries originate in the Lower Basin. In fact, 77% of the Mekong's total drainage is situated in the Lower Basin, 35–40% of which originates from watersheds in Laos (Elhance, 1999, p. 194). Owing to the number of tributaries it boasts, Laos has the largest available renewable freshwater per capita ratio in Asia (Hirsch and Cheong, 1996a, p. 9), making it a major contributor of the Basin's hydrological regime. A number of hydropolitical and hydrological variables are presented in Table CS1.1.

The Basin is subject to both interannual and intraannual fluctuation of water flow, mainly due to variation in monsoon rains. Mean annual rainfall in the Lower Mekong is 1672 mm/year, with the rainy season being April–October (Hori, 2000). Monsoon rains, mostly in the Lower Basin, account for roughly 75% of the Mekong's discharge and cause yearly flooding in the lowlands of Cambodia and Vietnam. Flow volume in the Mekong is represented by the gauging station in Kratie, Cambodia (Hori, 2000). Specifically, 45 years of flow measurement suggest an average annual flow of 441 BCM, based on average flow volume of 14,000 m^3/s, with a large variation ranging between a max of 66,700 and a min of 1,250 m^3/s (Hori, 2000, p. 32).

The cultivation of rice fields throughout the Mekong Delta depends on the seasonal increases in the river flow, though severe floods sometimes cause serious damage to rice crops. The importance of seasonal floods for agriculture stems

Table CS1.1: Area, population, and runoff by basin riparians.

Country	Share of area within the basin (%)[a]	Share of population within the basin (%)[a]	Percentage of runoff originating in local tributaries (%)[a]	GNP per capita (USD as of 2000)[b]
China (Yunnan)	20.8	12.9	16.0	565
Myanmar	3.0	1.2	2.0	na
Thailand	23.1	37.8	18.0	2,000
Laos	25.5	6.1	35.0	260
Cambodia	19.4	11.4	18.0	260
Vietnam	8.2	30.6	11.0	390
Total	100 (795,500 km^2)	100 (74.3 million)	100 (450–475 BCM/year)	NA

[a]World Bank (2006).
[b]Modified from Hori (2000, pp. 11, 30).
na = not available; NA = not applicable.
Note: Absolute total basin values are in parentheses.

from insufficient rainfall throughout the Lower Basin, which varies from less than adequate to just adequate for rice production from year to year. Another important feature of the Lower Basin's hydrological regime is the seasonal change in flow of the Tonle Sap ("Great Lake"). During the rainy season, this "river-lake" acts as a natural reservoir for excess Mekong River flow before reversing direction during the dry season, emptying much needed water into the Mekong Delta (Hori, 2000).

The Mekong Basin is characterized by a highly mountainous topography, a feature that has severely constrained the mobility of people and goods and limited agricultural development, to suitable flatlands, primarily those on the plateau shared by Thailand and Laos and in the southern Delta region. While a barrier to agricultural development, the river's steep incline both in China and in Laos presents significant opportunities for hydropower development and, by extension, water resource management (which will be elaborated later).

Because of centuries of underdevelopment, the result of past colonial rule, civil strife in the region, and intense historical enmities among the riparian states, the Mekong is one of the world's largest basins yet to realize its full development potential. Despite pledges to enhance regional management of its water resources in recent decades, the Mekong remains one of the least modified of major world rivers, both in terms of water impoundments and diversions (Hirsch and Cheong, 1996b, p. 4). It should be noted, moreover, that the majority of development in the Basin, to date, has been on the river's tributaries, particularly in Laos and Thailand. The main branch of the River itself has yet to undergo significant development.

HISTORY OF WATER AND OTHER DISPUTES IN THE MEKONG BASIN[1]

Several historical, political, and policy disagreements among the basin countries have led to a number of conflicts (some also leading to wars) in the region. Table CS1.2 provides a selected number of incidents, highlighting the role of domestic politics and policies in shaping the overall environment in the Mekong Basin. As can be gleaned, the economic structures in the six riparian countries are quite different, which may be a factor in explaining the likelihood for regional cooperation, discussed in the coming section. Both a weak regional economy and dependence on external funding characterize Myanmar, Laos, and Cambodia. A market economy links of China, Vietnam, and Thailand, although the former two riparians are still struggling with market adjustments.

---

[1] Based on Radosevich (1996), Elhance (1999), Browder (2000), and Gajaseni *et al.* (2006). Additional references are inserted in the text where relevant.

Table CS1.2: Domestic politics and policies in the riparian states of the Mekong.

Riparian	Domestic politics and policies
China	A centrally administered system but succumbing to political and economic regionalism. Basin-related development conducted largely at the provincial level in Yunnan province. Plans to build a series of dams along the main branch of the Mekong could either help or hurt the Basin wide regime. Market reforms w/ continued central planning; industrialization means energy demand growing rapidly, particularly in inland provinces
Myanmar	Military junta lacking popular support. Has neither the will nor the means to influence the Basin regime, but may pose a threat to future cooperation efforts should it take control of the Basin region (the "Golden Triangle") currently controlled by minority rebel forces, opium cartels, and drug traffickers. Weak regional economy
Lao PDR	Communist leadership is politically weak but has bargaining power given the country's natural endowment of water and terrain conducive to hydropower development. Economic development relies heavily on potential hydropower and agriculture production
Cambodia	Weakly structured coalition government under strict UN supervision struggling to establish sound political institutions. Isolated during Khmer Rouge era, Cambodia desperately wants to reenter the regional political and economic realm. Vietnam needs Cambodia's cooperation in maintaining the Tonle Sap hydrological regime intact. Cambodia is developing but still heavily dependent on foreign assistance; Agriculture drives the economy
Thailand	Pro-Western, market-based parliamentary monarchy. Save China, Thailand is the Basin powerhouse and tends to dictate the terms of regional cooperation. Largely at odds with Vietnam, its traditional rival, most recently due to its ambitious hydropower development plans. Industrialized, pro-capitalist economy; Domestic hydropower capacity already over-extended, necessitating power purchasing arrangements with other Basin riparians
Vietnam	Communist regime in Hanoi launched an ambitious economic reform program in the late 1980s, termed "*doi moi*," but has failed to match economic liberalizations with political freedom. Thus, Vietnam still embodies a central planning system. Vietnam has little bargaining power as the most downstream of the riparians, but does have certain "associative" influence over the behavior and decisions of its Indochina cohorts, Cambodia, and Laos. Eager to increase its regional influence vis-à-vis Thailand and China. Market reforms have modernized the economy, but Delta region still heavily dependent on agriculture

Sources: Based on Kirmani and Le Moigne (1997), Nguyen (1999), and Osborne (2000).

Historical Conflict and Cooperation

When examining the historical relations among the Mekong Basin riparians, one should bear in mind that clear demarcated national boundaries did not exist in the Basin until 1926, when the French colonial government in Indochina (encompassing present-day Vietnam, Cambodia, and Laos) and the government of Siam (now Thailand) came to an agreement delineating a territorial boundary between them. The border was based on the course of the main branch of the Mekong. In fact, the history of the region has been one of alternating contractions and expansions by the riparians, particularly the larger powers China, Vietnam, and Thailand (Cambodia and Laos to a lesser extent). Borders have therefore remained hotly contested even after 1954, when the French colonies gained their independence (Osborne, 2000).

Riparian Conflicts

Centuries-old rivalries among the Mekong riparians have not waned. The resentment of countries making up Indochina — Vietnam, Cambodia and Laos — have likewise not abated toward Thailand. The latter's ability to eschew European domination in the 19th century and its stable relations with the West since World War II has created much bitterness. The Chinese "diaspora" in Southeast Asia has created yet another source of tension, particularly during periods of heightened nationalistic sentiment.

When examined from the level of bilateral conflict, it is understandable that historical animosities in the Basin continue to fetter real cooperation. Thailand and Vietnam share the most intense rivalry, dating back to the pre-colonial period when the two countries vied for territories now constituting Laos and Cambodia. Tensions have been aggravated by more recent ideological disputes as well as growing disagreements over shared-water resources. Laos and Cambodia engaged in similar periods of territorial contraction and expansion during their earlier histories, but these territories mainly acted as a buffer zone for mitigating Thai-Vietnamese frictions.

Vietnam has had a similarly trying relationship with its northern neighbor China. Beyond historical aggression toward Vietnam during periods of territorial expansion, China became the source of intense Vietnamese resentment due to its involvement in the delineation of the border between North and South Vietnam following Vietnamese independence in 1954. China's invasion of Vietnam in 1979 in support of an opposition faction and the brief border war that ensued, fueled the fire of historical enmities once again. Moreover, China's support for the insurgent Khmer Rouge over the pro-Vietnamese government in Cambodia widened the ideological rift between the two countries. Vietnam and Cambodia share a similar history of aggression, though on a lesser scale. However, in the aftermath of the Vietnam War tempers flared as Vietnam sought to undermine the Khmer Rouge regime as it rapidly rose to power, culminating in an invasion of Cambodia in 1978 and a subsequent 11-year Vietnamese military presence in the Cambodian capital Phnom Penh.

Traditionally, relations between Thailand and Cambodia were somewhat less tumultuous than between Thailand and its other neighbors, though tempers flared in 1997 when the Thais provided refuge to former Khmer Rouge leader Pol Pot amid a countrywide purge of Khmer leaders by the Cambodian military. (While the Thai government continues to deny responsibility, some observers suggest that military and business elites in Thailand benefited from their collusion with Khmer leaders.) Meanwhile, a centuries-old border dispute between Thailand and Laos remains unresolved. Most recently, relations between these two countries have focused on hydropower development in Laos to fuel Thailand's growing energy demand.

Table CS1.3: Basin-specific agreements reached to date.

Year	Agreement
1926	French Indochina and Siam (Thailand) agree on river boundary
1952 Agreement	Mekong as an "international waterway"
1957 Mekong Statute	Mekong Committee and "Mekong cascade"
1975 Joint Declaration	Veto power removed
1995 Mekong Agreement	"Agreement to agree" on Basin development

Finally, Myanmar historically has had poor relations with the countries of Indochina, and more recently has been in confrontations with Thailand over incidents involving Burmese minority violence in the Thai-Burmese border region. Sino-Burmese relations, on the other hand, are improving as border trade between the two countries grows, but old hostilities remain.

The dynamics of postcolonial geopolitics throughout the region have until recently impeded any joint efforts to develop the hydraulic potential of the Lower Mekong Basin. Radoshevich (1996) indicates that there are nearly 30 agreements on the Lower Mekong dating from 1856 to 1978. Although several agreements have been reached among Lower Basin riparians, expressing cooperative intentions (see recent ones in Table CS1.3), cooperation has still been hamstrung by underdevelopment, "Cold War" instability, and a legacy of historical animosities, with hostility only beginning to yield to dialogue only in the 1990s. Still, the only existing achievements to date are largely a result of unilateral and bilateral initiatives partially or principally funded by international donors and agencies. A brief chronology of hydropolitical conflict and cooperation in the Basin closely reflects the geopolitical dynamics in the region. It should also be noted that Upper Mekong countries (China and Myanmar) have not been involved in any negotiation or cooperation plans.

COOPERATION ATTEMPTS

The first initiative to coordinate water-related issues on a regional basis came in 1949, when the United Nations Economic Commission for Asia and the Far East (ECAFE, now ESCAP) established the Bureau of Flood Control for the Basin. Three years later, in 1952, an agreement among the Lower Basin states recognized the Mekong as an "international waterway," creating a conceptual framework for future cooperation. The first formal attempt among Basin riparians to cooperate over water resources came in 1957 with the signing of the first Mekong Statute. The Mekong Committee was thus formally established, with the Mekong Secretariat — responsible for administration and implementation of joint Basin development plans — under the Mekong Committee's jurisdiction (Radosevich, 1996).

Modern hydropolitical relations among the riparians can be historically broken down into three phases of cooperative management (Browder, 2000, p. 5). The first period extended from 1957, when the first Mekong Statute was signed, to 1978, roughly when the United States completed its withdrawal from Vietnam. The second period was sparked by the withdrawal of Cambodia from the Mekong Committee after the isolationist Khmer Rouge took power in 1978. Cambodia's request for readmission to the Basin regime in 1991 marked the beginning of the third, and ongoing, period of cooperation. It should be noted that despite persistent efforts at cooperation on management of the Mekong's shared-water resources, the Basin regime has thus far produced little tangible evidence of such cooperation.

Mekong Committee Era (1957–1978)

With the 1957 Mekong Statute, the parties announced plans to build a "cascade" of reservoirs based on several new dam projects. Under the Statute, all four parties had to agree on Basin projects, with ultimate approval authority vested in the Mekong Committee. The Committee was funded through international grants primarily from the USA and United Nations Development Program (UNDP) in the early years, though the World Bank also began its involvement in 1969. Despite the political upheavals following the Vietnam War, which resulted in communist victories in the former Indochina states, the parties managed to preserve the regime as a conduit for foreign assistance until 1978, when the Khmer Rouge abruptly withdrew Cambodia from the Basin regime.

Interim Mekong Committee (IMC) Era (1978–1992)

From 1978 through the early 1990s, the Basin regime continued to operate despite Cambodia's absence under the weak supervision of the IMC, which had no substantive power to influence Basin development (Hirsch and Cheong, 1996a, pp. 10–11). Plans for the "cascade" were abandoned and joint development of main branch of the Mekong came to a halt (Hirsch and Cheong, 1996b, p. 3). The largest project completed in the Lower Basin during this period was the 150 MW Nam Ngum Dam in Thailand (1984) — the only truly international hydropower project to come to fruition under the Mekong Committee (or any of its other incarnations), involving 10 countries in the financing of the dam.

The Mekong River Commission (MRC) Era (1992–Present)

The post-Cold War era changed the political and economic landscape in the Mekong region, allowing countries to put aside ideological encumbrances and spur market reforms and regional economic integration. The first impetus for renewed Basin cooperation came in 1991 when Cambodia, emerging from the ravages of the Khmer Rouge era, requested readmission into the Mekong regime. Given the changing geopolitical circumstances, conflict emerged between Vietnam and Thailand over dry season water use. At the same time, China's announced plans to construct more than a dozen dams through 2010. Renegotiating the terms of the Mekong regime appeared necessary and negotiations between the Lower Basin riparians commenced in 1992. In 1994, deep into negotiations, Vietnam and the United States normalized relations, clearing the way for the former's entry into the Association of Southeast Asian Nations (ASEAN); ASEAN membership for Cambodia, and Laos followed soon thereafter. To some degree, these circumstances changed the nature of the balance of power in the region — and at the negotiating table. Ultimately, on April 5, 1995 representatives of Thailand, Vietnam, Cambodia, and Laos signed the "Agreement on the Cooperation for the Sustainable Development of the Mekong River Basin" in Chiang Rai, Thailand, marking the formal beginning of the current period of Lower Basin cooperation.

In addition to the involvement of UNDP and other international agencies, the great powers have likewise been interested in the region's stability. During the last 50 years, USA has been especially involved by sponsoring studies and modeling efforts and providing institutional support and capacity building to the Mekong Commission (Jacobs, 1998).

In the early 1990s, it has been felt however that the MRC had not exercised its real mandate over the basin water planning and management. Thus, despite international involvement, the full potential of exploiting the region's water resources had not been materialized (Kirmani and Le Moigne, 1997). Interestingly, and as of 2005, both the riparians and the international development community lead by the World Bank, and the Asian Development Bank have been involved in a Mekong Water Resources Assistance Strategy (World Bank, 2006), that is addressed later in the case study.

THE NEGOTIATION PROCESS OF THE 1995 MEKONG AGREEMENT[2]

It is somewhat remarkable that the Mekong regime has continued to operate for more than three decades — through the Vietnam War, civil war in Cambodia, and ideological conflicts between Vietnam and Thailand — when it appeared that no scope for amicable relations over water (or any other issues, for that matter) existed. Entering the post-Cold War era, therefore, it seemed entirely feasible, according to Browder (2000), that the Mekong riparians could find ways to overcome, or at the very least strategically ignore, their apparent differences in order to cooperate over water issues. In this respect, water constitutes a cooperation-inducing development resource, which 'transcends' common thinking about resource-related disputes."

Status Quo Situation Prior to 1991, Under the IMC

The lax IMC (1978–1992) rules did not require riparian states pursuing Basin development plans to seek the prior approval of other riparians. The primary uses of water by each riparian are presented in Table CS1.4 and further elaborated below.

---

[2]Based mainly on Radosevich (1996), Elhance (1999), and Browder (2000). Additional references are used as relevant.

Table CS1.4: Primary uses of water in the Mekong Basin prior to 1991.

Riparian	Primary use
Thailand	Industrial water uses and hydropower from the Mekong tributaries
Lao PDR	Hydropower from Mekong tributaries; navigation along the main branch of the river
Vietnam	Irrigation (Delta region agriculture); dry season "water quality" in the Delta area
Cambodia	Irrigation (agriculture); fisheries
China	No substantial use for Mekong waters
Myanmar	No substantial use for Mekong waters

Country Interests and Issues

Vietnam. Vietnam's most pressing issue in water resource management is the protection of its agricultural interests in the Mekong Delta. Vietnam is particularly keen on developing its rice-growing capacity, with plans to bring new land under cultivation to meet the demands of its fast-growing population. Vietnam's other primary concern is dry-season water allocation. Because of the sharp seasonal variations in river flow and a need to use the majority of that flow to prevent seawater damage, Vietnamese officials have advocated using traditional flooding techniques to meet future irrigation requirements in the Delta. Irrigation and hydropower having conflicting uses of water have to be addressed in a basin-wide integrated way. Therefore, the government has also explored the feasibility of building upstream reservoirs of its own to ensure adequate freshwater supply year-round. However, Vietnam's hydropower generation potential is limited and largely dependent on how Basin water resources are managed and developed upstream.

Thailand. Because of over-exploitation and over-development in the 1970s and 1980s, the country is now dealing with scarcity of natural resources — water resources chief among them. Policymakers have thus turned their attention to the Mekong and its tributaries, which presented a prime source of hydroelectric power and a solution for water scarcity concerns. Because of its geographical position and topography, however, Thailand has not been able to harness much of the Mekong's potential. The government had been considering diverting roughly $90\,\mathrm{m}^3/\mathrm{s}$ from the Mekong (and gradually up to $300\,\mathrm{m}^3/\mathrm{s}$) by the year 2005, to the more industrialized Chao Praya Basin, where both industry growth and public demand for potable water had already begun to outpace water availability, especially in the Bangkok metropolitan area.

Lao PDR. Laos' interests focus mainly on hydropower development capacity. The country's capacity for roughly half of the hydropower potential of the entire Mekong Basin and currently relies on hydroelectricity as a major source of revenue. A total of 28 projects (to be completed by 2010) had been proposed, and three dams have already underway.

Cambodia. Cambodia's interests in water resource management primarily revolve around future irrigation needs and the impact of upstream projects on the

Table CS1.5: Noncooperative basin development strategies prior to 1991.

Thailand	Plans to divert up to $300\,\mathrm{m^3/s}$ from the main branch of the Mekong to the Chao Praya Basin; bilateral hydropower projects with Laos on Mekong tributaries
Lao PDR	Bilateral hydropower projects with Thailand on Mekong tributaries
Vietnam	Plans to bring new lands under cultivation in the Delta area, relying on flooding cycles during the monsoon season for irrigation
Cambodia	Longer-term plans to bring new lands under cultivation and develop existing irrigation systems
China	Longer-term plans to build a cascade of 15 dams for hydropower generation; vaguely articulated plans to develop navigation along the Mekong mainstream for access to South China Sea
Myanmar	No articulated plans for Mekong water resources

seasonal shift in direction of the Tonle Sap. A summary of the issues and positions are presented in Table CS1.5.

Tables CS1.4 and CS1.5 point to similarities in noncooperative strategies Lower Mekong Riparians. Thailand and Laos are the upstream riparians and Cambodia and Vietnam are the downstream riparians. Therefore, one would expect some kind of sub-coalitional arrangements along these lines. However, this was not the case.

Because of the intense rivalry associated with Cold War enmities and ideological fault lines that characterized riparian relations throughout the IMC period, each riparian, but especially Thailand and Vietnam, considered any form of joint cooperation as submitting their national interests to the indirect authority of a neighboring rival. Riparians viewed their respective payoffs from a zero-sum perspective, where pursuing unilateral strategies maximized their utility, while "cooperating" was regarded as yielding to the opponent. The weakness of the IMC regime, particularly the absence of veto rights over water development projects in the Lower Basin, reflects this fact. Furthermore, the Basin-wide development schemes envisaged by the former Mekong Committee (1957–1978) were a series of large-scale projects, which considered the Lower Basin as a single hydrological unit. These development plans, however, were shelved during the IMC period. Indeed, following the Vietnam War, the regional balance of power over water resources was redefined, and the riparians viewed Basin-wide projects as impinging on their national sovereignty and as a means for external actors to coerce them into cooperation.[3]

Riparian relations during the IMC period help explain the lack of a full-basin (grand coalition) cooperation in the Basin. Benefits from unilateral strategies could therefore be expressed in terms of avoided ideological concessions (communism vs. free market regimes). For instance, Thailand was wary of the power other riparians, particularly Vietnam, would have been granted over joint projects if the aforementioned proposed Basin-wide cooperative plans were to be implemented. Instead, Thailand chose to develop the hydropower potential of its shared rivers with Laos,

---

[3]As suggested by Radosevich (2006) "The real cause for not pursuing the mainstream dams was advent of environmental era that caused donors to not fund such dams."

a much weaker riparian. While indeed a cooperative endeavor, these projects were implemented in accordance with Thailand's own national policies and goals and generally did not lessen Thailand's relative power. Vietnam, on the other hand, was extremely reluctant to submit to any joint development effort, which it viewed as an instrument of Western interference. Meanwhile, Cambodia's withdrawal from the Mekong regime clearly indicated the little value the country placed on "jointly developing" the Mekong.

Turning Point

The end of the Cold War paved the way for peace in Southeast Asia. Vietnam, shedding the ideological shackles of Communism, was experiencing rapid growth through its *doi moi* economic reform program. Thailand, the regional economic power, was emerging as one of Asia's newly industrialized countries and as a model for market-oriented industrialization in the Basin. Meanwhile, Laos and Cambodia, both recuperating from internal strife, were eager to cooperate with a view to accessing much-needed foreign capital investment.

At the same time, the negotiating parties realized that their unilateral policies would not be sustainable in the long run. The turning point, however, came in 1991, when Cambodia requested readmission into the Mekong regime. Yet while Cambodia's quest to rejoin the Mekong regime set the process of renewed Basin cooperation in motion, according to Browder (2000), the central issue driving the negotiations toward the 1995 Mekong Agreement was conflict between Thailand and Vietnam over dry season water use.

Incentives to Cooperate in the Lower Mekong

Browder (2000) identifies three relevant sets of fundamental interests, which motivated the parties to negotiate: water resources, foreign relations, and international assistance. The first synergy of interests concerned the desire for improved relations at the regional level. The main objective behind Vietnam and Thailand's push to reinstate the Mekong regime in the aftermath of the Cold War was the desire to build cordial relations with each other and transcend their ideological rivalry. Water resources were an ideal starting point for détente and relationship-building. Besides water resource issues, the post-Cold War relationship between Thailand and Vietnam had come to encompass other dimensions ranging from trade, investment, and fisheries development to transportation, migration, and boundary disputes.

Laos and Cambodia, on the other hand, were motivated by two tangible goals: the desire to reach an accord in order to attract foreign aid and technical assistance, and to promote their own economic development through regional cooperation.

Theoretically, where interdependencies exist, pooling the resource potential of an entire river system offers a wider range of technically feasible objectives. Furthermore, by avoiding duplication of investments, more optimal development schemes can be pursued at a region-wide level (see Chapter 4). Nonetheless, the efficient allocation of the water resources remains the ultimate challenge. When the aggregate demand for water is broken down according to how the resource could be used, one can essentially distinguish two competing ways of allocating the Mekong's water: agricultural uses and hydropower development.

Both forms of water utilization were predicted to significantly increase the demand for water resources due to several factors, among them, economic development, urbanization of the rural class and a projected population increase. Furthermore, ambitious resettlement and industrialization projects were competing for the available, yet untapped Mekong water resources. Below, we focus only on the issue of hydropower generation potential.

Power generation potential (upstream riparians in the Lower Mekong). If the Mekong is fully developed to generate hydropower, currently unutilized water could help produce 500,000 GW of electricity per year (Elhance, 1999, p. 194). In fact, the Lower Basin alone has a potential of generating 200,000 million kWh per year (Elhance, 1999, p. 198). Questions have been raised as to Southeast Asia's capacity to absorb this potential supply of hydroelectricity, especially since the existing infrastructure to export it is insufficient to cope with such volumes. Though these logistical challenges do not pose an insurmountable obstacle in the long run, they nonetheless need to be considered when assessing the net benefits of dam projects to upstream countries.

The development of the Mekong's hydropower potential is considered the key to reconstructing the economies of this war-torn region. Due to the untapped hydropower potential of its tributaries and the main branch of the Mekong, Laos has been the focal point of dam-building proposals. Meanwhile, demand for electricity in the Lower Basin had been increasing at approximately 10% per year throughout the early 1990s. Although hydroelectric dams had been part of formal plans for the main branch of the Mekong since the 1950s, it was not until four decades later that the first dam, the 1500 MW Manwan Dam, was completed in China's Yunnan province (Tangwisutijit, 1994, p. 1). According to Chinese estimates, the Upper Basin had additional generating potential of some 20 million kilowatts of hydroelectric power. The steepness of the river gradient in this area favors the construction of high-walled dams with relatively low-cost structures (Chapman and He, 2006, p. 5). China estimates that as many as 15 dams can be built on the main river within Chinese territory. By 2010, with the completion of the Xiaowan Dam, officers of the Mekong River Commission predict that the regulated dry-season flow of the river at the Yunnan–Laos border will be up to 50% greater than that under natural conditions (Chapman and He, 2006, p. 6). The immediate downstream benefit of China's dam-building would be for Laos, where the greater volume of water available for hydropower generation during the dry season — the peak season for electricity demand — will enhance the productivity of planned hydropower facilities in Laos itself (Chapman and He, 2006, p. 6).

While China provides only 16% of the total discharge of the Mekong system, the length and elevation of the river through remote areas of Yunnan Province has motivated Chinese plans for a set of main-stem dams on the main branch of the river built for power generation, meeting rapidly growing domestic demand. Since nearly the entire drop in elevation of the main branch occurs in Yunnan, it is logical that China is pursuing its hydropower dam program on the upper Mekong (Lancang), with firm plans for reservoirs of up to $23 \, \text{km}^3$ behind some of the world's highest concrete dams. In parallel, Yunnan province is also pursuing plans to construct a series of hydropower dams on the Nu, a tributary of the Salween River. The plans are currently subject to environmental reviews in China (World Bank, 2006, p. 15). Most of the remaining hydropower potential in the Lower Mekong Basin is on the tributaries of the Mekong. Demand for power in Thailand and Vietnam, and on the South China Grid, has been a major driver for hydropower planning not only on the tributaries in these countries, but also for Laos where domestic demand is low but power trade with neighboring countries is a major foreign exchange earning opportunity. The main branch of the Mekong River in Cambodia has potential for hydropower development, but even a run-of-the-river dam would inundate a large area and would have major impacts on fish migration in that stretch of the river. Such development would pose serious ecological, social, and economic risks that could outweigh the potential benefits from power generation. Cambodia's rapidly growing demands for power could alternatively be met through cooperation in cross-border hydropower sharing on tributaries that originate in Laos and Vietnam and pass through Cambodia to the main branch of the Mekong, such as in the Sesan, Serepok, and Sekong subcatchments. In the same vein, the headwaters of many of the tributaries are found within Vietnam where the hydropower potential is being developed. However, Vietnam will increasingly need to cooperate with the downstream countries (Cambodia or Laos) to avoid negative impacts. More importantly, this cooperation could open opportunities for investments with mutual benefits, where the design and operational schedule of the reservoirs could support downstream use of the resources (World Bank, 2006, p. 15).

THE NEGOTIATION PROCESS[4]

At the outset of negotiations in 1992, none of the parties had particularly attractive BATNAs ("Best Alternative to a Negotiated Settlement"). Furthermore, each state, but particularly Cambodia and Laos, felt they risked losing a valuable mechanism for accessing foreign aid if the negotiations were not successful.

The negotiation process, however, suffered several setbacks, which not only prolonged the formal negotiation stage, but also delayed the final outcome by almost two years. These delays were the result of the riparians' *claiming tactics*, which included attempts by individual countries to misrepresent their BATNAs, link issues for leverage, and mislead other parties (Browder, 2000, p. 3). As far as BATNAs are concerned the better a country's alternatives, the more demanding it can be during the negotiation process. That is, it will have less to lose if an agreement is not reached (Young, 1994, p. 134).

---

[4]Based mainly on Radosevich (1996) and Browder (2000).

At the onset of negotiations in early 1992, the Mekong Secretariat drafted a declaration reestablishing the Mekong Committee and dissolving the IMC. The reinstatement of the original Mekong Committee reintroduced the issue of veto power over water projects, prompting the first crisis, the so-called *1st Protocol Issue*. Thai officials felt that the mandate of the former body no longer served their interests, accusing the Committee of being too control-oriented. By the early 1990s, Thailand was no longer actively pursuing projects on the main branch of the Mekong, and did not want to give other member states veto power over Thai water projects. Other states, however, were concerned that devoid of veto power, they would be powerless to prevent Thailand from planned diversions of the Mekong (particularly the planned diversion of up to $300\,\mathrm{m}^3/\mathrm{s}$ of water from the main branch). Accordingly, they proposed modifying the Thai proposal to require member states to notify and obtain regime approval on any proposed projects while the negotiations were still in progress. The confrontation ended when the Thai foreign minister cancelled the first plenary session in Chiang Rai (Thailand).

After this initial debacle, Thailand organized a new meeting in March 1992. The Thai government suggested inviting China and Burma, as vital upstream parties, to join the discussions. However, Vietnam objected, fearing a shift in the balance of power (i.e., a Sino-Thai coalition) should the Upper Basin states come into the regime. The ensuing conflict — referred to as the *Representation Issue* — led Vietnam to boycott the meeting. As a result, little progress was made, since both Laos and Cambodia were reluctant to proceed without their neighbor.

Aside from the veto power issue, Thailand — the party with the most urgent need for water resource development — argued that the Mekong Secretariat, historically funded by international agencies and led by a UNDP-appointed official, had lost its neutrality. Consequently, it did not want the Secretariat to participate in the negotiations. In March 1992, following a confrontation with the Secretariat's foreign director over the neutrality matter — referred to as the *2nd Protocol Issue* — Thailand unilaterally dismissed him, and subsequently expelled him from the country. Vietnam, Laos, and Cambodia objected to this unilateral move, recognizing that the international presence would increase their bargaining power vis-à-vis Thailand.

Ultimately, the parties agreed to resume negotiations at the behest of the UNDP, which appointed George Radosevich to act as an official mediator. Negotiation assistance was largely provided by Radosevich thereafter, and was vital to the "successful" outcome of the three-year negotiation process. An informal meeting was held in Hong Kong in October 1992, and was instrumental in achieving the breakthroughs necessary to revitalize the negotiation process. The choice of a neutral meeting place provided a more relaxed atmosphere to the negotiations, and the four Lower Basin riparians were able to resolve their initial differences. Radosevich was accepted and respected by all participants, and all four Lower Basin countries agreed to continue the negotiations though contemplating a treaty that would allow Burma and China to join later. The culmination of this new impetus to cooperate came with the Kuala Lumpur Communiqué in December 1992, when the parties publicly committed themselves to restructuring the Mekong regime. This represented a critical shift in their respective BATNAs, because failing to reach a formal agreement now meant an unacceptable loss of "face" (Browder, 2000, p. 12).

The participation of the UNDP in the negotiation process and in the formulation of the 1995 Mekong Agreement was necessary to overcome the legacy of mistrust among the Basin riparians. Some would even argue that the successful conclusion of this process was yet another example of international will overcoming internal resistance in the region. Elhance (1999) perhaps giving too much credence to the efforts of external actors, confirms the significant role they played in shaping cooperation: "... the Mekong project was a classic example of external effort, external management, and external planning with little involvement of the (supposed) beneficiaries." (Elhance, 1999, p. 219).[5]

At this point in the negotiation process the parties agreed to extend the original deadline for agreement of December 1993, as additional time was needed to work out the more contentious issues. Foremost among these issues the highly disputed Article 5, relevant for determining the clauses relating to reasonable and equitable water utilization, and which pitted Vietnam directly against Thailand. Talks at the fourth Mekong Working Group meeting (MWG-IV), held in Phnom Penh in October 1993, broke down following a disagreement between the two countries over this issue. Strong political commitment from both the Thai and Vietnamese leadership enabled the negotiations to resume. The Vietnamese delegation then proposed a revised draft of Article 5, with the support of Laos and Cambodia, and submitted it through the UNDP to Thailand. This last breakthrough paved the way for the final text of the 1995 Mekong Agreement to be approved by the Mekong Working Group at its Fifth Meeting in Hanoi in November 1994.

FEATURES OF THE 1995 AGREEMENT[6]

The Mekong River Commission

The Commission's primary objective is to promote cooperation in all fields of sustainable development, utilization, management, and conservation of Basin water and related resources including but not limited to irrigation, hydropower, navigation, flood control, fisheries, and tourism. All planned programs and projects under the MRC are organized under one of four key categories: (i) Natural resources planning and development; (ii) Environmental and social cost management; (iii) Databases and information systems; and (iv) Organization management and cooperation.

As was the case with preceding institutions, the MRC depends on resources from member countries, international donors, and cooperating agencies. Grants primarily from UNDP fund the costs of maintaining the Mekong Secretariat, the

---

[5]Radosevich (2006) disagrees with this latter statement, arguing that he traveled to each capital numerous times for consultations with every riparian before a formal meeting was convened to discuss the issues at hand.
[6]Based mainly on Radosevich (1996), Browder (2000), and Gajaseni *et al.* (2006).

implementation arm of the MRC, as well as the investigations, studies, and planning for water and related resources executed by the Secretariat in conjunction with central government agencies in Laos, Thailand, Cambodia, and Vietnam. Investment costs for projects formulated through the Mekong regime are typically financed with assistance from bilateral aid agencies or through concessionary loans from development banks.

The Agreement

On 5 April 1995, after 21 months of negotiations, the four Lower Basin riparians signed the "Agreement on the Cooperation for the Sustainable Development of the Mekong River Basin," replacing the 1957, 1975, and 1978 agreements (Elhance, 1999, pp. 221–222). In the same year, the Asian Development Bank (ADB) launched the Greater Mekong Sub-region (GMS) initiative, thus ensuring international assistance for future Basin cooperation efforts. With the signing of the 1995 Agreement, the Mekong Committee, dissolved at the outset of negotiation at the request of Thailand, was reestablished as the Mekong River Commission (MRC). The key articles of the Agreement include:

1. notification and consultation procedures;
2. maintenance of dry season flows;
3. water quality protection;
4. monitoring; and
5. information exchange.

The Agreement also called for the preparation of a comprehensive Basin Development Plan (BDP) to serve as a framework for future development in the Basin. Furthermore, it contains an open invitation to China and Burma to join the Basin regime provided they accept all the rights and obligations reflected in the Agreement.

The newly incorporated notification/consultation procedures remove the power of riparian countries to veto projects undertaken unilaterally or by two or more of the other Basin riparians previously granted under the 1957 Mekong Statute and further elaborated in the 1975 Joint Declaration.[7] This was a hotly contested issue during the negotiation process, with many tense moments involving mainly Thailand and Vietnam. Vietnam feared Thailand's unilateral development intentions and wanted the right to prior approval of planned Basin projects, while Thailand opposed the inclusion of a veto power clause that would frustrate its development objectives and give the other riparians greater influence over the evolution of the Basin regime. The

---

[7]While in the Mekong Committee era (1957–1978) no veto power was in existence, the era of the Interim Mekong Committee (1978–1992) allowed for veto power. Both institutions paralyzed the joint management of the Basin because they were not based on cooperative principles. The institution that was put in place in the 1995 agreement, namely "consultation and notification" is essential for cooperation, and thus preferred.

compromise clause appears to have favored Thailand's position, but nevertheless lends greater transparency to Basin-related development activities, to the benefit of Vietnam, Laos, and Cambodia. In addition, the flow maintenance provisions introduced in the Agreement were especially significant for Vietnam, given both its agricultural needs and the need to combat saltwater intrusion into the Delta, Laos, whose future hydropower development program will rely on a constant and predictable flow of water from upstream also benefited from the flow maintenance provisions (Radosevich and Olson, 1999).

Beyond the 1995 Mekong Treaty — Auxiliary Agreements and Power Changes

The 1995 Mekong Treaty is a mutually cooperative framework allowing the riparians to agree on a number of important items. This seminal structure facilitated the negotiations of several auxiliary agreements since 1995. While some of the agreements are bilateral others are also multilateral (grand coalition).

Some of the achievements of the basin riparian as of 2004 include: adoption of an agreement on data and information sharing among the four Lower Mekong riparians; establishment and use of a web-based flood forecasting, and dry season river flow monitoring; historic hydrological data exchange agreement between China and MRC (signed April 2002); development and adoption of water utilization rules, the latest including the preliminary procedures for prior notification, prior consultation and agreement; formulation of a regional flood management program; basin-wide hydropower strategy; research coordination within the Mekong under Consultative Group on International Agricultural Research (CGIAR) Challenge Programme; communication strategies that have raised the profile and increased awareness of the organization, internet-communication, technical publication and media exposure; integrated training and junior riparian professional programs; implementation of the basin development planning process with a focus on a subarea approach; development of an integrated approach to agriculture, irrigation, and forestry; support for development of a navigation program; establishment of the inland fisheries research institute in Phnom Penh (MRC, 2004, p. 2).

The agreement on data and information sharing among the member countries in late 2001 was one of the concrete milestones achieved since the signing of the 1995 Agreement. Even after the 1995 Mekong Treaty was implemented, information has often been concealed by the member countries. Since data and information sharing is a pre-requisite for any effective regional cooperation, this agreement is an important step toward closer collaboration. In July 2003, the Joint Committee of the MRC adopted the Guidelines on Data Custodianship and Management of Information Systems to formalize the detailed procedures for data exchange among the MRC member countries, and for allowing access to MRC data and information by the users (MRC, 2004, p. 3).

In 2002, the four ministers in the MRC Council signed on behalf of their Governments, the Preliminary Procedures for Notification, Prior Consultation and

Agreement. In line with the provisions of the 1995 Agreement, these Procedures provide long awaited guidelines on the conduct of notification, prior consultation, and specific agreement before any proposed use of the Mekong River waters can be initiated (MRC, 2004, p. 4).

Dispute resolution practices have also developed in the basin. For example, in 1998–1999 the MRC served as a neutral broker in dispute between Vietnam and Cambodia over the Se San hydropower project. A couple of years later, the MRC was likewise involved in mediating a dispute over a proposed navigation improvement project in the upper Mekong (MRC, 2004, p. 4).

With both political and economic reforms taking place in the different basin states in recent years, one has to take relative economic power and into account. For example, in 2005, GDP per capita (in terms of 2005 Purchasing Power Parity (PPP)) values of the four Lower Mekong riparians [(in parentheses are the annual growth rates): Laos 2,000 (7.3); Thailand 8,600 (4.5); Vietnam 2,800 (8.5); Cambodia 2,500 (13.5)] suggests a decline in the relative power of Thailand and an increase in that of the rest of the basin states, especially Vietnam (CIA, 2006). In addition, the annual growth rates of GDP per capita indicate expected long-term trends that may likewise affect the balance of power in the basin.

Epilogue — The Mekong Water Resources Assistance Strategy

While there was substantial progress, the mushrooming of regional organizations dealing with the development of the Mekong could result in a duplication of efforts, splintering of resources, and conflicted agreements. To ensure efficiency in the parties' efforts, it will be necessary for the region to determine how best to coordinate activities. It would seem that since the FTA agreement encompasses all of the riparians, and specifically calls for greater cooperation in the development of the Mekong River Basin, it could potentially provide the best forum.

In general, the countries' shunning of basin wide development in favor of unilateral and bilateral schemes threatens the viability of the vision and expectations set forth in the 1995 Mekong Agreement. The problems and difficulties that persist in the MRC likewise don't bode well for the region. Specifically Thailand's planned water diversion from the Mekong and Salween basins, together with Vietnam's intentions to construct dam on the Ya Li (Se San) and Serepok rivers, signal the aims of these countries to move forward with development projects, irrespective of regional considerations. In addition, the construction of dams in the upstream reaches in Yunnan Province and the recent approval of the Nam Theun 2 project have alerted the public to the risks of uncoordinated development of the Mekong.

While the Lower Mekong countries are visibly more engaged in the MRC, there is also a growing tendency to view the MRC as an obstacle for trans-boundary water development in the region (with the organization being perceived as a regulatory agency imposing rules, instead of helping solve problems). Furthermore, the MRC has not yet acquired the expertise, organizational capacity or analytical tools needed to facilitate the negotiation process among the countries. Despite good progress in the past five years, the Commission has likewise not been able to put basic cooperative frameworks and an effective decision-support system together (World Bank, 2006, p. 5).

The World Bank and the Asian Development Bank have been working with other donors on the Mekong Water Resources Assistance Strategy designed to address the above concerns. While the past decade embodied risk- and investment-averse water development strategies, the current tactic of the Assistance Strategy emphasizes cooperative opportunities and benefit-sharing schemes. It highlights (a) achievements in the region that are essential and positive, (b) the fact that the achievements do, however, fall short of meeting challenges and capture future opportunities, and (c) that, unless serious attention is given by the development partners to the present institutional dynamics in the Mekong River basin, there is a high likelihood that the progress made in building cooperation among the riparian states will not materialize to its fullest potential (World Bank, 2006, pp. 5–6).

The MRC is a key regional institution, which has demonstrated major strengths but substantial flaws and weaknesses as well. If the MRC fails to live up to its members' expectations (capable of supporting the countries in making wise decisions for balanced investment and integrated management of the water resources), then the current, growing level of trust currently exemplifying regional cooperation will be undermined. It will require both will and capability of all the riparian countries and the different organs of the MRC to work assiduously and collaboratively in fulfilling the tasks of developing the basin, providing for watershed and environmental protection, developing the capabilities for integrated water resources management across countries and sub-basins, and strengthening governance in the collective stewardship of the Basin. Development partners have a special responsibility to foster and facilitate cooperation. Over the past year the Banks, World Bank and Asian Development Bank, have been perceived as effective champions of this aim, partly due to their professional resources and partly their potential to steer investments in appropriate directions (World Bank, 2006, p. 5).

ANNEX

Table CS1A.1: Time line of the negotiation process leading to the 1995 Mekong Agreement.

Negotiation phase	Date	Event	Significance
Initiation of the pre-negotiation phase	June 1991	Cambodian request for readmission into Mekong regime	Turning point: reactivates Mekong Committee
Pre-negotiation phase	February 1992 (Thailand)	Chiang Rai plenary session canceled by Thai foreign minister	1st Protocol Issue — rift widens over the terms by which the MC would be reactivated widens

(Continued)

Table CS1A.1: (*Continued*)

Negotiation phase	Date	Event	Significance
	March 1992 (Thailand)	Chiang Mai meeting hosted by the Thai government — boycotted by Vietnam	Rift over the representation issue
	March 1992	Thai government unilaterally expels UNDP head of the Mekong Committee	2nd Protocol Issue
Critical transition from pre-negotiation stage to full-fledged negotiations	October 1992 (Hong Kong)	UNDP-sponsored informal consultations between the four Lower Basin riparians	1993 Mekong Work approved — previous contentious issues resolved
	December 1992 (Kuala Lumpur)	Kuala Lumpur Meeting and Communiqué	The four Lower Basin riparians make a formal commitment to establish a new framework of cooperation
Negotiations	February 1993 (Hanoi)	MWG-I meeting	National negotiating teams formally established; negotiation protocol finalized
	April 1993, Bangkok	MWG-II meeting	Negotiation agenda adopted; agreement to produce National Position Papers
	June 1993 Vientiane	MWG-III meeting	Working draft agreement; organizational structure for the MRC established
	August 1993	Technical Drafting Meeting-I	Agreed on Article 6 and proposed new draft for Article 5 (water utilization)
	October 1993 Phnom Penh	MWG-IV meeting	Lack of agreement on Article 5 halts progress and jeopardizes negotiations
	January 1994 Vientiane	Technical Drafting Meeting-II	Vietnam introduces new Article 5; rift widens and MWG-V postponed
Final negotiation stage	April 1994, Hanoi	Thai and Vietnamese prime ministers meet	Political will to reach an agreement reaffirmed
	May 1994, Ho Chi Minh City	Vietnamese, Lao, and Cambodian teams meet	Indochina states formulate a revised proposal of Article 5 for Thailand's consideration

(*Continued*)

Table CS1A.1: (*Continued*)

Negotiation phase	Date	Event	Significance
	November 1994, Hanoi	MWG-V meeting	Draft agreement initiated by national negotiating teams
Agreement reached	April 1995, Chiang Rai	Signing ceremony for the Mekong Agreement	New framework for cooperation and Mekong River Commission established

Source: Adapted from Radosevich and Olson (1999, p. 10) and Browder (2000, p. 245).

REFERENCES

(CIA) Central Intelligence Agency USA (2006). World Fact Book. Available at https://www.cia.gov/cia/publications/factbook/index.html (Visited on December 2, 2006).

(MRC) Mekong River Commission (2004). Progress in water management at the river basin level: Mekong River Basin. Paper presented at the 3rd World Water Forum (International Network of Basin Organizations-INBO Session) March 20, Kyoto, Japan. (Also available at http://www.mrcmekong.org (Visited on December 2, 2006).

Browder, G. (2000). An analysis of the negotiation for the 1995 Mekong Agreement, *International Negotiation*, 5(2), 237–261.

Chapman, E.C. and D. He (2006). Downstream implications of China's dams on the Lancang Jiang (Upper Mekong) and their political significance for greater regional cooperation, basin-wide. http://asia.anu.edu.au/mekong/dams.html (Visited on November 25, 2006).

Elhance, A.P. (1999). The Mekong Basin. In: Elhance, A.P. (ed.), *Hydropolitics in the 3rd World*. Washington, DC: United States Institute of Peace Press.

Gajaseni, M., O.W. Heal and G. Edwards-Jones (2006). The Mekong River Basin: Comprehensive water governance. In: Finger, M., L. Tamiotti and J. Allouche (eds.), *The Multi-Governance of Water*. Albany, NY: State University of New York Press.

Hirsch, P. and G. Cheong (1996a). Country and regional perspectives on resource management, Part 5 of the final overview report to AusAID entitled *Natural Resource Management in the Mekong River Basin: Perspectives for Australian Development Cooperation*, University of Sydney, April 2. http://www.usyd.edu.au/su/geography/hirsch/5/5.htm (Visited on November 24, 2006).

Hirsch, P. and G. Cheong (1996b). Historical perspectives on Mekong Basin resource management, Part 4 of the final overview report to AusAID entitled *Natural Resource Management in the Mekong River Basin: Perspectives for Australian Development Cooperation*, University of Sydney, April 2. http://www.usyd.edu.au/su/geography/hirsch/4/4.htm (Visited on November 24, 2006).

Hori, H. (2000). *The Mekong Environment and Development*. New York: United Nations University Press.

Jacobs, J.W. (1998). The United States and the Mekong Project, *Water Policy*, 1, 587–603.

Kirmani, S. and G. Le Moigne (1997). Fostering riparian cooperation in international river basins. The World Bank at its best in development diplomacy. World Bank Technical Paper 349, Washington, DC: World Bank.

Nguyen, T.D. (1999). *The Mekong River and the Struggle for Indochina: Water, War, and Peace.* Westport, CT: Praeger.

Osborne, M. (2000). *The Mekong: Turbulent Past, Uncertain Future.* New York: Atlantic Monthly Press.

Radosevich, G.E. (1996). The Mekong — A new framework for development and management. In: Biswas, A.K. and T. Hashimoto (eds.), *Asian International Waters from Ganges-Brahmaputra to Mekong.* New Delhi: Oxford University Press.

Radosevich, G.E. (2006). Personal Communications on this case study, email exchange dated December 4, 2006.

Radosevich, G.E. and D.C. Olson (1999). Existing and emerging basin arrangements in Asia: Mekong River Commission case study. Paper presented at the Third Workshop on River Basin Institution Development, June 24, 1999, The World Bank, Washington, DC. Also available at http://siteresources.worldbank.org/INTWRD/918599-1112615943168/20431963/MekgongRiverComCaseStudy.pdf (Visited on 12/02. 206).

World Bank (WB) and Asian Development Bank (ADB) (2006). Future directions for water resources management in the Mekong River Basin, WB/ADB joint working paper — Mekong Water Resources Assistance Strategy (MWRAS), Draft document #36760, June, Washington, DC: World Bank.

Young, H.P. (ed.) (1994). *Negotiation Analysis.* Ann Arbor: The University of Michigan Press.

ADDITIONAL READING

Akatsuka, Y. and T. Asaeda (1996). Econo-political environments of the Mekong Basin: Development and related transport infrastructure. In: Biswas, A.K. and T. Hashimoto (eds.), *Asian International Waters From Ganges-Brahmaputra to Mekong.* New Delhi: Oxford University Press.

Barling, M. (1999). Mekong journey: Assessing the impacts of dams in Laos, *Geography Review January*, 12(3), 36–40.

Chenoweth, J.L., H.M. Malano and J.F. Bird (2001). Integrated river basin management in the multi-jurisdictional river basins: The case of the Mekong River Basin, *Water Resources Development*, 17(3), 365–377.

Hirsch, P. (1996). Large dams, restructuring and regional integration in Southeast Asia, *Asia Pacific Viewpoint*, 37(1), 1–20.

Jacobs, J.W. (2002). The Mekong River Commission: Transboundary water resources planning and regional security, *The Geographical Journal*, 168(4), 354.

Miller, M. (1996). Transformation of the river basin authority: The case of the Mekong Committee. In: Biswas, A.K. and T. Hashimoto (eds.), *Asian International Waters From Ganges-Brahmaputra to Mekong.* New Delhi: Oxford University Press.

Nakayama, M. (1999). Aspects behind differences in two agreements adopted by riparian countries of the lower Mekong River Basin, *Journal of Comparative Policy Analysis: Research and Practice*, 1, 293–308.

Öjendal, J. (1991). Mainland Southeast Asia: Cooperation or conflict over water? In: Ohlsson, L. (ed.), *Hydropolitics, Conflicts Over Water As a Development Constraint.* London: ZED Books.

Tangwisutijit, N. (1994). Choking the life out of the nine-tailed dragon, *World Rivers Review*, 9(4), 4th Quarter.

CASE STUDY 2: THE GANGES BASIN (WITH FOCUS ON INDIA AND BANGLADESH)*

One of the most studied international basins, the Ganges, has tremendous joint development potential that has not yet been realized by its riparian states. Rather, the Ganges Basin is more popularly known for its rich history of disputes. Conflicts and negotiations related to the Ganges have been ongoing for more than 50 years. Though it might seem a long duration, the relevant issues and positions have changed over time, as the number of riparians grew in the southern part of the system from one to three. Sharing (*per se*) of the Ganges water was a strictly domestic problem before the partition of India. With Eastern and Western Pakistan's independence from India in 1947, the conflict became international. With the independence of Bangladesh (former Eastern Pakistan) from Western Pakistan in 1971, the main parties to the conflict were Bangladesh and India and have remained so until now.

For all practical purposes, the Himalayan mountains separate Tibet from the rest of the Ganges riparians. In reality, Tibet was never part of the negotiations that took place. Tibet's geographical isolation, combined with the fact that Bhutan, and Nepal, are land locked, and Bangladesh is surrounded by Indian territory have major implications on the positions and dynamics of the basin's hydropolitics. The long history of disputes and negotiation largely took place between India and Bangladesh, as we shall see later. That has come to a sustainable end by the signing of the 1996 treaty between India and Bangladesh.

FEATURES OF THE BASIN

The Ganges or Ganges–Brahmaputra–Meghna/Barak (GBM) Basin comprise a river system that originates in the eastern Himalayas and spans over 1.758 million km^2, of which 8% lies in Bangladesh, 8% in Nepal, 4% in Bhutan, 62% in India, and 18% in the Tibetan region of China (the literature gives different estimates of the basin's regional distribution). The three rivers making up the basin meet in Bangladesh and flow to the Bay of Bengal as the Meghna River (Elhance, 1999; Nishat and Faisal, 2000; Wolf *et al.*, 1999, p. 401).

---

*This case study benefited from research by Kate Bernsohn, Niclas During, Markus Knigge, and Julia Tock. The case study benefited also from review comments by Islam M. Faisal. The case study is not aimed at covering all aspects and details.

Map CS2.1: The Ganges Basin.

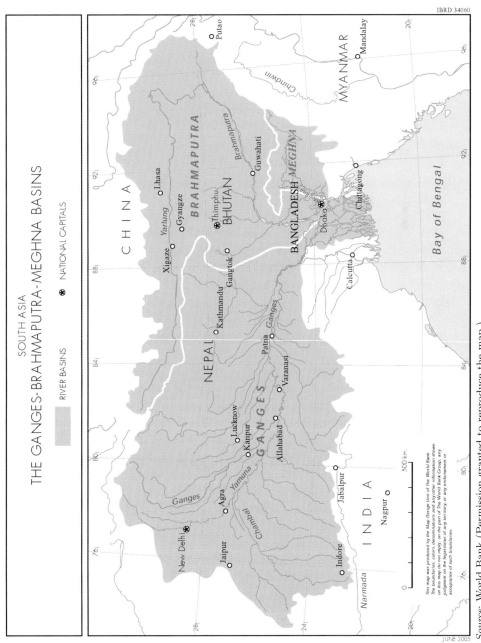

Source: World Bank (Permission granted to reproduce the map.)

Table CS2.1: Important tributaries of the GBM system.

Ganges	Brahmaputra		Meghna
	In India	In Bangladesh	
Yamuna	Subansiri	Tista	Barak
Mahakali	Jir Bhoreli	Jaldhaka	
Karnali	Manas	Torsa	
Gandak	Buri Dihang	Gumti	
Kosi	Dhansiri		
Mahanadra	Koppili		

Source: Upreti (1993).

A look at the tributaries flowing into the GBM (Table CS2.1) explains some of the complexities of managing this system, specially since most of the tributaries are international in nature.

The Himalayan glaciers and annual snow cover that accumulate in the winter and melt during the summer constitute the main water source of the GBM. In addition to the three main rivers of the GBM, there are more than 50 smaller rivers and tributaries that enter Bangladesh from India. Because the system is so interconnected, it is very difficult to distinguish how much water contributes to the entire system. The literature is likewise not conclusive about the issue and the best information available relates to the flow of the various rivers in major gauging stations, usually before the river in question merges with another one (Table CS2.2).

How much water is in the basin? This is a very difficult question to answer given the special nature of the region, the river system, and the climatic and weather conditions. The climate in the basin is a temperate subtropical Monsoon climate with annual rainfall ranging between 990 mm/year to 11,500 mm/year. The only problem with this abundant amount of rainfall is its uneven distribution over time, and especially during the summer (wet season — *kharif*) and winter (dry season — *rabi*) months. With the previous comments in mind, the long-term average annual flow of the Ganges and the Brahmaputra is 424 BCM and 555 BCM, respectively

Table CS2.2: Catchment area of the Ganges and Brahmaputra and contribution to flow.

Country	Ganges		Brahmaputra
	Area (km^2)	Contribution to flow (%)	
Tibet			292,670
Nepal	69,930	45	54,390
India	880,600	55	186,480
Bangladesh	3,885		72,520

Source: Based on Upreti (1993, pp. 41–56).
Note: Different estimates that are similar magnitude, estimates are provided in Shah (2001, pp. 19–21).

Table CS2.3: Annual water flow in the Ganges at Farakka during the period 1949–1985.

Year	Flow (BCM/year)	Year	Flow (BCM/year)	Year	Flow (BCM/year)	Year	Flow (BCM/year)
1949	400						
1950	400	1960	370	1970	350	1980	480
1951	305	1961	480	1971	535	1981	390
1952	340	1962	425	1972	240	1982	370
1953	380	1963	465	1973	420	1983	375
1954	460	1964	420	1974	340	1984	385
1955	535	1965	270	1975	465	1985	445
1956	470	1966	275	1976	380		
1957	330	1967	340	1977	400		
1958	410	1968	310	1978	510		
1959	360	1969	360	1979	250		

Source: London Economics (1995).

(these numbers are subject to large variations, depending on the source used). As such, this river system is the most important resource of economic activity in the basin countries, as will be elaborated below. Since our focus in this case study will be the dispute between India and Bangladesh, it is useful to consider the water flow at one of the main barrages: the Farakka Barrage, which is a contested water diversion structure that will be discussed in length in this case study (Table CS2.3).

Following this physical geography section, we will concentrate mainly on the Ganges River and the India–Bangladesh conflict, although we will relate to the rest of the river system and the other riparian — Nepal, when addressing possible cooperation among the three riparian states — Nepal, India, and Bangladesh.

Economic and Other Development Issues

The GBM is considered one of the richest basins in the world in terms of the potential of its natural resources (hydropower generation, fisheries, forestry, irrigated agriculture, navigation, environmental amenities, tourism, minerals, oil and gas). However, the three basin countries, called "the Poverty Triangle" are among the poorest nations in the world. Table CS2.4 provides several

Table CS2.4: Water-related economic indicators for the three basin riparians.

	Nepal		India		Bangladesh	
	1995	2005	1995	2005	1995	2005
Population (million)	25	28	900	1,095	120	147
GDP per capita (current $)	197	237	348	657	246	428
Share of agric in GDP (%)	42	38	29	19	31	20

Source: CIA (2006).

economic indicators that help to grasp the fundamental predicament of the basin's riparian states.

WATER ISSUES AMONG THE RIPARIANS OF THE GBM

The three riparian states in the GBM basin face common externality problems. Some of these problems have been around since the British rule, and others emerged since the independence of India and Bangladesh. A set of major issues are listed below.

Floods

One serious problem faced by all riparians is floods and other ecological disasters, such as sedimentation, soil erosion, and deforestation. Although Bangladesh is most prone to floods in the basin, India and Nepal are faced with similar problems of flood during the wet season, and especially between June and September. Management of the water flow and floods via adequate storage capacity could have solved some of these problems. In addition, information sharing and the establishment of an early warning system between India and Bangladesh are relatively simple cost-effective solutions (Kumra, 1995).

Drainage Congestion

India, the upstream riparian on many of the tributaries that flow into Bangladesh, suffers from the impact of drainage congestion and small-scale diversions in Bangladesh. By changing the slope or by affecting the lateral flow of drainage in the basin, even in downstream locations, the water table rises upstream. This is the case in India when development of roads and diversion of dames by farmers take place in Bangladesh (Kumra, 1995).

Water Availability and Water Quality

About 94% of Bangladesh's surface water sources originate outside its territory. Therefore, Bangladesh is vulnerable to any quantitative and qualitative impacts (externalities) caused by actions of upstream riparians. These impacts include shortage of water flow in the dry season affecting irrigated agriculture, and devastating floods in the wet season (Crow et al., 1995). The Farakka Barrage has contributed to a 50% decline in the dry season flow of the Ganges in Bangladesh (Mirza, 1998). This has caused serious economic (agriculture, industry) and ecological damage (the Sundarban and its biodiversity as well as on the agrarian ecosystem of South West Bangladesh).

At present, Bangladesh is facing similar issues with respect to sharing the Teesta and the Barak. In the near future, sharing the Brahmaputra may become the main contention between India and Bangladesh, as this river alone contributes 67% of the total dry season inflow into Bangladesh from India (Faisal, 2006).

Flow Regulation

Even if the region receives additional rain, the intertemporal and spatial distribution of this water is very uneven (dry and wet season floods, monsoons) and has become one of the key issues in the conflict. Most of Bangladesh's area (as well as India) is situated over a large aquifer system, which is part of the Indo-Gangetic Plain (and is used to augment water in scarce time periods and locations). Thirty percent of Bangladesh's land is below hide-tide level, making it very sensitive to seawater intrusion to groundwater aquifers. Therefore, during the dry season, intrusion of saline water makes even the little water available in Bangladesh's rivers (e.g., Meghna and Pasur, in the southern districts along the Bay of Bengal) of poor quality for both drinking and irrigation. Therefore, it is necessary for Bangladesh to maintain a minimum water flow in certain rivers for salinity control (Upreti, 1993).

Siltation and Creation of New Land

About 2.9 billion m^3 of silt deposited on yearly basis along the Bay of Bengal creates new land, which is also disputed locally between farmers in Bangladesh and India (Upreti, 1993).[1]

The Need for Minimum Flow in the Port of Calcutta (Kolkata)

Since British rule the Calcutta port has been one of the most important waterways in India. Siltation negatively affects the port and necessitates a steady water flow to flush the silt into the Bay of Bengal. The British planners found that a Barrage on the Ganges at Farakka (The Farakka Barrage) would allow to regulate the flow of water in the river downstream to Farakka and control the siltation level in the port. At that time, Bangladesh was still under British rule as was India. However, it was only after independence that, the Government of India initiated The Farakka Barrage project. The project began in 1961 and was concluded in 1971. Its main

---

[1]Faisal (2006) argues, however, that almost all of the sediments end up in the Meghna estuary, which is well inside Bangladeshi territory. There is only one island in the India–Bangladesh sea territory which is disputed.

purpose is to divert part of the water from the Ganges to the Bhagirati–Hooghly River Basin (Upreti, 1993; Crow *et al.*, 1995).

Environmental Amenities

Bangladesh part of basin is characterized by a long delta with very complicated environmental issues. They include Fauna and Flora, and Mangrove forest that are affected by the dry season shortage of water and by salinity intrusion because of low water flow in the river system (Upreti, 1993; Mirza, 1998; Kumra, 1995).

River Course Changes

The border between India and Bangladesh passes through the middle of shared rivers in many areas. Because of the erosion problems, the river changes its course which leads to farmers on both sides of the river to face situations where ownership of islands in the middle of the river is disputed (Upreti, 1993). Problems may also arise when one side of the banks of the river erodes and the other side experiences accretion crossing over the international border (Faisal, 2006).

POTENTIAL FOR COOPERATION

The Ganges riparian states make-up some of the least developed economies in the world and display the lowest per capita income (Table CS2.4). Interestingly, the Ganges–Brahmaputra–Barak Basin has immense potential in the areas of irrigation, power generation, fisheries, and navigation. Nonetheless, the region continues to experience rapid population growth, with a significant proportion of the people living in poverty (Table CS2.4; Elhance, 1999). Agriculture, farming, and cattle raising are the principal economic activities in the basin, employing up to 80% of the total population. Agriculture accounts for nearly one-half of all freshwater usage in the basin, making water supply one of the most significant barriers to economic development (Elhance, 1999).

The GBM is the most plentiful basin in the world in terms of water and other natural resources potential. In addition, the geography of the basin and the relative advantage of each of the riparian states offers many cooperative arrangements. Many studies demonstrated the potential in regional cooperation in the GBM basin (e.g., Rogers, 1993; Kishor, 1996; Eaton and Chaturvedi, 1993).

We will start by illustrating (Table CS2.5) the interrelations between the three riparians and the possible cooperative activities they could undertake.

Nepal and India both have a vast exploitable hydropower potential from other shared rivers, but presently only generate marginal amounts of energy. Nepal has the potential to produce 83,000 MW, 42,000 MW of which have been assessed to be technologically and economically feasible. Nonetheless, Nepal presently produces

Table CS2.5: Areas with cooperation potential in the GBM basin.

Cooperation issue	Nepal	India	Bangladesh
Flood control	✓	✓	✓
Hydropower generation	✓	✓	
Navigation		✓	✓
Irrigation	✓	✓	✓
Forestry	✓	✓	✓
Environment (sedimentation, fauna, flora)	✓	✓	✓
Fishery		✓	✓
Water quality		✓	✓
Data sharing	✓	✓	✓

Source: Authors' analysis.

about 250 MW and buys some of its power from India (Verghese, 1996, p. 38ff). Similarly, India exploits only 12% of the hydroelectric potential of the Ganges and 10% from the central Indian tributaries (Elhance, 1999, p. 163). Current exploitation of the Ganges has limited the river's navigation potential as a major waterway. With a large net of inland waterways, Bangladesh could likewise benefit substantially from an expansion of year-round navigable waterways in the basin (Elhance, 1999, p. 165).

As all of the basin countries attempt to modernize their economies, the need for freshwater and energy will increase significantly with industrial development exacerbating the environmental situation. Water will not only remain critical to economic development, but also increase in importance in the future.

CONFLICTS AND NEGOTIATIONS

The political landscape in South Asia changed radically in 1947 with the departure of the British colonial power from what was then British India (comprising today's India, Pakistan, and Bangladesh). The unresolved boundary disputes and the partition of British India into India and Pakistan in 1947, with little regard for the geography and integrity of the major river basin, play a critical role in the current constraints on water supply.

Currently, central governments in both India and Bangladesh are run by democratically elected administrations. India is the world's largest democracy, and regular elections have been held to choose central and state governments since independence. The relationship between central and provincial governments in India complicates the situation as the hydropolitics involves several states, such as Uttar Pradesh, Bihar, and West Bengal in India. Since the federal polity gives jurisdiction over all water matters to the state, conflicting needs and interests of the different states must be reconciled domestically before any international agreement can be reached. Bangladesh was ruled by one party and experienced a series of military coups after becoming a sovereign and secular state in 1971. When Bangladesh

declared itself an Islamic state in 1977, relations with India deteriorated considerably, with Bangladesh entering a period of political turmoil. Despite recent democratization, Bangladesh's political realm remains strained, in particular where India is
concerned. Political factions and interest groups continue to exploit any dispute with
their powerful neighbor to gain domestic political leverage and leaders are aware
that cooperation with India could be viewed as compromising national sovereignty
and interest (Elhance, 1999; Salman and Uprety, 2002).

The Driver of the Conflict[2]

India first considered distribution of the Ganges waters through a feasibility
study back in the mid-1900s, under British supervision. Eastern Pakistan (now
Bangladesh) was of course already a central party to the conflict at the time of its
inception in 1947, but did not state any clear policy over the issue until 1951. Investigations were under way and East Pakistan referenced this when encouraging India to
consider Bangladesh's interests before taking action (Rangachari and Ramaswamy,
1993). In 1951, the main interest of Eastern Pakistan as it is of Bangladesh today,
was securing access to fresh water during the dry season for its population. Over
the course of time, increasing salinization has negatively affected the agriculture —
while the population has increased, the quality of the soil has deteriorated. This
has affected the livelihoods of millions of people. For example, increased salinity
has forced hundreds of industries to close down in Khulna and Mongla, which had
the prospect of becoming thriving industrial zones in Bangladesh. Other agricultural
and ecological damages, mentioned earlier, were also paramount (Faisal, 2006).

India's main concern in the 1950s was the water levels in the Calcutta port. The
use of the port is made possible if a certain flow of water into and out of the port is
secured, and any increase in the water flow out of the port would be beneficial, for
this most important port in the eastern and northeastern part of the country. For
this reason, India had considered diverting water from the Ganges into the Calcutta
port. Consequently the Farakka Barrage was built and began operating in the 1970s,
considerably reducing the Bangladesh share of the Ganges waters flows. India has
increasingly come to realize that the prospect of keeping the Calcutta port open is
unsustainable. Nevertheless, India continues to divert a large share of the waters
to keep the port operational. In addition, the diversions continue to provide India's
population with fresh water and likewise help keep salinization under control.

Though environmental issues such as salinization, arsenic contamination of
ground water (in both countries), in addition to border disputes have occurred
throughout the history of the conflict, they never took central stage in the negotiations. Therefore, we have chosen to concentrate on the distribution of the water
flows in the following discussion (Kumra, 1995, p. 130; Elhance, 1999, p. 163).

---

[2]Based mainly on Elhance (1999), Nishat and Faisal (2000), Faisal (2002), and Tanzeema and
Faisal (2001).

We will address only issues that prevailed in the period after India's independence. The first conflict over the GBM basin took place in 1951 when the Farakka Barrage was planned.

Pakistan, at that time included Bangladesh as "East Pakistan," claimed that the project will harm East Pakistan, which already suffers from severe water scarcity. India responded that East Pakistan has sufficient amounts of water and suggested that the two countries collaborate on the development of the Ganges waters. However, when Pakistan suggested the countries collaborate on a particular project in East Pakistan and on a joint survey of the upper reaches of the Ganges and Brahmaputra, India objected and argued that Pakistan should survey rivers on its own territory.

When talks resumed in 1957, Pakistan made a few suggestions including:

1. The parties should seek assistance of a UN body in planning and developing eastern waters for their mutual benefits to both countries;
2. Individual projects on the Ganges be reviewed by experts of the two countries before implementation;
3. UN Secretary General be asked to appoint experts to participate in technical meetings in which various aspects of water resources development issues will be discussed.

India did not agree to these suggestions and the issue was discussed again in 1960, 1961, and 1962. With little progress on the Farakka issue, in 1967 Pakistan threatened to bring the matter before an international authority. In fast the issue was raised by Pakistan in the 1967 water peace conference held in Washington, DC, and during the discussions leading to the Tashkent Declaration that marked the formal end to the India–Pakistan war (over Kashmir). The issue was raised again in 1968 in an international meeting of the Afro-Asian Legal Consultative Committee, and again in 1969. At that time, Pakistan requested guarantee from India for a fixed quantity of water from the Ganges to East Pakistan. India rejected the request on the basis that it can be honored only after the parties exchanged data and agreed on basic technical issues.

In 1970, in the last meeting between Pakistan and India on the Farakka Barrage, the parties agreed that water would be discharged from the Farakka to East Pakistan. A year later, in 1971, the Farakka Barrage was completed and Bangladesh gained its independence.

Bangladesh, now an independent state, had several serious reservations about the Farakka Barrage. Its argued that at least $55,000\,\mathrm{m^3/s}$ (cumecs) be released at Farakka in the lean (dry) period so as to prevent water shortages in Bangladesh. Such shortages could affect fisheries production and result in river navigation and irrigation problems. Lowering of ground water levels could likewise result if water flows are reduced.

In 1972, the India-Bangladesh Treaty of Friendship was signed by Sheikh Mujib (Bangladesh) and Indira Gandhi (India), codifying the two countries' desire to collaborate over water issues in the GBM basin. The agreement established also the

Joint Rivers Commission (JRC). Over the years, the JRC has become a prominent body active in the facilitation of interim agreements between the two riparians on the water at Farakka.

THE FARAKKA AGREEMENTS[3]

Since the planing phase in the 1950s and through construction in the 1960s, the Farakka Barrage has been disputed between India and Pakistan. India eventually completed the project in 1971 (after a war with Pakistan on border-related issues in Kashmir and Jammu), the year Bangladesh became independent (after having uprising and hostile activities against Pakistan for more than five years). Therefore, the Farakka Barrage has become an integral part of the hydro political relations between India and Bangladesh.

As alluded earlier, the central disputed issue between India and Bangladesh over the Ganges has been the sharing of the waters at Farakka during the lean period of January–May (Bangladesh never challenged the existence of the Farakka Barrage). For that reason, we will discuss the history of the agreements over water-sharing at Farakka, mainly during the lean period. It should be mentioned that between 1971 and 1996, there have been about five agreements and this is an indication of the unsustainable allocation regime. The flow of water during the lean season in two gauging stations (Farakka and Harding Bridge) of the Ganges are presented in Fig. CS2.1.

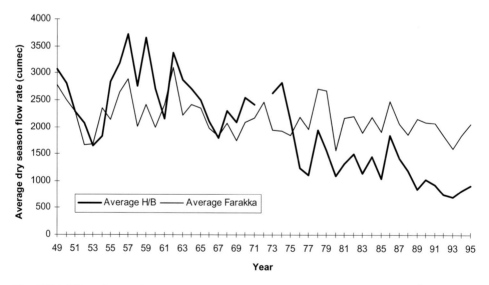

Fig. CS2.1: Water flow in the Harding Bridge and Farakka during the lean period (m^3/s). *Source*: JRC and the Hydrology Unit of the Bangladesh Water Development Board. Provided by Faisal (2006).

---

[3]Based mainly on Upreti (1993) and Salman and Uprety (2002).

The 18 April 1975 Temporary Allocation Agreement of the Ganges Waters at Farakka

This temporary agreement was the result of closer political understanding between the two new countries. It provided Bangladesh 75–80% of the water and leaves India with 25–20%, depending on the exact period. This very generous allocation (Tabled CS2.6) on the part of India may explain the reason for doubt in India regarding its permanent status.

However, in August 1975 after Sheikh Mujib was assassinated in Bangladesh and a military regime was established there, and relations between the two countries cooled, especially following allegations regarding the overuse of its sharing of the Ganges water. India, responded by unilaterally withdrawing water at Farakka, based on the fact that the 1975 agreement expired on 31 May, 1975.

Relatively weak compared to India, Bangladesh adopted a different strategy — internationalizing the dispute on water-sharing at Farakka. Between 1975 and 1976, Bangladesh raised the issue with about five international organizations, including the UN General Assembly.

The 5 November 1977 Water Sharing Agreement

This agreement was the result of the 1976 elections in India where by the Janata Party formed the government. The party implemented its policy for regional issues it had on its political platform during the election campaign. The 1977 agreement (Table CS2.7) was signed for a duration of five years and calls on the two riparians to find a long-term solution for the dry season water flow. The agreement was subject to extensions, based on mutual agreement between the two riparians. The agreement allows India to draw a small quantity of water, not to exceed 200 cusecs for local use downstream of Farakka. One of the key elements of the included a "80% minimum flow" guarantee clause for Bangladesh. It also called for finding a mutually agreeable means for flow augmentation in the dry season. The 1977 agreement was criticized in India.

In October 1982, the 1977 agreement was extended for two more years (with minor modifications — Salman and Uprety 2002, Table 7.4). By then, the October

Table CS2.6: The 1975 agreement for sharing of lean season flow at Farakka (Cusecs).

Period	Flow at Farakka	Diverted to Hooghly (India)	Remaining flow to Bangladesh
21–30 April 1975	55,000	11,000	44,000
1–10 May 1975	56,500	12,000	44,500
11–20 May 1975	59,250	15,000	44,250
21–31 May 1975	65,500	16,000	49,500

Source: Upreti (1993).

Table CS2.7: The 1977 agreement for sharing of lean season flow at Farakka (Cusecs).

Period	Flows reaching Farakka	Diverted to Hooghly (India)	Remaining flow to Bangladesh
January			
1–10	98,500	40,000	58,500
11–20	98,750	38,500	51,250
21–30	82,500	35,000	47,500
February			
1–10	79,250	33,000	46,250
11–20	74,000	31,500	42,500
21–28/9	70,000	30,750	39,250
March			
1–10	65,250	26,750	38,500
11–20	63,500	25,500	38,000
21–30	61,000	25,000	36,000
April			
1–10	59,000	24,000	35,000
11–20	55,500	20,750	34,750
21–30	55,000	20,500	34,500
May			
1–10	56,500	21,500	35,000
11–20	59,250	24,000	35,250
21–31	65,500	26,750	38,750

Source: Upreti (1993).

Table CS2.8: The 1985 agreement for sharing of lean season flow at Farakka (Cusecs).

Period	Diverted to Hooghly (India)	Remaining flow to Bangladesh
All dry season	40,000	35,000

Source: Upreti (1993).

1985 agreement was signed (Table CS2.8). Ratified in 1986 for a duration of three years, it was subject to extension.

The various allocation agreements of the waters at Farakka faced one major problem — low water volumes often not sufficient for the needs of the two riparians. Therefore, augmentation of the flow became an important issue for joint investigation. Some proposals included:

1. *The Ganges–Brahmaputra Link Canal*: proposed by India and rejected by Bangladesh for the following reasons: (i) the canal will divide Bangladesh; (ii) it will create a loss of 20,000 ha of agricultural land; and (iii) starting and end points of the canal will be on Indian land.
2. *Storage dams, on Nepalese and Indian territory*: proposed by Bangladesh and rejected by India on the ground of (i) very little water potential for storage; (ii) such storage is distant from Farakka and subject to large losses to seepage. This

proposal was favored by Nepal because (i) it extends its water-related relationships to include Bangladesh; (ii) it will make Nepal less dependent on India; and (iii) it will create an opportunity to fund hydropower projects.

The main problem was that India always insisted on keeping the dialogue bilateral. Nepal, on the other hand, had its own water issues to deal with and did not show much interest in complicating matters by bringing Bangladesh into the process (Faisal, 2006). In connection with the above proposals, Nepal was invited to participate in the discussions on the augmentation of the Ganges water flow at Farakka, but nothing came out of these talks.

The Road to a Treaty

In 1987 and 1988, severe floods that left an estimated 10 million people homeless obliged Bangladesh and India to commence further discussion about flood control. Bangladesh re-introduced the Farakka issue in international forums and again attempted to internationalize it in 1988. An Indo-Bangladesh Task Force of Experts was set up to jointly study the Ganges and Brahmaputra Rivers and set up an efficient flood management plan. Some limited but effective agreements were reached on monitoring and information sharing issues. In 1992, after several decades of coups and military rule, democracy triumphed in Bangladesh. In India, the United Front Movement (that consisted of 13 regional movements and were the basis for the United Front Government) declared that improved relations with India's neighbors were India's main priority. Both India's and Bangladesh's Prime Ministers agreed shortly thereafter that equitable, long-term, and comprehensive arrangements for sharing the flows of major rivers should be attained through mutual discussions. Several ministers (e.g., water, energy, foreign affairs) were asked to make a new effort to find a long-term solution to the sharing of water flows in the dry season and it was agreed that joint monitoring of releases at Farakka should be undertaken immediately (Salman and Uprety, 2002).

The 1996 Water Treaty Between India and Bangladesh

The treaty (this is the first time that an agreement between India and Bangladesh on the Ganges water is formally called a "Treaty"[4] (Salman and Uprety (2002)) was signed in November 1996 for 30 years. As in many cases, this treaty is mainly the result changes in the governments in both countries, and good relations chemistry between the Prime Ministers of both India and Bangladesh. The treaty allocation schedule is presented in Table CS2.9.

There is an important difference between the flow schedules in the 1977 Agreement and the 1996 Treaty. Specifically, the allocations in the 1996 Treaty are more

---

[4]There is a technical difference between an agreement and a treaty. The former is limited in scope and may be signed at the ministerial level. The latter requires a full cabinet level approval due to its more comprehensive scope or longer tenure (Faisal, 2006).

Table CS2.9: Ganges Treaty, 1996, Farakka Barrage Water Sharing, January–May.

Flow at Farakka (m³/s)	India's share	Bangladesh's share
< 70,000	50%	50%
70,000–75,000	Balance of flow	35,000 m³/s
> 75,000	40,000 m³/s	Balance of flow

Source: Salman and Uprety (2002).

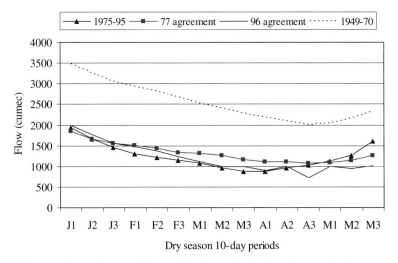

Fig. CS2.2: Historical and simulated flows at Hardinge Bridge (gauging station).
Source: Nishat and Faisal (2000, p. 198).

flexible, and based on shares rather than fixed amounts. Nonetheless, some claim that the schedule in the 1996 Treaty and the 1977 Agreement did not help alleviate the lean season water scarcity in Bangladesh, but rather validated the status quo. However, the 1996 Treaty also calls for augmentation solutions to the flow at Farakka in the dry season. Since the treaty is in force for 30 years, this allows the countries sometime to consider such panaceas. Performance of the schedules in the various agreements is presented in Fig. CS2.2.[5]

THE NEGOTIATION PROCESS IN RETROSPECT

In general, domestic politics is an important driver in explaining the outcomes of a negotiation process (Milner, 1997). The political instability in Bangladesh,

---

[5]Another feature that is lacking is the guarantee clause that was part of the 1977 Agreement. By 1996, however, India recognized that its upper riparian states were increasingly withdrawing water from the Ganges before the flow reached Farakka. Thus, it was politically difficult to commit to any guarantee clause.

for example, was a decisive factor in the negative outcomes of the negotiations. The military rulers of Bangladesh often attempted to gain domestic (and international) political support by bringing attention to its negotiations with India and arousing harsh public opinion. In fact, the military regime unnecessarily raised the issue of sharing water resources to increasingly charged levels, making it a major political goal. As a consequence, India's attitude in the negotiations also hardened and together with an atmosphere of political instability during the military junta in Bangladesh these factors contributed to a lack of progress in the negotiations (Upreti, 1993, p. 134).

Though domestic politics may explain the outcomes of negotiations, India's overwhelming power is another important variable. As the upper riparian and the regional super power, from both a political and economic perspective, India holds much more sway compared to Bangladesh. To some degree this has allowed India to make consistent use of stalling tactics throughout the conflict. Minor issues such as flow measurement were allowed to unnecessarily prolong or stall the negotiation process (Nishat and Faisal, 2000, p. 293; Asafuddowlah, 1995, p. 212).

While the main institutional mechanism in the basin, the Joint Rivers Commission, saw months and years of debate over minor technical details, the real progress was made only when the politicians showed strong will to reach a settlement. For example, the 1996 Treaty was negotiated, drafted, and signed in less than six months primarily due to the favorable political climate in both countries (Nishat and Faisal, 2000, p. 295). A phased chronology of the entire negotiation process is summarized in Table CS2.10.

ROLE OF THE JOINT RIVERS COMMISSION

The JRC was established in 1972 by the governments of India and Bangladesh, in response to potential water-related conflicts (Nishat and Faisal, 2000). The JRC met several times during the year in the period 1972–1996 mainly to address its mandate as shown in Table CS2.11. The JRC's main mission is to maximize benefits from the shared rivers by studying flood and cyclone pattern to formulate control works, flood forecasting and warning systems and; studying irrigation and flood control. While its success record is not impressing, the JRC played an important role in the inter-party dialogue and negotiations (Nishat and Faisal, 2000, p. 296).

ROLE OF INTERNATIONAL COMMUNITY

As a result of its inferior position in the conflict, Bangladesh has shown greater interest and taken more measures to bring external parties into the negotiations, whereas India has advocated a bilateral relationship, a situation in which India would most likely would have greater leverage.

In the 1970s, Bangladesh raised the issue at various international forums. Bangladesh water experts brought up the sharing of river waters in the US and

Table CS2.10: Historical phases of Indo-Bangladesh negotiation.

Phase	Main activities	Comment
Phase I: 1951–1974	Discussion centered on respective claims by India and Pakistan (later Bangladesh) on the Ganges water and their justifications	India assured that shares would be finalized before commissioning of the Barrage
	Pakistan/Bangladesh claimed the entire natural flow of the Ganges reaching Farakka and indicated that reservoir(s) upstream of Farakka should provide any additional flow required for the Calcutta Port	Bangladesh becomes an independent country in 1971
	India, on the other hand, argued that Bangladesh needs a small part of the historic flow as most of it is being wasted into the Bay of Bengal	Joint Rivers Commission was formulated in 1972 to facilitate water-related negotiations
Phase II: 1974–1976	The issue of flow augmentation was raised recognizing that after water withdrawal for the Calcutta Port, residual flow will not be enough for Bangladesh	The Farakka Barrage began operating in 1975 with a test withdrawal of 11,000 to 16,000 cusec through a feeder canal for 41 days
	Bangladesh proposed that a number of dams could be built in India and Nepal to tap large monsoon flows	
	India proposed diversion of flows from the Brahmaputra through a link canal to the Ganges	In 1976 and 1977, India withdrew water unilaterally causing a major water crisis in the southwest region of Bangladesh
	Bangladesh took the issue to the United Nations and the General Assembly adopted a resolution according to which both countries agreed to meet in Dhaka to arrive at a fair and expeditious settlement	
Phase III: 1977–1982	The first water-sharing agreement was signed on 5 November 1977 for a duration of 5 years. Water was distributed based on a 10-day basis schedule in the dry season (January–May)	The agreement expired in November 1982
	It was decided that a mutually agreeable flow augmentation method would be worked out within 3 years. However, no new alternatives could be found and both sides stuck with their initial positions	Because of lack of progress on flow augmentation, the agreement was not renewed after its expiration
Phase IV: 1982–1988	Two Memoranda of Understanding (MOU) were signed. The first one in 1982 for a duration of 18 months covering the dry seasons of 1983 and 1984	No progress could be made on the flow augmentation
	There was no agreement regarding 1985. In November 1985, the second MOU was signed for a 3-year period	The last MOU expired in May 1988

(*Continued*)

Table CS2.10: (*Continued*)

Phase	Main activities	Remark
	A joint team of experts from India and Bangladesh visited Nepal to collect data. Nepal showed keen interest in a tri-lateral initiative for resolving the water crisis	India objected to Nepal's involvement as a third party, emphasizing the bilateral nature of the negotiations between India and Bangladesh
Phase V: 1988–1996	Discussions continued. Heads of states met in Delhi in September 1988. Secretaries of Water Resources were assigned the task of working out a formula for long-term sharing of all the common rivers	India's precondition of having an augmentation plan prevented the signing of any agreement
	Between April 1990 and February 1992, six meetings were held in Dhaka and Delhi with little progress	
	Prime Ministers of the two countries met in 1992 and several rounds of talks were conducted in 1995 at the Foreign Secretaries level	
Phase VI: 1996–1997	After changes in governments in both India and Bangladesh, a 30-year Treaty was signed in December 1996. The treaty became effective on January 1, 1997	Prevailing political mood has always been the main factor in the successful conclusion of negotiations
	The treaty urges the parties to find ways to augment the flow of the Ganges in the dry season as well as devising sharing arrangements to be worked out for all common rivers	
	India is accused of withdrawing more water greater than the amounts stipulated in the treaty	
2005	In September 2005, during the 36th JRC meeting, Bangladesh proposed once again to open tripartite talks that would include Nepal. At stake were investments in reservoirs in Nepal for augmenting the dry season flow of the Ganges	

Source: Information for 1951–1995 is based on Nishat and Faisal (2000, p. 294). Information for 2005 is based on Rahaman (2006).

England in 1976, the same issue was raised before the Economic and Social Commission for Asia and the Pacific as well as before the 7th Islamic Foreign Ministers Conference at Islamabad in 1976. It was again discussed later the same year at the Summit Conference of the nonaligned countries in Colombo, and finally it was on the agenda of the 31st session of the UN General Assembly. The UN made declarations and encouraged the parties to solve the dispute through increased cooperation but the UN did not pass any resolutions. However, the UN did, along with the group

Bridges Over Water

Table CS2.11: Chronological summary of JRC activities (1972–1996).

Committee	Period	Scope	No. of MTGS
Joint River Commission	25 June 1972 to 10 April 1999	Formed in April 1972 to assist the governments of India and Bangladesh resolve common water issues	33
Meetings at the secretary level on sharing of waters of the common rivers between Bangladesh and India	19 April 1990 to 3 February 1992	Discussed water-sharing issues for six common rivers, namely Monu, Muhuri, Khowai, Gumti, Dharla, and Dudhkumar	6
JCE (Joint Committee of Experts)	16 January 1986 to 22 November 1987	First formulated in 1982 but remained inactive until reformulation in 1985 under the MOU of 1985 for sharing the Ganges	9 Secretary level 2 Minister level
Meetings on sharing of the Teesta Waters	16 January 1979 to 13 September 1987	Teesta issues discussed	4 Technical level 6 Secretary level
Joint Committee on sharing of the Ganges	24 December 1996 to 4 April 2000	Ganges issues discussed	15
Joint Committee on sharing of Teesta Waters	29 August 1997 to 30 January 2000	Meetings held between 1982 and 1988 focused on river erosion and border disputes	3
Indo-Bangladesh experts on flood forecasting and warning system	20 November 1997 to 24 October 1998 (meetings also took place during the early seventies and eighties)	Explored the possibilities of improving the accuracy of flood forecasting and warning	2
Standing Committee of JRC	13 April 1982 to 28 October 1999	A permanent committee of JRC	14
Indo-Bangladesh Joint Scientific Study Team	19 June 1998 to 22 December 1999	Formed to investigate the discrepancy in the shared flow after the 1996 Treaty	3
Honorable Prime Ministers' level meeting of Bangladesh and India	11–12 December 1996	Details of the 1996 Treaty were worked out	1

Source: Faisal and Nishat (2000).

of nonaligned countries play a role as a catalyst in the signing of the Ganges water agreement of 1977 (Upreti, 1993, p. 136).

India favored the countries' shared waters were a bilateral matter. Internationalizing the negotiations would only serve to deteriorate the relations between Bangladesh and India. India's view prevailed from at least the 1970s until the mid 1990s with Bangladesh's internationlization efforts only aggravating the situation. Consequently, the bilateral approach triumphed during this period (Upreti, 1993). The Ganges issue was raised once again in the UN General Assembly in 1993, when the Ganges flow reaches its lowest historic levels. The matter drew increased international attention and this time around indirect pressure was exerted on India to work toward a long-term settlement (Nishat and Faisal, 2000, p. 305).

At present, the ideas concerning external involvement point to the potential role for either the UN or the Group of Seven (G7) to provide institutional mechanisms for the monitoring of agreements and distribution of benefits and costs. The South Asian Association for Regional Cooperation (SAARC) has been involved in standardizing discussions among basin states of the Ganges and Brahmaputra, which has brought about an increased awareness of the gains that could come to each party from increased regional cooperation over the Basin. That being said, the situation has not advanced notably since the 30-year treaty was signed in 1996.[6]

REFERENCES

Asafuddowlah, M. (1995). Sharing of transboundary rivers: The Ganges tragedy. In: Blake, G.H., W.J. Hildesley, M.A. Pratt, R.J. Ridley and C.H. Schofield (eds.), *The Peaceful Management of Transboundary Resources*, London: Kluwer Academic Publishers.

(CIA) Central Intelligence Agency USA (2006). *World Fact Book*. Can be downloaded from https://www.cia.gov/cia/publications/factbook/index.html (Last visited on December 8, 2006).

Crow, B., A. Lindquist and D. Wilson (1995). *Sharing the Ganges — The Politics and Technology of River Development*. New Delhi: Sage Publications.

Eaton, J.D. and M.C. Chaturvedi (1993). Water resources cooperation in the Ganges-Brahmaputra river basin. Policy Research Project Report number 101, Lyndon B. Johnson School of Public Affairs, University of Texas at Austin.

Elhance, A.P. (1999). The Ganges-Brahmaputra-Barak basin. In: Elhance, A.P. (ed.), *Hydropolitics in the 3rd World, Conflict and Cooperation in International River Basins*. Washington, DC: United States Institute of Peace Press.

Faisal, I.M. (2006). Personal Communication, email sent on 12/18/2006.

Goldman, M. (1996). Sharing the Ganges: The politics and technology of river development, *Contemporary Sociology*, 25(5), 649–650.

Kishore D.C. (1996). The political economy of regional cooperation in South Asia, *Pacific Affairs*, 69(2), 196.

Kumra, V.K. (1995). Water quality in the river Ganges. In: Chapman, G.P. and M. Thompson (eds.), *Water and the Quest for Sustainable Development in the Ganges Valley*. London: Mansell Publishing Ltd.

---

[6]The World Bank has likewise been involved to a limited degree (Goldman, 1996).

London Economics (1995). India National Hydrology Project: An economic appraisal. London, UK, September.

Milner, H.V. (1997). *Interests, Institutions and Information, Domestic Politics and International Relations.* Princeton: Princeton University Press.

Mirza, M.M.Q. (1998). Research: Diversion of the Ganges water at Farakka and its effects on salinity in Bangladesh, *Environmental Management*, 22(5), 711–722.

Nishat, A. and I.M. Faisal (2000). An assessment of the institutional mechanisms for water negotiations in the Ganges-Brahmaputra Meghna basin, *International Negotiation*, 5(2), 289–310.

Rahaman, M.M. (2006). The Ganges Water Conflict: A comparative analysis of 1977 Agreement and 1996 Treaty, *Asteriskos - Journal of International & Peace Studies*, Vol 1/2, 195–208.

Rangachari, R. and R.I. Ramaswamy (1993). Indo-Bangladesh talks on the Ganga Waters issue. In: Verghese, B.G. and R.I. Ramaswamy (eds.), *Harnessing the Eastern Himalayan Rivers.* New Delhi: Konark Publishers Pvt Ltd.

Rogers, P. (1993). The value of cooperation in resolving international river basin disputes, *Natural Resources Forum*, 17(2), 117–131.

Salman M.A.S. and K. Uprety (2002). *Conflict and Cooperation on South Asia's International Rivers — A Legal Perspective.* (Part IV: India-Bangladesh Relations). Law, Justice and Development Series, Washington, DC: World Bank.

Shah, R.B. (2001). Ganges – Brahmaputra: The outlook for the twenty-first century. In: Biswas, A.K. and J.I. Vitto (eds.), *Sustainable Development of Ganges – Brahmaputra – Meghna Basins.* Tokyo: United Nations University Press.

Tanzeema, S. and I.M. Faisal (2001). Sharing the Ganges: A critical analysis of the water sharing treaties, *Water Policy*, 3, 13–28.

Upreti, B.C. (1993). *Politics of Himalayan River Waters.* Nirala Series 32. Jaipur, India: Nirala Publications.

Verghese, B.G. (1996). Towards an eastern Himalayan rivers concord. In: Biswas, A.K. and T. Hashimoto (eds.), *Asian International Waters.* Oxford: Oxford University Press.

Wolf, A., J.A. Natharius, J.J. Danielson, B.S. Ward and J.K. Pender (1999). International river basins of the world, *Water Resources Development*, 15(4), 387–427.

ADDITIONAL READING

Ahmad, Q.A. (2004). Regional cooperation in flood management in the Ganges-Brahmaputra-Meghna region: Bangladesh perspective, *Natural Hazards*, 28(1), 191–198.

Beach, H.L., J. Hamner, J. Hewitt, E. Kaufman, A. Kurki, J. Oppenheimer and A. Wolf (2000). *Transboundary Freshwater Dispute Resolution: Theory, Practice and Annotated References.* Tokyo and New York: United Nations University Press.

Bindra, S. (1985). India and Her Neighbors. New Delhi: Deep & Deep Publications.

Biswas, A.K. and J.I. Uitto (2001). *Sustainable Development of the Ganges-Brahmaputra-Meghna Basins.* Tokyo: United Nations University Press.

Blake, G.H., W.J. Hildesley, M.A. Pratt, R.J. Ridley and C.H. Schofield (eds.) (1993). *The Peaceful Management of Transboundary Resources.* New Delhi: Konark Publishers Pvt Ltd.

Briscoe, J. and R.P.S. Malik (2006). *India's Water Economy: Bracing for a Turbulent Future.* New Delhi: Oxford University Press.

Brojendra Nath Banerjee (1989). *Can the Ganga be Cleaned?* Delhi: B.R. Publishing Corporation.

Chapman, G.P. (1995). Environmental myth as international politics: The problem of the Bengal delta. In: Chapman, G.P. and M. Thompson (eds.), *Water and the Quest for Sustainable Development in the Ganges Valley.* London: Mansell Publishing Ltd.

Corell, E. and A. Swain (1991). India: The domestic and international politics of water scarcity. In: Ohlsson, L. (ed.), *Hydropolitics, Conflicts over Water as a Development Constraint.* London: ZED Books.

Faisal, M.I. (2002). Managing common waters in the Ganges-Brahmaputra-Meghna region: Looking ahead, *SAIS Review*, 22(2), 309–327.

Nishat, E. (1996). *Impacts of the Ganges Water Disputes on Bangladesh in Asian International Waters, From Ganges-Brahmaputra to Mekong.* London: Oxford University Press.

Postel, S. (1999). *Pillar of Sand: Can the Irrigation Miracle Last?* New York: W.W. Norton & Company.

Salman, M.A.S. and K. Uprety (1999). Hydro-politics in South Asia: A comparative analysis of the Mahakali and the Ganges Treaties, *Natural Resources Journal*, 39(Spring), 295–343.

Verghese, B.G. and I.R. Ramaswamy (eds.) (1993). *Harnessing the Eastern Himalayan Rivers.* New Delhi: Konark Publishers Pvt Ltd.

CASE STUDY 3: THE INDUS RIVER BASIN*

The Indus Waters Treaty, which arranges the use of the River Indus water between India and Pakistan, is praised as one of the most sophisticated international water agreements. It has proved stable despite several complications taking place during its negotiations and implementation. Among the multitude of water treaties, this is the only agreement that physically divides a river system between the riparian states. Finally, it is also the only water treaty whereby a third party, the World Bank, played not only a crucial role in brokering the specific arrangements but was also a signatory.

The treaty is now almost 50 years of age. The two signatory states face increasing water scarcity problems, mainly due to high inefficiency of water use in irrigation (80% of the water is used for low value agriculture production), increased levels of water pollution, and competing needs driven by high population growth (Briscoe and Malik, 2006; World Bank, 2005c). These "physical" aspects, coupled with the sometimes precarious political relations between the riparians, give rise to concerns regarding the sustainability of the treaty. In this case study, we describe the key issues that lead to the original dispute and played an important role during the negotiation process between the riparians. We also consider the variables that continue to affect the long-term sustainability of the agreement.

FEATURES OF THE BASIN

The Indus River system (Map CS3.1) consists of several tributaries that collect snowmelt and rain from the highest peaks of the Himalayas and carry it to the Arabian Sea, traveling 5,000 km. Seven of the rivers in this system (Table CS3.1) cover most of the system's drainage area of about 950,000 km^2 and a catchment area of nearly 470,000 km^2 in four countries, Afghanistan, China (Tibet), India, and Pakistan, and includes the Kuram, Swat, and Kabul that rise in Afghanistan, and the Indus and Sutlej that rise in Tibet. In the discussion below, we will refer only to the basin part that is shared by India and Pakistan, which comprises five rivers — the Indus, Beas, Ravi, Chenab, and Sutlej.

The Indus Basin is a geographically contained system that is characterized by huge water supply variations. The mean annual rainfall ranges from less than

---

*This case study benefited from research by Patrick Doyle, Ruby Khan, and Ashley Hubka. It benefited greatly from comments by Salman Salman and Undala Alam. Because of the interlinkages between the information and sources, citation may have been not appropriately provided. The case study is not aimed at covering all aspects and details.

Map CS3.1: The Indus Basin.

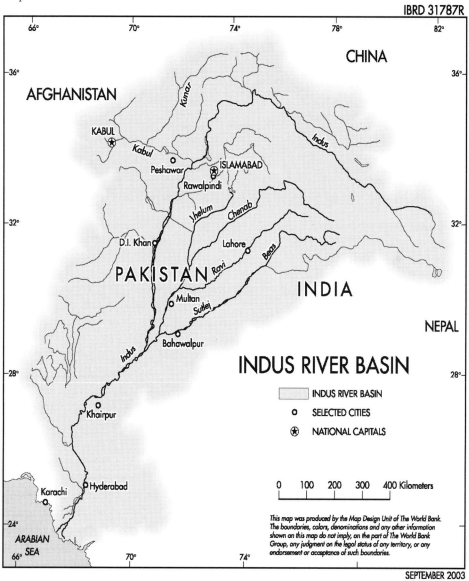

Source: World Bank (Permission granted to reproduce the map.)

100 mm in parts of the lower Indus region, above the Arabian Sea, to more than 750 mm in the northern foothills, below the Himalaya mountains. The area is subject to seasonal monsoons, which dump rainfall during the months of July and August, and severe droughts. Rainfall and water flow (from snowmelt) variability in the river is vast, with about 3/4 of the flow occurring between 4 months of the year — June and September (Alam, 1998; Salman and Uprety, 2002).

Table CS3.1: Catchment areas and runoff of the Indus river system.

River/tributary	Gauging station	Catchment area (km^2)[a]	Average annual runoff 1922–1961 (billion m^3)[b]
Sutlej (E)[c]	Rupar	48,300	17
Beas (E)	Mandi Plain	16,900	16
Ravi (E)	Madhopur	8,100	9
Chenab (W)	Marala	29,600	32
Jhelum (W)	Mangla	33,600	28
Kabul (W)	Warsak	67,600	21
Indus (W)	Attock	265,300	115
Total		469,400	217

[a,b]It should be noted that different sources provide different estimates of the area and the runoff of the Indus system.
[c]E = eastern rivers; W = western rivers.
Sources: Harza (1963); Kirmani (1959); and Bureau of Reclamation (1963).

The major economic activity in the basin is irrigated agriculture. Until the British annexation of Sind and Punjab regions in the 19th century, inundation irrigation was the main technology, depending on availability of water in the river. Had it not been for the modern irrigation network developed after the annexation, the basin would not prosper to the extent it had. Modern irrigation, at that time, provided the framework around which both Pakistani and Indian Punjab grew to their present economic importance (Alam, 1998; Kux, 2006). By 1947, the irrigation system in the basin consisted of 26 million acres of irrigated agriculture, 34,000 miles of major canals, and 50 million people relying on a system consisting of 13 additional canals that were already in place (Alam, 1998).

The dispute between India and Pakistan over the Indus water has to be addressed in the context of a broader set of issues. These issues go far beyond water and are rooted in a period before India and Pakistan became independent. While the Indus dispute was resolved by means of a treaty that has held for nearly 50 years, there are new issues that have recently emerged (see Epilogue section), which threaten the stability of the treaty (World Bank, 2005a, 2005b, 2005c). With population growth rates that more than doubled over the last 50 years (India grew from 400 million to over 1 billion and Pakistan grew from 40 to 150 million between 1950 and 2000), the demands on the Indus River are mounting.

HISTORY OF WATER AND OTHER DISPUTES IN THE INDUS BASIN

Disputes over water-sharing in British India were not uncommon, but they were also not the only issues among the various parties inhabiting British-ruled (Raj) India.

The British administered 2/3 of India's territory while the rest was ruled by more than 500 Indian Princes (Maharajas). Each of these principalities, including Jammu and Kashmir, were large enough to become nation states had they been independent (Kux, 2006). This partition of the land gave rise to differences in interests, over control and management of natural resources, leading to local disputes that were resolved locally (see below) with the intervention of the British administration (Salman and Uprety, 2002).

Another source of tension, escalating at times to bitter disputes, was the nationalistic differences and power struggle between Muslims and Hindus. While the Muslims had dominated most of the Indian subcontinent for nearly 600 years (1191–1757) they have been politically demoted by the British and faced difficulties adjusting to the new Raj realities. The Hindus on the other hand adapted relatively well to the new political and administrative opportunities (Kux, 2006, p. 4). Despite the political situation, the 215 million Hindu Indians and the 70 million Muslim Indians resided peacefully side by side.

It was not until the early 1900s when the Muslim League in the Indian Congress was pushing for Indian self-government, which both Muslims and Hindus could support, that socio-political and economic safeguards were secured. However, with the Hindu majority leaders not agreeing to all proposed safeguards, the Muslim–Hindu united front collapsed, leading to a long period of retaliations of both Hindus and Muslims against the British Raj (Kux, 2006). In 1935 the pressure for independence mounted, and the Government of India Act was approved. The decision facilitated self-rule at the provincial level and the central Indian Government. In essence, the 1935 Act led to the termination of the British Raj and eventually to the partition of British India into the independent states of India and Pakistan on 15 and 14 August 1947, respectively.[1] These events are an integral part of the Indus Basin water dispute and its resolution. They will be elaborated later.

Irrigation-Related Disputes and Their Resolution

Even before the partition of India and Pakistan, the Indus posed problems between states of British India, and between British India and Indian Princes. The problem became international only after partition, though, and the attendant increase in hostility and lack of supralegal authority exacerbated the issue. Pakistani territory, which had relied on the Indus waters for centuries, now found the water sources originating in another country, one with whom geopolitical relations were increasing in hostility.

Treaties negotiating resolution to early conflicts on the Indus Basin began as early as 1874, when Britain and Indian Maharajas agreed on the percentage of water each would receive from the Hathmatee Basin for irrigation purposes. At the time, the British and the Maharaja of Edur agreed to the construction of the weir,

---

[1]The reader could realize that by condensing the process some important omissions are unavoidable. For a short but more concise historical background, see also Kux (2006, pp. 3–18).

and the British agreed to pay for damages if the sites were flooded. In 1892, the State of Jind and the British government agreed to allocate water for irrigation in exchange for payment. The only problem with the above agreements was that the Indian parties had little, or no choice, in the matter since they were much weaker than their British counterparts. Such power asymmetry characterized much, or all, of the negotiations that took place during the pre-partition period (Salman and Uprety, 2002).

By the late 1940s, the irrigation works along the river were the most extensive in the world. These irrigation projects were developed over the years under one political authority, that of British India, and any water conflict was resolved by executive order (Salman and Uprety, 2002). The Government of India Act of 1935, however, placed water under provincial jurisdiction, and several disputes did occur, especially at the sites boasting more extensive works, notably between the provinces of Punjab and Sind.[2]

In 1942, a judicial commission was appointed by the British government to study Sind's concern over planned Punjabi development. The Commission recognized the claims of Sind, and called for the integrated management of the basin as a whole. The Commission's report was found unacceptable by both sides, and the chief engineers of the two sides met informally between 1943 and 1945 to try and reconcile their differences. Although a draft agreement was produced, neither of the two provinces accepted the terms and the dispute was referred to London for a final decision in 1947 (Gulhati, 1973).

Before a decision could be reached, the Indian Independence Act of June 1947 internationalized the dispute between the new countries of India and Pakistan. Partition was to be carried out in 73 days, and the full implications of dividing the Indus basin seem not to have been fully considered. That being said, Sir Cyril Radcliffe, who was responsible for the boundary delineation, did express his hope that, "some joint control and management of the irrigation system may be found" (Mehta, 1988, p. 4). Heightened political tensions, population displacements, and unresolved territorial issues, all served to exacerbate hostilities over the water dispute.

As the monsoon flows receded in the autumn of 1947, the chief engineers of Pakistan and India met and agreed to a "Standstill Agreement," which froze water allocations at two points on the river until 31 March 1948, allowing discharges from headworks in India to continue to flow into Pakistan. On 1 April 1948, the day that the "Standstill Agreement" expired, in the absence of a new agreement, the provincial government of East Punjab (India) discontinued the delivery of water to the Dipalpur Canal and the main branches of the Upper Bari Daab Canal. At an Inter-Dominion conference held in Delhi on 3–4 May 1948, India agreed to the resumption of flow, but maintained that Pakistan could

---

[2] As suggested by Undala Alam in her review of this case study (personal communication, October 30, 2006) "The provincial governments of Punjab and Sind developed their irrigation independently and in direct competition of one another. This was long before the 1935 Act made water a provincial responsibility. There were two commissions (Anderson and Rau) set up to resolve the Punjab-Sind dispute, neither of which were ultimately successful."

not claim any share of those waters as a matter of right. Pakistan contested India's position which was aggravated by the Indian claim that, since Pakistan had agreed to pay for water under the Standstill Agreement of 1947, Pakistan had recognized India's water rights. Pakistan countered that they had the rights of prior appropriation, and that payments to India were only to cover operation and maintenance costs (Gulhati, 1973; Salman and Uprety, 2002; Alam, 1998).

While these conflicting claims were not resolved, an agreement was signed, later referred to as the Delhi Agreement, in which India assured Pakistan that it will not withdraw water without allowing time for Pakistan to develop alternate sources. Pakistan later expressed its displeasure with the agreement in a note dated 16 June 1949, calling for the "equitable apportionment of all common waters," and suggesting the case be turned over to the World Court of Justice. India preferred rather that a commission of judges from each side attempt to resolve their differences before turning the problem over to a third party. Stalemate continued through 1950 (Gulhati, 1973).

In the early days of statehood, India and Pakistan had approached the World Bank with separate applications for loans to develop their portion of the Sutlej River, which was at the center of their dispute. The World Bank, a relatively new international institution in the late 1940s, had great interest in getting involved with such significant development investments. However, the requested loans by India and Pakistan were in essence incongruous. Nonetheless, if the Bank could successfully resolve the dispute between the two riparians, its reputation would be boosted in the international arena.

ATTEMPTS AT CONFLICT MANAGEMENT — THE NEGOTIATION PROCESS[3]

In 1951, Indian Prime Minister Nehru invited David Lilienthal, former chairperson of the Tennessee Valley Authority (TVA), to visit India and discuss the possibility of adapting the TVA regime to India's water problems. Lilienthal also visited Pakistan and, on his return to the US, wrote an article outlining his impressions and recommendations. His article was read by Lilienthal's friend Eugene Black, president of the World Bank (Bank), who contacted Lilienthal for recommendations on helping to resolve the Indus waters dispute (at the time it was known as the "Canal Waters Dispute" and only involved the Sutlej River). As a result, Black contacted the prime ministers of Pakistan and India, inviting both countries to accept the Bank's good offices. In a subsequent letter, Black outlined "essential principles" that might be followed for conflict resolution. These

---

[3]Based on Gulhati (1973); Mehta (1988); Biswas (1992); Alam (1998, 2002); Salman and Uprety (2002); Kux (2006).

principles included:

- that there was enough water in the Indus system for both countries;
- that the water resources of the Indus Basin should be managed cooperatively;
- that the problems of the Basin should be solved on a functional not political level, without relation to past negotiations and past claims.

Black suggested that India and Pakistan each appoint a senior engineer to work on a plan for development of the Indus Basin. A Bank engineer would be made available as a consultant. Both sides accepted Black's initiative. The first meeting of the Working Party included Indian and Pakistani engineers, along with a team from the Bank, which met for the first time in Washington, D.C. in May 1952.

When the two sides were unable to agree on a common development plan for the Basin in subsequent meetings in Karachi, November 1952, and Delhi, January 1953, the Bank suggested that each party submits its own plan. Both sides did submit plans on 6 October 1953, which largely agreed on the water supplies available for irrigation, yet varied tremendously on how these supplies should be allocated (Table CS3A.2).

The irrigation systems that have to be re-allocated among the two riparian states, not only infringe upon the political sovereignty but also made it impossible in years of less than average water flow in the rivers. The Bank carried out its own independent studies to examine the relevant issues and prepared an adequate set of works to provide alternatives to Pakistan's uses of the Eastern Rivers. The studies confirmed that there was not enough surplus water in the Western Rivers, particularly in the critical crop periods. In addition, storage reservoirs were necessary to meet the shortages.

The Bank concluded that not only was the stalemate likely to continue, but that the ideal goal of integrated watershed development for the benefit of both riparians was probably too elusive of a goal at this stage of political relations. On 5 February 1954, the Bank issued its own proposal, abandoning the strategy of integrated development in favor of one of separation (Table CS3A.2). The Bank proposal called for the entire flow of the eastern rivers (Ravi, Beas, and Sutlej) to be allocated to India, and all of the western rivers (Indus, Jhelum, and Chenab), except for a small amount from the Jhelum, to be allocated to Pakistan. According to the proposal, the two sides would agree to a transition period while Pakistan would complete link canals dividing the watershed, during which India would continue to allow the waters historically used by Pakistan to flow from the eastern rivers. The Bank also recognized that it was virtually impossible to resolve the dispute without additional sources for financing the replacement and construction of new storage works.

The Bank proposal was given to both parties simultaneously. On 25 March 1954, India accepted the proposal as the basis for agreement. Pakistan viewed the proposal with more trepidation, and gave only qualified acceptance on 28 July 1954. Pakistan considered the flow of the western rivers to be insufficient to replace their existing supplies from the eastern rivers, particularly given limited available storage capacity.

To help facilitate an agreement, the Bank issued an aide memoir in 1956, calling for more storage on the western rivers, and suggesting India's financial liability for "replacement facilities" — increased storage facilities and enlarged link canals in Pakistan, which could be recognized as the cost replacement of pre-partition canals (Table CS3A.2).

By 1959, the Bank recognized that the main obstacle to a final agreement was deciding which works would be considered "replacement" and which "development." In other words, the dispute lingered over India's financial responsibilities and the respective works. To circumvent this problem, Black suggested an alternative approach in a visit to India and Pakistan in May. Perhaps the parties could settle on a specific amount for which India is responsible, rather than squabbling over individual works. The Bank might then help raise additional funds for watershed development. India was offered financial help with construction of its Beas Dam. Pakistan's plan, including both proposed dams, would be considered favorably. With these conditions, both sides agreed to a fixed payment settlement, and to a 10-year transition period during which Pakistan would be able to continue using its historic flows from the eastern rivers.

In August 1959, Black organized a consortium of international donors to support development in the Indus Basin, which raised close to $900 million, in addition to India's commitment of $174 million (£62 million) in 10 installments. The Indus Waters Treaty (IWT) was signed in Karachi on 19 September 1960 and government ratifications were exchanged in Delhi in January 1961.

The Indus Waters Treaty addressed both the technical and financial concerns of each side, and included a timeline for transition. The main points of the treaty included:

- an agreement that Pakistan would receive unrestricted use of the western rivers, which India would allow to flow unimpeded, with minor exceptions[4];
- provisions for 3 dams, 8 link canals, 3 barrages, and 2500 tube wells to be built in Pakistan;
- a 10-year transition period, from 1 April 1960 to 31 March 1970, during which water would continue to be supplied to Pakistan according to a detailed schedule;
- a schedule for India to provide its fixed financial contribution of £62 million, in 10 annual installments during the transition period;
- additional provisions for data exchange and future cooperation.

The treaty also established the Permanent Indus Commission, made up of one Commissioner of Indus Waters from each country. The two Commissioners would

---

[4]This sentence does not suggest that the rivers, and water therein, belong to India, given that some of the rivers flow through territory (Kashmir) still claimed by each country.

meet annually in order to:

- establish and promote cooperative arrangements for the treaty implementation;
- promote cooperation between the Parties in the development of the waters of the Indus system;
- examine and resolve by agreement any question that may arise between the Parties concerning interpretation or implementation of the Treaty;
- submit an annual report to the two governments.

In case of a dispute, provisions were made to appoint a "neutral expert." If the neutral expert fails to resolve the dispute, negotiators can be appointed by each side to meet with one or more mutually agreed-upon mediators. If either side (or the mediator) views mediated agreement as unlikely, provisions are included for the convening of a Court of Arbitration. In addition, the treaty calls for either party, if it undertakes any engineering works on any of the tributaries, to notify the other of its plans and to provide any data that may be requested.

Since 1960, no projects have been submitted under the provisions for "future cooperation," nor have any issues of water quality been submitted at all. Other disputes have arisen, and handled in a variety of ways. The first issues arose when India did not deliver a set allocation of water between 1965–1966, but became instead a question of procedure and the legality of commission decisions. Negotiators agreed that each commissioner acted as government representatives and that their decisions were legally binding. Another controversy surrounding the design and construction of the Salal Dam was resolved through bilateral negotiations between the two governments. Other disputes, over new hydroelectric projects and the Wuller Barrage on the Jhelum tributary, have yet to be resolved.

EPILOGUE: THE CHENAB DAM DISPUTE

India plans to implement the Baglihar Hydropower Project on the Chenab River in the Indian state of Jammu and Kashmir. The project has been in planning since 1992. Pakistan government regards this as an abrogation of the Indus Water Treaty and raised objections to the design, height, storage capacity, and gates of the spillway structure of the Baglihar power plant. Furthermore, Pakistan has argued that the construction of the dam will temporarily deplete the flow in the river during the sowing season in Punjab province in Pakistan. The monsoons may further worsen the conditions. India continues to claim that Pakistan's arguments do not hold weight because the treaty clearly states that power generation projects can be built on any of these three western rivers of the Indus River system as long as they benefit the local people and generally do not interrupt the flow of the river.

Soon after bilateral talks in January 2004 failed, Pakistan asked for the intervention of the World Bank (World Bank, 2005a). The World Bank announced (World Bank, 2005b) that it would appoint a "neutral expert", Mr. Lafitte, to arbitrate. The neutral expert was selected after being approved by the two riparians. A report has been released. (Another hydroelectric project which is being objected to by Pakistan is the Kishan Ganga project being constructed on the Jhelum river by India, and is seen as contravening the Indus Waters Treaty.)

Pakistan's concerns in this dispute, which are expressed in terms of design parameters, surround the following points: (a) Pakistan feels that India will be able to store excessive amounts of water behind the dam, more than the Treaty permits, leading to control over irrigation water flow on one hand and ability to flood downstream areas; and (b) Pakistan takes issue with the fact that construction began before it granted approval. Pointing to the capricious nature of flood analysis and the possibility that climate change may increase future floods, Mr. Lafitte determined that it is sensible to use $16,500\,\mathrm{m}^3$/second. A related point contested between the two riparians was whether the Baglihar dam needed a gated or ungated spillway. To minimize India's ability to regulate the river's flow, Pakistan insisted that since the Baglihar was a run-of-the-river plant it required an ungated spillway. Drawing attention to its need to regulate floods and manage heavy sedimentation that would otherwise decrease the plant's useful life, India argued that a gated spillway is essential. Lafitte argues for the need to incorporate the latest available technology and standards that were not present at the time the IWT was negotiated. Given the new knowledge, Lafitte agreed with India's need for gated spillway. This decision, however, produced another disagreement, where should the gated spillway be located. Pakistan insisted it was not at the highest level as specified by the IWT. Lafitte argued that "sound and economic design and satisfactory construction and operation" confirm the position selected by India. Consistent with Pakistan's concern about India's increasing ability to control the Chenab River, it disagreed with the Baglihar dam's 37.5 Million Cubic Meters (MCM) of "pondage", or live storage capacity, used to generate power, arguing that it should be 6.22 MCM instead. Lafitte determined that the structure's pondage should be decreased to 32.5 MCM and the dead storage should be increased by one meter of its original design.

The neutral expert also settled the two remaining issues, the freeboard's height and power intake levels, with slight modification to their design. The Baglihar originally had a freeboard 4.5 meters high, but after consulting the latest technology, Lafitte decided that India should lower the freeboard by 1.5 meters. Finally, Pakistan argued that the intake level for the turbines were not at the highest level as specified under the IWT. The neutral expert determined that the height should be increased by three meters (Zawahri, 2007, most facts are cited).

The World Bank's Role in the Treaty and its Implementation

The World Bank has played an important role in the negotiation and implementation of the Indus Waters Treaty. As Salman puts it, was the World Bank a third party that mediated or only provided good offices to the negotiating riparians (Salman, 2002)? It can be further posed whether by being a signatory to the treaty was the World Bank, in many ways, a partner to the agreement? And if so, what were its motives for such deep involvement?

As Salman (2005, p. 191) cites the President of the World Bank at that time, Mr. Eugene Black: "Not only did the Indus issue stand in the way of constructive action by the Bank in the subcontinent, it was cause for concern in a wider sense. With two of the Bank's potentially largest customers so bitterly opposed, the world's investors might regard the Bank's own prospects with a skepticism that would cripple its ability to raise money through borrowing."

Indeed, the World Bank increased its lending to the two countries following the Treaty. For example, between 1960 and 1970 the World Bank approved five water-related projects in the Indus Basin, totaling US\$ 220.7 million in current prices or US\$ 10.7 billion in 2004/5 prices (World Bank, 2005c, p. 94).

Therefore, the Bank's reputation due to its role in resolving the dispute, and subsequently making loans to both countries, has been an important factor in this case. In addition, the World Bank acted as a mediator-party to the treaty. By being a signatory to the treaty, the World Bank has signaled (documented it in a special clause in the treaty) that it will continue to help settle "differences" and "disputes." The Treaty classifies the issues on which there is disagreement into three parts: (i) question to be dealt with by the Commission, (ii) difference to be dealt with by the Neutral Expert, and (iii) dispute to be dealt with by the Court of Arbitration. There is a role for the Bank in the appointment of the Neutral Expert, and a limited role in the establishment of the Court of Arbitration. Accordingly, the World Bank appointed a neutral expert in 2005 in the dispute over the Baglihar Hydropower Project on the Chenab River in India. The neutral expert has published the results in February 2007, as was discussed earlier.

ANNEX

Table CS3A.1: Time table of major events associated with the Indus Waters Treaty.

Month/Year	Event
1939	Punjab–Sind Dispute (Rau Commission)
1947	Partitioning (Radcliffe/Arbitral commission)
12/1947	Standstill agreement
3/1948	Standstill agreement expires
4/1948	Dispute formally began
5/1948	New agreement (The Delhi Agreement)
1950	Pakistan denounces agreement
1950/51	Negotiation continues
7/1951	Lilienthal article published
9/1951	World Bank offer of good offices
9/1951	World Bank offer accepted
1952	Standstill agreement
1952	World Bank approach proposed
1953	World Bank approach abandoned
1953	Plan 1 proposed by parties
1953	Plan 2 proposed by parties
1954	World Bank new proposal
1954	India accepts, Pakistan questions proposal
1956	World Bank modifies proposal
1958	Pakistan accepts proposal
1959	Outline of agreement negotiated
1960	Agreement concluded
2005	Chenab dispute

Sources: Compiled from Salman (2002, 2005); Alam (1998, 2002); and Gulhati (1973).

Table CS3A.2: Offers and counteroffers in the negotiation process of the Indus Treaty.

Initial Positions of India and Pakistan

India	Pakistan
Claims rights over water flowing/originating within its territory (Sovereignty)	Claims historical rights of water used originally by Punjab and Sind

The majority of the rich water sources are in India; 10 out of the 13 canal systems are in Pakistan; 2 are in India; and 1 is divided between India and Pakistan

World Bank First Proposal (Rejected)

Suggested the adoption of Lilienthal's original proposal where the two states will jointly operate existing irrigation schemes and develop new ones

(*Continued*)

Table CS3A.2: (*Continued*)

First Countries Plan (Rejected)

India	Pakistan
90 MAF[a] to Pakistan; 29 MAF to India; total water allocated 119 MAF	102.5 MAF to Pakistan; 15.5 MAF to India; total water allocated 118 MAF

Second Countries Plan (Rejected)

India	Pakistan
To India: 7% of the water of the Western rivers and all the water of the Eastern rivers	*To India*: 30% of the water of the Eastern rivers, and no water from the Western rivers
To Pakistan: 93% of the water of the Western rivers, and no water from the Eastern rivers	*To Pakistan*: 70% of the water of the Eastern Rivers, and all the water of the Western rivers

World Bank Second Proposal (Accepted)

To India:	*To Pakistan*:
Eastern rivers	Western rivers
Sutlej 13.5 MAF	Indus 90.0 MAF
Beas 12.7 MAF	Jhelum 23.0 MAF
Ravi 6.4 MAF	Chenab 23.0 MAF
Total 32.6 MAF	Total 136.0 MAF

Eastern rivers to India and Western rivers to Pakistan. In addition, a system of institutions and financial agreements to secure and develop water resources, recognizing the need for additional storage of water during the dry season, and additional funding for terminating Pakistan's use of Eastern rivers.

[a]Notes: MAF = million acre-feet. 1 acre-foot = 1235 m^3.
Sources: Based on Biswas (1992); Alam (2002); and Salman (2005).

REFERENCES

Alam, U.Z. (1998). Water rationality: Mediating the Indus Waters Treaty. Unpublished thesis, University of Durham.

Alam, U.Z. (2002). Questioning the water wars rationale: A case study of the Indus Waters Treaty, *Geographical Journal*, 168.

Biswas, A.K. (1992). Indus Water Treaty: The negotiating process, *Water International*, 17, 201–209.

Briscoe, J. and R.P.S. Malik (2006). *India's Water Economy: Bracing for a Turbulent Future*. New Delhi: Oxford University Press.

Bureau of Reclamation (1963). United States Department of the Interior, Evaluation, of Engineering and Economic Feasibility, Beas and Rajasthan Projects, Northern India. Report Prepared by the United States Department of the Interior, Bureau of Reclamation, of AID (Agency for International Development), Department of State (Washington, DC, USA), pp. 152–153.

Gulhati, N.D. (1973). *Indus Waters Treaty: An Exercise in International Mediation*. New York: Allied Publishers.

Harza Engineering (1963). A programme for water and power development in west Pakistan, 1963–1975. Prepared for Water and Power Development Authority of Pakistan (West Pakistan), *Supporting Studies — An Appraisal of Resources and Potential Development* (Lahore: Harza Engineering Company International), pp. 1–7.

Kirmani, S. (1959). Sediment problems in the Indus Basin, part I: Sedimentation in reservoirs, Proceedings of the West Pakistan Engineering Congress, 43. Lahore, West Pakistan Engineering Congress, Paper No. 336.

Kirmani, S. and G. LeMoigne (1997). *Fostering Riparian Cooperation in International River Basins.* World Bank Technical Paper No. 335.

Kux, D. (2006). *India Pakistan Negotiations: Is Past Still Prologue?* Perspective Series. Washington, DC: United States Institute of Peace.

Mehta, J.S. (1988). The Indus Water Treaty: A case study in the resolution of an international river basin conflict, *Natural Resources Forum*, 12(1), 69–77.

Salman, M.A.S. and K. Uprety (2002). *Conflict and Cooperation on South Asia's International Rivers—A Legal Perspective. (Part II: India-Pakistan Relations).* Law, Justice and Development Series, Washington, DC: World Bank.

Salman, M.A.S. (2002). Good offices and mediation on international water disputes. In: The International Bureau of the Permanent Court of Arbitration (ed.), *Resolution of International Water Disputes.* New York: Kluwer Law International, pp. 155–198.

Salman, M.A.S. (2005). Presentation on the Indus Water Treaty. Personal communication and data sharing. Washington, DC.

World Bank (2005a). World Bank reviews Indus Treaty correspondence, January 28. http://web.worldbank.org/WBSITE/EXTERNAL/NEWS/0,contentMDK:20334487~menuPK:34466~pagePK:34370~piPK:34424~theSitePK:4607,00.html (Last visited on May 20, 2006).

World Bank (2005b). World Bank names neutral expert on Baglihar, May 10. http://web.worldbank.org/WBSITE/EXTERNAL/NEWS/0,contentMDK:20485918~menuPK:34466~pagePK:34370~piPK:34424~theSitePK:4607,00.html (Last visited on May 20, 2006).

World Bank (2005c). Pakistan water resources assistance strategy. Report No. 34081-PK, November 14, 2005, South Asia Region Agriculture and Rural Development Unit, Washington, DC: World Bank.

World Bank (2007). The Nature of Law, April 2007 Edition. http://newsletters.worldbank.org/external/default/main?menuPK2363052&thesitePK=2363040&pagePK=64133601&contentMDK=21285727&piPK=64129599. (Last visited on April 27, 2007).

Zawahri, N.A. (2007). India, Pakistan, and Cooperation along the Indus River System, *Water Policy* (Accepted for Publication).

ADDITIONAL READING

Beach, H.L., J. Hamner, J. Hewitt, E. Kaufman, A. Kurki, J. Oppenheimer and A. Wolf (2000). *Transboundary Freshwater Dispute Resolution: Theory, Practice and Annotated References.* Tokyo and New York: United Nations University Press.

Biswas, A.K. (1996). Water for sustainable development of south and southeast Asia in the twenty-first century. In: Biswas, A.K. and T. Hashimoto (eds.), *Asian International Waters: From Ganges-Brahmaputra to Mekong.* Bombay and New York: Oxford University Press.

Blinkenberg, L. (1998). *India-Pakistan: The History of Unsolved Conflicts.* Denmark: Odense University Press.

Corell, E. and A. Swain (1991). India: The domestic and international politics of water scarcity. In: Ohlsson, L. (ed.), *Hydropolitics, Conflicts over Water as a Development Constraint.* London: ZED Books.

Michel, A.A. (1967). *The Indus Rivers, A Study of the Effects of Partition.* New Haven and London: Yale University Press.

Rao, K.L. (1979). *India's Water Wealth: Its Assessment, Uses and Projections.* New Delhi: Orient Longman.

CASE STUDY 4: THE ARAL SEA BASIN*

The year 1992 marks two distinct but likewise related events in the history of transboundary water. For one, the collapse of the Soviet Union introduced a new era in international relations accompanied by several opportunities for cooperation over transboundary water. At the same time, one of the biggest environmental and natural resources catastrophes — the degradation of the Aral Sea and the associated environmental problems — became an international concern after years of being managed domestically. The five newly independent states (republics) of Kazakhstan, Kyrgyz Republic (Kyrgyzstan), Tajikistan, Turkmenistan, and Uzbekistan were left to address the shrinking sea. Given that the grave deterioration of the Aral Sea is relatively a recent issue, it has yet to be dealt with in a serious manner. While numerous statements have been issued by the riparian countries, the river basin lacks a robust and comprehensive treaty. This case study will focus, therefore, on the factors and processes militating against full cooperation in the basin.

FEATURES OF THE BASIN

The Aral Sea extends over 690,000 km^2 (Kirmani and LeMoigne, 1997). The Basin is formed by two of the largest rivers of Central Asia — The Amu Darya and the Syr Darya. The source of the Amu Darya is largely in Tajikistan, with a few water-courses originating in northeastern Afghanistan. The Syr Darya originates mainly in Kyrgyzstan. The Aral Sea Basin has three distinct ecological zones: the mountains, the deserts, and the Aral Sea with its deltas. The Tian Shan and Pamir mountains in the south and southwest are characterized by high altitudes with peaks over 7,000 m and by an average annual high precipitation ranging from 800 to 1,600 mm/year. The mountains host large forest reserves and some national parks. In the foothills and valleys, soil and temperature conditions are favorable for agriculture. The low-land deserts of Karakum and Kyzylkum cover most of the basin area, and are characterized by low precipitation (under 100 mm/year) and high evaporation rates (Kirmani and LeMoigne, 1997, p. 10).

The Basin coincides with almost the entire area of Kyrgyz Republic, Tajikistan, Turkmenistan, and Uzbekistan. It covers also the southern part of Kazakhstan, and the northern part of Afghanistan and Iran (Dukhovny et al., 2006). The total mean

*This case study benefited from research by Tim Eestermans, Lola Gulomova, Benjamin Hengst, Pothik Chatterjee, Haik Gugarats, Elcin Caner, Max Du Jardin, Abigail Goss, Hamir K. Sahnai, Edward Anderson, Brigid Harris, Andrea Semaan Bissar, Marco Sampablo Lauro, Nicholas M. A. Smith, and Jeff Brez. It benefited greatly from comments by Masood Ahmad. The case study is not aimed at covering all aspects and details.

Map CS4.1: The Aral Sea Basin.

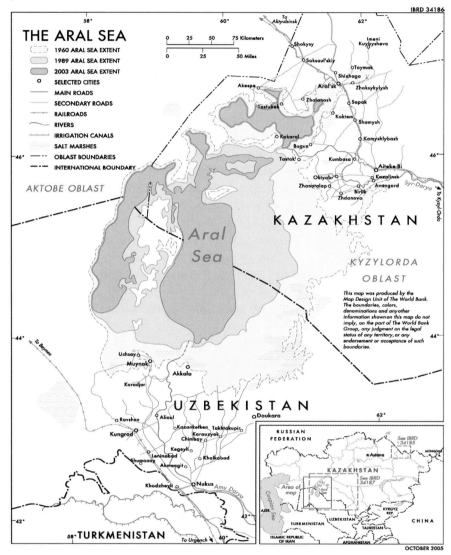

Source: World Bank (Permission granted to reproduce the map.)

annual flow of the two rivers is estimated at about 116 BCM (Central Asia Water
Information, 2006). Groundwater resources utilized in the basin amount to 35 BCM
(Water Resources Institute, 2003). While Afghanistan and Iran contribute 9% of the
basin's resources (Table CS4.1), they are not part of the Aral Sea Basin dispute.

The Aral Sea, which has no outlet, was the fourth largest inland (brackish) lake
in the world prior to 1960. It is shared by Uzbekistan and Kazakhstan. As indicated,
the Amu Darya and Syr Darya originate respectively in the Kyrgyz Republic and
Tajikistan, yet cross Turkmenistan, Kazakhstan, and Uzbekistan, before discharging
into the Aral Sea. In the 1950s the Aral Sea had a water volume exceeding $1,090 \, km^3$
$(1 \, km^3 = 1 \, billion \, m^3 = BCM)$, and a surface area of more than $67,900 \, km^2$. The

Table CS4.1: Aral Sea-mean annual runoff surface water contributions (BCM/year).

Country	Contribution to river		Total water contributions		Total water use (BCM)	Total water use for irrigation in 1994, BCM (% of total)[b]
	Syr Darya (BCM)	Amu Darya (BCM)	BCM	% of total		
Kazakhstan	2.516 [38.1][a]	0 [0.0]	2.516	2.2	11.0	9.7 (88)
Kyrgyzstan	27.542 [5.0]	1.654 [2.0]	29.196	25.2	5.1	4.6 (90)
Tajikistan	1.005 [6.2]	58.732 [12.0]	59.737	51.5	12.0	10.3 (86)
Turkmenistan	0 [0.0]	1.405 [43.0]	1.405	1.2	23.1	22.4 (97)
Uzbekistan	5.562 [51.7]	6.791 [43.0]	12.353	10.6	58.0	53.0 (91)
Afghanistan and Iran	0	10.814	10.814	9.3	0	0
Flows to the Aral Sea					7.9	
Total Aral Sea basin	36.625	79.396	116.021	100	116	100.0 (86)

Source: Central Asia Water Information (2006).
[a]Allocation during the Soviet regime Polat (2002).
[b]World Bank (1998).

water level in the Aral Sea ranged seasonally between 50 and 53 m above sea level (Glantz, 1999; Central Asia Water Information, 2006).

The region is largely arid and semi-arid and sparsely populated. It has a rich history of water resources development. For example, by 1900, 7–8 million people lived in Central Asia with about 3.5 million hectares of irrigated land and networks of channels forming the basis of the society's economy. At present the population of the region has increased seven times, exceeding 50 million people. Irrigated lands have reached 7.5–7.9 million hectares (IFAS-UNEP, 2001).

In its more glorious past, the Aral Sea played an important economic role as a north–south shipping route and as the source of an annual fishing catch of 45,000–50,000 tons of fish. The reed growth along the Sea's shores provided the raw material for cellulose and carton production. Sustained pastures and more than 250,000 hectares of tugay forests in the Amu delta, where migrant birds nested and rare animals lived, were a natural barrier against soil erosion.

The Aral Sea had an extremely complex ecological system. It had a dominant moderating effect on the local climate. The mass evaporation from the lake created a screen that kept the micro climate behind it moderate and stable. It protected Central Asia from the cold north winds. Upon meeting the immense column of evaporation, the cold air was lifted to great heights, traveled to far distances in the south and came down to replenish snow deposits and glaciers in the mountains of the Kyrgyz Republic and Tajikistan. Melting snows in these locations were the source for the Syr Darya and Amu Darya flowing back to the lake.

Basin development of irrigated agriculture during the 1950s did not reduce the rivers' runoff into the lake, because the areas developed were primarily in valleys and river deltas, areas with abundant water. Sufficient drainage provided appropriate conditions for irrigated agriculture with water consumption of the respective crops constituting less than the evapotranspiration of the preceding plants which grew in the area. Consequently, the water balance in the Aral Sea Basin was not affected (Dinar *et al.*, 1995).

The Problems

In the 1960s, the Soviet government initiated regional irrigation development projects aimed at improving economic conditions in the region and addressing food and fiber (cotton) security, which were a major priority for Moscow. A system of canals and pumps was constructed to withdraw water from the Amu Darya and Syr Darya before their discharge into the Aral Sea, and to convey the water to remote desert areas of Kazakhstan, Turkmenistan and Uzbekistan (the Karakum Canal, described in government publications as the "Eighth Wonder of the World" — Turkmenistan Ministry of Irrigation and Water Economy, 1995). The Karakum Canal is the largest canal in Central Asia. It diverts $500 \text{ m}^3/\text{s}$ from the middle of the Amu Darya to Turkmenistan. About 33% of the water used for irrigation in Turkmenistan percolates through the sandy soils of the canal. Furthermore, seepage losses are so significant that they have created an 800 km^2 lake alongside the Karakum Canal.

The long-term impact of these water diversions has been devastating to the Aral Sea, as can be seen from Table CS4.2. While the shrinking of the lake and the deterioration of its water quality were apparent prior to 1991, the associated environmental consequences became international, and gained serious attention, only after the collapse of the Soviet Union. The environmental damages caused by the diminishing lake have had direct and indirect health and economic consequences, such as loss of employment opportunities and elevated cancer occurrences.

Water management under the Soviets was centralized and coordinated by the Ministry of Water Management, which oversaw construction projects necessary for regional hydropower and agricultural needs (Langford and Vinogradov, 2001, p. 350), operation of the infrastructure and allocation of water quotas for different uses in the five Soviet republics. Of the total 116 BCM/year diverted from the Amu Darya and Syr Darya at the end of the Soviet legacy, nearly 90% was used for irrigation (Dukhovny *et al.*, 2006; Table CS4.1). The water was used mainly for growing cotton, wheat, and rice, using very inefficient irrigation technologies. Irrigation's share in riparian water use is estimated at 81, 94, 92, 98, and 94%, respectively for Kazakhstan, Kyrgyzstan, Tajikistan, Turkmenistan, and Uzbekistan, in 1990 (World Resource Institute, 2003; see also Table CS4.1).

Once the Soviet Union was dissolved, the downstream riparians, still utilizing generous water allocations, immediately became dependent on their upstream neighbors for water, dramatically increasing both the possibility for conflict in the region as well as the need for cooperation. Today the downstream nations, whose economies depend heavily on irrigated agriculture for hard currency income, view water management not only as an economic issue, but also as integral to their national security (ICG, 2006, p. 2).

With the subsequent independence of the five Central Asian republics, financial help from Moscow was likewise dashed. In the absence of major aid for solving the

Table CS4.2: Aral Sea — forty years of mining the Aral Sea and their consequences.

Year	Annual inflow into the Aral Sea (BCM)[b]	Water level (m)	Salinity (g/l)
1960	56.0	53.3	10
1970	38.5	51.6	11
1976[a]	10.3	48.3	14
1980	8.3	46.2	16
1985	0	44.0	20
1989	5.4	39.0	28
1994[a]	30.6	36.8	> 35
2000[a]	3.5	33.4	> 60

Source: IFAS-UNEP (2001); for 1989–2000: Sanigmii (2000).

[a] *Source for 1976, 1994, and 2000*: Glantz (1999). Values in 1994 and 2000 are for the Large Sea. The small, Northern Sea, has higher water levels and lower salinization levels.

[b] *Source*: Weinthal (2002); for 1989–2000: Sanigmii (2000).

Note: Flow measurements are made in the last weir station, about 150 km from the Aral Sea. Thus, the flow amounts do not necessarily mean that the quantity entered the Aral Sea, although it is a very good approximation. The year 1994 was an exceptionally wet year, where precipitation was sufficient to eliminate pumping of water from the rivers.

environmental consequences of the Sea's deterioration, the five republics needed to manage the problem in unison. Interestingly, their point of departure was the same water allocations which was in place during the Soviet era. The following sections will focus on the regional dispute that ensued and the various agreements negotiated among the basin states.

HISTORY OF WATER AND OTHER DISPUTES IN THE BASIN

Increasing demand for water in each of the post-independence republics, inadequate monitoring and measurement provisions, and lack of enforcement made the original allocations unsustainable. Tension over water allocations increased with the lack of a central coordinating authority. While outright resource wars have been avoided, the five nations have been at odds with each other (Table CS4.3) adopting a "zero-sum" attitude — each country acts to maximize its water allocation without reference to regional needs or planning. In addition, most of the states in the region have announced plans to build their own dams and reservoirs to increase internal water capacity. Verbal threats have been enunciated (Table CS4.3; see also Time Table Annex).

Two main reservoirs provide water for irrigated crops in the three downstream states, Kazakhstan, Turkmenistan, and Uzbekistan — the Karakum in

Bridges Over Water

Table CS4.3: Water-related and other disputes among the Aral Sea Basin riparian states.

	Kazakhstan	Tajikistan	Uzbekistan
Kazakhstan			In 1997 Kazakhstan repeatedly blames Uzbekistan for cutting the water flow by 70%. Border disputes. Uzbekistan attempts to shift the border twice during this year. Disagreements over the terms of an energy swap agreement. Uzbekistan introduces visa regime for citizens of other member countries in the Commonwealth of Independent States (CIS), which makes trade between the countries difficult due to border shifts.
Kyrgyzstan	Kazakhstan fails to deliver energy under an energy swap agreement. Kyrgyzstan closes Toktogul reservoir.		Kyrgyzstan cuts water flow from its reservoir when Uzbekistan does not agree to pay for water. In 1999 Uzbekistan deploys 130,000 troops on the Kyrgyz border to guard the reservoirs rid the area of 4000–10,000 Islamic Movement of Uzbekistan (IMU) and Taliban fighters who had infiltrated the area. Ownership dispute over the reservoir on the border of Kyrgyzstan and Uzbekistan. Border disputes. Dispute over energy swap agreement. Uzbekistan places mines along the border with Kyrgyzstan to prevent the illegal movement of IMU fighters from the territory of Kyrgyzstan. Uzbekistan introduces visa regime for citizens of other member countries in the CIS, which makes trade between the countries difficult due to border shifts.

(*Continued*)

Table CS4.3 (*Continued*)

	Kazakhstan	Tajikistan	Uzbekistan
Tajikistan	At the request of Kazakhstan, Tajikistan releases water every time Kazakhstan faced difficulties with irrigation of fields even though it suffered great losses.		Ethnic tensions rise in the north of Tajikistan where Uzbeks reside. Political tensions escalate due to civil war in Tajikistan. Uzbekistan imposes trade restrictions and repeatedly closes the border, blaming Tajikistan for aiding the IMU. Uzbekistan places mines along the border with Tajikistan to prevent the illegal movement of IMU fighters from the territory of Tajikistan. Uzbekistan introduces visa regime for citizens of other member countries in the CIS, which makes trade between the countries difficult due to border shifts.
Uzbekistan		Uzbekistan asks Tajikistan to release water downstream in exchange for electricity and gas in winter. Disputes erupt between Tajikistan and Uzbekistan due to Uzbekistan's failure to comply with agreed terms.	

northern Tajikistan and Toktogul on the Kyrgyz border with Uzbekistan. Unlike their downstream neighbors Kyrgyzstan and Tajikistan have no natural gas and oil reserves and consider the water originating on their territory to be their resource.[1]

---

[1]The Kyrgyz President signed an edict in October 1997 codifying the right of Kyrgyzstan to profit from water resources within its territories. Kyrgyzstan demonstrated a clear intent to follow through on its plans. It has also demanded compensation for lost revenues — rather than generating hydropower Kyrgyzstan releases water downstream to Uzbek farmers (Heltzer, 2003).

In 1998, Kazakhstan and Uzbekistan signed barter agreements (United Nations, 2006) with Kyrgyzstan, exchanging coal and electricity for water. The swap agreements do not specify the volume of water to be released in exchange for a given tonnage of coal nor do they indicate how water stored during wet years should be released in dry years. When the states fail to meet the targets, each country's experts disagree as to the volume of water to be received downstream. These disputes occur about the volume of energy swaps and not about the time of water release or other issues. As a result of these disputes, the agricultural sectors of Kazakhstan and Uzbekistan suffered dramatically due to the shortage of irrigation water. This in turn results in decrease of the water flow of the Syr Darya into the Aral Sea.

Regional Politics and Power

The disputes summarized above show how complicated the relationships between the Basin states are. The few indicators in Table CS4.4 suggest that there is an imbalance of regional power that could explain some of the behavior of the basin states.

It is extremely difficult to predict which state will play the regional leadership role. Kazakhstan, Kyrgyzstan, and Tajikistan have demonstrated their will to deal with regional issues, such as the problem of the Aral Sea, on a multilateral basis. However, Kyrgyzstan, with relatively little power to boast, acts primarily in its own interest. Tajikistan, another relatively weak riparian, strives to keep friendly relationships with all the basin states. It is an isolated country. Its infrastructure is completely linked with Uzbekistan and Kyrgyzstan and any disagreements with these states tend to exacerbate the economic situation in Tajikistan. Therefore, Tajikistan often responds favorably to requests of additional water from other states. Surprisingly, it is Tajikistan that is in desperate need of additional water resources.

Turkmenistan refuses to deal with regional issues due to its isolationist policy. Given its neutrality, and despite its water shortage and needs, Turkmenistan relies primarily on bilateral deals with the basin states and does not play an integral part in the overall water dispute (Table CS4.5). This policy may change with the

Table CS4.4: Demographic and economic indicators of the Basin states, 1990 (92), 1995, 2000.

Indicators	Kazakhstan	Kyrgyzstan	Tajikistan	Turkmenistan	Uzbekistan
Population[a]	16.7	4.4	5.3	3.7	20.5
(million)	16.7	4.6	6.0	4.6	23.1
	16.1	4.9	6.1	4.7	24.9
GDP per capita	1690	520	740	2088	517
(1995 US$)[a]	1263	331	407	940	446
	1515	399	386	1377	485

Source: World Bank (2003).
[a]Population and GDP values in each cell are respectively for 1990–1992, 1995, and 2000. GDP values are constant 1995 US$.

Table CS4.5: Regional power relations and behavioral pattern.

State	Political power within the region and behavioral pattern
Kazakhstan	Strong, often acts as mediator in basin disputes
Kyrgyzstan	Medium, but acts in its own benefit. Plagued by ethnic and political unrest since 1990
Tajikistan	Weak, adopts a friendship framework. Fell into civil war immediately upon gaining independence (among liberals, pro-Communists and Islamists)
Turkmenistan	Adopts an isolationist policy on regional issues
Uzbekistan	Strong, considers itself a regional leader yet often acts unilaterally on different regional matters

passing away of Turkmenistan's life-long ruler, Saparmurat Niyazov, or as he used to be called — Turkmenbashi (father of the Turkmens).

ATTEMPTS AT CONFLICT MANAGEMENT — THE NEGOTIATION PROCESS AND REGIONAL AGREEMENTS

Since some of the states' land and population shares in the basin range between 50% and 99% (Heltzer, 2003), it is clear why the riparians are eager to covet as much of the Basin's resources as possible. The desire of the upstream states to utilize river flows for hydropower during winter has been incompatible with the desire of the downstream states to store upstream water for irrigation during the dry season. During the Soviet era, the timing for releasing the water downstream was dictated and enforced by Moscow. After independence, however, the need for negotiations became much more critical. In fact, between 1991 and 1994, more than 300 informal agreements concerning the Aral Sea Basin were concluded as compared with only three formal agreements signed prior to the collapse of the Soviet Regime (Peachey, 2004).

Basin-Level Agreements and Plans

In 1986, the Soviet Union created the Syr Darya and Amu Darya Basin Management Organizations (BVO) mainly for internal coordination purposes. They were not forums for negotiation but rather management authorities to oversee plans approved by the Soviet Ministry of Water Management (Dukhovny *et al.*, 2006). Three international agreements were likewise concluded between the Soviet Union and Afghanistan.

The first Agreement — *The Frontier Agreement between Afghanistan and the USSR* — was signed in 1946. It established a joint commission aimed to discuss water issues related to the Amu Darya, which forms a border between the two countries. It also codified a water allocation regime, allotting 9 BCM of the Pyandj River to Afghanistan and the remainder to the USSR (Ahmad and Wasiq, 2004; Votrin, 2006).

The second Agreement between the two states — *Treaty Concerning the Regime to the Soviet-Afghan Frontier* — was signed in January 1958. It established water-related environmental and ecological standards. The two states agreed to refrain from actions that alter the course of frontier waters, and to restore the waterways if they do begin to diverge from their previous route. They also agreed to prevent water pollution and to exchange data and information regarding water levels and volume. In addition, they also agreed to establish a flood warning system.

In June 1958, the two countries concluded their third, and final water Agreement — *The Protocol between the USSR and Afghanistan Concerning the Joint Execution of Works for the Integrated Utilization of the Water Resources in the Frontier Section of the Amu Darya*. The treaty promoted the shared utilization of the waters of the Amu Darya between the two countries (Ahmad and Wasiq, 2004; Votrin, 2006).

The need for a dispute resolution framework became apparent when the Soviet Union was dissolved in December 1991. The path to such a framework has been anything but direct, however, and has required numerous agreements and institutional changes to arrive at the present structure (de Chazournes, 2006). The following section will trace the process leading to this structure and the agreements reached.[2]

The Almaty Agreement (1992) and the Interstate Commission for Water Cooperation

The creation of five new states necessitated the formation of a regional institution for dispute resolution. In February 1992, a mere three months after the official dissolution of the USSR, the Ministers of Water Resources for the five states signed the *Agreement on Cooperation in the Management, Utilization and Protection of Water Resources in Interstate Sources* in Almaty. This agreement established a framework to resolve water disputes, but also set water allocation levels at Soviet era quantities until the states could reach a solution amenable to all parties. This essentially favored downstream (agriculture intensive) states, and provided no allocation for Afghanistan (O'Hara, 2004).

Another result of the Almaty Agreement was the creation of the Interstate Commission for Water Cooperation (ICWC), comprised of the basin's Ministers of Water Resources. ICWC's objective has been to develop a single water policy that meets the interests of each state while sustaining the basin resources. ICWC is also responsible for managing and monitoring water allocations and serves as the

---

[2]Provisions to include Afghanistan in this framework once that country formulates a stable government and is better able to predict and insist its water needs, will have to be made.

reporting authority for the re-established Amu Darya and Syr Darya Basin Management Organizations (BVOs). The BVOs make recommendations to the ICWC for short-term and long-term water development for their respective basin, taking into account allocation, water quality, conservation, and environmental protection issues (Vinogradov, 2001).

The Agreement on Joint Activities in the Aral Sea (1993)

This new agreement, which was signed between all five heads of state on 26 March 1993, addresses the environmental, social, and economic issues of the Aral Sea Basin. While the treaty was non-binding and provided no dispute resolution mechanisms, it established regional institutions for water management in the basin. These organizations are discussed in detail in the next section. As stated by Article III of the agreement, Russia participated as an observer in addressing the Aral Sea crisis, and provided financial and technical assistance (IWL, 2006; Roll *et al.*, 2006).

The ICAS, the IFAS, and the SDC (1993–1995)

Additional organizations were created between 1993 and 1995 to support the management of the Aral Sea Basin. These included the *Interstate Council on the Aral Sea Basin* (ICAS) that was formed to develop policies and proposals for the management of the Aral Sea Basin (Peachey, 2004); the *International Fund for the Aral Sea* (IFAS), designed to manage contributions and to finance program activities (Mukhammadiev, 2001); the *Sustainable Development Commission* (SDC) formed to ensure that socio-economic issues were considered by ICAS when determining new policy, and the *Executive Committee of the ICAS* (EC-ICAS), which was given the responsibility of implementing programs set forth by the *Aral Sea Basin Program* (ASBP).

The (ASBP) International Involvement (1994)

The ASBP, initiated in 1994, is a consortium of international organizations such as UNDP, UNEP, the World Bank, and the EU. It is aimed at identifying long-term solutions for the basin's wide-ranging problems (environment, water management, rehabilitation of the disaster zone around the lake). It is also charged with improving the capacity of the riparian states to implement these programs (World Bank, 1998).

A review of the Aral Sea management framework structure, following the initiation of the ASBP, found that there was a lack of clarity in the roles and functions between the newly formed ICAS and the ICWC, as well as between the ICAS and the EC-ICAS (Vinogradov, 2001). In response, the five riparian states agreed in 1997 to restructure the institutional framework, leading to a new IFAS that combines the ICAS and the previous IFAS. The EC-ICAS was transformed into the EC-IFAS which, along with the SDC and the ICWC, were to report directly to the new IFAS board members. The revised institutional framework of the Aral Sea

Basin along with the ASBP are considered a major factor in improved cooperation in the basin (see also section on the North Sea restoration).

Main Declarations, Bilateral and Multilateral Agreements, and Unilateral Legal Initiatives (1995–2003)

Below we provide a very short review of major negotiated outcomes and unilateral initiatives. The details can be found in (IFAS, 2006) and (Roll *et al.*, 2006). They are also summarized in the Annex.

Between 1995 and 2003, four declarations were made by the riparian states pertaining to the improvement of the basin (IFAS, 2006). Following the formation of the ASBP, the Nukus Declaration (September 1995) discusses the sustainable development of the Aral Sea Basin and affirms the financial obligations of the states to the ICAS, IFAS, and the SDC. The Almaty Declaration (1997) proclaims 1998 as the *Year of Protection of the Environment* in the region. The declaration recognizes that an eco-system approach should be used in the region's water resource management. The Ashgabat Declaration (1999) emphasized the support for joint actions to address common environmental problems in the basin (Roll *et al.*, 2006) and announced the implementation of the *Water Resources and Environment Control Project* (improved use of water and other natural resources). The 2002 Dushanbe Declaration establishes major directions for solving the problems related to the Aral Sea, and for improving monitoring and information exchange on water and other natural resources.

Bilateral and Multilateral Water Agreements

As alluded to earlier, a complex water storage system had been built during the Soviet era on the Amu Darya and Syr Darya to store water in winter for use in the subsequent summer for irrigation and electricity generation. Since independence one of the lingering problems continues to be the operation and maintenance of infrastructure and hydraulic facilities. The issue was partly addressed by the Framework Agreement. The Agreement stated that the infrastructure would be owned by the state where it was located, though the liability for the management activities would be shared among them (de Chazournes, 2006).

To cope with the remaining problems, states reverted to short-term bilateral and trilateral agreements. Most of these agreements pertained to the Syr Darya as it suffers from greater water scarcity and requires additional attention. Furthermore, the upstream riparian on the Amu Darya, Tajikistan, had been engaged in a civil war in the mid-1990s, which hindered its ability to negotiate.

In truth, these informal arrangements have not been successful over time. The main issue of dispute has been the lack of long-term compensation mechanisms from the downstream states to the upper riparians. This has resulted in a more formalized and predictable framework, to avoid such disputes from arising, instead of the series of *ad hoc* agreements to establish energy and water trade-offs. An illustration of the result of such arrangements can be seen at the Toktogul hydropower station and reservoir, on the Syr Darya in Kyrgyzstan, which controls the release of water to the downstream riparian states.

The Syr Darya Framework Agreement. This agreement, also referred to as the Bishkek Agreement, was signed by the Prime Ministers of Kyrgyzstan, Uzbekistan, and Kazakhastan in 1998 (de Chazournes, 2006). Tajikistan became a signatory to the agreement only later, in 1999, as its civil war was coming to an end. The agreement demonstrated support for cooperative management of the basin's resources and was an attempt to resolve the issue of exchanging fuel for water, a point of contention among the upper and lower riparians.

The agreement specified that Kyrgyzstan should be compensated by the downstream riparians (Uzbekistan and Kazakhastan) for the costs of maintaining the infrastructure related to water storage, and subsequently the potential hydropower production it foregoes in the winter (McKinney, 2004). The agreement is based on the proposed management and maintenance of the five reservoirs: Toktogul, Kairakum, Charvak, Chardarya, and Andijan, in the Syr Darya Basin. The treaty also pertained to the timing of water storage releases from the Toktogul reservoir and the related compensation schemes among the riparians. In addition, the agreement takes into account the issue of the value of the water released.

Article IV of the agreement declares that energy losses, as a result of reduced water releases during the nonvegetative period (winter months), shall be compensated with coal, gas, and electricity, or their monetary equivalent. A tariff will be included in these exchanges based on costs of operation, maintenance, and reconstruction of hydrotechnical facilities.

The treaty also declares that the four nations will seek agreement on construction of new hydropower facilities, and promote the use of monetary exchange as a replacement for current energy exchanges. The riparians likewise agreed to reduce the amount of pollutants released into the river, and to develop water saving technologies.

Box CS4.1: The Syr Darya Water-Energy Swap Agreement in numbers.

Kyrgyzstan receives 1.1 million of kWh of power in electricity or coal, valued at \$22 million, and 400 million kWh of power plus 500 million m^3 of gas, valued at \$48.5 million, from Kazakhstan and Uzbekistan, respectively. In return Kyrgyzstan delivers 3.25 BCM of water from the Toktogul Reservoir in monthly flows and 1.1 billion kWh of summer hydroelectric power to both Kazakhstan and Uzbekistan.

Source: United Nations Treaty Collection (2006).

Overall, the 1998 Barter Agreement seems reasonable. Since Kazakhstan and Uzbekistan benefit from timely water releases from Kyrgyz dams, it is only fair that they pay for part of the maintenance and operation of the dams. However, the fact that Uzbekistan pays more than Kazakhstan for the same amount of water and power could be challenged. Furthermore, is it fair that Uzbekistan and Kazakhstan pay for the maintenance and operation of the dam and for the water released?

The Amu Darya River Basin Agreements. Barter agreements, codifying energy for water swaps, are also instituted among the Amu Darya riparian states. Tajikistan exports 3.4 billion kWh ($170 million) of hydroelectric power to Uzbekistan from the Amu Darya dams. In exchange, Tajikistan imports 3 billion kWh ($130 million) of electricity per year from Uzbekistan in the form of natural gas. Furthermore, while the Amu Darya does not flow within the borders of Kyrgyzstan, the ICWC allocates 0.15 BCM/year of Amu Darya water to Kyrgyzstan for additional energy production. By allocating Amu Darya water to Kyrgyzstan, the ICWC is able to alleviate some of the demands on the Syr Darya (Heltzer, 2003).

Kyrgyzstan's New Law and Its Impact

In 2001, the Kyrgyz Parliament passed a new law that allows Kyrgyzstan to demand monetary compensation from the downstream riparians for water storage and infrastructure maintenance undertaken by Kyrgyzstan. This law is considered by Kyrgyzstan a clarification of the 1998 Framework Agreement (Heltzer, 2003). Furthermore, the law reflects Kyrgyzstan's belief that while the downstream states are entitled to a percentage of the water, the amount they have historically used has been excessive. Specifically, the law introduces payments for storage infrastructure related services (to account for operation and maintenance of the storage and conveyance facilities) and for quantities of water released beyond what the downstream states actually need for irrigation (according to Kyrgyzstan's opinion). The law also accounts for the hydropower benefits Kyrgyzstan foregoes due to the storage of water in favor of downstream states.

Kyrgyzstan's law has expectedly impacted other riparians in the region. For example, Tajikistan, the second upstream riparian, has been contemplating a similar law. In November 2002, Tajikistan and Uzbekistan negotiated and adopted a Power-Trade Relations Agreement (de Chazournes, 2006). It established a framework for bilateral power-trade relations, and also instituted policy conditions for an integrated water and energy system. Other riparian states in the basin are expected to join this framework.

It is quite clear that Kyrgyzstan's law intends to bring the lower riparians back to the bargaining table, renegotiating the terms of the region's water allocation regime. Uzbekistan, which is a significant user of water, may realize that it is cheaper to reach an agreement on water allocation levels so that it only has to pay for the excess water it uses. This may aid the region in determining equitable and efficient water allocations.

International Agreements Involving the Basin States

The basin states are involved in various other international agreements that can contribute directly, or indirectly, to cooperation on the Aral Sea.

Central Asian Economic Community (CAEC)

Central Asia Cooperation Organization was established in 1994 by Kazakhstan, Uzbekistan, and Kyrgystan. Tajikistan joined in 1998 and Russia in 2004.

Commonwealth of Independent States (CIS) Collective Security Treaty

Established on 15 May 1992 with Armenia, Kazakhstan, Kyrgyzstan, Russia, Tajikistan, and Uzbekistan as signatories. Azerbaijan, Georgia, and Belarus joined in 1993. The regime entered into force on 20 April 1994. The treaty reaffirmed the desire of all participating states to abstain from the use or threat of force. Signatories are not allowed to join other military alliances. Similarly, aggression against one signatory would be perceived as an aggression against all.

Shanghai Cooperation Organization (SCO)

Began in 1996 with a treaty on *Deepening Military Trust in Border Regions* and signed, in Shanghai, by Kazakhstan, China, Kyrgyzstan, Russia, and Tajikistan. In 1997 the same countries signed the Treaty on *Reduction of Military Forces in Border Regions* in a meeting in Moscow. On 14 June 2001, the above treaties evolved into an intergovernmental organization which included Kazakhstan, Kyrgyzstan, Russia, China, Tajikistan, and Uzbekistan.

Observation on Conflict and Cooperation in the Aral Sea Basin

The agreements and declarations enumerated above have established an approach for limiting water consumption in the Amu Darya and Syr Darya basins, and on a common strategy for transboundary water resources management. The treaties have likewise set the basis for potential cooperation. Unfortunately, this collective corpus of agreements has only marginally ameliorated tension in the area.

The emergence of cooperation in the Aral Sea basin so soon after independence was especially striking, since most other attempts at rapid regional institutionalization and cross-border exchange have been useless. As explained by Weinthal (2002), the rapid cooperation in the region, in the form of new institutions, may be just as much about 'state making' as it is promoting regional cooperation.

On the other hand, the large number of regional agreements pertaining to the Aral Sea may be scrutinized, since they are devoid of meaningful content. Similarly, the riparian states have likewise shown little willingness to establish and participate in multilateral, multi-issue frameworks, which is required to prevent conflict and safeguard natural resources. Thus far, basin states have preferred bilateral, case-by-case solutions. Specifically, the lower riparians (economically and militarily more powerful than the upper riparians) have chosen to adopt these bilateral case-by-case solutions to mitigate the recurrent disputes over water. Such a strategy may have reduced the impact of regional cooperation initiatives that take advantage of economies of scale and respond appropriately the extrenalities present in the basin. On the other hand, case-by-case panaceas have also prevented interstate crises from escalating into open violent conflict (Just and Netanyahu, 1998).

Finally, the active and generous role of the international community in the form of international organizations and NGOs impel institution building at both the regional and domestic levels that induce cooperation and reinforce capacity.

EPILOGUE: RECENT DEVELOPMENTS

Two recent developments may affect the status and direction of regional affairs. First, the successful revival of the Northern Sea, and the second, the death of Turkmenistan's life-long ruler, Saparmurat Niyazov — Turkmenbashi.

The Northern Aral Sea Resurrection

The Southern Aral Sea continues to shrink as outflows from the sea surpass inflows. The level of the Northern Aral Sea, however, has been rising due to recent rehabilitation efforts (World Bank, 2001). During the period from 1991 to 1997 the Southern Aral Sea received an average of 13.2 BCM of water inflows from the Northern Aral Sea and the Amu Darya River, and 3.6 BCM from precipitation. It lost an average of 29.6 BCM due to evaporation. The Northern Sea is in a much better state. The average inflow from the Syr Darya River to the Northern Aral Sea was 5.8 BCM and the average inflow from precipitation was 0.4 BCM. Outflow from the Northern Sea averaged 3.4 BCM while losses due to evaporation were constant at 2.8 BCM (World Bank, 2001).

It is currently widely recognized that the goal of restoring the entire Aral Sea to previous levels is not achievable in the foreseeable future. It is estimated that to restore the sea in 25 years would require 75 BCM of water annually, which would be an unrealistic expectation as it would require, either billions of US dollars in investments to improve the efficiency of the existing irrigation systems upstream, or closing most of the irrigation systems. Funds for such large investments are not available and closing the irrigation systems would create even bigger economic and social hardships than the Aral Sea crisis ever did (World Bank, 2001).

However, the Northern Aral Sea, which is fed by the Syr Darya can be rehabilitated by building a dike in the Berg Strait. Simultaneously, the delta area, wetlands and lakes near the Sea could then be rehabilitated. Current projects aimed to rehabilitate the Aral Sea include the World Bank's Syr Darya Control and Northern Aral Sea Phase-I Project (World Bank, 2001) and the Aral Sea Basin Program (World Bank, 1998). The World Bank's project in Kazakhstan aims to rehabilitate the Northern Sea and rejuvenate fish yields; increase water levels and decrease salinity; improve air, soil, and water quality; improve irrigation and crop production; improve the water supply; and improve the health of the local population. Implementation of the project includes the construction of a dam between the Northern Sea and the Southern Sea with the goal of increasing the water level in the Northern Sea, and repairing old infrastructure such as the Chardara Dam on the border of Uzbekistan and Kazakhstan (World Bank, 2001).

When these rehabilitation schemes began, project managers assumed that it would take up to 10 years for the water to rise $3\,\mathrm{m}$ and cover $800\ \mathrm{km}^2$ of dry seabed. However, just 7 months after the dike's completion, the Northern Aral Sea has reached the target level, 42 m above the level of the Baltic Sea. Spare water is already flowing through the spillway — evidence of what may become one of the biggest reversals of an environmental catastrophe in history (Pala, 2006, p. 163).

The Death of Turkmeni leader, Saparmurat Niyazov Turkmenbashi on December 21, 2006

The passing away of the Turkmeni leader, Saparmurat Niyazov Turkmenbashi on December 21, 2006 shocked his nation, the region and many others that have interest in regional water and gas issues. How would that event affect the waves in the Aral Sea?

In this context, many, if not all, possible outcomes are unknown. The domestic power balance would probably dictate many of the answers to the following questions. What kind of a future is waiting for Turkmenistan? How will the opposition act? What kind of attitudes will Turkmenistan maintain towards regional issues? What would be the faith of the "isolationist" policy? While it is still too early to predict, it is clear that new power balances, domestic, regional and international, have now renewed stake and will affect Turkmenistan's role in the regional economy and politics (Erol, 2006). The Aral Sea and the gas reserves and plans are certainly part of this possible stake.

ANNEX

Time table of major events associated with the Aral Sea.

Year	Agreement/Declaration/Event	Accomplishment
1953	Treaty signed between Soviet Union and Afghanistan	Establishes precedent for transboundary cooperation
1986	Basin Water-Management Associations (BWAs) established: BWA Amu Darya and BWA Syr Darya	Regional boards to coordinate water management in respective river drainage basins; formed initial infrastructure
1991	All five nations agree to abide by Soviet era water allocations	First step in water management following Soviet breakup
1992	Almaty Agreement signed by all Central Asian nations	Interstate Coordinating Water Commission (ICWC) created to ensure quota implementation and protect resources, govern the two BWAs. Scientific Information center (SIC) created to monitor and measure water in region
1993	ICKKU/ICKKTU	Interstate Council of Kazakhstan, Kyrgyzstan, and Uzbekistan, and later, Tajikistan
1993	International Fund to Save the Aral Sea (IFAS) created by all five nations	Created to coordinate financial resources provided by member states and donors
1993	Interstate Council on the Aral Sea Basin (ICAS) set up by all five nations	Created to coordinate projects and set policy on Aral Basin efforts
1995	ICSDTEC (SCSD)	Sustainable Development Commission
1995	Nukus Declaration signed by all five nations	Nukus Declaration acknowledged the formulation of the Aral Sea Basin Sustainable Development Convention. All nations pledge commitment to Basin protection and fund-raising
1997	New IFAS created, merged with ICAS	Streamlined institutional structure New draft institutional agreement resulted, with improvements in legal content
09/1997		The four states of Kazakhstan, Kyrgyzstan, Tajikistan, and Uzbekistan signed an agreement on the use of the Syr Darya waters
1996–present	Various multi- and bilateral agreements (less than five nations)	Topics of these agreements include energy swaps, water flow and allocation, and water measurement
1998–present	Various multi-lateral conferences, including those sponsored by UN or other NGOs	Repeated commitments to environmental and regional planning; establishment of scientific monitoring regimes
03/1998		Agreement for Cooperation in the field of Environment and Rational Use of Nature.
04/1998	Central Asian Environment Ministerial Conference	The Ministers reaffirmed their commitment to environmental cooperation in accordance with previous agreements

REFERENCES

Ahmad, M. and M. Wasiq (2004). *Water Resource Development in Northern Afghanistan and its Implications for Amu Darya Basin.* Washington, DC: World Bank.

Cenral Asia Water Information (2006). http://www.cawater-info.net/aral/water_e.htm (Visited on October 26, 2006).

de Chazournes, L. B. (2006). The Aral Sea Basin: Legal and institutional aspects of governance. In: Finger, M., T. Ludivine and J. Allouche (eds.), *The Multigovernance of Water.* New York: State University of New York Press.

Dinar, A., P. Seidel, H. Olem, V. Jorden, A. Duda and R. Johnson (1995). Restoring and protecting the world's lakes and reservoirs. World Bank Technical Paper Number 289. Washington, DC: World Bank.

Dukhovny, V., V. Sokolov and B. Mukhamadiev (2006). Integrated water resources management in the Aral Area Basin: Science policy and practice. In: John, W. and P. Wouters (eds.), *Hydrology and Water Law—Bridging the Gap.* London: IWA Publishing, pp. 198–217.

Erol, M. S. (2006). Turkmenistan after Turkmenbashi. The Journal of Turkish Weekly Opinion. http://www.turkinshweekly.net/comments.php?id=2393 (Visited on April 22, 2006).

Glantz, M. H. (1999). Sustainable development and creeping environmental problems in the Aral Sea Region. In: Glantz, M. H. (ed.), *Creeping Environmental Problems and Sustainable Development in the Aral Sea Basin.* Cambridge: Cambridge University Press, pp. 1–25.

Heltzer, G. (2003). Stalemate in the Aral Sea Basin: Will Kyrgyzstan's new water law bring the downstream nations back to the multilateral bargaining table?, *Georgetown Environmental Law Review*, Winter, 15(2), 291–321.

IFAS (2006). Declarations. http://www.ec-ifas.org/English_version/About_IFAS_eng/ declaration_eng.htm (Visited on November 4, 2006).

IFAS–UNEP (2001). International Fund for the Aral Sea and the UN Environment Programme. Environment State of the Aral Sea Basin — Regional Report of the Central Asian States 2000. http://enrin.grida.no/aral/aralsea/english/obr/obr.htm (Visited on October 27, 2006).

International Crisis Group (ICG) (2006). Central Asia: Water and Conflict. http://www.intl-crisis-group.org/projects/showreport.cfm?reportid=668 (Visited on November 2, 2006).

International Water Law (IWL) (2006). Agreement of the Republic of Kazakhstan, Republic of Kyrgyzstan, Republic of Tajikistan, Turkmenistan, and Republic of Uzbekistan on joint activities in addressing the Aral Sea. http:// www.internationalwaterlaw.org/ RegionalDocs/Aral-Sea.htm (Visited on November 3, 2006).

Just, R. E. and S. Netanyahu (1998). International water resource conflicts: Experience and potential. In: Just, R. E. and S. Netanyahu (eds.), *Conflict and Cooperation on Trans-Boundary Water Resources.* Boston: Kluwer Academic Publishers, pp. 1–26.

Kirmani, S. and G. L. Moigne (1997). Fostering riparian cooperation in international river basins: The World Bank at its best in development diplomacy. World Bank Technical Paper 349, Washington, DC: World Bank.

Langford, V. P. E. and S. Vinogradov (2001). Managing transboundary water resources in the Aral Sea Basin: In search of a solution. *International Journal of Global Environmental Issues*, 1(3/4), 345–362.

McKinney, D. C. (2004). Cooperative management of transboundary water resources in Central Asia. In: Burghart, D. and T. Sabonis-Helf (eds.), *In the Tracks of Tamerlane—Central Asia's Path into the 21st Century.* National Defense University Press (Available online 2003: http://www.ce.utexas.edu/prof/mckinney/papers/aral/CentralAsiaWater-McKinney.pdf).

Mukhammadiev, B. (2001). Legal aspects of interstate cooperation for transboundary water resources management in the Aral Sea Basin. AWRA/IWLRI-University of Dundee International Specialty Conference, August 6–8, 2001.

O'Hara, S. L. (2004). *Central Asians Divided Over Use of Dwindling Water Supply.* Local Governance Brief, Summer, 2004.

Peachey, E. (2004). The Aral Sea Basin crisis and sustainable water resource management in central Asia. *Journal of Public and International Affairs* (Vol. 15), Spring, 2004.

Pala, C. (2006). Once a terminal case, the North Aral Sea shows new signs of life. *Science,* 312, 183, April 14.

Polat, N. (2002). *Boundary Issues in Central Asia.* Ardsley, NY: Translational Publishers, p. 137.

Roll, Gulnara, *et al.* (2006). Aral Sea: Experience and Lessons Learned Brief. http://www.ilec.or.jp/lbmi2/reports/01_Aral_Sea_27February2006.pdf (Visited on November 4, 2006).

Sanigmii (2000). Uzbekistan Scientific Institute of Hydrometeorology, Tashkent. Data made available to the authors.

Turkmenistan Ministry of Irrigation and Water Economy (Called also Ministry of Land Reclamation and Water Management), Irrigation in Turkmenistan, Ashgabat, March 1995 (in Turkmen, Russian, and English).

United Nations, United Nations Treaty Collection (2006). Protocol of the Bishkek Agreement. http://untreaty.un.org/ (Visited on November 6, 2006).

Vinogradov, S. (2001). Managing Transboundary Water Resources in the Aral Sea Basin: in search of a solution. *International Journal of Global Environmental Issues,* 1(3/4), 345–362.

Votrin, V. (2006). Transboundary water disputes in Central Asia: Using indicators of water conflict in identifying water conflict potential, Vrije Universiteit Brussel. http://www.transboundarywaters.orst.edu/publications/related_research/votrin/votrin_thesis.html (Visited on November 3, 2006).

Weinthal E. (2002). *State Making and Environmental Cooperation: Linking Domestic and International Politics in Central Asia.* Cambridge, MA: The MIT Press.

World Bank (1998). Aral Sea Basin Program (Kazakhstan, Kyrgyz Republic, Tajikistan, Turkimenistan and Uzbekistan) Water and Environmental Management Project. Project Document Volume I — Main Report, May 1998. Rural Development and Environment Sector Unit Europe and Central Asia Region. Washington, DC: GEF.

World Bank (2001). Project Appraisal Document on a Proposed Loan in The Amount of US$64.5 Million to The Republic of Kazakhstan for the Syr Darya Control and Northern Aral Sea Phase-I Project May 11, 2001. Rural Development and Environment Sector Unit Europe and Central Asia Region. Washington, DC: World Bank Report No. 22190-KZ.

World Bank (2003). Water Resources in the Europe and Central Asia Region, Volume II: Country Water Notes and Selected Transboundary Basins. Washington, DC: World Bank.

World Resources Institute (2003). *World Resources, Decisions for the Earth*. Washington, DC: World Resources Institute.

ADDITIONAL READING

Beach, H. L., J. Hamner, J. Hewitt, E. Kaufman, A. Kurki, J. Oppenheimer and A. Wolf (2000). *Transboundary Freshwater Dispute Resolution: Theory, Practice and Annotated References*. Tokyo and New York: United Nations University Press.

Bedford, D.P. (1996). International water management in the Aral Sea Basin, *Water International*, 21, 63–69.

De Chazournes, L. B. (2006). The Aral Sea Basin: Legal and institutional aspects of governance. In: Finger, M., T. Ludivine and J. Allouche (eds.), *The Multigovernance of Water*. New York: State University of New York Press, pp. 147–171.

Dinar, S. (2003). Treaty principles and patterns: Selected international water agreements as lessons for the resolution of the Syr Darya and Amu Darya water disputes. In: Hartmunt, V. and N. Dobretsov (eds.), *Transboundary Water Resources: Strategy for Regional Security and Ecological Stability*. NATO Science Series. Dordrecht: Springer, pp. 147–168.

Glantz, M. H. (ed.) (1999). *Creeping Environmental Problems and Sustainable Development in the Aral Sea Basin*. Cambridge: Cambridge University Press.

Gleason, G. (2001). Interstate cooperation in Central Asia from the CIS to the Shanghai forum. *Europe-Asia Studies*, 53(7), 1077–1095.

Heltzer, G. (2003). Stalemate in the Aral Sea Basin: Will Kyrgyzstan's new water law bring the downstream nations back to the multilateral bargaining table?, *Georgetown Environmental Law Review, Winter*, 15(2), 291–321.

Levintanus, A. (1992). Saving the Aral Sea, *Water Resources Development*, 8(1), 60–64.

Micklin, P. (1992). The Aral Sea crisis: Introduction to the special issue, *Post Soviet Geography*, 3(5), 269–270.

Micklin, P. (1998). Regional and international responses to the Aral crisis: An overview of efforts and accomplishments, *Post-Soviet Geography and Economics*, 39(7), 399–417.

O'Hara, S. L. (2000). Lessons from the Past: Water management in Central Asia, *Water Policy*, 2, 365–384.

O'Hara, S. L. (2000). Central Asia's water resources: Contemporary and future management issues, *Water Resources Development*, 16(3), 423–441.

Precoda, N. (1991). Requiem to the Aral Sea, *Ambio*, 20(3–4), 109–114.

Sergai, V. (1996). Transboundary water resources in the former Soviet Union: Between conflict and cooperation, *Natural Resources Journal*, 36, 393–414.

World Bank (2004). Water energy nexus, improving regional cooperation in the Syr-Darya Basin. Washington.

ANNEX 1: SAMPLE TREATIES

A1.1 The 1977 Ganges Agreement

No. 16210

———

BANGLADESH
and
INDIA

Agreement on sharing of the Ganges waters at Farakka and on augmenting its flows (with schedule). Signed at Dacca on 5 November 1977

Authentic texts: Bengali, Hindi and English.
Registered by Bangladesh on 12 January 1978.

————

BANGLADESH
et
INDE

Accord relatif au partage des eaux du Gange à Farakka et à l'augmentation de son débit (avec annexe). Signé à Dacca le 5 novembre 1977

Textes authentiques: bengali, hindi et anglais.
Enregistré par le Bangladesh le 12 janvier 1978.

---

*Full texts of treaties are reproduced herewith with the expressed permission from the United Nations Secretariat, 2006.

AGREEMENT* BETWEEN THE GOVERNMENT OF THE PEOPLE'S REPUB-
LIC OF BANGLADESH AND THE GOVERNMENT OF THE REPUBLIC
OF INDIA ON SHARING OF THE GANGES WATERS AT FARAKKA AND
ON AUGMENTING ITS FLOWS

———————

The Government of the People's Republic of Bangladesh and the Government
of the Republic of India,

Determined to promote and strengthen their relations of friendship and good
neighbourliness,

Inspired by the common desire of promoting the well-being of their peoples,

Being desirous of sharing by mutual agreement the waters of the international
rivers flowing through the territories of the two countries and of making the optimum
utilisation of the water resources of their region by joint efforts,

Recognising that the need of making an interim arrangement for sharing of the
Ganges waters at Farakka in a spirit of mutual accommodation and the need for a
solution of the long-term problem of augmenting the flows of the Ganges are in the
mutual interests of the peoples of the two countries,

Being desirous of finding a fair solution to the question before them, without
affecting the rights and entitlements of either country other than those covered by
this Agreement, or establishing any general principles of law or precedent,

Have agreed as follows:

A. ARRANGEMENTS FOR SHARING OF THE WATERS OF THE GANGES AT FARAKKA

Article I. The quantum of waters agreed to be released by India to Bangladesh
will be at Farakka.

Article II. (i) The sharing between Bangladesh and India of the Ganges waters
at Farakka from the 1st January to the 31st May every year will be with reference to
the quantum shown in column 2 of the Schedule annexed hereto which is based on
75 percent availability calculated from the recorded flows of the Ganges at Farakka
from 1948 to 1973.

(ii) India shall release to Bangladesh waters by 10-day periods in quantum
shown in column 4 of the Schedule:

– provided that if the actual availability at Farakka of the Ganges waters during
  a 10-day period is higher or lower than the quantum shown in column 2 of the
  Schedule it shall be shared in the proportion applicable to that period;
– provided further that if during a particular 10-day period, the Ganges flows at
  Farakka come down to such a level that the share of Bangladesh is lower than
  80 percent of the value shown in column 4, the release of waters to Bangladesh

———————
*Came into force on 5 November 1977 by signature, in accordance with Article XV.

during that 10-day period shall not fall below 80 percent of the value shown in column 4.

Article III. The waters released to Bangladesh at Farakka under Article I shall not be reduced below Farakka except for reasonable uses of waters, not exceeding 200 cusecs, by India between Farakka and the point on the Ganges where both its banks are in Bangladesh.

Article IV. A Committee consisting of the representatives nominated by the two Governments (hereinafter called the Joint Committee) shall be constituted. The Joint Committee shall set up suitable teams at Farakka and Hardinge Bridge to observe and record at Farakka the daily flows below Farakka Barrage and in the Feeder Canal, as well as at Hardinge Bridge.

Article V. The Joint Committee shall decide its own procedure and method of functioning.

Article VI. The Joint Committee shall submit to the two Governments all data collected by it and shall also submit a yearly report to both the Governments.

Article VII. The Joint Committee shall be responsible for implementing the arrangements contained in this part of the Agreement and examining any difficulty arising out of the implementation of the above arrangements and of the operation of Farakka Barrage. Any difference or dispute arising in this regard, if not resolved by the Joint Committee, shall be referred to a panel of an equal number of Bangladeshi and Indian experts nominated by the two Governments. If the difference or dispute still remains unresolved, it shall be referred to the two Governments which shall meet urgently at the appropriate level to resolve it by mutual discussion and failing that by such other arrangements as they may mutually agree upon.

B. LONG-TERM ARRANGEMENTS

Article VIII. The two Governments recognise the need to cooperate with each other in finding a solution to the long-term problem of augmenting the flows of the Ganges during the dry season.

Article IX. The Indo-Bangladesh Joint Rivers Commission established by the two Governments in 1972 shall carry out investigation and study of schemes relating to the augmentation of the dry season flows of the Ganges, proposed or to be proposed by either Government with a view to finding a solution which is economical and feasible. It shall submit its recommendations to the two Governments within a period of three years.

Article X. The two Governments shall consider and agree upon a scheme or schemes, taking into account the recommendations of the Joint Rivers Commission, and take necessary measures to implement them as speedily as possible.

Article XI. Any difficulty, difference or dispute arising from or with regard to this part of the Agreement, if not resolved by the Joint Rivers Commission, shall be referred to the two Governments which shall meet urgently at the appropriate level to resolve it by mutual discussion.

C. Review and Duration

Article XII. The provisions of this Agreement will be implemented by both Parties in good faith. During the period for which the Agreement continues to be in force in accordance with Article XV of the Agreement, the quantum of waters agreed to be released to Bangladesh at Farakka in accordance with this Agreement shall not be reduced.

Article XIII. The Agreement will be reviewed by the two Governments at the expiry of three years from the date of coming into force of this Agreement. Further reviews shall take place six months before the expiry of this Agreement or as may be agreed upon between the two Governments.

Article XIV. The review or reviews referred to in Article XIII shall entail consideration of the working, impact, implementation and progress of the arrangements contained in parts A and B of this Agreement.

Article XV. This Agreement shall enter into force upon signature and shall remain in force for a period of 5 years from the date of its coming into force. It may be extended further for a specified period by mutual agreement in the light of the review or reviews referred to in Article XIII.

IN WITNESS WHEREOF the undersigned, being duly authorised thereto by the respective Governments, have signed this Agreement.

DONE in duplicate at Dacca on the 5th November 1977 in the Bengali, Hindi and English languages. In the event of any conflict between the texts, the English text shall prevail.

Rear Admiral MUSHARRAF HUSAIN KHAN Chief of Naval Staff and Member, President's Council of Advisers in charge of the Ministry of Communications, Flood Control, Water Resources and Power, Government of the People's Republic of Bangladesh	SURJIT SINGH BARNALA Minister for Agriculture and Irrigation, Government of the Republic of India
For the Government of the People's Republic of Bangladesh	For the Government of the Republic of India

SCHEDULE
(vide *Article II (i)*)
SHARING OF WATERS AT FARAKKA BETWEEN THE 1ST JANUARY
AND THE 31ST MAY EVERY YEAR

1	2	3	4
Period	Flow reaching Farakka (based on 75% availability from observed data (1948-73))	Withdrawal by India at Farakka	Release to Bangladesh
	Cusecs	*Cusecs*	*Cusecs*
January			
1–10	98,500	40,000	58,500
11–20	89,750	38,500	51,250
21–31	82,500	35,000	47,500
February			
1–10	79,250	33,000	46,250
11–20	74,000	31,500	42,500
21–28/29	70,000	30,750	39,250
March			
1–10	65,250	26,750	38,500
11–20	63,500	25,500	38,000
21–31	61,000	25,000	36,000
April			
1–10	59,000	24,000	35,000
11–20	55,500	20,750	34,750
21–30	55,000	20,500	34,500
May			
1–10	56,500	21,500	35,000
11–20	59,250	24,000	35,250
21–31	65,500	26,750	38,750

A1.2 The 1975 Mekong Treaty

Volume 2069, 1-35844
[ENGLISH TEXT—TEXTE ANGLAIS]

AGREEMENT ON THE COOPERATION FOR THE SUSTAINABLE
DEVELOPMENT OF THE MEKONG RIVER BASIN

The Governments of the Kingdom of Cambodia, the Lao People's Democratic Republic, the Kingdom of Thailand, and the Socialist Republic of Viet Nam, being equally desirous of continuing to cooperate in a constructive and mutually beneficial manner for sustainable development, utilization, conservation and management of the Mekong River Basin water and related resources, have resolved to conclude this Agreement setting forth the framework for cooperation acceptable to all parties hereto to accomplish these ends, and for that purpose have appointed as their respective plenipotentiaries:

The Kingdom of Cambodia:
H.E. Mr. Ing Kieth,
Deputy Prime Minister and Minister of Public Works and Transport;
The Lao People's Democratic Republic:
H.E. Mr. Somsavat Lengsavad,
Minister of Foreign Affairs;
The Kingdom of Thailand:
H.E. Dr. Krasae Chanawongse,
Minister of Foreign Affairs;
The Socialist Republic of Viet Nam:
H.E. Mr. Nguyen Manh Cam,
Minister of Foreign Affairs,

Who, having communicated to each other their respective full powers and having found them in good and due form, have agreed to the following:

CHAPTER I. PREAMBLE

Recalling the establishment of the Committee for the Coordination of Investigations of the Lower Mekong Basin on 17 September 1957 by the Governments of these countries by Statute endorsed by the United Nations,

Noting the unique spirit of cooperation and mutual assistance that inspired the work of the Committee for the Coordination of Investigations of the Lower Mekong Basin and the many accomplishments that have been achieved through its efforts,

Acknowledging the great political, economic and social changes that have taken place in these countries of the region during this period of time which necessitate these efforts to re-assess, re-define and establish the future framework for cooperation,

Recognizing that the Mekong River Basin and the related natural resources and environment are natural assets of immense value to all the riparian countries for the economic and social well-being and living standards of their peoples,

Reaffirming the determination to continue to cooperate and promote in a constructive and mutually beneficial manner in the sustainable development, utilization, conservation and management of the Mekong River Basin water and related resources for navigational and non-navigational purposes, for social and economic development and the well-being of all riparian States, consistent with the needs to protect, preserve, enhance and manage the environmental and aquatic conditions and maintenance of the ecological balance exceptional to this river basin,

Affirming to promote or assist in the promotion of interdependent sub-regional growth and cooperation among the community of Mekong nations, taking into account the regional benefits that could be derived and/or detriments that could be avoided or mitigated from activities within the Mekong River Basin undertaken by this framework of cooperation,

Realizing the necessity to provide an adequate, efficient and functional joint organizational structure to implement this Agreement and the projects, programs and activities taken thereunder in cooperation and coordination with each member and the international community, and to address and resolve issues and problems that may arise from the use and development of the Mekong River Basin water and related resources in an amicable, timely and good neighborly manner,

Proclaiming further the following specific objectives, principles, institutional framework and ancillary provisions in conformity with the objectives and principles of the Charter of the United Nations and international law:

CHAPTER II. DEFINITIONS OF TERMS

For the purposes of this Agreement, it shall be understood that the following meanings to the underlined terms shall apply except where otherwise inconsistent with the context:

Agreement under Article 5: A decision of the Joint Committee resulting from prior consultation and evaluation on any proposed use for inter-basin diversions during the wet season from the mainstream as well as for intra-basin use or inter-basin diversions of these waters during the dry season. The objective of this agreement is to achieve an optimum use and prevention of waste of the waters through a dynamic and practical consensus in conformity with the Rules for Water Utilization and Inter-Basin Diversions set forth in Article 26.

Acceptable minimum monthly natural flow: The acceptable minimum monthly natural flow during each month of the dry season.

Acceptable natural reverse flow: The wet season flow level in the Mekong River at Kratie that allows the reverse flow of the Tonle Sap to an agreed upon optimum level of the Great Lake.

Basin Development Plan: The general planning tool and process that the Joint Committee would use as a blueprint to identify, categorize and prioritize the projects and programs to seek assistance for and to implement the plan at the basin level.

Environment: The conditions of water and land resources, air, flora, and fauna that exists in a particular region.

Notification: Timely providing information by a riparian to the Joint Committee on its proposed use of water according to the format, content and procedures set forth in the Rules for Water Utilization and Inter-Basin Diversions under Article 26.

Prior consultation: Timely notification plus additional data and information to the Joint Committee as provided in the Rules for Water Utilization and Inter-Basin Diversion under Article 26, that would allow the other member riparians to discuss and evaluate the impact of the proposed use upon their uses of water and any other affects, which is the basis for arriving at an agreement. Prior consultation is neither a right to veto the use nor unilateral right to use water by any riparian without taking into account other riparians' rights.

Proposed use: Any proposal for a definite use of the waters of the Mekong River system by any riparian, excluding domestic and minor uses of water not having a significant impact on mainstream flows.

Chapter III. Objectives and Principles of Cooperation

The parties agree:

Article 1. Areas of Cooperation

To cooperate in all fields of sustainable development, utilization, management and conservation of the water and related resources of the Mekong River Basin including, but not limited to irrigation, hydro-power, navigation, flood control, fisheries, timber floating, recreation and tourism, in a manner to optimize the multiple-use and mutual benefits of all riparians and to minimize the harmful effects that might result from natural occurrences and man-made activities.

Article 2. Projects, Programs and Planning

To promote, support, cooperate and coordinate in the development of the full potential of sustainable benefits to all riparian States and the prevention of wasteful use of Mekong River Basin waters, with emphasis and preference on joint and/or basin-wide development projects and basin programs through the formulation of a basin development plan, that would be used to identify, categorize and prioritize the projects and programs to seek assistance for and to implement at the basin level.

Article 3. Protection of the Environment and Ecological Balance

To protect the environment, natural resources, aquatic life and conditions, and ecological balance of the Mekong River Basin from pollution or other harmful effects resulting from any development plans and uses of water and related resources in the Basin.

Article 4. Sovereign Equality and Territorial Integrity

To cooperate on the basis of sovereign equality and territorial integrity in the utilization and protection of the water resources of the Mekong River Basin.

Article 5. Reasonable and Equitable Utilization

To utilize the waters of the Mekong River system in a reasonable and equitable manner in their respective territories, pursuant to all relevant factors and circumstances, the Rules for Water Utilization and Inter-Basin Diversion provided for under Article 26 and the provisions of A and B below:

A. On tributaries of the Mekong River, including Tonle Sap, intra-basin uses and inter-basin diversions shall be subject to notification to the Joint Committee.

B. On the mainstream of the Mekong River:

1. During the wet season:

a) Intra-basin use shall be subject to notification to the Joint Committee.

b) Inter-basin diversion shall be subject to prior consultation which aims at arriving at an agreement by the Joint Committee.

2. During the dry season:

a) Intra-basin use shall be subject to prior consultation which aims at arriving at an agreement by the Joint Committee.

b) Any inter-basin diversion project shall be agreed upon by the Joint Committee through a specific agreement for each project prior to any proposed diversion. However, should there be a surplus quantity of water available in excess of the proposed uses of all parties in any dry season, verified and unanimously confirmed as such by the Joint Committee, an inter-basin diversion of the surplus could be made subject to prior consultation.

Article 6. Maintenance of Flows on the Mainstream

To cooperate in the maintenance of the flows on the mainstream from diversions, storage releases, or other actions of a permanent nature; except in the cases of historically severe droughts and/or floods:

A. Of not less than the acceptable minimum monthly natural flow during each month of the dry season;

B. To enable the acceptable natural reverse flow of the Tonle Sap to take place during the wet season; and

C. To prevent average daily peak flows greater than what naturally occur on the average during the flood season.

The Joint Committee shall adopt guidelines for the locations and levels of the flows, and monitor and take action necessary for their maintenance as provided in Article 26.

Article 7. Prevention and Cessation of Harmful Effects

To make every effort to avoid, minimize and mitigate harmful effects that might occur to the environment, especially the water quantity and quality, the aquatic (eco-system) conditions, and ecological balance of the river system, from the development and use of the Mekong River Basin water resources or discharge of wastes and return flows. Where one or more States is notified with proper and valid evidence that it is causing substantial damage to one or more riparians from the use of and/or discharge to water of the Mekong River, that State or States shall cease immediately the alleged cause of harm until such cause of harm is determined in accordance with Article 8.

Article 8. State Responsibility for Damages

Where harmful effects cause substantial damage to one or more riparians from the use of and/or discharge to waters of the Mekong River by any riparian State, the party(ies) concerned shall determine all relative factors, the cause, extent of damage and responsibility for damages caused by that State in conformity with the principles of international law relating to state responsibility, and to address and resolve all issues, differences and disputes in an amicable and timely manner by peaceful means as provided in Articles 34 and 35 of this Agreement, and in conformity with the Charter of the United Nations.

Article 9. Freedom of Navigation

On the basis of equality of right, freedom of navigation shall be accorded throughout the mainstream of the Mekong River without regard to the territorial boundaries, for transportation and communication to promote regional cooperation and to satisfactorily implement projects under this Agreement. The Mekong River shall be kept free from obstructions, measures, conduct and actions that might directly or indirectly impair navigability, interfere with this right or permanently make it more difficult. Navigational uses are not assured any priority over other uses, but will be incorporated into any mainstream project. Riparians may issue regulations for the portions of the Mekong River within their territories, particularly in sanitary, customs and immigration matters, police and general security.

Article 10. Emergency Situations

Whenever a Party becomes aware of any special water quantity or quality problems constituting an emergency that requires an immediate response, it shall notify and consult directly with the party(ies) concerned and the Joint Committee without delay in order to take appropriate remedial action.

CHAPTER IV. INSTITUTIONAL FRAMEWORK
A. MEKONG RIVER COMMISSION
Article 11. Status

The institutional framework for cooperation in the Mekong River Basin under this Agreement shall be called the Mekong River Commission and shall, for the purpose of the exercise of its functions, enjoy the status of an international body, including entering into agreements and obligations with the donor or international community.

Article 12. Structure of Mekong River Commission

The Commission shall consist of three permanent bodies:
Council
Joint Committee, and
Secretariat

Article 13. Assumption of Assets, Obligations and Rights

The Commission shall assume all the assets, rights and obligations of the Committee for the Coordination of Investigations of the Lower Mekong Basin (Mekong Committee/Interim Mekong Committee) and Mekong Secretariat.

Article 14. Budget of the Mekong River Commission

The budget of the Commission shall be drawn up by the Joint Committee and approved by the Council and shall consist of contributions from member countries on an equal basis unless otherwise decided by the Council, from the international community (donor countries), and from other sources.

B. COUNCIL
Article 15. Composition of Council

The Council shall be composed of one member from each participating riparian State at the Ministerial and Cabinet level (no less than Vice-Minister level) who would be empowered to make policy decisions on behalf of his/her government.

Article 16. Chairmanship of Council

The Chairmanship of the Council shall be for a term of one year and rotate according to the alphabetical listing of the participating countries.

Article 17. Sessions of Council

The Council shall convene at least one regular session every year and may convene special sessions whenever it considers it necessary or upon the request of a member State. It may invite observers to its sessions as it deems appropriate.

Article 18. Functions of Council

The functions of the Council are:

A. To make policies and decisions and provide other necessary guidance concerning the promotion, support, cooperation and coordination in joint activities and projects in a constructive and mutually beneficial manner for the sustainable development, utilization, conservation and management of the Mekong River Basin waters and related resources, and protection of the environment and aquatic conditions in the Basin as provided for under this Agreement;

B. To decide any other policy-making matters and make decisions necessary to successfully implement this Agreement, including but not limited to approval of the Rules of Procedures of the Joint Committee under Article 25, Rules of Water Utilization and Inter-Basin Diversions proposed by the Joint Committee under Article 26, and the basin development plan and major component projects/programs; to establish guidelines for financial and technical assistance of development projects and programs; and if considered necessary, to invite the donors to coordinate their support through a Donor Consultative Group; and

C. To entertain, address and resolve issues, differences and disputes referred to it by any Council member, the Joint Committee, or any member State on matters arising under this Agreement.

Article 19. Rules of Procedures

The Council shall adopt its own Rules of Procedures, and may seek technical advisory services as it deems necessary.

Article 20. Decisions of Council

Decisions of the Council shall be by unanimous vote except as otherwise provided for in its Rules of Procedures.

C. JOINT COMMITTEE
Article 21. Composition of Joint Committee

The Joint Committee shall be composed of one member from each participating riparian State at no less than Head of Department level.

Article 22. Chairmanship of Joint Committee

The Chairmanship of the Joint Committee will rotate according to the reverse alphabetical listing of the member countries and the Chairperson shall serve a term of one year.

Article 23. Sessions of Joint Committee

The Joint Committee shall convene at least two regular sessions every year and may convene special sessions whenever it considers it necessary or upon the request of a member State. It may invite observers to its sessions as it deems appropriate.

Article 24. Functions of Joint Committee

The functions of the Joint Committee are:

A. To implement the policies and decisions of the Council and such other tasks as may be assigned by the Council.

B. To formulate a basin development plan, which would be periodically reviewed and revised as necessary; to submit to the Council for approval the basin development plan and joint development projects/programs to be implemented in connection with it; and to confer with donors, directly or through their consultative group, to obtain the financial and technical support necessary for project/program implementation.

C. To regularly obtain, update and exchange information and data necessary to implement this Agreement.

D. To conduct appropriate studies and assessments for the protection of the environment and maintenance of the ecological balance of the Mekong River Basin.

E. To assign tasks and supervise the activities of the Secretariat as is required to implement this Agreement and the policies, decisions, projects and programs adopted thereunder, including the maintenance of databases and information necessary for the Council and Joint Committee to perform their functions, and approval of the annual work program prepared by the Secretariat.

F. To address and make every effort to resolve issues and differences that may arise between regular sessions of the Council, referred to it by any Joint Committee member or member state on matters arising under this Agreement, and when necessary to refer the matter to the Council.

G. To review and approve studies and training for the personnel of the riparian member countries involved in Mekong River Basin activities as appropriate and necessary to strengthen the capability to implement this Agreement.

H. To make recommendations to the Council for approval on the organizational structure, modifications and restructuring of the Secretariat.

Article 25. Rules of Procedures

The Joint Committee shall propose its own Rules of Procedures to be approved by the Council. It may form ad hoc and/or permanent sub-committees or working groups as considered necessary, and may seek technical advisory services except as may be provided for in the Council's Rules of Procedures or decisions.

Article 26. Rules for Water Utilization and Inter-Basin Diversions

The Joint Committee shall prepare and propose for approval of the Council, inter alia, Rules for Water Utilization and Inter-Basin Diversions pursuant to Articles 5 and 6, including but not limited to: 1) establishing the time frame for the wet and dry seasons; 2) establishing the location of hydrological stations, and determining and maintaining the flow level requirements at each station; 3) setting out criteria for determining surplus quantities of water during the dry season on the mainstream; 4) improving upon the mechanism to monitor intra-basin use; and 5) setting up a mechanism to monitor inter-basin diversions from the mainstream.

Article 27. Decisions of the Joint Committee

Decisions of the Joint Committee shall be by unanimous vote except as otherwise provided for in its Rules of Procedures.

D. SECRETARIAT

Article 28. Purpose of Secretariat

The Secretariat shall render technical and administrative services to the Council and Joint Committee, and be under the supervision of the Joint Committee.

Article 29. Location of Secretariat

The location and structure of the permanent office of the Secretariat shall be decided by the Council, and if necessary, a headquarters agreement shall be negotiated and entered into with the host government.

Article 30. Functions of the Secretariat

The functions and duties of the Secretariat will be to:

A. Carry out the decisions and tasks assigned by the Council and Joint Committee under the direction of and directly responsible to the Joint Committee;

B. Provide technical services and financial administration and advise as requested by the Council and Joint Committee;

C. Formulate the annual work program, and prepare all other plans, project and program documents, studies and assessments as may be required;

D. Assist the Joint Committee in the implementation and management of projects and programs as requested;

E. Maintain databases of information as directed;

F. Make preparations for sessions of the Council and Joint Committee; and

G. Carry out all other assignments as may be requested.

Article 31. Chief Executive Officer

The Secretariat shall be under the direction of a Chief Executive Officer (CEO), who shall be appointed by the Council from a short-list of qualified candidates selected by the Joint Committee. The Terms of Reference of the CEO shall be prepared by the Joint Committee and approved by the Council.

Article 32. Assistant Chief Executive Officer

There will be one Assistant to the CEO, nominated by the CEO and approved by the Chairman of the Joint Committee. Such Assistant will be of the same nationality as the Chairman of the Joint Committee and shall serve for a co-terminus one-year term.

Article 33. Riparian Staff

Riparian technical staff of the Secretariat are to be recruited on a basis of technical competence, and the number of posts shall be assigned on an equal basis among the members. Riparian technical staff shall be assigned to the Secretariat for no more than two three-year terms, except as otherwise decided by the Joint Committee.

Chapter V. Addressing Differences and Disputes
Article 34. Resolution by Mekong River Commission

Whenever any difference or dispute may arise between two or more parties to this Agreement regarding any matters covered by this Agreement and/or actions taken by the implementing organization through its various bodies, particularly as to the interpretations of the Agreement and the legal rights of the parties, the Commission shall first make every effort to resolve the issue as provided in Articles 18.C and 24.F.

Article 35. Resolution by Governments

In the event the Commission is unable to resolve the difference or dispute within a timely manner, the issue shall be referred to the Governments to take cognizance of the matter for resolution by negotiation through diplomatic channels within a timely manner, and may communicate their decision to the Council for further proceedings as may be necessary to carry out such decision. Should the Governments find it necessary or beneficial to facilitate the resolution of the matter, they may, by mutual agreement, request the assistance of mediation through an entity or party mutually agreed upon, and thereafter to proceed according to the principles of international law.

Chapter VI. Final Provisions
Article 36. Entry into Force and Prior Agreements

This Agreement shall:

A. Enter into force among all parties, with no retroactive effect upon activities and projects previously existing, on the date of signature by the appointed plenipotentiaries.

B. Replace the Statute of the Committee for Coordination of Investigations of the Lower Mekong Basin of 1957 as amended, the Joint Declaration of Principles for Utilization of the Waters of the Lower Mekong Basin of 1975, the Declaration Concerning the Interim Committee for Coordination of Investigations of the Lower Mekong Basin of 1978, and all Rules of Procedures adopted under such agreements. This Agreement shall not replace or take precedence over any other treaties, acts or agreements entered into by and among any of the parties hereto, except that where a conflict in terms, areas of jurisdiction of subject matter or operation of any entities created under existing agreements occurs with any provisions of this Agreement, the issues shall be submitted to the respective governments to address and resolve.

Article 37. Amendments, Modification, Supersession and Termination

This Agreement may be amended, modified, superseded or terminated by the mutual agreement of all parties hereto at the time of such action.

Article 38. Scope of Agreement

This Agreement shall consist of the Preamble and all provisions thereafter and amendments thereto, the Annexes, and all other agreements entered into by the Parties under this Agreement. Parties may enter into bi- or multi-lateral special agreements or arrangements for implementation and management of any programs and projects to be undertaken within the framework of this Agreement, which agreements shall not be in conflict with this Agreement and shall not confer any rights or obligations upon the parties not signatories thereto, except as otherwise conferred under this Agreement.

Article 39. Additional Parties to Agreement

Any other riparian State, accepting the rights and obligations under this Agreement, may become a party with the consent of the parties.

Article 40. Suspension and Withdrawal

Any party to this Agreement may withdraw or suspend their participation under present Agreement by giving written notice to the Chairman of the Council of the Mekong River Commission, who shall acknowledge receipt thereof and immediately communicate it to the Council representatives of all remaining parties. Such notice of withdrawal or suspension shall take effect one year after the date of acknowledgment or receipt unless such notice is withdrawn beforehand or the parties mutually agree otherwise. Unless mutually agreed upon to the contrary by all remaining parties to this Agreement, such notice shall not be prejudicial to nor relieve the noticing party of any commitments entered into concerning programs, projects, studies or other recognized rights and interests of any riparians, or under international law.

Article 41. United Nations and International Community Involvement

The member countries to this Agreement acknowledge the important contribution in the assistance and guidance of the United Nations, donors and the international community and wish to continue the relationship under this Agreement.

Article 42. Registration of Agreement

This Agreement shall be registered and deposited, in English and French, with the Secretary General of the United Nations.

In witness whereof, the undersigned, duly authorized by their respective governments, have signed this Agreement. Done on 5 April 1995 at Chiang Rai, Thailand, in English and French, both texts being equally authentic. In the case of any inconsistency, the text in the English language, in which language the Agreement was drawn up, shall prevail.

For the Kingdom of Cambodia:
  ING KIETH
Deputy Prime Minister and Minister of Public Works and Transport

For the Lao People's Democratic Republic:
  SOMSAVAT LENGSAVAD
Minister of Foreign Affairs

For the Kingdom of Thailand:
  Dr. KRASAE CHANAWONGSE
Minister of Foreign Affairs

For the Socialist Republic of Vietnam:
  NGUYEN MANH CAM
Minister of Foreign Affairs

PROTOCOL TO THE AGREEMENT ON THE COOPERATION FOR THE SUSTAINABLE DEVELOPMENT OF THE MEKONG RIVER BASIN FOR THE ESTABLISHMENT AND COMMENCEMENT OF THE MEKONG RIVER COMMISSION

The Governments of the Kingdom of Cambodia, Lao People's Democratic Republic, Kingdom of Thailand, and Socialist Republic of Viet Nam, have signed on this day the Agreement on the Cooperation for the Sustainable Development of the Mekong River Basin.

Said Agreement provides for in Chapter IV the establishment of the Mekong River Commission as the institutional framework through which the Agreement will be implemented.

By this Protocol, the signatory parties to the Agreement do hereby declare the establishment and commencement of the Mekong River Commission, consisting of three permanent bodies, the Council, Joint Committee and Secretariat, effective on this date with the full authority and responsibility set forth under the Agreement.

In witness whereof, the undersigned, duly authorized by their respective governments have signed this Protocol. Done on 5 April 1995 at Chiang Rai, Thailand.

For the Kingdom of Cambodia:
  ING KIETH
Deputy Prime Minister and Minister of Public Works and Transport

For the Lao People's Democratic Republic:
  SOMSAVAT LENGSAVAD
Minister of Foreign Affairs

For the Kingdom of Thailand:
  DR. KRASAE CHANAWONGSE
Minister of Foreign Affairs

For the Socialist Republic of Vietnam:
  NGUYEN MANH CAM
Minister of Foreign Affairs

The 1960 Indus Treaty

Main Treaty

No. 6032

———

INDIA, PAKISTAN and INTERNATIONAL BANK FOR RECONSTRUCTION AND DEVELOPMENT

The Indus Waters Treaty 1960 (with annexes). Signed at Karachi, on 19 September 1960

Protocol to the above-mentioned Treaty. Signed on 27 November, 2 and 23 December 1960

Official text: English.

Registered by India on 16 January 1962.

————

INDE, PAKISTAN et BANQUE INTERNATIONALE POUR LA RECONSTRUCTION ET LE DÉVELOPPEMENT

Traité de 1960 sur les eaux de l'Indus (avec annexes). Signé à Karachi, le 19 septembre 1960

Protocole relatif au Traité susmentionné. Signé les 27 novembre, 2 et 23 décembre 1960

Texte officiel: anglais.

Enregistrés par l'Inde le 16 janvier 1962.

No. 6032. THE INDUS WATERS TREATY 1960[2] BETWEEN THE GOVERNMENT OF INDIA, THE GOVERNMENT OF PAKISTAN AND THE INTERNATIONAL BANK FOR RECONSTRUCTION AND DEVELOPMENT. SIGNED AT KARACHI, ON 19 SEPTEMBER 1960

PREAMBLE

The Government of India and the Government of Pakistan, being equally desirous of attaining the most complete and satisfactory utilisation of the waters of the Indus system of rivers and recognising the need, therefore, of fixing and delimiting, in a spirit of goodwill and friendship, the rights and obligations of each in relation to the other concerning the use of these waters and of making provision for the settlement, in a cooperative spirit, of all such questions as may hereafter arise in regard to the interpretation or application of the provisions agreed upon herein, have resolved to conclude a Treaty in furtherance of these objectives, and for this purpose have named as their plenipotentiaries:

The Government of India:

Shri Jawaharlal Nehru, Prime Minister of India, and

The Government of Pakistan:

Field Marshal Mohammad Ayub Khan, H.P., H.J., President of Pakistan;

who, having communicated to each other their respective Full Powers and having found them in good and due form, have agreed upon the following Articles and Annexures:

Article I

DEFINITIONS

As used in this Treaty:

(1) The terms "Article" and "Annexure" mean respectively an Article of, and an Annexure to, this Treaty. Except as otherwise indicated, references to Paragraphs are to the paragraphs in the Article or in the Annexure in which the reference is made.

(2) The term "Tributary" of a river means any surface channel, whether in continuous or intermittent flow and by whatever name called, whose waters in the natural course would fall into that river, e.g. a tributary, a torrent, a natural drainage, an artificial drainage, a *nadi*, a *nallah*, a *nai*, a *khad*, a *cho*. The term also includes any subtributary or branch or subsidiary channel, by whatever name called, whose

---

[2]Came into force on 12 January 1961, upon the exchange of the instruments of ratification at New Delhi, with retroactive effect from 1 April 1960, in accordance with Article XII (2).

The text printed herein incorporates the corrections effected by the Protocol signed on 27 November, 2 and 23 December 1960 (See p. 290 of this volume).

*All references in this treaty to specific page numbers in this volume are not included in our book but appear in the original treaty.

waters, in the natural course, would directly or otherwise flow into that surface channel.

(3) The term "The Indus," "The Jhelum," "The Chenab," "The Ravi," "The Beas" or "The Sutlej" means the named river (including Connecting Lakes, if any) and all its Tributaries: Provided however that

(i) none of the rivers named above shall be deemed to be a Tributary;
(ii) The Chenab shall be deemed to include the river Panjnad; and
(iii) the river Chandra and the river Bhaga shall be deemed to be Tributaries of The Chenab.

(4) The term "Main" added after Indus, Jhelum, Chenab, Sutlej, Beas or Ravi means the main stem of the named river excluding its Tributaries, but including all channels and creeks of the main stem of that river and such Connecting Lakes as form part of the main stem itself. The Jhelum Main shall be deemed to extend up to Verinag, and the Chenab Main up to the confluence of the river Chandra and the river Bhaga.

(5) The term "Eastern Rivers" means The Sutlej, The Beas and The Ravi taken together.

(6) The term "Western Rivers" means The Indus, The Jhelum and The Chenab taken together.

(7) The term "the Rivers" means all the rivers, The Sutlej, The Beas, The Ravi, The Indus, The Jhelum and The Chenab.

(8) The term "Connecting Lake" means any lake which receives water from, or yields water to, any of the Rivers; but any lake which occasionally and irregularly receives only the spill of any of the Rivers and returns only the whole or part of that spill is not a Connecting Lake.

(9) The term "Agricultural Use" means the use of water for irrigation, except for irrigation of household gardens and public recreational gardens.

(10) The term "Domestic Use" means the use of water for:

(a) drinking, washing, bathing, recreation, sanitation (including the conveyance and dilution of sewage and of industrial and other wastes), stock and poultry, and other like purposes;
(b) household and municipal purposes (including use for household gardens and public recreational gardens); and
(c) industrial purposes (including mining, milling and other like purposes);

but the term does not include Agricultural Use or use for the generation of hydro-electric power.

(11) The term "Non-Consumptive Use" means any control or use of water for navigation, floating of timber or other property, flood protection or flood control, fishing or fish culture, wild life or other like beneficial purposes, provided that, exclusive of seepage and evaporation of water incidental to the control or use, the water (undiminished in volume within the practical range of measurement) remains

in, or is returned to, the same river or its Tributaries; but the term does not include Agricultural Use or use for the generation of hydro-electric power.

(12) The term "Transition Period" means the period beginning and ending as provided in Article II (6).

(13) The term "Bank" means the International Bank for Reconstruction and Development.

(14) The term "Commissioner" means either of the Commissioners appointed under the provisions of Article VIII (1) and the term "Commission" means the Permanent Indus Commission constituted in accordance with Article VIII (3).

(15) The term "interference with the waters" means:

(a) Any act of withdrawal therefrom; or
(b) Any man-made obstruction to their flow which causes a change in the volume (within the practical range of measurement) of the daily flow of the waters: Provided however that an obstruction which involves only an insignificant and incidental change in the volume of the daily flow, for example, fluctuations due to afflux caused by bridge piers or a temporary by-pass, etc., shall not be deemed to be an interference with the waters.

(16) The term "Effective Date" means the date on which this Treaty takes effect in accordance with the provisions of Article XII, that is, the first of April 1960.

Article II
PROVISIONS REGARDING EASTERN RIVERS

(1) All the waters of the Eastern Rivers shall be available for the unrestricted use of India, except as otherwise expressly provided in this Article.

(2) Except for Domestic Use and Non-Consumptive Use, Pakistan shall be under an obligation to let flow, and shall not permit any interference with, the waters of the Sutlej Main and the Ravi Main in the reaches where these rivers flow in Pakistan and have not yet finally crossed into Pakistan. The points of final crossing are the following: (a) near the new Hasta Bund upstream of Suleimanke in the case of the Sutlej Main, and (b) about one and a half miles upstream of the syphon for the B-R-B-D Link in the case of the Ravi Main.

(3) Except for Domestic Use, Non-Consumptive Use and Agricultural (as specified in Annexure B),[3] Pakistan shall be under an obligation to let flow, and shall not permit any interference with, the waters (while flowing in Pakistan) of any Tributary which in its natural course joins the Sutlej Main or the Ravi Main before these rivers have finally crossed into Pakistan.

(4) All the waters, while flowing in Pakistan, of any Tributary which, in its natural course, joins the Sutlej Main or the Ravi Main after these rivers have finally crossed into Pakistan shall be available for the unrestricted use of Pakistan: Provided

---

[3]See p. 160 of this volume.

however that this provision shall not be construed as giving Pakistan any claim or right to any releases by India in any such Tributary. If Pakistan should deliver any of the waters of any such Tributary, which on the Effective Date joins the Ravi Main after this river has finally crossed into Pakistan, into a reach of the Ravi Main upstream of this crossing, India shall not make use of these waters; each Party agrees to establish such discharge observation stations and make such observations as may be necessary for the determination of the component of water available for the use of Pakistan on account of the aforesaid deliveries by Pakistan, and Pakistan agrees to meet the cost of establishing the aforesaid discharge observation stations and making the aforesaid observations.

(5) There shall be a Transition Period during which, to the extent specified in Annexure H,[4] India shall

   (i) limit its withdrawals for Agricultural Use,
  (ii) limit abstractions for storages, and
 (iii) make deliveries to Pakistan

from the Eastern Rivers.

(6) The Transition Period shall begin on 1st April 1960 and it shall end on 31st March 1970, or, if extended under the provisions of Part 8 of Annexure H, on the date up to which it has been extended. In any event, whether or not the replacement referred to in Article IV (1) has been accomplished, the Transition Period shall end not later than 31st March 1973.

(7) If the Transition Period is extended beyond 31st March 1970, the provisions of Article V (5) shall apply.

(8) If the Transition Period is extended beyond 31st March 1970, the provisions of Paragraph (5) shall apply during the period of extension beyond 31st March 1970.

(9) During the Transition Period, Pakistan shall receive for unrestricted use the waters of the Eastern Rivers which are to be released by India in accordance with the provisions of Annexure H. After the end of the Transition Period, Pakistan shall have no claim or right to releases by India of any of the waters of the Eastern Rivers. In case there are any releases, Pakistan shall enjoy the unrestricted use of the waters so released after they have finally crossed into Pakistan: Provided that in the event that Pakistan makes any use of these waters, Pakistan shall not acquire any right whatsoever, by prescription or otherwise, to a continuance of such releases or such use.

Article III
PROVISIONS REGARDING WESTERN RIVERS

(1) Pakistan shall receive for unrestricted use all those waters of the Western Rivers which India is under obligation to let flow under the provisions of Paragraph (2).

---

[4]See p. 222 of this volume.

(2) India shall be under an obligation to let flow all the waters of the Western Rivers, and shall not permit any interference with these waters, except for the following uses, restricted (except as provided in item (*c*) (ii) of Paragraph 5 of Annexure C)[5] in the case of each of the rivers, The Indus, The Jhelum and The Chenab, to the drainage basin thereof:

(*a*) Domestic Use;
(*b*) Non-Consumptive Use;
(*c*) Agricultural Use, as set out in Annexure C; and
(*d*) Generation of hydro-electric power, as set out in Annexure D.[6]

(3) Pakistan shall have the unrestricted use of all waters originating from sources other than the Eastern Rivers which are delivered by Pakistan into The Ravi or The Sutlej, and India shall not make use of these waters. Each Party agrees to establish such discharge observation stations and make such observations as may be considered necessary by the Commission for the determination of the component of water available for the use of Pakistan on account of the aforesaid deliveries by Pakistan.

(4) Except as provided in Annexures D and E,[7] India shall not store any water of, or construct any storage works on, the Western Rivers.

Article IV

PROVISIONS REGARDING EASTERN RIVERS AND WESTERN RIVERS

(1) Pakistan shall use its best endeavours to construct and bring into operation, with due regard to expedition and economy, that part of a system of works which will accomplish the replacement, from the Western Rivers and other sources, of water supplies for irrigation canals in Pakistan which, on 15th August 1947, were dependent on water supplies from the Eastern Rivers.

(2) Each Party agrees that any Non-Consumptive Use made by it shall be so made as not to materially change, on account of such use, the flow in any channel to the prejudice of the uses on that channel by the other Party under the provisions of this Treaty. In executing any scheme of flood protection or flood control each Party will avoid, as far as practicable, any material damage to the other Party, and any such scheme carried out by India on the Western Rivers shall not involve any use of water or any storage in addition to that provided under Article III.

(3) Nothing in this Treaty shall be construed as having the effect of preventing either Party from undertaking schemes of drainage, river training, conservation of soil against erosion and dredging, or from removal of stones, gravel or sand from the beds of the Rivers: Provided that

[5]See p. 162 of this volume.
[6]See p. 170 of this volume.
[7]See pp. 170 and 186 of this volume.

(*a*) in executing any of the schemes mentioned above, each Party will avoid, as far as practicable, any material damage to the other Party;

(*b*) any such scheme carried out by India on the Western Rivers shall not involve any use of water or any storage in addition to that provided under Article III;

(*c*) except as provided in Paragraph (5) and Article VII (1) (*b*), India shall not take any action to increase the catchment area, beyond the area on the Effective Date, of any natural or artificial drainage or drain which crosses into Pakistan, and shall not undertake such construction or remodelling of any drainage or drain which so crosses or falls into a drainage or drain which so crosses as might cause material damage in Pakistan or entail the construction of a new drain or enlargement of an existing drainage or drain in Pakistan; and

(*d*) should Pakistan desire to increase the catchment area, beyond the area on the Effective Date, of any natural or artificial drainage or drain, which receives drainage waters from India, or, except in an emergency, to pour any waters into it in excess of the quantities received by it as on the Effective Date, Pakistan shall, before undertaking any work for these purposes, increase the capacity of that drainage or drain to the extent necessary so as not to impair its efficacy for dealing with drainage waters received from India as on the Effective Date.

(4) Pakistan shall maintain in good order its portions of the drainages mentioned below with capacities not less than the capacities as on the Effective Date:

(i) Hudiara Drain
(ii) Kasur Nala
(iii) Salimshah Drain
(iv) Fazilka Drain.

(5) If India finds it necessary that any of the drainages mentioned in Paragraph (4) should be deepened or widened in Pakistan, Pakistan agrees to undertake to do so as a work of public interest, provided India agrees to pay the cost of the deepening or widening.

(6) Each Party will use its best endeavours to maintain the natural channels of the Rivers, as on the Effective Date, in such condition as will avoid, as far as practicable, any obstruction to the flow in these channels likely to cause material damage to the other Party.

(7) Neither Party will take any action which would have the effect of diverting the Ravi Main between Madhopur and Lahore, or the Sutlej Main between Harike and Suleimanke, from its natural channel between high banks.

(8) The use of the natural channels of the Rivers for the discharge of flood or other excess waters shall be free and not subject to limitation by either Party, and neither Party shall have any claim against the other in respect of any damage caused by such use. Each Party agrees to communicate to the other Party, as far in

advance as practicable, any information it may have in regard to such extraordinary discharges of water from reservoirs and flood flows as may affect the other Party.

(9) Each Party declares its intention to operate its storage dams, barrages and irrigation canals in such manner, consistent with the normal operations of its hydraulic systems, as to avoid, as far as feasible, material damage to the other Party.

(10) Each Party declares its intention to prevent, as far as practicable, undue pollution of the waters of the Rivers which might affect adversely uses similar in nature to those to which the waters were put on the Effective Date, and agrees to take all reasonable measures to ensure that, before any sewage or industrial waste is allowed to flow into the Rivers, it will be treated, where necessary, in such manner as not materially to affect those uses: Provided that the criterion of reasonableness shall be the customary practice in similar situations on the Rivers.

(11) The Parties agree to adopt, as far as feasible, appropriate measures for the recovery, and restoration to owners, of timber and other property floated or floating down the Rivers, subject to appropriate charges being paid by the owners.

(12) The use of water for industrial purposes under Articles II (2), II (3) and III (2) shall not exceed:

(a) in the case of an industrial process known on the Effective Date, such quantum of use as was customary in that process on the Effective Date;

(b) in the case of an industrial process not known on the Effective Date:

  (i) such quantum of use as was customary on the Effective Date in similar or in any way comparable industrial processes; or

  (ii) if there was no industrial process on the Effective Date similar or in any way comparable to the new process, such quantum of use as would not have a substantially adverse effect on the other Party.

(13) Such part of any water withdrawn for Domestic Use under the provisions of Articles II (3) and III (2) as is subsequently applied to Agricultural Use shall be accounted for as part of the Agricultural Use specified in Annexure B and Annexure C respectively; each Party will use its best endeavours to return to the same river (directly or through one of its Tributaries) all water withdrawn therefrom for industrial purposes and not consumed either in the industrial processes for which it was withdrawn or in some other Domestic Use.

(14) In the event that either Party should develop a use of the waters of the Rivers which is not in accordance with the provisions of this Treaty, that Party shall not acquire by reason of such use any right, by prescription or otherwise, to a continuance of such use.

(15) Except as otherwise required by the express provisions of this Treaty, nothing in this Treaty shall be construed as affecting existing territorial rights over the waters of any of the Rivers or the beds or banks thereof, or as affecting existing property rights under municipal law over such waters or beds or banks.

Article V

FINANCIAL PROVISIONS

(1) In consideration of the fact that the purpose of part of the system of works referred to in Article IV (1) is the replacement, from the Western Rivers and other sources, of water supplies for irrigation canals in Pakistan which, on 15th August 1947, were dependent on water supplies from the Eastern Rivers, India agrees to make a fixed contribution of Pounds Sterling 62,060,000 towards the costs of these works. The amount in Pounds Sterling of this contribution shall remain unchanged irrespective of any alteration in the par value of any currency.

(2) The sum of Pounds Sterling 62,060,000 specified in Paragraph (1) shall be paid in ten equal annual instalments on the 1st of November of each year. The first of such annual instalments shall be paid on 1st November 1960, or if the Treaty has not entered into force by that date, then within one month after the Treaty enters into force.

(3) Each of the instalments specified in Paragraph (2) shall be paid to the Bank for the credit of the Indus Basin Development Fund to be established and administered by the Bank, and payment shall be made in Pounds Sterling, or in such other currency or currencies as may from time to time be agreed between India and the Bank.

(4) The payments provided for under the provisions of Paragraph (3) shall be made without deduction or set-off on account of any financial claims of India on Pakistan arising otherwise than under the provisions of this Treaty: Provided that this provision shall in no way absolve Pakistan from the necessity of paying in other ways debts to India which may be outstanding against Pakistan.

(5) If, at the request of Pakistan, the Transition Period is extended in accordance with the provisions of Article II (6) and of Part 8 of Annexure H, the Bank shall thereupon pay to India out of the Indus Basin Development Fund the appropriate amount specified in the Table below:

Table

Period of Aggregate Extension of Transition Period	Payment to India £ Stg.
One year	3,125,000
Two years	6,406,250
Three years	9,850,000

(6) The provisions of Article IV (1) and Article V (1) shall not be construed as conferring upon India any right to participate in the decisions as to the system of works which Pakistan constructs pursuant to Article IV (1) or as constituting an assumption of any responsibility by India or as an agreement by India in regard to such works.

(7) Except for such payments as are specifically provided for in this Treaty, neither Party shall be entitled to claim any payment for observance of the provisions of this Treaty or to make any charge for water received from it by the other Party.

Article VI
EXCHANGE OF DATA

(1) The following data with respect to the flow in, and utilisation of the waters of, the Rivers shall be exchanged regularly between the Parties:

(*a*) Daily (or as observed or estimated less frequently) gauge and discharge data relating to flow of the Rivers at all observation sites.
(*b*) Daily extractions for or releases from reservoirs.
(*c*) Daily withdrawals at the heads of all canals operated by government or by a government agency (hereinafter in this Article called canals), including link canals.
(*d*) Daily escapages from all canals, including link canals.
(*e*) Daily deliveries from link canals.

These data shall be transmitted monthly by each Party to the other as soon as the data for a calendar month have been collected and tabulated, but not later than three months after the end of the months to which they relate: Provided that such of the data specified above as are considered by either Party to be necessary for operational purposes shall be supplied daily or at less frequent intervals, as may be requested. Should one Party request the supply of any of these data by telegram, telephone, or wireless, it shall reimburse the other Party for the cost of transmission.

(2) If, in addition to the data specified in Paragraph (1) of this Article, either Party requests the supply of any data relating to the hydrology of the Rivers, or to canal or reservoir operation connected with the Rivers, or to any provision of this Treaty, such data shall be supplied by the other Party to the extent that these are available.

Article VII
FUTURE CO-OPERATION

(1) The two Parties recognize that they have a common interest in the optimum development of the Rivers, and, to that end, they declare their intention to co-operate, by mutual agreement, to the fullest possible extent. In particular:

(*a*) Each Party, to the extent it considers practicable and on agreement by the other Party to pay the costs to be incurred, will, at the request of the other Party, set up or install such hydrologic observation stations within the drainage basins of the Rivers, and set up or install such meteorological observation stations relating thereto and carry out such observations thereat, as may be requested, and will supply the data so obtained.

(*b*) Each Party, to the extent it considers practicable and on agreement by the other Party to pay the costs to be incurred, will, at the request of the other Party, carry out such new drainage works as may be required in connection with new drainage works of the other Party.

(*c*) At the request of either Party, the two Parties may, by mutual agreement, co-operate in undertaking engineering works on the Rivers.

The formal arrangements, in each case, shall be as agreed upon between the Parties.

(2) If either Party plans to construct any engineering work which would cause interference with the waters of any of the Rivers and which, in its opinion, would affect the other Party materially, it shall notify the other Party of its plans and shall supply such data relating to the work as may be available and as would enable the other Party to inform itself of the nature, magnitude and effect of the work. If a work would cause interference with the waters of any of the Rivers but would not, in the opinion of the Party planning it, affect the other Party materially, nevertheless the Party planning the work shall, on request, supply the other Party with such data regarding the nature, magnitude and effect, if any, of the work as may be available.

Article VIII

PERMANENT INDUS COMMISSION

(1) India and Pakistan shall each create a permanent post of Commissioner for Indus Waters, and shall appoint to this post, as often as a vacancy occurs, a person who should ordinarily be a high-ranking engineer competent in the field of hydrology and water-use. Unless either Government should decide to take up any particular question directly with the other Government, each Commissioner will be the representative of his Government for all matters arising out of this Treaty, and will serve as the regular channel of communication on all matters relating to the implementation of the Treaty, and, in particular, with respect to

(*a*) the furnishing or exchange of information or data provided for in the Treaty; and

(*b*) the giving of any notice or response to any notice provided for in the Treaty.

(2) The status of each Commissioner and his duties and responsibilities towards his Government will be determined by that Government.

(3) The two Commissioners shall together form the Permanent Indus Commission.

(4) The purpose and functions of the Commission shall be to establish and maintain co-operative arrangements for the implementation of this Treaty, to promote co-operation between the Parties in the development of the waters of the Rivers and, in particular,

(*a*) to study and report to the two Governments on any problem relating to the development of the waters of the Rivers which may be jointly referred to the

Commission by the two Governments: in the event that a reference is made by one Government alone, the Commissioner of the other Government shall obtain the authorization of his Government before he proceeds to act on the reference;

(b) to make every effort to settle promptly, in accordance with the provisions of Article IX (1), any question arising thereunder;

(c) to undertake, once in every five years, a general tour of inspection of the Rivers for ascertaining the facts connected with various developments and works on the Rivers;

(d) to undertake promptly, at the request of either Commissioner, a tour of inspection of such works or sites on the Rivers as may be considered necessary by him for ascertaining the facts connected with those works or sites; and

(e) to take, during the Transition Period, such steps as may be necessary for the implementation of the provisions of Annexure H.

(5) The Commission shall meet regularly at least once a year, alternately in India and Pakistan. This regular annual meeting shall be held in November or in such other month as may be agreed upon between the Commissioners. The Commission shall also meet when requested by either Commissioner.

(6) To enable the Commissioners to perform their functions in the Commission, each Government agrees to accord to the Commissioner of the other Government the same privileges and immunities as are accorded to representatives of member States to the principal and subsidiary organs of the United Nations under Sections 11, 12 and 13 of Article IV of the Convention on the Privileges and Immunities of the United Nations[8] (dated 13th February, 1946) during the periods specified in those Sections. It is understood and agreed that these privileges and immunities are accorded to the Commissioners not for the personal benefit of the individuals themselves but in order to safeguard the independent exercise of their functions in connection with the Commission; consequently, the Government appointing the Commissioner not only has the right but is under a duty to waive the immunity of its Commissioner in any case where, in the opinion of the appointing Government, the immunity would impede the course of justice and can be waived without prejudice to the purpose for which the immunity is accorded.

(7) For the purposes of the inspections specified in Paragraph (4) (c) and (d), each Commissioner may be accompanied by two advisers or assistants to whom appropriate facilities will be accorded.

(8) The Commission shall submit to the Government of India and to the Government of Pakistan, before the first of June of every year, a report on its work for the year ended on the preceding 31st of March, and may submit to the two Governments other reports at such times as it may think desirable.

(9) Each Government shall bear the expenses of its Commissioner and his ordinary staff. The cost of any special staff required in connection with the work mentioned in Article VII (1) shall be borne as provided therein.

(10) The Commission shall determine its own procedures.

---

[8]See footnote 1, p. 38 of this volume.

Article IX
Settlement of Differences and Disputes

(1) Any question which arises between the Parties concerning the interpretation or application of this Treaty or the existence of any fact which, if established, might constitute a breach of this Treaty shall first be examined by the Commission, which will endeavour to resolve the question by agreement.

(2) If the Commission does not reach agreement on any of the questions mentioned in Paragraph (1), then a difference will be deemed to have arisen, which shall be dealt with as follows:

(a) Any difference which, in the opinion of either Commissioner, falls within the provisions of Part 1 of Annexure F[9] shall, at the request of either Commissioner, be dealt with by a Neutral Expert in accordance with the provisions of Part 2 of Annexure F;

(b) If the difference does not come within the provisions of Paragraph (2) (a), or if a Neutral Expert, in accordance with the provisions of Paragraph 7 of Annexure F, has informed the Commission that, in his opinion, the difference, or a part thereof, should be treated as a dispute, then a dispute will be deemed to have arisen which shall be settled in accordance with the provisions of Paragraphs (3), (4) and (5):

Provided that, at the discretion of the Commission, any difference may either be dealt with by a Neutral Expert in accordance with the provisions of Part 2 of Annexure F or be deemed to be a dispute to be settled in accordance with the provisions of Paragraphs (3), (4) and (5), or may be settled in any other way agreed upon by the Commission.

(3) As soon as a dispute to be settled in accordance with this and the succeeding paragraphs of this Article has arisen, the Commission shall, at the request of either Commissioner, report the fact to the two Governments, as early as practicable, stating in its report the points on which the Commission is in agreement and the issues in dispute, the views of each Commissioner on these issues and his reasons therefor.

(4) Either Government may, following receipt of the report referred to in Paragraph (3), or if it comes to the conclusion that this report is being unduly delayed in the Commission, invite the other Government to resolve the dispute by agreement. In doing so it shall state the names of its negotiators and their readiness to meet with the negotiators to be appointed by the other Government at a time and place to be indicated by the other Government. To assist in these negotiations, the two Governments may agree to enlist the services of one or more mediators acceptable to them.

(5) A court of Arbitration shall be established to resolve the dispute in the manner provided by Annexure G[10]

(a) upon agreement between the Parties to do so; or

---

[9]See p. 202 of this volume.
[10]See p. 210 of this volume.

(*b*) at the request of either Party, if, after negotiations have begun pursuant to Paragraph (4), in its opinion the dispute is not likely to be resolved by negotiation or mediation; or

(*c*) at the request of either Party, if, after the expiry of one month following receipt by the other Government of the invitation referred to in Paragraph (4), that Party comes to the conclusion that the other Government is unduly delaying the negotiations.

(6) The provisions of Paragraphs (3), (4) and (5) shall not apply to any difference while it is being dealt with by a Neutral Expert.

Article X
EMERGENCY PROVISION

If, at any time prior to 31st March 1965, Pakistan should represent to the Bank that, because of the outbreak of large-scale international hostilities arising out of causes beyond the control of Pakistan, it is unable to obtain from abroad the materials and equipment necessary for the completion, by 31st March 1973, of that part of the system of works referred to in Article IV (1) which related to the replacement referred to therein, (hereinafter referred to as the "replacement element") and if, after consideration of this representation in consultation with India, the Bank is of the opinion that

(*a*) these hostilities are on a scale of which the consequence is that Pakistan is unable to obtain in time such materials and equipment as must be procured from abroad for the completion, by 31st March 1973, of the replacement element, and

(*b*) since the Effective Date, Pakistan has taken all reasonable steps to obtain the said materials and equipment and, with such resources of materials and equipment as have been available to Pakistan both from within Pakistan and from abroad, has carried forward the construction of the replacement element with due diligence and all reasonable expedition,

the Bank shall immediately notify each of the Parties accordingly. The Parties undertake, without prejudice to the provisions of Article XII (3) and (4), that on being so notified, they will forthwith consult together and enlist the good offices of the Bank in their consultation, with a view to reaching mutual agreement as to whether or not, in the light of all the circumstances then prevailing, any modifications of the provisions of this Treaty are appropriate and advisable and, if so, the nature and the extent of the modifications.

Article XI
GENERAL PROVISIONS

(1) It is expressly understood that

(*a*) this Treaty governs the rights and obligations of each Party in relation to the other with respect only to the use of the waters of the Rivers and matters incidental thereto; and (*b*) nothing contained in this Treaty, and nothing arising out of the execution thereof, shall be construed as constituting a recognition or waiver (whether tacit, by implication or otherwise) of any rights or claims whatsoever of either of the Parties other than those rights or claims which are expressly recognized or waived in this Treaty.

Each of the Parties agrees that it will not invoke this Treaty, anything contained therein, or anything arising out of the execution thereof, in support of any of its own rights or claims whatsoever or in disputing any of the rights or claims whatsoever of the other Party, other than those rights or claims which are expressly recognized or waived in this Treaty.

(2) Nothing in this Treaty shall be construed by the Parties as in any way establishing any general principle of law or any precedent.

(3) The rights and obligations of each Party under this Treaty shall remain unaffected by any provisions contained in, or by anything arising out of the execution of, any agreement establishing the Indus Basin Development Fund.

Article XII
FINAL PROVISIONS

(1) This Treaty consists of the Preamble, the Articles hereof and Annexures A to H hereto, and may be cited as "The Indus Waters Treaty 1960".

(2) This Treaty shall be ratified and the ratifications thereof shall be exchanged in New Delhi. It shall enter into force upon the exchange of ratifications, and will then take effect retrospectively from the first of April 1960.

(3) The provisions of this Treaty may from time to time be modified by a duly ratified treaty concluded for that purpose between the two Governments.

(4) The provisions of this Treaty, or the provisions of this Treaty as modified under the provisions of Paragraph (3), shall continue in force until terminated by a duly ratified treaty concluded for that purpose between the two Governments.

IN WITNESS WHEREOF the respective Plenipotentiaries have signed this Treaty and have hereunto affixed their seals.

DONE in triplicate in English at Karachi on this Nineteenth day of September 1960.

For the Government of India:
(*Signed*) Jawaharlal NEHRU

For the Government of Pakistan:
(*Signed*) Mohammad Ayub KHAN
Field Marshal, H.P., H.J.

For the International Bank for Reconstruction and Development,
for the purposes specified in Articles V and X and Annexures F, G and H:
(*Signed*) W. A. B. ILIFF

ANNEXURE A — EXCHANGE OF NOTES BETWEEN GOVERNMENT OF INDIA AND GOVERNMENT OF PAKISTAN

I. NOTE DATED 19TH SEPTEMBER 1960, FROM THE HIGH COMMISSIONER FOR INDIA IN PAKISTAN, KARACHI, TO THE MINISTER FOR FOREIGN AFFAIRS AND COMMONWEALTH RELATIONS, GOVERNMENT OF PAKISTAN

19th September, 1960

Excellency:

I have been instructed by my Government to communicate to you the following:

"The Government of India agrees that, on the ratification of the Indus Waters Treaty 1960,[11] the Inter-Dominion Agreement on the Canal Water Dispute signed at New Delhi on 4th May 1948[12] (of which a copy is annexed hereto) and the rights and obligations of either party thereto claimed under, or arising out of, that Agreement shall be without effect as from 1st April 1960."

"The position of the Government of India stated above and Your Excellency's Note of to-day's date stating the position of the Government of Pakistan on this question will form part of Annexure A to the Indus Waters Treaty 1960."

Accept, Excellency, the renewed assurance of my highest consideration.

ANNEX

A dispute has arisen between the East and West Punjab Governments regarding the supply by East Punjab of water to the Central Bari Doab and the Depalpur canals in West Punjab. The contention of the East Punjab Government is that under the Punjab Partition (Apportionment of Assets and Liabilities) Order, 1947, and the Arbitral Award the proprietary rights in the waters of the rivers in East Punjab vest wholly in the East Punjab Government and that the West Punjab Government cannot claim any share of these waters as a right. The West Punjab Government disputes this contention, its view being that the point has conclusively been decided in its favour by implication by the Arbitral Award and that in accordance with international law and equity, West Punjab has a right to the waters of the East Punjab rivers.

2. The East Punjab Government has revived the flow of water into these canals on certain conditions of which two are disputed by West Punjab. One, which arises out of the contention in paragraph 1, is the right to the levy of seigniorage charges for water and the other is the question of the capital cost of the Madhavpur[*] Head Works and carrier channels to be taken into account.

---

[11] See p. 126 of this volume.
[12] United Nations, *Treaty Series*, Vol. 54, p. 45; Vol. 85, p. 356, and Vol. 128, p. 300.
[*] sic "Madhopur"

3.   The East and West Punjab Governments are anxious that this question should be settled in a spirit of goodwill and friendship. Without prejudice to its legal rights in the matter the East Punjab Government has assured the West Punjab Government that it has no intention suddenly to withhold water from West Punjab without giving it time to tap alternative sources. The West Punjab Government on its part recognise the natural anxiety of the East Punjab Government to discharge the obligation to develop areas where water is scarce and which were under-developed in relation to parts of West Punjab.

4.   Apart, therefore, from the question of law involved, the Governments are anxious to approach the problem in a practical spirit on the basis of the East Punjab Government progressively diminishing its supply to these canals in order to give reasonable time to enable the West Punjab Government to tap alternative sources.

5.   The West Punjab Government has agreed to deposit immediately in the Reserve Bank such *ad hoc* sum as may be specified by the Prime Minister of India. Out of this sum, that Government agrees to the immediate transfer to East Punjab Government of sums over which there is no dispute.

6.   After an examination by each party of the legal issues, of the method of estimating the cost of water to be supplied by the East Punjab Government and of the technical survey of water resources and the means of using them for supply to these canals, the two Governments agree that further meetings between their representatives should take place.

7.   The Dominion Governments of India and Pakistan accept the above terms and express the hope that a friendly solution will be reached.

Jawaharlal NEHRU	Ghulam MOHD
N. V. GADGIL	Shaukat Hyat KHAN
Swaran SINGH	Mumtaz DAULTANA

New Delhi, May 4, 1948

II.   NOTE DATED 19TH SEPTEMBER 1960, FROM THE MINISTER FOR FOREIGN AFFAIRS AND COMMONWEALTH RELATIONS, GOVERNMENT OF PAKISTAN, TO THE HIGH COMMISSIONER FOR INDIA IN PAKISTAN, KARACHI

19th September, 1960

Excellency:

I have been instructed by my Government to communicate to you the following:

"The Government of Pakistan agrees that, on the ratification of the Indus Waters Treaty 1960, the document on the Canal Water Dispute signed at New Delhi on 4th May 1948 (of which a copy is annexed hereto) and the rights and obligations of either party thereto claimed under, or arising out of, that document shall be without effect as from 1st April 1960."

"The position of the Government of Pakistan stated above and Your Excellency's Note of to-day's date stating the position of the Government of India on this question will form part of Annexure A to the Indus Waters Treaty 1960."

Accept, Excellency, the renewed assurance of my highest consideration.

ANNEX

[For the text of this annex, see p. 158 of this volume]

ANNEXURE B — AGRICULTURAL USE BY PAKISTAN FROM CERTAIN TRIBUTARIES OF THE RAVI

(Article II (3))

1.   The provisions of this Annexure shall apply with respect to the Agricultural Use by Pakistan from certain Tributaries of The Ravi under the provisions of Article II (3) and, subject to the provisions of this Annexure, such use shall be unrestricted.

2.   Pakistan may withdraw from the Basantar Tributary of the Ravi such waters as may be available and necessary for the irrigation of not more than 100 acres annually.

3.   In addition to the area specified in Paragraph 2, Pakistan may also withdraw such waters from each of the following Tributaries of The Ravi as may be available and as may be necessary for the irrigation of that part of the following areas cultivated on *sailab* as on the Effective Date which cannot be so cultivated after that date: Provided that the total area whether irrigated or cultivated on *sailab* shall not exceed the limits specified below, except during a year of exceptionally heavy floods when *sailab* may extend to areas which were not cultivated on *sailab* as on the Effective Date and when such areas may be cultivated in addition to the limits specified:

Name of Tributary	Maximum Annual Cultivation (acres)
Basantar	14,000
Bein	26,600
Tarnah	1,800
Ujh	3,000

4.   The provisions of Paragraphs 2 and 3 shall not be construed as giving Pakistan any claim or right to any releases by India in the Tributaries mentioned in these paragraphs.

5.   Not later than 31st March 1961, Pakistan shall furnish to India a statement by Districts and Tehsils showing (i) the area irrigated and (ii) the area cultivated on

sailab, as on the Effective Date, from the waters of each of the Tributaries specified in Paragraphs 2 and 3.

6.   As soon as the statistics for each crop year (commencing with the beginning of *kharif* and ending with the end of the following *rabi*) have been compiled at the District Headquarters, but not later than the 30th November following the end of that crop year, Pakistan shall furnish to India a statement arranged by Tributaries and showing for each of the Districts and Tehsils irrigated or cultivated on *sailab* from the Tributaries mentioned in Paragraphs 2 and 3:

(i) the area irrigated, and

(ii) the area cultivated on *sailab*.

ANNEXURE C — AGRICULTURAL USE BY INDIA FROM THE WESTERN RIVERS

(*Article III(2)(c)*)

1.   The provisions of this Annexure shall apply with respect to the Agricultural Use by India from the Western Rivers under the provisions of Article III (2) (*c*) and, subject to the provisions of this Annexure, such use shall be unrestricted.

2.   As used in this Annexure, the term "Irrigated Cropped Area" means the total area under irrigated crops in a year, the same area being counted twice if it bears different crops in *kharif* and *rabi*. The term shall be deemed to exclude small blocks of *ghair mumkim* lands in an irrigated field, lands on which cultivation is dependent on rain or snow and to which no irrigation water is applied, areas naturally inundated by river flow and cultivated on *sailab* thereafter, any area under floating gardens or *demb* lands in and along any lakes, and any area under water-plants growing within the water-spread of any lake or in standing water in a natural depression.

3.   India may withdraw from the Chenab Main such waters as India may need for Agricultural Use on the following canals limited to the maximum withdrawals noted against each:

Name of Canal	Maximum Withdrawals for Agricultural Use
(*a*) Ranbir Canal	1,000 cusecs from 15th April to 14th October, and 350 cusecs from 15th October to 14th April.
(*b*) Pratap Canal	400 cusecs from 15th April to 14th October, and 100 cusecs from 15th October to 14th April.

Provided that:

(i) The maximum withdrawals shown above shall be exclusive of any withdrawals which may be made through these canals for purposes of silt extraction on condition that the waters withdrawn for silt extraction are returned to The Chenab.

(ii) India may make additional withdrawals through the Ranbir Canal up to 250 cusecs for hydro-electric generation on condition that the waters so withdrawn are returned to The Chenab.

(iii) If India should construct a barrage across the Chenab Main below the head regulators of these two canals, the withdrawals to be then made, limited to the amounts specified in (*a*) and (*b*) above, during each 10-day period or subperiod thereof, shall be as determined by the Commission in accordance with sound irrigation practice and, in the absence of agreement between the Commissioners, by a Neutral Expert in accordance with the provisions of Annexure F.

4. Apart from the irrigation from the Ranbir and Pratap Canals under the provisions of Paragraph 3, India may continue to irrigate from the Western Rivers those areas which were so irrigated as on the Effective Date.

5. In addition to such withdrawals as may be made in accordance with the provisions of Paragraphs 3 and 4, India may, subject to the provisions of Paragraphs 6, 7, 8 and 9, make further withdrawals from the Western Rivers to the extent India may consider necessary to meet the irrigation needs of the areas specified below:

Particulars	*Maximum Irrigated Cropped Area (over and above the cropped area irrigated under the provisions of Paragraphs 3 and 4) (acres)*
(*a*) From The Indus, in its drainage basin	70,000
(*b*) From The Jhelum, in its drainage basin	400,000
(*c*) From The Chenab,	
(i) in its drainage basin	225,000 of which not more than 100,000 acres will be in the Jammu District.
(ii) outside its drainage basin in the area west of the Deg Nadi (also called Devak River), the aggregate capacity of irrigating channels leading out of the drainage basin of the Chenab to this area not to exceed 120 cusecs	6,000

Provided that

(i) in addition to the maximum Irrigated Cropped Area specified above, India may irrigate road-side trees from any source whatever;

(ii) the maximum Irrigated Cropped Area shown against items (*a*), (*b*) and (*c*) (i) above shall be deemed to include cropped areas, if any, irrigated from an open well, a tube-well, a spring, a lake (other than a Connecting lake) or a tank, in excess of the areas so irrigated as on the Effective Date; and

(iii) the aggregate of the areas specified against items (*a*), (*b*) and (*c*) (i) above may be redistributed among the three drainage basins in such manner as may be agreed upon between the Commissioners.

6. (*a*) Within the limits of the maximum Irrigated Cropped Areas specified against items (*b*) and (*c*) (i) in Paragraph 5, there shall be no restriction on the development of such of these areas as may be irrigated from an open well, a tube-well, a spring, a lake (other than a Connecting Lake) or a tank.

(*b*) Within the limits of the maximum Irrigated Cropped Areas specified against items (*b*) and (*c*) in Paragraph 5, there shall be no restriction on the development of such of these areas as may be irrigated from General Storage (as defined in Annexure E);[12] the areas irrigated from General Storage may, however, receive irrigation from river flow also, but, unless the Commissioners otherwise agree, only in the following periods:–

(i) from The Jhelum: 21st June to 20th August
(ii) from The Chenab: 21st June to 31st August:

Provided that withdrawals for such irrigation, whether from General Storage or from river flow, are controlled by Government.

7. Within the limits of the maximum Irrigated Cropped Areas specified against items (*b*) and (*c*) in Paragraph 5, the development of these areas by withdrawals from river flow (as distinct from withdrawals from General Storage *cum* river flow in accordance with Paragraph 6 (*b*) shall be regulated as follows:

(*a*) Until India can release water from Conservation Storage (as defined in Annexure E) in accordance with sub-paragraphs (*b*) and (*c*) below, the new area developed shall not exceed the following:
   (i) from The Jhelum: 150,000 acres
   (ii) from The Chenab: 25,000 acres during the Transition Period and 50,000 acres after the end of the Transition Period.

(*b*) In addition to the areas specified in (*a*) above, there may be developed from The Jhelum or The Chenab an aggregate area of 150,000 acres if there is released annually from Conservation Storage, in accordance with Paragraph 8, a volume of 0.2 MAF into The Jhelum and a volume of 0.1 MAF into The Chenab; provided that India shall have the option to store on and release into The Chenab the whole or a part of the volume of 0.2 MAF specified above for release into The Jhelum.

(*c*) Any additional areas over and above those specified in (*a*) and (*b*) above may be developed if there is released annually from Conservation Storage a volume of 0.2 MAF into The Jhelum or The Chenab, in accordance with Paragraph 8, in addition to the releases specified in (*b*) above.

8. The releases from Conservation Storage, as specified in Paragraphs 7 (*b*) and 7 (*c*), shall be made in accordance with a schedule to be determined by the Commission which shall keep in view, first, the effect, if any, on Agricultural Use by Pakistan consequent on the reduction in supplies available to Pakistan as a result

---

[12]See p. 186 of this volume.

of the withdrawals made by India under the provisions of Paragraph 7 and, then, the requirements, if any, of hydroelectric power to be developed by India from these releases. In the absence of agreement between the Commissioners, the matter may be referred under the provisions of Article IX (2) (*a*) for decision to a Neutral Expert.

9. On those Tributaries of The Jhelum on which there is any Agricultural Use or hydro-electric use by Pakistan, any new Agricultural Use by India shall be so made as not to affect adversely the then existing Agricultural Use or hydro-electric use by Pakistan on those Tributaries.

10. Not later than 31st March 1961, India shall furnish to Pakistan a statement showing, for each of the Districts and Tehsils irrigated from the Western Rivers, the Irrigated Cropped Area as on the Effective Date (excluding only the area irrigated under the provisions of Paragraph 3), arranged in accordance with items (*a*), (*b*) and (*c*)(i) of Paragraph 5: Provided that in the case of areas in the Punjab, the date may be extended to 30th September 1961.

11. (*a*) As soon as the statistics for each crop year (commencing with the beginning of *kharif* and ending with the end of the following *rabi*) have been compiled at the District Headquarters, but not later than the 30th November following the end of that crop year, India shall furnish to Pakistan a statement showing for each of the Districts and *Tehsils* irrigated from the Western Rivers, the total Irrigated Cropped Areas (excluding the area irrigated under the provisions of Paragraph 3) arranged in accordance with items (*a*), (*b*), (*c*) (i) and (*c*) (ii) of Paragraph 5: Provided that, in the case of areas in the Punjab, the 30th November date specified above may be extended to the following 30th June in the event of failure of communications.

(*b*) If the limits specified in Paragraph 7 (*a*) or 7 (*b*) are exceeded for any crop year, the statement shall also show the figures for Irrigated Cropped Areas falling under Paragraph 6 (*a*) and 6 (*b*) respectively, unless appropriate releases from Conservation Storage under the provisions of Paragraph 8 have already begun to be made.

ANNEXURE D — GENERATION OF HYDRO-ELECTRIC POWER BY INDIA ON THE WESTERN RIVERS
(Article III (2)(d)*))*

1.   The provisions of this Annexure shall apply with respect to the use by India of the waters of the Western Rivers for the generation of hydro-electric power under the provisions of Article III (2)(*d*) and, subject to the provisions of this Annexure, such use shall be unrestricted: Provided that the design, construction and operation of new hydroelectric plants which are incorporated in a Storage Work (as defined in Annexure E) shall be governed by the relevant provisions of Annexure E.[13]

---

[13]See p. 186 of this volume.

PART 1 — DEFINITIONS

2.   As used in this Annexure:

(a) "Dead Storage" means that portion of the storage which is not used for operational purposes and "Dead Storage Level" means the level corresponding to Dead Storage.
(b) "Live Storage" means all storage above Dead Storage.
(c) "Pondage" means Live Storage of only sufficient magnitude to meet fluctuations in the discharge of the turbines arising from variations in the daily and the weekly loads of the plant.
(d) "Full Pondage Level" means the level corresponding to the maximum Pondage provided in the design in accordance with Paragraph 8 (c).
(e) "Surcharge Storage" means uncontrollable storage occupying space above the Full Pondage Level.
(f) "Operating Pool" means the storage capacity between Dead Storage level and Full Pondage Level.
(g) "Run-of-River Plant" means a hydro-electric plant that develops power without Live Storage as an integral part of the plant, except for Pondage and Surcharge Storage.
(h) "Regulating Basin" means the basin whose only purpose is to even out fluctuations in the discharge from the turbines arising from variations in the daily and the weekly loads of the plant.
(i) "Firm Power" means the hydro-electric power corresponding to the minimum mean discharge at the site of a plant, the minimum mean discharge being calculated as follows:
   The average discharge for each 10-day period (1st to 10th, 11th to 20th and 21st to the end of the month) will be worked out for each year for which discharge data, whether observed or estimated, are proposed to be studied for purposes of design. The mean of the yearly values for each 10-day period will then be worked out. The lowest of the mean values thus obtained will be taken as the minimum mean discharge. The studies will be based on data for as long a period as available but may be limited to the latest 5 years in the case of Small Plants (as defined in Paragraph 18) and to the latest 25 years in the case of other Plants (as defined in Paragraph 8).
(j) "Secondary Power" means the power, other than Firm Power, available only during certain periods of the year.

PART 2 — HYDRO-ELECTRIC PLANTS IN OPERATION, OR UNDER
CONSTRUCTION, AS ON THE EFFECTIVE DATE

3.   There shall be no restriction on the operation of the following hydro-electric plants which were in operation as on the Effective Date:

Name of Plant	Capacity (exclusive of standby units) (kilowatts)
(i) Pahalgam	186
(ii) Bandipura	30
(iii) Dachhigam	40
(iv) Ranbir Canal	1,200
(v) Udhampur	640
(vi) Poonch	160

4. There shall be no restriction on the completion by India, in accordance with the design adopted prior to the Effective Date, or on the operation by India, of the following hydro-electric plants which were actually under construction on the Effective Date, whether or not the plant was on that date in partial operation:

Name of Plant	Designed capacity (exclusive of standby units) (kilowatts)
(i) Mahora	12,000
(ii) Ganderbal	15,000
(iii) Kupwara	150
(iv) Bhadarwah	600
(v) Kishtwar	350
(vi) Rajouri	650
(vii) Chinani	14,000
(viii) Nichalani Banihal	600

5. As soon as India finds it possible to do so, but not later than 31st March 1961, India shall communicate to Pakistan the Information specified in Appendix I[14] to this Annexure for each of the plants specified in Paragraphs 3 and 4. If any such information is not available or is not pertinent to the design of the plant or to the conditions at the site, it will be so stated.

6. (a) If any alteration proposed in the design of any of the plants specified in Paragraphs 3 and 4 would result in a material change in the information furnished to Pakistan under the provisions of Paragraph 5, India shall, at least 4 months in advance of making the alteration, communicate particulars of the change to Pakistan in writing and the provisions of Paragraph 7 shall then apply.

(b) In the event of an emergency arising which requires repairs to be undertaken to protect the integrity of any of the plants specified in Paragraphs 3 and 4, India may undertake immediately the necessary repairs or alterations and, if these repairs

---

[14]See p. 182 of this volume.

or alterations result in a change in the information furnished to Pakistan under the provisions of Paragraph 5, India shall as soon as possible communicate particulars of the change to Pakistan in writing. The provisions of Paragraph 7 shall then apply.

7. Within three months of the receipt of the particulars specified in Paragraph 6, Pakistan shall communicate to India in writing any objection it may have with regard to the proposed change on the ground that the change involves a material departure from the criteria set out in Paragraph 8 or 18 of this Annexure or Paragraph 11 of Annexure E as the case may be. If no objection is received by India from Pakistan within the specified period of three months, then Pakistan shall be deemed to have no objection. If a question arises as to whether or not the change involves a material departure from such of the criteria mentioned above as may be applicable, then either Party may proceed to have the question resolved in accordance with the provisions of Article IX(1) and (2).

PART 3 — NEW RUN-OF-RIVER PLANTS

8. Except as provided in Paragraph 18, the design of any new Run-of-River Plant (hereinafter in this Part referred to as a Plant) shall conform to the following criteria:

(a) The works themselves shall not be capable of raising artificially the water level in the Operating Pool above the Full Pondage Level specified in the design.

(b) The design of the works shall take due account of the requirements of Surcharge Storage and of Secondary Power.

(c) The maximum Pondage in the Operating Pool shall not exceed twice the Pondage required for Firm Power.

(d) There shall be no outlets below the Dead Storage Level, unless necessary for sediment control or any other technical purpose; any such outlet shall be of the minimum size, and located at the highest level, consistent with sound and economical design and with satisfactory operation of the works.

(e) If the conditions at the site of a Plant make a gated spillway necessary, the bottom level of the gates in normal closed position shall be located at the highest level consistent with sound and economical design and satisfactory construction and operation of the works.

(f) The intakes for the turbines shall be located at the highest level consistent with satisfactory and economical construction and operation of the Plant as a Run-of-River Plant and with customary and accepted practice of design for the designated range of the Plant's operation.

(g) If any Plant is constructed on the Chenab Main at a site below Kotru (Longitude 74°–59′ East and Latitude 33°–09′ North), a Regulating Basin shall be incorporated.

9. To enable Pakistan to satisfy itself that the design of a Plant conforms to the criteria mentioned in Paragraph 8, India shall, at least six months in advance of the beginning of construction of river works connected with the Plant, communicate

to Pakistan, in writing, the information specified in Appendix II[15] to this Annexure. If any such information is not available or is not pertinent to the design of the Plant or to the conditions at the site, it will be so stated.

10. Within three months of the receipt by Pakistan of the information specified in Paragraph 9, Pakistan shall communicate to India, in writing, any objection that it may have with regard to the proposed design on the ground that it does not conform to the criteria mentioned in Paragraph 8. If no objection is received by India from Pakistan within the specified period of three months, then Pakistan shall be deemed to have no objection.

11. If a question arises as to whether or not the design of a Plant conforms to the criteria set out in Paragraph 8, then either Party may proceed to have the question resolved in accordance with the provisions of Article IX(1) and (2).

12. (a) If any alteration proposed in the design of a Plant before it comes into operation would result in a material change in the information furnished to Pakistan under the provisions of Paragraph 9, India shall immediately communicate particulars of the change to Pakistan in writing and the provisions of Paragraphs 10 and 11 shall then apply, but the period of three months specified in Paragraph 10 shall be reduced to two months.

(b) If any alteration proposed in the design of a Plant after it comes into operation would result in a material change in the information furnished to Pakistan under the provisions of Paragraph 9, India shall, at least four months in advance of making the alteration, communicate particulars of the change to Pakistan in writing and the provisions of Paragraphs 10 and 11 shall then apply, but the period of three months specified in Paragraph 10 shall be reduced to two months.

13. In the event of an emergency arising which requires repairs to be undertaken to protect the integrity of a Plant, India may undertake immediately the necessary repairs or alterations; if these repairs or alterations result in a change in the information furnished to Pakistan under the provisions of Paragraph 9, India shall, as soon as possible, communicate particulars of the change to Pakistan in writing to enable Pakistan to satisfy itself that after such change the design of the Plant conforms to the criteria specified in Paragraph 8. The provisions of Paragraphs 10 and 11 shall then apply.

14. The filling of Dead Storage shall be carried out in accordance with the provisions of Paragraph 18 or 19 of Annexure E.

15. Subject to the provisions of Paragraph 17, the works connected with a Plant shall be so operated that (a) the volume of water received in the river upstream of the Plant, during any period of seven consecutive days, shall be delivered into the river below the Plant during the same seven-day period, and (b) in any one period of 24 hours within that seven-day period, the volume delivered into the river below the Plant shall be not less than 30%, and not more than 130%, of the volume

---

[15]See p. 182 of this volume.

received in the river above the Plant during the same 24-hour period: Provided however that:

(i) where a Plant is located at a site on the Chenab Main below Ramban, the volume of water received in the river upstream of the Plant in any one period of 24 hours shall be delivered into the river below the Plant within the same period of 24 hours;

(ii) where a Plant is located at a site on the Chenab Main above Ramban, the volume of water delivered into the river below the Plant in any one period of 24 hours shall not be less than 50% and not more than 130%, of the volume received above the Plant during the same 24-hour period; and

iii) where a Plant is located on a Tributary of The Jhelum on which Pakistan has any Agricultural use or hydro-electric use, the water released below the Plant may be delivered, if necessary, into another Tributary but only to the extent that the then existing Agricultural Use or hydro-electric use by Pakistan on the former Tributary would not be adversely affected.

16.   For the purpose of Paragraph 15, the period of 24 hours shall commence at 8 a.m. daily and the period of 7 consecutive days shall commence at 8 a.m. on every Saturday. The time shall be Indian Standard Time.

17.   The provisions of Paragraph 15 shall not apply during the period when the Dead Storage at a Plant is being filled in accordance with the provisions of Paragraph 14. In applying the provisions of Paragraph 15:

(*a*) a tolerance of 10% in volume shall be permissible; and
(*b*) Surcharge Storage shall be ignored.

18.   The provisions of Paragraphs 8, 9, 10, 11, 12 and 13 shall not apply to a new Run-of-River Plant which is located on a Tributary and which conforms to the following criteria (hereinafter referred to as a Small Plant):

(*a*) the aggregate designed maximum discharge through the turbines does not exceed 300 cusecs;
(*b*) no storage is involved in connection with the Small Plant, except the Pondage and the storage incidental to the diversion structure; and
(*c*) the crest of the diversion structure across the Tributary, or the top level of the gates, if any, shall not be higher than 20 feet above the mean bed of the Tributary at the site of the structure.

19.   The information specified in Appendix III[16] to this Annexure shall be communicated to Pakistan by India at least two months in advance of the beginning of construction of the river works connected with a Small Plant. If any such information is not available or is not pertinent to the design of the Small Plant or to the conditions at the site, it will be so stated.

---

[16]See p. 184 of this volume.

20. Within two months of the receipt by Pakistan of the information specified in Appendix III, Pakistan shall communicate to India, in writing, any objection that it may have with regard to the proposed design on the ground that it does not conform to the criteria mentioned in Paragraph 18. If no objection is received by India from Pakistan within the specified period of two months, then Pakistan shall be deemed to have no objection.

21. If a question arises as to whether or not the design of a Small Plant conforms to the criteria set out in Paragraph 18, then either Party may proceed to have the question resolved in accordance with the provisions of Article IX (1) and (2).

22. If any alteration in the design of a Small Plant, whether during the construction period or subsequently, results in a change in the information furnished to Pakistan under the provisions of Paragraph 19, then India shall immediately communicate the change in writing to Pakistan.

23. If, with any alteration proposed in the design of a Small Plant, the design would cease to comply with the criteria set out in Paragraph 18, then the provisions of Paragraphs 18 to 22 inclusive shall no longer apply and, in lieu thereof, the provisions of Paragraphs 8 to 13 inclusive shall apply.

PART 4 — NEW PLANTS ON IRRIGATION CHANNELS

24. Notwithstanding the foregoing provisions of this Annexure, there shall be no restriction on the construction and operation by India of new hydro-electric plants on any irrigation channel taking off the Western Rivers, provided that

(*a*) the works incorporate no storage other than Pondage and the Dead Storage incidental to the diversion structure, and
(*b*) no additional supplies are run in the irrigation channel for the purpose of generating hydro-electric power.

PART 5 — GENERAL

25. If the change referred to in Paragraphs 6 (*a*) and 12 is not material, India shall communicate particulars of the change to Pakistan, in writing, as soon as the alteration has been made or the repairs have been undertaken. The provisions of Paragraph 7 or Paragraph 23, as the case may be, shall then apply.

APPENDIX I TO ANNEXURE D
(*Paragraph 5*)

1. *Location of Plant*
   General map showing the location of the site; if on a Tributary, its situation with respect to the main river.

2. *Hydraulic Data*

    (*a*) Stage-area and stage-capacity curves of the reservoir, forebay and Regulating Basin.

    (*b*) Full Pondage Level, Dead Storage Level and Operating Pool.

    (*c*) Dead Storage capacity.

3. *Particulars of Design*

    (*a*) Type of spillway, length and crest level; size, number and top level of spillway gates.

    (*b*) Outlet works: function, type, size, number, maximum designed capacity and sill levels.

    (*c*) Aggregate designed maximum discharge through the turbines.

    (*d*) Maximum aggregate capacity of power units (exclusive of standby units) for Firm Power and Secondary Power.

    (*e*) Regulating Basin and its outlet works: dimensions and maximum discharge capacity.

4. *General*

    Probable date of completion of river works, and dates on which various stages of the plant would come into operation.

APPENDIX II TO ANNEXURE D

(*Paragraph 9*)

1.   *Location of Plant*

    General map showing the location of the site; if on a Tributary, its situation with respect to the main river.

2. *Hydrologic Data*

    (*a*) General map (Scale: 1/4 inch or more = 1 mile) showing the discharge observation site or sites or rainfall gauge stations on whose data the design is based. In case of a Plant on a Tributary, this map should also show the catchment area of the Tributary above the site.

    (*b*) Observed or estimated daily river discharge data on which the design is based (observed data will be given for as long a period as available; estimated data will be given for as long a period as possible; in both cases data may be limited to the latest 25 years).

    (*c*) Flood data, observed or estimated (with details of estimation).

    (*d*) Gauge-discharge curve or curves for site or sites mentioned in (*a*) above.

3. *Hydraulic Data*

    (*a*) Stage-area and stage-capacity curves of the reservoir, forebay and Regulating Basin, with contoured survey maps on which based.

    (*b*) Full Pondage Level, Dead Storage Level and Operating Pool together with the calculations for the Operating Pool.

(c) Dead Storage capacity.

(d) Estimated evaporation losses in the reservoir, Regulating Basin, head-race, forebay and tail-race.

(e) Maximum designed flood discharge, discharge-capacity curve for spillway and maximum designed flood level.

(f) Designated range of operation.

4. *Particulars of Design*

(a) Dimensioned plan showing dam, spillway, intake and outlet works, diversion works, head-race and forebay, powerhouse, tail-race and Regulating Basin.

(b) Type of dam, length and height above mean bed of river.

(c) Cross-section of the river at the site; mean bed level.

(d) Type of spillway, length and crest level; size, number and top level of spillway gates.

(e) Type of intake, maximum designed capacity, number and size, sill levels; diversion works.

(f) Head-race and tail-race: length, size, maximum designed capacity.

(g) Outlet works: function, type, size, number, maximum designed capacity and sill levels.

(h) Discharge proposed to be passed through the Plant, initially and ultimately, and expected variations in the discharge on account of the daily and the weekly load fluctuations.

(i) Maximum aggregate capacity of power units (exclusive of standby units) for Firm Power and Secondary Power.

(j) Regulating Basin and its outlet works: type, number, size, sill levels and designed maximum discharge capacity.

5. *General*

(a) Estimated effect of proposed development on the flow pattern below the last plant downstream (with details of estimation),

(b) Probable date of completion of river works, and dates on which various stages of the Plant would come into operation.

APPENDIX III TO ANNEXURE D
(*Paragraph 19*)

1. *Location of Small Plant*

General map showing the location of the site on the Tributary and its situation with respect to the main river.

2. *Hydrologic Data*

(a) Observed or estimated daily Tributary discharge (observed data will be given for as long a period as available; estimated data will be given for as long a period as possible; in both cases, data may be limited to the latest five years).

(b) Flood data, observed or estimated (with details of estimation).

(c) Gauge-discharge curve relating to discharge site.

3. *Hydraulic Data*

(a) Stage-area and stage-capacity curves of the forebay with survey map on which based.

(b) Full Pondage Level, Dead Storage Level and Operating Pool together with the calculations for the Operating Pool.

4. *Particulars of Design*

(a) Dimensioned plan showing diversion works, outlet works, head-race and fore-bay, powerhouse and tail-race.

(b) Type of diversion works, length and height of crest or top level of gates above the mean bed of the Tributary at the site.

(c) Cross-section of the Tributary at the site; mean bed level.

(d) Head-race and tail-race: length, size and designed maximum capacity.

(e) Aggregate designed maximum discharge through the turbines.

(f) Spillway, if any: type, length and crest level; size, number and top level of gates.

(g) Maximum aggregate capacity of power units (exclusive of standby units) for Firm Power and Secondary Power.

ANNEXURE E — STORAGE OF WATERS BY INDIA ON THE WESTERN RIVERS

(Article III (4))

1.   The provisions of this Annexure shall apply with respect to the storage of water on the Western Rivers, and to the construction and operation of Storage Works thereon, by India under the provisions of Article III (4).

2.   As used in this Annexure:

(a) "Storage Work" means a work constructed for the purpose of impounding the waters of a stream; but excludes

   (i) a Small Tank,

   (ii) the works specified in Paragraphs 3 and 4 of Annexure D,[17] and

   (iii) a new work constructed in accordance with the provisions of Annexure D.

(b) "Reservoir Capacity" means the gross volume of water which can be stored in the reservoir.

(c) "Dead Storage Capacity" means that portion of the Reservoir Capacity which is not used for operational purposes, and "Dead Storage" means the corresponding volume of water.

---

[17]See p. 170 of this volume.

(*d*) "Live Storage Capacity" means the Reservoir Capacity excluding Dead Storage Capacity, and "Live Storage" means the corresponding volume of water.

(*e*) "Flood Storage Capacity" means that portion of the Reservoir Capacity which is reserved for the temporary storage of flood waters in order to regulate downstream flows, and "Flood Storage" means the corresponding volume of water.

(*f*) "Surcharge Storage Capacity" means the Reservoir Capacity between the crest of an uncontrolled spillway or the top of the crest gates in normal closed position and the maximum water elevation above this level for which the dam is designed, and "Surcharge Storage" means the corresponding volume of water.

(*g*) "Conservation Storage Capacity" means the Reservoir Capacity excluding Flood Storage Capacity, Dead Storage Capacity and Surcharge Storage Capacity, and "Conservation Storage" means the corresponding volume of water.

(*h*) "Power Storage Capacity" means that portion of the Conservation Storage Capacity which is designated to be used for generating electric energy, and "Power Storage" means the corresponding volume of water.

(*i*) "General Storage Capacity" means the Conservation Storage Capacity excluding Power Storage Capacity, and "General Storage" means the corresponding volume of water.

(*j*) "Dead Storage Level" means the level of water in a reservoir corresponding to Dead Storage Capacity, below which level the reservoir does not operate.

(*k*) "Full Reservoir Level" means the level of water in a reservoir corresponding to Conservation Storage Capacity.

(*l*) "Multi-purpose Reservoir" means a reservoir capable of and intended for use for more than one purpose.

(*m*) "Single-purpose Reservoir" means a reservoir capable of and intended for use for only one purpose.

(*n*) "Small Tank" means a tank having a Live Storage of less than 700 acre-feet and fed only from a non-perennial small stream: Provided that the Dead Storage does not exceed 50 acre-feet.

3. There shall be no restriction on the operation as heretofore by India of those Storage Works which were in operation as on the Effective Date or on the construction and operation of Small Tanks.

4. As soon as India finds it possible to do so, but not later than 31st March 1961, India shall communicate to Pakistan in writing the information specified in the Appendix[18] to this Annexure for such Storage Works as were in operation as on the Effective Date. If any such information is not available or is not pertinent to the design of the Storage Work or to the conditions at the site, it will be so stated.

5. (*a*) If any alteration proposed in the design of any of the Storage Works referred to in Paragraph 3 would result in a material change in the information furnished to Pakistan under the provisions of Paragraph 4, India shall, at least 4 months in advance of making the alteration, communicate particulars of the change to Pakistan in writing and the provisions of Paragraph 6 shall then apply.

---

[18]See p. 198 of this volume.

(b) In the event of an emergency arising which requires repairs to be undertaken to p otect the integrity of any of the Storage Works referred to in Paragraph 3, India may undertake immediately the necessary repairs or alterations and, if these repairs or alterations result in a change in the information furnished to Pakistan under the provisions of Paragraph 4, India shall as soon as possible communicate particulars of the change to Pakistan in writing. The provisions of Paragraph 6 shall then apply.

6.   Within three months of the receipt of the particulars specified in Paragraph 5, Pakistan shall communicate to India in writing any objection it may have with regard to the proposed change on the ground that the change involves a material departure from the criteria set out in Paragraph 11. If no objection is received by India from Pakistan within the specified period of three months, then Pakistan shall be deemed to have no objection. If a question arises as to whether or not the change involves a material departure from such of the criteria mentioned above as may be applicable, then either Party may proceed to have the question resolved in accordance with the provisions of Article IX (1) and (2).

7.   The aggregate storage capacity of all Single-purpose and Multi-purpose Reservoirs which may be constructed by India after the Effective Date on each of the River Systems specified in Column (2) of the following table shall not exceed, for each of the categories shown in Columns (3), (4) and (5), the quantities specified therein:

		Conservation Storage Capacity		
		General Storage Capacity	Power Storage Capacity	Flood Storage Capacity
	River System			
(1)	*(2)*	*(3)*	*(4)*	*(5)*
		million acre-feet		
(a)	The Indus	0.25	0.50	Nil
(b)	The Jhelum (excluding the Jhelum Main).	0.15	0.25	0.75
(c)	The Jhelum Main	Nil	Nil	As provided in Paragraph 9
(d)	The Chenab (excluding the Chenab Main)	0.50	0.60	Nil
(e)	The Chenab Main	Nil	0.60	Nil

Provided that

  (i) the storage specified in Column (3) above may be used for any purpose whatever, including the generation of electric energy;

 (ii) the storage specified in Column (4) above may also be put to Non-Consumptive Use (other than flood protection or flood control) or to Domestic Use;

(iii) India shall have the option to increase the Power Storage Capacity specified against item (d) above by making a reduction by an equal amount in the Power Storage Capacity specified against items (b) or (e) above; and

(iv) Storage Works to provide the Power Storage Capacity on the Chenab Main specified against item (e) above shall not be constructed at a point below Naunut (Latitude 33° 19′ N. and Longitude 75° 59′ E.).

8. The figures specified in Paragraph 7 shall be exclusive of the following:

(*a*) Storage in any Small Tank.

(*b*) Any natural storage in a Connecting Lake, that is to say, storage not resulting from any man-made works.

(*c*) Waters which, without any man-made channel or works, spill into natural depressions or borrow-pits during floods.

(*d*) Dead Storage.

(*e*) The volume of Pondage for hydro-electric plants under Annexure D and under Paragraph 21 (*a*).

(*f*) Surcharge Storage.

(*g*) Storage in a Regulating Basin (as defined in Annexure D).

(*h*) Storage incidental to a barrage on the Jhelum Main or on the Chenab Main not exceeding 10,000 acre-feet.

9. India may construct on the Jhelum Main such works as it may consider necessary for flood control of the Jhelum Main and may complete any such works as were under construction on the Effective Date: Provided that

(i) any storage which may be effected by such works shall be confined to off-channel storage in side valleys, depressions or lakes and will not involve any storage in the Jhelum Main itself; and

(ii) except for the part held in lakes, borrow-pits or natural depressions, the stored waters shall be released as quickly as possible after the flood recedes and returned to the Jhelum Main lower down.

These works shall be constructed in accordance with the provisions of Paragraph 11 (*d*).

10. Notwithstanding the provisions of Paragraph 7, any Storage Work to be con structed on a Tributary of The Jhelum on which Pakistan has any Agricultural Use or hydro-electric use shall be so designed and operated as not to adversely affect the then existing Agricultural Use or hydro-electric use on that Tributary.

11. The design of any Storage Work (other than a Storage Work falling under Paragraph 3) shall conform to the following criteria:

(*a*) The Storage Work shall not be capable of raising artificially the water level in the reservoir higher than the designed Full Reservoir Level except to the extent necessary for Flood Storage, if any, specified in the design.

(*b*) The design of the works shall take due account of the requirements of Surcharge Storage.

(*c*) The volume between the Full Reservoir Level and the Dead Storage Level of any reservoir shall not exceed the Conservation Storage Capacity specified in the design.

(*d*) With respect to the Flood Storage mentioned in Paragraph 9, the design of the works on the Jhelum Main shall be such that no water can spill from the Jhelum Main into the off-channel storage except when the water level in the Jhelum Main rises above the low flood stage.

(*e*) Outlets or other works of sufficient capacity shall be provided to deliver into the river downstream the flow of the river received upstream of the Storage Work, except during freshets or floods. These outlets or works shall be located at the highest level consistent with sound and economical design and with satisfactory operation of the Storage Work.

(*f*) Any outlets below the Dead Storage Level necessary for sediment control or any other technical purpose shall be of the minimum size, and located at the highest level, consistent with sound and economical design and with satisfactory operation of the Storage Work.

(*g*) If a power plant is incorporated in the Storage Work, the intakes for the turbines shall be located at the highest level consistent with satisfactory and economical construction and operation of the plant and with customary and accepted practice of design for the designated range of the plant's operation.

12.   To enable Pakistan to satisfy itself that the design of a Storage Work (other than a Storage Work falling under Paragraph 3) conforms to the criteria mentioned in Paragraph 11, India shall, at least six months in advance of the beginning of construction of the Storage Work, communicate to Pakistan in writing the information specified in the Appendix to this Annexure; if any such information is not available or is not pertinent to the design of the Storage Work or to the conditions at the site, it will be so stated:

Provided that, in the case of a Storage Work falling under Paragraph 9,

(i) if the work is a new work, the period of six months shall be reduced to four months, and

(ii) if the work is a work under construction on the Effective Date, the information shall be furnished not later than 31st December 1960.

13.   Within three months (or two months, in the case of a Storage Work specified in Paragraph 9) of the receipt by Pakistan of the information specified in Paragraph 12, Pakistan shall communicate to India in writing any objection that it may have with regard to the proposed design on the ground that the design does not conform to the criteria mentioned in Paragraph 11. If no objection is received by India from Pakistan within the specified period of three months (or two months, in the case of a Storage Work specified in Paragraph 9), then Pakistan shall be deemed to have no objection.

14. If a question arises as to whether or not the design of a Storage Work (other than a Storage Work falling under Paragraph 3) conforms to the criteria set out in Paragraph 11, then either Party may proceed to have the question resolved in accordance with the provisions of Article IX (1) and (2).

15.   (*a*) If any alteration proposed in the design of a Storage Work (other than a Storage Work falling under Paragraph 3) before it comes into operation would result in a material change in the information furnished to Pakistan under the provisions of Paragraph 12, India shall immediately communicate particulars of the change to Pakistan in writing and the provisions of Paragraphs 13 and 14 shall then apply, but where a period of three months is specified in Paragraph 13, that period shall be reduced to two months.

(*b*) If any alteration proposed in the design of a Storage Work (other than a Storage Work falling under Paragraph 3), after it comes into operation would result in a material change in the information furnished to Pakistan under the provisions of Paragraph 12, India shall, at least four months in advance of making the alteration, communicate particulars of the change to Pakistan in writing and the provisions of Paragraphs 13 and 14 shall then apply, but where a period of three months is specified in Paragraph 13, that period shall be reduced to two months.

16.   In the event of an emergency arising which requires repairs to be undertaken to protect the integrity of a Storage Work (other than a Storage Work falling under Paragraph 3), India may undertake immediately the necessary repairs or alterations; if these repairs or alterations result in a change in the information furnished to Pakistan under the provisions of Paragraph 12, India shall, as soon as possible, communicate particulars of the change to Pakistan in writing to enable Pakistan to satisfy itself that after such change the design of the work conforms to the criteria specified in Paragraph 11. The provisions of Paragraphs 13 and 14 shall then apply.

17.   The Flood Storage specified against item (*b*) in Paragraph 7 may be effected only during floods when the discharge of the river exceeds the amount specified for this purpose in the design of the work; the storage above Full Reservoir Level shall be released as quickly as possible after the flood recedes.

18.   The annual filling of Conservation Storage and the initial filling below the Dead Storage Level, at any site, shall be carried out at such times and in accordance with such rules as may be agreed upon between the Commissioners. In case the Commissioners are unable to reach agreement, India may carry out the filling as follows:

(*a*) if the site is on The Indus, between 1st July and 20th August;
(*b*) if the site is on The Jhelum, between 21st June and 20th August; and
(*c*) if the site is on The Chenab, between 21st June and 31st August at such rate as not to reduce, on account of this filling, the flow in the Chenab Main above Merala to less than 55,000 cusecs.

19.   The Dead Storage shall not be depleted except in an unforeseen emergency. If so depleted, it will be refilled in accordance with the conditions of its initial filling.

20.   Subject to the provisions of Paragraph 8 of Annexure C,[19] India may make re leases from Conservation Storage in any manner it may determine.

21.   If a hydro-electric power plant is incorporated in a Storage Work (other than a Storage Work falling under Paragraph 3), the plant shall be so operated that:

(*a*) the maximum Pondage (as defined in Annexure D) shall not exceed the Pondage required for the firm power of the plant, and the water-level in the reservoir corresponding to maximum Pondage shall not, on account of this Pondage, exceed the Full Reservoir Level at any time; and

---

[19]See p. 162 of this volume.

(*b*) except during the period in which a filling is being carried out in accordance with the provisions of Paragraph 18 or 19, the volume of water delivered into the river below the work during any period of seven consecutive days shall not be less than the volume of water received in the river upstream of the work in that seven-day period.

22. In applying the provisions of Paragraph 21 (*b*):

(*a*) the period of seven consecutive days shall commence at 8 a.m. on every Saturday and the time shall be Indian Standard Time;

(*b*) a tolerance of 10% in volume shall be permissible and adjusted as soon as possible; and

(*c*) any temporary uncontrollable retention of water due to variation in river supply will be accounted for.

23. When the Live Storage Capacity of a Storage Work is reduced by sedimentation, India may, in accordance with the relevant provisions of this Annexure, construct new Storage Works or modify existing Storage Works so as to make up the storage capacity lost by sedimentation.

24. If a power plant incorporated in a Storage Work (other than a Storage Work falling under Paragraph 3) is used to operate a peak power plant and lies on any Tributary of The Jhelum on which there is any Agricultural Use by Pakistan, a Regulating Basin (as defined in Annexure D) shall be incorporated.

25. If the change referred to in Paragraph 5(*a*) or 15 is not material, India shall communicate particulars of the change to Pakistan, in writing, as soon as the alteration has been made or the repairs have been undertaken. The provisions of Paragraph 6 or Paragraphs 13 and 14, as the case may be, shall then apply.

APPENDIX TO ANNEXURE E

(*Paragraphs 4 and 12*)

1. *Location of Storage Work*

General map showing the location of the site; if on a Tributary, its situation with respect to the main river.

2. *Hydrologic Data*

(*a*) General map (Scale: 1/4 inch or more = 1 mile) showing the discharge observation site or sites or rainfall gauge stations, on whose data the design is based. In case of a work on a Tributary, this map should also show the catchment area of the Tributary above the site.

(*b*) Observed or estimated daily river discharge data on which the design is based (observed data will be given for as long a period as available; estimated data will be given for as long a period as possible; in both cases data may be limited to the latest 25 years).

(*c*) Flood data, observed or estimated (with details of estimation).

(*d*) Gauge-discharge curve or curves for site or sites mentioned in (*a*) above.

(*e*) Sediment data.

3. *Hydraulic Data*

(*a*) Stage-area and stage-capacity curves of the reservoir with contoured survey maps on which based.

(*b*) Reservoir Capacity, Dead Storage Capacity, Flood Storage Capacity, Conservation Storage Capacity, Power Storage Capacity, General Storage Capacity and Surcharge Storage Capacity.

(*c*) Full Reservoir Level, Dead Storage Level and levels corresponding to Flood Storage and Surcharge Storage.

(*d*) Estimated evaporation losses in the reservoir.

(*e*) Maximum designed flood discharge and discharge-capacity curve for spillway.

(*f*) If a power plant is incorporated in a Storage Work:

(i) Stage-area and stage-capacity curves of forebay and Regulating Basin, with contoured survey maps on which based,

(ii) Estimated evaporation losses in the Regulating Basin, head-race, forebay and tail-race,

(iii) Designated range of operation.

4. *Particulars of Design*

(*a*) Dimensioned plan showing dam, spillway, diversion works and outlet works.

(*b*) Type of dam, length and height above mean bed of the river.

(*c*) Cross-section of the river at the site and mean bed level.

(*d*) Type of spillway, length and crest level; size, number and top level of spillway gates.

(*e*) Type of diversion works, maximum designed capacity, number and size; sill levels.

(*f*) Outlet works: function, type, size, number, maximum designed capacity and sill levels.

(*g*) If a power plant is incorporated in a Storage Work,

(i) Dimensioned plan showing head-race and forebay, powerhouse, tail-race and Regulating Basin.

(ii) Type of intake, maximum designed capacity, size and sill level,

(iii) Head-race and tail-race, length, size and maximum designed capacity,

(iv) Discharge proposed to be passed through the plant, initially and ultimately, and expected variations in the discharge on account of the daily and the weekly load fluctuations.

(v) Maximum aggregate capacity of power units (exclusive of standby units) for firm power and secondary power.

(vi) Regulating Basin and its outlet works: type, number, size, sill levels and designed maximum discharge capacity.

5. *General*

   (*a*) Probable date of completion of river works and probable dates on which various stages of the work would come into operation.

   (*b*) Estimated effect of proposed Storage Work on the flow pattern of river supplies below the Storage Work or, if India has any other Storage Work or Run-of-River Plant (as defined in Annexure D)[20] below the proposed Storage Work, then on the flow pattern below the last Storage Work or Plant.

ANNEXURE F — NEUTRAL EXPERT

(Article IX (2))

PART 1 — QUESTIONS TO BE REFERRED TO A NEUTRAL EXPERT

   1. Subject to the provisions of Paragraph 2, either Commissioner may, under the provisions of Article IX (2)(*a*), refer to a Neutral Expert any of the following questions:

(1) Determination of the component of water available for the use of Pakistan

   (*a*) in the Ravi Main, on account of the deliveries by Pakistan under the provisions of Article II (4), and

   (*b*) at various points on The Ravi or The Sutlej, on account of the deliveries by Pakistan under the provisions of Article III (3).

(2) Determination of the boundary of the drainage basin of The Indus or The Jhelum or The Chenab for the purposes of Article III (2).

(3) Whether or not any use of water or storage in addition to that provided under Article III is involved in any of the schemes referred to in Article IV (2) or in Article IV (3)(*b*) and carried out by India on the Western Rivers.

(4) Questions relating to

   (*a*) obligations with respect to construction or remodelling of, or pouring of waters into, any drainage or drain as provided in Article IV (3)(*c*) and Article IV (3)(*d*); and

   (*b*) maintenance of drainages specified in Article IV (4).

(5) Questions arising under Article IV (7) as to whether any action taken by either Party is likely to have the effect of diverting the Ravi Main between Madhopur and Lahore, or the Sutlej Main between Harike and Suleimanke, from its natural channel between high banks.

(6) Determination of facts relating to questions arising under Article IV (11) or Article IV (12).

(7) Whether any of the data requested by either Party falls outside the scope of Article VI (2).

---

[20] See p. 170 of this volume.

(8) Determination of withdrawals to be made by India under proviso (iii) to Paragraph 3 of Annexure C.[21]

(9) Determination of schedule of releases from Conservation Storage under the provisions of Paragraph 8 of Annexure C.

(10) Whether or not any new Agricultural Use by India, on those Tributaries of The Jhelum on which there is any Agricultural Use or hydro-electric use by Pakistan, conforms to the provisions of Paragraph 9 of Annexure C.

(11) Questions arising under the provisions of Paragraph 7, Paragraph 11 or Paragraph 21 of Annexure D.[22]

(12) Whether or not the operation by India of any plant constructed in accordance with the provisions of Part 3 of Annexure D conforms to the criteria set out in Paragraphs 15, 16 and 17 of that Annexure.

(13) Whether or not any new hydro-electric plant on an irrigation channel taking off the Western Rivers conforms to the provisos to Paragraph 24 of Annexure D.

(14) Whether or not the operation of a Storage Work which was in operation as on the Effective Date substantially conforms to the provisions of Paragraph 3 of Annexure E.[23]

(15) Whether or not any part of the storage in a Connecting Lake is the result of man-made works constructed after the Effective Date (Paragraph 8 (*b*) of Annexure E).

(16) Whether or not any flood control work constructed on the Jhelum Main conforms to the provisions of Paragraph 9 of Annexure E.

(17) Whether or not any Storage Work to be constructed on a Tributary of The Jhelum on which Pakistan has any Agricultural Use or hydro-electric use conforms to the provisions of Paragraph 10 of Annexure E.

(18) Questions arising under the provisions of Paragraph 6 or 14 of Annexure E.

(19) Whether or not the operation of any Storage Work constructed by India, after the Effective Date, conforms to the provisions of Paragraphs 17, 18, 19, 21 and 22 of Annexure E and, to the extent necessary, to the provisions of Paragraph 8 of Annexure C.

(20) Whether or not the storage capacity proposed to be made up by India under Paragraph 23 of Annexure E exceeds the storage capacity lost by sedimentation.

(21) Determination of modifications to be made in the provisions of Parts 2, 4 or 5 of Annexure H[24] in accordance with Paragraphs 11, 31 or 38 thereof when the additional supplies referred to in Paragraph 66 of that Annexure become available.

(22) Modification of Forms under the provisions of Paragraph 41 of Annexure H.

(23) Revision of the figure for the conveyance loss from the head of the Madhopur Beas Link to the junction of the Chakki Torrent with the Beas Main under the provisions of Paragraph 45 (*c*) (ii) of Annexure H.

---

[21] See p. 162 of this volume.
[22] See p. 170 of this volume.
[23] See p. 186 of this volume.
[24] See p. 222 of this volume.

2.   If a claim for financial compensation has been raised with respect to any question specified in Paragraph 1, that question shall not be referred to a Neutral Expert unless the two Commissioners are agreed that it should be so referred.

3.   Either Commissioner may refer to a Neutral Expert under the provisions of Article IX (2) (*a*) any question arising with regard to the determination of costs under Article IV (5), Article IV (11), Article VII (1)(*a*) or Article VII (1)(*b*).

PART 2 — APPOINTMENT AND PROCEDURE

4.   A Neutral Expert shall be a highly qualified engineer, and, on the receipt of a request made in accordance with Paragraph 5, he shall be appointed, and the terms of his retainer shall be fixed, as follows:

(*a*) During the Transition Period, by the Bank.
(*b*) After the expiration of the Transition Period,
   (i) jointly by the Government of India and the Government of Pakistan, or
   (ii) if no appointment is made in accordance with (i) above within one month after the date of the request, then by such person or body as may have been agreed upon between the two Governments in advance, on an annual basis, or, in the absence of such agreement, by the Bank.

Provided that every appointment made in accordance with (*a*) or (6)(ii) above shall be made after consultation with each of the Parties.

The Bank shall be notified of every appointment, except when the Bank is itself the appointing authority.

5.   If a difference arises and has to be dealt with in accordance with the provisions of Article IX (2)(*a*), the following procedure will be followed:

(*a*) The Commissioner who is of the opinion that the difference falls within the provisions of Part 1 of this Annexure (hereinafter in this paragraph referred to as "the first Commissioner") shall notify the other Commissioner of his intention to ask for the appointment of a Neutral Expert. Such notification shall clearly state the paragraph or paragraphs of Part 1 of this Annexure under which the difference falls and shall also contain a statement of the point or points of difference.
(*b*) Within two weeks of the receipt by the other Commissioner of the notification specified in (*a*) above, the two Commissioners will endeavour to prepare a joint statement of the point or points of difference.
(*c*) After expiry of the period of two weeks specified in (*b*) above, the first Commissioner may request the appropriate authority specified in Paragraph 4 to appoint a Neutral Expert; a copy of the request shall be sent at the same time to the other Commissioner.
(*d*) The request under (*c*) above shall be accompanied by the joint statement specified in (*b*) above; failing this, either Commissioner may send a separate statement to the appointing authority and, if he does so, he shall at the same time send a copy of the separate statement to the other Commissioner.

6.   The procedure with respect to each reference to a Neutral Expert shall be deter mined by him, provided that:

(a) he shall afford to each Party an adequate hearing;
(b) in making his decision, he shall be governed by the provisions of this Treaty and by the compromis, if any, presented to him by the Commission; and
(c) without prejudice to the provisions of Paragraph 3, unless both Parties so request, he shall not deal with any issue of financial compensation.

7.   Should the Commission be unable to agree that any particular difference falls within Part 1 of this Annexure, the Neutral Expert shall, after hearing both Parties, decide whether or not it so falls. Should he decide that the difference so falls, he shall proceed to render a decision on the merits ; should he decide otherwise, he shall inform the Commission that, in his opinion, the difference should be treated as a dispute. Should the Neutral Expert decide that only a part of the difference so falls, he shall, at his discretion, either:

(a) proceed to render a decision on the part which so falls, and inform the Commission that, in his opinion, the part which does not so fall should be treated as a dispute, or
(b) inform the Commission that, in his opinion, the entire difference should be treated as a dispute.

8.   Each Government agrees to extend to the Neutral Expert such facilities as he may require for the discharge of his functions.

9.   The Neutral Expert shall, as soon as possible, render a decision on the question or questions referred to him, giving his reasons. A copy of such decision, duly signed by the Neutral Expert, shall be forwarded by him to each of the Commissioners and to the Bank.

10.   Each Party shall bear its own costs. The remuneration and the expenses of the Neutral Expert and of any assistance that he may need shall be borne initially as provided in Part 3 of this Annexure and eventually by the Party against which his decision is rendered, except as, in special circumstances, and for reasons to be stated by him, he may otherwise direct. He shall include in his decision a direction concerning the extent to which the costs of such remuneration and expenses are to be borne by either Party.

11.   The decision of the Neutral Expert on all matters within his competence shall be final and binding, in respect of the particular matter on which the decision is made, upon the Parties and upon any Court of Arbitration established under the provisions of Article IX (5).

12.   The Neutral Expert may, at the request of the Commission, suggest for the consideration of the Parties such measures as are, in his opinion, appropriate to compose a difference or to implement his decision.

13.   Without prejudice to the finality of the Neutral Expert's decision, if any question (including a claim, to financial compensation) which is not within the

competence of a Neutral Expert should arise out of his decision, that question shall, if it cannot be resolved by agreement, be settled in accordance with the provisions of Article IX (3), (4) and (5).

PART 3 — EXPENSES

14.   India and Pakistan shall, within 30 days after the Treaty enters into force, each pay to the Bank the sum of U.S. $5,000 to be held in trust by the Bank, together with any income therefrom and any other amounts payable to the Bank hereunder, on the terms and conditions hereinafter set forth in this Annexure.

15.   The remuneration and expenses of the Neutral Expert, and of any assistance that he may need, shall be paid or reimbursed by the Bank from the amounts held by it hereunder. The Bank shall be entitled to rely upon the statement of the Neutral Expert as to the amount of the remuneration and expenses of himself (determined in accordance with the terms of his retainer) and of any such assistance utilized by him.

16.   Within 30 days of the rendering of a decision by the Neutral Expert, the Party or Parties concerned shall, in accordance with that decision, refund to the Bank the amounts paid by the Bank pursuant to Paragraph 15.

17.   The Bank will keep amounts held by it hereunder separate from its other assets, in such form, in such banks or other depositories and in such accounts as it shall determine. The Bank may, but it shall not be required to, invest these amounts. The Bank will not be liable to the Parties for failure of any depository or other person to perform its obligations. The Bank shall be under no obligation to make payments hereunder of amounts in excess of those held by it hereunder.

18.   If at any time or times the amounts held by the Bank hereunder shall in its judgment be insufficient to meet the payments provided for in Paragraph 15, it will so notify the Parties, which shall, within 30 days thereafter, pay to the Bank, in equal shares, the amount specified in such notice as being the amount required to cover the deficiency. Any amounts so paid to the Bank may, by agreement between the Bank and the Parties, be refunded to the Parties.

ANNEXURE G — COURT OF ARBITRATION

(Article IX(5))

1.   If the necessity arises to establish a Court of Arbitration under the provisions of Article IX, the provisions of this Annexure shall apply.

2.   The arbitration proceeding may be instituted

(*a*) by the two Parties entering into a special agreement (*compromis*) specifying the issues in dispute, the composition of the Court and instructions to the Court concerning its procedures and any other matters agreed upon between the Parties; or

(b) at the request of either Party to the other in accordance with the provisions of Article IX (5) (b) or (c). Such request shall contain a statement setting forth the nature of the dispute or claim to be submitted to arbitration, the nature of the relief sought and the names of the arbitrators appointed under Paragraph 6 by the Party instituting the proceeding.

3.   The date of the special agreement referred to in Paragraph 2 (a), or the date on which the request referred to in Paragraph 2 (b) is received by the other Party, shall be deemed to be the date on which the proceeding is instituted.

4.   Unless otherwise agreed between the Parties, a Court of Arbitration shall consist of seven arbitrators appointed as follows:

(a) Two arbitrators to be appointed by each Party in accordance with Paragraph 6; and
(b) Three arbitrators (hereinafter sometimes called the umpires) to be appointed in accordance with Paragraph 7, one from each of the following categories:
    (i) Persons qualified by status and reputation to be Chairman of the Court of Arbitration who may, but need not, be engineers or lawyers.
    (ii) Highly qualified engineers.
    (iii) Persons well versed hi international law.

The Chairman of the Court shall be a person from category (b) (i) above.

5.   The Parties shall endeavour to nominate and maintain a Standing Panel of umpires (hereinafter called the Panel) in the following manner:

(a) The Panel shall consist of four persons in each of the three categories specified in Paragraph 4 (b).
(b) The Panel will be selected, as soon as possible after the Effective Date, by agreement between the Parties and with the consent of the persons whose names are included in the Panel.
(c) A person may at any time be retired from the Panel at the request of either Party: Provided however that he may not be so retired
    (i) during the period after arbitration proceedings have been instituted under Para graph 2 (b) and before the process described in Paragraph 7 (a) has been completed; or
    (ii) during the period after he has been appointed to a Court and before the proceedings are completed.
(d) If a member of the Panel should die, resign or be retired, his successor shall be selected by agreement between the Parties.

6.   The arbitrators referred to in Paragraph 4 (a) shall be appointed as follows:

The Party instituting the proceeding shall appoint two arbitrators at the time it makes a request to the other Party under Paragraph 2 (b). Within 30 days of the receipt of this request, the other Party shall notify the names of the arbitrators appointed by it.

7.   The umpires shall be appointed as follows:

(a) If a Panel has been nominated in accordance with the provisions of Paragraph 5, each umpire shall be selected as follows from the Panel, from his appropriate category, provided that the category has, at that time, at least three names on the Panel:

   The Parties shall endeavour to agree to place the names of the persons in each category in the order in which they shall be invited to serve on the Court. If such agreement cannot be reached within 30 days of the date on which the proceeding is instituted, the Parties shall promptly establish such an order by drawing lots. If, in any category, the person whose name is placed first in the order so established, on receipt of an invitation to serve on the Court, declines to do so, the person whose name is next on the list shall be invited. The process shall be repeated until the invitation is accepted or all names in the category are exhausted.

(b) If a Panel has not been nominated in accordance with Paragraph 5, or if there should be less than three names on the Panel in any category or if no person in a category accepts the invitation referred to in Paragraph 7 (a), the umpires, or the remaining umpires or umpire, as the case may be, shall be appointed as follows:

   (i) By agreement between the Parties.

   (ii) Should the Parties be unable to agree on the selection of any or all of the three umpires, they shall agree on one or more persons to help them in making the necessary selection by agreement; but if one or more umpires remain to be appointed 60 days after the date on which the proceeding is instituted, or 30 days after the completion of the process described in sub-paragraph (a) above, as the case may be, then the Parties shall determine by lot for each umpire remaining to be appointed, a person from the appropriate list set out in the Appendix[25] to this Annexure, who shall then be requested to make the necessary selection.

   (iii) A national of India or Pakistan, or a person who is, or has been, employed or retained by either of the Parties shall be disqualified from selection under sub-paragraph (ii) above:

   Provided that

      (1) the person making the selection shall be entitled to rely on a declaration from the appointee, before his selection, that he is not disqualified on any of the above grounds; and

      (2) the Parties may by agreement waive any or all of the above disqualifications in the case of any individual appointee.

   (iv) The lists in the Appendix to this Annexure may, from time to time, be modified or enlarged by agreement between the Parties.

---

[25]See p. 222 of this volume.

8.   In selecting umpires pursuant to Paragraph 7, the Chairman shall be selected first, unless the Parties otherwise agree.

9.   Should either Party fail to participate in the drawing of lots as provided in Paragraphs 7 and 10, the other Party may request the President of the Bank to nominate a person to draw the lots, and the person so nominated shall do so after giving due notice to the Parties and inviting them to be represented at the drawing of the lots.

10.   In the case of death, retirement or disability from any cause of one of the arbitrators or umpires his place shall be filled as follows:

(a)   In the case of one of the arbitrators appointed under Paragraph 6, his place shall be filled by the Party which appointed him. The Court shall, on request, suspend the proceedings but for not longer than 15 days pending such replacement.

(b)   In the case of an umpire, a new appointment shall be made by agreement between the Parties or, failing such agreement, by a person determined by lot from the appropriate list set out in the Appendix to this Annexure, who shall then be requested to make the necessary selection subject to the provisions of Paragraph 7 (b) (iii). Unless the Parties otherwise agree, the Court shall suspend the proceedings pending such replacement.

11.   As soon as the three umpires have accepted appointment, they together with such arbitrators as have been appointed by the two Parties under Paragraph 6 shall form the Court of Arbitration. Unless the Parties otherwise agree, the Court shall be competent to transact business only when all the three umpires and at least two arbitrators are present.

12.   Each Party shall be represented before the Court by an Agent and may have the assistance of Counsel.

13.   Within 15 days of the date of institution of a proceeding, each Party shall place sufficient funds at the disposal of its Commissioner to meet in equal shares the initial expenses of the umpires to enable them to attend the first meeting of the Court. If either Party should fail to do so, the other Party may initially meet the whole of such expenses.

14.   The Court of Arbitration shall convene, for its first meeting, on such date and at such place as shall be fixed by the Chairman.

15.   At its first meeting the Court shall

(a)   establish its secretariat and appoint a Treasurer;

(b)   make an estimate of the likely expenses of the Court and call upon each Party to pay to the Treasurer half of the expenses so estimated: Provided that, if either Party should fail to make such payment, the other Party may initially pay the whole of the estimated expenses;

(c)   specify the issues in dispute;

(d)   lay down a programme for submission by each side of legal pleadings and rejoinders; and

(e)   determine the time and place of reconvening the Court.

Unless special circumstances arise, the Court shall not reconvene until the pleadings and rejoinders have been closed. During the intervening period, at the request of either Party, the Chairman of the Court may, for sufficient reason, make changes in the arrangements made under (d) and (e) above.

16. Subject to the provisions of this Treaty and except as the Parties may otherwise agree, the Court shall decide all questions relating to its competence and shall determine its procedure, including the time within which each Party must present and conclude its arguments. All such decisions of the Court shall be by a majority of those present and voting. Each arbitrator, including the Chairman, shall have one vote. In the event of an equality of votes, the Chairman shall have a casting vote.

17. The proceedings of the Court shall be in English.

18. Two or more certified copies of every document produced before the Court by one Party shall be communicated by the Court to the other Party; the Court shall not take cognizance of any document or paper or fact presented by a Party unless so communicated.

19. The Chairman of the Court shall control the discussions. The discussions shall not be open to the public unless it is so decided by the Court with the consent of the Parties. The discussions shall be recorded in minutes drawn up by the Secretaries appointed by the Chairman. These minutes shall be signed by the Chairman and shall alone have an authentic character.

20. The Court shall have the right to require from the Agents of the Parties the production of all papers and other evidence it considers necessary and to demand all necessary explanations. In case of refusal, the Court shall take formal note of it.

21. The members of the Court shall be entitled to put questions to the Agents and Counsel of the Parties and to demand explanations from them on doubtful points. Neither the questions put nor the remarks made by the members of the Court during the discussions shall be regarded as an expression of an opinion of the Court or any of its members.

22. When the Agents and Counsel of the Parties have, within the time allotted by the Court, submitted all explanations and evidence in support of their case, the Court shall pronounce the discussions closed. The Court may, however, at its discretion reopen the discussions at any time before making its Award. The deliberations of the Court shall be in private and shall remain secret.

23. The Court shall render its Award, in writing, on the issues in dispute and on such relief, including financial compensation, as may have been claimed. The Award shall be accompanied by a statement of reasons. An Award signed by four or more members of the Court shall constitute the Award of the Court. A signed counterpart of the Award shall be delivered by the Court to each Party. Any such Award rendered in accordance with the provisions of this Annexure in regard to a particular dispute shall be final and binding upon the Parties with respect to that dispute.

24.   The salaries and allowances of the arbitrators appointed pursuant to Paragraph 6 shall be determined and, in the first instance, borne by their Governments; those of the umpires shall be agreed upon with them by the Parties or by the persons appointing them, and (subject to Paragraph 13) shall be paid, in the first instance, by the Treasurer. The salaries and allowances of the secretariat of the Court shall be determined by the Court and paid, in the first instance, by the Treasurer.

25.   Each Government agrees to accord to the members and officials of the Court of Arbitration and to the Agents and Counsel appearing before the Court the same privileges and immunities as are accorded to representatives of members states to the principal and subsidiary organs of the United Nations under Sections 11, 12 and 13 of Article IV of the Convention on the Privileges and Immunities of the United Nations (dated 13th February 1946) during the periods specified in these Sections. The Chairman of the Court, with the approval of the Court, has the right and the duty to waive the immunity of any official of the Court in any case where the immunity would impede the course of justice and can be waived without prejudice to the interests of the Court. The Government appointing any of the aforementioned Agents and Counsel has the right and the duty to waive the immunity of any of its said appointees in any case where in its opinion the immunity would impede the course of justice and can be waived without prejudice to the effective performance of the functions of the said appointees. The immunities and privileges provided for in this paragraph shall not be applicable as between an Agent or Counsel appearing before the Court and the Government which has appointed him.

26.   In its Award, the Court shall also award the costs of the proceedings, including those initially borne by the Parties and those paid by the Treasurer.

27.   At the request of either Party, made within three months of the date of the Award, the Court shall reassemble to clarify or interpret its Award. Pending such clarification or interpretation the Court may, at the request of either Party and if in the opinion of the Court circumstances so require, grant a stay of execution of its Award. After furnishing this clarification or interpretation, or if no request for such clarification or interpretation is made within three months of the date of the Award, the Court shall be deemed to have been dissolved.

28.   Either Party may request the Court at its first meeting to lay down, pending its Award, such interim measures as, in the opinion of that Party, are necessary to safeguard its interests under the Treaty with respect to the matter in dispute, or to avoid prejudice to the final solution or aggravation or extension of the dispute. The Court shall, thereupon, after having afforded an adequate hearing to each Party, decide, by a majority consisting of at least four members of the Court, whether any interim measures are necessary for the reasons hereinbefore stated and, if so, shall specify such measures: Provided that

(a) the Court shall lay down such interim measures only for such specified period as, in its opinion, will be necessary to render the Award: this period may, if necessary, be extended unless the delay in rendering the Award is due to any delay on the part of the Party which requested the interim measures in supplying such information as may be required by the other Party or by the Court in connection with the dispute; and

(*b*) the specification of such interim measures shall not be construed as an indication of any view of the Court on the merits of the dispute.

29.   Except as the Parties may otherwise agree, the law to be applied by the Court shall be this Treaty and, whenever necessary for its interpretation or application, but only to the extent necessary for that purpose, the following in the order in which they are listed:

(*a*) International conventions establishing rules which are expressly recognized by the Parties.

(*b*) Customary international law.

APPENDIX TO ANNEXURE G

(*Paragraph 7 (b)*)

List I for selection of Chairman	*List II* for selection of Engineer Member	*List III* for selection of Legal Member
(i) The Secretary-General of the United Nations	(i) The President of Massachusetts Institute of Technology, Cambridge, Mass., U.S.A.	(i) The Chief Justice of the United States
(ii) The President of the International Bank for Reconstruction and Development	(ii) The Rector of the Imperial College of Science and Technology, London, England	(ii) The Lord Chief Justice of England

ANNEXURE H — TRANSITIONAL ARRANGEMENTS

(*Article II (5)*)

PART 1 — PRELIMINARY

1.   The provisions of Article II (5) with respect to the distribution of the waters of the Eastern Rivers during the Transition Period shall be governed by the provisions of this Annexure. With the exception of the provisions of Paragraph 50, all the provisions of this Annexure shall lapse on the date on which the Transition Period ends. The provisions of Paragraphs 50 and 51 shall lapse as soon as the final refund or the additional payment referred to therein has been made for the last year of the Transition Period.

2.   For the purposes of this Annexure, the Transition Period shall be divided into two parts: Phase I and Phase II.

3.   Phase I shall begin on 1st April 1960 and it shall end on 31st March 1965, or, if the proposed Trimmu-Islam Link is not ready to operate by 31st March 1965 but is ready to operate prior to 31st March 1966 then, on the date on which the link is ready to operate. In any event, whether or not the Trimmu-Islam Link is ready to operate, Phase I shall end not later than 31st March 1966.

4.   Phase II shall begin on 1st April 1965, or, if Phase I has been extended under the provisions of Paragraph 3, then on the day following the end of Phase I but in any case not later than 1st April 1966. Phase II shall end on the same date as the Transition Period.

5.   As used in this Annexure:

(*a*) The term 'Central Ban Doab Channels' or 'C.B.D.C.' means the system of irrigation channels located in Pakistan which, prior to 15th August 1947, formed a part of the Upper Bari Doab Canal System.

(*b*) The terms '*kharif*' and '*rabi*' respectively mean the crop seasons extending from 1st April to 30th September (both days inclusive) and 1st October to 31st March (both days inclusive).

(*c*) The term 'Water-accounting Period' means the period which is treated as a unit for the purpose of preparing an account of the distribution of waters between India and Pakistan.

(*d*) The term 'Beas Component at Ferozepore' means the amount of flow water derived from The Beas which would have reached Ferozepore if there had been
   (i) no transfers from The Ravi or contribution from The Sutlej,
   (ii) no withdrawals by the canals at Harike,
   (iii) no abstraction of flow waters by, or release of stored waters from, any storage reservoir on The Beas or the pond at Harike,
   (iv) no withdrawals by the Shahnehr Canal in excess of those specified in Para graph 55, and
   (v) no withdrawal by any new canal from The Beas or from the Sutlej Main between Harike Below and Ferozepore constructed after the Effective Date with a capacity of more than 10 cusecs.

(*e*) The term 'Sutlej Component at Ferozepore' means the amount of flow water derived from The Sutlej which would have reached Ferozepore if there had been
   (i) no transfers from The Ravi or contribution from The Beas,
   (ii) no withdrawals, as at Rupar, in excess of those specified in Paragraph 21 (*a*), and
   (iii) no abstraction of flow waters by, or release of stored waters from, any storage reservoir on The Sutlej or the ponds at Nangal or Harike.

PART 2 — DISTRIBUTION OF THE WATERS OF THE RAVI

6.   Subject to the provisions of Paragraph 20 and to the payment by Pakistan, by due date, of the amounts to be specified under the provisions of Paragraph 48, India agrees to continue the supply of water to the C.B.D.C., during the transition Period, in accordance with the provisions of Paragraphs 7 to 19. The balance of the

waters of The Ravi, after India has made the deliveries specified in these Paragraphs or the releases specified in Paragraph 20, shall be available for unrestricted use by India.

7.   India will deliver supplies to the C.B.D.C. throughout *rabi* and during April 1–10 and September 21–30 in *kharif* (dates as at the points of delivery, no time-lag being allowed from Madhopur to these points), at the points noted in Column (3) of Table A below, according to indents to be placed by Pakistan, up to the maximum quantity noted against each point in Column (4) of Table A:

Table A

Item	Name of Channel	Point of Delivery (*Approximate*)	Maximum Quantity (*cusecs*)
Col. (1)	*Col.* (2)	*Col.* (3)	*Col.* (4)
1.	Lahore Branch	R.D. 196,455	615
2.	Main Branch Lower	R.D. 250,620	1,382
3.	Pull Distributary	R.D. 74,595	10
4.	Kohali Distributary	R.D. 67,245	26
5.	Khalra Distributary	R.D. 26,900	11
6.	Bhuchar Kahna Distributary	R.D. 15,705	317
		TOTAL:	2,361

8.   (*a*) The supply available in the Ravi Main, at Madhopur Above, after deducting the actual withdrawal (the deduction being limited to a maximum of 120 cusecs during April 1–10 and September 21–30 and to nil cusecs during *rabi*) for the Kashmir (Basantpur) Canal, will be taken as the 'gross supply available': Provided that any withdrawal from The Ravi upstream of Madhopur by a new canal constructed after the Effective Date with a capacity of more than 10 cusecs will be accounted for in working out the supply available in the Ravi Main at Madhopur Above.

(*b*) From the 'gross supply available' as determined in (*a*) above, the escapages, if any, from the Upper Bari Doab Canal into The Ravi will be deducted to get the 'net supply available'. India will use its best endeavours to limit these escapages to the minimum necessary for operational requirements.

(*c*) The 'net supply available' as determined in (*b*) above, limited to a daily ceiling of 6,800 cusecs during April 1–10 and 21st September to 15th October and of 5,770 cusecs during 16th October to 31st March, will be taken as the 'distributable supply'.

9.   If the 'distributable supply' falls below 6,800 cusecs during April 1–10 or 21st September to 15th October, the aggregate deliveries to the C.B.D.C. may be reduced to 34.7 per cent of the 'distributable supply'. If the 'distributable supply' falls below 5,770 cusecs during 16th October to 31st March, the aggregate deliveries to the C.B.D.C. may be reduced to 41 per cent of the 'distributable supply'.

10.   If in any year after the Rasul-Qadirabad and the Qadirabad-Balloki Links are ready to operate, the average discharge for a period of five consecutive days during 21st February to 6th April in the Jhelum Main at Rasul Above (including the supply in the tail-race of the Rasul hydro-electric plant) exceeds 20,000 cusecs and the daily discharge is not less than 17,000 cusecs on any of these five days, India may, from a date four days after the expiry of the said period of five days, discontinue deliveries to the C.B.D.C. from that date until 10th April in that year: Provided that, if India should decide to exercise this option, India shall notify Pakistan telegraphically three days in advance of the date proposed for the discontinuance of deliveries.

11.   As soon as the supplies specified in Paragraph 66 are available for reduction of deliveries by India during September 21–30 and *rabi*, the Commissioners will meet and agree upon suitable modifications in the provisions of this Part of this Annexure. In case the Commissioners are unable to agree, the difference shall be dealt with by a Neutral Expert in accordance with the provisions of Annexure F[26].

12.   A rotational programme will be followed for the distribution of supplies during 16th October lo 31st March; it will be extended, if necessary, for the distribution of supplies during 21st September to 15th October and April 1–10. This programme will be framed and, if necessary, modified by the Chief Engineer, Punjab, India, in such manner as will enable the C.B.D.C. to get the due percentage of the 'distributable supply' during each of the following Water-accounting Periods:

  (i)   21st September to 15th October,
 (ii)   16th October to 2nd December (*rabi* sowing period).
(iii)   3rd December to 12th February (*rabi* growing period).
 (iv)   13th February to 31st March (*rabi* maturing period),
  (v)   April 1–10.

In framing, operating and, if necessary, modifying the rotational programme, the Chief Engineer, Punjab, will make every effort to see that, within each of the Water-accounting Periods specified above, the supplies delivered to the C.B.D.C. are spread out over the period as fairly as the prevailing circumstances permit.

13.   The Chief Engineer, West Pakistan, will communicate to the Chief Engineer, Punjab (India) by 31st August each year, his suggestions, if any, for framing the next rotational programme and the Chief Engineer, Punjab, in framing that programme, will give due consideration to these suggestions. Copies of the programme shall be supplied by the Chief Engineer, Punjab, to the Chief Engineer, West Pakistan, and to the Com missioners, as early as possible but not later than 30th September each year. Copies of the modified programme shall similarly be supplied as soon as possible after the modifications have been made and the Chief Engineer, West Pakistan, and the Commissioners will be kept informed of the circumstances under which the modifications are made.

---

[26]See p. 202 of this volume.

14.   Neither Party shall have any claim for restitution of water not used by it when available to it.

15.   India will give Pakistan adequate prior notice of any closures at the head of the Upper Bari Doab Canal during the period 21st September to 10th April. If, however, on account of any operational emergency, India finds it necessary to suddenly close the Upper Bari Doab Canal at head, or any channel specified in Table A,[27] India will notify Pakistan telegraphically.

16.   No claim whatsoever shall lie against India for any interruption of supply to the C.B.D.C. due to a closure of the Upper Bari Doab Canal at head, or of any channel specified in Table A, if such closure is considered necessary by India in the interest of the safety or the maintenance of the Upper Bari Doab Canal system.

17.   India will use its best endeavours not to pass into any of the channels listed as Items 1, 2 and 6 of Table A, any supplies in excess of 110 per cent of the corresponding figure given in Column (4) of that Table. Any supplies passed into any of the aforesaid channels in excess of 105 per cent of the corresponding figure given in Column (4) of Table A will not be taken into account in drawing up the water-account. If however the indent of any channel is less than the corresponding figure given in Column (4) of Table A, the supplies passed into that channel up to 110 per cent of the indent will be taken into account in drawing up the water-account.

18.   If, because of unavoidable circumstances arising out of the inherent difficulties in the operation of the Upper Bari Doab Canal (U.B.D.C.) system, deliveries to C.B.D.C. are temporarily reduced below the amounts indented or due (whichever amounts are less), no claim for financial compensation shall lie against India on this account. India will make every effort to bring about at the earliest possible opportunity a resumption of deliveries to C.B.D.C. up to the amounts indented or due (whichever amounts are less).

19.   The delivery into each of the channels specified in Table A will be regulated by India in accordance with the discharge table current for that channel on the Effective Date until that table is revised, if necessary, on the basis of

(i) any discharge observation made by India whenever it may consider necessary to do so, but not more often than once in two months; or
(ii) any joint discharge observation by India and Pakistan which may be undertaken at the request of either Commissioner, but not more often than once in three months; the observation shall be made within a fortnight of the receipt of the request.

India will supply to Pakistan, for each channel specified in Table A, a copy of the discharge table current on the Effective Date and of any revised discharge table prepared thereafter in accordance with (i) or (ii) above.

---

[27] See p. 226 of this volume.

20. Pakistan shall have the option to request India to discontinue the deliveries to C.B.D.C. at the points specified in Table A and to release instead equal supplies (that is, those due under the provisions of Paragraphs 7 to 11) into the Ravi Main below Madhopur. This option may be exercised, effective 1st April in any year, by written notification delivered to India before 30th September preceding. On receipt of such notification, India shall comply with Pakistan's request and thereupon India shall have no obligation to make deliveries to C.B.D.C. at the points specified in Table A during the remaining part of the Transition Period, but will use its best endeavours to ensure that no abstraction is made by India below Madhopur from the supplies so released.

PART 3 — DISTRIBUTION OF THE WATERS OF THE SUTLEJ AND THE BEAS
IN KHARIF DURING PHASE I

21. Except as provided in Paragraphs 22, 23, 24 and 27, India agrees to limit its withdrawals during Phase I at Bhakra, Nangal, Rupar, Harike and Ferozepore (including abstractions for storage by the Bhakra Dam and for the ponds at Nangal and Harike) and by the Bachherewah Grey Canal from the flow waters (as distinct from stored waters) present in the Sutlej Main and from the 'Beas Component at Ferozepore', in each Water-accounting Period, to the equivalent of the following:

(a) 10,250 cusecs from April 1–10 to July 1–10; 12,000 cusecs from July 11–20 to August 21–31 and 10,500 cusecs during September 1–10 to 21–30 from the Sutlej Main, as at Rupar; *plus*

(b) 3,500 cusecs during April 1–10 to 21–30; 4,500 cusecs during May 1–10 to 21–31 and 5,500 cusecs from June 1–10 to September 21–30, as at Ferozepore, from the 'Sutlej Component at Ferozepore' and the 'Beas Component at Ferozepore', taken together: Provided that this withdrawal shall not exceed the sum of the 'Sutlej Component at Ferozepore' and 16 per cent of the 'Beas Component at Ferozepore'.

22. In addition to the withdrawals under Paragraph 21, India may make further withdrawals in each Water-accounting Period, equivalent to the amount related to Pakistan's ability to replace. This amount shall be determined as follows:

(a) For each Water-accounting Period, the 'average discharge at Merala Above' shall first be worked out as follows:

(i) The daily figures for the discharges at Merala Above shall be limited to a minimum equal to the figure for the appropriate Floor Discharge at Merala Above, as given in Column (2) of Table B[28] below, and to a maximum of M cusecs where M has the following values:

---

[28]See p. 236 of this volume.

Period		Value of M (cusecs)
April	1–10	28,000
	11–20	33,000
	21–30	35,000
May	1–10	41,000
	11–20	43,000
May 21–31 to Sept. 21–30	. . . .	45,000

(ii) The average of the daily figures, limited in accordance with (i) above, will be taken as the 'average discharge at Merala Above', for the Water-accounting Period.

(b) For each Water-accounting Period, the 'gross amount' as at Ferozepore, corresponding to the 'average discharge at Merala Above', as determined in (a) above, shall next be worked out from Table B, in the following manner:

When the 'average discharge at Merala Above' is equal to the Floor Discharge shown in Column (2) of Table B, the 'gross amount', as at Ferozepore, shall be zero. When the 'average discharge at Merala Above' equals or exceeds the Ceiling Discharge shown in Column (3) of Table B, the 'gross amount', as at Ferozepore, shall be the amount shown in Column (4) of Table B. For an 'average discharge at Merala Above' between those shown in Columns (2) and (3) of Table B, the 'gross amount', as at Ferozepore, shall be the proportional intermediate amount: Provided that

(i) if during April 1–10 in any year, the 'average discharge at Merala Above' is equal to 11,100 cusecs and the 'gross amount' for the whole of the preceding March, under the provisions of Paragraph 35, has been equal to zero, then for the succeeding April 11–20 the figures for Columns (2), (3) and (4) of Table B will be taken as 12,000; 23,400 and 8,600 respectively; no change will be made for calculating the 'gross amount' in any subsequent Water-accounting Period in that year, but if, in addition to the conditions already stated for April 1–10, the 'average discharge at Merala Above', during April 11–20, equals 12,000 cusecs, then for the succeeding April 21–30 the figures for Columns (2), (3) and (4) of Table B will be taken as 12,100; 23,500 and 8,600 respectively; no change will be made for calculating the 'gross amount' in any subsequent Water-accounting Period in that year;

(ii) if during March 21–31 in any year, the average discharge at Merala Above (obtained by limiting the daily values to a maximum of 27,000 cusecs) exceeds 22,000 cusecs, then for the succeeding April 1–10 the figures for Columns (2), (3) and (4) of Table B will be taken as 11,100; 26,700 and 12,900 respectively; no change will be made for any subsequent Water-accounting Period in that year; and

(iii) if, during any Water-accounting period from April 1–10 to September 21–30, the Upper Chenab Canal (U.C.C.) and M.R. Link are both closed at head (any day, on which some supplies are passed into U.C.C. in order that the head across the U.C.C. Head Regulator should not exceed 17 feet, being treated as a day of closure), on account of the discharge on any day in the Jammu Tawi having exceeded 30,000 cusecs, or on account of the discharge at Merala Above on any day having exceeded 200,000 cusecs, the 'gross amount', as at Ferozepore, will be worked out as follows:

For each of the days for which both U.C.C. and M.R. Link remain closed at head, the 'gross amount', as at Ferozepore, shall be taken as 108 per cent of Q during April 1–10 to August 21–31 and 100 per cent of Q during September 1–10 to 21–30, where Q equals 67 per cent of the corresponding actual river supply at Balloki Above (allowing three days time-lag from Merala to Balloki) *minus* 300 cusecs; Q being limited to 8,000 cusecs during April 1–10, to 11,000 cusecs during April 11–20, to 13,000 cusecs during April 21–30, and to 15,000 cusecs from May 1–10 to September 21–30. For the remaining days in the Water-accounting Period, the 'gross amount' shall be worked out on the basis of the average of the daily discharges at Merala Above for those days, the daily discharges being limited, where necessary, in accordance with (a) (i) above. The 'gross amount', for the Water-accounting Period taken as a whole, will be taken as equal to the sum of the 'gross amount' for each of the days of closure *plus* the 'gross amount' for the remaining days of the Water-accounting Period multiplied by the corresponding number of days, the aggregate being divided by the total number of days in the Water-accounting Period.

Pakistan will notify India about any such closure by telegram stating therein the discharge of Jammu Tawi, the discharge at Merala Above and the discharge of U.C.C. at head, and will continue to supply similar information daily by telegram till the U.C.C. and M. R. Link are re-opened.

(*c*) The 'gross amount', as at Ferozepore, as determined under (*b*) above, will then be multiplied by the corresponding factor in Column (5) of Table B to obtain the amount of further withdrawals by India, as at Ferozepore.

23. During September 11–20 and September 21–30, an adjustment shall be made in the withdrawals which India may make under the provisions of Paragraphs 21 and 22 by adding the actual gains in the Sutlej Main from Ferozepore to Islam to the value deter mined under the provisions of Paragraphs 21 and 22 and deducting from the resulting total 3,400 cusecs during September 11–20 and 2,900 cusecs during September 21–30.

24. If, in any Water-accounting Period, the sum of (i) and (ii) below exceeds 35,000 cusecs during April 1–10 to August 21–31, or 30,000 cusecs during September, then India may make further withdrawals, as at Ferozepore, from the flow waters of The Sutlej and The Beas to the extent of the excess over 35,000 cusecs or 30,000 cusecs, as the case may be.

(i) The supply available from the 'Sutlej Component at Ferozepore' and from the 'Beas Component at Ferozepore' *less* the withdrawals due to be made by India under the provisions of Paragraphs 21 (*b*), 22 and 23.

Table B

Period	Floor Discharge at Merala Above	Ceiling Discharge at Merala Above	'Gross amount' as at Ferogepore, corresponding to the Ceiling Discharge	Factor to be applied to the 'gross amount' As determined under Paragraph 22(b)
Col. (1)	Col. (2)	Col. (3)	Col. (4)	Col. (5)
			cusecs	
April 1–10	11,100	22,500	8,600	0.60
11–20	12,000	27,600	12,900	0.60
21–30	12,100	30,000	16,000	0.60
May 1–10	18,000	37,100	17,300	0.60
11–20	19,900	39,000	17,300	0.65
21–30	21,600	40,900	17,300	0.70
June 1–10	19,100	38,100	17,300	0.70
11–20	22,900	41,900	17,300	0.70
21–30	22,700	41,500	17,300	0.70
July 1–10	20,200	38,900	17,300	0.70
11–20	22,000	41,200	17,300	0.70
21–30	20,000	39,900	18,400	0.70
Aug. 1–10	14,100	33,700	18,400	0.70
11–20	15,000	34,500	18,400	0.70
21–30	18,300	37,300	18,400	0.70
Sept. 1–10	20,400	39,700	17,200	0.70
11–20	22,200	40,400	17,200	0.70
21–30	21,100	39,300	17,200	0.70

(ii) The appropriate 'gross amount', as at Ferozepore, determined in accordance with Paragraph 22 (b).

25.   After allowing for the withdrawals by India under the provisions of Paragraphs 21 (b), 22, 23 and 24, the balance of the 'Sutlej Component at Ferozepore' and of the 'Beas Component at Ferozepore' shall be delivered at Ferozepore for use by the Pakistan Sutlej Valley Canals.

26.   Pakistan undertakes that, between 1st April and 30th June, and between 11th and 30th September, when the flow at Merala Above on any day is less than the appropriate Ceiling Discharge shown in Column (3) of Table B, it will not allow surplus water to escape below Khanki or below Balloki (except in circumstances arising out of an operational emergency or out of inherent difficulties in the operation of the system of works) and will cause such surplus waters to be transferred to Suleimanke. If, however, there should be spill at Khanki or at Balloki because of the afore said circumstances, Pakistan will immediately inform India of the reasons for such spill and take steps to discontinue the spill as soon as possible.

27.   If the aggregate of (i) and (ii) below does not exceed 35,000 cusecs during any Water-accounting Period from April 1–10 to June 21–30, or 30,000 cusecs during

September 11–20 or 21–30, and if Pakistan expects at any time during any of these Water-accounting Periods, that on one or more days it would be unable to use in its Sutlej Valley Canals the supplies likely to be available to it under the provisions of Paragraph 25 and the probable transfers under Paragraph 26, and that there is, therefore, a likelihood of escapage below Islam, Pakistan agrees that it will give such timely information to India as will enable India to make such additional withdrawals at or above Ferozepore on the day or days to be specified as will reduce the escapage below Islam to a minimum.

(i) The likely delivery to Pakistan at Ferozepore under the provisions of Paragraph 25.

(ii) The probable appropriate 'gross amount', as at Ferozepore, determined in accordance with Paragraph 22 (*b*).

Provided that the above provisions shall not apply during any Water-accounting Period in which (i) above is zero.

28. Subject to the provisions of Paragraph 64 and to the payment by Pakistan, by due date, of the amounts to be specified under the provisions of Paragraph 49, India agrees to deliver into the Dipalpur Canal at Ferozepore, during each Water-accounting Period, such part of the supplies due to be released by India under the provisions of Paragraph 25, as Pakistan may request, limited to a maximum of 6,950 cusecs: Provided that no claim shall lie against India if, because of circumstances arising out of the inherent difficulties in feeding the Dipalpur Canal, the supply delivered into the Dipalpur Canal should at any time fall below the supply requested by Pakistan to be fed into this Canal out of the total supplies due to be released by India at Ferozepore.

PART 4 — DISTRIBUTION OF THE WATERS OF THE SUTLEJ AND THE BEAS
IN KHARIF DURING PHASE II

29. Subject to the provisions of Paragraphs 30 and 31 below, India agrees to deliver at Ferozepore for use by the Pakistan Sutlej Valley Canals the following minimum supplies during Phase II:

(*a*) In each Water-accounting Period during April 1–30: 74 per cent of the amount calculated for delivery at Ferozepore under the provisions of Paragraph 25 *minus* 21 per cent of the 'gross amount' determined in accordance with Paragraph 22 (*b*): Provided that, during April 1–10 in any year, if the discharge at Trimmu Above is less than 8,500 cusecs, the delivery during April 1–10 in that year shall be the same as under the provisions of Paragraph 25.

(*b*) In each Water-accounting Period during May 1–31: 71 per cent of the amount calculated for delivery at Ferozepore under the provisions of Paragraph 25 *minus* 24 per cent of the 'gross amount' determined in accordance with Paragraph 22 (*b*).

(*c*) In each Water-accounting Period during June 1–30: 58 per cent of the amount calculated for delivery at Ferozepore under the provisions of Paragraph 25 *minus* 36 per cent of the 'gross amount' determined in accordance with Paragraph 22 (*b*).

(*d*) July 1–10: 3,000 cusecs.

(*e*) July 11–20 to August 21–31: 4,000 cusecs.

(*f*) September 1–10: 3,000 cusecs.

(*g*) September 11–20 and 21–30: As under the provisions of Part 3 of this Annexure reduced by the following:

66 per cent of the amount by which the discharge at Trimmu Above (corrected for actual gains and losses between Trimmu and Panjnad, allowing a time-lag of three days from Trimmu to Panjnad) exceeds the smaller of the following two quantities:

 (i) the sum of the actual withdrawals by the Panjnad and Haveli canals; and
(ii) 19,600 cusecs:

Provided that the gains from Trimmu to Panjnad shall be deemed to be limited to the actual withdrawals at Panjnad and provided further that the reduction, as thus calculated, shall be limited to a daily maximum of 7,000 cusecs and shall not exceed one-third of the sum of the supply which would have been delivered at Ferozepore under the provisions of Paragraph 25 and the 'gross amount' determined in accordance with Paragraph 22 (*b*).

30. As soon as the Rasul-Qadirabad and the Qadirabad-Balloki Links are ready to operate, the deliveries at Ferozepore for use by the Pakistan Sutlej Valley Canals, as specified in Paragraph 29, may be reduced

(*a*) in each Water-accounting Period during April 1–10 to June 21–30, by (AX-AB) cusecs limited to (AY) cusecs where

X = the actual discharge at Rasul Above (including the supply in the tail-race of the Rasul hydro-electric plant),

Y = difference between 18,400 cusecs (limited during April 1–10 to 21–30 to the 'gross amount' as at Ferozepore corresponding to the Ceiling Discharge in Table B, read with provisos (i) and (ii) of Paragraph 22 (*b*) and the actual 'gross amount' worked out under Paragraph 22 (*b*),

A = a factor equal to 0.60 from April 1–10 to May 1–10, 0.65 for May 11–20, and 0.70 from May 21–31 to June 21–30, and

B = 24,000 cusecs from April 1–10 to 21–30,
32,000 cusecs from May 1–10 to 21–31 and
40,500 cusecs from June 1–10 to 21–30; and

(*b*) during July 1–10 and 11–20, by 1,000 cusecs.

31. As soon as the supplies specified in Paragraph 66 are available for reduction of deliveries by India during September, the Commissioners will meet and agree upon modifications in the provisions relating to the deliveries at Ferozepore during September 11–20 and 21–30. In case the Commissioners are unable to agree, the

difference shall be dealt with by a Neutral Expert in accordance with the provisions of Annexure F.

32.   Subject to the provisions of Paragraph 64 and to the payment by Pakistan, by due date, of the amounts to be specified under the provisions of Paragraph 49, India will arrange to deliver into the Dipalpur Canal at Ferozepore, during each Water-accounting Period, such part of the supplies due to be released for Pakistan under the provisions of Paragraphs 29, 30 and 31 as Pakistan may request, limited to a maximum of 6,950 cusecs: Provided that no claim shall lie against India if, because of circumstances arising out of the inherent difficulties in feeding the Dipalpur Canal, the supply delivered into the Dipalpur Canal should at any time fall below the supply requested by Pakistan to be fed into this canal out of the total supplies due to be released by India at Ferozepore.

33.   Subject to the provisions of Paragraphs 29 to 32 and Paragraph 57, there shall be no restriction on the use by India of the waters of The Sutlej and The Beas in *kharif* during Phase II.

PART 5 — DISTRIBUTION OF THE WATERS OF THE SUTLEJ AND THE BEAS IN RABI

34.   Subject to the provisions of Paragraphs 35 to 38, during the Transition Period India agrees to deliver at Ferozepore for use by the Pakistan Sutlej Valley Canals, the following minimum supplies during *rabi:*—

(a) October 1–10 and October 11–15: (i) 84 per cent of the 'Beas Component at Ferozepore' *plus* (ii) 1,670 cusecs *minus* (iii) the actual gains from Ferozepore to Islam.

(b) October 16–20: (i) 79 per cent of the 'Beas Component at Ferozepore' *plus* (ii) 960 cu secs *minus* (iii) the actual gains from Ferozepore to Islam.

(c) October 21–31: (i) 79 per cent of the 'Beas Component at Ferozepore' *plus* (ii) 640 cusecs *minus* (iii) the actual gains from Ferozepore to Islam.

(d) November 1–10: (i) 79 per cent of the 'Beas Component at Ferozepore' *plus* (ii) 570 cusecs *minus* (iii) the actual gains from Ferozepore to Islam.

(e) In each Water-accounting Period from November 11–20 to March 21–31: 79 per cent of the 'Beas Component at Ferozepore'.

35.   When the flow at Trimmu Above, during March 1–10, 11–20 and 21–31 in any year, exceeds the smaller of the following two quantities:

(i) the supplies required at Trimmu Above to meet the withdrawals of the Haveli and Panjnad Canals (after allowing a time-lag of five days from Trimmu to Panjnad), and

(ii) 7,500 cusecs during Phase I or 10,000 cusecs during Phase II,

the deliveries specified in Paragraph 34 (e) may be reduced, during March 1–10, 11–20 and 21–31 in that year, by amounts related to Pakistan's ability to replace.

For March 1–10, 11–20 and 21–31, these amounts shall be taken as equal to 60 per cent of the 'gross amount' determined as follows:

> When the sum of (*a*) the average discharge at Merala Above (obtained by limiting the daily values to a maximum of 25,000 cusecs during March 1–10, a maximum of 26,000 cusecs during March 11–20 and a maximum of 27,000 cusecs during March 21–31) and (*b*) the Ravi Component at Balloki Above (total supply at Balloki Above *minus* the delivery at U.C.C. tail *minus* the delivery at M.R. Link outfall *minus* the delivery into the Ravi Main through B.R.B.D. escapes, the result being limited to a minimum of zero) is less than or equal to the Floor Discharge shown in Column (2) of Table C below, the 'gross amount', as at Ferozepore, shall be zero. When this sum equals or exceeds the Ceiling Discharge shown in Column (3) of Table C, the 'gross amount', as at Ferozepore, shall be the amount shown in Column (4) of Table C. When the sum is between the values shown in the said Columns (2) and (3), the 'gross amount', as at Ferozepore, shall be the proportional intermediate amount.

Table C

Period	Floor Discharge	Ceiling Discharge	'Gross amount', as at Ferozepore, corresponding to the Ceiling Discharge
Col. (1)	*Col. (2)*	*Col. (3)*	*Col. (4)*
		cusecs	
March 1–10	14,500	21,200	5,000
11–20	14,500	22,000	6,000
21–31	14 500	24 000	8,000

36. If, during any Water-accounting Period, the aggregate of (i), (ii) and (iii) below exceeds 25,000 cusecs during October 1–10 and 11–15 or 10,000 cusecs from October 16–20 to March 21–31, the deliveries due to be made under the provisions of Paragraphs 34 and 35 may be reduced by the amount of such excess over 25,000 cusecs or 10,000 cusecs, as the case may be.

(i) Deliveries due to Pakistan at Ferozepore under the provisions of Paragraphs 34 and 35.
(ii) During March only, 60 per cent of the appropriate 'gross amount', as worked out under Paragraph 35.
(iii) During October 1–10 to November 1–10 only, the actual gains from Ferozepore to Islam, or, under the circumstances specified in Paragraph 62, the estimated gains agreed upon between the Commissioners.

37. In Phase II, during March, the deliveries to Pakistan, under the provisions of Paragraphs 34 to 36, may on any day be reduced by 60 per cent of the amount by

which the discharge at Trimmu Above two days earlier exceeds 10,000 cusecs, but the reduction on this account shall not exceed 12 per cent of the 'Beas Component at Ferozepore'.

38.   As soon as the supplies specified in Paragraph 66 are available for reduction of deliveries by India during *rabi*, the Commissioners will meet and agree upon modifications in the deliveries to be made by India at Ferozepore during *rabi*. In case the Commissioners are unable to agree, the difference shall be dealt with by a Neutral Expert in accordance with the provisions of Annexure F.

39.   Subject to the provision of Paragraph 64 and to the payment by Pakistan, by due date, of the amounts to be specified under the provisions of Paragraph 49, India agrees to deliver into the Dipalpur Canal at Ferozepore, during October 1–10 and 11–15 in each year, such part of the supplies due to be released for Pakistan under the provisions of Paragraphs 34 to 38 as Pakistan may request, limited to a maximum of 6,950 cusecs: Provided that no claim shall lie against India if, because of circumstances arising out of the inherent difficulties in feeding the Dipalpur Canal, the supply delivered into the Dipalpur Canal should at any time fall below the supply requested by Pakistan to be fed into this canal out of the total supplies due to be released by India at Ferozepore.

40.   Subject to the provisions of Paragraphs 34 to 38 and Paragraph 57, there shall be no restriction on the use by India of the waters of The Sutlej and The Beas during *rabi*.

PART 6 — WATER-ACCOUNTS AT FEROZEPORE

41.   An account of the distribution of waters, as at Ferozepore, under the provisions of Parts 3, 4 and 5 of this Annexure will be maintained by each Commissioner in accordance with the provisions of Paragraphs 42 to 46, and appropriate Forms will be used, both for Phase I and Phase II, in order to facilitate, and to provide a record of, the distribution of waters in accordance with the provisions of this Annexure. Such Forms for Phase I are set out in Appendix II[29] to this Annexure. Appropriate Forms for Phase II will be prepared by the Commission. The Forms (both for Phase I and Phase II) may, from time to time, be modified or added to by the Commission, but only to the extent that the Com mission finds it necessary to do so in order to further facilitate, and to maintain an appropriate record of, the distribution of waters in accordance with the provisions of this Annexure. In the absence of agreement in the Commission, the question shall be referred to a Neutral Expert for decision in accordance with the provisions of Annexure F.

42.   Each calendar month will be divided into three Water-accounting Periods, viz., 1st to 10th, 11th to 20th and 21st to the last day of the month, except the month of October which will be divided into four Water-accounting Periods, viz., 1st to 10th, 11th to 15th, 16th to 20th and 21st to 31st.

43.   For each Water-accounting Period, the river supplies or withdrawals or deliveries at any point will, unless otherwise specified in this Annexure, be taken as

---

[29]See p. 264 of this volume.

the average values of the daily figures for the days included in or corresponding to that Water-accounting Period.

44.   The water-accounts for the period April 1–10 to July 1–10 (Ferozepore dates) will be prepared with due allowance for time-lag as set out in Appendix I[30] to this Annexure.

45.   (*a*) The 'Sutlej Component at Ferozepore' during each Water-accounting Period from April 1–10 to September 21–30 and the 'Beas Component at Ferozepore' during each Water-accounting Period from April 1–10 to March 21–31 shall be worked out in accordance with Appendix I to this Annexure.

(*b*) During the Water-accounting Periods from September 11–20 to November 1–10, the gains and losses in the reach from Ferozepore to Islam shall be taken as the actual gains or losses calculated without allowance for time-lag.

(*c*) A conveyance loss of 6 per cent from the head of the Madhopur Beas Link to the junction of the Chakki Torrent with the Beas Main shall be adopted until revised, at the request of either Commissioner, as follows:

(i) The figure may be revised by agreement between the Commissioners, either after a study of available data and general considerations or after an analysis of discharge observations to be carried out jointly by the Commissioners, at the request of either Commissioner, or

(ii) if the Commissioners are unable to agree on a suitable figure (or figures) for the conveyance losses, the matter may be referred to a Neutral Expert for decision in accordance with the provisions of Annexure F.

(*d*) The procedure for working out the equivalents, at Mandi Plain, of any withdrawals from the Beas Main by any new canal constructed after the Effective Date, with a capacity of more than 10 cusecs, or of any abstractions from the flow waters by, or releases of stored waters from, any reservoir on The Beas will be determined by the Com mission at the appropriate time.

(*e*) An allowance for run-out (*Nikal*) shall be made in the water-account in respect of the waters passed into The Beas by the M.B. Link (including escapages from the U.B.D.C. into The Beas). This allowance shall equal the volume of water passed by the Link (including escapages from U.B.D.C.) into The Beas on the last two days of the operation of the Link during the period from 1st September to 15th October and it shall be accounted for at Mandi Plain during the ten days following the closure of the Link: Provided that this allowance shall be made only once and if the Link is re-opened thereafter, no further allowance on that account shall be made.

46.   Every effort will be made by India to balance the water-account at Ferozepore for each of the Water-accounting Periods, but any excess or deficit in deliveries due to Pakistan, in any Water-accounting Period, under the provisions of this Annexure, that may arise out of the inherent difficulties in determining these

---

[30]See p. 262 of this volume.

deliveries shall be carried over to the next Water-accounting Period for adjustment: Provided that:

(*a*) If, in any Water-accounting Period during Phase I, the sum of (i), (ii) and (iii) below exceeds 35,000 cusecs during April 1–10 to August 21–31, 30,000 cusecs during September 1–10 to 21–30, 25,000 cusecs during October 1–10 or 11–15, or 10,000 cusecs during October 16–20 to March 21–31, then there will be no carry-over from any such period to the next period.

   (i) The supply at Ferozepore Below (including withdrawals by the Dipalpur Canal, if any).

   (ii) During March 1–10 to September 21–30, the appropriate 'gross amount', as at Ferozepore, determined in accordance with Paragraph 22 (*b*) or Paragraph 35.

   (iii) During September 11–20 to November 1–10, the actual gains and losses from Ferozepore to Islam, losses being treated as negative gains; or, under the circum stances specified in Paragraph 62, the estimated gains agreed upon between the Commissioners.

(*b*) If, in any Water-accounting Period, the indents of the Indian Canals at Ferozepore and Harike have been fully met and there is an excess delivery to Pakistan at Feroze pore, then such excess shall not be carried forward to the next period.

(*c*) In each year, the water-account shall be finally closed at the end of the Water-accounting Period March 21–31 and any excess or deficit in the water-account, at the end of that Period, shall not be carried over to the succeeding Water-accounting Period, viz., April 1–10.

(*d*) If, during Phase I, in any Water-accounting Period from April 1–10 to June 21–30, the withdrawals computed as due to India under the provisions of Paragraphs 21 (*b*), 22, 23 and 24 exceed the supply available to India from the 'Sutlej Component at Ferozepore' and from the 'Beas Component at Ferozepore' taken together, then, in the water-account only 50 per cent of such excess shall be carried over for use by India.

(*e*) If, during Phase II, in any Water-accounting Period from April 1–10 to June 21–30, the withdrawals computed as due to India from the 'Sutlej Component at Ferozepore' and from the 'Beas Component at Ferozepore' after allowing for the deliveries due to Pakistan at Ferozepore under the provisions of Paragraphs 29 and 30 exceed the supply available to India from the 'Sutlej Component at Ferozepore' and from the 'Beas Component at Ferozepore', then such excess shall be treated separately and accounted for as below:

   (i) The excess may be carried over for adjustment to the succeeding Water-accounting Period and, where necessary, to the next succeeding Water-accounting Period, but shall be deemed to have lapsed if not adjusted by then.

   (ii) The cumulative excess carried over shall not exceed 2,000 cusecs from April 1–10 to May 21–31 and 3,000 cusecs during June 1–10 to 21–30.

   (iii) In no case shall the excess be carried over beyond June 21–30.

47.   As soon as possible after the end of each Water-accounting Period, each Commissioner will intimate to the other, by telegram, the excess or deficit carried over to the next Water-accounting Period. On receipt of this information, either Commissioner may. if he considers it necessary, ask for an exchange of the relevant water-accounts.

PART 7 — FINANCIAL PROVISIONS

48.   For each year for which Pakistan has not exercised the option under the provisions of Paragraph 20:

(a) India will, by 1st February preceding, communicate to Pakistan, in writing, the estimated proportionate working expenses payable by Pakistan for the Madhopur Headworks and the carrier channels calculated in accordance with Appendix III[31] to this Annexure; and

(b) Pakistan will pay to the Reserve Bank of India, New Delhi, for the credit of the Government of India, before 1st April of that year, the amount intimated by India.

49.   For each year for which Pakistan has not exercised the option under the provisions of Paragraph 64:

(a) India will, by 1st February preceding, communicate to Pakistan, in writing, the estimated proportionate working expenses payable by Pakistan for the Ferozepore Headworks (including the part of the Dipalpur Canal in India) calculated in accordance with Appendix IV[32] to this Annexure; and

(b) Pakistan will pay to the Reserve Bank of India, New Delhi, for the credit of the Government of India, before 1st April of that year, the amount intimated by India.

50.   As soon as the figures of actual audited expenditures on the Madhopur Headworks and the carrier channels and on the Ferozepore Headworks for each year are supplied by the Accountant General, Punjab (India), but not later than one year after the end of the year to which the expenditure relates, India will communicate to Pakistan, in writing, the actual expenditure corresponding to the estimated proportionate working expenses paid by Pakistan under the provisions of Paragraphs 48 (b) and 49 (b). If the actual proportionate expenditure is less than the amount paid by Pakistan under the provisions of Paragraphs 48 (b) and 49 (b), India shall, within one month, refund the difference to Pakistan and if the actual proportionate expenditure is more than the amount paid, Pakistan shall, within one month, make an additional payment to India to cover the difference.

51.   The payments by Pakistan to India under the provisions of Paragraphs 48, 49 and 50 and the refund by India under the provisions of Paragraph 50 shall

---

[31] See p. 286 of this volume.
[32] See p. 288 of this volume.

be made with out any set off against any other financial transaction between the Parties.

PART 8 — EXTENSION OF TRANSITION PERIOD

52.   In the event that Pakistan is of the opinion that the replacement referred to in Article IV (1) cannot be effected unless the Transition Period is extended beyond 31st March 1970, this period may be extended at the request of Pakistan

(a) by one, two or three years beyond 31st March 1970; or

(b) having been extended initially by one year beyond 31st March 1970, then by one or two years beyond 31st March 1971; or

(c) having been extended initially by two years beyond 31st March 1970, or having been extended by one year beyond 31st March 1971 under (b) above, then by one more year beyond 31st March 1972.

53.   A request by Pakistan for any extension under the provisions of Paragraph 52 shall be made to India by formal notice in writing, and any such notice shall specify the date up to which Pakistan requests an extension under the aforesaid provisions. On the receipt of such notice by India within the time-limit specified in Paragraph 54, the Transition Period shall be extended up to the date requested by Pakistan.

54.   A formal notice under Paragraph 53 shall be given as early as possible and, in any event, in such manner as to reach India at least twelve months before the due date for the expiration of the Transition Period. Unless such a notice is received by India within this time-limit, the Transition Period shall expire on the due date without any right of extension or further extension: Provided however that the Transition Period shall be extended, within the provisions of Paragraph 52, by an exceptional notice of request for an extension received by India not later than five months before the due date for expiration of the Transition Period, if, within the twelve months prior to such due date, heavy flood damage should have occurred which, in the opinion of Pakistan, cannot be repaired in time to operate the system of works as planned.

PART 9 — GENERAL

55.   India may continue to irrigate from the Eastern Rivers those areas which were so irrigated, as on the Effective Date, from The Sutlej, The Beas or The Ravi by means other than the canals taking off at Madhopur, Nangal, Rupar, Harike and Ferozepore: Provided that

(i) any withdrawals by the Shahnehr Canal in excess of 940 cusecs during any Water-accounting Period shall be accounted for in the estimation of the 'Beas Component at Ferozepore', and

(ii) the capacity of the Shahnehr Canal shall not be increased beyond its actual capacity as on the Effective Date (about 1,000 cusecs).

If India should construct a barrage across the Beas Main below the head of the Shahnehr Canal or undertake such other works as would enable the Canal to increase its withdrawals by more than 50 cusecs over and above those attained as on the Effective Date, the withdrawals during each Water-accounting Period in excess of the average withdrawals for each such period during the five years preceding the completion of the barrage or of such other works shall be accounted for in the estimation of the 'Beas Component at Ferozepore'.

56.   India agrees that, from 21st September to 31st March, it will not make any withdrawals for Agricultural Use by Government canals or by power pumps from the Ravi Main below Madhopur, in excess of the withdrawals as on the Effective Date.

57.   Subject to the provisions of Paragraph 55, India agrees that it will not make any withdrawals for Agricultural Use from the Sutlej Main below Ferozepore from the supplies delivered at Ferozepore for use by the Pakistan Sutlej Valley Canals.

58.   India shall be entitled to utilise without restriction the waters stored by it (in accordance with the provisions of this Annexure) in any reservoir on the Eastern Rivers or in the ponds at Nangal or Harike.

59.   Pakistan agrees that

(i) it will have filled the ponds at Suleimanke and Islam by 10th September in each year to the maximum extent possible without causing the maximum working head across the weirs and the maximum pond levels to exceed the values given in Table D below:

Table D

Weir	Maximum working head in feet	Maximum pond level (R. L)
Suleimanke	18.5	569.0
Islam	18.0 .	452.0

(ii) after the river has fallen to a stage at which the releases from the ponds will not result in a spill below Islam, it will lower the pond levels gradually to R. L. 565.5 at Suleimanke and R. L. 449.0, or lower if possible, at Islam, and complete the lowering, as far as possible, by 31st October, without spilling below Islam; and

(iii) it will use its best endeavours to fill the pond at Islam to R. L. 455.0, provided that this does not endanger the safety of the weir:

Provided that the above provisions in so far as they relate to the Islam Weir shall lapse on the date Pakistan discontinues the use of this weir. Instead, the pond at the new weir below Islam shall be filled by 10th September each year and lowered by 31st October in accordance with the above provisions, but the maximum working head in feet, the maxi mum pond level and the level to which the pond is to be lowered by 31st October shall be determined in accordance with the design of the new weir.

60. Pakistan agrees that it will not release any water below the barrage at Suleimanke between 13th October and 10th November, except when the supply reaching Suleimanke on any day (including the delivery, if any, from B. S. Link tail) is in excess of 6,000 cusecs, when the excess on that day over 4,000 cusecs may be released. If the supply reaching Islam falls below 350 cusecs, Pakistan may release supplies below Suleimanke provided that such releases shall be so regulated that the supply reaching Islam does not appreciably exceed 20 per cent of the sum of the withdrawals, at head, of the perennia Pakistan Sutlej Valley Canals.

61. Pakistan agrees that from 21st August to 15th September it will, except under unavoidable circumstances, run the B. S. Link with a discharge not less than 13,000 cusecs, at head.

62. If, for any reason, Pakistan is unable to adhere to the programme for filling and emptying the ponds at Suleimanke and Islam, as set out in Paragraph 59, the Commissioners will agree on an estimate of the gains which would have accrued in the reach from Ferozepore to Islam but for Pakistan's inability to adhere to the aforesaid programme and these estimated gains will be used in the water-account instead of the actual gains or losses.

63. In the event of an emergency, leading to circumstances under which Pakistan is unable to fulfil the provisions of Paragraph 61, the actual gains or losses will be used in the water-account, and the Pakistan Commissioner will immediately inform the Indian Commissioner of the emergency and take steps to restore normal conditions as soon as possible.

64. Pakistan shall have the option to request India to discontinue the deliveries into the Dipalpur Canal. This option may be exercised effective 1st April in any year by written notification delivered to India before 30th September preceding. On receipt of such notification, India will cease to have any obligation to make deliveries into the Di palpur Canal during the remaining part of the Transition Period.

65. If, owing to heavy floods,

(i) damage should occur to any of the Link Canals (including Headworks) specified in Column (1) below during the period specified for that particular Link Canal in Column (2) below, and

(ii) as a result of such damage, the ability of that Link Canal to transfer supplies should have been diminished to an extent causing serious interruption of supplies in irrigation canals dependent on that Link Canal,

then the two Commissioners will promptly enter into consultations, with the good offices of the Bank, to work out the steps to be taken to restore the situation to normal and to work out such temporary modifications of the relevant provisions of this Annexure as may be agreed upon as appropriate and desirable, taking equitably into consideration the consequences of such modifications on the cultivators concerned both in India and in Pakistan. Any modifications agreed upon shall lapse on the terminal date specified in Column (2) below.

	Column (1)	*Column* (2)
(a)	M. R. Link	Up to 31st March 1962
(b)	B. S. Link	Up to 31st March 1962
(c)	B. R. B. D. Link	Up to 31st March 1962
(d)	Trimmu-Islam Link (including the Headworks for this Link on the Ravi Main and the Sutlej Main).	Two years beginning from the date on which the Link is ready to operate, but not to extend beyond 31st March 1968.
(e)	Rasul-Qadirabad and Qadirabad-Balloki Links (including the Head-works for these Links).	Three years beginning from the date on which the Links extend beyond the end are ready to operate, but not to of the Transition Period.

66. If, at any time before the end of the Transition Period, the Bank is of the opinion that the part of the system of works referred to in Article IV (1) is ready to provide additional supplies during September 11–30 and *rabi*, over and above the replacements in these periods specifically provided for in Parts 2 to 5 of this Annexure, it shall so notify the Par ties. On receipt of such notification, Pakistan shall provide, towards a reduction of the deliveries by India during September 11–30 and *rabi* to the C.B.D.C. and at Ferozepore under the provisions of Parts 2 to 5 of this Annexure, the equivalent (at points of delivery) of 60 per cent of the total supplies made available by the whole of the above-mentioned system of works: Provided that, in computing the aforesaid total supplies, any contribution from the Indus and any supplies developed by tube-wells shall be excluded.

67. The provisions of this Annexure may be amended by agreement between the Commissioners. Any such amendment shall become effective when agreement thereto has been signified in an exchange of letters between the two Governments.

PART 10 — SPECIAL PROVISIONS FOR 1960 AND 1961

68. The actual withdrawals made by India and the actual deliveries made by India into the C.B.D.C., into the Dipalpur Canal and into the Sutlej Main at Ferozepore, during the period between the Effective Date and the date on which this Treaty enters into force, shall be deemed to be withdrawals and deliveries made in accordance with the provisions of this Annexure.

69. For the year commencing on 1st April 1960, (a) the communication by India of the amount of the estimated proportionate working expenses specified in Paragraphs 48 (a) and 49 (a) shall be made within one month of the date on which this Treaty enters into force and (b) the payment by Pakistan to India specified in Paragraphs 48 (b) and 49 (b) with respect to that year shall be made by Pakistan within three months of the date on which this Treaty enters into force and the provisions of Paragraph 50 shall then apply.

70. Subject to the provisions of Paragraph 28 and if the supplies due to be released for Pakistan at Ferozepore, during 1961 from April 1–10 to June 21–30,

are less than the amounts set out in Column (2) below and Pakistan is unable to deliver into the Dipalpur Canal from the B.R.B.D. Link during April, May or June amounts equal to the aggregate amounts specified for that month in Column (2) below, India will make additional deliveries into the Dipalpur Canal at Ferozepore to make up these aggregate amounts in such manner as to ensure that the canal is not closed for more than 10 days either in May or in June 1961.

Column (1)		*Column (2)*
April	1–10	Nil cusecs
	11–15	Nil ”
	16–20	1,000 ”
	21–30	800 ”
Aggregate for April		13,000 cusec-days
May	1–10	Nil cusecs
	11–20	1,000 ”
	21–31	800 ”
Aggregate for May		18,800 cusec-days
June	1–10	1,000 cusecs
	11–20	1,000 ”
	21–30	1,200 ”
Aggregate for April		32,000 cusec-days

APPENDIX I TO ANNEXURE H

PROVISIONS FOR TIME-LAG AND FOR DETERMINATION OF THE 'SUTLEJ COMPONENT AT FEROZEPORE' AND THE 'BEAS COMPONENT AT FEROZEPORE'

A. *Time-lag*

	Time-lag in days	
	April	*May 1 to July 10* (*Ferozepore Dates*)
Bhakra/Nangal to Rupar	1	1
Rupar to Ferozepore	4	3
Ferozepore to Suleimanke	3	2
Shahnehr Canal head to Mandi Plain	3	2
Mandi Plain to Ferozepore	1	1
Western Bein to Ferozepore	1	1
Madhopur to Mandi Plain via Beas	3	2
Mirthal to Mandi Plain	3	2

For other periods and reaches, unless otherwise specified in this Annexure, the dates will be taken to be the same as the dates at Ferozepore, with no allowance for time-lag.

B. *'Sutlej Component at Ferozepore' corresponding to assumed releases of flow waters below Rupar*

(i) The assumed releases of flow waters below Rupar shall be taken as equal to the Sutlej flow waters, as distinct from stored waters, which would have been released below Rupar if the aggregate of the net Indian withdrawals from these flow waters had been limited to the values specified in Paragraph 21 (a) of this Annexure.

(ii) For each of the Water-accounting Periods from April 1–10 to August 21–31 (Ferozepore dates) the values of the 'Sutlej Component at Ferozepore' corresponding to the assumed releases below Rupar shall be worked out from the following table:

Assumed releases below Rupar		*'Sutlej Component at Ferozepore'*
(Cusecs)		*(Cusecs)*
below 500	. . . .	Actual at Ferozepore
500	. . . .	320
1,000	. . . .	640
1,500	. . . .	960
2,000	. . . .	1,280
3,000	. . . .	1,920
5,000	. . . .	3,200
7,500	. . . .	5,400
10,000	. . . .	7,600
15,000	. . . .	12,000
20,000	. . . .	16,400
30,000	. . . .	25,200
40,000	. . . .	34,000
50,000	. . . .	42,800
100,000	. . . .	86,800
200,000	. . . .	174,800

For intermediate values of the assumed releases below Rupar, in excess of 500 cusecs, the 'Sutlej Component at Ferozepore' will be worked out proportionately.

(iii) During September 1–10 to 21–30, the 'Sutlej Component at Ferozepore' shall be taken as equal to 0.90 S *plus* 400 cusecs, where S equals the assumed releases of flow water below Rupar (allowing three days time-lag between Ferozepore and Rupar).

C. *'Beas Component at Ferozepore' (X) corresponding to the sum (Y) of the Beas Component at Mandi Plain and the discharge of the Western Bein*

For each Water-accounting Period, the 'Beas Component at Ferozepore' (X) shall be worked out by multiplying the sum (Y) of the Beas Component at Mandi

Plain and the discharge of the Western Bein by the appropriate factor given in the following table:

Water-accounting Periods	*Factor for converting Y to X*
(*Ferozepore Dates*)	
April 1–10 and 11–20	0.95
April 21–30 and May 1–10	0.89
May 11–20 to July 1–10	0.87
July 11–20 to August 11–20	0.89
August 21–31 and September 1–10	0.92
September 11–20 to October 21–31	0.98
November 1–10 to 21–30	0.95
December 1–10 to 21–31	0.97
January 1–10 to February 21–28/29	0.92
March 1–10 to 21–31	0.94

APPENDIX II TO ANNEXURE H

FORMS OF WATER-ACCOUNT

FORM NO. 1 (a)

WATER-ACCOUNT AS AT FEROZEPORE FOR THE PERIODS
APRIL 1–10 TO SEPTEMBER 21–30

Water-accounting Period (Ferozepore Dates) . . . . *19* . . . .

Item	*Particulars*	*Dates (with time-lag, if any)*	*Average value (cusecs)*
	Part A		
1.	Sutlej Component at Ferozepore = Item (15) or (26) of Form 5, as the case may be.		
2.	Beas Component at Ferozepore = Item (20) of Form 2.		
3.	Withdrawal due to India as at Ferozepore, under Paragraph 21 (b) = [(1) + 16% of (2)] limited to . . . . . .* cusecs.		
	Part B		
4.	'Gross amount', as at Ferozepore = Item (10) or (14) of Form 4.		
5.	Additional withdrawal due to India, as at Ferozepore, under Paragraph 22 = (4) × . .†		
6.	Withdrawals due to India, as at Ferozepore, under Paragraphs 21(b) and 22 = (3) + (5).		
	Part C		
	To be worked out for Sept. 11–20 and 21–30 only		
7.	River gains from Ferozepore to Islam = Item (7) of Form 6.		
8.	Deductions under Paragraph 23 (3,400 cusecs for Sept. 11–20; 2,900 cusecs for Sept. 21–30).		
9.	Adjusted withdrawal due to India, as at Ferozepore, under Paragraph 23 = (6) + (7) −(8).		
	Part D		
10.	Aggregate of Sutlej and Beas Components at Ferozepore = (1) + (2).		

---

* 3,500 cusecs during April 1–10 to 21–30
  4,500 cusecs during May 1–10 to 21–31
  5,500 cusecs during June 1–10 to Sept. 21–30.
† 0.60 for Apr. 1–10 to May 1–10
  0.65 for May 11–20
  0.70 for May 21–31 to Sept.21–30.

Item	Particulars	Dates (with time-lag, if any)	Average value (cusecs)
11.	Excess of (10) over (6) or (9), as the case may be = (10) − (6) for Apr. 1–10 to Sept. 1–10 and (10) − (9) for Sept. 11–20 and 21–30.		
12.	Aggregate of (4) and (11).		
13.	Further withdrawal due to India as at Ferozepore under Paragraph 24 = (12) − 35,000 cusecs, if positive, during Apr. 1–10 to Aug. 21–31 or (12) − 30,000 cusecs, if positive, during Sept. 1–10 to 21–30.		
14.	Delivery due to Pakistan at Ferozepore under Paragraph 25 = (11) − (13).		

Part E

15.	Additional withdrawals due to India at Ferozepore as per information given by Pakistan under Paragraph 27 (to be taken as zero if (18) below is positive).		
16.	Deliveries due to Pakistan at Ferozepore under Paragraphs 25 and 27 = (14) − (15).		

Part F

17.	Withdrawal due to India, as at Ferozepore, under Paragraphs 21(b), 22, 23 and 24 = (6) + (13) for Apr. 1–10 to Sept. 1–10 and (9) + (13) for Sept. 11–20 and 21–30.		
18.	Excess of withdrawals due to India, as at Ferozepore, over available supply = [(17) − (10)] if positive.		
19.	50% of (18).		
20.	Brought forward from preceding Period = (25) of preceding Period multiplied by number of days in preceding Period divided by number of days in the current Period (zero for Apr. 1–10).		
21.	Adjusted delivery due to Pakistan at Ferozepore = (16) − (19) − (20).		

Part G

22.	River supply at Ferozepore Below (actual).		
23.	Delivery into Dipalpur Canal at Ferozepore (actual).		

Item	Particulars	Dates (*with time-lag, if any*)	*Average value* (*cusecs*)
24.	Total actual delivery to Pakistan at Ferozepore = (22) + (23).		
25.	Excess (+) or deficit (−) in deliveries to Pakistan at Ferozepore carried over** to succeeding Period = (24) − (21).		

**The carry-over will be subject to the following:

1. If Item (13) of Form 3 is zero or positive, then no excess shall be carried over to the succeeding Period, but any deficit shall be so carried over.
2. Neither excess nor deficit shall be carried over to the succeeding Period in case
   (i) Item (24) of this Form *plus* Item (4) of this Form exceeds 35,000 cusecs during Apr. 1–10 to Aug. 21–31 or 30,000 cusecs during Sept. 1–10; or
   (ii) Item (24) of this Form *plus* Item (4) of this Form *plus* Item (7) of Form 6, or *minus* Item (8) of Form 6, as the case may be, exceeds 30,000 cusecs during Sept. 11–20 or 21–30.

FORM NO. 1(*b*)

WATER-ACCOUNT AS AT FEROZEPORE FOR THE PERIODS OCTOBER 1–10 TO FEBRUARY 21–28/29

Water-accounting Period (Ferozepore Dates) . . . . . . 19 . . . .

Item	Particulars	*Average value* (*cusecs*)
1.	Beas Component at Ferozepore = Item (20) of Form 2.	
2.	...* per cent of Beas Component = ...* × (1)/100. (*Items 3 and 4 are to be worked out for October 1–10 to November 1–10 only.*)	
3.	Additional fixed supply to be delivered to Pakistan under Paragraph 34.	
4.	River gains from Ferozepore to Islam = Item (7) of Form 6, or gains estimated in accordance with Paragraph 62.	
5.	Supply to be delivered to Pakistan under Paragraph 34 = (2) + (3) − (4).	
6.	Aggregate of (4) and (5).	
7.	Excess of (6) over 25,000 cusecs during October 1–10 or 11–15, or 10,000 cusecs during October 16–20 to February 21–28/29.	

---

*84 per cent during October 1–10 and 11–15 and 79 per cent during October 16–20 to February 21–28/29.

Item	Particulars	Average value (*cusecs*)
8.	Delivery due to Pakistan under Paragraphs 34 and 36 = $(5) - (7)$.	
9.	Brought over from preceding Period = $(14)^\dagger$ of preceding Period multiplied by the number of days in preceding Period divided by number of days in the current Period.	
10.	Total delivery due to Pakistan = $(8) - (9)$.	
11.	Ferozepore Below (actual).	
12.	Dipalpur Canal at Head.	
13.	Total actual delivery to Pakistan = $(11) + (12)$.	
14.	Excess $(+)$ or deficit $(-)$ in deliveries to Pakistan to be carried over** to the succeeding Period = $(13) - (10)$.	

$\dagger$ For October 1–10, this will be Item 25 of Form 1 (*a*) for September 21–30.

** The carry-over will be subject to the following:

1. If Item (13) of Form 3 is zero or positive, then no excess shall be carried over to the succeeding Period but any deficit shall be so carried over.

2. In case Item (13) of this Form *plus* Item (4) of this Form or *minus* Item (8) of Form 6, as the case may be, exceeds 25,000 cusecs during October 1–10 or 11–15 or 10,000 cusecs during October 16–20 to March 21–31, then neither excess nor deficit shall be carried over to the succeeding Period.

FORM NO. 1 (*c*)

WATER-ACCOUNT AS AT FEROZEPORE FOR THE PERIODS MARCH 1–10 TO MARCH 21–31

Water-accounting Period (Ferozepore Dates) . . . . . . *19* . . . .

Item	Particulars	Average value (*cusecs*)
1.	Beas Component at Ferozepore = Item (20) of Form 2.	
2.	Delivery to be made to Pakistan at Ferozepore under Paragraph 34 (*e*) = 79 per cent of (1).	
3.	River supply at Trimmu Above.	
4.	River supply at Trimmu Below.	
5.	River supply at Panjnad Below (with 5 days time-lag from Trimmu, the Trimmu dates being the same as Ferozepore dates).	

Item	Particulars	*Average value (cusecs)*
6.	Supply required at Trimmu to meet the actual withdrawals of Panjnad Canals = (4) − (5), limited to a minimum of zero.	
7.	Actual withdrawals of Haveli Canals at Head.	
8.	Supply required at Trimmu to meet the needs of Haveli and Panjnad Canals = (6) + (7).	
9.	Lesser of (8) and 7,500 cusecs. *[Items (10) and (11) are to be taken as zero if (3) does not exceed (9).]*	
10.	'Gross amount', as at Ferozepore = Item (10) of Form 4.	
11.	Reduction to be made in (2), in accordance with Paragraph 35 = 60 per cent of (10).	
12.	Delivery due to Pakistan under Paragraphs 34 (*e*) and 35 = (2) − (11).	
13.	Aggregate of (11) and (12).	
14.	Excess of (13) over 10,000 cusecs.	
15.	Delivery due to Pakistan under Paragraphs 34 (*e*), 35 and 36 = (12) − (14).	
16.	Brought over from preceding Period = Item (19)* of preceding Period multiplied by number of days in the preceding Period divided by number of days in the current Period.	
17.	Total delivery due to Pakistan = (15) — (16).	
18.	Actual delivery (i.e., River supply at Ferozepore Below).	
19.	Excess (+) or deficit (−) in deliveries to Pakistan to be carried over[†] to the succeeding Period = (18) − (17). *[There shall be no carry-over from March 21–31 to the succeeding April 1–10.]*	

---

[*] For March 1–10, this will be Item (14) of Form 1 (*b*) for February 21–28/29.

[†] The carry-over will be subject to the following:

1. If Item (13) of Form 3 is zero or positive, then no excess shall be carried over to the succeeding Period, but any deficit shall be so carried over.
2. In case Item (10) of this Form *plus* Item (18) of this Form exceeds 10,000 cusecs during March 1–10 or March 11–20, then neither nor deficit shall be carried over to the succeeding Period.

FORM NO. 2

ESTIMATION OF THE BEAS COMPONENT AT FEROZEPORE
(PARAGRAPH 5 (*d*))

Water-accounting Period (Ferozepore Dates) . . . .*19* . . . .

Item	Particulars	Dates at site (*with due allowance for time-lag*)	Average value (*cusecs*)
1.	M. B. Link at head.		
2.	U. B. D. C. escapages into The Beas.		
3.	Ravi water transferred to The Beas* = $[0.94 \times (1) + (2)]$.		
4.	Chakki torrent above junction with Beas Main. [N.B.: This includes (3)]		
5.	Beas at Mirthal (upstream of the junction with Chakki).		
6.	Aggregate of (4) and (5).		
7.	River supply at Mandi Plain.		
8.	Ravi Component at Mandi Plain = (3) or $[(3) \times (7) \div (6)]$ whichever is smaller,		
9.	M. B. Link run-out allowance = Item (7) of Form 9.		
10.	Beas Component at Mandi Plain = $(7) - (8) - (9)$.		
11.	Withdrawals by Shahnehr Canal.		
12.	Excess, if any, of Shahnehr Canal over 940 cusecs.		
13.	Withdrawals from The Beas by new canals constructed after the Effective Date, each with a capacity of more than 10 cusecs.		
14.	Equivalent of (13) at Mandi Plain,[†]		
15.	Abstraction (+) of flow waters by, or release (−) of stored waters from, reservoirs on The Beas.		
16.	Equivalent of (15) at Mandi Plain.[†]		

*A conveyance loss of 6% from the head of the Madhopur-Beas Link to the outfall of the Chakki Torrent into the Beas Main will be used until revised in accordance with the provisions of Paragraph 45 (*c*).

[†]As determined in accordance with the provisions of Paragraph 45 (*d*).

Item	Particulars	Dates at site (with due allowance for time-lag)	Average value (cusecs)
17.	Corrected Beas Component at Mandi Plain = (10) + (12) + (14) + (16).		
18.	Inflow from Western Bein.		
19.	Aggregate of (17) and (18).		
20.	Beas Component at Ferozepore = (19) multiplied by the appropriate factor for the period given in Paragraph C of Appendix I to this Annexure.		

FORM NO. 3

INDIAN CANAL INDENTS AND WITHDRAWALS AT HARIKE AND FEROZEPORE

(PARAGRAPH 46 (*b*))

Water-accounting Period (Ferozepore Dates) . . . . .19 . . . . .

Item	Particulars	Dates at site (with due allowance for time-lag)	Average value (cusecs)
1.	Withdrawal by Makhu Canal at Harike.		
2.	Withdrawal by Ferozepore Feeder at Harike.		
3.	Withdrawal by Rajasthan Feeder at Harike.		
4.	Withdrawal by Bikaner Canal at Ferozepore.		
5.	Withdrawal by Eastern Canal at Ferozepore.		
6.	Total withdrawals = (1) + (2) + (3) + (4) + (5).		
7.	Indent of Makhu Canal at Harike.		
8.	Indent of Ferozepore Feeder at Harike.		
9.	Indent of Rajasthan Feeder at Harike.		
10.	Indent of Bikaner Canal at Ferozepore.		
11.	Indent of Eastern Canal at Ferozepore.		
12.	Total Indents = (7) + (8) + (9) + (10) + (11).		
13.	(6) − (12).		

FORM NO. 4

DETERMINATION OF THE 'GROSS AMOUNT' AS AT FEROZEPORE
(MARCH 1–10 TO SEPTEMBER 21–30 ONLY)

(PARAGRAPHS 22 AND 35)

Water-accounting Period* (Ferozepore Dates) . . . . 19 . . . . .

Item	Particulars	Average value (cusecs)
1.	Chenab at Merala Above (average of daily values, in accordance with Paragraphs 22 (*a*) or 35).	
2.	Ravi Component at Balloki (for March 1–10 to 21–31 only) = Item (5) of Form 7.	
3.	Aggregate of (1) and (2).	
4.	Appropriate 'Floor Discharge' = Column (2) of Table B[†] or Column (2) of Table C, as the case may be.	
5.	Appropriate 'Ceiling Discharge' = Column (3) of Table B[†] or Column (3) of Table C, as the case may be.	
6.	Difference, Ceiling *minus* Floor = (5) − (4).	
7.	Appropriate 'Gross amount' as at Ferozepore corresponding to (5) = Column (4) of Table B[†] or Column (4) of Table C, as the case may be.	
8.	Ratio of (7) to (6) = (7) ÷ (6) (worked out to 3 decimals).	
9.	Supplies available in excess of Floor Discharge = [(3) − (4)], limited to a maximum of (6) and a minimum of zero.	
10.	'Gross amount', as at Ferozepore, corresponding to (3) = (9) × (8).	
	[*Items (11) to (14) to be worked out only if there has been a closure at Merala under the circumstances of Paragraph 22 (b) (iii).*	
11.	Total amount, as at Ferozepore, for the closure days = Item (9) of Form 8.	cusec-days
12.	Total amount, as at Ferozepore, for the remaining days = Item (10) multiplied by number of non-closure days	cusec-days
13.	Aggregate of (11) and (12)	cusec-days
14.	'Gross amount', as at Ferozepore, for the Water-accounting Period as a whole = (13) divided by number of days in the Period	cusecs

---

*In case of a closure at Merala under the circumstances mentioned in Paragraph 22 (*b*) (iii), Items (1) to (10) shall be worked out for the non-closure days only.

[†]Subject to the provisos (i) and (ii) of Paragraph 22 (*b*).

FORM NO. 5

ESTIMATION OF THE SUTLEJ COMPONENT AT FEROZEPORE
(APRIL 1–10 TO SEPTEMBER 21–30 ONLY)

(PARAGRAPH 5 (*e*))

Water-accounting Period (Ferozepore Dates) . . . . 19 . . . . . .

Item	Particulars	Dates at site (*with due allowance for time-lag*)	Average value (*cusecs*)
1.	Withdrawal by Bhakra Main Line at Rupar.		
2.	Withdrawal by Sirhind Canal at Rupar.		
3.	Withdrawal by Bist Doab Canal at Rupar.		
4.	Aggregate of (1), (2) and (3).		
5.	Abstraction of flow waters by Bhakra Reservoir.		
6.	Abstraction of flow waters by the Nangal Pond.		
7.	Release of stored waters from Bhakra Reservoir.		
8.	Release of stored waters from the Nangal Pond.		
9.	Net abstraction of flow waters by Bhakra Reservoir and Nangal Pond = [(5) + (6) − (7) − (8)], limited to a minimum of zero.		
10.	Net release of stored waters from Bhakra Reservoir and Nangal Pond = [(7) + (8) − (5) − (6)], limited to a minimum of zero.		
11.	River supply at Rupar Below (actual).		
12.	Flow water, as at Rupar Above = (11) + (4) + (9) − (10).		
13.	Withdrawal from flow water due to India under Paragraph 21 (*a*) = (12), limited to 10,250 cusecs during April 1–10 to July 1–10; 12,000 cusecs during July 11–20 to August 21–31 and 10,500 cusecs during September 1–10 to 21–30.		
14.	Sutlej at Rupar Below, if India's withdrawals from flow waters had been limited to (13) = (12) − (13).		

[*Item (15) is to be worked out for:*

(*I*) *Apr. 1–10 to Aug. 21–31, only if (14) equals or exceeds 500 cusecs, and*

Item	Particulars	Dates at site (*with due allowance for time-lag*)	*Average value* (*cusecs*)
	(*ii*) *Sept. 1–10 to Sept. 21–30, irrespective of the value of* (*14*).]		
15.	Sutlej Component at Ferozepore corresponding to (14) as determined from Paragraph B (ii) or Paragraph B (iii) of Appendix I to this Annexure.		
	[*Items* (*16*) *to* (*26*) *are to be worked out only for Apr. 1–10 to Aug. 21–31 and then also only if* (*14*) *is less than 500 cusecs.*		
16.	Actual Sutlej flow at Usafpur (including inflow from Eastern Bein).		
17.	River supply at Mandi Plain (actual) *plus* inflow from Western Bein = Item (7) of Form 2 + Item (18) of Form 2.		
18.	Aggregate of (16) and (17).		
19.	Withdrawal by Makhu Canal at Harike.		
20.	Withdrawal by Ferozepore Feeder at Harike.		
21.	Withdrawal by Rajasthan Feeder at Harike.		
22.	Abstraction (+) from flow waters by, or release (−) of stored waters from, the Harike Pond.		
23.	Total withdrawal at Harike = (19) + (20) + (21) + (22).		
24.	River supply at Ferozepore Above (actual).		
25.	Sutlej Component at Ferozepore (actual, corrected for withdrawals at Harike) = [(16) ÷ (18)] × [(24) + 0.90 (23)].		
26.	Sutlej Component at Ferozepore for the purposes of Paragraph 21 (*b*) = (25), if (11) is equal to or less than (14); and (25) × (14) ÷ (11), if (11) is more than 500 cusecs.		

FORM NO. 6

ESTIMATION OR THE RIVER GAINS AND LOSSES FROM FEROZEPORE TO ISLAM
(SEPTEMBER 11–20 TO NOVEMBER 1–10 ONLY)

(PARAGRAPHS 23 AND 34)

Water-accounting Period (Ferozepore Dates) . . . . *19* . . . . .

Item	Particulars	Average value (cusecs)
1.	River at Ferozepore Below.	
2.	B. S. Link at tail.	
3.	Total withdrawals by canals at Suleimanke.	
4.	Trimmu-Islam Link delivery into Sutlej Main.	
5.	Total withdrawals by canals at Islam.	
6.	River at Islam Below.	
7.	River gains from Ferozepore to Islam = $[(3) + (5) + (6) - (1) - (2) - (4)]$ if positive.	
8.	River losses from Ferozepore to Islam = $[(1) + (2) + (4) - (3) - (5) - (6)]$ if positive.	

FORM NO. 7

ESTIMATION OF THE RAVI COMPONENT AT BALLOKI ABOVE
(MARCH 1–10 TO 21–31 ONLY)

(PARAGRAPH 35)

Water-accounting Period (Ferozepore Dates) . . . . *19* . . . . .

Item	Particulars	Average value (cusecs)
1.	Delivery at tail of M. R. Link.	
2.	Delivery into Ravi from B.R.B.D. escapes.	
3.	Delivery at tail of U.C.C.	
4.	Total river supply at Balloki Above.	
5.	Ravi component at Balloki = $[(4) - (1) - (2) - (3)]$ limited to a minimum of zero.	

FORM NO. 8

DETERMINATION OF THE 'GROSS AMOUNT' AS AT FEROZEPORE
DURING DAYS OF CLOSURE AT MERALA (APRIL 1–10 TO
SEPTEMBER 21–30 ONLY)

(PARAGRAPH 22 (b) (iii))

Water-accounting Period (Ferozepore Dates) . . . . 19 . . . . .

Item	Particulars	Daily discharges (cusecs)			
	Dates at Merala *(Same as Ferozepore dates)*				
1.	Jammu Tawi Discharge near Merala.				
2.	Chenab flow at Merala Above.				
3.	M. R. Link at head.				
4.	U.C.C. at head.				
	Dates at Balloki *(allowing 3 days time-lag from Merala to Balloki)*				
5.	Supplies at Balloki Above.				
6.	Share of B. S. Link = 0.67 × (5).				
7.	Q = Item (6) — 300 cusecs, limited to A.*				
8.	Daily 'gross amount' at Ferozepore = N × (7) where N = 1.08 during April 1–10 to August 21–31 and 1.00 during September 1–10 to 21–30.				
9.	Sum of daily 'gross amounts' for the closure days = sum of daily figures for (8) cusec-days.				

---

* A equals: 8,000 cusecs, April 1–10;

11,000 cusecs, April 11–20;

13,000 cusecs, April 21–30 and

15,000 cusecs, May 1–10 to Sept. 21–30.

FORM NO. 9

M. B. LINK RUN-OUT (NIKAL) ALLOWANCE
(SEPTEMBER 1 TO OCTOBER 15 ONLY)

(PARAGRAPH 45 (*e*))

Water-accounting Period (*Ferozepore Dates*) . . . . *19* . . . . .

Item	Particulars	Value
1.	Date* of the last day of operation of the M. B. Link.	
2.	M. B. Link at Head	
	(*a*) for the last day of operation	cusecs
	(*b*) for the day preceding (*a*)	cusecs
3.	Total of (2) (*a*) and (2) (*b*)	cusec-days
4.	U.B.D.C. escapages into The Beas	
	(*a*) for the last day of operation of the M. B.	
	Link	cusecs
	(*b*) for the day preceding (*a*)	cusecs
5.	Total of (4) (*a*) and (4) (*b*)	cusec-days
6.	Run-out (*nikal*) = [0.94 × (3)] *plus* (5)	cusec-days
7.	Average run-out allowance on account of M. B. Link = (6)	
	divided by 10	cusecs

*If the Link has run continuously since 30th August, then this date will be the date preceding that on which the Link closes for the first time after 31st August. If the Link has not been in continuous operation since 30th August, there shall be no run-out allowance.

APPENDIX III TO ANNEXURE H

CALCULATIONS FOR DETERMINING PROPORTIONATE WORKING EXPENSES TO BE
PAID BY PAKISTAN UNDER THE PROVISIONS OF
PARAGRAPHS 48 AND 50 OF THIS ANNEXURE

1.   Until Pakistan exercises the option under the provisions of Paragraph 20 of this Annexure, the proportionate working expenses payable by it under the provisions of Paragraphs 48 and 50 of this Annexure shall be (X per cent of A) *plus* B, where

(*a*) For the year commencing on 1st April 1960, X equals 100; and from the year commencing 1st April 1961, $X = \dfrac{202}{365} \times 100$;

(*b*) A is the aggregate sum of the following:

(i) 45 per cent of the 'working expenses' during the year on Madhopur Headworks;

(ii) 65.5 per cent of the 'working expenses' during the year on 'II Main Canals and Branches' (carrier channels only); and

(iii) 66.8 per cent of the 'working expenses' during the year on 'III Distributaries' (carrier channels only); and

(*c*) B is a fixed over-head charge equal to Pounds Sterling 60,000 per year.

2. The 'working expenses' for the purpose of paragraph 1 above shall consist of:

(i) Expenditure under account heads Maintenance and Repairs, Extensions and Improvements, and Tools and Plant, and

(ii) Pro-rata establishment charges on account of Divisional and Circle Offices and Chief Engineers' Direction Charges.

3. The proportionate working expenses payable by Pakistan shall be modified, in accordance with paragraph 4 below, if

(*a*) India should bring into operation any new channel to irrigate any part of the areas which were irrigated, before the Effective Date, from the Lahore Branch and the Main Branch Lower; or

(*b*) Pakistan should desire to reduce

(i) the period specified in Paragraph 7 of this Annexure; or

(ii) the maximum quantities (in cusecs) specified in Paragraph 7 of this Annexure; or

(*c*) any change is made in the period or quantity of deliveries to the C.B.D.C. in accordance with the provisions of Paragraphs 10 or 11 of this Annexure.

In case of (*b*) above, Pakistan shall give India due notice of its intentions, such notice to reach India at least six months before the date from which the change is sought.

4. (*a*) Under the conditions envisaged in paragraph 3 (*a*) above, Pakistan shall pay 100 per cent of the 'working expenses' on such Branches or Distributaries as carry supplies for Pakistan only and for the remaining carrier channels the percentages given in paragraph 1 (*b*) (*ii*) or 1(*b*) (iii) above shall be re-calculated on the basis of ratio of cusec-miles to be delivered by the remaining channels to Pakistan (with pro-rata addition on account of absorption losses) to the aggregate of cusec-miles of the remaining channels (on the basis of 1948 capacities), the cusec-miles for each such channel being worked out separately.

(*b*) If there is a reduction in the period specified in Paragraph 7 of this Annexure, as envisaged under paragraph 3 (*b*) (i) or 3 (*c*) above, the factor X in paragraph 1 (*a*) above will be taken as equal to

$$\frac{\text{number of days during which C.B.D.C. is due to receive supplies from U.B.D.C.}}{\text{number of days in the year}}$$

(*c*) In the event that there is a reduction in the maximum quantities specified in Paragraph 7 of this Annexure as mentioned in paragraphs 3 (*b*) (ii) or 3 (*c*) above, the percentages in paragraphs 1 (*b*) (i), (*b*) (ii) and (*b*) (iii) above will be reduced pro-rata.

APPENDIX IV TO ANNEXURE H

CALCULATIONS FOR DETERMINING PROPORTIONATE WORKING EXPENSES TO BE PAID BY PAKISTAN UNDER THE PROVISIONS OF PARAGRAPHS 49 AND 50 OF THIS ANNEXURE

1. Until Pakistan exercises the option under the provisions of Paragraph 64 of this Annexure, the proportionate working expenses payable by it under the provisions of Paragraphs 49 and 50 of this Annexure shall be X per cent of (A *plus* B) where:

(a) For each of the three years commencing on 1st April 1960, 1st April 1961 and 1st April 1962, X equals 51; and from the year commencing 1st April 1963, X equals 80;

(b) A is the aggregate sum of the 'working expenses' during the year; and

(c) B is a fixed overhead charge equal to Pounds Sterling 110,000.

2. The 'working expenses' for the purpose of paragraph 1 above shall consist of:

(i) expenditure on the Ferozepore Headworks (including the part of the Dipalpur Canal in India) under account heads Maintenance and Repairs, Extensions and Improvements, and Tools and Plant;

(ii) pro-rata establishment charges on account of the Divisional and Circle Offices and Chief Engineers' Direction Charges; and

(iii) expenditure on 'Minor Works 18A (2) Miscellaneous' (discharge observations at Ferozepore).

———

PROTOCOL TO THE INDUS WATERS TREATY 1960.[33] SIGNED ON 27 NOVEMBER, 2 AND 23 DECEMBER 1960

———

The Government of India, the Government of Pakistan and the International Bank for Reconstruction and Development, having found that certain textual errors have occurred in The Indus Waters Treaty 1960,[33] as signed by their duly authorised Plenipotentiaries at Karachi on the nineteenth day of September in the year one thousand nine hundred and sixty, hereby agree as follows:

The corrections specified in the schedule hereunder shall be carried out in the text of The Indus Waters Treaty 1960 and the said Treaty shall be read subject to the said corrections.

———

[33]See p. 126 of this volume.

THE SCHEDULE

Serial No.	Reference	Page	Paragraph	Line	Particulars
1	Annexure C	4	6(*b*)	5	For colon read semicolon.
2	Annexure D	3	6(*a*)	5–6	For "communiate" read "communicate".
3	Annexure E	12	2(*b*)	5	For "case" read "cases".
4	Annexure F	3	1(22)	2	For "Annxure" read "Annexure".
5	Annexure H	1	title	2	For "Article II (5)" read "(Article II (5))".
6	Do.	3	title above paragraph	6	For "the Ravi" read "The Ravi".
7	Do.	3	Table A Column Numbers.		For "(Col. 2)" read "Col. (2)".
8	Annexure H	15	27(*ii*)	1	For "'gross amount,' " read "'gross amount' ".
9	Do.	20	35(*i*)	1	For "above" read "Above".
10	Do.	23		1	For "42–46" read "42 to 46".
11	Do.	24	45(*e*)	3	For "the Beas" read "The Beas".
12	Do.	25	46	7	For "Water-accounting" read "Water-accounting".
13	Do.	26	46(*d*)	7	For "Water-account" read "water-account".
14	Appendix I to Annexure H	1	title	2	For "time-Lag" read "Time-lag".
15	Appendix II to Annexure H	4	Item 2	1	For "Compoment" read "Componment".
16	Appendix II to Annexure H	6	Item 5	1	For "below" read "Below".
17	Do.	11	Footnote	1	For "circumsances" read "circumstances".
18	Do.	14	Item 15	3	For "C (*ii*)" and "C (*iii*) read "B (*ii*)" and "B (*iii*)" respectively.
19	Do.	19	Footnote	2	For "link" read "Link".

Serial No.	Reference	Page	Paragraph	Line	Particulars
20	Do.	19	Do.	3	For "link" read "Link".
21	Appendix III to Annexure H	2	3(c)	3	For "and" read "or".
22	Do.	3	4(b)	3	For "and" read "or".
23	Do.	3	4(c)	3	For "3 (b) (ii) and (c)" read "3 (b) (ii) or 3 (c)".
24	Appendix IV to Annexure H	1	2(iii)	1	For "Miscellaneous," read "Miscellaneous"'.

IN WITNESS WHEREOF the respective Plenipotentiaries of the Parties hereto, being signatories to The Indus Waters Treaty 1960, have affixed their signatures to this Protocol, which shall be called the "Protocol to The Indus Waters Treaty 1960", on the day appearing below their respective signatures.

DONE in triplicate in English.

For the Government of India:

(*Signed*) Jawaharlal NEHRU
27th November, 1960

For the Government of Pakistan:

(*Signed*) Mohammad Ayub KHAN
Field Marshal, H.P., H.J.
2nd December, 1960

For the International Bank for Reconstruction and Development:

(*Signed*) W. A. B. ILIFF
23rd December, 1960

Development and Fund Agreement

No. 6371

INTERNATIONAL BANK FOR
RECONSTRUCTION AND DEVELOPMENT
and
AUSTRALIA, CANADA, FEDERAL REPUBLIC OF
GERMANY, NEW ZEALAND, PAKISTAN, UNITED
KINGDOM OF GREAT BRITAIN AND NORTHERN
IRELAND and UNITED STATES OF AMERICA

Indus Basin Development Fund Agreement (with annexes). Signed at Karachi, on 19 September 1960

Official text: English.

Registered by the International Bank for Reconstruction and Development on 23 November 1962.

BANQUE INTERNATIONALE POUR
LA RECONSTRUCTION ET LE DÉVELOPPEMENT
et
AUSTRALIE, CANADA, RÉPUBLIQUE FÉDÉRALE
D'ALLEMAGNE, NOUVELLE-ZÉLANDE, PAKISTAN,
ROYAUME-UNI DE GRANDE-BRETAGNE ET D'IRLANDE
DU NORD et ÉTATS-UNIS D'AMÉRIQUE

Accord (avec annexes) relatif au Fonds de développement du bassin de l'Indus. Signé à Karachi, le 19 septembre 1960

Texte officiel anglais.

Enregistré par la Banque Internationale pour la reconstruction et le développement le 23 novembre 1962.

No. 6371. INDUS BASIN DEVELOPMENT FUND AGREEMENT[1] BETWEEN THE GOVERNMENTS OF THE COMMONWEALTH OF AUSTRALIA, CANADA, THE FEDERAL REPUBLIC OF GERMANY, NEW ZEALAND, PAKISTAN, THE UNITED KINGDOM OF GREAT BRITAIN AND NORTHERN IRELAND AND THE UNITED STATES OF AMERICA AND THE INTERNATIONAL BANK FOR RECONSTRUCTION AND DEVELOPMENT. SIGNED AT KARACHI, ON 19 SEPTEMBER 1960

AGREEMENT, dated this 19th day of September, 1960 between the Governments of the COMMONWEALTH OF AUSTRALIA (Australia), CANADA (Canada), the FEDERAL REPUBLIC OF GERMANY (Germany), NEW ZEALAND (New Zealand), PAKISTAN (Pakistan), the UNITED KINGDOM OF GREAT BRITAIN and NORTHERN IRELAND (United Kingdom) and the UNITED STATES OF AMERICA (United States) and the INTERNATIONAL BANK FOR RECONSTRUCTION AND DEVELOPMENT (hereinafter sometimes called the Bank).

WHEREAS the Government of India (India) and Pakistan have concluded (subject to exchange of ratifications) the Indus Waters Treaty 1960[2] (hereinafter called the Treaty, and of which a copy is annexed hereto as Annexure A) providing *inter alia,* for the sharing between India and Pakistan of the use of the waters of the Indus Basin;

AND WHEREAS the effective utilization by Pakistan of the waters assigned to it by the Treaty entails the construction of a system of works part of which will accomplish the replacement of water supplies for irrigation canals in Pakistan which hitherto have been dependent on water supplies from the waters assigned by the Treaty to India;

AND WHEREAS, by the terms of Article V of the Treaty, India has undertaken to make a payment of £62,060,000 towards the costs of the replacement part of such works, such sum to be paid to an Indus Basin Development Fund to be established and administered by the Bank;

AND WHEREAS, in concluding the Treaty, Pakistan has been influenced by the consideration that financial assistance of the nature and amounts specified hereinafter will be made available to Pakistan;

AND WHEREAS Australia, Canada, Germany, New Zealand, the United Kingdom, the United States and the Bank, in view of the importance which they attach to a settlement of the Indus Waters problem from the point of view both of the economic development of the area and of the promotion of peace and stability therein, have agreed as hereinafter set forth, to make a contribution towards the costs of such system of works and also to make such contribution available through the above-mentioned Indus Basin Development Fund;

---

[1] Came into force on 12 January 1961, the date of entry into force of the Indus Water Treaty 1960, with retroactive effect as from 1 April 1960, in accordance with the provisions of Article XIII.

[2] United Nations, *Treaty Series,* Vol. 419, p. 125.

Now THEREFORE, the Parties hereto agree as follows:

Article I
ESTABLISHMENT OF INDUS BASIN DEVELOPMENT FUND

Section 1.01. There is hereby established the Indus Basin Development Fund (hereinafter called the Fund), constituted by the monies which the contracting parties shall from time to time transfer to the Fund in accordance with Articles II and III of this Agreement, together with the monies to be paid to the Fund by India under the provisions of Article V of the Treaty, and any other assets and receipts therein, to be held in trust and administered by the Bank and used only for the purposes, and in accordance with the provisions, of this Agreement.

Section 1.02. The Fund and its assets and accounts shall be kept separate and apart from all other assets and accounts of the Bank and shall be separately designated in such appropriate manner as the Bank shall determine.

Section 1.03. The Bank is hereby designated Administrator of the Fund. The term Administrator will hereinafter be used to refer to the Bank acting in that capacity.

Article II
CONTRIBUTIONS TO FUND

Section 2.01. Each of the Governments specified below undertakes, as a party to this Agreement, subject to such parliamentary or congressional action as may be necessary, to make a contribution to the Fund in its own currency of the nature and in the amount specified opposite its name below:

		Grant	*Loan*
Australia	£A	6,965,000	—
Canada	Can.$	22,100,000	—
Germany	DM.	126,000,000	—
New Zealand	£NZ	1,000,000	—
United Kingdom	£	20,860,000	—
United States	U.S.$	177,000,000	Proceeds of a U.S. dollar loan to Pakistan (repayable in rupees) in an amount not exceeding U.S.$70,000,000 (hereinafter referred to as the United States loan).

Section 2.02. The following contribution (hereinafter referred to as the Bank loan) will also be made to the Fund:

The proceeds of a loan to Pakistan from the Bank in an amount not exceeding U.S.$80,000,000 equivalent, of which the terms and conditions are set out in the Loan Agreement annexed hereto as Annexure B.[3]

---

[3]See p. 280 of this volume.

Section 2.03. The United States, in addition to its contributions specified in Section 2.01 above, undertakes, subject to any necessary Congressional action, to make a contribution to the Fund of an amount in Pakistan rupees (hereinafter called rupees) equivalent to U.S.$235 million. This contribution shall be in the form of grants or loans or both to Pakistan in amounts and under conditions to be agreed between the United States and Pakistan.

Section 2.04. Pakistan undertakes to make the following contributions to the Fund:

(*a*) a contribution in pounds sterling of £440,000, and
(*b*) a contribution in rupees in an amount equivalent to £9,850,000.

Article III
PROVISIONS REGARDING PAYMENT OF CONTRIBUTIONS

Section 3.01. Upon the entry into force of this Agreement the Administrator shall promptly notify each Party of the amount required to be contributed by it to the Fund to cover estimated disbursements of the Fund during the half-year period commencing 1st October 1960, and shall before the beginning of each succeeding half-year period commencing 1st April or 1st October thereafter (at a time to be agreed in each case between the Administrator and the Party concerned) notify each Party of the amount so required to be contributed by it for such period. Each Party undertakes to make the payment specified in such notice at the time and in the amounts specified therein. The payments of the contributions under Section 2.01 hereof shall be made in the currency of the Party concerned, freely useable or convertible for purchases anywhere, or in such other currency or currencies as may be agreed between the Party and the Administrator. Each payment to the Fund shall be made to or on the order of the Administrator as specified in the notice covering the same.

Section 3.02. It is understood and agreed that:

(*a*) the payment to be made to the Fund by Pakistan in pounds sterling shall be £22,000 in each half-year,
(*b*) the payment to be made to the Fund by New Zealand shall be £NZ. 50,000 in each half-year,
(*c*) in each half-year the amount called up for payment to the Fund from the sources specified in Sections 2.01 and 2.02 hereof shall (after leaving out of account the payment by Pakistan under (*a*) above and the payment by New Zealand under (*b*) above) be divided between grants and loans in the ratio of 65 to 35:

Provided that:

(i) the aggregate payments from grants, as so determined, shall be apportioned among the contributing Parties according to the percentages set out below:

	%
Australia.	5.13
Canada	7.63
Germany	9.86
United Kingdom	19.20
United States.	58.18
	100.00

and

(ii) the aggregate payments from loans, as so determined, shall be apportioned between the Bank loan and the United States loan in the ratio of 80 to 70, or in such other ratio as the Bank and the United States may, from time to time, agree.

Section 3.03. It is understood and agreed that the aggregate rupee requirements of the Fund during each half-year shall be met as follows:

(a) By a payment to the Fund by Pakistan in rupees in the equivalent of £492,500.
(b) The balance thereof:

(i) as to 60%, from contributions to the Fund under Section 2.03 hereof, and
(ii) as to 40%, from rupees which the Administrator shall cause the Fund to purchase, against foreign exchange, from the State Bank of Pakistan.

Section 3.04. A preliminary estimate of the annual amounts to be contributed to the Fund by each Party to this Agreement is annexed hereto as Annexure C.[4] The Administrator will keep such estimate as up to date as possible and will promptly notify the Parties of any material changes therein.

Section 3.05. The Parties hereto agree to accept the Administrator's decision as to estimated requirements and receipts of the Fund for the purposes of Sections 3.01, 3.02 and 3.03 hereof, and as to the best practical method of accomplishing the apportionment provided for in Sections 3.02 and 3.03 hereof, using approximate amounts and estimates; provided, however, that no Party shall be obligated to make any payment to the Fund except to the extent it shall have undertaken so to do either by the provisions of this Agreement or otherwise. By agreement among the Parties, changes may be made in the apportionment, including changes to take account of any contributions arising under Article XII.

---

[4]See p. 282 of this volume.

Article IV

SPECIAL RESERVE

Section 4.01. It is understood and agreed that the Administrator shall retain in the Fund, out of each payment to the Fund by India, such amount as the Administrator may estimate to be necessary to build up a special reserve in pounds sterling (hereinafter called the Special Reserve) to meet the maximum obligations of the Fund under Article V (5) of the Treaty.

Section 4.02. If, at the request of Pakistan, the Transition Period provided for in the Treaty is extended in accordance with the provisions of Part 8 of Annexure H thereto, the Administrator shall pay to India in pounds sterling out of the Special Reserve such amounts as shall be payable to India pursuant to the provisions of Article V (5) of the Treaty. After the amounts, if any, payable to India pursuant to this Section shall have been finally determined, the Administrator shall pay to Pakistan in pounds sterling the amount of the Special Reserve, less such amounts, if any, as shall have become so payable to India.

Section 4.03. Income from investments of the Special Reserve shall be used by the Administrator to purchase rupees from the State Bank of Pakistan, and such rupees shall be treated as payments to the Fund pursuant to Section 3.03 (*a*).

Article V

DISBURSEMENTS FROM FUND

Section 5.01. Amounts in the Fund may be disbursed to Pakistan by the Administrator, and shall be used by Pakistan, exclusively to finance the cost of equipment, supplies, other property and services (hereinafter called "goods") required to construct the system of works described in Annexure D[5] to this Agreement, such system of works being herein collectively called the Project. The specific items to be financed from the Fund shall from time to time be determined by agreement between Pakistan and the Administrator, and the agreed list thereof may be changed from time to time by agreement between them.

Section 5.02. (*a*) Subject to the provisions of this Agreement, there shall be disbursed from the Fund: (i) such amounts as shall be required by Pakistan to reimburse it for the reasonable cost of goods to be financed from the Fund and (ii), if the Administrator shall so agree, such amounts as shall be required to meet the reasonable cost of such items.

(*b*) Except as otherwise provided herein or as shall be otherwise agreed between Pakistan and the Administrator, no disbursement shall be made on account of: (i) expenditures prior to April 1, 1960, or (ii) expenditures in the territories of any country which is not a member of the Bank (except New Zealand and Switzerland) or for goods produced in, or services supplied from, such territories.

---

[5] See p. 286 of this volume.

Section 5.03. Disbursements from the Fund shall be in such currencies as the Administrator shall elect: Provided that disbursements on account of expenditures in rupees or for goods produced in, or services supplied from, Pakistan shall be in rupees, except as the Administrator may otherwise agree.

Article VI
APPLICATIONS FOR DISBURSEMENTS

Section 6.01. When Pakistan shall desire to receive any disbursement from the Fund, Pakistan shall deliver to the Administrator a written application in such form, and containing such statements and agreements, as the Administrator shall reasonably request in accordance with the Bank's usual procedures, and as may be necessary or desirable to enable the Administrator to furnish the information and make the reports provided for in Section 8.01 of this Agreement.

Section 6.02. Pakistan shall furnish to the Administrator such documents and other evidence in support of each such application as the Administrator shall reasonably request in accordance with the Bank's usual procedures, whether before or after the Administrator shall have permitted any withdrawal requested in the application.

Section 6.03. Each application and the accompanying documents must be sufficient in form and substance to satisfy the Administrator that Pakistan is entitled to receive from the Fund the amount applied for, that the amount to be disbursed by the Fund is to be used only for the purposes specified in this Agreement, that the goods on account of which disbursement is requested are suitable for the Project, and that the cost thereof is not unreasonable.

Article VII
UNDERTAKINGS OF PAKISTAN

Section 7.01. (a) Pakistan shall cause the Project to be carried out with due diligence and efficiency and in conformity with sound engineering and financial practices, and shall accord appropriate priority, satisfactory to the Administrator, to that part of the Project whose purpose is replacement.

(b) All goods required for the Project shall be procured on the basis of international competition under arrangements satisfactory to the Administrator, except as the Administrator shall otherwise agree on grounds of efficiency or economy.

Section 7.02. Pakistan shall cause all goods financed out of monies disbursed by the Fund to be used exclusively in the carrying out of the Project, except as the Administrator may otherwise agree in respect of goods no longer required for the Project.

Section 7.03. (a) Pakistan shall cause to be furnished to the Administrator, promptly upon their preparation, the plans and specifications, cost estimates and constructions schedules for the Project, and any material modifications subsequently made therein, in such detail as the Administrator shall from time to time request.

(*b*) Pakistan shall maintain or cause to be maintained records adequate to identify the goods financed out of monies disbursed by the Fund, to disclose the use thereof in the Project, to record the progress of the Project (including the cost thereof) and to reflect in accordance with consistently maintained sound accounting practices the operations and financial condition of the agency or agencies of Pakistan responsible for the construction of the Project or any part thereof; shall enable the Administrator's representatives to inspect the Project, the goods used or acquired for the Project, and any relevant records and documents; and shall furnish to the Administrator all such information as the Administrator shall reasonably request concerning the expenditure of the monies disbursed by the Fund, the Project, and the operations and financial condition of the agency or agencies of Pakistan responsible for the construction of the Project or any part thereof.

Section 7.04. (*a*) Pakistan and the Administrator shall cooperate fully to assure that the purposes of this Agreement will be accomplished. To that end, each of them shall furnish to the other all such information as it shall reasonably request with regard to the general status of the Project.

(*b*) Pakistan and the Administrator shall from time to time exchange views through their representatives with regard to matters relating to the purposes of this Agreement. Pakistan shall promptly inform the Administrator of any condition which interferes with, or threatens to interfere with, the accomplishment of the purposes of this Agreement and the Administrator shall forward a report thereon to each of the other Parties to this Agreement.

Section 7.05. Without detracting from the obligations assumed under this Agreement by the Central Government of Pakistan, Pakistan may, from time to time, designate a government agency or agencies to carry out on behalf of the Central Government such duties incidental to the implementation of this Agreement as the Central Government may deem appropriate.

Article VIII

THE ADMINISTRATOR

Section 8.01. The Administrator shall, within 30 days after 31st December 1960 and after each 30th June and 31st December thereafter, send to each Party a report containing appropriate information with respect to the receipts and disbursements of, and balances in, the Fund, the progress of the Project, and other matters relating to the Fund, the Project and this Agreement. The administrator will consult with the respective Parties from time to time concerning the form and substance of such reports.

Section 8.02. The Administrator may invest monies held by the Fund pending disbursement in such short-term securities as it shall deem appropriate. This provision will apply primarily to the Special Reserve. The Administrator will, however, have power to invest on a short-term basis any monies from the contributors which are surplus to its immediate requirements on the understanding that the Administrator will take all reasonable steps under Article III of this Agreement to avoid building up balances in the Fund in excess of the amounts necessary to enable disbursements for the Project to be made as required. Subject to the provisions of Section 4.03, the income from such investments shall become part of the assets of the Fund.

Section 8.03. Whenever it shall be necessary for the purposes of this Agreement to value one currency in terms of another currency, such value shall be as reasonably determined by the Administrator in accordance with the Bank's usual procedures.

Section 8.04. The Administrator shall receive no compensation other than for expenses incurred solely because of services rendered under this Agreement, for which it shall be entitled to reimburse itself out of the Fund.

Section 8.05. The Bank, in acting as Administrator, shall exercise the same care in the administration and management of the Fund and in the discharge of its other functions under this Agreement, as it exercises in respect of the administration and management of its own affairs.

Article IX

CONSULTATION

Section 9.01. The following are hereby specified as Events for the purposes of this Article IX:

(*a*) an extraordinary situation shall have arisen, which shall make it improbable that Pakistan will be able to complete the Project;

(*b*) at any time amounts likely to be available for the Project shall not be sufficient to complete the Project;

(*c*) a default shall have occurred in the performance of any undertaking on the part of Pakistan under this Agreement.

Section 9.02. (*a*) If any of the Events specified in Section 9.01 shall have happened and in the judgment of the Administrator shall be likely to continue, the Administrator shall promptly notify the other Parties hereto and, in the case of an Event specified in Section 9.01 (*c*), may by notice to Pakistan suspend disbursements from the Fund.

(*b*) The Parties hereto shall forthwith consult with one another concerning the measures to be taken to correct the Event or Events. A majority of the Parties shall have the power to decide that any suspension imposed by the Administrator pursuant to sub-section (*a*) of this Section shall be continued or removed. The Administrator shall act in accordance with any such decision.

(*c*) If any such Event shall continue, and a majority of the Parties hereto shall decide that it is not likely to be corrected and that the purposes of this Agreement are not likely to be substantially fulfilled, and so inform the Administrator, the obligations of the Parties hereto to make contributions to the Fund shall cease and, subject to the provisions of Section 11.03 hereof, this Agreement shall terminate.

Article X
SETTLEMENT OF DISPUTES

Section 10.01. Any dispute between any of the Parties hereto concerning the interpretation or application of this Agreement, or of any supplementary arrangement or agreement, which cannot be resolved by agreement of such Parties, shall be submitted for final decision to an arbitrator selected by such Parties, or, failing such selection, to an arbitrator appointed by the Secretary General of the United Nations.

Article XI
TERMINATION

Section 11.01. Subject to the provisions of Section 11.03 hereof this Agreement, unless sooner terminated pursuant to Section 9.02 (*c*) hereof, shall terminate upon the completion of the Project or upon the disbursement from the Fund of all amounts due to be disbursed from it for the Project, whichever is the earlier.

Section 11.02. (*a*) If at termination there shall remain in the Fund any amounts derived from the contributions of the Parties (including interest), the Parties shall consult together as to their disposal.

(*b*) Any amounts remaining in the Fund which shall not have been derived from the contributions of the Parties, other than the Special Reserve, shall be paid at termination by the Administrator to Pakistan.

Section 11.03. Notwithstanding any termination pursuant to the provisions of Sections 9.02 (*c*) and 11.01 hereof, this Agreement shall remain in force for the purpose of receiving into the Fund any amounts due from India under the provisions of the Treaty, which amounts, except such part thereof as shall be retained for the Special Reserve, shall be paid to Pakistan by the Administrator as they are received. The provisions of Article IV shall continue to apply to the Special Reserve.

Article XII
ADDITIONAL PARTIES

Section 12.01. Any other Government or institution may, with the prior approval of the Parties hereto and in accordance with such arrangements as they shall agree, become a Party to this Agreement, upon deposit with the Bank of an instrument stating that it accepts all the provisions hereof and that it agrees to be bound thereby.

Section 12.02. The Administrator may receive on behalf of the Fund from any Government or institution, whether or not a party hereto, amounts not provided for herein to be held and used as part of the Fund subject to the provisions hereof, in accordance with such arrangements, not inconsistent herewith, as the Parties hereto may approve.

Article XIII
ENTRY INTO FORCE

Section 13.01. This Agreement shall enter into force on the date on which the Treaty enters into force pursuant to the provisions thereof, and will then take effect retrospectively as from the 1st April, 1960.

Article XIV
TITLE

Section 14.01. This Agreement may be cited as "The Indus Basin Development Fund Agreement, 1960."

DONE AT Karachi, this 19th day of September, 1960, in a single original to be deposited in the archives of the International Bank for Reconstruction and Development, which shall communicate certified copies thereof to each of the Governments signatory to this Agreement.

For the Government of the Commonwealth of Australia:
(*Signed*) A. R. CUTLER

For the Government of Canada:
(*Signed*) V. C. MOORE

For the Government of the Federal Republic of Germany:
(*Signed*) Heinz VON TRÜTZSCHLER

For the Government of New Zealand:
(*Signed*) G. R. POWLES

For the Government of Pakistan:
(*Signed*) M. SHOAIB

For the Government of the United Kingdom of Great Britain
and Northern Ireland:
(*Signed*) RICHARD THOMPSON

For the Government of the United States of America:
(*Signed*) William M. ROUNTREE

For the International Bank for Reconstruction and Development:
(*Signed*) W. A. B. ILIFF

A N N E X U R E   A
THE INDUS WATERS TREATY 1960[6]

A N N E X U R E   B
LOAN AGREEMENT BETWEEN REPUBLIC OF PAKISTAN AND INTERNATIONAL
BANK FOR RECONSTRUCTION and DEVELOPMENT[7]

---

[6]For the text of this Treaty, see United Nations, *Treaty Series,* Vol. 419, p. 125.
[7]For the text of this Agreement, see p. 207 of this volume.

ANNEXURE C
ESTIMATED DISBURSEMENTS
A. FOREIGN EXCHANGE
(Amounts in U.S. $ m. equivalents)

	(Total)	Year 1	Year 2	Year 3	Year 4	Year 5	Year 6	Year 7	Year 8	Year 9	Year 10	Year 11	Year 12
1. Direct Costs	(424)	21.54	47.46	44	59	68	45	38	26	28	31	13	3
2. Purchase of Rupees from State Bank (See line 5, table B)	(154.6)	5.7	12.1	17.7	21.3	22.5	20.9	13.7	12.1	12.5	8.5	4.8	2.8
3. 1 *plus* 2	(578.6)	27.24	59.56	61.7	80.3	90.5	65.9	51.7	38.1	40.5	39.5	17.8	5.8
4. Provision for Special Reserve[a]	(27.6)	2.76	2.76	2.76	2.76	2.76	2.76	2.76	2.76	2.76	2.76	—	—
5. 3 *plus* 4 (Total Foreign Exchange Requirements)	(606.2)	30.00	62.32	64.46	83.06	93.26	68.66	54.46	40.86	43.26	42.26	17.8	5.8
6. Indian Contribution	(173.8)	17.38	17.38	17.38	17.38	17.38	17.38	17.38	17.38	17.38	17.38	—	—
7. 5 *minus* 6	(432.4)	12.62	44.94	47.08	65.68	75.88	51.28	37.08	23.48	25.88	24.88	17.8	5.8
8. Pakistan Contribution	(1.2)	0.12	0.12	0.12	0.12	0.12	0.12	0.12	0.12	0.12	0.12	—	—
9. 7 *minus* 8	(431.2)	12.50	44.82	46.96	65.56	75.76	51.16	39.96	23.36	25.76	24.76	17.8	5.8
10. New Zealand Contribution	(2.8)	0.28	0.28	0.28	0.28	0.28	0.28	0.28	0.28	0.28	0.28	—	—
11. Amounts to be apportioned between Grants and Loans	(428.4)	12.22	44.54	46.68	65.28	75.48	50.88	36.68	23.08	25.48	24.48	17.8	5.8
Grants — 65%[b]	(278.4)	7.92	28.97	30.34	42.43	49.06	33.07	23.84	15.00	16.56	15.91	11.57	3.77
Loans — 35%	(150.0)	4.30	15.57	16.34	22.85	26.42	17.81	12.84	8.08	8.92	8.57	6.23	2.03

NOTES: [a]Under Section 4.01.*

    [b]The incidence on the contributing governments will be as set out in Section 3.02 (b)(i).

* All section references in this Annexure are to Sections of the Indus Basin Development Fund Agreement.

B. LOCAL CURRENCY
(Amounts in U.S. $ m. equivalents)

	(Total)	Year 1	Year 2	Year 3	Year 4	Year 5	Year 6	Year 7	Year 8	Year 9	Year 10	Year 11	Year 12
1 Direct Costs	(414)	17	33	47	56	59	55	37	33	34	24	12	7
2. From Pakistan Budget[a]	(27.6)	2.76	2.76	2.76	2.76	2.76	2.76	2.76	2.76	2.76	2.76	—	—
3. 1 *minus* 2	(386.4)	14.24	30.24	44.24	53.24	56.24	52.24	34.24	30.24	31.24	21.24	12	
4. From U.S. Govt.[b] 60% of Line 3	(231.8)	8.54	18.14	26.54	31.94	33.74	31.34	20.54	18.14	18.74	12.74	7.2	4.2
5. From Purchase of Rupees from State Bank[c] 40% of Line 3	(154.6)	5.7	12.1	17.7	21.3	22.5	20.9	13.7	12.1	12.5	8.5	4.8	2.8

NOTES: [a]Under Section 3.03 (a).
[b] Under Section 3.03 (b)(i).
[c]Under Section 3.03 (b)(ii).

A N N E X U R E   D
Project Description

1. The Project consists of a system of works to be constructed by Pakistan which will:

(*a*) transfer water from the three Western Rivers of the Indus system (Indus, Jhelum an Chenab), to meet existing irrigation uses in Pakistan which have hitherto depended upon the waters of the three Eastern Rivers (Ravi, Beas and Sutlej), thereby releasing the whole flow of the three Eastern Rivers for irrigation developments in India;

(*b*) provide substantial additional irrigation development in West Pakistan;

(*c*) develop 300,000 KW of hydro-electric potential for West Pakistan;

(*d*) make an important contribution to soil reclamation and drainage in West Pakistan by lowering ground water levels in water-logged and saline areas, and

(*e*) afford a measure of flood protection in West Pakistan.

2. The system of works includes:

	Location	*Capacity*
A. Dams and Related Works	(1) Jhelum River	Live storage of 4.75 million acre feet
	(a) Hydro-electric generating facilities	300,000 KW
	(2) Indus River	Live storage of 4.2 million acre feet
B. Link Canals (Construction and remodeling)	Rasul-Qadirabad	19,000 cusecs
	Qadirabad-Balloki	18,600 cusecs
	Balloki-Suleimanke	18,500 cusecs
	Marala-Ravi	22,000 cusecs
	Bambanwala-Ravi-Bedian-Dipalpur	5,000 cusecs
	Trimmu-Islam	11,000 cusecs
	Kalabagh-Jhelum	22,000 cusecs
	Taunsa-Panjnad	12,000 cusecs
C. Barrages	Qadirabad	
	Ravi River	
	Sutlej River	
D. Tubewells and Drainage Works		

(1) About 2,500 tubewells to contribute to a lowering of the water-table, some of which will yield additional water supplies for irrigation use; and

(2) A system of open drains to lower the water-table in about 2.5 million acres of land now under cultivation but seriously threatened by water-logging and salinity.

E. Other Works

Ancillary irrigation works directly related to the foregoing, including remodeling of existing works.

ANNEX 2: THE GENERICA — AN OUTLINE FOR PREPARING A BASIN CASE STUDY

This Annex is aimed at demonstrating how we may approach international water Conflict-Negotiation-Cooperation (CNC) either as analysts, as mediators, or as *ex-post* auditors, using the concepts and frameworks discussed throughout the book. In the following we will introduce a framework that may be used with adaptations and modifications to describe and analyze international water CNC case studies. Our case studies follow this framework as well.

We call our stylized river basin "GENERICA" and build a framework that attempts to be as general as possible. In recognizing the difficulty to suggest a generic framework for the analysis of CNC problems in general, the discussion will be based mainly on interaction and input from the students to the suggested framework provided by the teacher.

THE GENERICA RIVER BASIN CNC OUTLINE

1. Background

1.1. Physical Background on the River Basin and the Riparian States

1.1.1. Geography and hydrogeography of the basin

1.1.1.1. Map of the basin
1.1.1.2. Flow regime

1.1.1.2.1. Inter annual fluctuations, Intra annual distribution

1.1.1.3. Riparians' dependency on the basin water — are there other sources each riparian can develop unilaterally?
1.1.1.4. Riparians' situation in the basin that grants special 'power'

1.1.1.4.1. For example, use the geography of 'border creator' and 'through border'

1.2. Economic Background on the Riparian States

1.2.1. Economies of the riparian states

1.2.1.1. Population and population growth
1.2.1.2. Economic indicators of the riparians' economies
1.2.1.3. International agreements that affect the basin economies
1.2.1.4. Level of development, ability to adjust

1.2.1.5. Relative advantages and disadvantages

1.2.1.5.1. Financial, Human, Technological, and Organizational resources

1.2.2. Water related (directly and indirectly) sectors, projects, etc....

1.2.2.1. Past, present, future water utilization plans

1.2.2.2. Sectoral water use patterns (seasonality, shares, Water use efficiency)

1.2.2.3. Sectoral water demands

1.2.2.4. National water demand

1.3 Political Background on the Riparian States

1.3.1. History of relations among riparian states

1.3.1.1. Past and present sovereignty issues

1.3.1.1.1. Borders, Central government, etc...

1.3.1.2. Interaction among the riparian states

1.3.1.3. Past conflicts/cooperation among states, over water or other issues

1.3.1.3.1. History cooperation/hostility over water resources

1.3.1.3.2. History of cooperation/hostility over issues other than water

1.3.1.3.3. Existing agreements on any issue

1.3.2. Culture and religion of the riparian states

1.3.2.1. Social customs, values and beliefs influencing the relation's between the basin riparians

1.3.3. Domestic politics

1.3.3.1. Political regimes and central government structure

1.3.3.2. Comparative military and economic strengths of the riparian states

1.3.3.3. Active rebellion and separatist groups

1.3.4. Political stability of the riparian states

1.3.4.1. Existing institutions in the water sector of the riparian states

1.3.4.2. Internal conflicts

1.3.4.2.1. Inter-sectoral

1.3.4.2.2. Inter-regional

1.3.4.2.3. Casts, religions, tribes, etc....

2. The Status Quo Situation in the Basin

2.1 Conflict or Potential Conflict

2.1.1. Actual use of the basin resources

2.1.1.1. Unequal or asymmetric use of water

2.1.1.2. Any noticeable externality

2.1.1.2.1. Impact on downstream

2.1.1.2.2. Impact on other sectors (fishery, forestry, environment, etc...)

2.1.2. Development plans that will aggravate the status quo

2.1.3. The issues important to each riparian (list)

2.1.4. View point of each riparian on his and the other riparian positions (table)

2.1.5. Actions in the past or intent of actions by the riparian states

2.1.5.1. Legislation, declaration

2.1.5.2. Settlement

2.1.5.3. Mobilizing army

2.2 Initiation of Past Negotiations

2.2.1. The components of the negotiation process (use Table 1 with emphasis on the past)

Table 1: A guide to the negotiation process.

Steps in the negotiation process	Examples of key issues
Pre-negotiation Stage	
Convening	How is the decision made to begin negotiating? Who takes the initiative? Has a conflict erupted or are the parties trying to avoid a future conflict?
Representation	Which groups should participate in the negotiations? Who will represent those groups? Do the representatives have the authority to commit the groups they purport to represent?
Negotiation protocol	Will the negotiators use the services of a facilitator or mediator, and if so, who? Where and how often will meetings take place? How the press be handled?
Agenda setting	What issues will be discussed during the negotiations? Can the issues be productively addressed within the context of the negotiations? Are the most important issues for each party on the agenda?
Fact-finding	What is known and not known about the issues, contexts, and experiences relevant to dispute? Can the negotiators develop a common understanding of the facts of the dispute?

Table 1: (*Continued*).

Steps in the negotiation process	Examples of key issues
Formal Negotiation Stage	
Sharing interests and inventing options	Can the negotiators identify and share their main interests on each agenda issue? Can they develop a list of options for addressing each item on the agenda?
Packaging agreements	Which options from each agenda item should be included in the final agreement? Are the negotiators able to trade across issues that they value differently? Is it possible to develop an overall package which is acceptable to all parties?
Producing a written agreement	How will informal understandings be translated into a written agreement? Who drafts and makes modifications to the agreement?
Binding the parties to commitments	Should there be explicit performance measures and guarantees? Should the agreement be legally binding? Should there be financial penalties when non-compliance occurs?
Ratification	Will the involved interest groups formally approve the agreement negotiated by their representatives?

Source: Browder (2000).

2.3. Time Line of the Negotiation Process

2.3.1. Events external to the negotiation process

2.3.1.1. Possible relationship between external events and the direction and the speed of the process

2.3.2. Tactics used by the riparian states

2.4. Existing Treaty Between the All Riparian States or a Sub Group

2.4.1. Issues in the treaty

2.4.2. Enforcement and monitoring mechanisms

2.4.3. Is the treaty respected, is it stable?

2.4.3.1. Incidents of not respecting the treaty

2.4.3.1.1. "Justification" by the non-respecting state
2.4.3.1.2. Responses by other riparian states

2.4.4. Mediation efforts

2.4.4.1. Nature of the mediation process
2.4.4.2. International mediation
2.4.4.3. Regional mediation

3. An Alternative Solution or a Better Way to Negotiate an Agreed Treaty

3.1. Potential for Regional Cooperation

3.1.1. Water-related regional projects

3.1.1.1. The entire set of the riparian countries of the basin

3.1.1.1.1. Possible investment projects among subgroups — probably affected by geography

3.1.1.1.2. Sharing of information on hydrogeography

3.1.1.1.3. Exchange of water-related technologies and know how

3.1.2. Other issues for possible cooperation

3.1.2.1. Trade water-related products (electricity and agricultural products)

3.1.2.1.1. Long-term contractual agreements to utilize relative advantages

3.1.2.2. Industrial development

3.1.2.3. Environmental issues

Follow the Steps in Section 2. However, Include Justification for New Ideas

3.1.3. Issues ignored or overlooked

3.1.4. Interpretation of acts and positions of one riparian by others

3.1.5. Regional developments that can be used for opening the process

Criticize the Present Solution of the Conflict. Pay Attention to:

3.1.6. Fairness

3.1.7. Efficiency

3.1.8. Stability

3.1.9. Monitoring and enforcement

ANNEX 3: RIVER BASIN COOPERATIVE GAME THEORY EXAMPLE[1]

INTRODUCTION

In this Annex we consider the cooperative Game Theory analysis of a transboundary river basin and explore the extent to which cooperation may exist between riparian countries under various circumstances and what the value of that cooperation may be. The hypothetical Lara River basin is shown in Fig. A3.1, with the river flowing through three riparian countries along the river. The geography of the basin is that of a cross-border river; the river flows across each country and does not form the border between any of them. In future editions, we will consider other geographies. The flow of water in the river is subject to eliminate fluctuations that will be captured by referring to normal, dry and wet years.

Country A is a mountainous, upstream country where the majority of flow in the basin is generated from snow and glacier melt runoff. This country has a small, relative to the demands of the other two countries, demand for municipal and agricultural water and uses the river mainly to generate energy from a large hydroelectric facility associated with Reservoir A. Country A is experiencing increasing population and energy demand and is concerned about meeting winter energy needs once the demand exceeds the hydroelectric capacity of Reservoir A. Thus, this country is interested in negotiating with Countries B and C to receive compensation (in the form of cash payment or equivalent energy sources — electricity or fossil fuels) for providing irrigation water in the irrigation period.

Country B is a middle basin country with an agricultural economy that has a large irrigation water demand. This country is dependent on the multi-year storage capacity of Reservoir A to supply its irrigation water demand during drier than average years. Thus, Country B is interested in negotiating with Country A for an appropriate storage and release regime for the reservoir to meet its irrigation water needs and it has adequate energy resources to make payments of fuel to Country A in the winter in compensation for the irrigation season releases. Under low to normal flow conditions in the river, Country B has the ability to divert all of the water out of the river and use it for irrigation, thus leaving no water in the river for Country C. However, under high flow conditions, because of channel capacity constraints, it can be necessary to allow some flow to pass downstream to Country C.

---

[1] This river basin example benefitted from research by Rebecca L. Teasley. The software provided in the accompanying CD-ROM and used to compute the results for the example river basin was generously provided by the GAMS Development Corporation (http://www.gams.com). Any interested reader may use the software on the CD-ROM or download the latest version of the software from the GAMS website.

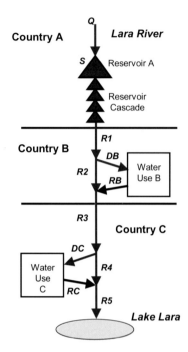

Fig. A3.1: Illustration of the Lara River basin shared between three countries A, B and C.
Source: Authors.

Country C is the downstream riparian of the basin. It also has an agricultural economy with an associated irrigation water demand. Country C receives water from releases out of Reservoir A storage (when they are allowed to bypass Country B) as well as agricultural return flows from Country B. Country C would like to negotiate with Countries A and B for adequate flows to supply its irrigation needs and it has adequate energy resources to make payments of fuel to Country A in the winter in compensation for the irrigation season releases.

Downstream of Country C, the river terminates in Lake Lara which has a delta region that is sensitive to the freshwater inflows from the river and needs an adequate hydrograph of environmental flows to ensure its ecosystem health. The international community has shown a great desire to see environmental flows reach this delta and lake.

The purpose of the exercise outlined in this Annex is to determine the value of cooperation between the countries if it exists. Each country has some options that it can exercise depending on the degree of trust and cooperation with the neighboring countries. For instance, given reasonable assurance of an adequate water supply, Country B could decide to expand its irrigated area. On the other hand, if there is poor cooperation Country A could decide to release increased wintertime flows to generate electricity. As a result, Country B could consider building additional storage in the middle section of the basin to capture these flows for use in the growing period. Country C is likewise dependent on the strategy of upstream Country A as well as the plans of Country B. It can also consider building additional storage to capture releases that occur in times and volumes that exceed irrigation water demands.

In the remainder of this Annex, we describe the basic equations and data of a simple river basin model to calculate the value of various strategies of the countries in their negotiations. Then the various coalitions of a cooperative game theory application in this basin are presented with the characteristic values to the countries based on the results of the model. Finally, several exercises for the student to expand their knowledge and experience with the game theory approach to river basin negotiation are presented.

THE RIVER BASIN MODEL

In this section, we describe the basic information and equations necessary to model the situation in the Lara River basin described above. The model considers the allocation of water to various uses in the basin (energy and agricultural production) for one year with monthly time steps beginning on January 1 and ending on December 31 of a typical year. An average climatic year is illustrated in the calculations, but wet and dry year inflow data are provided in the model so the student can consider the effects of different conditions on water allocation and the value of cooperation in the basin.

The river network illustrated in Fig. A3.1 contains a storage reservoir located in Country A with capacity for over-year storage or multi-year regulation of the river. The capacity of Reservoir A is 19.5 billion m^3; however, of that capacity, 5.5 billion m^3 is reserved for sediment accumulation and is not usable (known as "dead" storage), so the effective (or "active") storage volume of the reservoir is 14.5 billion m^3. Reservoir A is accompanied by a cascade of reservoirs (also owned by Country A) whose volume and water elevation do not change over time (these are "pass-through" or "run-of-the-river" reservoirs).

Neglecting evaporation of water from the surface of Reservoir A and seepage of water through the soils in the bottom of the reservoir, the volume of water in storage in the reservoir in any month t, S^t, is a function of the volume stored in the previous month, S^{t-1}, the inflows to the reservoir in the month, Q^t, and the releases from the reservoir in the month, $R1^t$:

$$\text{Reservoir Balance:} \quad S^t = S^{t-1} + Q^t - R1^t \qquad \text{(A3.1)}$$

At each junction point in the river basin where water is diverted from, or returned to, the river, a balance of flow must exist for each month. Thus, the following equations exist for the system illustrated in Fig. A3.1 and must be satisfied in each month, $t = 1, 2, \ldots, 12$:

$$\text{Balance1:} \quad R1^t = DB^t + R2^t \qquad \text{(A3.2)}$$

$$\text{LimitB:} \quad DB^t \leq \alpha * R1^t \qquad \text{(A3.3)}$$

$$\text{WaterB:} \quad water\_B^t/10^6 * Area_B \leq DB^t \qquad \text{(A3.4)}$$

$$\text{Return\_B:} \quad RB^t = RetB * DB^t \tag{A3.5}$$

$$\text{Balance2:} \quad R2^t + RB^t = R3^t \tag{A3.6}$$

$$\text{Balance3:} \quad R3^t = DC^t + R4^t \tag{A3.7}$$

$$\text{WaterC:} \quad water\_C^t / 10^6 * Area_C \le DC^t \tag{A3.8}$$

$$\text{Return\_C:} \quad RC^t = RetC * DC^t \tag{A3.9}$$

$$\text{Balance4:} \quad R4^t + RC^t = R5^t \tag{A3.10}$$

where $R1^t$, $R2^t$, $R3^t$, $R4^t$, and $R5^t$ are the monthly flows in the main river channel, DB^t and DC^t are the diversions of water to water use areas B and C, respectively, and RB^t and RC^t are the returns from water use areas B and C, respectively. All of the flows in the model are expressed in units of million m^3 per month. The return flow coefficients $RetB$ and $RetC$, represent the fraction of the water diverted to the water use areas in each country that is returned to the river. The parameters $water\_B$ and $water\_C$ are the aggregated crop water requirements and $Area_B$ and $Area_C$ are the cropped areas in Countries B and C, respectively (discussed below). There are a number of crops grown in Countries B and C, but only an aggregate measure of water requirement is used here, representing a cropping pattern but not individual crops. The fraction α is the maximum portion of the flow that is allowed to be diverted to Country B (the remaining portion being available to Country C).

Reservoir A is the only reservoir in the cascade for which the elevation of the water surface varies over time, depending on the volume of water in storage. For Reservoir A, the energy generated, E_{hydro} (kWh), is given in Eq. 10.2. For the constant volume (or "run of the river") reservoirs in the cascade below Reservoir A, the effective hydraulic head on hydropower plants does not vary with time.

The energy demand for Country A is satisfied by hydropower from Reservoir A with energy being purchased for any deficit of hydroelectric energy (sometimes fuels can be obtained through energy — water exchanges with Countries B and C). The total annual energy demand is 11,220 million kWh and it is higher in the winter months than in the summer months (the monthly distribution is shown in the model).

Irrigation is the primary consumptive water use in the Lara River basin and there are two large irrigation areas; one area in Country B (1.6 million ha) and another area in Country C (1.0 million ha). A number of different crops can be grown in each irrigation zone, but here we only consider an aggregate of the crops. The annual irrigation water requirements are 11,900 and 11,100 m^3/ha for Countries B and C, respectively (the monthly distribution is shown in the model). The profit ($/ha) for growing crops in each country varies, with Country B receiving $449 per ha and Country C receiving $208 per ha. The return flow coefficient (the fraction of applied irrigation water returning to the river) for each country is 0.40. The annual inflow to Reservoir A, Q in Fig. A3.1, is 8.90 (dry), 11.9 (average), and 14.9 (wet) billion m^3 per year (the monthly distribution is shown in the model).

An objective function for determining the tradeoffs between supplying power to Country A and irrigation water to Countries B and C can be formulated as

$$\text{Objective:} \quad Z = -w_A \sum_{t=1}^{12} \left(\frac{E_{demand}^t + E_{hydro}^t}{E_{demand}^t} \right)^2 + w_B * \frac{P_B * Area_B}{Max\_Profit\_B}$$

$$+ w_C * \frac{P_C * Area_C}{Max\_Profit\_B} \tag{A3.11}$$

where w_A, w_B, and w_C are weights representing the relative importance of satisfying the objectives of Country A (minimizing energy deficits), Country B (maximize profit from irrigated agriculture), and Country C (maximize profit from irrigated agriculture). In addition, the weights satisfy $0 < w_i < 1$, $i = A, B, C$, and $w_A + w_B + w_C = 1$. This objective function anticipates that Country A wants to minimize deviations of generated energy from the energy demand, and Countries B and C want to maximize their profits from irrigated agriculture.

The equations presented above have been programmed into the General Algebraic Modeling System (GAMS) language (Brooke *et al.*, 2006). A brief introduction to this system and the model are available with the model.

SOLVING THE RIVER BASIN MODEL

Using the objective weights[2] $w_A = 0.99999$, $w_B = 0.00005$, and $w_C = 0.00005$, the following results are obtained (detailed results of solving this model can be found in the output file from the model). This set of weights emphasizes the top priority energy production interests of Country A (with the largest weight w_A), but it also includes the profit maximizing behavior of Countries B and C (with small, but positive, weights w_B and w_C) utilizing the flows that they receive in the middle and downstream regions of the basin. The solution is actually the result for Coalition A discussed in the next section. Country A receives no payment if it generates surplus energy, so there is no incentive to release excess water over what is needed to meet its national energy demand. This fact is reflected in the model through the choice of the objective function weights. In addition, Country A has to purchase any energy deficit on the open market at a cost of $0.08 per kWh, and they must pay for the operation, maintenance and replacement costs on the hydropower generation equipment at Reservoir A — estimated at $0.01 per kWh. If Country A did not own the hydroelectric facility at Reservoir A, then they would have to satisfy all of their energy needs through purchases on the energy market, so this foregone cost is their gross benefit.

The benefit that Country A receives is the market value of the energy demand — cost of purchasing energy to make up any deficit — cost of hydro-energy generation O&M (see Table A3.1). In this case, the downstream countries receive only the

---

[2]The small positive weights of Countries B and C tend to keep their interests in the objective so that the solution includes, but is not dominated by, the maximization of agricultural production.

Table A3.1: Results for Coalitions {A}, {B} and {C}.

Entity	Category	Unit	Amount
Country A	Foregone energy cost	million $	898
	Hydro-energy cost	million $	112
	Deficit energy cost	million $	0
	Total energy cost	million $	112
	Total energy benefit	million $	785
Country B	Available area	1000 ha	1,600
	Irrigated area	1000 ha	170
	Agricultural Profit	million $	83
	Total Benefit	million $	83
Country C	Available area	1000 ha	1,000
	Irrigated area	1000 ha	166
	Agricultural Profit	million $	35
	Total Benefit	million $	35
Lake Lara	Inflow	billion m^3	6.3

water that is released to meet the energy demand of Country A. Country B is the first country to receive the water and by existing treaty can use no more than 58% of it to produce as much profit as possible from irrigated agriculture. Country C receives the remainder of the flow plus the return flow from Country B's agriculture. The agricultural profits to Countries B and C are shown in Table A3.1. The value of Coalition {A} is $785 million.

THE GAME — INTRODUCTION

Consider the game with 3 players: Countries A, B, and C, and the following 7 possible coalitions: {A}; {B}; {C}; {A, B}; {A, C}; {B, C}, and {A, B, C}. The river basin model described in the previous section can be used to calculate, for each of the possible coalitions, a value that is the net payoff from any of these possible arrangements. First, we will consider alternatives with no new projects and, later we will consider several unilateral and/or joint projects. Let us consider each coalition in turn.

Coalition {A}

Coalition {A} represents the situation in which Country A acts alone, without any cooperation with countries B and C. However, there are some physical phenomena that cause the actions of Country A to affect countries B and C in this situation. Under Coalition {A}, Country A releases sufficient water to cover only its internal power demands. Countries B and C receive the resulting water from these power releases — named "residual" water (see Fig. A3.2). Assume that Country B receives

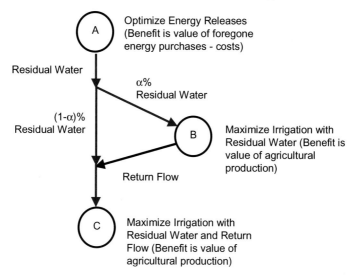

Fig. A3.2: Logic of Coalition {A}, {B}, and {C}.
Source: Authors.

$\alpha\%$ (say, 58%) of the residual water and shares the other $(1-\alpha)\%$ with Country C. Countries B and C would then use this water in irrigation for agricultural production. Country C also receives any agricultural return flows from Country B and uses this water in irrigation for agricultural production. Table A3.1 shows the costs and benefits to the countries. The value of Coalition {A} is \$785 million.

Coalition {B}

Coalition {B} represents the situation in which Country B acts alone, without any cooperation with Countries A and C, who each act to serve their own needs with the water available to them. Country A releases sufficient water to cover its power demand (see Fig. A3.2). Country B receives $\alpha\%$ (say, 58%) of the residual water and uses this water in irrigation for agricultural production. Country C receives the other $(1-\alpha)\%$ of the residual water. Since the optimizing behavior of the individual countries is the same, the same objective weights are used as with Coalition {A}, and the same results are obtained. The energy costs and benefits for Coalition {B} are the same as Coalition {A} (see Table A3.1). The value of Coalition {B} is \$83 million.

Coalition {C}

Coalition {C} represents the situation in which Country C acts alone, without any cooperation with Countries A and B, who each act to serve their own needs with the water available to them. Country A releases sufficient water to cover its power demand (see Fig. A3.2). Country B receives $\alpha\%$ (say, 58%) and Country C receives the other $(1 - \alpha)\%$ of the residual water. Since the optimizing behavior of the individual countries is the same, we can use the same objective weights as with Coalition $\{A\}$, and the same results are obtained. The energy costs and benefits for Coalition $\{C\}$ are the same as Coalitions $\{A\}$ and $\{B\}$ (see Table A3.1). The value of Coalition $\{C\}$ is \$35 million.

Coalition $\{A, B\}$

Coalition $\{A, B\}$ represents the situation in which Countries A and B cooperate. This cooperation takes the form of Country B compensating Country A for its energy deficit. In this example, we assume that this compensation is in cash, but it could be in the form of fuels (say, natural gas, coal, etc.). In return for this compensating payment, Country B receives irrigation water according to its needs plus any surplus energy generated by Country A during the release of the irrigation flows. Country B is then able to sell this surplus energy at a price of \$0.08 per kWh (see Fig. A3.3) either through an internal or external electricity market. Under this coalition, Country C still receives return flows from Country B, and it acts to maximize its agricultural production with these flows.

Using the objective weights $w_A = 0.00005$, $w_B = 0.49997$, and $w_C = 0.49997$ in the model, the results shown in Table A3.2 are obtained (detailed results of solving this model can be found in the output file from the model). These weights emphasize the top priority agricultural production interests of Country B (with large weight w_B), the energy deficit minimization behavior of Country A (with small, but positive, weight w_A), and the profit maximizing behavior of Country C (with large weight w_C). The surplus energy transferred from Country A to Country B is sold by

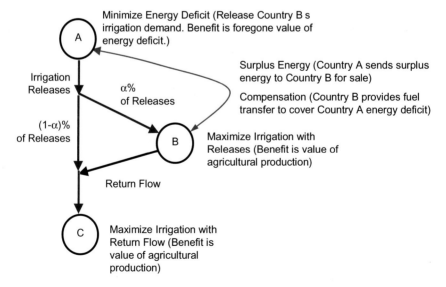

Fig. A3.3: Logic of Coalition $\{A, B\}$.

Source: Authors.

Table A3.2: Results for Coalition {A, B}.

Entity	Category	Unit	Amount
Country A	Foregone energy cost	million $	898
	Hydro-energy cost	million $	113
	Deficit energy cost	million $	400
	Total energy cost	million $	113
	Total energy benefit	million $	785
Country B	Available area	1000 ha	1,600
	Irrigated area	1000 ha	695
	Agricultural Profit	million $	340
	Surplus Energy	million $	406
	Compensation to Country A	million $	400
	Total Benefit to Country B	million $	345
Country C	Available area	1000 ha	1,000
	Irrigated area	1000 ha	680
	Agricultural Profit	million $	142
	Surplus Energy	million $	0
	Compensation to Country A	million $	0
	Total Benefit to Country C	million $	142
Lake Lara	Inflow	billion m^3	3.5

Country B for a value of $406 million. The compensating payment from Country B to Country A to cover the energy deficit is $400 million. The environmental flows entering the delta of Lake Lara are 1.8 billion m^3. The value of Coalition {A, B} is $1,130 million.

Coalition {A, C}

Coalition {A, C} represents the situation in which Countries A and C cooperate. This cooperation takes the form of Country C compensating Country A for its energy deficit. In return for this compensating payment, Country C receives irrigation water according to its needs plus any surplus energy generated by Country A during the release of the irrigation flows. Country C is then able to sell this surplus energy at a price of $0.08 per kWh (see Fig. A3.4). Under this coalition, Country B does not receive any flows from Country A.

Using the objective weights $w_A = 0.00005$, $w_B = 0.49997$, and $w_C = 0.49997$ in the model, the results shown in Table A3.3 are obtained (detailed results of solving this model can be found in the output file from the model). These weights emphasize the downstream, agricultural production interests of Country C, but they also include the energy deficit minimization behavior of Country A (hence, the very small, but positive, weight w_A), considering the compensation payments received from Country C, and the profit maximizing behavior of Country C utilizing the flows that it receives. The surplus energy transferred from Country A to Country C is sold by Country C for a value of $328 million. The compensating payment from

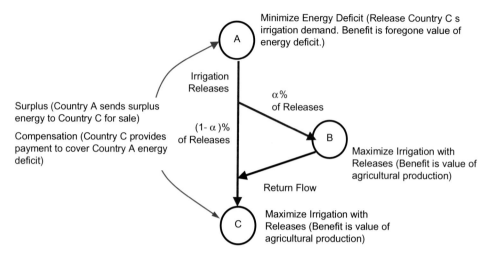

Fig. A3.4: Logic of Coalition $\{A, C\}$.

Source: Authors.

Table A3.3: Results for Coalition $\{A, C\}$.

Entity	Category	Unit	Amount
Country A	Foregone energy cost	million $	898
	Hydro-energy cost	million $	113
	Deficit energy cost	million $	385
	Compensation Received	million $	400
	Total energy cost	million $	113
	Total energy benefit	million $	785
Country B	Available area	1000 ha	1,600
	Irrigated area	1000 ha	695
	Agricultural Profit	million $	339
	Surplus Energy	million $	0
	Compensation to Country A	million $	0
	Total Benefit to Country B	million $	339
Country C	Available area	1000 ha	1,000
	Irrigated area	1000 ha	680
	Agricultural Profit	million $	142
	Surplus Energy	million $	406
	Compensation to Country A	million $	400
	Total Benefit to Country C	million $	147
Lake Lara	Inflow	billion m^3	3.5

Country C to Country A to cover the energy deficit is $435 million. The environmental flows entering the delta of Lake Lara are 4.6 billion m^3. The value of Coalition $\{AC\}$ is $932 million.

Coalition {B, C}

This coalition represents the situation in which Countries B and C cooperate, but A acts alone without any cooperation with the other countries. Under Coalition {B, C}, Country A releases sufficient water to cover only its internal power demands. Countries B and C receive the resulting water from these power releases — named "residual" water (see Fig. A3.2). Country B receives $\alpha\%$ (say, 58%) of the residual water and shares the other $(1-\alpha)\%$ with Country C. Countries B and C use their shares of the water in irrigation for agricultural production. Country C also receives any agricultural return flows from Country B and uses this water in irrigation for agricultural production. The objective function weights for this Coalition {B, C} are the same as for Coalition {A}. Table A3.4 shows the costs and benefits to countries B and C. The value of the Coalition {B, C} is $118 million.

Coalition {A, B, C}

This coalition represents the situation in which Countries A, B and C all cooperate. This cooperation takes the form of Countries B and C compensating Country A for its energy deficit. The amount of compensation payment is shared equally between Countries B and C (see Fig. A3.5). In return for these compensating payments, Countries B and C receive irrigation water according to their needs plus any surplus energy generated by Country A during the release of the irrigation flows. Country B receives $\alpha\%$ (say, 50%) of the surplus energy and shares the other $(1-\alpha)\%$ with

Table A3.4: Results for Coalition {B, C}.

Entity	Category	Unit	Amount
Country A	Foregone energy cost	million $	898
	Hydro-energy cost	million $	112
	Deficit energy cost	million $	0
	Compensation Received	million $	0
	Total energy cost	million $	211
	Total energy benefit	million $	785
Country B	Available area	1000 ha	1,600
	Irrigated area	1000 ha	170
	Agricultural Profit	million $	83
	Surplus Energy	million $	0
	Compensation to Country A	million $	0
	Total Benefit to Country B	million $	83
Country C	Available area	1000 ha	1,000
	Irrigated area	1000 ha	166
	Agricultural Profit	million $	35
	Surplus Energy	million $	0
	Compensation to Country A	million $	0
	Total Benefit to Country C	million $	35
Lake Lara	Inflows	billion m^3	6.3

Bridges Over Water

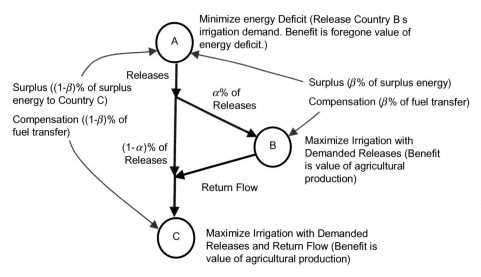

Fig. A3.5: Logic of Coalition {A, B, C}.

Source: Authors.

Country C. Country B receives β% (say, 50%) of the surplus energy and shares the other $(1-\beta)$% with Country C. Countries B and C are then able to sell their shares of the surplus energy at a price of $0.08 per kWh. Under this coalition, Country C still receives return flows from Country B.

Using the objective weights $w_A = 0.00005$, $w_B = 0.499975$, and $w_C = 0.499975$ in the model, the results shown in Table A3.5 are obtained (detailed results of solving

Table A3.5: Results for Coalition {A, B, C}.

Entity	Category	Unit	Amount
Country A	Foregone energy cost	million $	898
	Hydro-energy cost	million $	112
	Deficit energy cost	million $	400
	Compensation received	million $	400
	Total energy cost	million $	112
	Total energy benefit	million $	785
Country B	Available area	1000 ha	1,600
	Irrigated area	1000 ha	695
	Agricultural Profit	million $	339
	Surplus Energy	million $	203
	Compensation to Country A	million $	200
	Total Benefit to Country B	million $	342
Country C	Available area	1000 ha	1,000
	Irrigated area	1000 ha	680
	Agricultural Profit	million $	142
	Surplus Energy	million $	203
	Compensation to Country A	million $	200
	Total Benefit to Country C	million $	145
Lake Lara	Inflow	billion m^3	3.5

this model can be found in the output file from the model). These weights emphasize the agricultural production interests of Countries B and C (and their sharing of the releases from Country A), but they also include the energy deficit minimization behavior of Country A, and the compensation payments received from Countries B and C. The results are shown in Table A3.5. The surplus energy transferred from Country A is sold by Countries B and C for a value of $203 million each. The compensating payment from Countries B and C to Country A to cover the energy deficit is $200 million each. The value of Coalition {A, B, C} is $1,272 million.

CHARACTERISTIC FUNCTION OF THE GAME

The Characteristic function of the game, v, assigns to each coalition the maximum value of the game between the coalition under consideration and the other countries that are not in that coalition. For the non-cooperative coalitions, $v(A)$, $v(B)$, and $v(C)$ are what each country may obtain acting on its own; $v(AB)$ and $v(BC)$ are the values that the partial coalitions may obtain if they form these subgroups; and $v(ABC)$ is the value of the grand coalition of all countries in the negotiation. The characteristic function values for all possible coalitions are presented in Table A3.6.

From Table A3.6, we see that Countries A and B can gain an additional $262 million per year if they cooperate. Similarly, Countries A and C can gain an additional $165 million and all three countries can gain $369 million is they form the Grand Coalition. The main question remaining for the countries is how to divide up these additional gains, should they decide to cooperate and join one of the coalitions.

THE CORE

The Core is a set of gains from allocating the resource among the players that is not dominated by any other allocation set; that is, it provides a range for the possible allocation solutions. The core provides a bound for the maximum allocation each player may request in the negotiation. The system of equations defining the Core

Table A3.6: Characteristic function values for coalitions.

Coalition	Marginal contribution of Country to Coalition (million $)			Value of coalition	$\sum v\{j\}$	Incremental gains for coalition
	A	B	C			
{A}	785			785	746	0
{B}		83		83	83	0
{C}			35	35	35	0
{AB}	785	83		1,130	868	262
{AC}	785		35	932	767	165
{BC}		83	35	118	118	0
{ABC}	785	83	35	1,272	903	369

Bridges Over Water

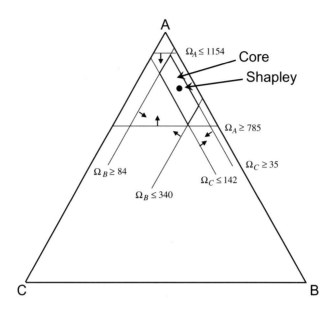

Fig. A3.6: The Core of the Game.

Source: Authors.

for the Lara River basin example is:

$$\Omega_A \geq \nu(A) = 785$$
$$\Omega_A \leq \nu(ABC) - \nu(BC) = 1154$$
$$\Omega_B \geq \nu(B) = 83$$
$$\Omega_B \leq \nu(ABC) - \nu(AC) = 340$$
$$\Omega_C \geq \nu(C) = 35$$
$$\Omega_C \leq \nu(ABC) - \nu(AB) = 142$$
$$\Omega_A + \Omega_B + \Omega_C = \nu(ABC) = 1272$$

where Ω_j; $j = A, B, C$ are each country's allocation of the gains from a coalition. We can plot this information on a simplex with the distance to the side opposite any vertex $i = \Omega_i$. The distance from any vertex to the opposite side is 1272 in the example (see Fig. A3.6).

THE SHAPLEY ALLOCATION

The Core represents the set of non-dominated imputations in the game. The question remains as to which point inside this set may represent the most reasonable allocation of the gains form the game. Several methods have been developed to identify point allocations which are within the core of the game. We will consider the Shapley value here. Considering the sequence of establishment of each coalition and the allocation of the incremental gain generated by each country's entry into

Table A3.7: Value of various permutations of coalition formation.

Permutation	Unit	Marginal contribution of Country to the coalition		
		A	B	C
ABC	Million $	785	345	142
ACB	Million $	785	340	147
BAC	Million $	1,047	83	142
BCA	Million $	1,154	83	35
CAB	Million $	897	340	35
CBA	Million $	1,154	83	35
Total	Million $	5,822	1,274	536
Shapley value	Million $	970	212	89
Percent of profit	%	0.76	0.17	0.07

an existing coalition allows us to calculate the Shapley value. Consider Table A3.7 where the countries are assumed to form the grand coalitions $\{A, B, C\}$ step by step, starting with one country and then adding the second and finally the third (the permutations in Table A3.7). As each country joins, we award that country the value that they add to the growing coalition (Straffin, 2004).

From the results of computing the values of the coalitions described above, we know that without cooperating with any of the other countries, Countries A, B, and C can expect to gain $785, $83 and $35 million per year, respectively. Can they do better than this through cooperation with the other riparian countries? From Table A3.7 we see that the gain for Country A is in the range ($785, $1,154) million per year with an average value of $970 million per year. Similarly, the gain for Country B is in the range ($83, $345) million per year with an average value of $212 million per year, and the gain for Country C is in the range ($35, $142) million per year with an average value of $89 million per year. The average value gives the imputation known as the Shapley value (see Fig. A3.6 and Table A3.7) $\Omega_A = 970$, $\Omega_B = 212$, $\Omega_C = 89$.

From the Grand Coalition $\{A, B, C\}$, Country A might try to negotiate to receive $1,154 million ($v(ABC) - v(BC)$) out of the $1,272 million value of the grand coalition (a major improvement over non-cooperation of $785 million), but they would be unlikely to receive more than the Shapley value of $970 million. In this coalition, Country A gets to take advantage of the compensating energy deliveries from the other countries (but this coalition is not the first choice of the other countries who prefer to join coalitions with Country A independently of the other, see below). Country A's second choice is Coalition $\{A, B\}$ where it might receive $1,047 million out of $1,272 million.

From Coalition $\{A, B\}$, Country B could negotiate to receive $345 million out of the $1,272 million value of the coalition (a definite improvement over the non-cooperative value of $83 million). In this coalition, Country B gets to take advantage of the irrigation releases and the surplus energy sales. Its second choice, the

Table A3.8: Gately propensity to disrupt and Loehman power index.

Country	Gately propensity to disrupt	Loehman power index
A	0.99	0.50
B	0.99	0.35
C	0.97	0.15

Grand Coalition $\{A, B, C\}$ is still an improvement over non-cooperation ($340 out of $1,272). Similar logic can be used to describe the position of Country C.

STABILITY INDICES

For a given allocation Ω_j to Country j in an imputation, the Gately "propensity to disrupt" of country j is calculated as (Gately, 1974; see Eq. 6.18):

$$d_j = \frac{\sum\limits_{i \neq j} \Omega_i - v(\{N - j\})}{\Omega_j - v(\{j\})}$$

When this ratio is positive and large, Country j has a tendency to disrupt the grand coalition unless his allocation is improved. This equation represents the ratio of what the countries in coalition $N - j$ would lose if Country j disrupted the grand coalition, to what the Country would lose. This concept is often used to reduce the set of core imputations by eliminating those imputations for which a Country's propensity to disrupt is higher than a specified value. The Loehman *et al.* (1979) power index (α_j) compares the gains to a country with the gains to the coalition is (Loehman *et al.* 1979; see Eq. 6.16):

$$\alpha_j = \frac{\Omega_j - v(\{j\})}{\sum\limits_{j \in N} (\Omega_j - v(\{j\}))}$$

Values of the Gately propensity to disrupt and the Loehman power index are shown in Table A3.8. For the Lara basin example the Shapley imputation is in the Core and gives small propensities to disrupt; thus, the Shapley allocation leaves each country equally satisfied, in terms of propensity to disrupt. The Loehman power index shows that Country A has the largest power in the basin, followed by Country B and the Country C.

SUMMARY

In this chapter we demonstrated how a transboundary water situation is analyzed using game theory concepts and computational software. Many questions and issues related to the game of the Lara River basin remain for the student to explore through the exercises and with the software continued on the CD-ROM.

Practice Questions

1. Some of the model parameters in the model of the example basin are uncertain or poorly estimated. What are the effects of these uncertainties on water allocation and the value of cooperation in the example basin? One way of examining this is to perturb the values of the parameters by a small amount from their given values and recalculate the results and compare these to the unperturbed results. Some of these parameters include: (1) C_Hydro, the cost to operate and maintain the hydroelectric generating equipment ($ per kWh); (2) P_Energy, the market price to purchase energy ($ per kWh); (3) PB and PC, the profit margins from agricultural production in Countries B and C, respectively ($ per ha); (4) RetB and RetC, the return flow coefficients for Countries B and C, respectively. Change the values of these parameters, independently, by 5% and determine which, if any, of the parameters the results seem most sensitive to.

2. The model results described in this annex were derived for normal year inflows to Reservoir A. Based on the hydrological record, the inflows to the reservoir, Q_Total (million m^3) in the model, could be 8,900 in a dry year, 11,900 in an average year, or 14,900 in a wet year. What is the result on water allocation and the value of cooperation in the basin if dry or wet year inflows are used, instead of normal year inflows?

3. Country A's energy demand, E_Dem_Total in the model, depends on the size of the population in that country. What is the effect on the model results of increasing population resulting in an increase in energy demand by 10% from the 11,220 million kWh assumed in the model? Does this have an impact on the water allocation and cooperation positions of the downstream countries?

4. The demand for water in the downstream countries B and C depend on the irrigation technology used there. What is the effect on the model results of increasing the efficiency of the irrigation technology by 10% in Country B (thus reducing the water demand Water_B_Total by a corresponding percentage)? This increased efficiency comes at a cost to Country B of $10/ha (this reduces the profit of water use in agriculture PB by a corresponding amount). Does this have an impact on the water allocation and cooperation position of the downstream country B or upstream country A?

5. The model illustrated in this annex assumes a particular ending storage for the year, end_S in the model. According to the treaty negotiations ongoing in the basin, in an normal inflow year the reservoir volume should be required to increase by 400 million m^3, similarly, in a dry year the decrease in the reservoir storage should be limited to 3,300 million m^3, and in a wet year the increase in storage should be required to be 3,900 million m^3. What is the effect on water allocation and the value of cooperation in the basin if these values in the dry or wet year conditions? Do you agree with the long-term arrangement of water in storage in the reservoir?

6. Country B has the option of constructing a new reservoir (see Fig. A3.7) with a capacity of 1.64 billion m^3. The main purpose of this reservoir is to capture winter releases from Country A and store them for use in summer irrigation. The cost of the new Reservoir B is \$250 million. What is the effect on water allocation and the value of cooperation in the basin if Country B has the option of constructing and operating this new reservoir?

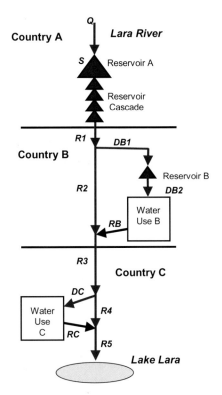

Fig. A3.7: Lara River basin with Reservoir B included.

Source: Authors.

REFERENCES

Brooke, A., D. Kendrick, A. Meeraus and R. Raman (2006). *GAMS Language Guide.* Washington DC: Gams Development Corporation.

Gately, D. (1974). Sharing the gains from regional cooperation: A game theoretic application to planning investment in electric power, *International Economic Review* 15(1), 195–208.

Loehman, E., J. Orlando, J. Tschirhart and A. Winstion (1979). Cost allocation for a regional wastewater treatment system, *Water Resources Research* 15, 193–202.

Straffin, P.D. (2004). *Game Theory and Strategy.* Washington DC: Mathematical Society of America.

INDEX